# THE HARBRACE ANTHOLOGY OF SHORT FICTION

Rushton

# THE HARBRACE ANTHOLOGY OF SHORT FICTION

## SECOND EDITION

SENIOR EDITORS

Jon C. Stott
Raymond E. Jones
Rick Bowers

CONTRIBUTING EDITORS

Glenn Burger
William Connor
Katherine Koller
James Nelson
Daphne Read
Glennis Stephenson
Bruce Stovel

UNIVERSITY OF ALBERTA

HARCOURT
BRACE
CANADA

Harcourt Brace & Company, Canada

Toronto  Montreal  Fort Worth  New York  Orlando
Philadelphia  San Diego  London  Sydney  Tokyo

**Canadian Cataloguing in Publication Data**

Main entry under title:

The Harbrace anthology of short fiction

2nd ed.
Includes bibliographical references and index.
ISBN 0-7747-3609-7

1. Short stories, English. I. Bowers, Rick.
II. Jones, Raymond E. III. Stott, Jon C., 1939– .

PN6120.2.H37 1998        823'.0108        C97-931847-5


Acquisitions Editor: Kelly V. Cochrane
Developmental Editor: Su Mei Ku
Supervising Editor: Semareh Al-Hillal
Production Co-ordinator: Sheila Barry

Copy Editor: Margaret Allen
Permissions Editor: Martina van de Velde
Cover and Interior Design: The Brookview Group Inc.
Typesetting and Assembly: MacTrix DTP
Printing and Binding: Best Book Manufacturers, Inc.

Cover Art: Helen D'Souza, "They Feed My Soul." Reproduced by permission of Shelley Brown & Associates on behalf of the artist.

This book was printed in Canada.

1  2  3  4  5    02  01  00  99  98

# PREFACE

"We imagine ourselves, we create ourselves, we touch ourselves into being with words, words that are important to us," writes Native North American author Gerald Vizenor. One means by which we imagine or create ourselves is through the reading of literature.

The Harbrace Anthology of Literature uses three approaches to encourage its readers in this activity. First, it presents significant and representative works from the increasingly widening canon of literature in English. Second, it provides strategies to assist readers in their appreciation of works of literature. Third, by introducing readers to the language of literature, both simple and complex, and by suggesting methods for articulating responses, it provides opportunities to explore literature and to respond to language in its rich and varied forms.

Although no anthology can include all of its readers' favourite works, the editors have attempted to make their selections as varied and diverse as possible. Thus, The Harbrace Anthology of Literature offers many contemporary poems, plays, and short stories, by men and women alike, from a variety of cultures and backgrounds, in addition to many of those works that have always formed an integral part of the accepted canon of literature in English. It also includes a large sampling of English-Canadian literature in the belief that Canadian students should have the opportunity to experience the major works of their literary tradition both on their own terms and within the larger context of literature written in English.

Individual works in The Harbrace Anthology of Literature mirror the diversity of backgrounds and interests of Canadian students as well as reflecting an expanded canon. The poems, plays, and short stories reveal many of the characteristic themes and artistic techniques of their authors; they also reflect the cultural and social contexts in which they were written. In particular, they embody, as the eighteenth-century poet Alexander Pope observed, "what oft was thought but ne'er so well expressed." Most readers of this anthology will find its works speaking directly to them and addressing their most deeply felt concerns.

The Harbrace Anthology of Literature is organized by genre, beginning with poetry. Its poetry selections span eleven hundred years, the longest period of the three genres presented in the anthology. It continues with drama and concludes with short stories, the most recent of the three genres to develop. Selections within each genre are chronological, according to the birth dates of their authors. Following a selection, its date of publication is printed in parentheses on the right; when it differs significantly and is known, the date of composition appears in parentheses on the left. Such an organizational pattern, based on chronology rather than on pedagogical or theoretical concerns, invites a broad range of responses to a work, unencumbered by artificial or purely technical groupings based on content or theme. It does, of course, implicitly suggest a historical continuity in literature: that works from a specific period often have technical and thematic similarities; and that earlier works and authors can influence later ones.

The book's Introduction considers the reading of literature both as a personal, necessary lifelong activity and as a discipline. It explores how reading poems, plays, and short stories allows individuals to understand their own lives and responses to literature in relation to those of other people. It also demonstrates how readers can engage more deeply with a text, experiencing it more fully and relating it more completely to their own lives.

The introduction to each genre focusses directly on the characteristics and conventions of the genre, using examples from the literature presented in *The Harbrace Anthology of Literature*. Discussions of individual characteristics are intended not to offer explanations or explications, but to indicate ways in which authors have used the various elements of the genre. For the reader, an awareness of these characteristics may assist in engagement with the text and lead to a broader range of responses.

Each work or, in the case of poetry, each group of poems by the same author is prefaced by a brief headnote establishing a biographical and literary context. The headnote may also touch on technique or theme. Explanatory footnotes identify historical, fictional, and mythological personages; literary and artistic works; real and fictional places; and terms not usually found in standard dictionaries. This material provides resources to assist readers in the personal creation of meaning — not to impose a critical viewpoint or to force interpretation in a specific, narrow direction.

Reading literature invites writing about it. The chapter entitled "Writing Essays about Literature" explores some of the challenges that writing about literature poses, without prescribing a recipe or rigid format for writing. It offers constructive suggestions to assist readers and writers in articulating responses — intellectual, aesthetic, or emotional — to works of literature.

The Glossary offers definitions of key terms, providing for readers both an awareness of essential concepts and a standard vocabulary for use in discussing literature.

## ACKNOWLEDGEMENTS

The compilation of this anthology was a co-operative venture of the ten colleagues whose names appear on the title page; however, no book, even one developed by ten people, is ever created in a vacuum. During the planning, compiling, writing, and editing stages of *The Harbrace Anthology of Literature*, many people offered suggestions and made valuable comments. We wish to acknowledge the contributions and suggestions of our colleagues from the University of Alberta and reviewers from other universities:

Claude G. Arnold
Richard Arnold
Diana Austin

Faith Balish
Ed Balsom
S. Bell

William Benzie
William Blackburn
Sylvia Bowerbank
Sally J. Braun
J. Brigham
Mervin Butovsky
George J. Casey
Lorelei Cederstrom
Stephen Cloutier
Jonathan Cutmore
Susan Drodge
Diane T. Edwards
Ian W. Fairclough
Noreen Golfman
Nat Hardy
James Hart
A. Howey
Susan Ingersoll
K. James-Cavan
Ron Johnson
W.B. Lambert
Edward Lobb
Jean MacIntyre
Sandra Mallett
T.J. Matheson
Lee McLeod
Craig W. McLuckie
Edward Mullaly

M. Murray
C. Nelson-McDermott
Victor A. Neufeldt
Andrew Parkin
Don Perkins
Richard Pickard
E.W. Pitcher
Victor Ramraj
Greg Randall
Christian Riegel
Constance Rooke
Eric J. Savoy
Steven Scott
John F. Secker
Graham Shorrocks
Stephen Slemon
Tony Steele
S. Warren Stevenson
Janis Svilpis
Peter A. Taylor
P. Tyndell
B.F. Tyson
Paul S. Upton
Karys A. Van de Pitte
Aritha van Herk
Linda Vecchi
Lorraine York
Edward R. Zietlow

As well, we thank Heather McWhinney, Kelly Cochrane, Su Mei Ku, Martina van de Velde, Jeannine Maxfield, and Semareh Al-Hillal at Harcourt Brace. These people have made this a better anthology; the responsibility for its limitations is our own.

## A Note from the Publisher

Thank you for selecting *The Harbrace Anthology of Literature*, Second Edition, edited by Jon C. Stott, Raymond E. Jones, and Rick Bowers. The editors and publisher have devoted considerable time and care to the development of this book. We appreciate your recognition of this effort and accomplishment.

We want to hear what you think about *The Harbrace Anthology of Literature*. Please take a few minutes to fill in the stamped reader reply card at the back of the book. Your comments and suggestions will be valuable to us as we prepare new editions and other books.

## A Note to the Reader

We would like to draw your attention to three elements of this text:

1. *Pagination:* This anthology was originally conceived as a three-genre collection: poetry, drama, and short fiction. In response to requests from instructors and students, however, we have produced the poetry and short fiction in separate volumes: *The Harbrace Anthology of Poetry* and *The Harbrace Anthology of Short Fiction.* (We do not have a new edition for the drama section, but the first edition of *The Harbrace Anthology of Drama* is available.) The split versions provide students with a more portable book, and offer instructors more alternatives in the way the text is used. You will find, however, that the pagination in these smaller volumes is exactly the same as in the main anthology. Unlike changing page numbers in a simple wordprocessed document, repaginating a book is an involved process that would result in a higher-priced text. When weighing these two options — raising the price of the text or keeping the pagination as is — we chose to keep the price of the text as low as possible.

2. *Dates at the end of poems:* One or two dates follow each poem in the poetry section. The date on the left is the date of the poem's original composition, and the date on the right is the date of the poem's first publication. Where the date of the poem's creation is unknown or where it is the same as the date of the poem's first publication, the date on the left has been omitted.

3. *Stanza continuation icon (* ⟶ *):* We have introduced a unique feature in the poetry section of this text. Because stanzas often flow onto a new page, it is sometimes difficult for the reader to establish whether a stanza ends at the bottom of the page or continues on the next page. Stanza breaks often have significant implications for the interpretation of poems. To avoid confusion about where stanzas end or continue, we have placed the symbol " ⟶ " below the last line on a page to indicate that a stanza continues on the next page. We hope this will assist your reading of the poetry.

# CONTENTS

# DRAMA

# SHORT FICTION

# INTRODUCTION

"Part of the beauty of all literature," commented novelist and short story writer F. Scott Fitzgerald, is that "you discover that your longings are universal longings, that you're not lonely and isolated from anyone. You belong." Sharing experience through the creation and reception of stories, poems, and plays is a very old, basic, and necessary human activity, as necessary to human existence as food, shelter, and clothing. The literary critic Northrop Frye further emphasized the importance of literature, observing that "whenever a society is reduced to the barest primary requirements of food and sex and shelter, the arts, including poetry, stand out sharply in relief as ranking with those primary requirements." The need to bring order, through language and stories, to human experience seems to be fundamental to all societies and cultures.

While some literature may simply entertain or allow escape from everyday lives, the works that ultimately stay with their readers are those that challenge, engage, or make demands. Well-crafted literature invites its readers to laugh, to cry, to wonder, to analyze, to explore, to understand.

Throughout our lives, we seek to understand ourselves, our emotions, our experiences, and our relationships with others. We also attempt to define our connections to larger social and cultural institutions. One way that we can do so is through literature, for works of literature are the records of individual response to the world in which we live.

Because of our own experiences, we are able to understand the self-doubts and uncertainties expressed in T.S. Eliot's "The Love Song of J. Alfred Prufrock," the wonder of first love experienced by Ferdinand and Miranda in William Shakespeare's *The Tempest*, the disillusionment and disappointment of returning to a family home after a prolonged absence in Greg Hollingshead's "The Naked Man," and the anguish of Phyllis Webb's "Treblinka Gas Chamber." The specific experiences may be different from our own, but we recognize similarities in the thoughts and emotions of the characters; examination and reflection may lead to clearer insights into our own lives.

Because works of literature are often demanding, they offer great rewards. Readers come to fuller awareness of themselves and others. They discover both the uniqueness and the universality of human experience; they explore both their own world and worlds they may never otherwise see. Through critical response to literature, readers question a work, examine their relationship to the author, consider the author's role, and develop an appreciation of the work, both on its own terms and as an expression of the author's vision of life. Readers may also explore a work in the context of its times, whether social, historical, or ideological.

Until fairly recently, much of the literature studied in English courses was chosen from a list of works deemed important by a majority of critics and scholars, a list referred to as the canon of English literature. Like most of these

1

critics and scholars, most of the writers were white, male, and British or of British descent. The list usually began with the anonymous creator of the Anglo-Saxon epic "Beowulf" and ended with such earlier twentieth-century writers as T.S. Eliot, W.H. Auden, and Dylan Thomas. Because it included very few works by women, members of ethnic minorities, or writers from the British colonies, however, it could not be said to reflect the diversity of writing in English.

The past 25 years have seen a remarkable change in our society as a whole: the recognition of the equal place of all people in it, regardless of gender or ethnic origin. As a consequence, many literary scholars and critics have vigorously sought to expand the canon so that it speaks to everyone. They have demanded the inclusion of the many voices whose stories, poems, and dramas are worthy of study, both on their own merits and because of the insights they offer into a very large segment of the population of the English-speaking world. Such critics have argued that literature should certainly present universal human concerns but should also help readers understand how gender, cultural background, and social position influence responses to life. The works in this anthology reflect this expanded canon.

Reading and reflecting on works of literature reveal human similarities as well as differences. Aphra Behn's drama *The Rover* makes us aware of the position of women in the male-dominated upper-class English society of the late seventeenth century. Athol Fugard's *"MASTER HAROLD"* . . . *and the boys* delineates the political and racial tensions of mid-twentieth-century South Africa. The poetry of Oodgeroo of the tribe Noonuccal (Kath Walker) reveals a modern Australian aboriginal woman examining her people's past and its troubled relationships with both government and newcomers.

Readers who come actively to such works with an open, questioning mind will be able to join with their authors in making explicit the implicit. They will appreciate that an author has used language connotatively, choosing words that, in addition to their dictionary meanings, suggest a range of emotions, ideas, or associations. They will recognize the symbolic nature of actions, characters, and objects. As the German literary critic Wolfgang Iser has commented, literary texts are incomplete; they contain gaps that readers fill in or bridge to create meaning. Readers anticipate, make inferences, draw conclusions; in short, they actively work with the language of a piece of literature to arrive at meaning.

Reading for meaning is a very personal act. It is not simply a matter of paraphrasing or summarizing a story or play, of transforming poetry into prose, or of examining literary technique or metaphorical language. Each reader is unique and will, therefore, respond differently — perhaps slightly, perhaps dramatically — to a work. A Dubliner will no doubt react differently to James Joyce's "Araby" than will a Winnipegger; a man about to retire will react differently to Shakespeare's *The Tempest* than will a young woman who has just left home for first-year college or university; a woman will react differently to Margaret Atwood's "The Resplendent Quetzal" than will a man. People who have read widely in each of these three authors or who have a well-developed knowledge of literature would likely have a different and broader interpretation of these three works than someone who seldom reads. Readers draw on personal experience, knowledge, and awareness of both specific literature and literary techniques to appreciate and interpret a literary work.

There is no one simple process for interpreting literature; different readers develop different approaches, some of which will be more useful for some works than for others. That said, interpretation of a literary work begins with the words of the text themselves. Readers question the choice and arrangement of details and ponder their significance. Such active inquiry may commence on reading the title or during a first reading. Individual interpretation will change with each rereading as readers observe more details, acquire more information about them, and perceive new relationships among them.

Readers bring their own experiences to their interpretation of literature. Basing interpretation on the words of the text, they can compare and contrast their own responses to life with those of authors and characters. Readers who have had intense family conflicts will be able to make inferences about the domestic arguments in Eudora Welty's "Why I Live at the P.O." Reciprocally, interpretation of literature can enrich experiences of life. Younger readers will not have had the experiences of the middle-aged women in Jane Rule's "Inland Passage," but a reading of that story may bring empathy for problems different from theirs. Recalling personal experience while reading a work for the first time can assist in its interpretation.

Readers also bring considerable literary experience to their reading of literature: an understanding of the ways in which authors use language and the general patterns of the major literary genres (poetry, drama, and fiction), awareness of important themes, and, frequently, familiarity with other works by the same writer. For example, knowledge of Shakespeare's use of blank verse, his creation of patterns of imagery, and the structure of his earlier comedies will make a study of *The Tempest* more rewarding. Reflection on the myths surrounding men and women will aid in the interpretation of Adrienne Rich's "Diving into the Wreck." Readers draw on what they already know and on critical literature to expand their interpretation of a literary work.

While readers bring considerable knowledge and experience to a literary work, they must also be conscious of the creative intelligence behind the selection and arrangement of its elements. General techniques and genre characteristics, as well as cultural or other forces at play during the writing, may influence some of the selection and arrangement, but most choices arise from the author's purpose in writing the work. Although readers may not find this purpose apparent on first reading, speculation on purpose, based on attention to details and their sequence, may reveal potentially deeper meanings in a work.

Understanding is enhanced as readers acquire more relevant background information and apply it to the text. Knowledge of the actual people and literary or mythological characters mentioned in the text, of allusions to historical events and episodes in other works, and of geographical or architectural settings will clarify their function in a work. In "Fogbound in Avalon," for example, Annie, the narrator, reads a magazine article about the painter Edvard Munch. Examining that artist's works may reveal a clearer picture of Annie's state of mind.

Literary works often reflect events and conflicts in the lives of their authors; awareness of such personal details can enhance a reader's understanding of how and why authors have written as they have. For example, James Joyce, in "Araby," William Wordsworth, in "Lines Composed a Few Miles above Tintern Abbey," and Amy Tan, in "Two Kinds," drew on facts from their own lives. What is perhaps most interesting is the way in which an author has taken such raw materials of life and shaped them to meet the needs of the work.

Literary works are also products of the times in which they were written, for nearly all writers have been sensitive to and influenced by the literary, intellectual, political, and social forces around them. Ernest Hemingway's attitude toward the rejection by many of traditional moral and religious values during and after World War I helps to explain the actions of the two waiters and the elderly man in "A Clean, Well-Lighted Place." Familiarity with Margaret Atwood's musings on being a woman writer will enrich interpretations of her poetry and such short stories as "The Resplendent Quetzal."

Finally, readers should remember that just as it is impossible to understand completely another person or even oneself, so there is no such thing as a final, complete, or totally correct interpretation of a work of literature. To successive readings of a work readers bring different frames of mind, other personal experiences, new literary or other factual knowledge, and greater familiarity with the work. Thus, with each reading, fuller, more rewarding, and potentially new interpretations are possible.

To assist readers in the creation of meaning, the introductions to the three genres in this anthology — poetry, drama, and short stories — discuss technical aspects of literary works. Headnotes and footnotes provide information about authors and their works and about names, places, and obscure terms mentioned in the texts. The Glossary defines terms frequently used in discussing literature.

Critical response to literature often involves writing about poems, stories, and dramas. Through writing, readers explore the parts and the whole of a work, examine their previous interpretations and test their validity, evaluate the significance of relationships among parts of a work, and create new meanings. Of course, new interpretations may not be final ones; indeed, they may be modified several times during the writing process. Exploration of apparently contradictory information may provide fresh insights into a work. If, in creating an interpretation, the writer has based the statements on the text, has provided evidence and not ignored contradictory evidence, and has argued logically and clearly, then the interpretation is valid. For those seeking assistance in the writing of interpretive essays, the chapter entitled "Writing Essays about Literature" offers a number of suggestions and guidelines.

What are the rewards of becoming active readers and interpreters? An answer can be found by returning to this introduction's opening discussion of essential human needs. Poems, plays, and short stories are artistic and articulate responses to life that offer emotional, intellectual, and imaginative nourishment to their readers. Anthologies such as this provide exposure to literature that enhances the readers' knowledge of themselves and the world outside of themselves. Such experiences can lead to self-discovery and a lifelong love of reading.

# SHORT FICTION

# INTRODUCTION

The daily lives of most people are full of stories, sometimes written down but, more often, not. People imagine, develop plans for a successful day, relate accounts (sometimes true and sometimes embroidered) about what they have done, or gossip about other people. They personalize, modify, and extend stories they have heard or read; retell and sometimes add variations to jokes and anecdotes; read newspaper stories; listen to country and western ballads; watch movies, television programs, and commercials (which are often mini-dramas). They receive some of their religious and political messages in the form of stories included in sermons and election speeches.

The processes of creating, transmitting, and receiving stories are among the most basic human activities. "One wants to tell a story, like Scheherazade," novelist Carlos Fuentes wrote, "in order not to die. It's one of the oldest urges of mankind. It's a way of stalling death." Like eating, sleeping, and breathing, it is a necessary human activity, and like breathing, so natural that we are often unaware that it is occurring. In *Tellers and Listeners: The Narrative Imagination*, the noted British critic Barbara Hardy has written:

> Nature, not art, makes us all story-tellers. Daily and nightly we devise fictions and chronicles, calling some of them daydreams or dreams, some of them nightmares, some of them truths, records, reports, and plans. Some of them we call, or refuse to call lies. Narrative imagination is a common human possession, differentiating us ... from the animals.

The creation of all stories involves the selection and structuring of details that assist the storytellers in achieving their intended purposes. While in the types of stories described by Hardy these activities may be casual and haphazard, in those written as short stories and novels they are usually very deliberate and precise. Authors include only those characters, events, objects, and details that they consider to be necessary for their stories, and they arrange them in artistically satisfying and meaningful patterns. As an example, we know that in their day-to-day lives people spend much time on routine activities such as obtaining, preparing, and eating food. Although some people have transformed them into highly entertaining events, authors describe these only when they are important to their stories in some way: to development of plot and conflict, perhaps, or to portray character.

Some stories make few demands on their readers, offering light entertainment. Others require attentive readers, not only because their characters and themes are more complex and involved, but also because their authors frequently imply, rather than explain, elements of character and theme. Authors may, for example, leave the significance of actions, dialogue, and objects for readers to discover. They may create narrators who are not reliable reporters or interpreters. Moreover, they may present events in other than chronological order or may not supply clear links or bridges between sections of a story.

Readers easily recognize the basic elements of most stories — characters, actions, and settings — and the basic organizing pattern, which is the introduction, development, and resolution of one or more conflicts. An understanding of the varied and complex ways in which both these elements and the pattern of conflict are used by authors, along with an awareness of the significance of such techniques as narrative point of view, symbolism, and irony will bring to readers fuller, richer comprehension of the stories they encounter. Careful attention to these elements is especially important in the reading of short stories, in which authors must achieve their purposes within a limited space, generally a few thousand words. Like lyric poets, to whom they have been frequently compared, they cannot waste words and must make each word contribute to their stories' total effect and meaning.

## PLOT AND CONFLICT

Key to many stories are the incidents they contain; readers want to know what happens next and how a story ends. Authors select and organize events and then add details that contribute to the **plot** and lead toward a satisfying conclusion. The plot of a story provides more than factual information about who did what and when; it helps readers understand why these events occurred.

In most short stories, the plot begins with an **exposition** and then is organized around the introduction, development, and **resolution** of one or more **conflicts**. The exposition provides necessary background about characters, settings, and events. Those stories told or narrated in the same order in which the events occurred, or chronological order, usually introduce the conflict near the beginning. The events that follow form the **rising action**, or sequence of actions, leading to the **climax** or turning point, which is the most significant moment in the story. The **dénouement**, or final outcome or consequence of events, and the resolution of the conflict usually follow quickly. "The Naked Man," "Rappaccini's Daughter," and "Bliss" present events in chronological order, helping to reveal both the relationships between actions and the nature of the characters' responses to them.

Many writers use **flashbacks**, interrupting the chronological presentation of events to introduce earlier actions that clarify the immediate present of the narrative. For example, during a Christmas vacation in Mexico, Sarah and Edward, the childless couple in "The Resplendent Quetzal," think about their courtship and unhappy married life in Toronto. By presenting these thoughts, which neither communicates to the other, the author clarifies the significance of their actions during an excursion to some Aztec ruins. Other writers use **foreshadowing**, providing clues which hint at significant events that occur later in the story. In "A Rose for Emily," the reasons for the title character's purchase of arsenic are not explained. Only at the conclusion are her motivations and the ironic significance of the notation on the package, "For rats," made clear.

Most readers demand more than an exciting plot to stimulate their imaginations or develop their understanding of themselves and the world around them. This is particularly the case in many modern short stories, where the plot is minimal, there are few, if any, physical actions, and the events may initially appear to be almost trivial. Interest in the motivations of characters and their responses frequently leads to a rereading of such stories. Do they develop during the course of a plot? Do they gain clearer understandings of themselves and their situations? What are the causes of the changes or insights, or the failure to achieve them?

When they change, the central characters, or **protagonists**, often do so as a result of conflicts with one or more of three kinds of opposing characters or forces, often referred to as **antagonists**. First, individuals may be in conflict with themselves. In "Rappacini's Daughter," Giovanni must wrestle with his conflicting opinions about Beatrice, attitudes that reveal more about different sides of his own nature than they do about the young woman. In contrast, the narrator's mother in "Borders" is in conflict with the immigration officials who demand that she declare herself either a Canadian or an American citizen. Her struggle symbolizes that between Native peoples and colonial powers that will not allow the subjects to define themselves in their own terms.

Second, characters find themselves in conflict with those around them — quite often brothers and sisters, parents and children, husbands and wives. Because family conflicts are among the most intense and intimate that most people experience, the frequency with which these occur in stories is not surprising. Often, in quarrelling with those closest to them, individuals are trying to define themselves and to define their positions in the relationships. In "The Naked Man," the members of a family are reunited when the son returns from a year-long trip to Australia. From the parents' surprise over his call from the airport, to the mother's anxiety to get to her hair appointment, to the welcome-home party at which the young man considers himself an outsider, the lack of family cohesiveness becomes increasingly apparent. The reclusive heroine of "A Rose for Emily," the last member of a once-proud and wealthy Southern family, asserts her own status by defying the townspeople, refusing to pay taxes, and flaunting her Northern lover before them.

Third, conflict may place the central characters in opposition to natural or supernatural forces. In "The Open Boat," four men attempt to survive a violent storm, while in "The Lamp at Noon," a husband and wife are virtually helpless in the face of drought and dust storms that are destroying their farm. In both stories, characters respond differently to the struggle with nature. While they have little chance of success against the elements, those who display courage and determination, like the Oiler in "The Open Boat," achieve a kind of moral victory.

Most stories present conflicts of more than one type and usually examine the interrelationships between them. In "The Conversion of the Jews," for example, Ozzie seeks to define himself while attempting to deal with the conflicting expectations of his mother, the rabbi, and his peers. The narrator of "Bartleby, the Scrivener," while attempting to understand the motives behind Bartleby's behaviour, is also wrestling with his own opposing attitudes and with the dehumanizing effect of life in New York.

Not all stories conclude with conflicts resolved. In some, the characters confront forces or realities they cannot alter, as is the case in "A Clean, Well-Lighted Place." In others, their own inner flaws do not permit resolution. The narrator of "Why I Live at the P.O." believes she has triumphed over her family by leaving home. Although she does not appear to realize it, it is she who has created many of the situations that have made conditions intolerable at the house, and, in her account of events, she unconsciously reveals that her anger and hostility, the sources of much of the conflict, remain. At the end of "Dulse," we do not know if the narrator will achieve a fuller understanding of her relationships and, as a result, a measure of happiness.

## CHARACTER AND CHARACTERIZATION

Short stories generally focus on one or two major **characters**. These are almost always **rounded**; that is, they possess the complexities, contradictions, and depths of personality associated with actual human beings. They are distinguished from **flat characters**, whose personalities are presented briefly and in little depth. They may also be **dynamic**, changing during the course of a story. The change may be positive, as it is for Fido in "Inside Passage." At first suspicious and resentful of her cabin mate, Fido reveals her own insecurities and vulnerabilities. However, she is able both to understand and accept the other woman's weakness and to control her own vulnerability sufficiently to declare her new-found love. Character change may also be negative, as in the case of Giovanni in "Rappaccini's Daughter." At first he is merely a naïve young man in a strange city. But the uncertainties he develops about Beatrice are based on his own self-centred concerns, and he must bear a great deal of responsibility for the disastrous outcome of the events.

In some modern short stories, characters are **static**, undergoing no development. Lack of change may be a result of the brevity of a story; there simply may not be the space to portray development. It may also be a reflection of the characters' inability to grow or to develop, or it may represent a thematic and philosophical position that views people as subject to outside forces that they can neither understand nor control. In "A Clean, Well-Lighted Place," for example, the older waiter, who is sympathetic to the old man who frequents the café, does not change as a result of his knowledge of the meaninglessness of life, a condition he cannot change. He merely accepts what is.

At the conclusion of many short stories, one or more of the major characters may experience what James Joyce called an "**epiphany**," a moment of revelation that brings understanding of a character's situation in life. In "Araby," the boy, while standing in the darkness, perceives the truth of his motivations for coming to the bazaar and the nature of his feelings for his friend's older sister. Annie, the narrator of "Fogbound in Avalon," finally realizes that returning to her home town has not helped her to overcome the unhappiness of her adult life.

In presenting characters confronting the conflicts in their lives, authors seldom engage in direct character analysis. Instead, they employ a variety of devices, especially **dialogue** and **action**, that reveal character implicitly. The conversation of the two waiters in "A Clean, Well-Lighted Place" consists of short, often abrupt phrases and sentences that seem very similar in style; however, the younger man asks a number of questions that reveal his lack of understanding of either his fellow worker or their customer. His partner gives simple answers without elaboration; these are the facts he accepts without questioning or resistance. In "The Naked Man," Dennis's and his parents' attitudes toward his Studebaker car indicate his new and somewhat awkward relationship in his family.

In these stories, the contrasting actions of people in the same situations reveal character. "Bartleby, the Scrivener" and "Cages" also use this method, and there are many other examples. In the former story, the work patterns of Turkey and Nippers, two copyists for a New York lawyer, represent contrasts that the cautious narrator is able to keep in balance. While each exhibits some extreme behaviours, the fact that their personalities complement each other allows the lawyer to maintain the calmness of his daily routine. However, the arrival of the title character upsets both his routine and peace of mind. The brothers in the latter story attend the same school, frequent the same places, and deal with their overbearing father. The elder is rebellious, confronting his father and peers at every opportunity; the younger, although resenting his father's favouritism toward his sibling, tries to avoid conflicts. Readers are led to wonder what there is in their personalities that causes such different responses to their environments.

Characters' thoughts and statements about themselves and other people also cast light on their own personalities. Their analyses and judgements should not necessarily be taken at face value. Rather, the reasons for them should be analyzed to discover what there is about particular characters that makes them view themselves and other people the way they do. For example, the narrator of "Why I Live at the P.O.," in expressing her negative opinion of her sister, reveals her own insecurity and resentment. In "Bartleby, the Scrivener," the narrator's satisfaction with his occupation and his position in New York legal circles may help to explain why he reacts to Bartleby as he does.

Physical objects, such as possessions or clothing, can reveal character. The items belonging to the dead priest in "Araby" reveal a great deal about both him and the young narrator. The two women sharing a cabin in "Inland Passage" dress differently, a reflection of how they are coping with the events of their pasts. By wearing her best silk dress to travel into the United States to visit her daughter, the mother of the narrator in "Borders" is indicating elements of her character that will become more evident in her confrontation with the officials.

Finally, authors' descriptions of the physical appearance of individuals assist in the delineation of character. Melville carefully describes not only the clothing, but also the faces of the three scriveners in "Bartleby." While Turkey and Nippers are obvious, simple contrasts in looks and behaviour, Bartleby, considered in relation to them, is far more ambiguous. Hawthorne makes careful use of physical description in "Rappaccini's Daughter." Rappaccini's "sickly and sallow hue," his "stooping posture," and his fixity of gaze are all intended to symbolize the negative effects of his intense, almost total preoccupation with his scientific pursuits.

## SETTING

**Settings** of stories, the locations and times in which the actions occur, can be specific social or cultural contexts, such as a character's home, neighbourhood, or place of work; larger, more generalized geographical regions, such as the Canadian Prairies, or the coastline of eastern Florida; specific times of the day or of the year; and historical periods. Even weather conditions may be an important part of setting. In addition to assisting readers in visualizing events, settings provide contexts for the actions and contribute to the delineation of character, the creation of mood, and the development of theme. Settings are frequently symbolic, representing internal emotional states of characters. Readers who interpret settings rather than simply read them literally, who question why authors have selected particular times and places for their stories, will gain fuller understanding of the works they encounter.

In Sinclair Ross's "The Lamp at Noon," set on a Saskatchewan farm during the drought of the 1930s, the use made of buildings, landscape, and weather contributes to the development of the theme. Although the summer season and the time of day should bring both brightness and hope, a three-day dust storm has obscured the sun and blown away the precious topsoil needed to grow crops. The dust settling over everything in the dimly lit kitchen symbolizes the hopelessness the farm wife experiences.

A major setting in many stories is the home of the central character, a place that should represent security, stability, and nurturance. Frequently, characters leave homes that do not possess these qualities. In "The Motor Car," Calvin departs from Barbados because his life there seems unfulfilling compared with the lives of the Canadian tourists who visit the island. He believes that Toronto will be everything for him that his home is not. In "The Naked Man," Dennis expects to return to a place that is emotionally, as well as physically, the same as when he left it. However, not only is his prized car missing, he is displaced from his own bedroom by a stranger, and his parents seem to resent his return as an intrusion into the new routines of their lives. "The Horse Dealer's Daughter" takes place on the last day a bankrupt family spends in its home. The story begins on a dull November morning as three brothers and their sister sit around the "desolate breakfast-table" looking out the window as the last of their horses are taken away. At the story's conclusion, Mabel is rescued from an attempted suicide by the local doctor, with whom she falls in love; however, there is no sense that she will ever find happiness in a secure home.

Even though the characters in many stories have dwellings to which they can return, these places do not always offer them security. In "The Resplendent Quetzal," the fact that Sarah and Edward spend Christmas, a time associated with home and family, on vacation in Mexico implies much about their lives back in Canada. Unlike his younger colleague, the older waiter in "A Clean, Well-Lighted Place" is not anxious to return to his lodgings, preferring to stay until dawn in a bar where he can better endure his life.

## POINT OF VIEW

The narrator of a story, the person reporting on the characters, actions, and settings of a story, is as important as these elements themselves. While authors write their stories, they do not tell them directly; they create **narrators,** through whose voices the stories are related. By the choice of narrative **point of view**, the perspective from which a story is told, an author influences its interpretation. Third-person narrators are not characters in the stories they tell. They may be objective, reporting only the observable facts of the story without direct comment; omniscient, delving into the minds of several or all of the characters; or limited, delving only into the mind of the central character. First-person narrators are present in the stories they tell, either as observers or minor participants, or as major characters. It is interesting, after reading a story, to speculate how its meaning might have been altered had the author selected a different point of view or narrator.

Each type of narrator provides specific advantages to an author. Immediately observable in objective third-person narrators is their detachment from the scenes they recount. During most of Hemingway's "A Clean, Well-Lighted Place," the narrator describes, without comment, the bar and café, the actions of the old man, and the conversations between the two waiters. Only at the conclusion of the story does the narrator present the thoughts of the older waiter. This shift from objective to limited third-person narration casts light on the "facts" of the earlier part of the narration. Knowing the attitude of the waiter, readers can perceive that the apparently objective reporting earlier in the story consisted of elements carefully selected to reveal the characters' attitudes toward life.

Choosing a third-person omniscient narrator who reports on the emotions and thoughts of several characters allows an author to develop comparisons between individuals and to portray more fully the nature of the relationships between them. Atwood's "The Resplendent Quetzal" consists of five sections. In the first four, the narrator reports alternately on the thoughts of Sarah and her husband, Edward, each of whom is in a different part of the Aztec ruins they are touring. Even in the concluding section, when Edward returns to his wife, the narrator presents the thoughts first of one and then the other. The abruptly shifting point of view indicates the nature of the couple's relationship.

Although able to enter into the mind of only one character, a limited third-person narrator is able to explore that character fully, often exposing the character's failure to perceive the nature of the situations in which she finds herself, as is the case in "Bliss," or presenting aspects of the character not understood by those around her, as in "The Story of an Hour." In the latter story, other people attribute the heroine's death to her shock of joy on discovering that her husband, presumed dead, is still alive. The narrator, in presenting the woman's thoughts as she sits alone after receiving the news of her husband's supposed death, provides readers with information that explains the true cause of her death.

Because they are characters in the stories they report on, first-person narrators usually have access to less information than do third-person narrators. The words of first-person narrators raise such questions as: "How reliably does the narrator interpret events, his or her own character, and the characters of other people?" The observer narrator, a representative of the townspeople in "A Rose for Emily," recounts incidents he has heard of or seen from a distance. Using such phrases as "we believed," "we said," and "we were sure," he also presents hypotheses about the recluse. Only after her death, when he, along with other townsmen, has entered her bedroom, does he make a discovery that provides an explanation of the elderly woman's life and casts light on the accuracy of her neighbours' suppositions about it. Through the use of this type of narrator, Faulkner creates a story that is as much about the townspeople who interpret and judge Emily Grierson as it is about her life itself.

First-person narrators who are the main characters in a story are also limited by the extent of the knowledge they possess. Moreover, qualities of their personalities may cause them to ignore, overlook, or misinterpret the significance of the actions in which they are involved and the characters with whom they interact. In the opening paragraph of "The Black Cat," the narrator states that he is presenting a "homely," that is, a plain, direct account of events. Later he notes, "I am above the weakness of seeking to establish a sequence of cause and effect." He does not seem to be aware that several personality defects, which he reveals during his account, may explain his actions. Other narrators may be more aware of themselves, and their narratives may present their consciousness of character change, as in "Bartleby, the Scrivener," in which the narrator seems to be as interested in explaining how the young man influenced him as he is in analyzing Bartleby himself.

## SYMBOLISM

Through an author's careful employment of **symbols** — objects, characters, or actions that stand for something beyond themselves — specific elements of many stories assume greater significance. Universal symbols, often called **archetypes**, are interpreted in much the same way in many different cultures. The use of the cycles of day and night and of the seasons to present the phases of human life is a familiar example. Cultural symbols hold special meanings for a specific group. For example, the cross embodies a number of complex spiritual beliefs for Christians. **Contextual symbols** are given or take on meaning only within the stories that contain them.

When employing universal or cultural symbols, authors usually assume their readers' general knowledge of the relationship between the literal objects, events, and characters and their symbolic meanings. Readers use this knowledge to interpret the symbols and hence to understand the stories they read more fully. For example, early in "Rappaccini's Daughter," Giovanni looks at the enclosed garden outside his window. Considering the garden in relation to the biblical Garden of Eden, readers may come to a fuller understanding of the theme of the fall from innocence and of the author's view of the character of the young man.

In "The Resplendent Quetzal," a cultural symbol takes on contextual meanings unique to the story. A sacred bird, whose feathers symbolize the souls of unborn babies to the Aztecs, it is the only bird Sarah decides she wishes to see. Edward, who "felt he was allowed to see birds only when they wanted him to," does not think there are any in the area they are visiting.

He is correct: neither one sees a quetzal. An understanding of what the bird symbolizes for each of them illuminates aspects of their characters.

In "Borders" and "The Loons," the titles introduce the major contextual symbols, which acquire additional meanings each time they appear. In the former story, the international boundary between Canada and the United States, the "border," comes to represent divisions, not only between countries, but also between cultures and even between members of a family. In "The Loons," the calls of the shy, elusive birds were "plaintive, and yet with a quality of chilling mockery ... [and] belonged to a world separated by aeons from our neat world of summer cottages and the lighted lamps of home." To the teenage narrator of the story, they stand for Piquette, a young, lonely Métis woman whom she had tried unsuccessfully to befriend.

## IRONY

**Irony**, one of the most frequently used techniques in stories, is of three types. Verbal irony is created when there is a difference between the apparent and actual meanings of a speaker's words. In "Rappaccini's Daughter," Baglioni offers Giovanni a cure for the sickness affecting him, heartily announcing, "Be of good cheer, son of my friend! It is not yet too late for the rescue." However, to himself he admits his true motivation: "We will thwart Rappaccini yet!" In dramatic irony, readers have clearer perceptions of situations than do the characters involved in them. In "Araby," the narrator is so involved in his emotions about Mangin's sister that he does not see how his thoughts and actions are indications of infatuation and sexual arousal, emotions that Joyce makes clear to the reader. Again, "Rappaccini's Daughter" provides an example. Giovanni offers Beatrice what he believes will be an antidote and thinks that, once cured of her toxic qualities, the two will live happily together. What results is not what he expected.

In some stories, the situational irony is of cosmic dimensions, as characters struggle against natural or supernatural forces that frequently defeat them. In "The Open Boat," the Oiler, who has been presented as the strongest and most courageous of the four men in the lifeboat, is the only person to die. Merit is of no importance in a harsh and impersonal universe, one that may have no guiding powers, as the Correspondent has vaguely realized during the ordeal.

Katherine Mansfield's "Bliss" contains all three types of irony. Harry practises verbal irony when speaking of Miss Fulton, a dinner guest, in terms that conceal his true attitude about her. The situational irony is introduced in the title, "Bliss," which refers to the emotion Bertha experiences for the first time. Because of it, she is "waiting for something ... divine to happen ... that she knew must happen ... infallibly." However, the events of the evening result in her feeling far from blissful. Bertha perceives the blossoming pear tree as a visual embodiment of her emotion and believes that Miss Fulton does as well. She is correct, but does not realize the cause of the other woman's feelings. On first reading, an attentive reader may notice in "Bliss" several instances of dramatic irony that subtly foreshadow the story's conclusion. These hints provide an undercurrent that contrasts Bertha's perceptions and anticipations with the realities of her situation.

## INTERPRETATION AND PERSONAL RESPONSE

Because of differences in gender, age, cultural backgrounds, and personal experiences, readers respond individually to short stories. Their interpretation begins with the words of the works themselves, for as creations of other individuals, these are influenced by their authors' gender, age, cultural and literary background, and personal experience. Full, informed response to a work requires that readers initially relinquish freedom of response, giving consideration to the contexts out of which a story emerged and the technical aspects of language used in writing it. Careful, analytical attention to a story will lead to speculation on an author's purpose in writing. Based on such inquiry, readers can engage in more informed evaluation of a work, considering how clearly and artistically the author has communicated and judging the validity of the work's theme. Then, having responded to it on its own terms, they can respond to it personally, relating it to their own lives, identifying with or reacting against the characters, accepting or rejecting the author's attitudes toward or interpretation of life, or modifying their own views in the light of those presented. In making informed personal responses, readers achieve a new freedom, one that helps them to enjoy stories more fully and to make the creating, telling, and reading of stories an integral part of their lives.

# Nathaniel Hawthorne (1804–1864)

A native of Salem, Massachusetts, where an ancestor was a judge in the seventeenth-century witch trials, Nathaniel Hawthorne set many of his short stories and *The Scarlet Letter*, his best-known novel, in colonial New England. He was more than a creator of historical fiction, however, describing himself as a writer who delved into "the depths of our common human nature." "Rappaccini's Daughter," for example, is set in sixteenth-century Italy, but does not deal with Renaissance history. Instead, it presents a common plot structure and theme: a young man's journey from country to city, symbolic of his coming of age. Hawthorne uses the garden as his central setting, introducing into the story the idea of a moral fall from innocence to experience. In addition to presenting Giovanni's ambiguous response to adult sexuality, as seen in the youth's shifting reactions to Beatrice and the garden, Hawthorne examines the profound effect that professional jealousies between the older authority figures, Baglioni and Rappaccini, have on the lives of Giovanni and Beatrice.

# RAPPACCINI'S DAUGHTER
## From the Writings of Aubépine [1]

A young man, named Giovanni Guasconti, came, very long ago, from the more southern region of Italy, to pursue his studies at the University of Padua. Giovanni, who had but a scanty supply of gold ducats in his pocket, took lodgings in a high and gloomy chamber of an old edifice, which looked not unworthy to have been the palace of a Paduan noble, and which, in fact, exhibited over its entrance the armorial bearings of a family long since extinct. The young stranger, who was not unstudied in the great poem of his country,[2] recollected that one of the ancestors of this family, and perhaps an occupant of this very mansion, had been pictured by Dante as a partaker of the immortal agonies of his Inferno. These reminiscences and associations, together with the tendency to heart-break natural to a young man for the first time out of his native sphere, caused Giovanni to sigh heavily, as he looked around the desolate and ill-furnished apartment.

"Holy Virgin, Signor," cried old dame Lisabetta, who, won by the youth's remarkable beauty of person, was kindly endeavoring to give the chamber a habitable air, "what a sigh was that to come out of a young man's heart! Do you find this old mansion gloomy? For the love of heaven, then, put your head out of the window, and you will see as bright sunshine as you have in Naples."

Guasconti mechanically did as the old woman advised, but could not quite agree with her that the Paduan sunshine was as cheerful as that of southern Italy. Such as it was, however, it fell upon a garden beneath the window, and expended its fostering influences on a variety of plants, which seemed to have been cultivated with exceeding care.

1 French for Hawthorn (tree). 2 *The Divine Comedy*, by Dante Alighieri. In this early-fourteenth-century Italian poem, the narrator is guided in a dream vision through Hell and Purgatory by the classical Roman poet Virgil, and through Heaven by a young maiden, Beatrice.

"Does this garden belong to the house?" asked Giovanni.

"Heaven forbid, Signor! — unless it were fruitful of better pot-herbs than any that grow there now," answered old Lisabetta. "No; that garden is cultivated by the own hands of Signor Giacomo Rappaccini, the famous Doctor, who, I warrant him, has been heard of as far as Naples. It is said that he distils these plants into medicines that are as potent as a charm. Oftentimes you may see the Signor Doctor at work, and perchance the Signora his daughter, too, gathering the strange flowers that grow in the garden."

The old woman had now done what she could for the aspect of the chamber, and, commending the young man to the protection of the saints, took her departure.

Giovanni still found no better occupation than to look down into the garden beneath his window. From its appearance, he judged it to be one of those botanic gardens, which were of earlier date in Padua than elsewhere in Italy, or in the world. Or, not improbably, it might once have been the pleasure-place of an opulent family; for there was the ruin of a marble fountain in the centre, sculptured with rare art, but so wofully shattered that it was impossible to trace the original design from the chaos of remaining fragments. The water, however, continued to gush and sparkle into the sunbeams as cheerfully as ever. A little gurgling sound ascended to the young man's window, and made him feel as if the fountain were an immortal spirit, that sung its song unceasingly, and without heeding the vicissitudes around it; while one century embodied it in marble, and another scattered the perishable garniture on the soil. All about the pool into which the water subsided, grew various plants, that seemed to require a plentiful supply of moisture for the nourishment of gigantic leaves, and, in some instances, flowers gorgeously magnificent. There was one shrub in particular, set in a marble vase in the midst of the pool, that bore a profusion of purple blossoms, each of which had the lustre and richness of a gem; and the whole together made a show so resplendent that it seemed enough to illuminate the garden, even had there been no sunshine. Every portion of the soil was peopled with plants and herbs, which, if less beautiful, still bore tokens of assiduous care; as if all had their individual virtues, known to the scientific mind that fostered them. Some were placed in urns, rich with old carving, and others in common garden-pots; some crept serpent-like along the ground, or climbed on high, using whatever means of ascent was offered them. One plant had wreathed itself round a statue of Vertumnus,[3] which was thus quite veiled and shrouded in a drapery of hanging foliage, so happily arranged that it might have served a sculptor for a study.

While Giovanni stood at the window, he heard a rustling behind a screen of leaves, and became aware that a person was at work in the garden. His figure soon emerged into view, and showed itself to be that of no common laborer, but a tall, emaciated, sallow, and sickly-looking man, dressed in a scholar's garb of black. He was beyond the middle term of life, with grey hair, a thin grey beard, and a face singularly marked with intellect and cultivation, but which could never, even in his more youthful days, have expressed much warmth of heart.

3 the Roman god of vegetation who seduced Pomona, goddess of fruits.

Nothing could exceed the intentness with which this scientific gardener examined every shrub which grew in his path; it seemed as if he was looking into their inmost nature, making observations in regard to their creative essence, and discovering why one leaf grew in this shape, and another in that, and wherefore such and such flowers differed among themselves in hue and perfume. Nevertheless, in spite of this deep intelligence on his part, there was no approach to intimacy between himself and these vegetable existences. On the contrary, he avoided their actual touch, or the direct inhaling of their odors, with a caution that impressed Giovanni most disagreeably; for the man's demeanor was that of one walking among malignant influences, such as savage beasts, or deadly snakes, or evil spirits, which, should he allow them one moment of license, would wreak upon him some terrible fatality. It was strangely frightful to the young man's imagination, to see this air of insecurity in a person cultivating a garden, that most simple and innocent of human toils, and which had been alike the joy and labor of the unfallen parents of the race. Was this garden, then, the Eden of the present world? — and this man, with such a perception of harm in what his own hands caused to grow, was he the Adam?

10    The distrustful gardener, while plucking away the dead leaves or pruning the too luxuriant growth of the shrubs, defended his hands with a pair of thick gloves. Nor were these his only armor. When, in his walk through the garden, he came to the magnificent plant that hung its purple gems beside the marble fountain, he placed a kind of mask over his mouth and nostrils, as if all this beauty did but conceal a deadlier malice. But finding his task still too dangerous, he drew back, removed the mask, and called loudly, but in the infirm voice of a person affected with inward disease:

"Beatrice! — Beatrice!"

"Here am I, my father! What would you?" cried a rich and youthful voice from the window of the opposite house; a voice as rich as a tropical sunset, and which made Giovanni, though he knew not why, think of deep hues of purple or crimson, and of perfumes heavily delectable. — "Are you in the garden?"

"Yes, Beatrice," answered the gardener, "and I need your help."

Soon there emerged from under a sculptured portal the figure of a young girl, arrayed with as much richness of taste as the most splendid of the flowers, beautiful as the day, and with a bloom so deep and vivid that one shade more would have been too much. She looked redundant with life, health, and energy; all of which attributes were bound down and compressed, as it were, and girdled tensely, in their luxuriance, by her virgin zone.[4] Yet Giovanni's fancy must have grown morbid, while he looked down into the garden; for the impression which the fair stranger made upon him was as if here were another flower, the human sister of those vegetable ones, as beautiful as they — more beautiful than the richest of them — but still to be touched only with a glove, nor to be approached without a mask. As Beatrice came down the garden path, it was observable that she handled and inhaled the odor of several of the plants, which her father had most sedulously avoided.

15    "Here, Beatrice," said the latter, — "see how many needful offices require to be done to our chief treasure. Yet, shattered as I am, my life might pay the

4 outer girdle-type garment worn on a woman's lower hips.

penalty of approaching it so closely as circumstances demand. Henceforth, I fear, this plant must be consigned to your sole charge."

"And gladly will I undertake it," cried again the rich tones of the young lady, as she bent towards the magnificent plant, and opened her arms as if to embrace it. "Yes, my sister, my splendor, it shall be Beatrice's task to nurse and serve thee; and thou shalt reward her with thy kisses and perfumed breath, which to her is as the breath of life!"

Then, with all the tenderness in her manner that was so strikingly expressed in her words, she busied herself with such attentions as the plant seemed to require; and Giovanni, at his lofty window, rubbed his eyes, and almost doubted whether it were a girl tending her favorite flower, or one sister performing the duties of affection to another. The scene soon terminated. Whether Doctor Rappaccini had finished his labors in the garden, or that his watchful eye had caught the stranger's face, he now took his daughter's arm and retired. Night was already closing in; oppressive exhalations seemed to proceed from the plants, and steal upward past the open window; and Giovanni, closing the lattice, went to his couch, and dreamed of a rich flower and beautiful girl. Flower and maiden were different and yet the same, and fraught with some strange peril in either shape.

But there is an influence in the light of morning that tends to rectify whatever errors of fancy, or even of judgment, we may have incurred during the sun's decline, or among the shadows of the night, or in the less wholesome glow of moonshine. Giovanni's first movement on starting from sleep, was to throw open the window, and gaze down into the garden which his dreams had made so fertile of mysteries. He was surprised, and a little ashamed, to find how real and matter-of-fact an affair it proved to be, in the first rays of the sun, which gilded the dew-drops that hung upon leaf and blossom, and, while giving a brighter beauty to each rare flower, brought everything within the limits of ordinary experience. The young man rejoiced, that, in the heart of the barren city, he had the privilege of overlooking this spot of lovely and luxuriant vegetation. It would serve, he said to himself, as a symbolic language, to keep him in communion with Nature. Neither the sickly and thought-worn Doctor Giacomo Rappaccini, it is true, nor his brilliant daughter, were now visible; so that Giovanni could not determine how much of the singularity which he attributed to both, was due to their own qualities, and how much to his wonder-working fancy. But he was inclined to take a most rational view of the whole matter.

In the course of the day, he paid his respects to Signor Pietro Baglioni, professor of medicine in the University, a physician of eminent repute, to whom Giovanni had brought a letter of introduction. The Professor was an elderly personage, apparently of genial nature, and habits that might almost be called jovial; he kept the young man to dinner, and made himself very agreeable by the freedom and liveliness of his conversation, especially when warmed by a flask or two of Tuscan wine. Giovanni, conceiving that men of science, inhabitants of the same city, must needs be on familiar terms with one another, took an opportunity to mention the name of Doctor Rappaccini. But the Professor did not respond with so much cordiality as he had anticipated.

"Ill would it become a teacher of the divine art of medicine," said Professor Pietro Baglioni, in answer to a question of Giovanni, "to withhold due and well-considered praise of a physician so eminently skilled as Rappaccini. But, on the other hand, I should answer it but scantily to my conscience, were I to permit a worthy youth like yourself, Signor Giovanni, the son of an ancient friend, to imbibe erroneous ideas respecting a man who might hereafter chance to hold your life and death in his hands. The truth is, our worshipful Doctor Rappaccini has as much science as any member of the faculty — with perhaps one single exception — in Padua, or all Italy. But there are certain grave objections to his professional character."

"And what are they?" asked the young man.

"Has my friend Giovanni any disease of body or heart, that he is so inquisitive about physicians?" said the Professor, with a smile. "But as for Rappaccini, it is said of him — and I, who know the man well, can answer for its truth — that he cares infinitely more for science than for mankind. His patients are interesting to him only as subjects for some new experiment. He would sacrifice human life, his own among the rest, or whatever else was dearest to him, for the sake of adding so much as a grain of mustard-seed to the great heap of his accumulated knowledge."

"Methinks he is an awful man, indeed," remarked Guasconti, mentally recalling the cold and purely intellectual aspect of Rappaccini. "And yet, worshipful Professor, is it not a noble spirit? Are there many men capable of so spiritual a love of science?"

"God forbid," answered the Professor, somewhat testily — "at least, unless they take sounder views of the healing art than those adopted by Rappaccini. It is his theory, that all medicinal virtues are comprised within those substances which we term vegetable poisons. These he cultivates with his own hands, and is said even to have produced new varieties of poison, more horribly deleterious than Nature, without the assistance of this learned person, would ever have plagued the world withal. That the Signor Doctor does less mischief than might be expected, with such dangerous substances, is undeniable. Now and then, it must be owned, he has effected — or seemed to effect — a marvellous cure. But, to tell you my private mind, Signor Giovanni, he should receive little credit for such instances of success — they being probably the work of chance — but should be held strictly accountable for his failures, which may justly be considered his own work."

25　　　The youth might have taken Baglioni's opinions with many grains of allowance, had he known that there was a professional warfare of long continuance between him and Doctor Rappaccini, in which the latter was generally thought to have gained the advantage. If the reader be inclined to judge for himself, we refer him to certain black-letter tracts on both sides, preserved in the medical department of the University of Padua.

"I know not, most learned Professor," returned Giovanni, after musing on what had been said of Rappaccini's exclusive zeal for science — "I know not how dearly this physician may love his art; but surely there is one object more dear to him. He has a daughter."

"Aha!" cried the Professor with a laugh. "So now our friend Giovanni's secret is out. You have heard of this daughter, whom all the young men in Padua are wild about, though not half a dozen have ever had the good hap to see her face. I know little of the Signora Beatrice, save that Rappaccini is said to have instructed her deeply in his science, and that, young and beautiful as fame reports her, she is already qualified to fill a professor's chair. Perchance her father destines her for mine! Other absurd rumors there be, not worth talking about, or listening to. So now, Signor Giovanni, drink off your glass of Lacryma."[5]

Guasconti returned to his lodgings somewhat heated with the wine he had quaffed, and which caused his brain to swim with strange fantasies in reference to Doctor Rappaccini and the beautiful Beatrice. On his way, happening to pass by a florist's, he bought a fresh bouquet of flowers.

Ascending to his chamber, he seated himself near the window, but within the shadow thrown by the depth of the wall, so that he could look down into the garden with little risk of being discovered. All beneath his eye was a solitude. The strange plants were basking in the sunshine, and now and then nodding gently to one another, as if in acknowledgment of sympathy and kindred. In the midst, by the shattered fountain, grew the magnificent shrub, with its purple gems clustering all over it; they glowed in the air, and gleamed back again out of the depths of the pool, which thus seemed to overflow with colored radiance from the rich reflection that was steeped in it. At first, as we have said, the garden was a solitude. Soon, however, — as Giovanni had half-hoped, half-feared, would be the case, — a figure appeared beneath the antique sculptured portal, and came down between the rows of plants, inhaling their various perfumes, as if she were one of those beings of old classic fable, that lived upon sweet odors. On again beholding Beatrice, the young man was even startled to perceive how much her beauty exceeded his recollection of it; so brilliant, so vivid was its character, that she glowed amid the sunlight, and, as Giovanni whispered to himself, positively illuminated the more shadowy intervals of the garden path. Her face being now more revealed than on the former occasion, he was struck by its expression of simplicity and sweetness; qualities that had not entered into his idea of her character, and which made him ask anew, what manner of mortal she might be. Nor did he fail again to observe, or imagine, an analogy between the beautiful girl and the gorgeous shrub that hung its gem-like flowers over the fountain; a resemblance which Beatrice seemed to have indulged a fantastic humor in heightening, both by the arrangement of her dress and the selection of its hues.

30    Approaching the shrub, she threw open her arms, as with a passionate ardor, and drew its branches into an intimate embrace; so intimate, that her features were hidden in its leafy bosom, and her glistening ringlets all intermingled with the flowers.

"Give me thy breath, my sister," exclaimed Beatrice; "for I am faint with common air! And give me this flower of thine, which I separate with gentlest fingers from the stem, and place it close beside my heart."

With these words, the beautiful daughter of Rappaccini plucked one of the richest blossoms of the shrub, and was about to fasten it in her bosom. But now, unless Giovanni's draughts of wine had bewildered his senses, a singular incident occurred. A small orange-colored reptile, of the lizard or chameleon species, chanced to be creeping along the path, just at the feet of Beatrice. It appeared to Giovanni — but, at the distance from which he gazed, he could

5 strong, sweet red wine named after the blood of Christ.

scarcely have seen anything so minute — it appeared to him, however, that a drop or two of moisture from the broken stem of the flower descended upon the lizard's head. For an instant, the reptile contorted itself violently, and then lay motionless in the sunshine. Beatrice observed this remarkable phenomenon, and crossed herself, sadly, but without surprise; nor did she therefore hesitate to arrange the fatal flower in her bosom. There it blushed, and almost glimmered with the dazzling effect of a precious stone, adding to her dress and aspect the one appropriate charm, which nothing else in the world could have supplied. But Giovanni, out of the shadow of his window, bent forward and shrank back, and murmured and trembled.

"Am I awake? Have I my senses?" said he to himself. "What is this being?— beautiful, shall I call her?— or inexpressibly terrible?"

Beatrice now strayed carelessly through the garden, approaching closer beneath Giovanni's window, so that he was compelled to thrust his head quite out of its concealment in order to gratify the intense and painful curiosity which she excited. At this moment, there came a beautiful insect over the garden wall; it had perhaps wandered through the city and found no flowers nor verdure among those antique haunts of men, until the heavy perfumes of Doctor Rappaccini's shrubs had lured it from afar. Without alighting on the flowers, this winged brightness seemed to be attracted by Beatrice, and lingered in the air and fluttered about her head. Now, here it could not be but that Giovanni Guasconti's eyes deceived him. Be that as it might, he fancied that while Beatrice was gazing at the insect with childish delight, it grew faint and fell at her feet;— its bright wings shivered; it was dead — from no cause that he could discern, unless it were the atmosphere of her breath. Again Beatrice crossed herself and sighed heavily, as she bent over the dead insect.

35 An impulsive movement of Giovanni drew her eyes to the window. There she beheld the beautiful head of the young man — rather a Grecian than an Italian head, with fair, regular features, and a glistening of gold among his ringlets — gazing down upon her like a being that hovered in mid-air. Scarcely knowing what he did, Giovanni threw down the bouquet which he had hitherto held in his hand.

"Signora," said he, "there are pure and healthful flowers. Wear them for the sake of Giovanni Guasconti!"

"Thanks, Signor," replied Beatrice, with her rich voice, that came forth as it were like a gush of music; and with a mirthful expression half childish and half woman-like. "I accept your gift, and would fain recompense it with this precious purple flower; but if I toss it into the air, it will not reach you. So Signor Guasconti must even content himself with my thanks."

She lifted the bouquet from the ground, and then as if inwardly ashamed at having stepped aside from her maidenly reserve to respond to a stranger's greeting, passed swiftly homeward through the garden. But, few as the moments were, it seemed to Giovanni when she was on the point of vanishing beneath the sculptured portal, that his beautiful bouquet was already beginning to wither in her grasp. It was an idle thought; there could be no possibility of distinguishing a faded flower from a fresh one at so great a distance.

For many days after this incident, the young man avoided the window that looked into Doctor Rappaccini's garden, as if something ugly and monstrous would have blasted his eye-sight, had he been betrayed into a glance. He felt conscious of having put himself, to a certain extent, within the influence of an unintelligible power, by the communication which he had opened with Beatrice. The wisest course would have been, if his heart were in any real danger, to quit his lodgings and Padua itself, at once; the next wiser, to have accustomed himself, as far as possible, to the familiar and day-light view of Beatrice; thus bringing her rigidly and systematically within the limits of ordinary experience. Least of all, while avoiding her sight, ought Giovanni to have remained so near this extraordinary being, that the proximity and possibility even of intercourse, should give a kind of substance and reality to the wild vagaries which his imagination ran riot continually in producing. Guasconti had not a deep heart — or at all events, its depths were not sounded now — but he had a quick fancy, and an ardent southern temperament, which rose every instant to a higher fever-pitch. Whether or no Beatrice possessed those terrible attributes — that fatal breath — the affinity with those so beautiful and deadly flowers — which were indicated by what Giovanni had witnessed, she had at least instilled a fierce and subtle poison into his system. It was not love, although her rich beauty was a madness to him; nor horror, even while he fancied her spirit to be imbued with the same baneful essence that seemed to pervade her physical frame; but a wild offspring of both love and horror that had each parent in it, and burned like one and shivered like the other. Giovanni knew not what to dread; still less did he know what to hope; yet hope and dread kept a continual warfare in his breast, alternately vanquishing one another and starting up afresh to renew the contest. Blessed are all simple emotions, be they dark or bright! It is the lurid intermixture of the two that produces the illuminating blaze of the infernal regions.

40    Sometimes he endeavored to assuage the fever of his spirit by a rapid walk through the streets of Padua, or beyond its gates; his footsteps kept time with the throbbings of his brain, so that the walk was apt to accelerate itself to a race. One day, he found himself arrested; his arm was seized by a portly personage who had turned back on recognizing the young man, and expended much breath in overtaking him.

"Signor Giovanni! — stay, my young friend!" cried he. "Have you forgotten me? That might well be the case, if I were as much altered as yourself."

It was Baglioni, whom Giovanni had avoided, ever since their first meeting, from a doubt that the Professor's sagacity would look too deeply into his secrets. Endeavoring to recover himself, he stared forth wildly from his inner world into the outer one, and spoke like a man in a dream:

"Yes; I am Giovanni Guasconti. You are Professor Pietro Baglioni. Now let me pass!"

"Not yet — not yet, Signor Giovanni Guasconti," said the Professor, smiling, but at the same time scrutinizing the youth with an earnest glance. — "What; did I grow up side by side with your father, and shall his son pass me like a stranger, in these old streets of Padua? Stand still, Signor Giovanni; for we must have a word or two, before we part."

45    "Speedily, then, most worshipful Professor, speedily!" said Giovanni, with feverish impatience. "Does not your worship see that I am in haste?"

Now, while he was speaking, there came a man in black along the street, stooping and moving feebly, like a person in inferior health. His face was all overspread with a most sickly and sallow hue, but yet so pervaded with an expression of piercing and active intellect, that an observer might easily have overlooked the merely physical attributes, and have seen only this wonderful energy. As he passed, this person exchanged a cold and distant salutation with Baglioni, but fixed his eyes upon Giovanni with an intentness that seemed to bring out whatever was within him worthy of notice. Nevertheless, there was a peculiar quietness in the look, as if taking merely a speculative, not a human, interest in the young man.

"It is Doctor Rappaccini!" whispered the Professor, when the stranger had passed. — "Has he ever seen your face before?"

"Not that I know," answered Giovanni, starting at the name.

"He *has* seen you! — he must have seen you!" said Baglioni, hastily. "For some purpose or other, this man of science is making a study of you. I know that look of his! It is the same that coldly illuminates his face, as he bends over a bird, a mouse, or a butterfly, which, in pursuance of some experiment, he has killed by the perfume of a flower; — a look as deep as Nature itself, but without Nature's warmth of love. Signor Giovanni, I will stake my life upon it, you are the subject of one of Rappaccini's experiments!"

50 "Will you make a fool of me?" cried Giovanni, passionately. "*That*, Signor Professor, were an untoward experiment."

"Patience, patience!" replied the imperturbable Professor. — "I tell thee, my poor Giovanni, that Rappaccini has a scientific interest in thee. Thou hast fallen into fearful hands! And the Signora Beatrice? What part does she act in this mystery?"

But Guasconti, finding Baglioni's pertinacity intolerable, here broke away, and was gone before the Professor could again seize his arm. He looked after the young man intently, and shook his head.

"This must not be," said Baglioni to himself. "The youth is the son of my old friend, and shall not come to any harm from which the arcana of medical science can preserve him. Besides, it is too insufferable an impertinence in Rappaccini, thus to snatch the lad out of my own hands, as I may say, and make use of him for his infernal experiments. This daughter of his! It shall be looked to. Perchance, most learned Rappaccini, I may foil you where you little dream of it!"

Meanwhile, Giovanni had pursued a circuitous route, and at length found himself at the door of his lodgings. As he crossed the threshold, he was met by old Lisabetta, who smirked and smiled, and was evidently desirous to attract his attention; vainly, however, as the ebullition of his feelings had momentarily subsided into a cold and dull vacuity. He turned his eyes full upon the withered face that was puckering itself into a smile, but seemed to behold it not. The old dame, therefore, laid her grasp upon his cloak.

55 "Signor! — Signor!" whispered she, still with a smile over the whole breadth of her visage, so that it looked not unlike a grotesque carving in wood, darkened by centuries — "Listen, Signor! There is a private entrance into the garden!"

"What do you say?" exclaimed Giovanni, turning quickly about, as if an inanimate thing should start into feverish life. — "A private entrance into Doctor Rappaccini's garden!"

"Hush! hush! — not so loud!" whispered Lisabetta, putting her hand over his mouth. "Yes; into the worshipful Doctor's garden, where you may see all his fine shrubbery. Many a young man in Padua would give gold to be admitted among those flowers."

Giovanni put a piece of gold into her hand.

"Show me the way," said he.

60      A surmise, probably excited by his conversation with Baglioni, crossed his mind, that this interposition of old Lisabetta might perchance be connected with the intrigue, whatever were its nature, in which the Professor seemed to suppose that Doctor Rappaccini was involving him. But such a suspicion, though it disturbed Giovanni, was inadequate to restrain him. The instant that he was aware of the possibility of approaching Beatrice, it seemed an absolute necessity of his existence to do so. It mattered not whether she were angel or demon; he was irrevocably within her sphere, and must obey the law that whirled him onward, in ever lessening circles, towards a result which he did not attempt to foreshadow. And yet, strange to say, there came across him a sudden doubt, whether this intense interest on his part were not delusory — whether it were really of so deep and positive a nature as to justify him in now thrusting himself into an incalculable position — whether it were not merely the fantasy of a young man's brain, only slightly, or not at all, connected with his heart!

He paused — hesitated — turned half about — but again went on. His withered guide led him along several obscure passages, and finally undid a door, through which, as it was opened, there came the sight and sound of rustling leaves, with the broken sunshine glimmering among them. Giovanni stepped forth, and forcing himself through the entanglement of a shrub that wreathed its tendrils over the hidden entrance, he stood beneath his own window, in the open area of Doctor Rappaccini's garden.

How often is it the case, that, when impossibilities have come to pass, and dreams have condensed their misty substance into tangible realities, we find ourselves calm, and even coldly self-possessed, amid circumstances which it would have been a delirium of joy or agony to anticipate! Fate delights to thwart us thus. Passion will choose his own time to rush upon the scene, and lingers sluggishly behind, when an appropriate adjustment of events would seem to summon his appearance. So was it now with Giovanni. Day after day, his pulses had throbbed with feverish blood, at the improbable idea of an interview with Beatrice, and of standing with her, face to face, in this very garden, basking in the Oriental sunshine of her beauty, and snatching from her full gaze the mystery which he deemed the riddle of his own existence. But now there was a singular and untimely equanimity within his breast. He threw a glance around the garden to discover if Beatrice or her father were present, and perceiving that he was alone, began a critical observation of the plants.

The aspect of one and all of them dissatisfied him; their gorgeousness seemed fierce, passionate, and even unnatural. There was hardly an individual shrub which a wanderer, straying by himself through a forest, would not have been startled to find growing wild, as if an unearthly face had glared at him out of the thicket. Several, also, would have shocked a delicate instinct by an appearance of artificialness, indicating that there had been such commixture, and, as it were, adultery of various vegetable species, that the production was no longer of God's making, but the monstrous offspring of man's depraved fancy, glowing with only an evil mockery of beauty. They were probably the result of experiment, which, in one or two cases, had succeeded in mingling plants individually lovely into a compound possessing the questionable and ominous character that distinguished the whole growth of the garden. In fine, Giovanni recognized but two or three plants in the collection, and those of a kind that he well knew to be poisonous. While busy with these contemplations, he heard the rustling of a silken garment, and turning, beheld Beatrice emerging from beneath the sculptured portal.

Giovanni had not considered with himself what should be his deportment; whether he should apologize for his intrusion into the garden, or assume that he was there with the privity, at least, if not by the desire, of Doctor Rappaccini or his daughter. But Beatrice's manner placed him at his ease, though leaving him still in doubt by what agency he had gained admittance. She came lightly along the path, and met him near the broken fountain. There was surprise in her face, but brightened by a simple and kind expression of pleasure.

65 "You are a connoisseur in flowers, Signor," said Beatrice with a smile, alluding to the bouquet which he had flung her from the window. "It is no marvel, therefore, if the sight of my father's rare collection has tempted you to take a nearer view. If he were here, he could tell you many strange and interesting facts as to the nature and habits of these shrubs, for he has spent a lifetime in such studies, and this garden is his world."

"And yourself, lady" — observed Giovanni — "if fame says true — you, likewise, are deeply skilled in the virtues indicated by these rich blossoms, and these spicy perfumes. Would you deign to be my instructress, I should prove an apter scholar than if taught by Signor Rappaccini himself."

"Are there such idle rumors?" asked Beatrice, with the music of a pleasant laugh. "Do people say that I am skilled in my father's science of plants? What a jest is there! No; though I have grown up among these flowers, I know no more of them than their hues and perfume; and sometimes, methinks I would fain rid myself of even that small knowledge. There are many flowers here, and those not the least brilliant, that shock and offend me, when they meet my eye. But, pray, Signor, do not believe these stories about my science. Believe nothing of me save what you see with your own eyes."

"And must I believe all that I have seen with my own eyes?" asked Giovanni pointedly, while the recollection of former scenes made him shrink. "No, Signora, you demand too little of me. Bid me believe nothing, save what comes from your own lips."

It would appear that Beatrice understood him. There came a deep flush to her cheek; but she looked full into Giovanni's eyes, and responded to his gaze of uneasy suspicion with a queen-like haughtiness.

70 "I do so bid you, Signor!" she replied. "Forget whatever you may have fancied in regard to me. If true to the outward senses, still it may be false in its

essence. But the words of Beatrice Rappaccini's lips are true from the depths of the heart outward. Those you may believe!"

A fervor glowed in her whole aspect, and beamed upon Giovanni's consciousness like the light of truth itself. But while she spoke, there was a fragrance in the atmosphere around her, rich and delightful, though evanescent, yet which the young man, from an indefinable reluctance, scarcely dared to draw into his lungs. It might be the odor of the flowers. Could it be Beatrice's breath, which thus embalmed her words with a strange richness, as if by steeping them in her heart? A faintness passed like a shadow over Giovanni, and flitted away; he seemed to gaze through the beautiful girl's eyes into her transparent soul, and felt no more doubt or fear.

The tinge of passion that had colored Beatrice's manner vanished; she became gay, and appeared to derive a pure delight from her communion with the youth, not unlike what the maiden of a lonely island might have felt, conversing with a voyager from the civilized world.[6] Evidently her experience of life had been confined within the limits of that garden. She talked now about matters as simple as the daylight or summer-clouds, and now asked questions in reference to the city, or Giovanni's distant home, his friends, his mother, and his sisters; questions indicating such seclusion, and such lack of familiarity with modes and forms, that Giovanni responded as if to an infant. Her spirit gushed out before him like a fresh rill, that was just catching its first glimpse of the sunlight, and wondering at the reflections of earth and sky which were flung into its bosom. There came thoughts, too, from a deep source, and fantasies of a gem-like brilliancy, as if diamonds and rubies sparkled upward among the bubbles of the fountain. Ever and anon, there gleamed across the young man's mind a sense of wonder, that he should be walking side by side with the being who had so wrought upon his imagination — whom he had idealized in such hues of terror — in whom he had positively witnessed such manifestations of dreadful attributes — that he should be conversing with Beatrice like a brother, and should find her so human and so maiden-like. But such reflections were only momentary; the effect of her character was too real, not to make itself familiar at once.

In this free intercourse, they had strayed through the garden, and now, after many turns among its avenues, were come to the shattered fountain, beside which grew the magnificent shrub with its treasury of glowing blossoms. A fragrance was diffused from it, which Giovanni recognized as identical with that which he had attributed to Beatrice's breath, but incomparably more powerful. As her eyes fell upon it, Giovanni beheld her press her hand to her bosom, as if her heart were throbbing suddenly and painfully.

"For the first time in my life," murmured she, addressing the shrub, "I had forgotten thee!"

"I remember, Signora," said Giovanni, "that you once promised to reward me with one of these living gems for the bouquet, which I had the happy boldness to fling to your feet. Permit me now to pluck it as a memorial of this interview."

6 implicit reference to the meeting of Miranda and Ferdinand in William Shakespeare's *The Tempest* (see page 478).

He made a step towards the shrub, with extended hand. But Beatrice darted forward, uttering a shriek that went through his heart like a dagger. She caught his hand, and drew it back with the whole force of her slender figure. Giovanni felt her touch thrilling through his fibres.

"Touch it not!" exclaimed she, in a voice of agony. "Not for thy life! It is fatal!"

Then, hiding her face, she fled from him, and vanished beneath the sculptured portal. As Giovanni followed her with his eyes, he beheld the emaciated figure and pale intelligence of Doctor Rappaccini, who had been watching the scene, he knew not how long, within the shadow of the entrance.

No sooner was Guasconti alone in his chamber, than the image of Beatrice came back to his passionate musings, invested with all the witchery that had been gathering around it ever since his first glimpse of her, and now likewise imbued with a tender warmth of girlish womanhood. She was human: her nature was endowed with all gentle and feminine qualities; she was worthiest to be worshipped; she was capable, surely, on her part, of the height and heroism of love. Those tokens, which he had hitherto considered as proofs of a frightful peculiarity in her physical and moral system, were now either forgotten, or, by the subtle sophistry of passion, transmuted into a golden crown of enchantment, rendering Beatrice the more admirable, by so much as she was the more unique. Whatever had looked ugly, was now beautiful; or, if incapable of such a change, it stole away and hid itself among those shapeless half-ideas, which throng the dim region beyond the daylight of our perfect consciousness. Thus did he spend the night, nor fell asleep, until the dawn had begun to awake the slumbering flowers in Doctor Rappaccini's garden, whither Giovanni's dreams doubtless led him. Up rose the sun in his due season, and flinging his beams upon the young man's eyelids, awoke him to a sense of pain. When thoroughly aroused, he became sensible of a burning and tingling agony in his hand — in his right hand — the very hand which Beatrice had grasped in her own, when he was on the point of plucking one of the gem-like flowers. On the back of that hand there was now a purple print, like that of four small fingers, and the likeness of a slender thumb upon his wrist.

Oh, how stubbornly does love — or even that cunning semblance of love which flourishes in the imagination, but strikes no depth of root into the heart — how stubbornly does it hold its faith, until the moment come, when it is doomed to vanish into thin mist! Giovanni wrapt a handkerchief about his hand, and wondered what evil thing had stung him, and soon forgot his pain in a reverie of Beatrice.

After the first interview, a second was in the inevitable course of what we call fate. A third; a fourth; and a meeting with Beatrice in the garden was no longer an incident in Giovanni's daily life, but the whole space in which he might be said to live; for the anticipation and memory of that ecstatic hour made up the remainder. Nor was it otherwise with the daughter of Rappaccini. She watched for the youth's appearance, and flew to his side with confidence as unreserved as if they had been playmates from early infancy — as if they were such playmates still. If, by any unwonted chance, he failed to come at the appointed moment, she stood beneath the window, and sent up the rich sweetness of her tones to float around him in his chamber, and echo and reverberate throughout his heart — "Giovanni! Giovanni! Why tarriest thou? Come down!" — And down he hastened into that Eden of poisonous flowers.

But, with all this intimate familiarity, there was still a reserve in Beatrice's demeanor, so rigidly and invariably sustained, that the idea of infringing it scarcely occurred to his imagination. By all appreciable signs, they loved; they had looked love, with eyes that conveyed the holy secret from the depths of one soul into the depths of the other, as if it were too sacred to be whispered by the way; they had even spoken love, in those gushes of passion when their spirits darted forth in articulated breath, like tongues of long-hidden flame; and yet there had been no seal of lips, no clasp of hands, nor any slightest caress, such as love claims and hallows. He had never touched one of the gleaming ringlets of her hair; her garment — so marked was the physical barrier between them — had never been waved against him by a breeze. On the few occasions when Giovanni had seemed tempted to overstep the limit, Beatrice grew so sad, so stern, and withal wore such a look of desolate separation, shuddering at itself, that not a spoken word was requisite to repel him. At such times, he was startled at the horrible suspicions that rose, monster-like, out of the caverns of his heart, and stared him in the face; his love grew thin and faint as the morning-mist; his doubts alone had substance. But when Beatrice's face brightened again, after the momentary shadow, she was transformed at once from the mysterious, questionable being, whom he had watched with so much awe and horror; she was now the beautiful and unsophisticated girl, whom he felt that his spirit knew with a certainty beyond all other knowledge.

A considerable time had now passed since Giovanni's last meeting with Baglioni. One morning, however, he was disagreeably surprised by a visit from the Professor, whom he had scarcely thought of for whole weeks, and would willingly have forgotten still longer. Given up, as he had long been, to a pervading excitement, he could tolerate no companions, except upon condition of their perfect sympathy with his present state of feeling. Such sympathy was not to be expected from Professor Baglioni.

The visitor chatted carelessly, for a few moments, about the gossip of the city and the University, and then took up another topic.

"I have been reading an old classic author lately," said he, "and met with a story that strangely interested me. Possibly you may remember it. It is of an Indian prince, who sent a beautiful woman as a present to Alexander the Great. She was as lovely as the dawn, and gorgeous as the sunset; but what especially distinguished her was a certain rich perfume in her breath — richer than a garden of Persian roses. Alexander, as was natural to a youthful conqueror, fell in love at first sight with this magnificent stranger. But a certain sage physician, happening to be present, discovered a terrible secret in regard to her."

"And what was that?" asked Giovanni, turning his eyes downward to avoid those of the Professor.

"That this lovely woman," continued Baglioni, with emphasis, "had been nourished with poisons from her birth upward, until her whole nature was so imbued with them, that she herself had become the deadliest poison in existence. Poison was her element of life. With that rich perfume of her breath, she blasted the very air. Her love would have been poison! — her embrace death! Is not this a marvelous tale?"

"A childish fable," answered Giovanni, nervously starting from his chair. "I marvel how your worship finds time to read such nonsense, among your graver studies."

"By the bye," said the Professor, looking uneasily about him, "what singular fragrance is this in your apartment? Is it the perfume of your gloves? It is faint, but delicious, and yet, after all, by no means agreeable. Were I to breathe it long, methinks it would make me ill. It is like the breath of a flower — but I see no flowers in the chamber."

90      "Nor are there any," replied Giovanni, who had turned pale as the Professor spoke; "nor, I think, is there any fragrance, except in your worship's imagination. Odors, being a sort of element combined of the sensual and the spiritual, are apt to deceive us in this manner. The recollection of a perfume — the bare idea of it — may easily be mistaken for a present reality."

"Aye; but my sober imagination does not often play such tricks," said Baglioni; "and were I to fancy any kind of odor, it would be that of some vile apothecary drug, wherewith my fingers are likely enough to be imbued. Our worshipful friend Rappaccini, as I have heard, tinctures his medicaments with odors richer than those of Araby.[7] Doubtless, likewise, the fair and learned Signora Beatrice would minister to her patients with draughts as sweet as a maiden's breath. But wo to him that sips them!"

Giovanni's face evinced many contending emotions. The tone in which the Professor alluded to the pure and lovely daughter of Rappaccini was a torture to his soul; and yet, the intimation of a view of her character, opposite to his own, gave instantaneous distinctness to a thousand dim suspicions, which now grinned at him like so many demons. But he strove hard to quell them, and to respond to Baglioni with a true lover's perfect faith.

"Signor Professor," said he, "you were my father's friend — perchance, too, it is your purpose to act a friendly part towards his son. I would fain feel nothing towards you, save respect and deference. But I pray you to observe, Signor, that there is one subject on which we must not speak. You know not the Signora Beatrice. You cannot, therefore, estimate the wrong — the blasphemy, I may even say — that is offered to her character by a light or injurious word."

"Giovanni! — my poor Giovanni!" answered the Professor, with a calm expression of pity, "I know this wretched girl far better than yourself. You shall hear the truth in respect to the poisoner Rappaccini, and his poisonous daughter. Yes; poisonous as she is beautiful! Listen; for even should you do violence to my grey hairs, it shall not silence me. That old fable of the Indian woman has become a truth, by the deep and deadly science of Rappaccini, and in the person of the lovely Beatrice!"

95      Giovanni groaned and hid his face.

"Her father," continued Baglioni, "was not restrained by natural affection from offering up his child, in this horrible manner, as the victim of his insane zeal for science. For — let us do him justice — he is as true a man of science as ever distilled his own heart in an alembic. What, then, will be your fate? Beyond a doubt, you are selected as the material of some new experiment. Perhaps the

---

7 the Middle East, a source of perfumes and spices popular in Europe.

result is to be death — perhaps a fate more awful still! Rappaccini, with what he calls the interest of science before his eyes, will hesitate at nothing."

"It is a dream!" muttered Giovanni to himself, "surely it is a dream!"

"But," resumed the Professor, "be of good cheer, son of my friend! It is not yet too late for the rescue. Possibly, we may even succeed in bringing back this miserable child within the limits of ordinary nature, from which her father's madness has estranged her. Behold this little silver vase! It was wrought by the hands of the renowned Benvenuto Cellini,[8] and is well worthy to be a love-gift to the fairest dame in Italy. But its contents are invaluable. One little sip of this antidote would have rendered the most virulent poisons of the Borgias innocuous. Doubt not that it will be as efficacious against those of Rappaccini. Bestow the vase, and the precious liquid within it, on your Beatrice, and hopefully await the result."

Baglioni laid a small, exquisitely wrought silver phial on the table, and withdrew, leaving what he had said to produce its effect upon the young man's mind.

"We will thwart Rappaccini yet!" thought he, chuckling to himself, as he descended the stairs. "But, let us confess the truth of him, he is a wonderful man! — a wonderful man indeed! A vile empiric, however, in his practice, and therefore not to be tolerated by those who respect the good old rules of the medical profession!"

Throughout Giovanni's whole acquaintance with Beatrice, he had occasionally, as we have said, been haunted by dark surmises as to her character. Yet, so thoroughly had she made herself felt by him as a simple, natural, most affectionate and guileless creature, that the image now held up by Professor Baglioni, looked as strange and incredible, as if it were not in accordance with his own original conception. True, there were ugly recollections connected with his first glimpses of the beautiful girl; he could not quite forget the bouquet that withered in her grasp, and the insect that perished amid the sunny air, by no ostensible agency, save the fragrance of her breath. These incidents, however, dissolving in the pure light of her character, had no longer the efficacy of facts, but were acknowledged as mistaken fantasies, by whatever testimony of the senses they might appear to be substantiated. There is something truer and more real, than what we can see with the eyes, and touch with the finger. On such better evidence, had Giovanni founded his confidence in Beatrice, though rather by the necessary force of her high attributes, than by any deep and generous faith, on his part. But, now, his spirit was incapable of sustaining itself at the height to which the early enthusiasm of passion had exalted it; he fell down, grovelling among earthly doubts, and defiled therewith the pure whiteness of Beatrice's image. Not that he gave her up; he did but distrust. He resolved to institute some decisive test that should satisfy him, once for all, whether there were those dreadful peculiarities in her physical nature, which could not be supposed to exist without some corresponding monstrosity of soul. His eyes, gazing down afar, might have deceived him as to the lizard, the insect, and the flowers. But if he could witness, at the distance of a few paces, the sudden blight of one fresh and healthful flower in Beatrice's

8 sixteenth-century Italian sculptor and goldsmith.

hand, there would be room for no further question. With this idea, he hastened to the florist's, and purchased a bouquet that was still gemmed with the morning dew-drops.

It was now the customary hour of his daily interview with Beatrice. Before descending into the garden, Giovanni failed not to look at his figure in the mirror; a vanity to be expected in a beautiful young man, yet, as displaying itself at that troubled and feverish moment, the token of a certain shallowness of feeling and insincerity of character. He did gaze, however, and said to himself, that his features had never before possessed so rich a grace, nor his eyes such vivacity, nor his cheeks so warm a hue of superabundant life.

"At least," thought he, "her poison has not yet insinuated itself into my system. I am no flower to perish in her grasp!"

With that thought, he turned his eyes on the bouquet, which he had never once laid aside from his hand. A thrill of indefinable horror shot through his frame, on perceiving that those dewy flowers were already beginning to droop; they wore the aspect of things that had been fresh and lovely, yesterday. Giovanni grew white as marble, and stood motionless before the mirror, staring at his own reflection there, as at the likeness of something frightful. He remembered Baglioni's remark about the fragrance that seemed to pervade the chamber. It must have been the poison in his breath! Then he shuddered — shuddered at himself! Recovering from his stupor, he began to watch, with curious eye, a spider that was busily at work, hanging its web from the antique cornice of the apartment, crossing and re-crossing the artful system of interwoven lines, as vigorous and active a spider as ever dangled from an old ceiling. Giovanni bent towards the insect, and emitted a deep, long breath. The spider suddenly ceased its toil; the web vibrated with a tremor originating in the body of the small artizan. Again Giovanni sent forth a breath, deeper, longer, and imbued with a venomous feeling out of his heart; he knew not whether he were wicked or only desperate. The spider made a convulsive gripe with his limbs, and hung dead across the window.

105 "Accursed! Accursed!" muttered Giovanni, addressing himself. "Hast thou grown so poisonous, that this deadly insect perishes by thy breath?"

At that moment, a rich, sweet voice came floating up from the garden: —

"Giovanni! Giovanni! It is past the hour! Why tarriest thou! Come down!"

"Yes," muttered Giovanni again. "She is the only being whom my breath may not slay! Would that it might!"

He rushed down, and in an instant, was standing before the bright and loving eyes of Beatrice. A moment ago, his wrath and despair had been so fierce that he could have desired nothing so much as to wither her by a glance. But, with her actual presence, there came influences which had too real an existence to be at once shaken off; recollections of the delicate and benign power of her feminine nature, which had so often enveloped him in a religious calm; recollections of many a holy and passionate outgush of her heart, when the pure fountain had been unsealed from its depths, and made visible in its transparency to his mental eye; recollections which, had Giovanni known how to estimate them, would have assured him that all this ugly mystery was but an earthly illusion, and that, whatever mist of evil might seem to have gathered over her, the real Beatrice was a heavenly angel. Incapable as he was of such high faith, still her presence had not utterly lost its magic. Giovanni's rage was quelled into an aspect of sullen insensibility. Beatrice, with a quick spiritual sense, immediately felt that there was a gulf of blackness between them, which neither he nor she could pass. They walked on together, sad and silent, and came thus to the marble fountain, and to its pool of water on the ground, in the midst of which grew the shrub that bore gem-like blossoms. Giovanni was affrighted at the eager enjoyment — the appetite, as it were — with which he found himself inhaling the fragrance of the flowers.

110    "Beatrice," asked he abruptly, "whence came this shrub?"

"My father created it," answered she, with simplicity.

"Created it! created it!" repeated Giovanni. "What mean you, Beatrice?"

"He is a man fearfully acquainted with the secrets of nature," replied Beatrice; "and, at the hour when I first drew breath, this plant sprang from the soil, the offspring of his science, of his intellect, while I was but his earthly child. Approach it not!" continued she, observing with terror that Giovanni was drawing nearer to the shrub. "It has qualities that you little dream of. But I, dearest Giovanni, — I grew up and blossomed with the plant, and was nourished with its breath. It was my sister, and I loved it with a human affection: for — alas! hast thou not suspected it? there was an awful doom."

Here Giovanni frowned so darkly upon her that Beatrice paused and trembled. But her faith in his tenderness reassured her, and made her blush that she had doubted for an instant.

115    "There was an awful doom," she continued, — "the effect of my father's fatal love of science — which estranged me from all society of my kind. Until Heaven sent thee, dearest Giovanni, Oh! how lonely was thy poor Beatrice!"

"Was it a hard doom?" asked Giovanni, fixing his eyes upon her.

"Only of late have I known how hard it was," answered she tenderly. "Oh, yes; but my heart was torpid, and therefore quiet."

Giovanni's rage broke forth from his sullen gloom like a lightning-flash out of a dark cloud.

"Accursed one!" cried he, with venomous scorn and anger. "And finding thy solitude wearisome, thou hast severed me, likewise, from all the warmth of life, and enticed me into thy region of unspeakable horror!"

120    "Giovanni!" exclaimed Beatrice, turning her large bright eyes upon his face. The force of his words had not found its way into her mind; she was merely thunder-struck.

"Yes, poisonous thing!" repeated Giovanni, beside himself with passion. "Thou hast done it! Thou hast blasted me! Thou hast filled my veins with poison! Thou hast made me as hateful, as ugly, as loathsome and deadly a creature as thyself, — a world's wonder of hideous monstrosity! Now — if our breath be happily as fatal to ourselves as to all others — let us join our lips in one kiss of unutterable hatred, and so die!"

"What has befallen me?" murmured Beatrice, with a low moan out of her heart. "Holy Virgin pity me, a poor heart-broken child!"

"Thou! Dost thou pray?" cried Giovanni, still with the same fiendish scorn. "Thy very prayers, as they come from thy lips, taint the atmosphere with death. Yes, yes; let us pray! Let us to church, and dip our fingers in the holy water at the portal! They that come after us will perish as by a pestilence. Let us sign crosses in the air! It will be scattering curses abroad in the likeness of holy symbols!"

"Giovanni," said Beatrice calmly, for her grief was beyond passion, "why dost thou join thyself with me thus in those terrible words? I, it is true, am the horrible thing thou namest me. But thou! — what hast thou to do, save with one other shudder at my hideous misery, to go forth out of the garden and mingle with thy race, and forget that there ever crawled on earth such a monster as poor Beatrice?"

125     "Dost thou pretend ignorance?" asked Giovanni, scowling upon her. "Behold! This power have I gained from the pure daughter of Rappaccini!"

There was a swarm of summer-insects flitting through the air, in search of the food promised by the flower-odors of the fatal garden. They circled round Giovanni's head, and were evidently attracted towards him by the same influence which had drawn them, for an instant, within the sphere of several of the shrubs. He sent forth a breath among them, and smiled bitterly at Beatrice, as at least a score of the insects fell dead upon the ground.

"I see it! I see it!" shrieked Beatrice. "It is my father's fatal science! No, no, Giovanni; it was not I! Never, never! I dreamed only to love thee, and be with thee a little time, and so to let thee pass away, leaving but thine image in mine heart. For, Giovanni — believe it — though my body be nourished with poison, my spirit is God's creature, and craves love as its daily food. But my father! — he has united us in this fearful sympathy. Yes; spurn me! — tread upon me! — kill me! Oh, what is death, after such words as thine? But it was not I! Not for a world of bliss would I have done it!"

Giovanni's passion had exhausted itself in its outburst from his lips. There now came across him a sense, mournful, and not without tenderness, of the intimate and peculiar relationship between Beatrice and himself. They stood, as it were, in an utter solitude, which would be made none the less solitary by the densest throng of human life. Ought not, then, the desert of humanity around them to press this insulated pair closer together? If they should be cruel to one another, who was there to be kind to them? Besides, thought Giovanni, might there not still be a hope of his returning within the limits of ordinary nature, and leading Beatrice — the redeemed Beatrice — by the hand? Oh, weak, and selfish, and unworthy spirit, that could dream of an earthly union and earthly happiness as possible, after such deep love had been so bitterly wronged as was Beatrice's love by Giovanni's blighting words! No, no; there could be no such hope. She must pass heavily, with that broken heart, across the borders of Time — she must bathe her hurts in some fount of Paradise, and forget her grief in the light of immortality — and *there* be well!

But Giovanni did not know it.

130     "Dear Beatrice," said he, approaching her, while she shrank away, as always at his approach, but now with a different impulse — "dearest Beatrice, our fate is not yet so desperate. Behold! There is a medicine, potent, as a wise physician has assured me, and almost divine in its efficacy. It is composed of ingredients the most opposite to those by which thy awful father has brought this calamity upon thee and me. It is distilled of blessed herbs. Shall we not quaff it together, and thus be purified from evil?"

"Give it me!" said Beatrice, extending her hand to receive the little silver phial which Giovanni took from his bosom. She added, with a peculiar emphasis: "I will drink — but do thou await the result."

She put Baglioni's antidote to her lips; and, at the same moment, the figure of Rappaccini emerged from the portal, and came slowly towards the marble fountain. As he drew near, the pale man of science seemed to gaze with a triumphant expression at the beautiful youth and maiden, as might an artist who should spend his life in achieving a picture or a group of statuary, and finally be satisfied with his success. He paused — his bent form grew erect with conscious power, he spread out his hands over them, in the attitude of a father imploring a blessing upon his children. But those were the same hands that had thrown poison into the stream of their lives! Giovanni trembled. Beatrice shuddered nervously, and pressed her hand upon her heart.

"My daughter," said Rappaccini, "thou art no longer lonely in the world! Pluck one of those precious gems from thy sister shrub, and bid thy bridegroom wear it in his bosom. It will not harm him now! My science, and the sympathy between thee and him, have so wrought within his system, that he now stands apart from common men, as thou dost, daughter of my pride and triumph, from ordinary women. Pass on, then, through the world, most dear to one another, and dreadful to all besides!"

"My father," said Beatrice, feebly — and still, as she spoke, she kept her hand upon her heart — "wherefore didst thou inflict this miserable doom upon thy child?"

135 "Miserable!" exclaimed Rappaccini. "What mean you, foolish girl? Dost thou deem it misery to be endowed with marvellous gifts, against which no power nor strength could avail an enemy? Misery, to be able to quell the mightiest with a breath? Misery, to be as terrible as thou art beautiful? Wouldst thou, then, have preferred the condition of a weak woman, exposed to all evil, and capable of none?"

"I would fain have been loved, not feared," murmured Beatrice, sinking down upon the ground. — "But now it matters not; I am going, father, where the evil, which thou hast striven to mingle with my being, will pass away like a dream — like the fragrance of these poisonous flowers, which will no longer taint my breath among the flowers of Eden. Farewell, Giovanni! Thy words of hatred are like lead within my heart — but they, too, will fall away as I ascend. Oh, was there not, from the first, more poison in thy nature than in mine?"

To Beatrice — so radically had her earthly part been wrought upon by Rappaccini's skill — as poison had been life, so the powerful antidote was death. And thus the poor victim of man's ingenuity and of thwarted nature, and of the fatality that attends all such efforts of perverted wisdom, perished there, at the feet of her father and Giovanni. Just at that moment, Professor Pietro Baglioni looked forth from the window, and called loudly, in a tone of triumph mixed with horror, to the thunder-stricken man of science:

"Rappaccini! Rappaccini! And is *this* the upshot of your experiment?"

(1844)

# Edgar Allan Poe  (1809–1849)

Born in Boston and raised by foster parents in Richmond, Virginia, Edgar Allan Poe struggled all his adult life to earn a living as a professional author, serving as a magazine editor and writing poetry, short stories, and reviews. A controversial figure before and after his death, he is remembered as a poet whose works influenced late-nineteenth- and early-twentieth-century French, British, and American poets, and as one of the first major writers of the short story. He developed a theory of the short story as a brief prose piece, capable of being read in no more than an hour, in which all details are selected and arranged to create a unified effect. Poe applied this theory skilfully in his story "The Black Cat." The narrator makes his "deathbed confession" to clarify for his audience the sequence of events that led to his present situation; however, his account reveals to readers aspects of his character of which he seems unaware and creates a sense of horror at his depravity.

# THE BLACK CAT

For the most wild, yet most homely narrative which I am about to pen, I neither expect nor solicit belief. Mad indeed would I be to expect it, in a case where my very senses reject their own evidence. Yet, mad am I not — and very surely do I not dream. But to-morrow I die, and to-day I would unburthen my soul. My immediate purpose is to place before the world, plainly, succinctly, and without comment, a series of mere household events. In their consequences, these events have terrified — have tortured — have destroyed me. Yet I will not attempt to expound them. To me, they have presented little but Horror — to many they will seem less terrible than *barroques*.[1] Hereafter, perhaps, some intellect may be found which will reduce my phantasm to the common-place — some intellect more calm, more logical, and far less excitable than my own, which will perceive, in the circumstances I detail with awe, nothing more than an ordinary succession of very natural causes and effects.

From my infancy I was noted for the docility and humanity of my disposition. My tenderness of heart was even so conspicuous as to make me the jest of my companions. I was especially fond of animals, and was indulged by my parents with a great variety of pets. With these I spent most of my time, and never was so happy as when feeding and caressing them. This peculiarity of character grew with my growth, and, in my manhood, I derived from it one of my principal sources of pleasure. To those who have cherished an affection for a faithful and sagacious dog, I need hardly be at the trouble of explaining the nature or the intensity of the gratification thus derivable. There is something in the unselfish and self-sacrificing love of a brute, which goes directly to the heart of him who has had frequent occasion to test the paltry friendship and gossamer fidelity of mere *Man*.

1 bizarre.

I married early, and was happy to find in my wife a disposition not uncongenial with my own. Observing my partiality for domestic pets, she lost no opportunity of procuring those of the most agreeable kind. We had birds, gold-fish, a fine dog, rabbits, a small monkey, and *a cat.*

This latter was a remarkably large and beautiful animal, entirely black, and sagacious to an astonishing degree. In speaking of his intelligence, my wife, who at heart was not a little tinctured with superstition, made frequent allusion to the ancient popular notion, which regarded all black cats as witches in disguise. Not that she was ever *serious* upon this point — and I mention the matter at all for no better reason than that it happens, just now, to be remembered.

Pluto[2] — this was the cat's name — was my favorite pet and playmate. I alone fed him, and he attended me wherever I went about the house. It was even with difficulty that I could prevent him from following me through the streets.

Our friendship lasted, in this manner, for several years, during which my general temperament and character — through the instrumentality of the Fiend Intemperance[3] — had (I blush to confess it) experienced a radical alteration for the worse. I grew, day by day, more moody, more irritable, more regardless of the feelings of others. I suffered myself to use intemperate language to my wife. At length, I even offered her personal violence. My pets, of course, were made to feel the change in my disposition. I not only neglected, but ill-used them. For Pluto, however, I still retained sufficient regard to restrain me from maltreating him, as I made no scruple of maltreating the rabbits, the monkey, or even the dog, when by accident, or through affection, they came in my way. But my disease grew upon me — for what disease is like Alcohol! — and at length even Pluto, who was now becoming old, and consequently somewhat peevish — even Pluto began to experience the effects of my ill temper.

One night, returning home, much intoxicated, from one of my haunts about town, I fancied that the cat avoided my presence. I seized him; when, in his fright at my violence, he inflicted a slight wound upon my hand with his teeth. The fury of a demon instantly possessed me. I knew myself no longer. My original soul seemed, at once, to take its flight from my body; and a more than fiendish malevolence, gin-nurtured, thrilled every fibre of my frame. I took from my waistcoat-pocket a pen-knife, opened it, grasped the poor beast by the throat, and deliberately cut one of its eyes from the socket! I blush, I burn, I shudder, while I pen the damnable atrocity.

When reason returned with the morning — when I had slept off the fumes of the night's debauch — I experienced a sentiment half of horror, half of remorse, for the crime of which I had been guilty; but it was, at best, a feeble and equivocal feeling, and the soul remained untouched. I again plunged into excess, and soon drowned in wine all memory of the deed.

In the meantime the cat slowly recovered. The socket of the lost eye presented, it is true, a frightful appearance, but he no longer appeared to suffer any pain. He went about the house as usual, but, as might be expected, fled in extreme terror at my approach. I had so much of my old heart left, as to be at first grieved by this evident dislike on the part of a creature which had once so

2 in Roman mythology, the god of the underworld.   3 alcoholism.

loved me. But this feeling soon gave place to irritation. And then came, as if to my final and irrevocable overthrow, the spirit of PERVERSENESS. Of this spirit philosophy takes no account. Yet I am not more sure that my soul lives, than I am that perverseness is one of the primitive impulses of the human heart — one of the indivisible primary faculties, or sentiments, which give direction to the character of Man. Who has not, a hundred times, found himself committing a vile or a silly action, for no other reason than because he knows he should *not*? Have we not a perpetual inclination, in the teeth of our best judgment, to violate that which is *Law*, merely because we understand it to be such? This spirit of perverseness, I say, came to my final overthrow. It was this unfathomable longing of the soul *to vex itself* — to offer violence to its own nature — to do wrong for the wrong's sake only — that urged me to continue and finally to consummate the injury I had inflicted upon the unoffending brute. One morning, in cool blood, I slipped a noose about its neck and hung it to the limb of a tree; — hung it with the tears streaming from my eyes, and with the bitterest remorse at my heart; — hung it *because* I knew that it had loved me, and *because* I felt it had given me no reason of offence; — hung it *because* I knew that in so doing I was committing a sin — a deadly sin that would so jeopardize my immortal soul as to place it — if such a thing were possible — even beyond the reach of the infinite mercy of the Most Merciful and Most Terrible God.

10     On the night of the day on which this cruel deed was done, I was aroused from sleep by the cry of fire. The curtains of my bed were in flames. The whole house was blazing. It was with great difficulty that my wife, a servant, and myself, made our escape from the conflagration. The destruction was complete. My entire worldly wealth was swallowed up, and I resigned myself thenceforward to despair.

I am above the weakness of seeking to establish a sequence of cause and effect, between the disaster and the atrocity. But I am detailing a chain of facts — and wish not to leave even a possible link imperfect. On the day succeeding the fire, I visited the ruins. The walls, with one exception, had fallen in. This exception was found in a compartment wall, not very thick, which stood about the middle of the house, and against which had rested the head of my bed. The plastering had here, in great measure, resisted the action of the fire — a fact which I attributed to its having been recently spread. About this wall a dense crowd were collected, and many persons seemed to be examining a particular portion of it with very minute and eager attention. The words "strange!" "singular!" and other similar expressions, excited my curiosity. I approached and saw, as if graven in *bas relief* upon the white surface, the figure of a gigantic *cat*. The impression was given with an accuracy truly marvellous. There was a rope about the animal's neck.

When I first beheld this apparition — for I could scarcely regard it as less — my wonder and my terror were extreme. But at length reflection came to my aid. The cat, I remembered, had been hung in a garden adjacent to the house. Upon the alarm of fire, this garden had been immediately filled by the crowd — by some one of whom the animal must have been cut from the tree and thrown, through an open window, into my chamber. This had probably been done with the view of arousing me from sleep. The falling of other walls had compressed the victim of my cruelty into the substance of the freshly-spread plaster; the lime of which, with the flames, and the *ammonia* from the carcass, had then accomplished the portraiture as I saw it.

Although I thus readily accounted to my reason, if not altogether to my conscience, for the startling fact just detailed, it did not the less fail to make a deep impression upon my fancy. For months I could not rid myself of the phantasm of the cat; and, during this period, there came back into my spirit a half-sentiment that seemed, but was not, remorse. I went so far as to regret the loss of the animal, and to look about me, among the vile haunts which I now habitually frequented, for another pet of the same species, and of somewhat similar appearance, with which to supply its place.

One night as I sat, half stupified, in a den of more than infamy, my attention was suddenly drawn to some black object, reposing upon the head of one of the immense hogsheads of Gin, or of Rum, which constituted the chief furniture of the apartment. I had been looking steadily at the top of this hogshead for some minutes, and what now caused me surprise was the fact that I had not sooner perceived the object thereupon. I approached it, and touched it with my hand. It was a black cat — a very large one — fully as large as Pluto, and closely resembling him in every respect but one. Pluto had not a white hair upon any portion of his body; but this cat had a large, although indefinite splotch of white, covering nearly the whole region of the breast.

15    Upon my touching him, he immediately arose, purred loudly, rubbed against my hand, and appeared delighted with my notice. This, then, was the very creature of which I was in search. I at once offered to purchase it of the landlord; but this person made no claim to it — knew nothing of it — had never seen it before.

I continued my caresses, and, when I prepared to go home, the animal evinced a disposition to accompany me. I permitted it to do so; occasionally stooping and patting it as I proceeded. When it reached the house it domesticated itself at once, and became immediately a great favorite with my wife.

For my own part, I soon found a dislike to it arising within me. This was just the reverse of what I had anticipated; but — I know not how or why it was — its evident fondness for myself rather disgusted and annoyed. By slow degrees, these feelings of disgust and annoyance rose into the bitterness of hatred. I avoided the creature; a certain sense of shame, and the remembrance of my former deed of cruelty, preventing me from physically abusing it. I did not, for some weeks, strike, or otherwise violently ill use it; but gradually — very gradually — I came to look upon it with unutterable loathing, and to flee silently from its odious presence, as from the breath of a pestilence.

What added, no doubt, to my hatred of the beast, was the discovery, on the morning after I brought it home, that, like Pluto, it also had been deprived of one of its eyes. This circumstance, however, only endeared it to my wife, who, as I have already said, possessed, in a high degree, that humanity of feeling which had once been my distinguishing trait, and the source of many of my simplest and purest pleasures.

With my aversion to this cat, however, its partiality for myself seemed to increase. It followed my footsteps with a pertinacity which it would be difficult to make the reader comprehend. Whenever I sat, it would crouch beneath my chair, or spring upon my knees, covering me with its loathsome caresses. If I arose to walk it would get between my feet and thus nearly throw me down, or, fastening its long and sharp claws in my dress, clamber, in this manner, to my breast. At such times, although I longed to destroy it with a blow, I was yet withheld from so doing, partly by a memory of my former crime, but chiefly — let me confess it at once — by absolute *dread* of the beast.

20      This dread was not exactly a dread of physical evil — and yet I should be at a loss how otherwise to define it. I am almost ashamed to own — yes, even in this felon's cell, I am almost ashamed to own — that the terror and horror with which the animal inspired me, had been heightened by one of the merest chimaeras it would be possible to conceive. My wife had called my attention, more than once, to the character of the mark of white hair, of which I have spoken, and which constituted the sole visible difference between the strange beast and the one I had destroyed. The reader will remember that this mark, although large, had been originally very indefinite; but, by slow degrees — degrees nearly imperceptible, and which for a long time my Reason struggled to reject as fanciful — it had, at length, assumed a rigorous distinctness of outline. It was now the representation of an object that I shudder to name — and for this, above all, I loathed, and dreaded, and would have rid myself of the monster *had I dared*— it was now, I say, the image of a hideous — of a ghastly thing — of the GALLOWS! — oh, mournful and terrible engine of Horror and of Crime — of Agony and of Death!

And now was I indeed wretched beyond the wretchedness of mere Humanity. And *a brute beast*— whose fellow I had contemptuously destroyed — *a brute beast* to work out for *me*— for me a man, fashioned in the image of the High God — so much of insufferable wo! Alas! neither by day nor by night knew I the blessing of Rest any more! During the former the creature left me no moment alone; and, in the latter, I started, hourly, from dreams of unutterable fear, to find the hot breath of *the thing* upon my face, and its vast weight — an incarnate Night-Mare that I had no power to shake off— incumbent eternally upon my *heart*!

Beneath the pressure of torments such as these, the feeble remnant of the good within me succumbed. Evil thoughts became my sole intimates — the darkest and most evil of thoughts. The moodiness of my usual temper increased to hatred of all things and of all mankind; while, from the sudden, frequent, and ungovernable outbursts of a fury to which I now blindly abandoned myself, my uncomplaining wife, alas! was the most usual and the most patient of sufferers.

One day she accompanied me, upon some household errand, into the cellar of the old building which our poverty compelled us to inhabit. The cat followed me down the steep stairs, and, nearly throwing me headlong, exasperated me to madness. Uplifting an axe, and forgetting, in my wrath, the childish dread which had hitherto stayed my hand, I aimed a blow at the animal which, of course, would have proved instantly fatal had it descended as I wished. But this blow was arrested by the hand of my wife. Goaded, by the interference, into a rage more than demoniacal, I withdrew my arm from her grasp and buried the axe in her brain. She fell dead upon the spot, without a groan.

This hideous murder accomplished, I set myself forthwith, and with entire deliberation, to the task of concealing the body. I knew that I could not remove it from the house, either by day or by night, without the risk of being observed by the neighbors. Many projects entered my mind. At one period I thought of cutting the corpse into minute fragments, and destroying them by fire. At another, I resolved to dig a grave for it in the floor of the cellar. Again, I deliberated about casting it in the well in the yard — about packing it in a box, as if merchandize, with the usual arrangements, and so getting a porter to take it from the house. Finally I hit upon what I considered a far better expedient than either of these. I determined to wall it up in the cellar — as the monks of the middle ages are recorded to have walled up their victims.

For a purpose such as this the cellar was well adapted. Its walls were loosely constructed, and had lately been plastered throughout with a rough plaster, which the dampness of the atmosphere had prevented from hardening. Moreover, in one of the walls was a projection, caused by a false chimney, or fireplace, that had been filled up, and made to resemble the rest of the cellar. I made no doubt that I could readily displace the bricks at this point, insert the corpse, and wall the whole up as before, so that no eye could detect any thing suspicious.

And in this calculation I was not deceived. By means of a crow-bar I easily dislodged the bricks, and, having carefully deposited the body against the inner wall, I propped it in that position, while, with little trouble, I re-laid the whole structure as it originally stood. Having procured mortar, sand, and hair, with every possible precaution, I prepared a plaster which could not be distinguished from the old, and with this I very carefully went over the new brick-work. When I had finished, I felt satisfied that all was right. The wall did not present the slightest appearance of having been disturbed. The rubbish on the floor was picked up with the minutest care. I looked around triumphantly, and said to myself — "Here at least, then, my labor has not been in vain."

My next step was to look for the beast which had been the cause of so much wretchedness; for I had, at length, firmly resolved to put it to death. Had I been able to meet with it, at the moment, there could have been no doubt of its fate; but it appeared that the crafty animal had been alarmed at the violence of my previous anger, and forebore to present itself in my present mood. It is impossible to describe, or to imagine, the deep, the blissful sense of relief which the absence of the detested creature occasioned in my bosom. It did not make its appearance during the night — and thus for one night at least, since its introduction into the house, I soundly and tranquilly slept; aye, *slept* even with the burden of murder upon my soul!

The second and the third day passed, and still my tormentor came not. Once again I breathed as a freeman. The monster, in terror, had fled the premises forever! I should behold it no more! My happiness was supreme! The guilt of my dark deed disturbed me but little. Some few inquiries had been made, but these had been readily answered. Even a search had been instituted — but of course nothing was to be discovered. I looked upon my future felicity as secured.

Upon the fourth day of the assassination, a party of the police came, very unexpectedly, into the house, and proceeded again to make rigorous

25

investigation of the premises. Secure, however, in the inscrutability of my place of concealment, I felt no embarrassment whatever. The officers bade me accompany them in their search. They left no nook or corner unexplored. At length, for the third or fourth time, they descended into the cellar. I quivered not in a muscle. My heart beat calmly as that of one who slumbers in innocence. I walked the cellar from end to end. I folded my arms upon my bosom, and roamed easily to and fro. The police were thoroughly satisfied and prepared to depart. The glee at my heart was too strong to be restrained. I burned to say if but one word, by way of triumph, and to render doubly sure their assurance of my guiltlessness.

30      "Gentlemen," I said at last, as the party ascended the steps, "I delight to have allayed your suspicions. I wish you all health, and a little more courtesy. By the bye, gentlemen, this — this is a very well constructed house." [In the rabid desire to say something easily, I scarcely knew what I uttered at all.] — "I may say an *excellently* well constructed house. These walls — are you going, gentlemen?— these walls are solidly put together;" and here, through the mere phrenzy of bravado, I rapped heavily, with a cane which I held in my hand, upon that very portion of the brick-work behind which stood the corpse of the wife of my bosom.

But may God shield and deliver me from the fangs of the Arch-Fiend! No sooner had the reverberation of my blows sunk into silence, than I was answered by a voice from within the tomb! — by a cry, at first muffled and broken, like the sobbing of a child, and then quickly swelling into one long, loud, and continuous scream, utterly anomalous and inhuman — a howl — a wailing shriek, half of horror and half of triumph, such as might have arisen only out of hell, conjointly from the throats of the damned in their agony and of the demons that exult in the damnation.

Of my own thoughts it is folly to speak. Swooning, I staggered to the opposite wall. For one instant the party upon the stairs remained motionless, through extremity of terror and of awe. In the next, a dozen stout arms were toiling at the wall. It fell bodily. The corpse, already greatly decayed and clotted with gore, stood erect before the eyes of the spectators. Upon its head, with red extended mouth and solitary eye of fire, sat the hideous beast whose craft had seduced me into murder, and whose informing voice had consigned me to the hangman. I had walled the monster up within the tomb!

(1843)

# Herman Melville   (1819–1891)

Born in New York City, Herman Melville spent many years as a sailor, including a cruise on a whaling ship, before becoming a writer. His most famous book, *Moby-Dick*, combined factual details about whaling with a symbolic examination about the nature of reality, particularly the conflict between good and evil. It is narrated by Ishmael, a quiet, thoughtful crew member, and presents the monomaniacal quest of Captain Ahab to slay a great white whale. Although "Bartleby, the Scrivener," written shortly after the novel, is much shorter and is set in a large city, it bears many similarities to *Moby-Dick*. The unnamed narrator is fascinated by a character who is much different from him, as Ishmael was fascinated by Ahab. The realistic and mundane details of a law office are given symbolic meanings, particularly the blank wall at which Bartleby stares. The lonely scrivener represents the condition of many human beings, orphans and "isolatoes," as Melville termed them, in a world where the significance of life, if there is any, cannot usually be understood. The short story also satirizes nineteenth-century Americans' preoccupation with the acquisition of wealth.

# BARTLEBY, THE SCRIVENER
## A Story of Wall-Street

I am a rather elderly man. The nature of my avocations for the last thirty years has brought me into more than ordinary contact with what would seem an interesting and somewhat singular set of men, of whom as yet nothing that I know of has ever been written: — I mean the law-copyists or scriveners. I have known very many of them, professionally and privately, and if I pleased, could relate divers histories, at which good-natured gentlemen might smile, and sentimental souls might weep. But I waive the biographies of all other scriveners for a few passages in the life of Bartleby, who was a scrivener the strangest I ever saw or heard of. While of other law-copyists I might write the complete life, of Bartleby nothing of that sort can be done. I believe that no materials exist for a full and satisfactory biography of this man. It is an irreparable loss to literature. Bartleby was one of those beings of whom nothing is ascertainable, except from the original sources, and in his case those are very small. What my own astonished eyes saw of Bartleby, *that* is all I know of him, except, indeed, one vague report which will appear in the sequel.

Ere introducing the scrivener, as he first appeared to me, it is fit I make some mention of myself, my *employés*, my business, my chambers, and general surroundings; because some such description is indispensable to an adequate understanding of the chief character about to be presented.

Imprimis: I am a man who, from his youth upwards, has been filled with a profound conviction that the easiest way of life is the best. Hence, though I belong to a profession proverbially energetic and nervous, even to turbulence, at times, yet nothing of that sort have I ever suffered to invade my peace. I am one of those unambitious lawyers who never addresses a jury, or in any way draws down public applause; but in the cool tranquillity of a snug retreat, do a snug business among rich men's bonds and mortgages and title-deeds. All who know me, consider me an eminently *safe* man. The late John Jacob Astor,[1] a personage little given to poetic enthusiasm, had no hesitation in pronouncing my first grand point to be prudence; my next, method. I do not speak it in vanity, but simply record the fact, that I was not unemployed in my profession by the late John Jacob Astor; a name which, I admit, I love to repeat, for it hath a rounded and orbicular sound to it, and rings like unto bullion. I will freely add, that I was not insensible to the late John Jacob Astor's good opinion.

Some time prior to the period at which this little history begins, my avocations had been largely increased. The good old office, now extinct in the State of New-York, of a Master in Chancery,[2] had been conferred upon me. It was not a very arduous office, but very pleasantly remunerative. I seldom lose my temper; much more seldom indulge in dangerous indignation at wrongs and outrages; but I must be permitted to be rash here and declare, that I consider the sudden and violent abrogation of the office of Master in Chancery, by the new Constitution, as a — premature act; inasmuch as I had counted upon a life-lease of the profits, whereas I only received those of a few short years. But this is by the way.

5     My chambers were up stairs at No. — Wall-street.[3] At one end they looked upon the white wall of the interior of a spacious sky-light shaft, penetrating the building from top to bottom. This view might have been considered rather tame than otherwise, deficient in what landscape painters call "life." But if so, the view from the other end of my chambers offered, at least, a contrast, if nothing more. In that direction my windows commanded an unobstructed view of a lofty brick wall, black by age and everlasting shade; which wall required no spy-glass to bring out its lurking beauties, but for the benefit of all near-sighted spectators, was pushed up to within ten feet of my window panes. Owing to the great height of the surrounding buildings, and my chambers being on the second floor, the interval between this wall and mine not a little resembled a huge square cistern.

At the period just preceding the advent of Bartleby, I had two persons as copyists in my employment, and a promising lad as an office-boy. First, Turkey; second, Nippers; third, Ginger Nut. These may seem names, the like of which are not usually found in the Directory. In truth they were nicknames, mutually conferred upon each other by my three clerks, and were deemed expressive of their respective persons or characters. Turkey was a short, pursy Englishman of about my own age, that is, somewhere not far from sixty. In the morning, one might say, his face was of a fine florid hue, but after twelve o'clock, meridian — his dinner hour — it blazed like a grate full of Christmas coals; and continued blazing — but, as it were, with a gradual wane — till 6 o'clock, P.M. or thereabouts, after which I saw no more of the proprietor of the face, which gaining its meridian with the sun, seemed to set with it, to rise, culminate, and decline the following day, with the like regularity and undiminished glory.

---

1 at the time of his death in 1848, Astor was the richest man in the United States. 2 officer of the court whose duties included taking testimonies, administering oaths, and acknowledging deeds. 3 located in New York City, the financial centre of the United States.

There are many singular coincidences I have known in the course of my life, not the least among which was the fact, that exactly when Turkey displayed his fullest beams from his red and radiant countenance, just then, too, at that critical moment, began the daily period when I considered his business capacities as seriously disturbed for the remainder of the twenty-four hours. Not that he was absolutely idle, or averse to business then; far from it. The difficulty was, he was apt to be altogether too energetic. There was a strange, inflamed, flurried, flighty recklessness of activity about him. He would be incautious in dipping his pen into his inkstand. All his blots upon my documents, were dropped there after twelve o'clock, meridian. Indeed, not only would he be reckless and sadly given to making blots in the afternoon, but some days he went further, and was rather noisy. At such times, too, his face flamed with augmented blazonry, as if cannel coal had been heaped on anthracite. He made an unpleasant racket with his chair; spilled his sandbox; in mending his pens, impatiently split them all to pieces, and threw them on the floor in a sudden passion; stood up and leaned over his table, boxing his papers about in a most indecorous manner, very sad to behold in an elderly man like him. Nevertheless, as he was in many ways a most valuable person to me, and all the time before twelve o'clock, meridian, was the quickest, steadiest creature too, accomplishing a great deal of work in a style not easy to be matched — for these reasons, I was willing to overlook his eccentricities, though indeed, occasionally, I remonstrated with him. I did this very gently, however, because, though the civilest, nay, the blandest and most reverential of men in the morning, yet in the afternoon he was disposed, upon provocation, to be slightly rash with his tongue, in fact, insolent. Now, valuing his morning services as I did, and resolved not to lose them; yet, at the same time made uncomfortable by his inflamed ways after twelve o'clock; and being a man of peace, unwilling by my admonitions to call forth unseemly retorts from him; I took upon me, one Saturday noon (he was always worse on Saturdays), to hint to him, very kindly, that perhaps now that he was growing old, it might be well to abridge his labors; in short, he need not come to my chambers after twelve o'clock, but, dinner over, had best go home to his lodgings and rest himself till tea-time. But no; he insisted upon his afternoon devotions. His countenance became intolerably fervid, as he oratorically assured me — gesticulating with a long ruler at the other end of the room — that if his services in the morning were useful, how indispensable, then, in the afternoon?

"With submission, sir," said Turkey on this occasion, "I consider myself your right-hand man. In the morning I but marshal and deploy my columns; but in the afternoon I put myself at their head, and gallantly charge the foe, thus!" — and he made a violent thrust with the ruler.

"But the blots, Turkey," intimated I.

"True, — but, with submission, sir, behold these hairs! I am getting old. Surely, sir, a blot or two of a warm afternoon is not to be severely urged against gray hairs. Old age — even if it blot the page — is honorable. With submission, sir, we *both* are getting old."

10     This appeal to my fellow-feeling was hardly to be resisted. At all events, I saw that go he would not. So I made up my mind to let him stay, resolving, nevertheless, to see to it, that during the afternoon he had to do with my less important papers.

Nippers, the second on my list, was a whiskered, sallow, and, upon the whole, rather piratical-looking young man of about five and twenty. I always deemed him the victim of two evil powers — ambition and indigestion. The ambition was evinced by a certain impatience of the duties of a mere copyist, an unwarrantable usurpation of strictly professional affairs, such as the original drawing up of legal documents. The indigestion seemed betokened in an occasional nervous testiness and grinning irritability, causing the teeth to audibly grind together over mistakes committed in copying; unnecessary maledictions, hissed, rather than spoken, in the heat of business; and especially by a continual discontent with the height of the table where he worked. Though of a very ingenious mechanical turn, Nippers could never get this table to suit him. He put chips under it, blocks of various sorts, bits of pasteboard, and at last went so far as to attempt an exquisite adjustment by final pieces of folded blotting-paper. But no invention would answer. If, for the sake of easing his back, he brought the table lid at a sharp angle well up towards his chin, and wrote there like a man using the steep roof of a Dutch house for his desk: — then he declared that it stopped the circulation in his arms. If now he lowered the table to his waistbands, and stooped over it in writing, then there was a sore aching in his back. In short, the truth of the matter was, Nippers knew not what he wanted. Or, if he wanted any thing, it was to be rid of a scrivener's table altogether. Among the manifestations of his diseased ambition was a fondness he had for receiving visits from certain ambiguous-looking fellows in seedy coats, whom he called his clients. Indeed I was aware that not only was he, at times, considerable of a ward-politician,[4] but he occasionally did a little business at the Justices' courts, and was not unknown on the steps of the Tombs.[5] I have good reason to believe, however, that one individual who called upon him at my chambers, and who, with a grand air, he insisted was his client, was no other than a dun, and the alleged title-deed, a bill. But with all his failings, and the annoyances he caused me, Nippers, like his compatriot Turkey, was a very useful man to me; wrote a neat, swift hand; and, when he chose, was not deficient in a gentlemanly sort of deportment. Added to this, he always dressed in a gentlemanly sort of way; and so, incidentally, reflected credit upon my chambers. Whereas with respect to Turkey, I had much ado to keep him from being a reproach to me. His clothes were apt to look oily and smell of eating-houses. He wore his pantaloons very loose and baggy in summer. His coats were execrable; his hat not to be handled. But while the hat was a thing of indifference to me, inasmuch as his natural civility and deference, as a dependent Englishman, always led him to doff it the moment he entered the room, yet his coat was another matter. Concerning his coats, I reasoned with him; but with no effect. The truth was, I suppose, that a man with so small an income, could not afford to sport such a lustrous face and a lustrous coat at one and the same time. As Nippers once observed, Turkey's money went chiefly for red ink. One winter day I presented Turkey with a highly-respectable looking coat of my own, a padded gray coat, of a most comfortable warmth, and which buttoned straight up from the knee to the neck. I thought Turkey would appreciate the favor, and abate his rashness and obstreperousness of afternoons. But no. I verily believe that buttoning himself up in so downy and blanket-like a coat had a pernicious effect upon him; upon the same principle that too much oats are bad for horses. In fact, precisely as a rash, restive horse is said to feel his oats, so Turkey felt his coat. It made him insolent. He was a man whom prosperity harmed.

Though concerning the self-indulgent habits of Turkey I had my own private surmises, yet touching Nippers I was well persuaded that whatever might be his faults in other respects, he was, at least, a temperate young man. But indeed, nature herself seemed to have been his vintner, and at his birth charged him so thoroughly with an irritable, brandy-like disposition, that all subsequent potations were needless. When I consider how, amid the stillness of my chambers, Nippers would sometimes impatiently rise from his seat, and stooping over his table, spread his arms wide apart, seize the whole desk, and move it, and jerk it, with a grim, grinding motion on the floor, as if the table were a perverse voluntary agent, intent on thwarting and vexing him; I plainly perceive that for Nippers, brandy and water were altogether superfluous.

It was fortunate for me that, owing to its peculiar cause — indigestion — the irritability and consequent nervousness of Nippers, were mainly observable in the morning, while in the afternoon he was comparatively mild. So that Turkey's paroxysms only coming on about twelve o'clock, I never had to do with their eccentricities at one time. Their fits relieved each other like guards. When Nippers' was on, Turkey's was off; and *vice versa*. This was a good natural arrangement under the circumstances.

Ginger Nut, the third on my list, was a lad some twelve years old. His father was a carman,[6] ambitious of seeing his son on the bench instead of a cart, before he died. So he sent him to my office as student at law, errand boy, and cleaner and sweeper, at the rate of one dollar a week. He had a little desk to himself, but he did not use it much. Upon inspection, the drawer exhibited a great array of the shells of various sorts of nuts. Indeed, to this quick-witted youth the whole noble science of the law was contained in a nut-shell. Not the least among the employments of Ginger Nut, as well as one which he discharged with the most alacrity, was his duty as cake and apple purveyor for Turkey and Nippers. Copying law papers being proverbially a dry, husky sort of business, my two scriveners were fain to moisten their mouths very often with Spitzenbergs[7] to be had at the numerous stalls nigh the Custom House and Post Office. Also, they sent Ginger Nut very frequently for that peculiar cake — small, flat, round, and very spicy — after which he had been named by them. Of a cold morning when business was but dull, Turkey would gobble up scores of these cakes, as if they were mere wafers — indeed they sell them at the rate of six or eight for a penny — the scrape of his pen blending with the crunching of the crisp particles in his mouth. Of all the fiery afternoon blunders and flurried rashnesses of Turkey, was his once moistening a ginger-cake between his lips, and clapping it on to a mortgage for a seal. I came within an ace of dismissing him then. But he mollified me by making an oriental bow, and saying — "With submission, sir, it was generous of me to find you in stationery on my own account."

6 driver of a cart.  7 variety of apple.

15     Now my original business — that of a conveyancer[8] and title hunter, and drawer-up of recondite documents of all sorts — was considerably increased by receiving the master's office. There was now great work for scriveners. Not only must I push the clerks already with me, but I must have additional help. In answer to my advertisement, a motionless young man one morning, stood upon my office threshold, the door being open, for it was summer. I can see that figure now — pallidly neat, pitiably respectable, incurably forlorn! It was Bartleby.

    After a few words touching his qualifications, I engaged him, glad to have among my corps of copyists a man of so singularly sedate an aspect, which I thought might operate beneficially upon the flighty temper of Turkey, and the fiery one of Nippers.

    I should have stated before that ground glass folding-doors divided my premises into two parts, one of which was occupied by my scriveners, the other by myself. According to my humor I threw open these doors, or closed them. I resolved to assign Bartleby a corner by the folding-doors, but on my side of them, so as to have this quiet man within easy call, in case any trifling thing was to be done. I placed his desk close up to a small side-window in that part of the room, a window which originally had afforded a lateral view of certain grimy back-yards and bricks, but which, owing to subsequent erections, commanded at present no view at all, though it gave some light. Within three feet of the panes was a wall, and the light came down from far above, between two lofty buildings, as from a very small opening in a dome. Still further to a satisfactory arrangement, I procured a high green folding screen, which might entirely isolate Bartleby from my sight, though not remove him from my voice. And thus, in a manner, privacy and society were conjoined.

    At first Bartleby did an extraordinary quantity of writing. As if long famishing for something to copy, he seemed to gorge himself on my documents. There was no pause for digestion. He ran a day and night line, copying by sun-light and by candle-light. I should have been quite delighted with his application, had he been cheerfully industrious. But he wrote on silently, palely, mechanically.

    It is, of course, an indispensable part of a scrivener's business to verify the accuracy of his copy, word by word. Where there are two or more scriveners in an office, they assist each other in this examination, one reading from the copy, the other holding the original. It is a very dull, wearisome, and lethargic affair. I can readily imagine that to some sanguine temperaments it would be altogether intolerable. For example, I cannot credit that the mettlesome poet Byron[9] would have contentedly sat down with Bartleby to examine a law document of, say five hundred pages, closely written in a crimpy hand.

20     Now and then, in the haste of business, it had been my habit to assist in comparing some brief document myself, calling Turkey or Nippers for this purpose. One object I had in placing Bartleby so handy to me behind the screen, was to avail myself of his services on such trivial occasions. It was on the third day, I think, of his being with me, and before any necessity had arisen for having his own writing examined, that, being much hurried to complete a

8 person who prepares documents for property transfers.  9 an English poet of the early nineteenth century, Byron was known for his flamboyant temperament.

small affair I had in hand, I abruptly called to Bartleby. In my haste and natural expectancy of instant compliance, I sat with my head bent over the original on my desk, and my right hand sideways, and somewhat nervously extended with the copy, so that immediately upon emerging from his retreat, Bartleby might snatch it and proceed to business without the least delay.

In this very attitude did I sit when I called to him, rapidly stating what it was I wanted him to do — namely, to examine a small paper with me. Imagine my surprise, nay, my consternation, when without moving from his privacy, Bartleby in a singularly mild, firm voice, replied, "I would prefer not to."

I sat awhile in perfect silence, rallying my stunned faculties. Immediately it occurred to me that my ears had deceived me, or Bartleby had entirely misunderstood my meaning. I repeated my request in the clearest tone I could assume. But in quite as clear a one came the previous reply, "I would prefer not to."

"Prefer not to," echoed I, rising in high excitement, and crossing the room with a stride. "What do you mean? Are you moon-struck? I want you to help me compare this sheet here — take it," and I thrust it towards him.

"I would prefer not to," said he.

25    I looked at him steadfastly. His face was leanly composed; his gray eye dimly calm. Not a wrinkle of agitation rippled him. Had there been the least uneasiness, anger, impatience or impertinence in his manner; in other words, had there been any thing ordinarily human about him, doubtless I should have violently dismissed him from the premises. But as it was, I should have as soon thought of turning my pale plaster-of-paris bust of Cicero out of doors. I stood gazing at him awhile, as he went on with his own writing, and then reseated myself at my desk. This is very strange, thought I. What had one best do? But my business hurried me. I concluded to forget the matter for the present, reserving it for my future leisure. So calling Nippers from the other room, the paper was speedily examined.

A few days after this, Bartleby concluded four lengthy documents, being quadruplicates of a week's testimony taken before me in my High Court of Chancery. It became necessary to examine them. It was an important suit, and great accuracy was imperative. Having all things arranged I called Turkey, Nippers and Ginger Nut from the next room, meaning to place the four copies in the hands of my four clerks, while I should read from the original. Accordingly Turkey, Nippers and Ginger Nut had taken their seats in a row, each with his document in hand, when I called to Bartleby to join this interesting group.

"Bartleby! quick, I am waiting."

I heard a slow scrape of his chair legs on the uncarpeted floor, and soon he appeared standing at the entrance of his hermitage.

"What is wanted?" said he mildly.

30    "The copies, the copies," said I hurriedly. "We are going to examine them. There" — and I held towards him the fourth quadruplicate.

"I would prefer not to," he said, and gently disappeared behind the screen.

For a few moments I was turned into a pillar of salt,[10] standing at the head of my seated column of clerks. Recovering myself, I advanced towards the screen, and demanded the reason for such extraordinary conduct.

---

10 in Genesis 19, Lot's wife was turned into a pillar of salt for disobeying God's orders not to look at the evil city of Sodom, which He was destroying.

"*Why* do you refuse?"

"I would prefer not to."

With any other man I should have flown outright into a dreadful passion, scorned all further words, and thrust him ignominiously from my presence. But there was something about Bartleby that not only strangely disarmed me, but in a wonderful manner touched and disconcerted me. I began to reason with him.

"These are your own copies we are about to examine. It is labor saving to you, because one examination will answer for your four papers. It is common usage. Every copyist is bound to help examine his copy. Is it not so? Will you not speak? Answer!"

"I prefer not to," he replied in a flute-like tone. It seemed to me that while I had been addressing him, he carefully revolved every statement that I made; fully comprehended the meaning; could not gainsay the irresistible conclusion; but, at the same time, some paramount consideration prevailed with him to reply as he did.

"You are decided, then, not to comply with my request — a request made according to common usage and common sense?"

He briefly gave me to understand that on that point my judgment was sound. Yes: his decision was irreversible.

It is not seldom the case that when a man is browbeaten in some unprecedented and violently unreasonable way, he begins to stagger in his own plainest faith. He begins, as it were, vaguely to surmise that, wonderful as it may be, all the justice and all the reason is on the other side. Accordingly, if any distinterested persons are present, he turns to them for some reinforcement for his own faltering mind.

"Turkey," said I, "what do you think of this? Am I not right?"

"With submission, sir," said Turkey, with his blandest tone, "I think that you are."

"Nippers," said I, "what do *you* think of it?"

"I think I should kick him out of the office."

(The reader of nice perceptions will here perceive that, it being morning, Turkey's answer is couched in polite and tranquil terms, but Nippers replies in ill-tempered ones. Or, to repeat a previous sentence, Nippers's ugly mood was on duty, and Turkey's off.)

"Ginger Nut," said I, willing to enlist the smallest suffrage in my behalf, "what do *you* think of it?"

"I think, sir, he's a little *luny*," replied Ginger Nut, with a grin.

"You hear what they say," said I, turning towards the screen, "come forth and do your duty."

But he vouchsafed no reply. I pondered a moment in sore perplexity. But once more business hurried me. I determined again to postpone the consideration of this dilemma to my future leisure. With a little trouble we made out to examine the papers without Bartleby, though at every page or two, Turkey deferentially dropped his opinion that this proceeding was quite out of the common; while Nippers, twitching in his chair with a dyspeptic nervousness, ground out between his set teeth occasional hissing maledictions against the stubborn oaf behind the screen. And for his (Nippers's) part, this was the first and the last time he would do another man's business without pay.

50    Meanwhile Bartleby sat in his hermitage, oblivious to every thing but his own peculiar business there.

Some days passed, the scrivener being employed upon another lengthy work. His late remarkable conduct led me to regard his ways narrowly. I observed that he never went to dinner; indeed that he never went any where. As yet I had never of my personal knowledge known him to be outside of my office. He was a perpetual sentry in the corner. At about eleven o'clock though, in the morning, I noticed that Ginger Nut would advance toward the opening in Bartleby's screen, as if silently beckoned thither by a gesture invisible to me where I sat. The boy would then leave the office jingling a few pence, and reappear with a handful of ginger-nuts which he delivered in the hermitage, receiving two of the cakes for his trouble.

He lives, then, on ginger-nuts, thought I; never eats a dinner, properly speaking; he must be a vegetarian then; but no; he never eats even vegetables, he eats nothing but ginger-nuts. My mind then ran on in reveries concerning the probable effects upon the human constitution of living entirely on ginger-nuts. Ginger-nuts are so called because they contain ginger as one of their peculiar constituents, and the final flavoring one. Now what was ginger? A hot, spicy thing. Was Bartleby hot and spicy? Not at all. Ginger, then, had no effect upon Bartleby. Probably he preferred it should have none.

Nothing so aggravates an earnest person as a passive resistance. If the individual so resisted be of a not inhumane temper, and the resisting one perfectly harmless in his passivity; then, in the better moods of the former, he will endeavor charitably to construe to his imagination what proves impossible to be solved by his judgment. Even so, for the most part, I regarded Bartleby and his ways. Poor fellow! thought I, he means no mischief; it is plain he intends no insolence; his aspect sufficiently evinces that his eccentricities are involuntary. He is useful to me. I can get along with him. If I turn him away, the chances are he will fall in with some less indulgent employer, and then he will be rudely treated, and perhaps driven forth miserably to starve. Yes. Here I can cheaply purchase a delicious self-approval. To befriend Bartleby; to humor him in his strange wilfulness, will cost me little or nothing, while I lay up in my soul what will eventually prove a sweet morsel for my conscience. But this mood was not invariable with me. The passiveness of Bartleby sometimes irritated me. I felt strangely goaded on to encounter him in new opposition, to elicit some angry spark from him answerable to my own. But indeed I might as well have essayed to strike fire with my knuckles against a bit of Windsor soap.[11] But one afternoon the evil impulse in me mastered me, and the following little scene ensued:

"Bartleby," said I, "when those papers are all copied, I will compare them with you."

55    "I would prefer not to."

"How? Surely you do not mean to persist in that mulish vagary?"

No answer.

I threw open the folding-doors near by, and turning upon Turkey and Nippers, exclaimed:

11 brown-coloured, scented soap.

"Bartleby a second time says, he won't examine his papers. What do you think of it, Turkey?"

60 It was afternoon, be it remembered. Turkey sat glowing like a brass boiler, his bald head steaming, his hands reeling among his blotted papers.

"Think of it?" roared Turkey; "I think I'll just step behind his screen, and black his eyes for him!"

So saying, Turkey rose to his feet and threw his arms into a pugilistic position. He was hurrying away to make good his promise, when I detained him, alarmed at the effect of incautiously rousing Turkey's combativeness after dinner.

"Sit down, Turkey," said I, "and hear what Nippers has to say. What do you think of it, Nippers? Would I not be justified in immediately dismissing Bartleby?"

"Excuse me, that is for you to decide, sir. I think his conduct quite unusual, and indeed unjust, as regards Turkey and myself. But it may only be a passing whim."

65 "Ah," exclaimed I, "you have strangely changed your mind then — you speak very gently of him now."

"All beer," cried Turkey; "gentleness is effects of beer — Nippers and I dined together to-day. You see how gentle I am, sir. Shall I go and black his eyes?"

"You refer to Bartleby, I suppose. No, not to-day, Turkey," I replied; "pray, put up your fists."

I closed the doors, and again advanced towards Bartleby. I felt additional incentives tempting me to my fate. I burned to be rebelled against again. I remembered that Bartleby never left the office.

"Bartleby," said I, "Ginger Nut is away; just step round to the Post Office, won't you? (it was but a three minutes walk,) and see if there is any thing for me."

70 "I would prefer not to."

"You *will* not?"

"I *prefer* not."

I staggered to my desk, and sat there in a deep study. My blind inveteracy returned. Was there any other thing in which I could procure myself to be ignominiously repulsed by this lean, penniless wight?— my hired clerk? What added thing is there, perfectly reasonable, that he will be sure to refuse to do?

"Bartleby!"

75 No answer.

"Bartleby," in a louder tone.

No answer.

"Bartleby," I roared.

Like a very ghost, agreeably to the laws of magical invocation, at the third summons, he appeared at the entrance of his hermitage.

80 "Go to the next room, and tell Nippers to come to me."

"I prefer not to," he respectfully and slowly said, and mildly disappeared.

"Very good, Bartleby," said I, in a quiet sort of serenely severe self-possessed tone, intimating the unalterable purpose of some terrible retribution very close at hand. At the moment I half intended something of the kind. But upon the whole, as it was drawing towards my dinner-hour, I thought it best to put on my hat and walk home for the day, suffering much from perplexity and distress of mind.

Shall I acknowledge it? The conclusion of this whole business was, that it soon became a fixed fact of my chambers, that a pale young scrivener, by the name of Bartleby, had a desk there; that he copied for me at the usual rate of four cents a folio (one hundred words); but he was permanently exempt from examining the work done by him, that duty being transferred to Turkey and Nippers, out of compliment doubtless to their superior acuteness; moreover, said Bartleby was never on any account to be dispatched on the most trivial errand of any sort; and that even if entreated to take upon him such a matter, it was generally understood that he would prefer not to — in other words, that he would refuse point-blank.

As days passed on, I became considerably reconciled to Bartleby. His steadiness, his freedom from all dissipation, his incessant industry (except when he chose to throw himself into a standing revery behind his screen), his great stillness, his unalterableness of demeanor under all circumstances, made him a valuable acquisition. One prime thing was this, — *he was always there;* — first in the morning, continually through the day, and the last at night. I had a singular confidence in his honesty. I felt my most precious papers perfectly safe in his hands. Sometimes to be sure I could not, for the very soul of me, avoid falling into sudden spasmodic passions with him. For it was exceeding difficult to bear in mind all the time those strange peculiarities, privileges, and unheard of exemptions, forming the tacit stipulations on Bartleby's part under which he remained in my office. Now and then, in the eagerness of dispatching pressing business, I would inadvertently summon Bartleby, in a short, rapid tone, to put his finger, say, on the incipient tie of a bit of red tape with which I was about compressing some papers. Of course, from behind the screen the usual answer, "I prefer not to," was sure to come; and then, how could a human creature with the common infirmities of our nature, refrain from bitterly exclaiming upon such perverseness — such unreasonableness. However, every added repulse of this sort which I received only tended to lessen the probability of my repeating the inadvertence.

85  Here it must be said, that according to the custom of most legal gentlemen occupying chambers in densely-populated law buildings, there were several keys to my door. One was kept by a woman residing in the attic, which person weekly scrubbed and daily swept and dusted my apartments. Another was kept by Turkey for convenience sake. The third I sometimes carried in my own pocket. The fourth I knew not who had.

Now, one Sunday morning I happened to go to Trinity Church, to hear a celebrated preacher, and finding myself rather early on the ground, I thought I would walk round to my chambers for a while. Luckily I had my key with me; but upon applying it to the lock, I found it resisted by something inserted from the inside. Quite surprised, I called out; when to my consternation a key was turned from within; and thrusting his lean visage at me, and holding the door ajar, the apparition of Bartleby appeared, in his shirt sleeves, and otherwise in a strangely tattered dishabille, saying quietly that he was sorry, but he was deeply engaged just then, and — preferred not admitting me at present.

In a brief word or two, he moreover added, that perhaps I had better walk round the block two or three times, and by that time he would probably have concluded his affairs.

Now, the utterly unsurmised appearance of Bartleby, tenanting my law-chambers of a Sunday morning, with his cadaverously gentlemanly *nonchalance*, yet withal firm and self-possessed, had such a strange effect upon me, that incontinently I slunk away from my own door, and did as desired. But not without sundry twinges of impotent rebellion against the mild effrontery of this unaccountable scrivener. Indeed, it was his wonderful mildness chiefly, which not only disarmed me, but unmanned me, as it were. For I consider that one, for the time, is a sort of unmanned when he tranquilly permits his hired clerk to dictate to him, and order him away from his own premises. Furthermore, I was full of uneasiness as to what Bartleby could possibly be doing in my office in his shirt sleeves, and in an otherwise dismantled condition of a Sunday morning. Was any thing amiss going on? Nay, that was out of the question. It was not to be thought of for a moment that Bartleby was an immoral person. But what could he be doing there?— copying? Nay again, whatever might be his eccentricities, Bartleby was an eminently decorous person. He would be the last man to sit down to his desk in any state approaching to nudity. Besides, it was Sunday; and there was something about Bartleby that forbade the sup-position that he would by any secular occupation violate the proprieties of the day.

Nevertheless, my mind was not pacified; and full of a restless curiosity, at last I returned to the door. Without hindrance I inserted my key, opened it, and entered. Bartleby was not to be seen. I looked round anxiously, peeped behind his screen; but it was very plain that he was gone. Upon more closely examining the place, I surmised that for an indefinite period Bartleby must have ate, dressed, and slept in my office, and that too without plate, mirror, or bed. The cushioned seat of a ricketty old sofa in one corner bore the faint impress of a lean, reclining form. Rolled away under his desk, I found a blanket; under the empty grate, a blacking box and brush; on a chair, a tin basin, with soap and a ragged towel; in a newspaper a few crumbs of ginger-nuts and a morsel of cheese. Yes, thought I, it is evident enough that Bartleby has been making his home here, keeping bachelor's hall all by himself. Immediately then the thought came sweeping across me, What miserable friendlessness and loneli-ness are here revealed! His poverty is great; but his solitude, how horrible! Think of it. Of a Sunday, Wall-street is deserted as Petra;[12] and every night of every day it is an emptiness. This building too, which of week-days hums with industry and life, at nightfall echoes with sheer vacancy, and all through Sunday is forlorn. And here Bartleby makes his home; sole spectator of a soli-tude which he has seen all populous — a sort of innocent and transformed Marius[13] brooding among the ruins of Carthage![14]

For the first time in my life a feeling of overpowering stinging melan-choly seized me. Before, I had never experienced aught but a not-unpleasing sadness. The bond of a common humanity now drew me irresistibly to gloom.

12 destroyed and abandoned city in north Africa.  13 Roman military commander who fled to Africa in the first century B.C.  14 north African city destroyed by the Romans in the second century B.C.

A fraternal melancholy! For both I and Bartleby were sons of Adam. I remembered the bright silks and sparkling faces I had seen that day, in gala trim, swan-like sailing down the Mississippi of Broadway; and I contrasted them with the pallid copyist, and thought to myself, Ah, happiness courts the light, so we deem the world is gay; but misery hides aloof, so we deem that misery there is none. These sad fancyings — chimeras, doubtless, of a sick and silly brain — led on to other and more special thoughts, concerning the eccentricities of Bartleby. Presentiments of strange discoveries hovered round me. The scrivener's pale form appeared to me laid out, among uncaring strangers, in its shivering winding sheet.

90      Suddenly I was attracted by Bartleby's closed desk, the key in open sight left in the lock.

I mean no mischief, seek the gratification of no heartless curiosity, thought I; besides, the desk is mine, and its contents too, so I will make bold to look within. Every thing was methodically arranged, the papers smoothly placed. The pigeon holes were deep, and removing the files of documents, I groped into their recesses. Presently I felt something there, and dragged it out. It was an old bandanna handkerchief, heavy and knotted. I opened it, and saw it was a savings' bank.

I now recalled all the quiet mysteries which I had noted in the man. I remembered that he never spoke but to answer; that though at intervals he had considerable time to himself, yet I had never seen him reading — no, not even a newspaper; that for long periods he would stand looking out, at his pale window behind the screen, upon the dead brick wall; I was quite sure he never visited any refectory or eating house; while his pale face clearly indicated that he never drank beer like Turkey, or tea and coffee even, like other men; that he never went any where in particular that I could learn; never went out for a walk, unless indeed that was the case at present; that he had declined telling who he was, or whence he came, or whether he had any relatives in the world; that though so thin and pale, he never complained of ill health. And more than all, I remembered a certain unconscious air of pallid — how shall I call it? — of pallid haughtiness, say, or rather an austere reserve about him, which had positively awed me into my tame compliance with his eccentricities, when I had feared to ask him to do the slightest incidental thing for me, even though I might know, from his long-continued motionlessness, that behind his screen he must be standing in one of those dead-wall reveries of his.

Revolving all these things, and coupling them with the recently discovered fact that he made my office his constant abiding place and home, and not forgetful of his morbid moodiness; revolving all these things, a prudential feeling began to steal over me. My first emotions had been those of pure melancholy and sincerest pity; but just in proportion as the forlornness of Bartleby grew and grew to my imagination, did that same melancholy merge into fear, that pity into repulsion. So true it is, and so terrible too, that up to a certain point the thought or sight of misery enlists our best affections; but, in certain special cases, beyond that point it does not. They err who would assert that invariably this is owing to the inherent selfishness of the human heart. It rather proceeds from a certain hopelessness of remedying excessive and organic ill. To a sensitive being, pity is not seldom pain. And when at last it is perceived that such pity cannot lead to effectual succor, common sense bids the soul be rid of it. What I saw that morning persuaded me that the scrivener was the victim of innate and incurable disorder. I might give alms to his body; but his body did not pain him; it was his soul that suffered, and his soul I could not reach.

I did not accomplish the purpose of going to Trinity Church that morning. Somehow, the things I had seen disqualified me for the time from church-going. I walked homeward, thinking what I would do with Bartleby. Finally, I resolved upon this; — I would put certain calm questions to him the next morning, touching his history, &c., and if he declined to answer them openly and unreservedly (and I supposed he would prefer not), then to give him a twenty dollar bill over and above whatever I might owe him, and tell him his services were no longer required; but that if in any other way I could assist him, I would be happy to do so, especially if he desired to return to his native place, wherever that might be, I would willingly help to defray the expenses. Moreover, if, after reaching home, he found himself at any time in want of aid, a letter from him would be sure of a reply.

95     The next morning came.

"Bartleby," said I, gently calling to him behind his screen.

No reply.

"Bartleby," said I, in a still gentler tone, "come here; I am not going to ask you to do any thing you would prefer not to do — I simply wish to speak to you."

Upon this he noiselessly slid into view.

100     "Will you tell me, Bartleby, where you were born?"

"I would prefer not to."

"Will you tell me *any thing* about yourself?"

"I would prefer not to."

"But what reasonable objection can you have to speak to me? I feel friendly towards you."

105     He did not look at me while I spoke, but kept his glance fixed upon my bust of Cicero,[15] which as I then sat, was directly behind me, some six inches above my head.

"What is your answer, Bartleby?" said I, after waiting a considerable time for a reply, during which his countenance remained immovable, only there was the faintest conceivable tremor of the white attenuated mouth.

"At present I prefer to give no answer," he said, and retired into his hermitage.

It was rather weak in me I confess, but his manner on this occasion nettled me. Not only did there seem to lurk in it a certain calm disdain, but his perverseness seemed ungrateful, considering the undeniable good usage and indulgence he had received from me.

Again I sat ruminating what I should do. Mortified as I was at his behavior, and resolved as I had been to dismiss him when I entered my office, nevertheless I strangely felt something superstitious knocking at my heart, and forbidding me to carry out my purpose, and denouncing me for a villain if I dared to breathe one bitter word against this forlornest of mankind. At last,

15 renowned Roman orator of the first century B.C.

familiarly drawing my chair behind his screen, I sat down and said: "Bartleby, never mind then about revealing your history; but let me entreat you as a friend, to comply as far as may be with the usages of this office. Say now you will help to examine papers to-morrow or next day: in short, say now that in a day or two you will begin to be a little reasonable:— say so, Bartleby."

110    "At present I would prefer not to be a little reasonable," was his mildly cadaverous reply.

Just then the folding-doors opened, and Nippers approached. He seemed suffering from an unusually bad night's rest, induced by severer indigestion than common. He overheard those final words of Bartleby.

"*Prefer not*, eh?" gritted Nippers — "I'd *prefer* him, if I were you, sir," addressing me — "I'd *prefer* him; I'd give him preferences, the stubborn mule! What is it, sir, pray, that he *prefers* not to do now?"

Bartleby moved not a limb.

"Mr. Nippers," said I, "I'd prefer that you would withdraw for the present."

115    Somehow, of late I had got into the way of involuntarily using this word "prefer" upon all sorts of not exactly suitable occasions. And I trembled to think that my contact with the scrivener had already and seriously affected me in a mental way. And what further and deeper aberration might it not yet produce? This apprehension had not been without efficacy in determining me to summary measures.

As Nippers, looking very sour and sulky, was departing, Turkey blandly and deferentially approached.

"With submission, sir," said he, "yesterday I was thinking about Bartleby here, and I think that if he would but prefer to take a quart of good ale every day, it would do much towards mending him, and enabling him to assist in examining his papers."

"So you have got the word too," said I, slightly excited.

"With submission, what word, sir," asked Turkey, respectfully crowding himself into the contracted space behind the screen, and by so doing, making me jostle the scrivener. "What word, sir?"

120    "I would prefer to be left alone here," said Bartleby, as if offended at being mobbed in his privacy.

"*That's* the word, Turkey," said I — "*that's* it."

"Oh, *prefer?* oh yes — queer word. I never use it myself. But, sir, as I was saying, if he would but prefer —"

"Turkey," interrupted I, "you will please withdraw."

"Oh certainly, sir, if you prefer that I should."

125    As he opened the folding-doors to retire, Nippers at his desk caught a glimpse of me, and asked whether I would prefer to have a certain paper copied on blue paper or white. He did not in the least roguishly accent the word prefer. It was plain that it involuntarily rolled from his tongue. I thought to myself, surely I must get rid of a demented man, who already has in some degree turned the tongues, if not the heads of myself and clerks. But I thought it prudent not to break the dismission at once.

The next day I noticed that Bartleby did nothing but stand at his window in his dead-wall revery. Upon asking him why he did not write, he said that he had decided upon doing no more writing.

"Why, how now? what next?" exclaimed I, "do no more writing?"

"No more."

"And what is the reason?"

130    "Do you not see the reason for yourself," he indifferently replied.

I looked steadfastly at him, and perceived that his eyes looked dull and glazed. Instantly it occurred to me, that his unexampled diligence in copying by his dim window for the first few weeks of his stay with me might have temporarily impaired his vision.

I was touched. I said something in condolence with him. I hinted that of course he did wisely in abstaining from writing for a while; and urged him to embrace that opportunity of taking wholesome exercise in the open air. This, however, he did not do. A few days after this, my other clerks being absent, and being in a great hurry to dispatch certain letters by the mail, I thought that, having nothing else earthly to do, Bartleby would surely be less inflexible than usual, and carry these letters to the post-office. But he blankly declined. So, much to my inconvenience, I went myself.

Still added days went by. Whether Bartleby's eyes improved or not, I could not say. To all appearance, I thought they did. But when I asked him if they did, he vouchsafed no answer. At all events, he would do no copying. At last, in reply to my urgings, he informed me that he had permanently given up copying.

"What!" exclaimed I; "suppose your eyes should get entirely well — better than ever before — would you not copy then?"

135    "I have given up copying," he answered, and slid aside.

He remained as ever, a fixture in my chamber. Nay — if that were possible — he became still more of a fixture than before. What was to be done? He would do nothing in the office: why should he stay there? In plain fact, he had now become a millstone to me, not only useless as a necklace, but afflictive to bear. Yet I was sorry for him. I speak less than truth when I say that, on his own account, he occasioned me uneasiness. If he would but have named a single relative or friend, I would instantly have written, and urged their taking the poor fellow away to some convenient retreat. But he seemed alone, absolutely alone in the universe. A bit of wreck in the mid Atlantic. At length, necessities connected with my business tyrannized over all other considerations. Decently as I could, I told Bartleby that in six days' time he must unconditionally leave the office. I warned him to take measures, in the interval, for procuring some other abode. I offered to assist him in this endeavor, if he himself would but take the first step towards a removal. "And when you finally quit me, Bartleby," added I, "I shall see that you go not away entirely unprovided. Six days from this hour, remember."

At the expiration of that period, I peeped behind the screen, and lo! Bartleby was there.

I buttoned up my coat, balanced myself; advanced slowly towards him, touched his shoulder, and said, "The time has come; you must quit this place; I am sorry for you; here is money, but you must go."

"I would prefer not," he replied, with his back still towards me.

140    "You *must*."

He remained silent.

Now I had an unbounded confidence in this man's common honesty. He had frequently restored to me sixpences and shillings carelessly dropped upon the floor, for I am apt to be very reckless in such shirt-button affairs. The proceeding then which followed will not be deemed extraordinary.

"Bartleby," said I, "I owe you twelve dollars on account; here are thirty-two; the odd twenty are yours. — Will you take it?" and I handed the bills towards him.

But he made no motion.

145    "I will leave them here then," putting them under a weight on the table. Then taking my hat and cane and going to the door I tranquilly turned and added — "After you have removed your things from these offices, Bartleby, you will of course lock the door — since every one is now gone for the day but you — and if you please, slip your key underneath the mat, so that I may have it in the morning. I shall not see you again; so good-bye to you. If hereafter in your new place of abode I can be of any service to you, do not fail to advise me by letter. Good-bye, Bartleby, and fare you well."

But he answered not a word; like the last column of some ruined temple, he remained standing mute and solitary in the middle of the otherwise deserted room.

As I walked home in a pensive mood, my vanity got the better of my pity. I could not but highly plume myself on my masterly management in getting rid of Bartleby. Masterly I call it, and such it must appear to any dispassionate thinker. The beauty of my procedure seemed to consist in its perfect quietness. There was no vulgar bullying, no bravado of any sort, no choleric hectoring, and striding to and fro across the apartment, jerking out vehement commands for Bartleby to bundle himself off with his beggarly traps. Nothing of the kind. Without loudly bidding Bartleby depart — as an inferior genius might have done — I *assumed* the ground that depart he must; and upon that assumption built all I had to say. The more I thought over my procedure, the more I was charmed with it. Nevertheless, next morning, upon awakening, I had my doubts, — I had somehow slept off the fumes of vanity. One of the coolest and wisest hours a man has, is just after he wakes in the morning. My procedure seemed as sagacious as ever, — but only in theory. How it would prove in practice — there was the rub. It was truly a beautiful thought to have assumed Bartleby's departure; but, after all, that assumption was simply my own, and none of Bartleby's. The great point was, not whether I had assumed that he would quit me, but whether he would prefer so to do. He was more a man of preferences than assumptions.

After breakfast, I walked down town, arguing the probabilities *pro* and *con.* One moment I thought it would prove a miserable failure, and Bartleby would be found all alive at my office as usual; the next moment it seemed certain that I should find his chair empty. And so I kept veering about. At the corner of Broadway and Canal-street, I saw quite an excited group of people standing in earnest conversation.

"I'll take odds he doesn't," said a voice as I passed.

150    "Doesn't go? — done!" said I, "put up your money."

I was instinctively putting my hand in my pocket to produce my own, when I remembered that this was an election day. The words I had overheard bore no reference to Bartleby, but to the success or non-success of some candidate for the mayoralty. In my intent frame of mind, I had, as it were, imagined that all Broadway shared in my excitement, and were debating the same question with me. I passed on, very thankful that the uproar of the street screened my momentary absent-mindedness.

As I had intended, I was earlier than usual at my office door. I stood listening for a moment. All was still. He must be gone. I tried the knob. The door was locked. Yes, my procedure had worked to a charm; he indeed must be vanished. Yet a certain melancholy mixed with this: I was almost sorry for my brilliant success. I was fumbling under the door mat for the key, which Bartleby was to have left there for me, when accidentally my knee knocked against a panel, producing a summoning sound, and in response a voice came to me from within — "Not yet; I am occupied."

It was Bartleby.

I was thunderstruck. For an instant I stood like the man who, pipe in mouth, was killed one cloudless afternoon long ago in Virginia, by summer lightning; at his own warm open window he was killed, and remained leaning out there upon the dreamy afternoon, till some one touched him, when he fell.

155 "Not gone!" I murmured at last. But again obeying that wondrous ascendancy which the inscrutable scrivener had over me, and from which ascendancy, for all my chafing, I could not completely escape, I slowly went down stairs and out into the street, and while walking round the block, considered what I should next do in this unheard-of perplexity. Turn the man out by an actual thrusting I could not; to drive him away by calling him hard names would not do; calling in the police was an unpleasant idea; and yet, permit him to enjoy his cadaverous triumph over me, — this too I could not think of. What was to be done? or, if nothing could be done, was there any thing further that I could *assume* in the matter? Yes, as before I had prospectively assumed that Bartleby would depart, so now I might retrospectively assume that departed he was. In the legitimate carrying out of this assumption, I might enter my office in a great hurry, and pretending not to see Bartleby at all, walk straight against him as if he were air. Such a proceeding would in a singular degree have the appearance of a home-thrust. It was hardly possible that Bartleby could withstand such an application of the doctrine of assumptions. But upon second thoughts the success of the plan seemed rather dubious. I resolved to argue the matter over with him again.

"Bartleby," said I, entering the office, with a quietly severe expression, "I am seriously displeased. I am pained, Bartleby. I had thought better of you. I had imagined you of such a gentlemanly organization, that in any delicate dilemma a slight hint would suffice — in short, an assumption. But it appears I am deceived. Why," I added, unaffectedly starting, "you have not even touched that money yet," pointing to it, just where I had left it the evening previous.

He answered nothing.

"Will you, or will you not, quit me?" I now demanded in a sudden passion, advancing close to him.

"I would prefer *not* to quit you," he replied, gently emphasizing the *not*.

160 "What earthly right have you to stay here? Do you pay any rent? Do you pay my taxes? Or is this property yours?"

He answered nothing.

"Are you ready to go on and write now? Are your eyes recovered? Could you copy a small paper for me this morning? or help examine a few lines? or step round to the post-office? In a word, will you do any thing at all, to give a coloring to your refusal to depart the premises?"

He silently retired into his hermitage.

I was now in such a state of nervous resentment that I thought it but prudent to check myself at present from further demonstrations. Bartleby and I were alone. I remembered the tragedy of the unfortunate Adams and the still more unfortunate Colt[16] in the solitary office of the latter; and how poor Colt, being dreadfully incensed by Adams, and imprudently permitting himself to get wildly excited, was at unawares hurried into his fatal act — an act which certainly no man could possibly deplore more than the actor himself. Often it had occurred to me in my ponderings upon the subject, that had that altercation taken place in the public street, or at a private residence, it would not have terminated as it did. It was the circumstance of being alone in a solitary office, up stairs, of a building entirely unhallowed by humanizing domestic associations — an uncarpeted office, doubtless, of a dusty, haggard sort of appearance; — this it must have been, which greatly helped to enhance the irritable desperation of the hapless Colt.

165      But when this old Adam[17] of resentment rose in me and tempted me concerning Bartleby, I grappled him and threw him. How? Why, simply by recalling the divine injunction: "A new commandment give I unto you, that ye love one another." Yes, this it was that saved me. Aside from higher considerations, charity often operates as a vastly wise and prudent principle — a great safeguard to its possessor. Men have committed murder for jealousy's sake, and anger's sake, and hatred's sake, and selfishness' sake, and spiritual pride's sake; but no man that ever I heard of, ever committed a diabolical murder for sweet charity's sake. Mere self-interest, then, if no better motive can be enlisted, should, especially with high-tempered men, prompt all beings to charity and philanthropy. At any rate, upon the occasion in question, I strove to drown my exasperated feelings towards the scrivener by benevolently construing his conduct. Poor fellow, poor fellow! thought I, he don't mean any thing; and besides, he has seen hard times, and ought to be indulged.

I endeavored also immediately to occupy myself, and at the same time to comfort my despondency. I tried to fancy that in the course of the morning, at such time as might prove agreeable to him, Bartleby, of his own free accord, would emerge from his hermitage, and take up some decided line of march in the direction of the door. But no. Half-past twelve o'clock came; Turkey began to glow in the face, overturn his inkstand, and become generally obstreperous; Nippers abated down into quietude and courtesy; Ginger Nut munched his noon apple; and Bartleby remained standing at his window in one of his profoundest dead-wall reveries. Will it be credited? Ought I to acknowledge it? That afternoon I left the office without saying one further word to him.

16 Samuel Adams was killed in 1841 in a fight with John Colt, a brother of the manufacturer of guns.
17 reference to the biblical first man, whose temperament was believed to have been passed on to all the human race.

Some days now passed, during which, at leisure intervals I looked a little into "Edwards on the Will,"[18] and "Priestley on Necessity."[19] Under the circumstances, those books induced a salutary feeling. Gradually I slid into the persuasion that these troubles of mine touching the scrivener, had been all predestinated from eternity, and Bartleby was billeted upon me for some mysterious purpose of an all-wise Providence, which it was not for a mere mortal like me to fathom. Yes, Bartleby, stay there behind your screen, thought I; I shall persecute you no more; you are harmless and noiseless as any of these old chairs; in short, I never feel so private as when I know you are here. At last I see it, I feel it; I penetrate to the predestinated purpose of my life. I am content. Others may have loftier parts to enact; but my mission in this world, Bartleby, is to furnish you with office-room for such period as you may see fit to remain.

I believe that this wise and blessed frame of mind would have continued with me, had it not been for the unsolicited and uncharitable remarks obtruded upon me by my professional friends who visited the rooms. But thus it often is, that the constant friction of illiberal minds wears out at last the best resolves of the more generous. Though to be sure, when I reflected upon it, it was not strange that people entering my office should be struck by the peculiar aspect of the unaccountable Bartleby, and so be tempted to throw out some sinister observations concerning him. Sometimes an attorney having business with me, and calling at my office, and finding no one but the scrivener there, would undertake to obtain some sort of precise information from him touching my whereabouts; but without heeding his idle talk, Bartleby would remain standing immovable in the middle of the room. So after contemplating him in that position for a time, the attorney would depart, no wiser than he came.

Also, when a Reference[20] was going on, and the room full of lawyers and witnesses and business was driving fast; some deeply occupied legal gentleman present, seeing Bartleby wholly unemployed, would request him to run round to his (the legal gentleman's) office and fetch some papers for him. Thereupon, Bartleby would tranquilly decline, and yet remain idle as before. Then the lawyer would give a great stare, and turn to me. And what could I say? At last I was made aware that all through the circle of my professional acquaintance, a whisper of wonder was running round, having reference to the strange creature I kept at my office. This worried me very much. And as the idea came upon me of his possibly turning out a long-lived man, and keep occupying my chambers, and denying my authority; and perplexing my visitors; and scandalizing my professional reputation; and casting a general gloom over the premises; keeping soul and body together to the last upon his savings (for doubtless he spent but half a dime a day), and in the end perhaps outlive me, and claim possession of my office by right of his perpetual occupancy: as all these dark anticipations crowded upon me more and more, and my friends continually intruded their relentless remarks upon the apparition in my room;

18 eighteenth-century American philosopher who believed that human beings' will was controlled by God. 19 eighteenth-century English philosopher who believed that, to prevent revolution, rulers should act in the interests of those they govern. 20 legal hearing in which two parties submit their differences to an arbitrator.

a great change was wrought in me. I resolved to gather all my faculties together, and for ever rid me of this intolerable incubus.

170 Ere revolving any complicated project, however, adapted to this end, I first simply suggested to Bartleby the propriety of his permanent departure. In a calm and serious tone, I commended the idea to his careful and mature consideration. But having taken three days to meditate upon it, he apprised me that his original determination remained the same; in short, that he still preferred to abide with me.

What shall I do? I now said to myself, buttoning up my coat to the last button. What shall I do? what ought I to do? what does conscience say I *should* do with this man, or rather ghost? Rid myself of him, I must; go, he shall. But how? You will not thrust him, the poor, pale, passive mortal, — you will not thrust such a helpless creature out of your door? you will not dishonor yourself by such cruelty? No, I will not, I cannot do that. Rather would I let him live and die here, and then mason up his remains in the wall. What then will you do? For all your coaxing, he will not budge. Bribes he leaves under your own paper-weight on your table; in short, it is quite plain that he prefers to cling to you.

Then something severe, something unusual must be done. What! surely you will not have him collared by a constable, and commit his innocent pallor to the common jail? And upon what ground could you procure such a thing to be done? — a vagrant, is he? What! he a vagrant, a wanderer, who refuses to budge? It is because he will *not* be a vagrant, then, that you seek to count him *as a* vagrant. That is too absurd. No visible means of support: there I have him. Wrong again: for undubitably he *does* support himself, and that is the only unanswerable proof that any man can show of his possessing the means so to do. No more then. Since he will not quit me, I must quit him. I will change my offices; I will move elsewhere; and give him fair notice, that if I find him on my new premises I will then proceed against him as a common trespasser.

Acting accordingly, next day I thus addressed him: "I find these chambers too far from the City Hall; the air is unwholesome. In a word, I propose to remove my offices next week, and shall no longer require your services. I tell you this now, in order that you may seek another place."

He made no reply, and nothing more was said.

175 On the appointed day I engaged carts and men, proceeded to my chambers, and having but little furniture, every thing was removed in a few hours. Throughout, the scrivener remained standing behind the screen, which I directed to be removed the last thing. It was withdrawn; and being folded up like a huge folio, left him the motionless occupant of a naked room. I stood in the entry watching him a moment, while something from within me upbraided me.

I re-entered, with my hand in my pocket — and — and my heart in my mouth.

"Good-bye, Bartleby; I am going — good-bye, and God some way bless you; and take that," slipping something in his hand. But it dropped upon the floor, and then, — strange to say — I tore myself from him whom I had so longed to be rid of.

Established in my new quarters, for a day or two I kept the door locked, and started at every footfall in the passages. When I returned to my rooms after any little absence, I would pause at the threshold for an instant, and attentively listen, ere applying my key. But these fears were needless. Bartleby never came nigh me.

I thought all was going well, when a perturbed looking stranger visited me, inquiring whether I was the person who had recently occupied rooms at No.— Wall-street.

180 Full of forebodings, I replied that I was.

"Then sir," said the stranger, who proved a lawyer, "you are responsible for the man you left there. He refuses to do any copying; he refuses to do any thing; he says he prefers not to; and he refuses to quit the premises."

"I am very sorry, sir" said I, with assumed tranquillity, but an inward tremor, "but, really, the man you allude to is nothing to me — he is no relation or apprentice of mine, that you should hold me responsible for him."

"In mercy's name, who is he?"

"I certainly cannot inform you. I know nothing about him. Formerly I employed him as a copyist; but he has done nothing for me now for some time past."

185 "I shall settle him then,— good morning, sir."

Several days passed, and I heard nothing more; and though I often felt a charitable prompting to call at the place and see poor Bartleby, yet a certain squeamishness of I know not what withheld me.

All is over with him, by this time, thought I at last, when through another week no further intelligence reached me. But coming to my room the day after, I found several persons waiting at my door in a high state of nervous excitement.

"That's the man — here he comes," cried the foremost one, whom I recognized as the lawyer who had previously called upon me alone.

"You must take him away, sir, at once," cried a portly person among them, advancing upon me, and whom I knew to be the landlord of No.— Wall-street. "These gentlemen, my tenants, cannot stand it any longer; Mr. B——" pointing to the lawyer, "has turned him out of his room, and he now persists in haunting the building generally, sitting upon the banisters of the stairs by day, and sleeping in the entry by night. Every body is concerned; clients are leaving the offices; some fears are entertained of a mob; something you must do, and that without delay."

190 Aghast at this torrent, I fell back before it, and would fain have locked myself in my new quarters. In vain I persisted that Bartleby was nothing to me — no more than to any one else. In vain:— I was the last person known to have any thing to do with him, and they held me to the terrible account. Fearful then of being exposed in the papers (as one person present obscurely threatened) I considered the matter, and at length said, that if the lawyer would give me a confidential interview with the scrivener, in his (the lawyer's) own room, I would that afternoon strive my best to rid them of the nuisance they complained of.

Going up stairs to my old haunt, there was Bartleby silently sitting upon the banister at the landing.

"What are you doing here, Bartleby?" said I.

"Sitting upon the banister," he mildly replied.

I motioned him into the lawyer's room, who then left us.

195     "Bartleby," said I, "are you aware that you are the cause of great tribulation to me, by persisting in occupying the entry after being dismissed from the office?"

No answer.

"Now one of two things must take place. Either you must do something, or something must be done to you. Now what sort of business would you like to engage in? Would you like to re-engage in copying for some one?"

"No; I would prefer not to make any change."

"Would you like a clerkship in a dry-goods store?"

200     "There is too much confinement about that. No, I would not like a clerkship; but I am not particular."

"Too much confinement," I cried, "why you keep yourself confined all the time!"

"I would prefer not to take a clerkship," he rejoined, as if to settle that little item at once.

"How would a bar-tender's business suit you? There is no trying of the eyesight in that."

"I would not like it at all; though, as I said before, I am not particular."

205     His unwonted wordiness inspirited me. I returned to the charge.

"Well then, would you like to travel through the country collecting bills for the merchants? That would improve your health."

"No, I would prefer to be something else."

"How then would going as a companion to Europe, to entertain some young gentleman with your conversation, — how would that suit you?"

"Not at all. It does not strike me that there is any thing definite about that. I like to be stationary. But I am not particular."

210     "Stationary you shall be then," I cried, now losing all patience, and for the first time in all my exasperating connection with him fairly flying into a passion. "If you do not go away from these premises before night, I shall feel bound — indeed I *am* bound — to — to — to quit the premises myself!" I rather absurdly concluded, knowing not with what possible threat to try to frighten his immobility into compliance. Despairing of all further efforts, I was precipitately leaving him, when a final thought occurred to me — one which had not been wholly unindulged before.

"Bartleby," said I, in the kindest tone I could assume under such exciting circumstances, "will you go home with me now — not to my office, but my dwelling — and remain there till we can conclude upon some convenient arrangement for you at our leisure? Come, let us start now, right away."

"No: at present I would prefer not to make any change at all."

I answered nothing; but effectually dodging every one by the suddenness and rapidity of my flight, rushed from the building, ran up Wall-street towards Broadway, and jumping into the first omnibus was soon removed from pursuit. As soon as tranquillity returned I distinctly perceived that I had now done all that I possibly could, both in respect to the demands of the landlord and his tenants, and with regard to my own desire and sense of duty, to benefit Bartleby, and shield him from rude persecution. I now strove to be entirely care-free and quiescent; and my conscience justified me in the attempt; though indeed it was not so successful as I could have wished. So fearful was I of being again hunted out by the incensed landlord and his exasperated tenants, that, surrendering my business to Nippers, for a few days I drove about the upper part of the town and through the suburbs, in my rockaway;[21] crossed over to Jersey City and Hoboken, and paid fugitive visits to Manhattanville and Astoria. In fact I almost lived in my rockaway for the time.

When again I entered my office, lo, a note from the landlord lay upon the desk. I opened it with trembling hands. It informed me that the writer had sent to the police, and had Bartleby removed to the Tombs as a vagrant. Moreover, since I knew more about him than any one else, he wished me to appear at that place, and make a suitable statement of the facts. These tidings had a conflicting effect upon me. At first I was indignant; but at last almost approved. The landlord's energetic, summary disposition, had led him to adopt a procedure which I do not think I would have decided upon myself; and yet as a last resort, under such peculiar circumstances, it seemed the only plan.

215   As I afterwards learned, the poor scrivener, when told that he must be conducted to the Tombs, offered not the slightest obstacle, but in his pale unmoving way, silently acquiesced.

Some of the compassionate and curious bystanders joined the party; and headed by one of the constables arm in arm with Bartleby, the silent procession filed its way through all the noise, and heat, and joy of the roaring thoroughfares at noon.

The same day I received the note I went to the Tombs, or to speak more properly, the Halls of Justice. Seeking the right officer, I stated the purpose of my call, and was informed that the individual I described was indeed within. I then assured the functionary that Bartleby was a perfectly honest man, and greatly to be compassionated, however unaccountably eccentric. I narrated all I knew, and closed by suggesting the idea of letting him remain in as indulgent confinement as possible till something less harsh might be done — though indeed I hardly knew what. At all events, if nothing else could be decided upon, the alms-house must receive him. I then begged to have an interview.

Being under no disgraceful charge, and quite serene and harmless in all his ways, they had permitted him freely to wander about the prison, and especially in the inclosed grass-platted yards thereof. And so I found him there, standing all alone in the quietest of the yards, his face towards a high wall, while all around, from the narrow slits of the jail windows, I thought I saw peering out upon him the eyes of murderers and thieves.

"Bartleby!"

220   "I know you," he said, without looking round, — "and I want nothing to say to you."

"It was not I that brought you here, Bartleby," said I, keenly pained at his implied suspicion. "And to you, this should not be so vile a place. Nothing reproachful attaches to you by being here. And see, it is not so sad a place as one might think. Look, there is the sky, and here is the grass."

"I know where I am," he replied, but would say nothing more, and so I left him.

As I entered the corridor again, a broad meat-like man, in an apron, accosted me, and jerking his thumb over his shoulder said — "Is that your friend?"

21 luxury carriage.

"Yes."

225 "Does he want to starve? If he does, let him live on the prison fare, that's all."

"Who are you?" asked I, not knowing what to make of such an unofficially speaking person in such a place.

"I am the grub-man. Such gentlemen as have friends here, hire me to provide them with something good to eat."

"Is this so?" said I, turning to the turnkey.

He said it was.

230 "Well then," said I, slipping some silver into the grub-man's hands (for so they called him). "I want you to give particular attention to my friend there; let him have the best dinner you can get. And you must be as polite to him as possible."

"Introduce me, will you?" said the grub-man, looking at me with an expression which seemed to say he was all impatience for an opportunity to give a specimen of his breeding.

Thinking it would prove of benefit to the scrivener, I acquiesced; and asking the grub-man his name, went up with him to Bartleby.

"Bartleby, this is Mr. Cutlets; you will find him very useful to you."

"Your sarvant, sir, your sarvant," said the grub-man, making a low salutation behind his apron. "Hope you find it pleasant here, sir; nice grounds — cool apartments, sir — hope you'll stay with us some time — try to make it agreeable. May Mrs. Cutlets and I have the pleasure of your company to dinner, sir, in Mrs. Cutlet's private room?"

235 "I prefer not to dine to-day," said Bartleby, turning away. "It would disagree with me; I am unused to dinners." So saying he slowly moved to the other side of the inclosure, and took up a position fronting the dead-wall.

"How's this?" said the grub-man, addressing me with a stare of astonishment. "He's odd, aint he?"

"I think he is a little deranged," said I, sadly.

"Deranged? deranged is it? Well now, upon my word, I thought that friend of yourn was a gentleman forger; they are always pale and genteel-like, them forgers. I can't help pity 'em — can't help it, sir. Did you know Monroe Edwards?" he added touchingly, and paused. Then, laying his hand pityingly on my shoulder, sighed, "he died of consumption at Sing-Sing.[22] So you weren't acquainted with Monroe?"

"No, I was never socially acquainted with any forgers. But I cannot stop longer. Look to my friend yonder. You will not lose by it. I will see you again."

240 Some few days after this, I again obtained admission to the Tombs, and went through the corridors in quest of Bartleby; but without finding him.

"I saw him coming from his cell not long ago," said a turnkey, "may be he's gone to loiter in the yards."

So I went in that direction.

"Are you looking for the silent man?" said another turnkey passing me. "Yonder he lies — sleeping in the yard there. 'Tis not twenty minutes since I saw him lie down."

22 state prison north of New York City.

The yard was entirely quiet. It was not accessible to the common prisoners. The surrounding walls, of amazing thickness, kept off all sounds behind them. The Egyptian character of the masonry weighed upon me with its gloom. But a soft imprisoned turf grew under foot. The heart of the eternal pyramids, it seemed, wherein, by some strange magic, through the clefts, grass-seed, dropped by birds, had sprung.

245 Strangely huddled at the base of the wall, his knees drawn up, and lying on his side, his head touching the cold stones, I saw the wasted Bartleby. But nothing stirred. I paused; then went close up to him; stooped over, and saw that his dim eyes were open; otherwise he seemed profoundly sleeping. Something prompted me to touch him. I felt his hand, when a tingling shiver ran up my arm and down my spine to my feet.

The round face of the grub-man peered upon me now. "His dinner is ready. Won't he dine to-day, either? Or does he live without dining?"

"Lives without dining," said I, and closed the eyes.

"Eh! — He's asleep, aint he?"

"With kings and counsellors,"[23] murmured I.

*****

250 There would seem little need for proceeding further in this history. Imagination will readily supply the meagre recital of poor Bartleby's interment. But ere parting with the reader, let me say, that if this little narrative has sufficiently interested him, to awaken curiosity as to who Bartleby was, and what manner of life he led prior to the present narrator's making his acquaintance, I can only reply, that in such curiosity I fully share, but am wholly unable to gratify it. Yet here I hardly know whether I should divulge one little item of rumor, which came to my ear a few months after the scrivener's decease. Upon what basis it rested, I could never ascertain; and hence, how true it is I cannot now tell. But inasmuch as this vague report has not been without a certain strange suggestive interest to me, however sad, it may prove the same with some others; and so I will briefly mention it. The report was this: that Bartleby had been a subordinate clerk in the Dead Letter Office at Washington, from which he had been suddenly removed by a change in the administration. When I think over this rumor, hardly can I express the emotions which seize me. Dead letters! does it not sound like dead men? Conceive a man by nature and misfortune prone to a pallid hopelessness, can any business seem more fitted to heighten it than that of continually handling these dead letters, and assorting them for the flames? For by the cart-load they are annually burned. Sometimes from out the folded paper the pale clerk takes a ring: — the finger it was meant for, perhaps, moulders in the grave; a bank-note sent in swiftest charity: — he whom it would relieve, nor eats nor hungers any more; pardon for those who died despairing; hope for those who died unhoping; good tidings for those who died stifled by unrelieved calamities. On errands of life, these letters speed to death.

Ah Bartleby! Ah humanity!

(1853)

23 see Job 3:14. A reference to death as a condition of tranquillity.

# Kate Chopin   (1851–1904)

Kate Chopin, who received a traditional Catholic upbringing and moved in the society circles of her native city, St. Louis, Missouri, began a career as an author after the death of her husband. She stated that she strove to present "human existence in its subtle, complex, true meaning, stripped of the veil with which ethical and conventional standards have draped it." Her novel *The Awakening* (1899), now considered a classic, is the story of a young mother's escape from her socially imposed roles; it was condemned as immoral and was mostly ignored until the 1960s, as were such stories as "A Shameful Affair" and "The Storm." "The Story of an Hour," which is praised for its conciseness and its presentation of "daring" themes, focusses on the surface and the secret life of the central character. Chopin's use of the limited third-person narrator and the surprise ending enables readers to understand the conventional attitudes of the other characters and Mrs. Mallard's own, unspoken views.

# THE STORY OF AN HOUR

Knowing that Mrs. Mallard was afflicted with a heart trouble, great care was taken to break to her as gently as possible the news of her husband's death.

It was her sister Josephine who told her, in broken sentences; veiled hints that revealed in half concealing. Her husband's friend Richards was there, too, near her. It was he who had been in the newspaper office when intelligence of the railroad disaster was received, with Brently Mallard's name leading the list of "killed." He had only taken the time to assure himself of its truth by a second telegram, and had hastened to forestall any less careful, less tender friend in bearing the sad message.

She did not hear the story as many women have heard the same, with a paralyzed inability to accept its significance. She wept at once, with sudden, wild abandonment, in her sister's arms. When the storm of grief had spent itself she went away to her room alone. She would have no one follow her.

There stood, facing the open window, a comfortable, roomy armchair. Into this she sank, pressed down by a physical exhaustion that haunted her body and seemed to reach into her soul.

5      She could see in the open square before her house the tops of trees that were all aquiver with the new spring life. The delicious breath of rain was in the air. In the street below a peddler was crying his wares. The notes of a distant song which some one was singing reached her faintly, and countless sparrows were twittering in the eaves.

There were patches of blue sky showing here and there through the clouds that had met and piled one above the other in the west facing her window.

She sat with her head thrown back upon the cushion of the chair, quite motionless, except when a sob came up into her throat and shook her, as a child who has cried itself to sleep continues to sob in its dreams.

She was young, with a fair, calm face, whose lines bespoke repression and even a certain strength. But now there was a dull stare in her eyes, whose gaze was fixed away off yonder on one of those patches of blue sky. It was not a glance of reflection, but rather indicated a suspension of intelligent thought.

There was something coming to her and she was waiting for it, fearfully. What was it? She did not know; it was too subtle and elusive to name. But she felt it, creeping out of the sky, reaching toward her through the sounds, the scents, the color that filled the air.

10    Now her bosom rose and fell tumultuously. She was beginning to recognize this thing that was approaching to possess her, and she was striving to beat it back with her will — as powerless as her two white slender hands would have been.

When she abandoned herself a little whispered word escaped her slightly parted lips. She said it over and over under her breath: "free, free, free!" The vacant stare and the look of terror that had followed it went from her eyes. They stayed keen and bright. Her pulses beat fast, and the coursing blood warmed and relaxed every inch of her body.

She did not stop to ask if it were or were not a monstrous joy that held her. A clear and exalted perception enabled her to dismiss the suggestion as trivial.

She knew that she would weep again when she saw the kind, tender hands folded in death; the face that had never looked save with love upon her, fixed and gray and dead. But she saw beyond that bitter moment a long procession of years to come that would belong to her absolutely. And she opened and spread her arms out to them in welcome.

There would be no one to live for her during those coming years; she would live for herself. There would be no powerful will bending hers in that blind persistence with which men and women believe they have a right to impose a private will upon a fellow-creature. A kind intention or a cruel intention made the act seem no less a crime as she looked upon it in that brief moment of illumination.

15    And yet she had loved him — sometimes. Often she had not. What did it matter! What could love, the unsolved mystery, count for in face of this possession of self-assertion which she suddenly recognized as the strongest impulse of her being!

"Free! Body and soul free!" she kept whispering.

Josephine was kneeling before the closed door with her lips to the keyhole, imploring for admission. "Louise, open the door! I beg; open the door — you will make yourself ill. What are you doing, Louise? For heaven's sake open the door."

"Go away. I am not making myself ill." No; she was drinking in a very elixir of life through that open window.

Her fancy was running riot along those days ahead of her. Spring days, and summer days, and all sorts of days that would be her own. She breathed a quick prayer that life might be long. It was only yesterday she had thought with a shudder that life might be long.

20    She arose at length and opened the door to her sister's importunities. There was a feverish triumph in her eyes, and she carried herself unwittingly like a goddess of Victory. She clasped her sister's waist, and together they descended the stairs. Richards stood waiting for them at the bottom.

Some one was opening the front door with a latchkey. It was Brently Mallard who entered, a little travel-stained, composedly carrying his grip-sack and umbrella. He had been far from the scene of accident, and did not even know there had been one. He stood amazed at Josephine's piercing cry; at Richards' quick motion to screen him from the view of his wife.

But Richards was too late.

When the doctors came they said she had died of heart disease — of joy that kills.

(1894)

# Joseph Conrad (1857–1924)

Born in the Ukraine of Polish parents, Joseph Conrad worked at sea for twenty years before settling in England. There he began writing novels and short stories, all in his third language, English, which he did not learn until he was an adult. His novels, such as *Lord Jim* and *Nostromo*, are dominated by a concern with the complexities of character and motivation, and focus on the degeneration and corruption of the human spirit. Like *Heart of Darkness* (1902), his best-known short novel, the story "An Outpost of Progress" presents a bleak view of civilization in its portrayal of the two white administrators of an isolated African trading post. Without the support of their own familiar world, Kayerts and Carlier are defeated by their own weaknesses.

# AN OUTPOST OF PROGRESS

I

There were two white men in charge of the trading station. Kayerts, the chief, was short and fat; Carlier, the assistant, was tall, with a large head and a very broad trunk perched upon a long pair of thin legs. The third man on the staff was a Sierra Leone nigger, who maintained that his name was Henry Price. However, for some reason or other, the natives down the river had given him the name of Makola, and it stuck to him through all his wanderings about the country. He spoke English and French with a warbling accent, wrote a beautiful hand, understood bookkeeping, and cherished in his innermost heart the worship of evil spirits. His wife was a negress from Loanda, very large and very noisy. Three children rolled about in sunshine before the door of his low, shed-like dwelling. Makola, taciturn and impenetrable, despised the two white men. He had charge of a small clay storehouse with a dried-grass roof, and pretended to keep a correct account of beads, cotton cloth, red kerchiefs, brass wire, and other trade goods it contained. Besides the storehouse and Makola's hut, there was only one large building in the cleared ground of the station. It was built neatly of reeds, with a verandah on all the four sides. There were three rooms in it. The one in the middle was the living-room, and had two rough tables and a few stools in it. The other two were the bedrooms for the white men. Each had a bedstead and a mosquito net for all furniture. The plank floor was littered with the belongings of the white men; open half-empty boxes, town wearing apparel, old boots; all the things dirty, and all the things broken, that accumulate mysteriously round untidy men. There was also another dwelling-place some distance away from the buildings. In it, under a tall cross much out of the perpendicular, slept the man who had seen the beginning of all this; who had planned and had watched the construction of this outpost of progress. He had been, at home, an unsuccessful painter who, weary of pursuing fame on an empty stomach, had gone out there through high protections. He had been the first chief of that station. Makola had watched the energetic artist die of fever in the just finished house with his usual kind of "I told you so" indifference. Then, for a time, he dwelt alone with his family, his account books, and the Evil Spirit that rules the lands under the equator. He got on very well with his god. Perhaps he had propitiated him by a promise of more white men to play with, by and by. At any rate the director of the Great Trading Company, coming up in a steamer that resembled an enormous sardine box with a flat-roofed shed erected on it, found the station in good order, and Makola as usual quietly diligent. The director had the cross put up over the first agent's grave, and appointed Kayerts to the post. Carlier was told off as second in charge. The director was a man ruthless and efficient, who at times, but very imperceptibly, indulged in grim humour. He made a speech to Kayerts and Carlier, pointing out to them the promising aspect of their station. The nearest trading-post was about three hundred miles away. It was an exceptional opportunity for them to distinguish themselves and to earn percentages on the trade. This appointment was a favour done to beginners. Kayerts was moved almost to tears by his director's kindness. He would, he said, by doing his best, try to justify the flattering confidence, &c., &c. Kayerts had been in the Administration of the Telegraphs, and knew how to express himself correctly. Carlier, an ex-non-commissioned officer of cavalry in an army guaranteed from harm by several European Powers, was less impressed. If there were commissions to get, so much the better; and, trailing a sulky glance over the river, the forests, the impenetrable bush that seemed to cut off the station from the rest of the world, he muttered between his teeth, "We shall see, very soon."

Next day, some bales of cotton goods and a few cases of provisions having been thrown on shore, the sardine-box steamer went off, not to return for another six months. On the deck the director touched his cap to the two agents, who stood on the bank waving their hats, and turning to an old servant of the Company on his passage to headquarters, said, "Look at those two imbeciles. They must be mad at home to send me such specimens. I told those fellows to plant a vegetable garden, build new storehouses and fences, and construct a landing-stage. I bet nothing will be done! They won't know how to begin. I always thought the station on this river useless, and they just fit the station!"

"They will form themselves there," said the old stager with a quiet smile.

"At any rate, I am rid of them for six months," retorted the director.

5      The two men watched the steamer round the bend, then, ascending arm in arm the slope of the bank, returned to the station. They had been in this vast and dark country only a very short time, and as yet always in the midst of other white men, under the eye and guidance of their superiors. And now, dull as they were to the subtle influences of surroundings, they felt themselves very much alone, when suddenly left unassisted to face the wilderness; a wilderness rendered more strange, more incomprehensible by the mysterious glimpses of the vigorous life it contained. They were two perfectly insignificant and incapable individuals, whose existence is only rendered possible through the high organization of civilized crowds. Few men realize that their life, the very essence of their character, their capabilities and their audacities, are only the expression of their belief in the safety of their surroundings. The courage, the composure, the confidence; the emotions and principles; every great and every insignificant thought belongs not to the individual but to the crowd: to

the crowd that believes blindly in the irresistible force of its institutions and of its morals, in the power of its police and of its opinion. But the contact with pure unmitigated savagery, with primitive nature and primitive man, brings sudden and profound trouble into the heart. To the sentiment of being alone of one's kind, to the clear perception of the loneliness of one's thoughts, of one's sensations — to the negation of the habitual, which is safe, there is added the affirmation of the unusual, which is dangerous; a suggestion of things vague, uncontrollable, and repulsive, whose discomposing intrusion excites the imagination and tries the civilized nerves of the foolish and the wise alike.

Kayerts and Carlier walked arm in arm, drawing close to one another as children do in the dark; and they had the same, not altogether unpleasant, sense of danger which one half suspects to be imaginary. They chatted persistently in familiar tones. "Our station is prettily situated," said one. The other assented with enthusiasm, enlarging volubly on the beauties of the situation. Then they passed near the grave. "Poor devil!" said Kayerts. "He died of fever, didn't he?" muttered Carlier, stopping short. "Why," retorted Kayerts, with indignation, "I've been told that the fellow exposed himself recklessly to the sun. The climate here, everybody says, is not at all worse than at home, as long as you keep out of the sun. Do you hear that, Carlier? I am chief here, and my orders are that you should not expose yourself to the sun!" He assumed his superiority jocularly, but his meaning was serious. The idea that he would, perhaps, have to bury Carlier and remain alone, gave him an inward shiver. He felt suddenly that this Carlier was more precious to him here, in the centre of Africa, than a brother could be anywhere else. Carlier, entering into the spirit of the thing, made a military salute and answered in a brisk tone, "Your orders shall be attended to, chief!" Then he burst out laughing, slapped Kayerts on the back and shouted, "We shall let life run easily here! Just sit still and gather in the ivory those savages will bring. This country has its good points, after all!" They both laughed loudly while Carlier thought: That poor Kayerts; he is so fat and unhealthy. It would be awful if I had to bury him here. He is a man I respect.... Before they reached the verandah of their house they called one another "my dear fellow."

The first day they were very active, pottering about with hammers and nails and red calico, to put up curtains, make their house habitable and pretty; resolved to settle down comfortably to their new life. For them an impossible task. To grapple effectually with even purely material problems requires more serenity of mind and more lofty courage than people generally imagine. No two beings could have been more unfitted for such a struggle. Society, not from any tenderness, but because of its strange needs, had taken care of those two men, forbidding them all independent thought, all initiative, all departure from routine; and forbidding it under pain of death. They could only live on condition of being machines. And now, released from the fostering care of men with pens behind the ears, or of men with gold lace on the sleeves, they were like those lifelong prisoners who, liberated after many years, do not know what use to make of their freedom. They did not know what use to make of their faculties, being both, through want of practice, incapable of independent thought.

At the end of two months Kayerts often would say, "If it was not for my Melie, you wouldn't catch me here." Melie was his daughter. He had thrown up his post in the Administration of the Telegraphs, though he had been for seventeen years perfectly happy there, to earn a dowry for his girl. His wife was dead, and the child was being brought up by his sisters. He regretted the streets, the pavements, the cafés, his friends of many years; all the things he used to see, day after day; all the thoughts suggested by familiar things — the thoughts effortless, monotonous, and soothing of a Government clerk; he regretted all the gossip, the small enmities, the mild venom, and the little jokes of Government offices. "If I had had a decent brother-in-law," Carlier would remark, "a fellow with a heart, I would not be here." He had left the army and had made himself so obnoxious to his family by his laziness and impudence, that an exasperated brother-in-law had made superhuman efforts to procure him an appointment in the Company as a second-class agent. Having not a penny in the world he was compelled to accept this means of livelihood as soon as it became quite clear to him that there was nothing more to squeeze out of his relations. He, like Kayerts, regretted his old life. He regretted the clink of sabre and spurs on a fine afternoon, the barrack-room witticisms, the girls of garrison towns; but, besides, he had also a sense of grievance. He was evidently a much ill-used man. This made him moody, at times. But the two men got on well together in the fellowship of their stupidity and laziness. Together they did nothing, absolutely nothing, and enjoyed the sense of idleness for which they were paid. And in time they came to feel something resembling affection for one another.

They lived like blind men in a large room, aware only of what came in contact with them (and of that only imperfectly), but unable to see the general aspect of things. The river, the forest, all the great land throbbing with life, were like a great emptiness. Even the brilliant sunshine disclosed nothing intelligible. Things appeared and disappeared before their eyes in an unconnected and aimless kind of way. The river seemed to come from nowhere and flow nowhither. It flowed through a void. Out of that void, at times, came canoes, and men with spears in their hands would suddenly crowd the yard of the station. They were naked, glossy black, ornamented with snowy shells and glistening brass wire, perfect of limb. They made an uncouth babbling noise when they spoke, moved in a stately manner, and sent quick, wild glances out of their startled, never-resting eyes. Those warriors would squat in long rows, four or more deep, before the verandah, while their chiefs bargained for hours with Makola over an elephant tusk. Kayerts sat on his chair and looked down on the proceedings, understanding nothing. He stared at them with his round blue eyes, called out to Carlier, "Here, look! look at that fellow there — and that other one, to the left. Did you ever see such a face? Oh, the funny brute!"

Carlier, smoking native tobacco in a short wooden pipe, would swagger up twirling his moustaches, and surveying the warriors with haughty indulgence, would say —

"Fine animals. Brought any bone? Yes? It's not any too soon. Look at the muscles of that fellow — third from the end. I wouldn't care to get a punch on the nose from him. Fine arms, but legs no good below the knee. Couldn't make cavalry men of them." And after glancing down complacently at his own shanks, he always concluded: "Pah! Don't they stink! You, Makola! Take that herd over to the fetish" (the storehouse was in every station called the fetish, perhaps because of the spirit of civilization it contained) "and give them up some of the rubbish you keep there. I'd rather see it full of bone than full of rags."

Kayerts approved.

"Yes, yes! Go and finish that palaver over there, Mr. Makola. I will come round when you are ready, to weigh the tusk. We must be careful." Then turning to his companion: "This is the tribe that lives down the river; they are rather aromatic. I remember, they had been once before here. D'ye hear that row? What a fellow has got to put up with in this dog of a country! My head is split."

Such profitable visits were rare. For days the two pioneers of trade and progress would look on their empty courtyard in the vibrating brilliance of vertical sunshine. Below the high bank, the silent river flowed on glittering and steady. On the sands in the middle of the stream, hippos and alligators sunned themselves side by side. And stretching away in all directions, surrounding the insignificant cleared spot of the trading post, immense forests, hiding fateful complications of fantastic life, lay in the eloquent silence of mute greatness. The two men understood nothing, cared for nothing but for the passage of days that separated them from the steamer's return. Their predecessor had left some torn books. They took up these wrecks of novels, and, as they had never read anything of the kind before, they were surprised and amused. Then during long days there were interminable and silly discussions about plots and personages. In the centre of Africa they made acquaintance of Richelieu and of d'Artagnan, of Hawk's Eye and of Father Goriot, and of many other people.[1] All these imaginary personages became subjects for gossip as if they had been living friends. They discounted their virtues, suspected their motives, decried their successes; were scandalized at their duplicity or were doubtful about their courage. The accounts of crimes filled them with indignation, while tender or pathetic passages moved them deeply. Carlier cleared his throat and said in a soldierly voice, "What nonsense!" Kayerts, his round eyes suffused with tears, his fat cheeks quivering, rubbed his bald head, and declared, "This is a splendid book. I had no idea there were such clever fellows in the world." They also found some old copies of a home paper. That print discussed what it was pleased to call "Our Colonial Expansion" in high-flown language. It spoke much of the rights and duties of civilization, of the sacredness of the civilizing work, and extolled the merits of those who went about bringing light, and faith and commerce to the dark places of the earth. Carlier and Kayerts read, wondered, and began to think better of themselves. Carlier said one evening, waving his hand about, "In a hundred years, there will be perhaps a town here. Quays, and warehouses, and barracks, and — and — billiard-rooms. Civilization, my boy, and virtue — and all. And then, chaps will read that two good fellows, Kayerts and Carlier, were the first civilized men to live in this very spot!" Kayerts nodded, "Yes, it is a consolation to think of that." They seemed to forget their dead predecessor; but, early one day, Carlier went out and replanted the cross firmly. "It used to make me squint whenever I walked that way," he explained to Kayerts over the morning coffee. "It made me squint,

1 heroes in popular adventure novels by Alexandre Dumas, James Fenimore Cooper, and Honoré de Balzac, respectively.

leaning over so much. So I just planted it upright. And solid, I promise you! I suspended myself with both hands to the cross-piece. Not a move. Oh, I did that properly."

15    At times Gobila came to see them. Gobila was the chief of the neighbouring villages. He was a gray-headed savage, thin and black, with a white cloth round his loins and a mangy panther skin hanging over his back. He came up with long strides of his skeleton legs, swinging a staff as tall as himself, and, entering the common room of the station, would squat on his heels to the left of the door. There he sat, watching Kayerts, and now and then making a speech which the other did not understand. Kayerts, without interrupting his occupation, would from time to time say in a friendly manner: "How goes it, you old image?" and they would smile at one another. The two whites had a liking for that old and incomprehensible creature, and called him Father Gobila. Gobila's manner was paternal, and he seemed really to love all white men. They all appeared to him very young, indistinguishably alike (except for stature), and he knew that they were all brothers, and also immortal. The death of the artist, who was the first white man whom he knew intimately, did not disturb this belief, because he was firmly convinced that the white stranger had pretended to die and got himself buried for some mysterious purpose of his own, into which it was useless to inquire. Perhaps it was his way of going home to his own country? At any rate, these were his brothers, and he transferred his absurd affection to them. They returned it in a way. Carlier slapped him on the back, and recklessly struck off matches for his amusement. Kayerts was always ready to let him have a sniff at the ammonia bottle. In short, they behaved just like that other white creature that had hidden itself in a hole in the ground. Gobila considered them attentively. Perhaps they were the same being with the other — or one of them was. He couldn't decide — clear up that mystery; but he remained always very friendly. In consequence of that friendship the women of Gobila's village walked in single file through the reedy grass, bringing every morning to the station, fowls, and sweet potatoes, and palm wine, and sometimes a goat. The Company never provisions the stations fully, and the agents required those local supplies to live. They had them through the good-will of Gobila, and lived well. Now and then one of them had a bout of fever, and the other nursed him with gentle devotion. They did not think much of it. It left them weaker, and their appearance changed for the worse. Carlier was hollow-eyed and irritable. Kayerts showed a drawn, flabby face above the rotundity of his stomach, which gave him a weird aspect. But being constantly together, they did not notice the change that took place gradually in their appearance, and also in their dispositions.

Five months passed in that way.

Then, one morning, as Kayerts and Carlier, lounging in their chairs under the verandah, talked about the approaching visit of the steamer, a knot of armed men came out of the forest and advanced towards the station. They were strangers to that part of the country. They were tall, slight, draped classically from neck to heel in blue fringed cloths, and carried percussion muskets over their bare right shoulders. Makola showed signs of excitement, and ran out of the storehouse (where he spent all his days) to meet these visitors. They came into the courtyard and looked about them with steady, scornful glances. Their leader, a powerful and determined-looking negro with bloodshot eyes, stood in front of the verandah and made a long speech. He gesticulated much, and ceased very suddenly.

There was something in his intonation, in the sounds of the long sentences he used, that startled the two whites. It was like a reminiscence of something not exactly familiar, and yet resembling the speech of civilized men. It sounded like one of those impossible languages which sometimes we hear in our dreams.

"What lingo is that?" said the amazed Carlier. "In the first moment I fancied the fellow was going to speak French. Anyway, it is a different kind of gibberish to what we ever heard."

20 "Yes," replied Kayerts. "Hey, Makola, what does he say? Where do they come from? Who are they?

But Makola, who seemed to be standing on hot bricks, answered hurriedly, "I don't know. They come from very far. Perhaps Mrs. Price will understand. They are perhaps bad men."

The leader, after waiting for a while, said something sharply to Makola, who shook his head. Then the man, after looking round, noticed Makola's hut and walked over there. The next moment Mrs. Makola was heard speaking with great volubility. The other strangers — they were six in all — strolled about with an air of ease, put their heads through the door of the storeroom, congregated round the grave, pointed understandingly at the cross, and generally made themselves at home.

"I don't like those chaps — and, I say, Kayerts, they must be from the coast; they've got firearms," observed the sagacious Carlier.

Kayerts also did not like those chaps. They both, for the first time, became aware that they lived in conditions where the unusual may be dangerous, and that there was no power on earth outside of themselves to stand between them and the unusual. They became uneasy, went in and loaded their revolvers. Kayerts said, "We must order Makola to tell them to go away before dark."

25 The strangers left in the afternoon, after eating a meal prepared for them by Mrs. Makola. The immense woman was excited, and talked much with the visitors. She rattled away shrilly, pointing here and there at the forests and at the river. Makola sat apart and watched. At times he got up and whispered to his wife. He accompanied the strangers across the ravine at the back of the station-ground, and returned slowly looking very thoughtful. When questioned by the white men he was very strange, seemed not to understand, seemed to have forgotten French — seemed to have forgotten how to speak altogether. Kayerts and Carlier agreed that the nigger had had too much palm wine.

There was some talk about keeping a watch in turn, but in the evening everything seemed so quiet and peaceful that they retired as usual. All night they were disturbed by a lot of drumming in the villages. A deep, rapid roll near by would be followed by another far off — then all ceased. Soon short appeals would rattle out here and there, then all mingle together, increase, become vigorous and sustained, would spread out over the forest, roll through the night, unbroken and ceaseless, near and far, as if the whole land had been one immense drum booming out steadily an appeal to heaven. And through the deep and tremendous noise sudden yells that resembled snatches of songs from a madhouse darted shrill and high in discordant jets of sound which seemed to rush far above the earth and drive all peace from under the stars.

Carlier and Kayerts slept badly. They both thought they had heard shots fired during the night — but they could not agree as to the direction. In the morning Makola was gone somewhere. He returned about noon with one of yesterday's strangers, and eluded all Kayerts' attempts to close with him: had become deaf apparently. Kayerts wondered. Carlier, who had been fishing off the bank, came back and remarked while he showed his catch, "The niggers seem to be in a deuce of a stir; I wonder what's up. I saw about fifteen canoes cross the river during the two hours I was there fishing." Kayerts, worried, said, "Isn't this Makola very queer to-day?" Carlier advised, "Keep all our men together in case of some trouble."

## II

There were ten station men who had been left by the Director. Those fellows, having engaged themselves to the Company for six months (without having any idea of a month in particular and only a very faint notion of time in general), had been serving the cause of progress for upwards of two years. Belonging to a tribe from a very distant part of the land of darkness and sorrow, they did not run away, naturally supposing that as wandering strangers they would be killed by the inhabitants of the country; in which they were right. They lived in straw huts on the slope of a ravine overgrown with reedy grass, just behind the station buildings. They were not happy, regretting the festive incantations, the sorceries, the human sacrifices of their own land; where they also had parents, brothers, sisters, admired chiefs, respected magicians, loved friends, and other ties supposed generally to be human. Besides, the rice rations served out by the Company did not agree with them, being a food unknown to their land, and to which they could not get used. Consequently they were unhealthy and miserable. Had they been of any other tribe they would have made up their minds to die — for nothing is easier to certain savages than suicide — and so have escaped from the puzzling difficulties of existence. But belonging, as they did, to a warlike tribe with filed teeth, they had more grit, and went on stupidly living through disease and sorrow. They did very little work, and had lost their splendid physique. Carlier and Kayerts doctored them assiduously without being able to bring them back into condition again. They were mustered every morning and told off to different tasks — grass-cutting, fence-building, tree-felling, &c., &c., which no power on earth could induce them to execute efficiently. The two whites had practically very little control over them.

In the afternoon Makola came over to the big house and found Kayerts watching three heavy columns of smoke rising above the forests. "What is that?" asked Kayerts. "Some villages burn," answered Makola, who seemed to have regained his wits. Then he said abruptly: "We have got very little ivory; bad six months' trading. Do you like get a little more ivory?"

"Yes," said Kayerts, eagerly. He thought of percentages which were low.

"Those men who came yesterday are traders from Loanda who have got more ivory than they can carry home. Shall I buy? I know their camp."

"Certainly," said Kayerts. "What are those traders?"

"Bad fellows," said Makola, indifferently. "They fight with people, and catch women and children. They are bad men, and got guns. There is a great disturbance in the country. Do you want ivory?"

"Yes," said Kayerts. Makola said nothing for a while. Then: "Those workmen of ours are no good at all," he muttered, looking round. "Station in very bad order, sir. Director will growl. Better get a fine lot of ivory, then he say nothing."

35 "I can't help it; the men won't work," said Kayerts. "When will you get that ivory?"

"Very soon," said Makola. "Perhaps to-night. You leave it to me, and keep indoors, sir. I think you had better give some palm wine to our men to make a dance this evening. Enjoy themselves. Work better to-morrow. There's plenty palm wine — gone a little sour."

Kayerts said yes, and Makola, with his own hands, carried big calabashes to the door of his hut. They stood there till the evening, and Mrs. Makola looked into every one. The men got them at sunset. When Kayerts and Carlier retired, a big bonfire was flaring before the men's huts. They could hear their shouts and drumming. Some men from Gobila's village had joined the station hands, and the entertainment was a great success.

In the middle of the night, Carlier waking suddenly, heard a man shout loudly; then a shot was fired. Only one. Carlier ran out and met Kayerts on the verandah. They were both startled. As they went across the yard to call Makola, they saw shadows moving in the night. One of them cried, "Don't shoot! It's me, Price." Then Makola appeared close to them. "Go back, go back, please," he urged, "you spoil all." "There are strange men about," said Carlier. "Never mind; I know," said Makola. Then he whispered, "All right. Bring ivory. Say nothing! I know my business." The two white men reluctantly went back to the house, but did not sleep. They heard footsteps, whispers, some groans. It seemed as if a lot of men came in, dumped heavy things on the ground, squabbled a long time, then went away. They lay on their hard beds and thought: "This Makola is invaluable." In the morning Carlier came out, very sleepy, and pulled at the cord of the big bell. The station hands mustered every morning to the sound of the bell. That morning nobody came. Kayerts turned out also, yawning. Across the yard they saw Makola come out of his hut, a tin basin of soapy water in his hand. Makola, a civilized nigger, was very neat in his person. He threw the soapsuds skilfully over a wretched little yellow cur he had, then turning his face to the agent's house, he shouted from the distance, "All the men gone last night!"

They heard him plainly, but in their surprise they both yelled out together: "What!" Then they stared at one another. "We are in a proper fix now," growled Carlier. "It's incredible!" muttered Kayerts. "I will go to the huts and see," said Carlier, striding off. Makola coming up found Kayerts standing alone.

40 "I can hardly believe it," said Kayerts, tearfully. "We took care of them as if they had been our children."

"They went with the coast people," said Makola after a moment of hesitation.

"What do I care with whom they went — the ungrateful brutes!" exclaimed the other. Then with sudden suspicion, and looking hard at Makola, he added: "What do you know about it?"

Makola moved his shoulders, looking down on the ground. "What do I know? I think only. Will you come and look at the ivory I've got there? It is a fine lot. You never saw such."

He moved towards the store. Kayerts followed him mechanically, thinking about the incredible desertion of the men. On the ground before the door of the fetish lay six splendid tusks.

45    "What did you give for it?" asked Kayerts, after surveying the lot with satisfaction.

"No regular trade," said Makola. "They brought the ivory and gave it to me. I told them to take what they most wanted in the station. It is a beautiful lot. No station can show such tusks. Those traders wanted carriers badly, and our men were no good here. No trade, no entry in books; all correct."

Kayerts nearly burst with indignation. "Why!" he shouted, "I believe you have sold our men for these tusks!" Makola stood impassive and silent. "I — I — will — I," stuttered Kayerts. "You fiend!" he yelled out.

"I did the best for you and the Company," said Makola, imperturbably. "Why you shout so much? Look at this tusk."

"I dismiss you! I will report you — I won't look at the tusk. I forbid you to touch them. I order you to throw them into the river. You — you!"

50    "You very red, Mr. Kayerts. If you are so irritable in the sun, you will get fever and die — like the first chief!" pronounced Makola impressively.

They stood still, contemplating one another with intense eyes, as if they had been looking with effort across immense distances. Kayerts shivered. Makola had meant no more than he said, but his words seemed to Kayerts full of ominous menace! He turned sharply and went away to the house. Makola retired into the bosom of his family; and the tusks, left lying before the store, looked very large and valuable in the sunshine.

Carlier came back on the verandah. "They're all gone, hey?" asked Kayerts from the far end of the common room in a muffled voice. "You did not find anybody?"

"Oh, yes," said Carlier, "I found one of Gobila's people lying dead before the huts — shot through the body. We heard that shot last night."

Kayerts came out quickly. He found his companion staring grimly over the yard at the tusks, away by the store. They both sat in silence for a while. Then Kayerts related his conversation with Makola. Carlier said nothing. At the midday meal they ate very little. They hardly exchanged a word that day. A great silence seemed to lie heavily over the station and press on their lips. Makola did not open the store; he spent the day playing with his children. He lay full-length on a mat outside his door, and the youngsters sat on his chest and clambered all over him. It was a touching picture. Mrs. Makola was busy cooking all day as usual. The white men made a somewhat better meal in the evening. Afterwards, Carlier smoking his pipe strolled over to the store; he stood for a long time over the tusks, touched one or two with his foot, even tried to lift the largest one by its small end. He came back to his chief, who had not stirred from the verandah, threw himself in the chair and said —

55     "I can see it! They were pounced upon while they slept heavily after drinking all that palm wine you've allowed Makola to give them. A put-up job! See? The worst is, some of Gobila's people went there, and got carried off too, no doubt. The least drunk woke up, and got shot for his sobriety. This is a funny country. What will you do now?"

"We can't touch it, of course," said Kayerts.

"Of course not," assented Carlier.

"Slavery is an awful thing," stammered out Kayerts in an unsteady voice.

"Frightful — the sufferings," grunted Carlier with conviction.

60     They believed their words. Everybody shows a respectful deference to certain sounds that he and his fellows can make. But about feelings people really know nothing. We talk with indignation or enthusiasm; we talk about oppression, cruelty, crime, devotion, self-sacrifice, virtue, and we know nothing real beyond the words. Nobody knows what suffering or sacrifice mean — except, perhaps the victims of the mysterious purpose of these illusions.

Next morning they saw Makola very busy setting up in the yard the big scales used for weighing ivory. By and by Carlier said: "What's that filthy scoundrel up to?" and lounged out into the yard. Kayerts followed. They stood watching. Makola took no notice. When the balance was swung true, he tried to lift a tusk into the scale. It was too heavy. He looked up helplessly without a word, and for a minute they stood round that balance as mute and still as three statues. Suddenly Carlier said: "Catch hold of the other end, Makola — you beast!" and together they swung the tusk up. Kayerts trembled in every limb. He muttered, "I say! O! I say!" and putting his hand in his pocket found there a dirty bit of paper and the stump of a pencil. He turned his back on the others, as if about to do something tricky, and noted stealthily the weights which Carlier shouted out to him with unnecessary loudness. When all was over Makola whispered to himself: "The sun's very strong here for the tusks." Carlier said to Kayerts in a careless tone: "I say, chief, I might just as well give him a lift with this lot into the store."

As they were going back to the house Kayerts observed with a sigh: "It had to be done." And Carlier said: "It's deplorable, but, the men being Company's men the ivory is Company's ivory. We must look after it." "I will report to the Director, of course," said Kayerts. "Of course; let him decide," approved Carlier.

At midday they made a hearty meal. Kayerts sighed from time to time. Whenever they mentioned Makola's name they always added to it an opprobrious epithet. It eased their conscience. Makola gave himself a half-holiday, and bathed his children in the river. No one from Gobila's villages came near the station that day. No one came the next day, and the next, nor for a whole week. Gobila's people might have been dead and buried for any sign of life they gave. But they were only mourning for those they had lost by the witchcraft of white men, who had brought wicked people into their country. The wicked people were gone, but fear remained. Fear always remains. A man may destroy everything within himself, love and hate and belief, and even doubt; but as long as he clings to life he cannot destroy fear: the fear, subtle, indestructible, and terrible, that pervades his being; that tinges his thoughts; that lurks in his heart; that watches on his lips the struggle of his last breath. In his fear, the mild old Gobila offered extra human sacrifices to all the Evil Spirits that had taken possession of his white friends. His heart was heavy. Some warriors spoke about burning and killing, but the cautious old savage dissuaded them. Who could foresee the woe those mysterious creatures, if irritated, might bring? They should be left alone. Perhaps in time they would disappear into the earth as the first one had disappeared. His people must keep away from them, and hope for the best.

Kayerts and Carlier did not disappear, but remained above on this earth, that, somehow, they fancied had become bigger and very empty. It was not the absolute and dumb solitude of the post that impressed them so much as an inarticulate feeling that something from within them was gone, something that worked for their safety, and had kept the wilderness from interfering with their hearts. The images of home; the memory of people like them, of men that thought and felt as they used to think and feel, receded into distances made indistinct by the glare of unclouded sunshine. And out of the great silence of the surrounding wilderness, its very hopelessness and savagery seemed to approach them nearer, to draw them gently, to look upon them, to envelop them with a solicitude irresistible, familiar, and disgusting.

65     Days lengthened into weeks, then into months. Gobila's people drummed and yelled to every new moon, as of yore, but kept away from the station. Makola and Carlier tried once in a canoe to open communications, but were received with a shower of arrows, and had to fly back to the station for dear life. That attempt set the country up and down the river into an uproar that could be very distinctly heard for days. The steamer was late. At first they spoke of delay jauntily, then anxiously, then gloomily. The matter was becoming serious. Stores were running short. Carlier cast his lines off the bank, but the river was low, and the fish kept out in the stream. They dared not stroll far away from the station to shoot. Moreover, there was no game in the impenetrable forest. Once Carlier shot a hippo in the river. They had no boat to secure it, and it sank. When it floated up it drifted away, and Gobila's people secured the carcase. It was the occasion for a national holiday, but Carlier had a fit of rage over it and talked about the necessity of exterminating all the niggers before the country could be made habitable. Kayerts mooned about silently; spent hours looking at the portrait of his Melie. It represented a little girl with long bleached tresses and a rather sour face. His legs were much swollen, and he could hardly walk. Carlier, undermined by fever, could not swagger any more, but kept tottering about, still with a devil-may-care air, as became a man who remembered his crack regiment. He had become hoarse, sarcastic, and inclined to say unpleasant things. He called it "being frank with you." They had long ago reckoned their percentages on trade, including in them that last deal of "this infamous Makola." They had also concluded not to say anything about it. Kayerts hesitated at first — was afraid of the Director.

"He has seen worse things done on the quiet," maintained Carlier, with a hoarse laugh. "Trust him! He won't thank you if you blab. He is no better than you or me. Who will talk if we hold our tongues? There is nobody here."

That was the root of the trouble! There was nobody there; and being left there alone with their weakness, they became daily more like a pair of accomplices than like a couple of devoted friends. They had heard nothing from home for eight months. Every evening they said, "To-morrow we shall see the steamer." But one of the Company's steamers had been wrecked, and the Director was busy with the other, relieving very distant and important stations on the main river. He thought that the useless station, and the useless men, could wait. Meantime Kayerts and Carlier lived on rice boiled without salt, and cursed the Company, all Africa, and the day they were born. One must have lived on such diet to discover what ghastly trouble the necessity of swallowing one's food may become. There was literally nothing else in the station but rice and coffee; they drank the coffee without sugar. The last fifteen lumps Kayerts had solemnly locked away in his box, together with a half-bottle of Cognâc, "in case of sickness," he explained. Carlier approved. "When one is sick," he said, "any little extra like that is cheering."

They waited. Rank grass began to sprout over the courtyard. The bell never rang now. Days passed, silent, exasperating, and slow. When the two men spoke, they snarled; and their silences were bitter, as if tinged by the bitterness of their thoughts.

One day after a lunch of boiled rice, Carlier put down his cup untasted, and said: "Hang it all! Let's have a decent cup of coffee for once. Bring out that sugar, Kayerts!"

70      "For the sick," muttered Kayerts, without looking up.

"For the sick," mocked Carlier. "Bosh! . . . Well! I am sick."

"You are no more sick than I am, and I go without," said Kayerts in a peaceful tone.

"Come! out with that sugar, you stingy old slave-dealer."

Kayerts looked up quickly. Carlier was smiling with marked insolence. And suddenly it seemed to Kayerts that he had never seen that man before. Who was he? He knew nothing about him. What was he capable of? There was a surprising flash of violent emotion within him, as if in the presence of something undreamt-of, dangerous, and final. But he managed to pronounce with composure —

75      "That joke is in very bad taste. Don't repeat it."

"Joke!" said Carlier, hitching himself forward on his seat. "I am hungry — I am sick — I don't joke! I hate hypocrites. You are a hypocrite. You are a slave-dealer. I am a slave-dealer. There's nothing but slave-dealers in this cursed country. I mean to have sugar in my coffee to-day, anyhow!"

"I forbid you to speak to me in that way," said Kayerts with a fair show of resolution.

"You! — What?" shouted Carlier, jumping up.

Kayerts stood up also. "I am your chief," he began, trying to master the shakiness of his voice.

80      "What?" yelled the other. "Who's chief? There's no chief here. There's nothing here: there's nothing but you and I. Fetch the sugar — you potbellied ass."

"Hold your tongue. Go out of this room," screamed Kayerts. "I dismiss you — you scoundrel!"

Carlier swung a stool. All at once he looked dangerously in earnest. "You flabby, good-for-nothing civilian — take that!" he howled.

Kayerts dropped under the table, and the stool struck the grass inner wall of the room. Then, as Carlier was trying to upset the table, Kayerts in desperation made a blind rush, head low, like a cornered pig would do, and over-turning his friend, bolted along the verandah, and into his room. He locked the door, snatched his revolver, and stood panting. In less than a minute, Carlier was kicking at the door furiously, howling, "If you don't bring out that sugar, I will shoot you at sight, like a dog. Now then — one — two — three. You won't? I will show you who's the master."

Kayerts thought the door would fall in, and scrambled through the square hole that served for a window in his room. There was then the whole breadth of the house between them. But the other was apparently not strong enough to break in the door, and Kayerts heard him running round. Then he also began to run laboriously on his swollen legs. He ran as quickly as he could, grasping the revolver, and unable yet to understand what was happening to him. He saw in succession Makola's house, the store, the river, the ravine, and the low bushes; and he saw all those things again as he ran for the second time round the house. Then again they flashed past him. That morning he could not have walked a yard without a groan.

85      And now he ran. He ran fast enough to keep out of sight of the other man.

Then as, weak and desperate, he thought, "Before I finish the next round I shall die," he heard the other man stumble heavily, then stop. He stopped also. He had the back and Carlier the front of the house, as before. He heard him drop into a chair cursing, and suddenly his own legs gave way, and he slid down into a sitting posture with his back to the wall. His mouth was as dry as a cinder, and his face was wet with perspiration — and tears. What was it all about? He thought it must be a horrible illusion; he thought he was dreaming; he thought he was going mad! After a while he collected his senses. What did they quarrel about? That sugar! How absurd! He would give it to him — didn't want it himself. And he began scrambling to his feet with a sudden feeling of security. But before he had fairly stood upright, a common-sense reflection occurred to him and drove him back into despair. He thought: If I give way now to that brute of a soldier, he will begin this horror again to-morrow — and the day after — every day — raise other pretensions, trample on me, torture me, make me his slave — and I will be lost! Lost! The steamer may not come for days — may never come. He shook so that he had to sit down on the floor again. He shivered forlornly. He felt he could not, would not move any more. He was completely distracted by the sudden perception that the position was without issue — that death and life had in a moment become equally difficult and terrible.

All at once he heard the other push his chair back; and he leaped to his feet with extreme facility. He listened and got confused. Must run again! Right or left? He heard footsteps. He darted to the left, grasping his revolver, and at the very same instant, as it seemed to him, they came into violent collision. Both shouted with surprise. A loud explosion took place between them; a roar of red fire, thick smoke; and Kayerts, deafened and blinded, rushed back thinking: I am hit — it's all over. He expected the other to come round — to gloat over his agony. He caught hold of an upright of the roof — "All over!" Then he heard a crashing fall on the other side of the house, as if somebody had tumbled headlong over a chair — then silence. Nothing more happened. He did not die. Only his shoulder felt as if it had been badly wrenched, and he had lost his revolver. He was disarmed and helpless! He waited for his fate. The other man made no sound. It was a stratagem. He was stalking him now! Along what side? Perhaps he was taking aim this very minute!

After a few moments of an agony frightful and absurd, he decided to go and meet his doom. He was prepared for every surrender. He turned the corner, steadying himself with one hand on the wall; made a few paces, and nearly swooned. He had seen on the floor, protruding past the other corner, a pair of turned-up feet. A pair of white naked feet in red slippers. He felt deadly sick, and stood for a time in profound darkness. Then Makola appeared before him, saying quietly: "Come along, Mr. Kayerts. He is dead." He burst into tears of gratitude; a loud, sobbing fit of crying. After a time he found himself sitting in a chair and looking at Carlier, who lay stretched on his back. Makola was kneeling over the body.

"Is this your revolver?" asked Makola, getting up.

90      "Yes," said Kayerts; then he added very quickly, "He ran after me to shoot me — you saw!"

"Yes, I saw," said Makola. "There is only one revolver; where's his?"

"Don't know," whispered Kayerts in a voice that had become suddenly very faint.

"I will go and look for it," said the other, gently. He made the round along the verandah, while Kayerts sat still and looked at the corpse. Makola came back empty-handed, stood in deep thought, then stepped quietly into the dead man's room, and came out directly with a revolver, which he held up before Kayerts. Kayerts shut his eyes. Everything was going round. He found life more terrible and difficult than death. He had shot an unarmed man.

After meditating for a while, Makola said softly, pointing at the dead man who lay there with his right eye blown out —

95      "He died of fever." Kayerts looked at him with a stony stare. "Yes," repeated Makola, thoughtfully, stepping over the corpse, "I think he died of fever. Bury him to-morrow."

And he went away slowly to his expectant wife, leaving the two white men alone on the verandah.

Night came, and Kayerts sat unmoving on his chair. He sat quiet as if he had taken a dose of opium. The violence of the emotions he had passed through produced a feeling of exhausted serenity. He had plumbed in one short afternoon the depths of horror and despair, and now found repose in the conviction that life had no more secrets for him: neither had death! He sat by the corpse thinking; thinking very actively, thinking very new thoughts. He seemed to have broken loose from himself altogether. His old thoughts, convictions, likes and dislikes, things he respected and things he abhorred, appeared in their true light at last! Appeared contemptible and childish, false and ridiculous. He revelled in his new wisdom while he sat by the man he had killed. He argued with himself about all things under heaven with that kind of wrong-headed lucidity which may be observed in some lunatics. Incidentally he reflected that the fellow dead there had been a noxious beast anyway; that men died every day in thousands; perhaps in hundreds of thousands — who could tell? — and that in the number, that one death could not possibly make any difference; couldn't have any importance, at least to a thinking creature.

He, Kayerts, was a thinking creature. He had been all his life, till that moment, a believer in a lot of nonsense like the rest of mankind — who are fools; but now he thought! He knew! He was at peace; he was familiar with the highest wisdom! Then he tried to imagine himself dead, and Carlier sitting in his chair watching him; and his attempt met with such unexpected success, that in a very few moments he became not at all sure who was dead and who was alive. This extraordinary achievement of his fancy startled him, however, and by a clever and timely effort of mind he saved himself just in time from becoming Carlier. His heart thumped, and he felt hot all over at the thought of that danger. Carlier! What a beastly thing! To compose his now disturbed nerves — and no wonder! — he tried to whistle a little. Then, suddenly, he fell asleep, or thought he had slept; but at any rate there was a fog, and somebody had whistled in the fog.

He stood up. The day had come, and a heavy mist had descended upon the land: the mist penetrating, enveloping, and silent; the morning mist of tropical lands; the mist that clings and kills; the mist white and deadly, immaculate and poisonous. He stood up, saw the body, and threw his arms above his head with a cry like that of a man who, waking from a trance, finds himself immured forever in a tomb. "*Help! . . . My God!*"

A shriek inhuman, vibrating and sudden, pierced like a sharp dart the white shroud of that land of sorrow. Three short, impatient screeches followed, and then, for a time, the fog-wreaths rolled on, undisturbed, through a formidable silence. Then many more shrieks, rapid and piercing, like the yells of some exasperated and ruthless creature, rent the air. Progress was calling to Kayerts from the river. Progress and civilization and all the virtues. Society was calling to its accomplished child to come, to be taken care of, to be instructed, to be judged, to be condemned; it called him to return to that rubbish heap from which he had wandered away, so that justice could be done.

100    Kayerts heard and understood. He stumbled out of the verandah, leaving the other man quite alone for the first time since they had been thrown there together. He groped his way through the fog, calling in his ignorance upon the invisible heaven to undo its work. Makola flitted by in the mist, shouting as he ran —

"Steamer! Steamer! They can't see. They whistle for the station. I go ring the bell. Go down to the landing, sir. I ring."

He disappeared. Kayerts stood still. He looked upwards; the fog rolled low over his head. He looked round like a man who has lost his way; and he saw a dark smudge, a cross-shaped stain, upon the shifting purity of the mist. As he began to stumble towards it, the station bell rang in a tumultuous peal its answer to the impatient clamour of the steamer.

The Managing Director of the Great Civilizing Company (since we know that civilization follows trade) landed first, and incontinently lost sight of the steamer. The fog down by the river was exceedingly dense; above, at the station, the bell rang unceasing and brazen.

The Director shouted loudly to the steamer:

105    "There is nobody down to meet us; there may be something wrong, though they are ringing. You had better come, too!"

And he began to toil up the steep bank. The captain and the engine-driver of the boat followed behind. As they scrambled up the fog thinned, and they could see their Director a good way ahead. Suddenly they saw him start forward, calling to them over his shoulder:—"Run! Run to the house! I've found one of them. Run, look for the other!"

He had found one of them! And even he, the man of varied and startling experience, was somewhat discomposed by the manner of this finding. He stood and fumbled in his pockets (for a knife) while he faced Kayerts, who was hanging by a leather strap from the cross. He had evidently climbed the grave, which was high and narrow, and after tying the end of the strap to the arm, had swung himself off. His toes were only a couple of inches above the ground; his arms hung stiffly down; he seemed to be standing rigidly at attention, but with one purple cheek playfully posed on the shoulder. And, irreverently, he was putting out a swollen tongue at his Managing Director.

(1897)

# Charlotte Perkins Gilman (1860–1935)

Although "The Yellow Wallpaper" has recently been praised as a major feminist short story, it was virtually unknown until the early 1960s, and its author, a native of Hartford, Connecticut, was remembered chiefly as an important theorist in the women's movement during the early decades of this century. In such book-length tracts as *Women and Economics* (1898) and short stories as "If I Were a Man" and "The Widow's Might," she studied the nature of women's lives and their relationships with men. "The Yellow Wallpaper," one of her first short stories, was based on the extreme mental depression she suffered in part as the result of psychiatric treatments prescribed after the birth of her daughter. It was written, she later stated, "not... to drive people crazy, but to save people from being driven crazy...." Often compared to Edgar Allan Poe's tales that examine the narrator's descent into madness, the story, with its depiction of the prison-like room and its grotesquely designed wallpaper, is often interpreted as a presentation of the destructive effects on women of the repressive patriarchal society of the nineteenth century.

# THE YELLOW WALLPAPER

It is very seldom that mere ordinary people like John and myself secure ancestral halls for the summer.

A colonial mansion, a hereditary estate, I would say a haunted house and reach the height of romantic felicity — but that would be asking too much of fate!

Still I will proudly declare that there is something queer about it.

Else, why should it be let so cheaply? And why have stood so long untenanted?

5  John laughs at me, of course, but one expects that.

John is practical in the extreme. He has no patience with faith, an intense horror of superstition, and he scoffs openly at any talk of things not to be felt and seen and put down in figures.

John is a physician, and *perhaps*— (I would not say it to a living soul, of course, but this is dead paper and a great relief to my mind) —*perhaps* that is one reason I do not get well faster.

You see, he does not believe I am sick! And what can one do?

If a physician of high standing, and one's own husband, assures friends and relatives that there is really nothing the matter with one but temporary nervous depression — a slight hysterical tendency — what is one to do?

10  My brother is also a physician, and also of high standing, and he says the same thing.

So I take phosphates or phosphites — whichever it is — and tonics, and air and exercise, and journeys, and am absolutely forbidden to "work" until I am well again.

Personally, I disagree with their ideas.

Personally, I believe that congenial work, with excitement and change, would do me good.

But what is one to do?

15     I did write for a while in spite of them; but it *does* exhaust me a good deal — having to be so sly about it, or else meet with heavy opposition.

    I sometimes fancy that in my condition, if I had less opposition and more society and stimulus — but John says the very worst thing I can do is to think about my condition, and I confess it always makes me feel bad.

    So I will let it alone and talk about the house.

    The most beautiful place! It is quite alone, standing well back from the road, quite three miles from the village. It makes me think of English places that you read about, for there are hedges and walls and gates that lock, and lots of separate little houses for the gardeners and people.

    There is a *delicious* garden! I never saw such a garden — large and shady, full of box-bordered paths, and lined with long grape-covered arbors with seats under them.

20     There were greenhouses, but they are all broken now.

    There was some legal trouble, I believe, something about the heirs and co-heirs; anyhow, the place has been empty for years.

    That spoils my ghostliness, I am afraid, but I don't care — there is something strange about the house — I can feel it.

    I even said so to John one moonlight evening, but he said what I felt was a draught, and shut the window.

    I get unreasonably angry with John sometimes. I'm sure I never used to be so sensitive. I think it is due to this nervous condition.

25     But John says if I feel so I shall neglect proper self-control; so I take pains to control myself — before him, at least, and that makes me very tired.

    I don't like our room a bit. I wanted one downstairs that opened onto the piazza and had roses all over the window, and such pretty old-fashioned chintz hangings! But John would not hear of it.

    He said there was only one window and not room for two beds, and no near room for him if he took another.

    He is very careful and loving, and hardly lets me stir without special direction.

    I have a schedule prescription for each hour in the day; he takes all care from me, and so I feel basely ungrateful not to value it more.

30     He said he came here solely on my account, that I was to have perfect rest and all the air I could get. "Your exercise depends on your strength, my dear," said he, "and your food somewhat on your appetite; but air you can absorb all the time." So we took the nursery at the top of the house.

    It is a big, airy room, the whole floor nearly, with windows that look all ways, and air and sunshine galore. It was nursery first, and then playroom and gymnasium, I should judge, for the windows are barred for little children, and there are rings and things in the walls.

    The paint and paper look as if a boys' school had used it. It is stripped off — the paper — in great patches all around the head of my bed, about as far as I can reach, and in a great place on the other side of the room low down. I never saw a worse paper in my life. One of those sprawling, flamboyant patterns committing every artistic sin.

    It is dull enough to confuse the eye in following, pronounced enough constantly to irritate and provoke study, and when you follow the lame uncertain curves for a little distance they suddenly commit suicide — plunge off at outrageous angles, destroy themselves in unheard-of contradictions.

The color is repellent, almost revolting: a smouldering unclean yellow, strangely faded by the slow-turning sunlight. It is a dull yet lurid orange in some places, a sickly sulphur tint in others.

No wonder the children hated it! I should hate it myself if I had to live in this room long.

There comes John, and I must put this away — he hates to have me write a word.

We have been here two weeks, and I haven't felt like writing before, since that first day.

I am sitting by the window now, up in this atrocious nursery, and there is nothing to hinder my writing as much as I please, save lack of strength.

John is away all day, and even some nights when his cases are serious.

I am glad my case is not serious!

But these nervous troubles are dreadfully depressing.

John does not know how much I really suffer. He knows there is no reason to suffer, and that satisfies him.

Of course it is only nervousness. It does weigh on me so not to do my duty in any way!

I meant to be such a help to John, such a real rest and comfort, and here I am a comparative burden already!

Nobody would believe what an effort it is to do what little I am able — to dress and entertain, and order things.

It is fortunate Mary is so good with the baby. Such a dear baby!

And yet I *cannot* be with him, it makes me so nervous.

I suppose John never was nervous in his life. He laughs at me so about this wallpaper!

At first he meant to repaper the room, but afterward he said that I was letting it get the better of me, and that nothing was worse for a nervous patient than to give way to such fancies.

He said that after the wallpaper was changed it would be the heavy bedstead, and then the barred windows, and then that gate at the head of the stairs, and so on.

"You know the place is doing you good," he said, "and really, dear, I don't care to renovate the house just for a three months' rental."

"Then do let us go downstairs," I said. "There are such pretty rooms there."

Then he took me in his arms and called me a blessed little goose, and said he would go down cellar, if I wished, and have it whitewashed into the bargain.

But he is right enough about the beds and windows and things.

It is as airy and comfortable a room as anyone need wish, and, of course, I would not be so silly as to make him uncomfortable just for a whim.

I'm really getting quite fond of the big room, all but that horrid paper.

Out of one window I can see the garden — those mysterious deep-shaded arbors, the riotous old-fashioned flowers, and bushes and gnarly trees.

Out of another I get a lovely view of the bay and a little private wharf belonging to the estate. There is a beautiful shaded lane that runs down there from the house. I always fancy I see people walking in these numerous paths and arbors, but John has cautioned me not to give way to fancy in the least. He says that with my imaginative power and habit of story-making, a nervous weakness like mine is sure to lead to all manner of excited fancies, and that I ought to use my will and good sense to check the tendency. So I try.

I think sometimes that if I were only well enough to write a little it would relieve the press of ideas and rest me.

But I find I get pretty tired when I try.

It is so discouraging not to have any advice and companionship about my work. When I get really well, John says we will ask Cousin Henry and Julia down for a long visit; but he says he would as soon put fireworks in my pillow-case as to let me have those stimulating people about now.

I wish I could get well faster.

But I must not think about that. This paper looks to me as if it *knew* what a vicious influence it had!

There is a recurrent spot where the pattern lolls like a broken neck and two bulbous eyes stare at you upside down.

I get positively angry with the impertinence of it and the everlastingness. Up and down and sideways they crawl, and those absurd unblinking eyes are everywhere. There is one place where two breadths didn't match, and the eyes go all up and down the line, one a little higher than the other.

I never saw so much expression in an inanimate thing before, and we all know how much expression they have! I used to lie awake as a child and get more entertainment and terror out of blank walls and plain furniture than most children could find in a toy-store.

I remember what a kindly wink the knobs of our big old bureau used to have, and there was one chair that always seemed like a strong friend.

I used to feel that if any of the other things looked too fierce I could always hop into that chair and be safe.

The furniture in this room is no worse than inharmonious, however, for we had to bring it all from downstairs. I suppose when this was used as a play-room they had to take the nursery things out, and no wonder! I never saw such ravages as the children have made here.

The wallpaper, as I said before, is torn off in spots, and it sticketh closer than a brother — they must have had perseverance as well as hatred.

Then the floor is scratched and gouged and splintered, the plaster itself is dug out here and there, and this great heavy bed, which is all we found in the room, looks as if it had been through the wars.

But I don't mind it a bit — only the paper.

There comes John's sister. Such a dear girl as she is, and so careful of me! I must not let her find me writing.

She is a perfect and enthusiastic housekeeper, and hopes for no better profession. I verily believe she thinks it is the writing which made me sick!

But I can write when she is out, and see her a long way off from these windows.

There is one that commands the road, a lovely shaded winding road, and one that just looks off over the country. A lovely country, too, full of great elms and velvet meadows.

This wallpaper has a kind of sub-pattern in a different shade, a particularly irritating one, for you can only see it in certain lights, and not clearly then.

But in the places where it isn't faded and where the sun is just so — I can see a strange, provoking, formless sort of figure that seems to skulk about behind that silly and conspicuous front design.

There's sister on the stairs!

80    Well, the Fourth of July[1] is over! The people are all gone, and I am tired out. John thought it might do me good to see a little company, so we just had Mother and Nellie and the children down for a week.

Of course I didn't do a thing. Jennie sees to everything now.

But it tired me all the same.

John says if I don't pick up faster he shall send me to Weir Mitchell[2] in the fall.

But I don't want to go there at all. I had a friend who was in his hands once, and she says he is just like John and my brother, only more so!

85    Besides, it is such an undertaking to go so far.

I don't feel as if it was worthwhile to turn my hand over for anything, and I'm getting dreadfully fretful and querulous.

I cry at nothing, and cry most of the time.

Of course I don't when John is here, or anybody else, but when I am alone.

And I am alone a good deal just now. John is kept in town very often by serious cases, and Jennie is good and lets me alone when I want her to.

90    So I walk a little in the garden or down that lovely lane, sit on the porch under the roses, and lie down up here a good deal.

I'm getting really fond of the room in spite of the wallpaper. Perhaps *because* of the wallpaper.

It dwells in my mind so!

I lie here on this great immovable bed — it is nailed down, I believe — and follow that pattern about by the hour. It is as good as gymnastics, I assure you. I start, we'll say, at the bottom, down in the corner over there where it has not been touched, and I determine for the thousandth time that I *will* follow that pointless pattern to some sort of a conclusion.

I know a little of the principle of design, and I know this thing was not arranged on any laws of radiation, or alternation, or repetition, or symmetry, or anything else that I ever heard of.

95    It is repeated, of course, by the breadths, but not otherwise.

Looked at in one way, each breadth stands alone; the bloated curves and flourishes — a kind of "debased Romanesque"[3] with delirium tremens — go waddling up and down in isolated columns of fatuity.

---

1 American Independence Day. 2 Gilman's own physician, Silas Weir Mitchell, popularized the "rest cure" for people suffering from nervous disorders. 3 style of architecture prevalent from the ninth to the twelfth century in Europe, when the Gothic style began to replace it. It is characterized by thick walls and plain, rounded arches supported by columns.

But, on the other hand, they connect diagonally, and the sprawling outlines run off in great slanting waves of optic horror, like a lot of wallowing sea-weeds in full chase.

The whole thing goes horizontally, too, at least it seems so, and I exhaust myself trying to distinguish the order of its going in that direction.

They have used a horizontal breadth for a frieze, and that adds wonderfully to the confusion.

100 There is one end of the room where it is almost intact, and there, when the crosslights fade and the low sun shines directly upon it, I can almost fancy radiation after all — the interminable grotesque seems to form around a common center and rush off in headlong plunges of equal distraction.

It makes me tired to follow it. I will take a nap, I guess.

I don't know why I should write this.

I don't want to.

I don't feel able.

105 And I know John would think it absurd. But I *must* say what I feel and think in some way — it is such a relief!

But the effort is getting to be greater than the relief.

Half the time now I am awfully lazy, and lie down ever so much. John says I mustn't lose my strength, and has me take cod liver oil and lots of tonics and things, to say nothing of ale and wine and rare meat.

Dear John! He loves me very dearly, and hates to have me sick. I tried to have a real earnest reasonable talk with him the other day, and tell him how I wish he would let me go and make a visit to Cousin Henry and Julia.

But he said I wasn't able to go, nor able to stand it after I got there; and I did not make out a very good case for myself, for I was crying before I had finished.

110 It is getting to be a great effort for me to think straight. Just this nervous weakness, I suppose.

And dear John gathered me up in his arms, and just carried me upstairs and laid me on the bed, and sat by me and read to me till it tired my head.

He said I was his darling and his comfort and all he had, and that I must take care of myself for his sake, and keep well.

He says no one but myself can help me out of it, that I must use my will and self-control and not let any silly fancies run away with me.

There's one comfort — the baby is well and happy, and does not have to occupy this nursery with the horrid wallpaper.

115 If we had not used it, that blessed child would have! What a fortunate escape! Why, I wouldn't have a child of mine, an impressionable little thing, live in such a room for worlds.

I never thought of it before, but it is lucky that John kept me here after all; I can stand it so much easier than a baby, you see.

Of course I never mention it to them any more — I am too wise — but I keep watch for it all the same.

There are things in that wallpaper that nobody knows about but me, or ever will.

Behind that outside pattern the dim shapes get clearer every day.

120 It is always the same shape, only very numerous.

And it is like a woman stooping down and creeping about behind that pattern. I don't like it a bit. I wonder — I begin to think — I wish John would take me away from here!

It is so hard to talk with John about my case, because he is so wise, and because he loves me so.

But I tried it last night.

It was moonlight. The moon shines in all around just as the sun does.

125 I hate to see it sometimes, it creeps so slowly, and always comes in by one window or another.

John was asleep and I hated to waken him, so I kept still and watched the moonlight on that undulating wallpaper till I felt creepy.

The faint figure behind seemed to shake the pattern, just as if she wanted to get out.

I got up softly and went to feel and see if the paper *did* move, and when I came back John was awake.

"What is it, little girl?" he said. "Don't go walking about like that — you'll get cold."

130 I thought it was a good time to talk, so I told him that I really was not gaining here, and that I wished he would take me away.

"Why, darling!" said he. "Our lease will be up in three weeks, and I can't see how to leave before.

"The repairs are not done at home, and I cannot possibly leave town just now. Of course, if you were in any danger, I could and would, but you really are better, dear, whether you can see it or not. I am a doctor, dear, and I know. You are gaining flesh and color, you appetite is better, I feel really much easier about you."

"I don't weigh a bit more," said I, "nor as much; and my appetite may be better in the evening when you are here but it is worse in the morning when you are away!"

"Bless her little heart!" said he with a big hug. "She shall be as sick as she pleases! But now let's improve the shining hours by going to sleep, and talk about it in the morning!"

135 "And you won't go away?" I asked gloomily.

"Why, how can I, dear? It is only three weeks more and then we will take a nice little trip of a few days while Jennie is getting the house ready. Really, dear, you are better!"

"Better in body perhaps —" I began, and stopped short, for he sat up straight and looked at me with such a stern, reproachful look that I could not say another word.

"My darling," said he, "I beg of you, for my sake and for our child's sake, as well as for your own, that you will never for one instant let that idea enter your mind! There is nothing so dangerous, so fascinating, to a temperament like yours. It is a false and foolish fancy. Can you not trust me as a physician when I tell you so?"

So of course I said no more on that score, and we went to sleep before long. He thought I was asleep first, but I wasn't, and lay there for hours trying to decide whether that front pattern and the back pattern really did move together or separately.

140 On a pattern like this, by daylight, there is a lack of sequence, a defiance of law, that is a constant irritant to a normal mind.

The color is hideous enough, and unreliable enough, and infuriating enough, but the pattern is torturing.

You think you have mastered it, but just as you get well under way in following, it turns a back-somersault and there you are. It slaps you in the face, knocks you down, and tramples upon you. It is like a bad dream.

The outside pattern is a florid arabesque,[4] reminding one of a fungus. If you can imagine a toadstool in joints, an interminable string of toadstools, budding and sprouting in endless convolutions — why, that is something like it.

That is, sometimes!

145 There is one marked peculiarity about this paper, a thing nobody seems to notice but myself, and that is that it changes as the light changes.

When the sun shoots in through the east window — I always watch for that first long, straight ray — it changes so quickly that I never can quite believe it.

That is why I watch it always.

By moonlight — the moon shines in all night when there is a moon — I wouldn't know it was the same paper.

At night in any kind of light, in twilight, candlelight, lamplight, and worst of all by moonlight, it becomes bars! The outside pattern, I mean, and the woman behind it is as plain as can be.

150 I didn't realize for a long time what the thing was that showed behind, that dim sub-pattern, but now I am quite sure it is a woman.

By daylight she is subdued, quiet. I fancy it is the pattern that keeps her so still. It is so puzzling. It keeps me quiet by the hour.

I lie down ever so much now. John says it is good for me, and to sleep all I can.

Indeed he started the habit by making me lie down for an hour after each meal.

It is a very bad habit, I am convinced, for you see, I don't sleep.

155 And that cultivates deceit, for I don't tell them I'm awake — oh, no!

The fact is I am getting a little afraid of John.

He seems very queer sometimes, and even Jennie has an inexplicable look.

It strikes me occasionally, just as a scientific hypothesis, that perhaps it is the paper!

I have watched John when he did not know I was looking, and come into the room suddenly on the most innocent excuses, and I've caught him several times *looking at the paper*! And Jennie too. I caught Jennie with her hand on it once.

160 She didn't know I was in the room, and when I asked her in a quiet, a very quiet voice, with the most restrained manner possible, what she was doing with the paper, she turned around as if she had been caught stealing, and looked quite angry — asked me why I should frighten her so!

---

4 interwoven pattern of flowers and designs.

Then she said that the paper stained everything it touched, that she had found yellow smooches on all my clothes and John's and she wished we would be more careful!

Did not that sound innocent? But I know she was studying that pattern, and I am determined that nobody shall find it out but myself!

Life is very much more exciting now than it used to be. You see, I have something more to expect, to look forward to, to watch. I really do eat better, and am more quiet than I was.

John is so pleased to see me improve! He laughed a little the other day, and said I seemed to be flourishing in spite of my wallpaper.

165    I turned it off with a laugh. I had no intention of telling him it was *because* of the wallpaper — he would make fun of me. He might even want to take me away.

I don't want to leave now until I have found it out. There is a week more, and I think that will be enough.

I'm feeling so much better!

I don't sleep much at night, for it is so interesting to watch developments; but I sleep a good deal during the daytime.

In the daytime it is tiresome and perplexing.

170    There are always new shoots on the fungus, and new shades of yellow all over it. I cannot keep count of them, though I have tried conscientiously.

It is the strangest yellow, that wallpaper! It makes me think of all the yellow things I ever saw — not beautiful ones like buttercups, but old, foul, bad yellow things.

But there is something else about that paper — the smell! I noticed it the moment we came into the room, but with so much air and sun it was not bad. Now we have had a week of fog and rain, and whether the windows are open or not, the smell is here.

It creeps all over the house.

I find it hovering in the dining-room, skulking in the parlor, hiding in the hall, lying in wait for me on the stairs.

175    It gets into my hair.

Even when I go to ride, if I turn my head suddenly and surprise it — there is that smell!

Such a peculiar odor, too! I have spent hours in trying to analyze it, to find what it smelled like.

It is not bad — at first — and very gentle, but quite the subtlest, most enduring odor I ever met.

In this damp weather it is awful. I wake up in the night and find it hanging over me.

180    It used to disturb me at first. I thought seriously of burning the house — to reach the smell.

But now I am used to it. The only thing I can think of that it is like is the *color* of the paper! A yellow smell.

There is a very funny mark on this wall, low down, near the mopboard. A streak that runs round the room. It goes behind every piece of furniture, except the bed, a long, straight, even *smooch*, as if it had been rubbed over and over.

I wonder how it was done and who did it, and what they did it for. Round and round and round — round and round and round — it makes me dizzy!

I really have discovered something at last.

185 Through watching so much at night, when it changes so, I have finally found out.

The front pattern *does* move — and no wonder! The woman behind shakes it!

Sometimes I think there are a great many women behind, and sometimes only one, and she crawls around fast, and her crawling shakes it all over.

Then in the very bright spots she keeps still, and in the very shady spots she just takes hold of the bars and shakes them hard.

And she is all the time trying to climb through. But nobody could climb through that pattern — it strangles so; I think that is why it has so many heads.

190 They get through, and then the pattern strangles them off and turns them upside down, and makes their eyes white!

If those heads were covered or taken off it would not be half so bad.

I think that woman gets out in the daytime!

And I'll tell you why — privately — I've seen her!

I can see her out of every one of my windows!

195 It is the same woman, I know, for she is always creeping, and most women do not creep by daylight.

I see her in that long shaded lane, creeping up and down. I see her in those dark grape arbors, creeping all around the garden.

I see her on that long road under the trees, creeping along, and when a carriage comes she hides under the blackberry vines.

I don't blame her a bit. It must be very humiliating to be caught creeping by daylight!

I always lock the door when I creep by daylight. I can't do it at night, for I know John would suspect something at once.

200 And John is so queer now that I don't want to irritate him. I wish he would take another room! Besides, I don't want anybody to get that woman out at night but myself.

I often wonder if I could see her out of all the windows at once.

But, turn as fast as I can, I can only see out of one at one time.

And though I always see her, she *may* be able to creep faster than I can turn! I have watched her sometimes away off in the open country, creeping as fast as a cloud shadow in a wind.

If only that top pattern could be gotten off from the under one! I mean to try it, little by little.

205 I have found out another funny thing, but I shan't tell it this time! It does not do to trust people too much.

There are only two more days to get this paper off, and I believe John is beginning to notice. I don't like the look in his eyes.

And I heard him ask Jennie a lot of professional questions about me. She had a very good report to give.

She said I slept a good deal in the daytime.

John knows I don't sleep very well at night, for all I'm so quiet!

He asked me all sorts of questions, too, and pretended to be very loving and kind.

As if I couldn't see through him!

Still, I don't wonder he acts so, sleeping under this paper for three months.

It only interests me, but I feel sure John and Jennie are affected by it.

Hurrah! This is the last day, but it is enough. John is to stay in town over night, and won't be out until this evening.

Jennie wanted to sleep with me — the sly thing; but I told her I should undoubtedly rest better for a night all alone.

That was clever, for really I wasn't alone a bit! As soon as it was moonlight and that poor thing began to crawl and shake the pattern, I got up and ran to help her.

I pulled and she shook. I shook and she pulled, and before morning we had peeled off yards of that paper.

A strip about as high as my head and half around the room.

And then when the sun came and that awful pattern began to laugh at me, I declared I would finish it today!

We go away tomorrow, and they are moving all my furniture down again to leave things as they were before.

Jennie looked at the wall in amazement, but I told her merrily that I did it out of pure spite at the vicious thing.

She laughed and said she wouldn't mind doing it herself, but I must not get tired.

How she betrayed herself that time!

But I am here, and no person touches this paper but Me — not *alive*!

She tried to get me out of the room — it was too patent! But I said it was so quiet and empty and clean now that I believed I would lie down again and sleep all I could, and not to wake me even for dinner — I would call when I woke.

So now she is gone, and the servants are gone, and the things are gone, and there is nothing left but that great bedstead nailed down, with the canvas mattress we found on it.

We shall sleep downstairs tonight, and take the boat home tomorrow.

I quite enjoy the room, now it is bare again.

How those children did tear about here!

This bedstead is fairly gnawed!

But I must get to work.

I have locked the door and thrown the key down into the front path.

I don't want to go out, and I don't want to have anybody come in, till John comes.

I want to astonish him.

I've got a rope up here that even Jennie did not find. If that woman does get out, and tries to get away, I can tie her!

But I forgot I could not reach far without anything to stand on!

This bed will *not* move!

I tried to lift and push it until I was lame, and then I got so angry I bit off a little piece at one corner — but it hurt my teeth.

Then I peeled off all the paper I could reach standing on the floor. It sticks horribly and the pattern just enjoys it! All those strangled heads and bulbous eyes and waddling fungus growths just shriek with derision!

240 I am getting angry enough to do something desperate. To jump out of the window would be admirable exercise, but the bars are too strong even to try.

Besides I wouldn't do it. Of course not. I know well enough that a step like that is improper and might be misconstrued.

I don't like to *look* out of the windows even — there are so many of those creeping women, and they creep so fast.

I wonder if they all come out of that wallpaper as I did?

But I am securely fastened now by my well-hidden rope — you don't get *me* out in the road there!

245 I suppose I shall have to get back behind the pattern when it comes night, and that is hard!

It is so pleasant to be out in this great room and creep around as I please!

I don't want to go outside. I won't, even if Jennie asks me to.

For outside you have to creep on the ground, and everything is green instead of yellow.

But here I can creep smoothly on the floor, and my shoulder just fits in that long smooch around the wall, so I cannot lose my way.

250 Why, there's John at the door!

It is no use, young man, you can't open it!

How he does call and pound!

Now he's crying to Jennie for an axe.

It would be a shame to break down that beautiful door!

255 "John, dear!" said I in the gentlest voice. "The key is down by the front steps, under a plantain leaf!"

That silenced him for a few moments.

Then he said, very quietly indeed, "Open the door, my darling!"

"I can't," said I. "The key is down by the front door under a plantain leaf!" And then I said it again, several times, very gently and slowly, and said it so often that he had to go and see, and he got it of course, and came in. He stopped short by the door.

"What is the matter?" he cried. "For God's sake, what are you doing!"

260 I kept on creeping just the same, but I looked at him over my shoulder.

"I've got out at last," said I, "in spite of you and Jane. And I've pulled off most of the paper, so you can't put me back!"

Now why should that man have fainted? But he did, and right across my path by the wall, so that I had to creep over him every time!

(1892)

# Stephen Crane   (1871–1900)

Before his death from tuberculosis at age 28, New Jersey–born Stephen Crane had published short stories, poetry, and a novel, *The Red Badge of Courage* (1896). One of a group of authors now known as naturalists, who rejected traditional social and religious beliefs as invalid, Crane examined the courage of individuals living in a world in which victory or defeat in struggles was a matter of chance. "The Open Boat," which was highly praised by both Joseph Conrad and Ernest Hemingway, is based on personal experience. Travelling to Cuba as a newspaper correspondent, Crane had been one of three survivors of a shipwreck off the Atlantic coast of Florida. In a newspaper account published a few days after his rescue, Crane focussed on the events leading to the sinking of the vessel, giving only a few sentences in the final paragraph to the time spent in the lifeboat and the rescue. Subtitled "A Tale Intended to Be after the Fact," "The Open Boat" explores the four men's 30 hours in the three-metre dinghy, examining their growing camaraderie and the correspondent's developing awareness of the impersonality of nature.

# THE OPEN BOAT

*A Tale Intended to Be after the Fact. Being the Experience of Four Men from the Sunk Steamer 'Commodore'*

I

None of them knew the colour of the sky. Their eyes glanced level, and were fastened upon the waves that swept toward them. These waves were of the hue of slate, save for the tops, which were of foaming white, and all of the men knew the colours of the sea. The horizon narrowed and widened, and dipped and rose, and at all times its edge was jagged with waves that seemed thrust up in points like rocks.

Many a man ought to have a bath-tub larger than the boat which here rode upon the sea. These waves were most wrongfully and barbarously abrupt and tall, and each froth-top was a problem in small boat navigation.

The cook squatted in the bottom and looked with both eyes at the six inches of gunwale which separated him from the ocean. His sleeves were rolled over his fat forearms, and the two flaps of his unbuttoned vest dangled as he bent to bail out the boat. Often he said: "Gawd! That was a narrow clip." As he remarked it he invariably gazed eastward over the broken sea.

The oiler, steering with one of the two oars in the boat, sometimes raised himself suddenly to keep clear of water that swirled in over the stern. It was a thin little oar and it seemed often ready to snap.

5    The correspondent, pulling at the other oar, watched the waves and wondered why he was there.

The injured captain, lying in the bow, was at this time buried in that profound dejection and indifference which comes, temporarily at least, to even the bravest and most enduring when, willy nilly, the firm fails, the army loses, the ship goes down. The mind of the master of a vessel is rooted deep in the timbers of her, though he commanded for a day or a decade, and this captain had on him the stern impression of a scene in the greys of dawn of seven turned faces, and later a stump of a top-mast with a white ball on it that slashed to and fro at the waves, went low and lower, and down. Thereafter there was something strange in his voice. Although steady, it was deep with mourning, and of a quality beyond oration or tears.

"Keep 'er a little more south, Billie," said he.

"'A little more south,' sir," said the oiler in the stern.

A seat in this boat was not unlike a seat upon a bucking broncho, and, by the same token, a broncho is not much smaller. The craft pranced and reared, and plunged like an animal. As each wave came, and she rose for it, she seemed like a horse making at a fence outrageously high. The manner of her scramble over these walls of water is a mystic thing, and, moreover, at the top of them were ordinarily these problems in white water, the foam racing down from the summit of each wave, requiring a new leap, and a leap from the air. Then, after scornfully bumping a crest, she would slide, and race, and splash down a long incline, and arrive bobbing and nodding in front of the next menace.

10    A singular disadvantage of the sea lies in the fact that after successfully surmounting one wave you discover that there is another behind it just as important and just as nervously anxious to do something effective in the way of swamping boats. In a ten-foot dingey one can get an idea of the resources of the sea in the line of waves that is not probable to the average experience which is never at sea in a dingey. As each salty wall of water approached, it shut all else from the view of the men in the boat, and it was not difficult to imagine that this particular wave was the final outburst of the ocean, the last effort of the grim water. There was a terrible grace in the move of the waves, and they came in silence, save for the snarling of the crests.

In the wan light, the faces of the men must have been grey. Their eyes must have glinted in strange ways as they gazed steadily astern. Viewed from a balcony, the whole thing would doubtlessly have been weirdly picturesque. But the men in the boat had no time to see it, and if they had had leisure there were other things to occupy their minds. The sun swung steadily up the sky, and they knew it was broad day because the colour of the sea changed from slate to emerald-green, streaked with amber lights, and the foam was like tumbling snow. The process of the breaking day was unknown to them. They were aware only of this effect upon the colour of the waves that rolled toward them.

In disjointed sentences the cook and the correspondent argued as to the difference between a life-saving station and a house of refuge. The cook had said: "There's a house of refuge just north of the Mosquito Inlet Light,[1] and as soon as they see us, they'll come off in their boat and pick us up."

"As soon as who see us?" said the correspondent.

"The crew," said the cook.

---

1 located on the Atlantic coast of northern Florida.

15    "Houses of refuge don't have crews," said the correspondent. "As I understand them, they are only places where clothes and grub are stored for the benefit of shipwrecked people. They don't carry crews."

"Oh, yes, they do," said the cook.

"No, they don't," said the correspondent.

"Well, we're not there yet, anyhow," said the oiler, in the stern.

"Well," said the cook, "perhaps it's not a house of refuge that I'm thinking of as being near Mosquito Inlet Light. Perhaps it's a life-saving station."

20    "We're not there yet," said the oiler, in the stern.


## II

As the boat bounced from the top of each wave, the wind tore through the hair of the hatless men, and as the craft plopped her stern down again the spray slashed past them. The crest of each of these waves was a hill, from the top of which the men surveyed, for a moment, a broad tumultuous expanse, shining and wind-riven. It was probably splendid. It was probably glorious, this play of the free sea, wild with lights of emerald and white and amber.

"Bully good thing it's an on-shore wind," said the cook. "If not, where would we be? Wouldn't have a show."

"That's right," said the correspondent.

The busy oiler nodded his assent.

25    Then the captain, in the bow, chuckled in a way that expressed humour, contempt, tragedy, all in one. "Do you think we've got much of a show now, boys?" said he.

Whereupon the three were silent, save for a trifle of hemming and hawing. To express any particular optimism at this time they felt to be childish and stupid, but they all doubtless possessed this sense of the situation in their mind. A young man thinks doggedly at such times. On the other hand, the ethics of their condition was decidedly against any open suggestion of hopelessness. So they were silent.

"Oh, well," said the captain, soothing his children, "we'll get ashore all right."

But there was that in his tone which made them think, so the oiler quoth: "Yes! If this wind holds!"

The cook was bailing: "Yes! If we don't catch hell in the surf."

30    Canton flannel gulls flew near and far. Sometimes they sat down on the sea, near patches of brown seaweed that rolled over the waves with a movement like carpets on a line in a gale. The birds sat comfortably in groups, and they were envied by some in the dingey, for the wrath of the sea was no more to them than it was to a covey of prairie chickens a thousand miles inland. Often they came very close and stared at the men with black bead-like eyes. At these times they were uncanny and sinister in their unblinking scrutiny, and the men hooted angrily at them, telling them to be gone. One came, and evidently decided to alight on the top of the captain's head. The bird flew parallel to the boat and did not circle, but made short sidelong jumps in the air in

chicken-fashion. His black eyes were wistfully fixed upon the captain's head. "Ugly brute," said the oiler to the bird. "You look as if you were made with a jack-knife." The cook and the correspondent swore darkly at the creature. The captain naturally wished to knock it away with the end of the heavy painter; but he did not dare do it, because anything resembling an emphatic gesture would have capsized this freighted boat, and so with his open hand, the captain gently and carefully waved the gull away. After it had been discouraged from the pursuit the captain breathed easier on account of his hair, and others breathed easier because the bird struck their minds at this time as being somehow grewsome and ominous.

In the meantime the oiler and the correspondent rowed. And also they rowed.

They sat together in the same seat, and each rowed an oar. Then the oiler took both oars; then the correspondent took both oars; then the oiler; then the correspondent. They rowed and they rowed. The very ticklish part of the business was when the time came for the reclining one in the stern to take his turn at the oars. By the very last star of truth, it is easier to steal eggs from under a hen than it was to change seats in the dingey. First the man in the stern slid his hand along the thwart and moved with care, as if he were of Sèvres.[2] Then the man in the rowing seat slid his hand along the other thwart. It was all done with the most extraordinary care. As the two sidled past each other, the whole party kept watchful eyes on the coming wave, and the captain cried: "Look out now! Steady there!"

The brown mats of sea-weed that appeared from time to time were like islands, bits of earth. They were travelling, apparently, neither one way nor the other. They were, to all intents, stationary. They informed the men in the boat that it was making progress slowly toward the land.

The captain, rearing cautiously in the bow, after the dingey soared on a great swell, said that he had seen the lighthouse at Mosquito Inlet. Presently the cook remarked that he had seen it. The correspondent was at the oars then, and for some reason he too wished to look at the lighthouse, but his back was toward the far shore and the waves were important, and for some time he could not seize an opportunity to turn his head. But at last there came a wave more gentle than the others, and when at the crest of it he swiftly scoured the western horizon.

35    "See it?" said the captain.

"No," said the correspondent slowly, "I didn't see anything."

"Look again," said the captain. He pointed. "It's exactly in that direction."

At the top of another wave, the correspondent did as he was bid, and this time his eyes chanced on a small still thing on the edge of the swaying horizon. It was precisely like the point of a pin. It took an anxious eye to find a lighthouse so tiny.

"Think we'll make it, captain?"

40    "If this wind holds and the boat don't swamp, we can't do much else," said the captain.

---

2 beautiful, delicate porcelain made in the commune of the same name on the Seine River in northern France.

The little boat, lifted by each towering sea, and splashed viciously by the crests, made progress that in the absence of seaweed was not apparent to those in her. She seemed just a wee thing wallowing, miraculously top-up, at the mercy of five oceans. Occasionally, a great spread of water, like white flames, swarmed into her.

"Bail her, cook," said the captain serenely.

"All right, captain," said the cheerful cook.

## III

It would be difficult to describe the subtle brotherhood of men that was here established on the seas. No one said that it was so. No one mentioned it. But it dwelt in the boat, and each man felt it warm him. They were a captain, an oiler, a cook, and a correspondent, and they were friends, friends in a more curiously iron-bound degree than may be common. The hurt captain, lying against the water-jar in the bow, spoke always in a low voice and calmly, but he could never command a more ready and swiftly obedient crew than the motley three of the dingey. It was more than a mere recognition of what was best for the common safety. There was surely in it a quality that was personal and heart-felt. And after this devotion to the commander of the boat there was this comradeship that the correspondent, for instance, who had been taught to be cynical of men, knew even at the time was the best experience of his life. But no one said that it was so. No one mentioned it.

45        "I wish we had a sail," remarked the captain. "We might try my overcoat on the end of an oar and give you two boys a chance to rest." So the cook and the correspondent held the mast and spread wide the overcoat. The oiler steered, and the little boat made good way with her new rig. Sometimes the oiler had to scull sharply to keep a sea from breaking into the boat, but otherwise sailing was a success.

Meanwhile the lighthouse had been growing slowly larger. It had now almost assumed colour, and appeared like a little grey shadow on the sky. The man at the oars could not be prevented from turning his head rather often to try for a glimpse of this little grey shadow.

At last, from the top of each wave the men in the tossing boat could see land. Even as the lighthouse was an upright shadow on the sky, this land seemed but a long black shadow on the sea. It certainly was thinner than paper. "We must be about opposite New Smyrna,"[3] said the cook, who had coasted this shore often in schooners. "Captain, by the way, I believe they abandoned that life-saving station there about a year ago."

"Did they?" said the captain.

The wind slowly died away. The cook and the correspondent were not now obliged to slave in order to hold high the oar. But the waves continued their old impetuous swooping at the dingey, and the little craft, no longer under way, struggled woundily over them. The oiler or the correspondent took the oars again.

3 located 25 kilometres south of Daytona Beach.

50      Shipwrecks are *à propos* of nothing. If men could only train for them and have them occur when the men had reached pink condition, there would be less drowning at sea. Of the four in the dingey none had slept any time worth mentioning for two days and two nights previous to embarking in the dingey, and in the excitement of clambering about the deck of a foundering ship they had also forgotten to eat heartily.

For these reasons, and for others, neither the oiler nor the correspondent was fond of rowing at this time. The correspondent wondered ingenuously how in the name of all that was sane could there be people who thought it amusing to row a boat. It was not an amusement; it was a diabolical punishment, and even a genius of mental aberrations could never conclude that it was anything but a horror to the muscles and a crime against the back. He mentioned to the boat in general how the amusement of rowing struck him, and the weary-faced oiler smiled in full sympathy. Previously to the foundering, by the way, the oiler had worked double-watch in the engine-room of the ship.

"Take her easy, now, boys," said the captain. "Don't spend yourselves. If we have to run a surf you'll need all your strength, because we'll sure have to swim for it. Take your time."

Slowly the land arose from the sea. From a black line it became a line of black and a line of white, trees and sand. Finally, the captain said that he could make out a house on the shore. "That's the house of refuge, sure," said the cook. "They'll see us before long, and come out after us."

The distant lighthouse reared high. "The keeper ought to be able to make us out now, if he's looking through a glass," said the captain. "He'll notify the life-saving people."

55      "None of those other boats could have got ashore to give word of the wreck," said the oiler, in a low voice. "Else the lifeboat would be out hunting us."

Slowly and beautifully the land loomed out of the sea. The wind came again. It had veered from the north-east to the south-east. Finally, a new sound struck the ears of the men in the boat. It was the low thunder of the surf on the shore. "We'll never be able to make the lighthouse now," said the captain. "Swing her head a little more north, Billie," said he.

"'A little more north,' sir," said the oiler.

Whereupon the little boat turned her nose once more down the wind, and all but the oarsman watched the shore grow. Under the influence of this expansion doubt and direful apprehension was leaving the minds of the men. The management of the boat was still most absorbing, but it could not prevent a quiet cheerfulness. In an hour, perhaps, they would be ashore.

Their backbones had become thoroughly used to balancing in the boat, and they now rode this wild colt of a dingey like circus men. The correspondent thought that he had been drenched to the skin, but happening to feel in the top pocket of his coat, he found therein eight cigars. Four of them were soaked with sea-water; four were perfectly scatheless. After a search, somebody produced three dry matches, and thereupon the four waifs rode impudently in their little boat, and with an assurance of an impending rescue shining in their eyes, puffed at the big cigars and judged well and ill of all men. Everybody took a drink of water.

## IV

60 "Cook," remarked the captain, "there don't seem to be any signs of life about your house of refuge."

"No," replied the cook. "Funny they don't see us!"

A broad stretch of lowly coast lay before the eyes of the men. It was of dunes topped with dark vegetation. The roar of the surf was plain, and sometimes they could see the white lip of a wave as it spun up the beach. A tiny house was blocked out black upon the sky. Southward, the slim lighthouse lifted its little grey length.

Tide, wind, and waves were swinging the dingey northward. "Funny they don't see us," said the men.

The surf's roar was here dulled, but its tone was, nevertheless, thunderous and mighty. As the boat swam over the great rollers, the men sat listening to this roar. "We'll swamp sure," said everybody.

65 It is fair to say here that there was not a life-saving station within twenty miles in either direction, but the men did not know this fact, and in consequence they made dark and opprobrious remarks concerning the eyesight of the nation's life-savers. Four scowling men sat in the dingey and surpassed records in the invention of epithets.

"Funny they don't see us."

The light-heartedness of a former time had completely failed. To their sharpened minds it was easy to conjure pictures of all kinds of incompetency and blindness and, indeed, cowardice. There was the shore of the populous land, and it was bitter and bitter to them that from it came no sign.

"Well," said the captain, ultimately, "I suppose we'll have to make a try for ourselves. If we stay out here too long, we'll none of us have strength left to swim after the boat swamps."

And so the oiler, who was at the oars, turned the boat straight for the shore. There was a sudden tightening of muscles. There was some thinking.

70 "If we don't all get ashore —" said the captain. "If we don't all get ashore, I suppose you fellows know where to send news of my finish?"

They then briefly exchanged some addresses and admonitions. As for the reflections of the men, there was a great deal of rage in them. Perchance they might be formulated thus: "If I am going to be drowned — if I am going to be drowned — if I am going to be drowned, why, in the name of the seven mad gods who rule the sea, was I allowed to come thus far and contemplate sand and trees? Was I brought here merely to have my nose dragged away as I was about to nibble the sacred cheese of life? It is preposterous. If this old ninny-woman, Fate, cannot do better than this, she should be deprived of the management of men's fortunes. She is an old hen who knows not her intention. If she has decided to drown me, why did she not do it in the beginning and save me all this trouble? The whole affair is absurd. . . . But no, she cannot mean to drown me. She dare not drown me. She cannot drown me. Not after all this work." Afterward the man might have had an impulse to shake his fist at the clouds: "Just you drown me, now, and then hear what I call you!"

The billows that came at this time were more formidable. They seemed always just about to break and roll over the little boat in a turmoil of foam.

There was a preparatory and long growl in the speech of them. No mind unused to the sea would have concluded that the dingey could ascend these sheer heights in time. The shore was still afar. The oiler was a wily surfman. "Boys," he said swiftly, "she won't live three minutes more, and we're too far out to swim. Shall I take her to sea again, captain?"

"Yes! Go ahead!" said the captain.

This oiler, by a series of quick miracles, and fast and steady oarsmanship, turned the boat in the middle of the surf and took her safely to sea again.

75   There was a considerable silence as the boat bumped over the furrowed sea to deeper water. Then somebody in gloom spoke. "Well, anyhow, they must have seen us from the shore by now."

The gulls went in slanting flight up the wind toward the grey desolate east. A squall, marked by dingy clouds, and clouds brick-red, like smoke from a burning building, appeared from the south-east.

"What do you think of those life-saving people? Ain't they peaches?"

"Funny they haven't seen us."

"Maybe they think we're out here for sport! Maybe they think we're fishin'. Maybe they think we're damned fools."

80   It was a long afternoon. A changed tide tried to force them southward, but wind and wave said northward. Far ahead, where coast-line, sea, and sky formed their mighty angle, there were little dots which seemed to indicate a city on the shore.

"St. Augustine?"[4]

The captain shook his head. "Too near Mosquito Inlet."

And the oiler rowed, and then the correspondent rowed. Then the oiler rowed. It was a weary business. The human back can become the seat of more aches and pains than are registered in books for the composite anatomy of a regiment. It is a limited area, but it can become the theatre of innumerable muscular conflicts, tangles, wrenches, knots, and other comforts.

"Did you ever like to row, Billie?" asked the correspondent.

85   "No," said the oiler. "Hang it."

When one exchanged the rowing-seat for a place in the bottom of the boat, he suffered a bodily depression that caused him to be careless of everything save an obligation to wiggle one finger. There was cold sea-water swashing to and fro in the boat, and he lay in it. His head, pillowed on a thwart, was within an inch of the swirl of a wave crest, and sometimes a particularly obstreperous sea came in-board and drenched him once more. But these matters did not annoy him. It is almost certain that if the boat had capsized he would have tumbled comfortably out upon the ocean as if he felt sure that it was a great soft mattress.

"Look! There's a man on the shore!"

"Where?"

"There! See 'im? See 'im?"

90   "Yes, sure! He's walking along."

"Now he's stopped. Look! He's facing us!"

"He's waving at us!"

4 city on the Atlantic coast of northern Florida.

"So he is! By thunder!"

"Ah, now we're all right! Now we're all right! There'll be a boat out here for us in half-an-hour."

95 "He's going on. He's running. He's going up to that house there."

The remote beach seemed lower than the sea, and it required a searching glance to discern the little black figure. The captain saw a floating stick and they rowed to it. A bath-towel was by some weird chance in the boat, and, tying this on the stick, the captain waved it. The oarsman did not dare turn his head, so he was obliged to ask questions.

"What's he doing now?"

"He's standing still again. He's looking, I think.... There he goes again. Towards the house.... Now he's stopped again."

"Is he waving at us?"

100 "No, not now! he was, though."

"Look! There comes another man!"

"He's running."

"Look at him go, would you."

"Why, he's on a bicycle. Now he's met the other man. They're both waving at us. Look!"

105 "There comes something up the beach."

"What the devil is that thing?"

"Why, it looks like a boat."

"Why, certainly it's a boat."

"No, it's on wheels."

110 "Yes, so it is. Well, that must be the life-boat. They drag them along shore on a wagon."

"That's the life-boat, sure."

"No, by —, it's — it's an omnibus."

"I tell you it's a life-boat."

"It is not! It's an omnibus. I can see it plain. See? One of these big hotel omnibuses."

115 "By thunder, you're right. It's an omnibus, sure as fate. What do you suppose they are doing with an omnibus? Maybe they are going around collecting the life-crew, hey?"

"That's it, likely. Look! There's a fellow waving a little black flag. He's standing on the steps of the omnibus. There come those other two fellows. Now they're all talking together. Look at the fellow with the flag. Maybe he ain't waving it."

"That ain't a flag, is it? That's his coat. Why certainly, that's his coat."

"So it is. It's his coat. He's taken it off and is waving it around his head. But would you look at him swing it."

"Oh, say, there isn't any life-saving station there. That's just a winter resort hotel omnibus that has brought over some of the boarders to see us drown."

120 "What's that idiot with the coat mean? What's he signaling, anyhow?"

"It looks as if he were trying to tell us to go north. There must be a life-saving station up there."

"No! He thinks we're fishing. Just giving us a merry hand. See? Ah, there, Willie."

"Well, I wish I could make something out of those signals. What do you suppose he means?"

"He don't mean anything. He's just playing."

"Well, if he'd just signal us to try the surf again, or to go to sea and wait, or go north, or go south, or go to hell — there would be some reason in it. But look at him. He just stands there and keeps his coat revolving like a wheel. The ass!"

"There come more people."

"Now there's quite a mob. Look! Isn't that a boat?"

"Where? Oh, I see where you mean. No, that's no boat."

"That fellow is still waving his coat."

"He must think we like to see him do that. Why don't he quit it? It don't mean anything."

"I don't know. I think he is trying to make us go north. It must be that there's a life-saving station there somewhere."

"Say, he ain't tired yet. Look at 'im wave."

"Wonder how long he can keep that up. He's been revolving his coat ever since he caught sight of us. He's an idiot. Why aren't they getting men to bring a boat out? A fishing boat — one of those big yawls — could come out here all right. Why don't he do something?"

"Oh, it's all right, now."

"They'll have a boat out here for us in less than no time, now that they've seen us."

A faint yellow tone came into the sky over the low land. The shadows on the sea slowly deepened. The wind bore coldness with it, and the men began to shiver.

"Holy smoke!" said one, allowing his voice to express his impious mood, "if we keep on monkeying out here! If we've got to flounder out here all night!"

"Oh, we'll never have to stay here all night! Don't you worry. They've seen us now, and it won't be long before they'll come chasing out after us."

The shore grew dusky. The man waving a coat blended gradually into this gloom, and it swallowed in the same manner the omnibus and the group of people. The spray, when it dashed uproariously over the side, made the voyagers shrink and swear like men who were being branded.

"I'd like to catch the chump who waved the coat. I feel like soaking him one, just for luck."

"Why? What did he do?"

"Oh, nothing, but then he seemed so damned cheerful."

In the meantime the oiler rowed, and then the correspondent rowed, and then the oiler rowed. Grey-faced and bowed forward, they mechanically, turn by turn, plied the leaden oars. The form of the lighthouse had vanished from the southern horizon, but finally a pale star appeared, just lifting from the sea. The streaked saffron in the west passed before the all-merging darkness, and the sea to the east was black. The land had vanished, and was expressed only by the low and drear thunder of the surf.

"If I am going to be drowned — if I am going to be drowned — if I am going to be drowned, why, in the name of the seven mad gods who rule the sea, was I allowed to come thus far and contemplate sand and trees? Was I brought here merely to have my nose dragged away as I was about to nibble the sacred cheese of life?"

145 The patient captain, drooped over the water-jar, was sometimes obliged to speak to the oarsman.

"Keep her head up! Keep her head up!"

"'Keep her head up,' sir." The voices were weary and low.

This was surely a quiet evening. All save the oarsman lay heavily and listlessly in the boat's bottom. As for him, his eyes were just capable of noting the tall black waves that swept forward in a most sinister silence, save for an occasional subdued growl of a crest.

The cook's head was on a thwart, and he looked without interest at the water under his nose. He was deep in other scenes. Finally he spoke. "Billie," he murmured, dreamfully, "what kind of pie do you like best?"


## V

150 "Pie," said the oiler and the correspondent, agitatedly. "Don't talk about those things, blast you!"

"Well," said the cook, "I was just thinking about ham sandwiches, and —"

A night on the sea in an open boat is a long night. As darkness settled finally, the shine of the light, lifting from the sea in the south, changed to full gold. On the northern horizon a new light appeared, a small bluish gleam on the edge of the waters. These two lights were the furniture of the world. Otherwise there was nothing but waves.

Two men huddled in the stern, and distances were so magnificent in the dingey that the rower was enabled to keep his feet partly warmed by thrusting them under his companions. Their legs indeed extended far under the rowing-seat until they touched the feet of the captain forward. Sometimes, despite the efforts of the tired oarsman, a wave came piling into the boat, an icy wave of the night, and the chilling water soaked them anew. They would twist their bodies for a moment and groan, and sleep the dead sleep once more, while the water in the boat gurgled about them as the craft rocked.

The plan of the oiler and the correspondent was for one to row until he lost the ability, and then arouse the other from his sea-water couch in the bottom of the boat.

155 The oiler plied the oars until his head drooped forward, and the over-powering sleep blinded him. And he rowed yet afterward. Then he touched a man in the bottom of the boat, and called his name. "Will you spell me for a little while?" he said, meekly.

"Sure, Billie," said the correspondent, awakening and dragging himself to a sitting position. They exchanged places carefully, and the oiler, cuddling down in the sea-water at the cook's side, seemed to go to sleep instantly.

The particular violence of the sea had ceased. The waves came without snarling. The obligation of the man at the oars was to keep the boat headed so that the tilt of the rollers would not capsize her, and to preserve her from filling when the crests rushed past. The black waves were silent and hard to be seen in the darkness. Often one was almost upon the boat before the oarsman was aware.

In a low voice the correspondent addressed the captain. He was not sure that the captain was awake, although this iron man seemed to be always awake. "Captain, shall I keep her making for that light north, sir?"

The same steady voice answered him. "Yes. Keep it about two points off the port bow."

160   The cook had tied a life-belt around himself in order to get even the warmth which this clumsy cork contrivance could donate, and he seemed almost stove-like when a rower, whose teeth invariably chattered wildly as soon as he ceased his labour, dropped down to sleep.

The correspondent, as he rowed, looked down at the two men sleeping under-foot. The cook's arm was around the oiler's shoulders, and, with their fragmentary clothing and haggard faces, they were the babes of the sea, a grotesque rendering of the old babes in the wood.[5]

Later he must have grown stupid at his work, for suddenly there was a growling of water, and a crest came with a roar and a swash into the boat, and it was a wonder that it did not set the cook afloat in his life-belt. The cook continued to sleep, but the oiler sat up, blinking his eyes and shaking with the new cold.

"Oh, I'm awful sorry, Billie," said the correspondent contritely.

"That's all right, old boy," said the oiler, and lay down again and was asleep.

165   Presently it seemed that even the captain dozed, and the correspondent thought that he was the one man afloat on all the oceans. The wind had a voice as it came over the waves, and it was sadder than the end.

There was a long, loud swishing astern of the boat, and a gleaming trail of phosphorescence, like blue flame, was furrowed on the black waters. It might have been made by a monstrous knife.

Then there came a stillness, while the correspondent breathed with the open mouth and looked at the sea.

Suddenly there was another swish and another long flash of bluish light, and this time it was alongside the boat, and might almost have been reached with an oar. The correspondent saw an enormous fin speed like a shadow through the water, hurling the crystalline spray and leaving the long glowing trail.

The correspondent looked over his shoulder at the captain. His face was hidden, and he seemed to be asleep. He looked at the babes of the sea. They certainly were asleep. So, being bereft of sympathy, he leaned a little way to one side and swore softly into the sea.

170   But the thing did not then leave the vicinity of the boat. Ahead or astern, on one side or the other, at intervals long or short, fled the long sparkling streak, and there was to be heard the whiroo of the dark fin. The speed and power of the thing was greatly to be admired. It cut the water like a gigantic and keen projectile.

5 popular nineteenth-century children's story about children who become lost and die in a forest.

The presence of this biding thing did not affect the man with the same horror that it would if he had been a picnicker. He simply looked at the sea dully and swore in an undertone.

Nevertheless, it is true that he did not wish to be alone. He wished one of his companions to awaken by chance and keep him company with it. But the captain hung motionless over the water-jar, and the oiler and the cook in the bottom of the boat were plunged in slumber.

## VI

"If I am going to be drowned — if I am going to be drowned — if I am going to be drowned, why, in the name of the seven mad gods who rule the sea, was I allowed to come thus far and contemplate sand and trees?"

During this dismal night, it may be remarked that a man would conclude that it was really the intention of the seven mad gods to drown him, despite the abominable injustice of it. For it was certainly an abominable injustice to drown a man who had worked so hard, so hard. The man felt it would be a crime most unnatural. Other people had drowned at sea since galleys swarmed with painted sails, but still —

175 When it occurs to a man that nature does not regard him as important, and that she feels she would not maim the universe by disposing of him, he at first wishes to throw bricks at the temple, and he hates deeply the fact that there are no bricks and no temples. Any visible expression of nature would surely be pelleted with his jeers.

Then, if there be no tangible thing to hoot he feels, perhaps, the desire to confront a personification and indulge in pleas, bowed to one knee, and with hands supplicant, saying: "Yes, but I love myself."

A high cold star on a winter's night is the word he feels that she says to him. Thereafter he knows the pathos of his situation.

The men in the dingey had not discussed these matters, but each had, no doubt, reflected upon them in silence and according to his mind. There was seldom any expression upon their faces save the general one of complete weariness. Speech was devoted to the business of the boat.

To chime the notes of his emotion, a verse mysteriously entered the correspondent's head. He had even forgotten that he had forgotten this verse, but it suddenly was in his mind.

> "A soldier of the Legion lay dying in Algiers,
> There was lack of woman's nursing, there was dearth of woman's tears;
> But a comrade stood beside him, and he took that comrade's hand,
> And he said: 'I shall never see my own, my native land.'"

180 In his childhood, the correspondent had been made acquainted with the fact that a soldier of the Legion lay dying in Algiers, but he had never regarded the fact as important. Myriads of his school-fellows had informed him of the soldier's plight, but the dinning had naturally ended by making him perfectly indifferent. He had never considered it his affair that a soldier of the Legion lay dying in Algiers, nor had it appeared to him as a matter for sorrow. It was less to him than the breaking of a pencil's point.

Now, however, it quaintly came to him as a human, living thing. It was no longer merely a picture of a few throes in the breast of a poet, meanwhile drinking tea and warming his feet at the grate; it was an actuality — stern, mournful, and fine.

The correspondent plainly saw the soldier. He lay on the sand with his feet out straight and still. While his pale left hand was upon his chest in an attempt to thwart the going of his life, the blood came between his fingers. In the far Algerian distance, a city of low square forms was set against a sky that was faint with the last sunset hues. The correspondent, plying the oars and dreaming of the slow and slower movements of the lips of the soldier, was moved by a profound and perfectly impersonal comprehension. He was sorry for the soldier of the Legion who lay dying in Algiers.

The thing which had followed the boat and waited, had evidently grown bored at the delay. There was no longer to be heard the slash of the cut-water, and there was no longer the flame of the long trail. The light in the north still glimmered, but it was apparently no nearer to the boat. Sometimes the boom of the surf rang in the correspondent's ears, and he turned the craft seaward then and rowed harder. Southward, some one had evidently built a watch-fire on the beach. It was too low and too far to be seen, but it made a shimmering, roseate reflection upon the bluff back of it, and this could be discerned from the boat. The wind came stronger, and sometimes a wave suddenly raged out like a mountain-cat, and there was to be seen the sheen and sparkle of a broken crest.

The captain, in the bow, moved on his water-jar and sat erect. "Pretty long night," he observed to the correspondent. He looked at the shore. "Those life-saving people take their time."

185     "Did you see that shark playing around?"

"Yes, I saw him. He was a big fellow, all right."

"Wish I had known you were awake."

Later the correspondent spoke into the bottom of the boat.

"Billie!" There was a slow and gradual disentanglement. "Billie, will you spell me?"

190     "Sure," said the oiler.

As soon as the correspondent touched the cold comfortable sea-water in the bottom of the boat, and had huddled close to the cook's life-belt he was deep in sleep, despite the fact that his teeth played all the popular airs. This sleep was so good to him that it was but a moment before he heard a voice call his name in a tone that demonstrated the last stages of exhaustion. "Will you spell me?"

"Sure, Billie."

The light in the north had mysteriously vanished, but the correspondent took his course from the wide-awake captain.

Later in the night they took the boat farther out to sea, and the captain directed the cook to take one oar at the stern and keep the boat facing the seas. He was to call out if he should hear the thunder of the surf. This plan enabled the oiler and the correspondent to get respite together. "We'll give those boys a chance to get into shape again," said the captain. They curled down and, after a few preliminary chatterings and trembles, slept once more the dead sleep. Neither knew they had bequeathed to the cook the company of another shark, or perhaps the same shark.

195     As the boat caroused on the waves, spray occasionally bumped over the side and gave them a fresh soaking, but this had no power to break their repose. The ominous slash of the wind and the water affected them as it would have affected mummies.

"Boys," said the cook, with the notes of every reluctance in his voice, "she's drifted in pretty close. I guess one of you had better take her to sea again." The correspondent, aroused, heard the crash of the toppled crests.

As he was rowing, the captain gave him some whisky-and-water, and this steadied the chills out of him. "If I ever get ashore and anybody shows me even a photograph of an oar —"

At last there was a short conversation.

"Billie.... Billie, will you spell me?"

200     "Sure," said the oiler.

## VII

When the correspondent again opened his eyes, the sea and the sky were each of the grey hue of the dawning. Later, carmine and gold was painted upon the waters. The morning appeared finally, in its splendour, with a sky of pure blue, and the sunlight flamed on the tips of the waves.

On the distant dunes were set many little black cottages, and a tall white windmill reared above them. No man, nor dog, nor bicycle appeared on the beach. The cottages might have formed a deserted village.

The voyagers scanned the shore. A conference was held in the boat. "Well," said the captain, "if no help is coming we might better try a run through the surf right away. If we stay out here much longer we will be too weak to do anything for ourselves at all." The others silently acquiesced in this reasoning. The boat was headed for the beach. The correspondent wondered if none ever ascended the tall wind-tower, and if then they never looked seaward. This tower was a giant, standing with its back to the plight of the ants. It represented in a degree, to the correspondent, the serenity of nature amid the struggles of the individual — nature in the wind, and nature in the vision of men. She did not seem cruel to him then, nor beneficent, nor treacherous, nor wise. But she was indifferent, flatly indifferent. It is, perhaps, plausible that a man in this situation, impressed with the unconcern of the universe, should see the innumerable flaws of his life, and have them taste wickedly in his mind and wish for another chance. A distinction between right and wrong seems absurdly clear to him, then, in this new ignorance of the grave-edge, and he understands that if he were given another opportunity he would mend his conduct and his words, and be better and brighter during an introduction or at a tea.

"Now, boys," said the captain, "she is going to swamp, sure. All we can do is to work her in as far as possible, and then when she swamps, pile out and scramble for the beach. Keep cool now, and don't jump until she swamps sure."

205     The oiler took the oars. Over his shoulders he scanned the surf. "Captain," he said, "I think I'd better bring her about, and keep her head-on to the seas and back her in."

"All right, Billie," said the captain. "Back her in." The oiler swung the boat then and, seated in the stern, the cook and the correspondent were obliged to look over their shoulders to contemplate the lonely and indifferent shore.

The monstrous in-shore rollers heaved the boat high until the men were again enabled to see the white sheets of water scudding up the slanted beach. "We won't get in very close," said the captain. Each time a man could wrest his attention from the rollers, he turned his glance toward the shore, and in the expression of the eyes during this contemplation there was a singular quality. The correspondent, observing the others, knew that they were not afraid, but the full meaning of their glances was shrouded.

As for himself, he was too tired to grapple fundamentally with the fact. He tried to coerce his mind into thinking of it, but the mind was dominated at this time by the muscles, and the muscles said they did not care. It merely occurred to him that if he should drown it would be a shame.

There were no hurried words, no pallor, no plain agitation. The men simply looked at the shore. "Now, remember to get well clear of the boat when you jump," said the captain.

210    Seaward the crest of a roller suddenly fell with a thunderous crash, and the long white comber came roaring down upon the boat.

"Steady now," said the captain. The men were silent. They turned their eyes from the shore to the comber and waited. The boat slid up the incline, leaped at the furious top, bounced over it, and swung down the long back of the wave. Some water had been shipped and the cook bailed it out.

But the next crest crashed also. The tumbling boiling flood of white water caught the boat and whirled it almost perpendicular. Water swarmed in from all sides. The correspondent had his hands on the gunwale at this time, and when the water entered at that place he swiftly withdrew his fingers, as if he objected to wetting them.

The little boat, drunken with this weight of water, reeled and snuggled deeper into the sea.

"Bail her out, cook! Bail her out," said the captain.

215    "All right, captain," said the cook.

"Now, boys, the next one will do for us, sure," said the oiler. "Mind to jump clear of the boat."

The third wave moved forward, huge, furious, implacable. It fairly swallowed the dingey, and almost simultaneously the men tumbled into the sea. A piece of lifebelt had lain in the bottom of the boat, and as the correspondent went overboard he held this to his chest with his left hand.

The January water was icy, and he reflected immediately that it was colder than he had expected to find it off the coast of Florida. This appeared to his dazed mind as a fact important enough to be noted at the time. The coldness of the water was sad; it was tragic. This fact was somehow so mixed and confused with his opinion of his own situation that it seemed almost a proper reason for tears. The water was cold.

When he came to the surface he was conscious of little but the noisy water. Afterward he saw his companions in the sea. The oiler was ahead in the race. He was swimming strongly and rapidly. Off to the correspondent's left, the cook's great white and corked back bulged out of the water, and in the rear the captain was hanging with his one good hand to the keel of the overturned dingey.

220   There is a certain immovable quality to a shore, and the correspondent wondered at it amid the confusion of the sea.

It seemed also very attractive, but the correspondent knew that it was a long journey, and he paddled leisurely. The piece of life-preserver lay under him, and sometimes he whirled down the incline of a wave as if he were on a hand-sled.

But finally he arrived at a place in the sea where travel was beset with difficulty. He did not pause swimming to inquire what manner of current had caught him, but there his progress ceased. The shore was set before him like a bit of scenery on a stage, and he looked at it and understood with his eyes each detail of it.

As the cook passed, much farther to the left, the captain was calling to him, "Turn over on your back, cook! Turn over on your back and use the oar."

"All right, sir." The cook turned on his back, and, paddling with an oar, went ahead as if he were a canoe.

225   Presently the boat also passed to the left of the correspondent with the captain clinging with one hand to the keel. He would have appeared like a man raising himself to look over a board fence, if it were not for the extraordinary gymnastics of the boat. The correspondent marvelled that the captain could still hold to it.

They passed on, nearer to shore — the oiler, the cook, the captain — and following them went the water-jar, bouncing gaily over the seas.

The correspondent remained in the grip of this strange new enemy — a current. The shore, with its white slope of sand and its green bluff, topped with little silent cottages, was spread like a picture before him. It was very near to him then, but he was impressed as one who in a gallery looks at a scene from Brittany[6] or Holland.

He thought: "Am I going to drown? Can it be possible? Can it be possible? Can it be possible?" Perhaps an individual must consider his own death to be the final phenomenon of nature.

But later a wave perhaps whirled him out of this small deadly current, for he found suddenly that he could again make progress toward the shore. Later still, he was aware that the captain, clinging with one hand to the keel of the dingey, had his face turned away from the shore and toward him, and was calling his name. "Come to the boat! Come to the boat!"

230   In his struggle to reach the captain and the boat, he reflected that when one gets properly wearied, drowning must really be a comfortable arrangement, a cessation of hostilities accompanied by a large degree of relief, and he was glad of it, for the main thing in his mind for some moments had been horror of the temporary agony. He did not wish to be hurt.

Presently he saw a man running along the shore. He was undressing with most remarkable speed. Coat, trousers, shirt, everything flew magically off him.

"Come to the boat," called the captain.

6 rural region in northwestern France.

"All right, captain." As the correspondent paddled, he saw the captain let himself down to the bottom and leave the boat. Then the correspondent performed his one little marvel of the voyage. A large wave caught him and flung him with ease and supreme speed completely over the boat and far beyond it. It struck him even then as an event in gymnastics, and a true miracle of the sea. An overturned boat in the surf is not a plaything to a swimming man.

The correspondent arrived in water that reached only to his waist, but his condition did not enable him to stand for more than a moment. Each wave knocked him into a heap, and the under-tow pulled at him.

235      Then he saw the man who had been running and undressing, and undressing and running, come bounding into the water. He dragged ashore the cook, and then waded towards the captain, but the captain waved him away, and sent him to the correspondent. He was naked, naked as a tree in winter, but a halo was about his head, and he shone like a saint. He gave a strong pull, and a long drag, and a bully heave at the correspondent's hand. The correspondent, schooled in the minor formulæ, said: "Thanks, old man." But suddenly the man cried: "What's that?" He pointed a swift finger. The correspondent said: "Go."

In the shallows, face downward, lay the oiler. His forehead touched sand that was periodically, between each wave, clear of the sea.

The correspondent did not know all that transpired afterward. When he achieved safe ground he fell, striking the sand with each particular part of his body. It was as if he had dropped from a roof, but the thud was grateful to him.

It seems that instantly the beach was populated with men with blankets, clothes, and flasks, and women with coffee-pots and all the remedies sacred to their minds. The welcome of the land to the men from the sea was warm and generous, but a still and dripping shape was carried slowly up the beach, and the land's welcome for it could only be the different and sinister hospitality of the grave.

When it came night, the white waves paced to and fro in the moonlight, and the wind brought the sound of the great sea's voice to the men on shore, and they felt that they could then be interpreters.

(1897)

# James Joyce   (1882–1941)

Although Dublin-born, James Joyce lived most of his adult life in Europe, including twenty years in Paris, where he wrote most of his books about Dublin and
its people: *Dubliners*, a collection of short stories; and three novels, *A Portait of
the Artist as a Young Man, Ulysses,* and *Finnegans Wake.* The first three of these
were filled with minutely depicted presentations of scenes and characters of
Dublin. In *Dubliners*, from which "Araby" is taken, the details are given symbolic
meanings that transform specific aspects of late-nineteenth-century Irish life
into the universal. Many of the characters experience what Joyce called an
"epiphany," a moment of insight in which they understand the nature of their
lives. At the edge of adolescence, the young narrator experiences a profound
conflict between his emerging sexuality and his strict religious upbringing.
From the opening sentence's reference to a "blind" street to the concluding
one's references to the darkness of the bazaar, Joyce carefully selects and
arranges details to emphasize the boy's movement from innocence and ignorance to insight.

# ARABY[1]

North Richmond Street, being blind,[2] was a quiet street except at the hour
when the Christian Brothers' School set the boys free. An uninhabited house
of two storeys stood at the blind end, detached from its neighbours in a square
ground. The other houses of the street, conscious of decent lives within them,
gazed at one another with brown imperturbable faces.

　　The former tenant of our house, a priest, had died in the back drawing-
room. Air, musty from having been long enclosed, hung in all the rooms, and
the waste room behind the kitchen was littered with old useless papers. Among
these I found a few paper-covered books, the pages of which were curled and
damp: *The Abbot*,[3] by Walter Scott, *The Devout Communicant*[4] and *The Memoirs
of Vidocq*.[5] I liked the last best because its leaves were yellow. The wild garden
behind the house contained a central apple-tree and a few straggling bushes
under one of which I found the late tenant's rusty bicycle-pump. He had been
a very charitable priest; in his will he had left all his money to institutions
and the furniture of his house to his sister.

　　When the short days of winter came dusk fell before we had well eaten our
dinners. When we met in the street the houses had grown sombre. The space
of sky above us was the colour of ever-changing violet and towards it the
lamps of the street lifted their feeble lanterns. The cold air stung us and we
played till our bodies glowed. Our shouts echoed in the silent street. The
career of our play brought us through the dark muddy lanes behind the houses
where we ran the gantlet of the rough tribes from the cottages, to the back doors

---

1 Dublin charity bazaar with a name evoking the romance and mystery of Arabia. 2 dead-end street.
3 in Sir Walter Scott's 1820 novel set in the eighteenth century, a young man loyally serves Mary Queen of
Scots. 4 nineteenth-century religious tract. 5 François Vidocq was an early-nineteenth-century French
thief turned detective.

of the dark dripping gardens where odours arose from the ashpits, to the dark odorous stables where a coachman smoothed and combed the horse or shook music from the buckled harness. When we returned to the street light from the kitchen windows had filled the areas. If my uncle was seen turning the corner we hid in the shadow until we had seen him safely housed. Or if Mangan's sister came out on the doorstep to call her brother in to his tea we watched her from our shadow peer up and down the street. We waited to see whether she would remain or go in and, if she remained, we left our shadow and walked up to Mangan's steps resignedly. She was waiting for us, her figure defined by the light from the half-opened door. Her brother always teased her before he obeyed and I stood by the railings looking at her. Her dress swung as she moved her body and the soft rope of her hair tossed from side to side.

Every morning I lay on the floor in the front parlour watching her door. The blind was pulled down to within an inch of the sash so that I could not be seen. When she came out on the doorstep my heart leaped. I ran to the hall, seized my books and followed her. I kept her brown figure always in my eye and, when we came near the point at which our ways diverged, I quickened my pace and passed her. This happened morning after morning. I had never spoken to her, except for a few casual words, and yet her name was like a summons to all my foolish blood.

5      Her image accompanied me even in places the most hostile to romance. On Saturday evenings when my aunt went marketing I had to go to carry some of the parcels. We walked through the flaring streets, jostled by drunken men and bargaining women, amid the curses of labourers, the shrill litanies of shop-boys who stood on guard by the barrels of pigs' cheeks, the nasal chanting of street-singers, who sang a *come-all-you* about O'Donovan Rossa,[6] or a ballad about the troubles in our native land. These noises converged in a single sensation of life for me: I imagined that I bore my chalice safely through a throng of foes. Her name sprang to my lips at moments in strange prayers and praises which I myself did not understand. My eyes were often full of tears (I could not tell why) and at times a flood from my heart seemed to pour itself out into my bosom. I thought little of the future. I did not know whether I would ever speak to her or not or, if I spoke to her, how I could tell her of my confused adoration. But my body was like a harp and her words and gestures were like fingers running upon the wires.

One evening I went into the back drawing-room in which the priest had died. It was a dark rainy evening and there was no sound in the house. Through one of the broken panes I heard the rain impinge upon the earth, the fine incessant needles of water playing in the sodden beds. Some distant lamp or lighted window gleamed below me. I was thankful that I could see so little. All my senses seemed to desire to veil themselves and, feeling that I was about to slip from them, I pressed the palms of my hands together until they trembled, murmuring: *O love! O love!* many times.

At last she spoke to me. When she addressed the first words to me I was so confused that I did not know what to answer. She asked me was I going to

6 popular street ballad about a nineteenth-century Irish revolutionary.

*Araby*. I forget whether I answered yes or no. It would be a splendid bazaar, she said; she would love to go.

— And why can't you? I asked.

While she spoke she turned a silver bracelet round and round her wrist. She could not go, she said, because there would be a retreat that week in her convent. Her brother and two other boys were fighting for their caps and I was alone at the railings. She held one of the spikes, bowing her head towards me. The light from the lamp opposite our door caught the white curve of her neck, lit up her hair that rested there and, falling, lit up the hand upon the railing. It fell over one side of her dress and caught the white border of a petticoat, just visible as she stood at ease.

10 — It's well for you, she said.

— If I go, I said, I will bring you something.

What innumerable follies laid waste my waking and sleeping thoughts after that evening! I wished to annihilate the tedious intervening days. I chafed against the work of school. At night in my bedroom and by day in the classroom her image came between me and the page I strove to read. The syllables of the word *Araby* were called to me through the silence in which my soul luxuriated and cast an Eastern enchantment over me. I asked for leave to go to the bazaar on Saturday night. My aunt was surprised and hoped it was not some Freemason[7] affair. I answered few questions in class. I watched my master's face pass from amiability to sternness; he hoped I was not beginning to idle. I could not call my wandering thoughts together. I had hardly any patience with the serious work of life which, now that it stood between me and my desire, seemed to me child's play, ugly monotonous child's play.

On Saturday morning I reminded my uncle that I wished to go to the bazaar in the evening. He was fussing at the hallstand, looking for the hat-brush, and answered me curtly:

— Yes, boy, I know.

15 As he was in the hall I could not go into the front parlour and lie at the window. I left the house in bad humour and walked slowly towards the school. The air was pitilessly raw and already my heart misgave me.

When I came home to dinner my uncle had not yet been home. Still it was early. I sat staring at the clock for some time and, when its ticking began to irritate me, I left the room. I mounted the staircase and gained the upper part of the house. The high cold empty gloomy rooms liberated me and I went from room to room singing. From the front window I saw my companions playing below in the street. Their cries reached me weakened and indistinct and, leaning my forehead against the cool glass, I looked over at the dark house where she lived. I may have stood there for an hour, seeing nothing but the brown-clad figure cast by my imagination, touched discreetly by the lamplight at the curved neck, at the hand upon the railings and at the border below the dress.

When I came downstairs again I found Mrs Mercer sitting at the fire. She was an old garrulous woman, a pawnbroker's widow, who collected used stamps for some pious purpose. I had to endure the gossip of the tea-table.

7 the Protestant Masons were considered enemies of Irish Roman Catholics.

The meal was prolonged beyond an hour and still my uncle did not come. Mrs Mercer stood up to go: she was sorry she couldn't wait any longer, but it was after eight o'clock and she did not like to be out late, as the night air was bad for her. When she had gone I began to walk up and down the room, clenching my fists. My aunt said:

— I'm afraid you may put off your bazaar for this night of Our Lord.

At nine o'clock I heard my uncle's latchkey in the halldoor. I heard him talking to himself and heard the hallstand rocking when it had received the weight of his overcoat. I could interpret these signs. When he was midway through his dinner I asked him to give me the money to go to the bazaar. He had forgotten.

20      — The people are in bed and after their first sleep now, he said.

I did not smile. My aunt said to him energetically:

— Can't you give him the money and let him go? You've kept him late enough as it is.

My uncle said he was very sorry he had forgotten. He said he believed in the old saying: *All work and no play makes Jack a dull boy*. He asked where I was going and, when I had told him a second time he asked me did I know *The Arab's Farewell to his Steed*.[8] When I left the kitchen he was about to recite the opening lines of the piece to my aunt.

I held a florin[9] tightly in my hand as I strode down Buckingham Street towards the station. The sight of the streets thronged with buyers and glaring with gas recalled to me the purpose of my journey. I took my seat in a third-class carriage of a deserted train. After an intolerable delay the train moved out of the station slowly. It crept onward among ruinous houses and over the twinkling river. At Westland Row Station a crowd of people pressed to the carriage doors; but the porters moved them back, saying that it was a special train for the bazaar. I remained alone in the bare carriage. In a few minutes the train drew up beside an improvised wooden platform. I passed out on to the road and saw by the lighted dial of a clock that it was ten minutes to ten. In front of me was a large building which displayed the magical name.

25      I could not find any sixpenny entrance and, fearing that the bazaar would be closed, I passed in quickly through a turnstile, handing a shilling to a weary-looking man. I found myself in a big hall girdled at half its height by a gallery. Nearly all the stalls were closed and the greater part of the hall was in darkness. I recognized a silence like that which pervades a church after a service. I walked into the centre of the bazaar timidly. A few people were gathered about the stalls which were still open. Before a curtain, over which the words *Café Chantant* were written in coloured lamps, two men were counting money on a salver. I listened to the fall of the coins.

Remembering with difficulty why I had come I went over to one of the stalls and examined porcelain vases and flowered tea-sets. At the door of the stall a young lady was talking and laughing with two young gentlemen. I remarked their English accents and listened vaguely to their conversation.

— Oh, I never said such a thing!

8 sentimental nineteenth-century poem about a man who, disconsolate at selling his horse, reclaims it.
9 two-shilling coin worth about 50 cents at that time.

— O, but you did!

— O, but I didn't!

— Didn't she say that?

— Yes. I heard her.

— O, there's a . . . fib!

Observing me the young lady came over and asked me did I wish to buy anything. The tone of her voice was not encouraging; she seemed to have spoken to me out of a sense of duty. I looked humbly at the great jars that stood like eastern guards at either side of the dark entrance to the stall and murmured:

— No, thank you.

The young lady changed the position of one of the vases and went back to the two young men. They began to talk of the same subject. Once or twice the young lady glanced at me over her shoulder.

I lingered before her stall, though I knew my stay was useless, to make my interest in her wares seem the more real. Then I turned away slowly and walked down the middle of the bazaar. I allowed the two pennies to fall against the sixpence in my pocket. I heard a voice call from one end of the gallery that the light was out. The upper part of the hall was now completely dark.

Gazing up into the darkness I saw myself as a creature driven and derided by vanity; and my eyes burned with anguish and anger.

(1914)

# D.H. Lawrence (1885–1930)

Born in Eastwood, Nottinghamshire, England, in the industrial Midlands, D.H. Lawrence published ten novels, as well as travel books and collections of short stories, poems, and literary criticism. He spent much of his adult life travelling and lived in Europe, the United States, and Australia, in which places many of his works were written. Although his novels often aroused controversy because of their detailed examination of sexual tensions and conflicts, literary critics have frequently defended them, particularly his best-known novel, *Sons and Lovers*, for their highly moralistic treatment of the emotional relationships between men and women. In "The Horse Dealer's Daughter," Mabel sees the sale of the family home as the end of her life. However, after the local doctor saves her from committing suicide, she experiences symbolic rebirth to love and human relationship.

# THE HORSE DEALER'S DAUGHTER

"Well, Mabel, and what are you going to do with yourself?" asked Joe, with foolish flippancy. He felt quite safe himself. Without listening for an answer, he turned aside, worked a grain of tobacco to the tip of his tongue, and spat it out. He did not care about anything, since he felt safe himself.

The three brothers and the sister sat round the desolate breakfast-table, attempting some sort of desultory consultation. The morning's post had given the final tap to the family fortunes, and all was over. The dreary dining-room itself, with its heavy mahogany furniture, looked as if it were waiting to be done away with.

But the consultation amounted to nothing. There was a strange air of ineffectuality about the three men, as they sprawled at table, smoking and reflecting vaguely on their own condition. The girl was alone, a rather short, sullen-looking young woman of twenty-seven. She did not share the same life as her brothers. She would have been good-looking, save for the impressive fixity of her face, 'bull-dog', as her brothers called it.

There was a confused tramping of horses' feet outside. The three men all sprawled round in their chairs to watch. Beyond the dark holly bushes that separated the strip of lawn from the high-road, they could see a cavalcade of shire horses swinging out of their own yard, being taken for exercise. This was the last time. These were the last horses that would go through their hands. The young men watched with critical, callous look. They were all frightened at the collapse of their lives, and the sense of disaster in which they were involved left them no inner freedom.

5 Yet they were three fine, well-set fellows enough. Joe, the eldest, was a man of thirty-three, broad and handsome in a hot, flushed way. His face was red, he twisted his black moustache over a thick finger, his eyes were shallow and restless. He had a sensual way of uncovering his teeth when he laughed, and his bearing was stupid. Now he watched the horses with a glazed look of helplessness in his eyes, a certain stupor of downfall.

The great draught-horses swung past. They were tied head to tail, four of them, and they heaved along to where a lane branched off from the high-road, planting their great hoofs floutingly in the fine black mud, swinging their great rounded haunches sumptuously, and trotting a few sudden steps as they were led into the lane, round the corner. Every movement showed a massive, slumbrous strength, and a stupidity which held them in subjection. The groom at the head looked back, jerking the leading rope. And the cavalcade moved out of sight up the lane, the tail of the last horse, bobbed up tight and stiff, held out taut from the swinging great haunches as they rocked behind the hedges in a motion-like sleep.

Joe watched with glazed hopeless eyes. The horses were almost like his own body to him. He felt he was done for now. Luckily he was engaged to a woman as old as himself, and therefore her father, who was steward of a neighbouring estate, would provide him with a job. He would marry and go into harness. His life was over, he would be a subject animal now.

He turned uneasily aside, the retreating steps of the horses echoing in his ears. Then, with foolish restlessness, he reached for the scraps of bacon-rind from the plates, and making a faint whistling sound, flung them to the terrier that lay against the fender. He watched the dog swallow them, and waited till the creature looked into his eyes. Then a faint grin came on his face, and in a high, foolish voice he said:

"You won't get much more bacon, shall you, you little b — ?"

10    The dog faintly and dismally wagged its tail, then lowered its haunches, circled round, and lay down again.

There was another helpless silence at the table. Joe sprawled uneasily in his seat, not willing to go till the family conclave was dissolved. Fred Henry, the second brother, was erect, clean-limbed, alert. He had watched the passing of the horses with more *sang-froid*.[1] If he was an animal, like Joe, he was an animal which controls, not one which is controlled. He was master of any horse, and he carried himself with a well-tempered air of mastery. But he was not master of the situations of life. He pushed his coarse brown moustache upwards, off his lip, and glanced irritably at his sister, who sat impassive and inscrutable.

"You'll go and stop with Lucy for a bit, shan't you?" he asked. The girl did not answer.

"I don't see what else you can do," persisted Fred Henry.

"Go as a skivvy,"[2] Joe interpolated laconically.

15    The girl did not move a muscle.

"If I was her, I should go in for training for a nurse," said Malcolm, the youngest of them all. He was the baby of the family, a young man of twenty-two, with a fresh, jaunty *museau*.[3]

But Mabel did not take any notice of him. They had talked at her and round her for so many years, that she hardly heard them at all.

The marble clock on the mantelpiece softly chimed the half-hour, the dog rose uneasily from the hearth-rug and looked at the party at the breakfast-table. But still they sat on in ineffectual conclave.

1 cool indifference. 2 female servant. 3 face.

"Oh, all right," said Joe suddenly, apropos of nothing. "I'll get a move on."

20 He pushed back his chair, straddled his knees with a downward jerk, to get them free, in horsey fashion, and went to the fire. Still he did not go out of the room; he was curious to know what the others would do or say. He began to charge his pipe, looking down at the dog and saying in a high, affected voice:

"Going wi' me? Going wi' me are ter? Tha'rt goin' further than tha counts on just now, dost hear?"

The dog faintly wagged its tail, the man stuck out his jaw and covered his pipe with his hands, and puffed intently, losing himself in the tobacco, looking down all the while at the dog with an absent brown eye. The dog looked up at him in mournful distrust. Joe stood with his knees stuck out, in real horsey fashion.

"Have you had a letter from Lucy?" Fred Henry asked of his sister.

"Last week," came the neutral reply.

25 "And what does she say?"

There was no answer.

"Does she *ask* you to go and stop there?" persisted Fred Henry.

"She says I can if I like."

"Well, then, you'd better. Tell her you'll come on Monday."

30 This was received in silence.

"That's what you'll do then, is it?" said Fred Henry, in some exasperation.

But she made no answer. There was a silence of futility and irritation in the room. Malcolm grinned fatuously.

"You'll have to make up your mind between now and next Wednesday," said Joe loudly, "or else find yourself lodgings on the kerbstone."

The face of the young woman darkened, but she sat on immutable.

35 "Here's Jack Fergusson!" exclaimed Malcolm, who was looking aimlessly out of the window.

"Where?" exclaimed Joe loudly.

"Just gone past."

"Coming in?"

Malcolm craned his neck to see the gate.

40 "Yes," he said.

There was a silence. Mabel sat on like one condemned, at the head of the table. Then a whistle was heard from the kitchen. The dog got up and barked sharply. Joe opened the door and shouted:

"Come on."

After a moment a young man entered. He was muffled up in an overcoat and a purple woollen scarf, and his tweed cap, which he did not remove, was pulled down on his head. He was of medium height, his face was rather long and pale, his eyes looked tired.

"Hello, Jack! Well, Jack!" exclaimed Malcolm and Joe. Fred Henry merely said: "Jack."

45 "What's doing?" asked the newcomer, evidently addressing Fred Henry.

"Same. We've got to be out by Wednesday. Got a cold?"

"I have — got it bad, too."

"Why don't you stop in?"

"Me stop in? When I can't stand on my legs, perhaps I shall have a chance." The young man spoke huskily. He had a slight Scotch accent.

"It's a knock-out, isn't it," said Joe, boisterously, "if a doctor goes round croaking with a cold. Looks bad for the patients, doesn't it?"

The young doctor looked at him slowly.

"Anything the matter with *you*, then?" he asked sarcastically.

"Not as I know of. Damn your eyes, I hope not. Why?"

"I thought you were very concerned about the patients, wondered if you might be one yourself."

"Damn it, no, I've never been patient to no flaming doctor, and hope I never shall be," returned Joe.

At this point Mabel rose from the table, and they all seemed to become aware of her existence. She began putting the dishes together. The young doctor looked at her, but did not address her. He had not greeted her. She went out of the room with the tray, her face impassive and unchanged.

"When are you off then, all of you?" asked the doctor.

"I'm catching the eleven-forty," replied Malcolm. "Are you goin' down wi' th' trap, Joe?"

"Yes, I've told you I'm going down wi' th' trap, haven't I?"

"We'd better be getting her in then. So long, Jack, if I don't see you before I go," said Malcolm, shaking hands.

He went out, followed by Joe, who seemed to have his tail between his legs.

"Well, this is the devil's own," exclaimed the doctor, when he was left alone with Fred Henry. "Going before Wednesday, are you?"

"That's the orders," replied the other.

"Where, to Northampton?"[4]

"That's it."

"The devil!" exclaimed Fergusson, with quiet chagrin.

And there was silence between the two.

"All settled up, are you?" asked Fergusson.

"About."

There was another pause.

"Well, I shall miss yer, Freddy, boy," said the young doctor.

"And I shall miss thee, Jack," returned the other.

"Miss you like hell," mused the doctor.

Fred Henry turned aside. There was nothing to say. Mabel came in again, to finish clearing the table.

"What are *you* going to do, then, Miss Pervin?" asked Fergusson. "Going to your sister's, are you?"

Mabel looked at him with her steady, dangerous eyes, that always made him uncomfortable, unsettling his superficial ease.

"No," she said.

"Well, what in the name of fortune *are* you going to do? Say what you mean to do," cried Fred Henry, with futile intensity.

But she only averted her head, and continued her work. She folded the white table-cloth, and put on the chenille cloth.

4 city in central England.

80 "The sulkiest bitch that ever trod!" muttered her brother.

But she finished her task with perfectly impassive face, the young doctor watching her interestedly all the while. Then she went out.

Fred Henry stared after her, clenching his lips, his blue eyes fixing in sharp antagonism, as he made a grimace of sour exasperation.

"You could bray her into bits, and that's all you'd get out of her," he said, in a small, narrowed tone.

The doctor smiled faintly.

85 "What's she *going* to do, then?" he asked.

"Strike me if *I* know!" returned the other.

There was a pause. Then the doctor stirred.

"I'll be seeing you to-night, shall I?" he said to his friend.

"Ay — where's it to be? Are we going over to Jessdale?"

90 "I don't know. I've got such a cold on me. I'll come round to the 'Moon and Stars', anyway."

"Let Lizzie and May miss their night for once, eh?"

"That's it — if I feel as I do now."

"All's one —"

The two young men went through the passage and down to the back door together. The house was large, but it was servantless now, and desolate. At the back was a small bricked house-yard and beyond that a big square, gravelled fine and red, and having stables on two sides. Sloping, dank, winter-dark fields stretched away on the open sides.

95 But the stables were empty. Joseph Pervin, the father of the family, had been a man of no education, who had become a fairly large horse dealer. The stables had been full of horses, there was a great turmoil and come-and-go of horses and of dealers and grooms. Then the kitchen was full of servants. But of late things had declined. The old man had married a second time, to retrieve his fortunes. Now he was dead and everything was gone to the dogs, there was nothing but debt and threatening.

For months, Mabel had been servantless in the big house, keeping the home together in penury for her ineffectual brothers. She had kept house for ten years. But previously it was with unstinted means. Then, however brutal and coarse everything was, the sense of money had kept her proud, confident. The men might be foul-mouthed, the women in the kitchen might have bad reputations, her brothers might have illegitimate children. But so long as there was money, the girl felt herself established, and brutally proud, reserved.

No company came to the house, save dealers and coarse men. Mabel had no associates of her own sex, after her sister went away. But she did not mind. She went regularly to church, she attended to her father. And she lived in the memory of her mother, who had died when she was fourteen, and whom she had loved. She had loved her father, too, in a different way, depending upon him, and feeling secure in him, until at the age of fifty-four he married again. And then she had set hard against him. Now he had died and left them all hopelessly in debt.

She had suffered badly during the period of poverty. Nothing, however, could shake the curious, sullen, animal pride that dominated each member of the family. Now, for Mabel, the end had come. Still she would not cast about her. She would follow her own way just the same. She would always hold the keys of her own situation. Mindless and persistent, she endured from day to day. Why should she think? Why should she answer anybody? It was enough that this was the end, and there was no way out. She need not pass any more darkly along the main street of the small town, avoiding every eye. She need not demean herself any more, going into the shops and buying the cheapest food. This was at an end. She thought of nobody, not even of herself. Mindless and persistent, she seemed in a sort of ecstasy to be coming nearer to her fulfilment, her own glorification, approaching her dead mother, who was glorified.

In the afternoon she took a little bag, with shears and sponge and a small scrubbing-brush, and went out. It was a grey, wintry day, with saddened, dark green fields and an atmosphere blackened by the smoke of foundries not far off. She went quickly, darkly along the causeway, heeding nobody, through the town to the churchyard.

100    There she always felt secure, as if no one could see her, although as a matter of fact she was exposed to the stare of everyone who passed along under the churchyard wall. Nevertheless, once under the shadow of the great looming church, among the graves, she felt immune from the world, reserved within the thick churchyard wall as in another country.

Carefully she clipped the grass from the grave, and arranged the pinky white, small chrysanthemums in the tin cross. When this was done, she took an empty jar from a neighbouring grave, brought water, and carefully, most scrupulously sponged the marble headstone and the coping-stone.

It gave her sincere satisfaction to do this. She felt in immediate contact with the world of her mother. She took minute pains, went through the park in a state bordering on pure happiness, as if in performing this task she came into a subtle, intimate connection with her mother. For the life she followed here in the world was far less real than the world of death she inherited from her mother.

The doctor's house was just by the church. Fergusson, being a mere hired assistant, was slave to the country-side. As he hurried now to attend to the out-patients in the surgery, glancing across the graveyard with his quick eye, he saw the girl at her task at the grave. She seemed so intent and remote, it was like looking into another world. Some mystical element was touched in him. He slowed down as he walked, watching her as if spellbound.

She lifted her eyes, feeling him looking. Their eyes met. And each looked again at once, each feeling, in some way, found out by the other. He lifted his cap and passed on down the road. There remained distinct in his con-sciousness, like a vision, the memory of her face, lifted from the tombstone in the churchyard, and looking at him with slow, large, portentous eyes. It *was* por-tentous, her face. It seemed to mesmerise him. There was a heavy power in her eyes which laid hold of his whole being, as if he had drunk some powerful drug. He had been feeling weak and done before. Now the life came back into him, he felt delivered from his own fretted, daily self.

105    He finished his duties at the surgery as quickly as might be, hastily filling up the bottles of the waiting people with cheap drugs. Then, in perpetual haste, he set off again to visit several cases in another part of his round, before tea-time. At all times he preferred to walk if he could, but particularly when he was not well. He fancied the motion restored him.

The afternoon was falling. It was grey, deadened, and wintry, with a slow, moist, heavy coldness sinking in and deadening all the faculties. But why should he think or notice? He hastily climbed the hill and turned across the dark green fields, following the black cinder-track. In the distance, across a shallow dip in the country, the small town was clustered like smouldering ash, a tower, a spire, a heap of low, raw, extinct houses. And on the nearest fringe of the town, sloping into the dip, was Oldmeadow, the Pervins' house. He could see the stables and the outbuildings distinctly, as they lay towards him on the slope. Well, he would not go there many more times! Another resource would be lost to him, another place gone: the only company he cared for in the alien, ugly little town he was losing. Nothing but work, drudgery, constant hastening from dwelling to dwelling among the colliers and the iron-workers. It wore him out, but at the same time he had a craving for it. It was a stimulant to him to be in the homes of the working people, moving, as it were, through the innermost body of their life. His nerves were excited and gratified. He could come so near, into the very lives of the rough, inarticulate, powerfully emotional men and women. He grumbled, he said he hated the hellish hole. But as a matter of fact it excited him, the contact with the rough, strongly-feeling people was a stimulant applied direct to his nerves.

Below Oldmeadow, in the green, shallow, soddened hollow of fields, lay a square, deep pond. Roving across the landscape, the doctor's quick eye detected a figure in black passing through the gate of the field, down towards the pond. He looked again. It would be Mabel Pervin. His mind suddenly became alive and attentive.

Why was she going down there? He pulled up on the path on the slope above, and stood staring. He could just make sure of the small black figure moving in the hollow of the failing day. He seemed to see her in the midst of such obscurity, that he was like a clairvoyant, seeing rather with the mind's eye than with ordinary sight. Yet he could see her positively enough, whilst he kept his eye attentive. He felt, if he looked away from her, in the thick, ugly falling dusk, he would lose her altogether.

He followed her minutely as she moved, direct and intent, like something transmitted rather than stirring in voluntary activity, straight down the field towards the pond. There she stood on the bank for a moment. She never raised her head. Then she waded slowly into the water.

He stood motionless as the small black figure walked slowly and deliberately towards the centre of the pond, very slowly, gradually moving deeper into the motionless water, and still moving forward as the water got up to her breast. Then he could see her no more in the dusk of the dead afternoon.

"There!" he exclaimed. "Would you believe it?"

And he hastened straight down, running over the wet, soddened fields, pushing through the hedges, down into the depression of callous wintry obscurity. It took him several minutes to come to the pond. He stood on the bank, breathing heavily. He could see nothing. His eyes seemed to penetrate the dead water. Yes, perhaps that was the dark shadow of her black clothing beneath the surface of the water.

He slowly ventured into the pond. The bottom was deep, soft clay, he sank in, and the water clasped dead cold round his legs. As he stirred he could smell the cold, rotten clay that fouled up into the water. It was objectionable in his lungs. Still, repelled and yet not heeding, he moved deeper into the pond. The cold water rose over his thighs, over his loins, upon his abdomen. The lower part of his body was all sunk in the hideous cold element. And the bottom was so deeply soft and uncertain, he was afraid of pitching with his mouth underneath. He could not swim, and was afraid.

He crouched a little, spreading his hands under the water and moving them round, trying to feel for her. The dead cold pond swayed upon his chest. He moved again, a little deeper, and again, with his hands underneath, he felt all around under the water. And he touched her clothing. But it evaded his fingers. He made a desperate effort to grasp it.

115     And so doing he lost his balance and went under, horribly, suffocating in the foul earthy water, struggling madly for a few moments. At last, after what seemed an eternity, he got his footing, rose again into the air and looked around. He gasped, and knew he was in the world. Then he looked at the water. She had risen near him. He grasped her clothing, and drawing her nearer, turned to take his way to land again.

He went very slowly, carefully, absorbed in the slow progress. He rose higher, climbing out of the pond. The water was now only about his legs; he was thankful, full of relief to be out of the clutches of the pond. He lifted her and staggered on to the bank, out of the horror of wet, grey clay.

He laid her down on the bank. She was quite unconscious and running with water. He made the water come from her mouth, he worked to restore her. He did not have to work very long before he could feel the breathing begin again in her; she was breathing naturally. He worked a little longer. He could feel her live beneath his hands; she was coming back. He wiped her face, wrapped her in his overcoat, looked round into the dim, dark grey world, then lifted her and staggered down the bank and across the fields.

It seemed an unthinkably long way, and his burden so heavy he felt he would never get to the house. But at last he was in the stable-yard, and then in the house-yard. He opened the door and went into the house. In the kitchen he laid her down on the hearth-rug and called. The house was empty. But the fire was burning in the grate.

Then again he kneeled to attend to her. She was breathing regularly, her eyes were wide open and as if conscious, but there seemed something missing in her look. She was conscious in herself, but unconscious of her surroundings.

120     He ran upstairs, took blankets from a bed, and put them before the fire to warm. Then he removed her saturated, earthy-smelling clothing, rubbed her dry with a towel, and wrapped her naked in the blankets. Then he went into the dining-room, to look for spirits. There was a little whisky. He drank a gulp himself, and put some into her mouth.

The effect was instantaneous. She looked full into his face, as if she had been seeing him for some time, and yet had only just become conscious of him.

"Dr. Fergusson?" she said.

"What?" he answered.

He was divesting himself of his coat, intending to find some dry clothing upstairs. He could not bear the smell of the dead, clayey water, and he was mortally afraid for his own health.

125    "What did I do?" she asked.

"Walked into the pond," he replied. He had begun to shudder like one sick, and could hardly attend to her. Her eyes remained full on him, he seemed to be going dark in his mind, looking back at her helplessly. The shuddering became quieter in him, his life came back to him, dark and unknowing, but strong again.

"Was I out of my mind?" she asked, while her eyes were fixed on him all the time.

"Maybe, for the moment," he replied. He felt quiet, because his strength had come back. The strange fretful strain had left him.

"Am I out of my mind now?" she asked.

130    "Are you?" he reflected a moment. "No," he answered truthfully, "I don't see that you are." He turned his face aside. He was afraid now, because he felt dazed, and felt dimly that her power was stronger than his, in this issue. And she continued to look at him fixedly all the time. "Can you tell me where I shall find some dry things to put on?" he asked.

"Did you dive into the pond for me?" she asked.

"No," he answered. "I walked in. But I went in overhead as well."

There was silence for a moment. He hesitated. He very much wanted to go upstairs to get into dry clothing. But there was another desire in him. And she seemed to hold him. His will seemed to have gone to sleep, and left him, standing there slack before her. But he felt warm inside himself. He did not shudder at all, though his clothes were sodden on him.

"Why did you?" she asked.

135    "Because I didn't want you to do such a foolish thing," he said.

"It wasn't foolish," she said, still gazing at him as she lay on the floor, with a sofa cushion under her head. "It was the right thing to do. I knew best, then."

"I'll go and shift these wet things," he said. But still he had not the power to move out of her presence, until she sent him. It was as if she had the life of his body in her hands, and he could not extricate himself. Or perhaps he did not want to.

Suddenly she sat up. Then she became aware of her own immediate condition. She felt the blankets about her, she knew her own limbs. For a moment it seemed as if her reason were going. She looked round, with wild eye, as if seeking something. He stood still with fear. She saw her clothing lying scattered.

"Who undressed me?" she asked, her eyes resting full and inevitable on his face.

140    "I did," he replied, "to bring you round."

For some moments she sat and gazed at him awfully, her lips parted.

"Do you love me, then?" she asked.

He only stood and stared at her, fascinated. His soul seemed to melt.

She shuffled forward on her knees, and put her arms round him, round his legs, as he stood there, pressing her breasts against his knees and thighs, clutching him with strange, convulsive certainty, pressing his thighs against her, drawing him to her face, her throat, as she looked up at him with flaring, humble eyes of transfiguration, triumphant in first possession.

145    "You love me," she murmured, in strange transport, yearning and triumphant and confident. "You love me. I know you love me, I know."

And she was passionately kissing his knees, through the wet clothing, passionately and indiscriminately kissing his knees, his legs, as if unaware of everything.

He looked down at the tangled wet hair, the wild, bare, animal shoulders. He was amazed, bewildered, and afraid. He had never thought of loving her. He had never wanted to love her. When he rescued her and restored her, he was a doctor, and she was a patient. He had had no single personal thought of her. Nay, this introduction of the personal element was very distasteful to him, a violation of his professional honour. It was horrible to have her there embracing his knees. It was horrible. He revolted from it, violently. And yet — and yet — he had not the power to break away.

She looked at him again, with the same supplication of powerful love, and that same transcendent, frightening light of triumph. In view of the delicate flame which seemed to come from her face like a light, he was powerless. And yet he had never intended to love her. He had never intended. And something stubborn in him could not give way.

"You love me," she repeated, in a murmur of deep, rhapsodic assurance. "You love me."

150

Her hands were drawing him, drawing him down to her. He was afraid, even a little horrified. For he had, really, no intention of loving her. Yet her hands were drawing him towards her. He put out his hand quickly to steady himself, and grasped her bare shoulder. A flame seemed to burn the hand that grasped her soft shoulder. He had no intention of loving her: his whole will was against his yielding. It was horrible. And yet wonderful was the touch of her shoulders, beautiful the shining of her face. Was she perhaps mad? He had a horror of yielding to her. Yet something in him ached also.

He had been staring away at the door, away from her. But his hand remained on her shoulder. She had gone suddenly very still. He looked down at her. Her eyes were now wide with fear, with doubt, the light was dying from her face, a shadow of terrible greyness was returning. He could not bear the touch of her eyes' question upon him, and the look of death behind the question.

With an inward groan he gave way, and let his heart yield towards her. A sudden gentle smile came on his face. And her eyes, which never left his face, slowly, slowly filled with tears. He watched the strange water rise in her eyes, like some slow fountain coming up. And his heart seemed to burn and melt away in his breast.

He could not bear to look at her any more. He dropped on his knees and caught her head with his arms and pressed her face against his throat. She was very still. His heart, which seemed to have broken, was burning with a kind of agony in his breast. And he felt her slow, hot tears wetting his throat. But he could not move.

He felt the hot tears wet his neck and the hollows of his neck, and he remained motionless, suspended through one of man's eternities. Only now it had become indispensable to him to have her face pressed close to him; he could never let her go again. He could never let her head go away from the close clutch of his arm. He wanted to remain like that for ever, with his heart hurting him in a pain that was also life to him. Without knowing, he was looking down on her damp, soft brown hair.

155      Then, as it were suddenly, he smelt the horrid stagnant smell of that water. And at the same moment she drew away from him and looked at him. Her eyes were wistful and unfathomable. He was afraid of them, and he fell to kissing her, not knowing what he was doing. He wanted her eyes not to have that terrible, wistful, unfathomable look.

When she turned her face to him again, a faint delicate flush was glowing, and there was again dawning that terrible shining of joy in her eyes, which really terrified him, and yet which he now wanted to see, because he feared the look of doubt still more.

"You love me?" she said, rather faltering.

"Yes." The word cost him a painful effort. Not because it wasn't true. But because it was too newly true, the *saying* seemed to tear open again his newly-torn heart. And he hardly wanted it to be true, even now.

She lifted her face to him, and he bent forward and kissed her on the mouth, gently, with the one kiss that is an eternal pledge. And as he kissed her his heart strained again in his breast. He never intended to love her. But now it was over. He had crossed over the gulf to her, and all that he had left behind had shrivelled and become void.

160      After the kiss, her eyes again slowly filled with tears. She sat still, away from him, with her face drooped aside, and her hands folded in her lap. The tears fell very slowly. There was complete silence. He too sat there motionless and silent on the hearth-rug. The strange pain of his heart that was broken seemed to consume him. That he should love her? That this was love! That he should be ripped open in this way! Him, a doctor! How they would all jeer if they knew! It was agony to him to think they might know.

In the curious naked pain of the thought he looked again to her. She was sitting there drooped into a muse. He saw a tear fall, and his heart flared hot. He saw for the first time that one of her shoulders was quite uncovered, one arm bare, he could see one of her small breasts; dimly, because it had become almost dark in the room.

"Why are you crying?" he asked, in an altered voice.

She looked up at him, and behind her tears the consciousness of her situation for the first time brought a dark look of shame to her eyes.

"I'm not crying, really," she said, watching him, half frightened.

165      He reached his hand, and softly closed it on her bare arm.

"I love you! I love you!" he said in a soft, low vibrating voice, unlike himself.

She shrank, and dropped her head. The soft, penetrating grip of his hand on her arm distressed her. She looked up at him.

"I want to go," she said. "I want to go and get you some dry things."

"Why?" he said. "I'm all right."

170      "But I want to go," she said. "And I want you to change your things."

He released her arm, and she wrapped herself in the blanket, looking at him rather frightened. And still she did not rise.

"Kiss me," she said wistfully.

He kissed her, but briefly, half in anger.

Then, after a second, she rose nervously, all mixed up in the blanket. He watched her in her confusion as she tried to extricate herself and wrap herself up so that she could walk. He watched her relentlessly, as she knew. And as she went, the blanket trailing, and as he saw a glimpse of her feet and her white leg, he tried to remember her as she was when he had wrapped her in the blanket. But then he didn't want to remember, because she had been nothing to him then, and his nature revolted from remembering her as she was when she was nothing to him.

175　A tumbling, muffled noise from within the dark house startled him. Then he heard her voice: "There are clothes." He rose and went to the foot of the stairs, and gathered up the garments she had thrown down. Then he came back to the fire, to rub himself down and dress. He grinned at his own appearance when he had finished.

The fire was sinking, so he put on coal. The house was now quite dark, save for the light of a street-lamp that shone in faintly from beyond the holly trees. He lit the gas with matches he found on the mantelpiece. Then he emptied the pockets of his own clothes, and threw all his wet things in a heap into the scullery. After which he gathered up her sodden clothes, gently, and put them in a separate heap on the coppertop in the scullery.

It was six o'clock on the clock. His own watch had stopped. He ought to go back to the surgery. He waited, and still she did not come down. So he went to the foot of the stairs and called:

"I shall have to go."

Almost immediately he heard her coming down. She had on her best dress of black voile, and her hair was tidy, but still damp. She looked at him — and in spite of herself, smiled.

180　"I don't like you in those clothes," she said.

"Do I look a sight?" he answered.

They were shy of one another.

"I'll make you some tea," she said.

"No, I must go."

185　"Must you?" And she looked at him again with the wide, strained, doubtful eyes. And again, from the pain of his breast, he knew how he loved her. He went and bent to kiss her, gently, passionately, with his heart's painful kiss.

"And my hair smells so horrible," she murmured in distraction. "And I'm so awful, I'm so awful! Oh no, I'm too awful." And she broke into bitter, heartbroken sobbing. "You can't want to love me. I'm horrible."

"Don't be silly, don't be silly," he said, trying to comfort her, kissing her, holding her in his arms. "I want you, I want to marry you, we're going to be married, quickly, quickly — to-morrow if I can."

But she only sobbed terribly, and cried:

"I feel awful. I feel awful. I feel I'm horrible to you."

190　"No, I want you, I want you," was all he answered, blindly, with that terrible intonation which frightened her almost more than her horror lest he should *not* want her.

(1922)

# Katherine Mansfield (1888–1923)

Born in Wellington, New Zealand, Katherine Mansfield (the pseudonym of Kathleen Beauchamp) moved to London when she was twenty and shortly after began her career as a writer. Critics have compared her works to those of Russian author Anton Chekhov, whose ironic view of life and whose technical innovations, particularly the use of small details to reveal character, she greatly admired. In her collections of short stories, three of which—*In a German Pension*, *Bliss*, and *The Garden Party*—were published during her life, she examined the nature of childhood and the troubled relationships between men and women. The description of the heroine's activities in the early pages of "Bliss" reveals the happiness Bertha feels as she prepares for a dinner party, while later details indicate her changing emotions. Events of the narrative and her emotions and feelings subtly foreshadow the story's conclusion.

# BLISS

Although Bertha Young was thirty she still had moments like this when she wanted to run instead of walk, to take dancing steps on and off the pavement, to bowl a hoop, to throw something up in the air and catch it again, or to stand still and laugh at — nothing — at nothing, simply.

What can you do if you are thirty and, turning the corner of your own street, you are overcome, suddenly, by a feeling of bliss — absolute bliss! — as though you'd suddenly swallowed a bright piece of that late afternoon sun and it burned in your bosom, sending out a little shower of sparks into every particle, into every finger and toe?...

Oh, is there no way you can express it without being "drunk and disorderly"? How idiotic civilization is! Why be given a body if you have to keep it shut up in a case like a rare, rare fiddle?

"No, that about the fiddle is not quite what I mean," she thought, running up the steps and feeling in her bag for the key — she's forgotten it, as usual — and rattling the letter-box. "It's not what I mean, because — Thank you, Mary"—she went into the hall. "Is nurse back?"

5     "Yes, M'm."

"And has the fruit come?"

"Yes, M'm. Everything's come."

"Bring the fruit up to the dining-room, will you? I'll arrange it before I go upstairs."

It was dusky in the dining-room and quite chilly. But all the same Bertha threw off her coat; she could not bear the tight clasp of it another moment, and the cold air fell on her arms.

10     But in her bosom there was still that bright glowing place — that shower of little sparks coming from it. It was almost unbearable. She hardly dared to breathe for fear of fanning it higher, and yet she breathed deeply, deeply. She hardly dared to look into the cold mirror — but she did look, and it gave her back a woman, radiant, with smiling, trembling lips, with big, dark eyes and an

air of listening, waiting for something...divine to happen...that she knew must happen...infallibly.

Mary brought in the fruit on a tray and with it a glass bowl, and a blue dish, very lovely, with a strange sheen on it as though it had been dipped in milk.

"Shall I turn on the light, M'm?"

"No, thank you. I can see quite well."

There were tangerines and apples stained with strawberry pink. Some yellow pears, smooth as silk, some white grapes covered with a silver bloom and a big cluster of purple ones. These last she had bought to tone in with the new dining-room carpet. Yes, that did sound rather far-fetched and absurd, but it was really why she had bought them. She had thought in the shop: "I must have some purple ones to bring the carpet up to the table." And it had seemed quite sense at the time.

15 When she had finished with them and had made two pyramids of these bright round shapes, she stood away from the table to get the effect — and it really was most curious. For the dark table seemed to melt into the dusky light and the glass dish and the blue bowl to float in the air. This, of course in her present mood, was so incredibly beautiful.... She began to laugh.

"No, no. I'm getting hysterical." And she seized her bag and coat and ran upstairs to the nursery.

Nurse sat at a low table giving Little B her supper after her bath. The baby had on a white flannel gown and a blue woollen jacket, and her dark, fine hair was brushed up into a funny little peak. She looked up when she saw her mother and began to jump.

"Now, my lovey, eat it up like a good girl," said Nurse, setting her lips in a way that Bertha knew, and that meant she had come into the nursery at another wrong moment.

"Has she been good, Nanny?"

20 "She's been a little sweet all the afternoon," whispered Nanny. "We went to the park and I sat down on a chair and took her out of the pram and a big dog came along and put his head on my knee and she clutched its ear, tugged it. Oh, you should have seen her."

Bertha wanted to ask if it wasn't rather dangerous to let her clutch at a strange dog's ear. But she did not dare to. She stood watching them, her hands by her side, like the poor little girl in front of the rich little girl with the doll.

The baby looked up at her again, stared, and then smiled so charmingly that Bertha couldn't help crying:

"Oh, Nanny, do let me finish giving her her supper while you put the bath things away."

"Well, M'm, she oughtn't to be changed hands while she's eating," said Nanny, still whispering. "It unsettles her; it's very likely to upset her."

25 How absurd it was. Why have a baby if it has to be kept — not in a case like a rare, rare fiddle — but in another woman's arms?

"Oh, I must!" said she.

Very offended, Nanny handed her over.

"Now, don't excite her after her supper. You know you do, M'm. And I have such a time with her after!"

Thank heaven! Nanny went out of the room with the bath towels.

30 "Now I've got you to myself, my little precious," said Bertha, as the baby leaned against her.

She ate delightfully, holding up her lips for the spoon and then waving her hands. Sometimes she wouldn't let the spoon go; and sometimes, just as Bertha had filled it, she waved it away to the four winds.

When the soup was finished Bertha turned round to the fire.

"You're nice — you're very nice!" said she, kissing her warm baby. "I'm fond of you. I like you."

And, indeed, she loved Little B so much — her neck as she bent forward, her exquisite toes as they shone transparent in the firelight — that all her feeling of bliss came back again, and again she didn't know how to express it — what to do with it.

35 "You're wanted on the telephone," said Nanny, coming back in triumph and seizing *her* Little B.

Down she flew. It was Harry.

"Oh, is that you, Ber? Look here. I'll be late. I'll take a taxi and come along as quickly as I can, but get dinner put back ten minutes — will you? All right?"

"Yes, perfectly. Oh, Harry!"

"Yes?"

40 What had she to say? She'd nothing to say. She only wanted to get in touch with him for a moment. She couldn't absurdly cry: "Hasn't it been a divine day!"

"What is it?" rapped out the little voice.

"Nothing. *Entendu*,"[1] said Bertha, and hung up the receiver, thinking how more than idiotic civilization was.

They had people coming to dinner. The Norman Knights — a very sound couple — he was about to start a theatre, and she was awfully keen on interior decoration, a young man, Eddie Warren, who had just published a little book of poems and whom everybody was asking to dine, and a "find" of Bertha's called Pearl Fulton. What Miss Fulton did, Bertha didn't know. They had met at the club and Bertha had fallen in love with her, as she always did fall in love with beautiful women who had something strange about them.

The provoking thing was that, though they had been about together and met a number of times and really talked, Bertha couldn't yet make her out. Up to a certain point Miss Fulton was rarely, wonderfully frank, but the certain point was there, and beyond that she would not go.

45 Was there anything beyond it? Harry said "No." Voted her dullish, and "cold like all blond women, with a touch, perhaps, of anaemia of the brain." But Bertha wouldn't agree with him; not yet, at any rate.

"No, the way she has of sitting with her head a little on one side, and smiling, has something behind it, Harry, and I must find out what that something is."

1 understood, agreed.

"Most likely it's a good stomach," answered Harry.

He made a point of catching Bertha's heels with replies of that kind... "liver frozen, my dear girl," or "pure flatulence," or "kidney disease,"... and so on. For some strange reason Bertha liked this, and almost admired it in him very much.

She went into the drawing-room and lighted the fire; then, picking up the cushions, one by one, that Mary had disposed so carefully, she threw them back on to the chairs and the couches. That made all the difference; the room came alive at once. As she was about to throw the last one she surprised herself by suddenly hugging it to her, passionately, passionately. But it did not put out the fire in her bosom. Oh, on the contrary!

The windows of the drawing-room opened on to a balcony overlooking the garden. At the far end, against the wall, there was a tall, slender pear tree in fullest, richest bloom; it stood perfect, as though becalmed against the jade-green sky. Bertha couldn't help feeling, even from this distance, that it had not a single bud or a faded petal. Down below, in the garden beds, the red and yellow tulips, heavy with flowers, seemed to lean upon the dusk. A grey cat, dragging its belly, crept across the lawn, and a black one, its shadow, trailed after. The sight of them, so intent and so quick, gave Bertha a curious shiver.

"What creepy things cats are!" she stammered, and she turned away from the window and began walking up and down....

How strong the jonquils smelled in the warm room. Too strong? Oh, no. And yet, as though overcome, she flung down on a couch and pressed her hands to her eyes.

"I'm too happy — too happy!" she murmured.

And she seemed to see on her eyelids the lovely pear tree with its wide open blossoms as a symbol of her own life.

Really — really — she had everything. She was young. Harry and she were as much in love as ever, and they got on together splendidly and were really good pals. She had an adorable baby. They didn't have to worry about money. They had this absolutely satisfactory house and garden. And friends — modern, thrilling friends, writers and painters and poets or people keen on social questions — just the kind of friends they wanted. And then there were books, and there was music, and she had found a wonderful little dressmaker, and they were going abroad in the summer, and their new cook made the most superb omelettes....

"I'm absurd! Absurd!" She sat up; but she felt quite dizzy, quite drunk. It must have been the spring.

Yes, it was the spring. Now she was so tired she could not drag herself upstairs to dress.

A white dress, a string of jade beads, green shoes and stockings. It wasn't intentional. She had thought of this scheme hours before she stood at the drawing-room window.

Her petals rustled softly into the hall, and she kissed Mrs. Norman Knight, who was taking off the most amusing orange coat with a procession of black monkeys round the hem and up the fronts.

"... Why! Why! Why is the middle-class so stodgy — so utterly without a sense of humour! My dear, it's only by a fluke that I am here at all — Norman being the protective fluke. For my darling monkeys so upset the train that it rose to a man and simply ate me with its eyes. Didn't laugh — wasn't amused — that I should have loved. No, just stared — and bored me through and through."

"But the cream of it was," said Norman, pressing a large tortoiseshell-rimmed monocle into his eye, "you don't mind me telling this, Face, do you?" (In their home and among their friends they called each other Face and Mug.) "The cream of it was when she, being full fed, turned to the woman beside her and said: 'Haven't you ever seen a monkey before?'"

"Oh, yes!" Mrs. Norman Knight joined in the laughter. "Wasn't that too absolutely creamy?"

And a funnier thing still was that now her coat was off she did look like a very intelligent monkey — who had even made that yellow silk dress out of scraped banana skins. And her amber ear-rings; they were like little dangling nuts.

"This is a sad, sad fall!" said Mug, pausing in front of Little B's perambulator. "When the perambulator comes into the hall —" and he waved the rest of the quotation away.

65  The bell rang. It was lean, pale Eddie Warren (as usual) in a state of acute distress.

"It *is* the right house, *isn't* it?" he pleaded.

"Oh, I think so — I hope so," said Bertha brightly.

"I have had such a *dreadful* experience with a taxi-man; he was *most* sinister. I couldn't get him to *stop*. The *more* I knocked and called the *faster* he went. And *in* the moonlight this *bizarre* figure with the *flattened* head *crouching* over the *lit-tle* wheel...."

He shuddered, taking off an immense white silk scarf. Bertha noticed that his socks were white, too — most charming.

70  "But how dreadful!" she cried.

"Yes, it really was," said Eddie, following her into the drawing-room. "I saw myself *driving* through Eternity in a *timeless* taxi."

He knew the Norman Knights. In fact, he was going to write a play for N.K. when the theatre scheme came off.

"Well, Warren, how's the play?" said Norman Knight, dropping his monocle and giving his eye a moment in which to rise to the surface before it was screwed down again.

And Mrs. Norman Knight: "Oh, Mr. Warren, what happy socks?"

75  "I *am* so glad you like them," said he, staring at his feet. "They seem to have got so *much* whiter since the moon rose." And he turned his lean sorrowful young face to Bertha. "There *is* a moon, you know."

She wanted to cry: "I am sure there is — often — often!"

He really was a most attractive person. But so was Face, crouched before the fire in her banana skins, and so was Mug, smoking a cigarette and saying as he flicked the ash: "Why doth the bridegroom tarry?"

"There he is, now."

Bang went the front door open and shut. Harry shouted: "Hullo, you people. Down in five minutes." And they heard him swarm up the stairs. Bertha couldn't help smiling; she knew how he loved doing things at high pressure. What, after all, did an extra five minutes matter? But he would pretend to himself that they mattered beyond measure. And then he would make a great point of coming into the drawing-room, extravagantly cool and collected.

80      Harry had such a zest for life. Oh, how she appreciated it in him. And his passion for fighting — for seeking in everything that came up against him another test of his power and of his courage — that, too, she understood. Even when it made him just occasionally, to other people, who didn't know him well, a little ridiculous perhaps. . . . For there were moments when he rushed into battle where no battle was. . . . She talked and laughed and positively forgot until he had come in (just as she had imagined) that Pearl Fulton had not turned up.

"I wonder if Miss Fulton has forgotten?"

"I expect so," said Harry. "Is she on the 'phone?"

"Ah! There's a taxi, now." And Bertha smiled with that little air of proprietorship that she always assumed while her women finds were new and mysterious. "She lives in taxis."

"She'll run to fat if she does," said Harry coolly, ringing the bell for dinner. "Frightful danger for blond women."

85      "Harry — don't," warned Bertha, laughing up at him.

Came another tiny moment, while they waited, laughing and talking, just a trifle too much at their ease, a trifle too unaware. And then Miss Fulton, all in silver, with a silver fillet binding her pale blond hair, came in smiling, her head a little on one side.

"Am I late?"

"No, not at all," said Bertha. "Come along." And she took her arm and they moved into the dining-room.

What was there in the touch of that cool arm that could fan — fan — start blazing — blazing — the fire of bliss that Bertha did not know what to do with?

90      Miss Fulton did not look at her; but then she seldom did look at people directly. Her heavy eyelids lay upon her eyes and the strange half smile came and went upon her lips as though she lived by listening rather than seeing. But Bertha knew, suddenly, as if the longest, most intimate look had passed between them — as if they had said to each other: "You, too?" — that Pearl Fulton, stirring the beautiful red soup in the grey plate, was feeling just what she was feeling.

And the others? Face and Mug, Eddie and Harry, their spoons rising and falling — dabbing their lips with their napkins, crumbling bread, fiddling with the forks and glasses and talking.

"I met her at the Alpha shore — the weirdest little person. She'd not only cut off her hair, but she seemed to have taken a dreadfully good snip off her legs and arms and her neck and her poor little nose as well."

"Isn't she very *liée* [2] with Michael Oat?"

"The man who wrote *Love in False Teeth*?"

95      "He wants to write a play for me. One act. One man. Decides to commit suicide. Gives all the reasons why he should and why he shouldn't. And just

2 attached (involved).

as he has made up his mind either to do it or not to do it — curtain. Not half a bad idea."

"What's he going to call it —'Stomach Trouble'?"

"I *think* I've come across the *same* idea in a lit-tle French review, *quite* unknown in England."

No, they didn't share it. They were dears — dears — and she loved having them there, at her table, and giving them delicious food and wine. In fact, she longed to tell them how delightful they were, and what a decorative group they made, how they seemed to set one another off and how they reminded her of a play by Tchekof![3]

Harry was enjoying his dinner. It was part of his — well, not his nature, exactly, and certainly not his pose — his — something or other — to talk about food and to glory in his "shameless passion for the white flesh of the lobster" and "the green of pistachio ices — green and cold like the eyelids of Egyptian dancers."

100     When he looked up at her and said: "Bertha, this is a very admirable *soufflée!*" she almost could have wept with child-like pleasure.

Oh, why did she feel so tender towards the whole world tonight? Everything was good — was right. All that happened seemed to fill again her brimming cup of bliss.

And still, in the back of her mind, there was the pear tree. It would be silver now, in the light of poor dear Eddie's moon, silver as Miss Fulton, who sat there turning a tangerine in her slender fingers that were so pale a light seemed to come from them.

What she simply couldn't make out — what was miraculous — was how she should have guessed Miss Fulton's mood so exactly and so instantly. For she never doubted for a moment that she was right, and yet what had she to go on? Less than nothing.

"I believe this does happen very, very rarely between women. Never between men," thought Bertha. "But while I am making the coffee in the drawing-room perhaps she will 'give a sign.'"

105     What she meant by that she did not know, and what would happen after that she could not imagine.

While she thought like this she saw herself talking and laughing. She had to talk because of her desire to laugh.

"I must laugh or die."

But when she noticed Face's funny little habit of tucking something down the front of her bodice — as if she kept a tiny, secret hoard of nuts there, too — Bertha had to dig her nails into her hands — so as not to laugh too much.

It was over at last. And: "Come and see my new coffee machine," said Bertha.

110     "We only have a new coffee machine once a fortnight," said Harry. Face took her arm this time; Miss Fulton bent her head and followed after.

The fire had died down in the drawing-room to a red, flickering "nest of baby phoenixes," said Face.

3 Anton Chekhov, nineteenth-century Russian writer of ironic dramas and short stories.

"Don't turn up the light for a moment. It is so lovely." And down she crouched by the fire again. She was always cold ... "without her little red flannel jacket, of course," thought Bertha.

At that moment Miss Fulton "gave the sign."

"Have you a garden?" said the cool, sleepy voice.

115     This was so exquisite on her part that all Bertha could do was to obey. She crossed the room, pulled the curtains apart, and opened those long windows.

"There!" she breathed.

And the two women stood side by side looking at the slender, flowering tree. Although it was so still it seemed, like the flame of a candle, to stretch up, to point, to quiver in the bright air, to grow taller and taller as they gazed — almost to touch the rim of the round, silver moon.

How long did they stand there? Both, as it were, caught in that circle of unearthly light, understanding each other perfectly, creatures of another world, and wondering what they were to do in this one with all this blissful treasure that burned in their bosoms and dropped, in silver flowers, from their hair and hands?

For ever — for a moment? And did Miss Fulton murmur: "Yes. Just *that*." Or did Bertha dream it?

120     Then the light was snapped on and Face made the coffee and Harry said: "My dear Mrs. Knight, don't ask me about my baby. I never see her. I shan't feel the slightest interest in her until she has a lover," and Mug took his eye out of the conservatory for a moment and then put it under glass again and Eddie Warren drank his coffee and set down the cup with a face of anguish as though he had drunk and seen the spider.

"What I want to do is to give the young men a show. I believe London is simply teeming with first-chop, unwritten plays. What I want to say to 'em is: 'Here's the theatre. Fire ahead.'"

"You know, my dear, I am going to decorate a room for the Jacob Nathans. Oh, I am so tempted to do a fried-fish scheme, with the backs of the chairs shaped like frying pans and lovely chip potatoes embroidered all over the curtains."

"The trouble with our young writing men is that they are still too romantic. You can't put out to sea without being seasick and wanting a basin. Well, why won't they have the courage of those basins?"

"A *dreadful* poem about a *girl* who was *violated* by a beggar *without* a nose in a lit-tle wood. ... "

125     Miss Fulton sank into the lowest, deepest chair and Harry handed round the cigarettes.

From the way he stood in front of her shaking the silver box and saying abruptly: "Egyptian? Turkish? Virginian? They're all mixed up," Bertha realized that she not only bored him; he really disliked her. And she decided from the way Miss Fulton said: "No, thank you, I won't smoke," that she felt it, too, and was hurt.

"Oh, Harry, don't dislike her. You are quite wrong about her. She's wonderful, wonderful. And, besides, how can you feel so differently about some one who means so much to me. I shall try to tell you when we are in bed tonight what has been happening. What she and I have shared."

At those last words something strange and almost terrifying darted into Bertha's mind. And this something blind and smiling whispered to her: "Soon these people will go. The house will be quiet — quiet. The lights will be out. And you and he will be alone together in the dark room — the warm bed. . . ."

She jumped up from her chair and ran over to the piano.

130 "What a pity some one does not play!" she cried. "What a pity somebody does not play."

For the first time in her life Bertha Young desired her husband.

Oh, she'd loved him — she'd been in love with him, of course, in every other way, but just not in that way. And, equally, of course, she'd understood that he was different. They'd discussed it so often. It had worried her dreadfully at first to find that she was so cold, but after a time it had not seemed to matter. They were so frank with each other — such good pals. That was the best of being modern.

But now — ardently! ardently! The word ached in her ardent body! Was this what that feeling of bliss had been leading up to? But then — then —

"My dear," said Mrs. Norman Knight, "you know our shame. We are the victims of time and train. We live in Hampstead. It's been so nice."

135 "I'll come with you into the hall," said Bertha. "I love having you. But you must not miss the last train. That's so awful, isn't it?"

"Have a whisky, Knight, before you go?" called Harry.

"No, thanks, old chap."

Bertha squeezed his hand for that as she shook it.

"Good night, good-bye," she cried from the top step, feeling that this self of hers was taking leave of them for ever.

140 When she got back into the drawing-room the others were on the move.

". . . Then you can come part of the way in my taxi."

"I shall be so thankful not to have to face another drive alone after my dreadful experience."

"You can get a taxi at the rank just at the end of the street. You won't have to walk more than a few yards."

"That's comfort. I'll go and put on my coat."

145 Miss Fulton moved towards the hall and Bertha was following when Harry almost pushed past.

"Let me help you."

Bertha knew that he was repenting his rudeness — she let him go. What a boy he was in some ways — so impulsive — so — simple.

And Eddie and she were left by the fire.

"I wonder if you have seen Bilks' new poem called Table d'Hôte," said Eddie softly. "It's so wonderful. In the last Anthology. Have you got a copy? I'd so like to show it to you. It begins with an incredibly beautiful line: 'Why Must it Always be Tomato Soup?'"

150 "Yes," said Bertha. And she moved noiselessly to a table opposite the drawing-room door and Eddie glided noiselessly after her. She picked up the little book and gave it to him; they had not made a sound.

While he looked it up she turned her head towards the hall. And she saw . . . Harry with Miss Fulton's coat in his arms and Miss Fulton with her back turned to him and her head bent. He tossed the coat away, put his hands on her shoulders and turned her violently to him. His lips said: "I adore you," and Miss Fulton laid her moonbeam fingers on his cheeks and smiled her sleepy smile. Harry's nostrils quivered; his lips curled back in a hideous grin while he whispered: "Tomorrow," and with her eyelids Miss Fulton said "Yes."

"Here it is," said Eddie. "'Why Must it Always be Tomato Soup?' It's so *deeply* true, don't you feel? Tomato soup is so *dreadfully* eternal."

"If you prefer," said Harry's voice, very loud, from the hall, "I can 'phone you a cab to come to the door."

"Oh, no. It's not necessary," said Miss Fulton, and she came up to Bertha and gave her the slender fingers to hold.

155 "Good-bye. Thank you so much."

"Good-bye," said Bertha.

Miss Fulton held her hand a moment longer.

"Your lovely pear tree!" she murmured.

And then she was gone, with Eddie following, like the black cat following the grey cat.

160 "I'll shut up shop," said Harry, extravagantly cool and collected.

"Your lovely pear tree — pear tree — pear tree!"

Bertha simply ran over to the long windows.

"Oh, what is going to happen now?" she cried.

But the pear tree was as lovely as ever and as full of flower and as still.

(1918)

# Katherine Anne Porter (1890–1980)

Born in Indian Creek, Texas, Katherine Anne Porter lived and worked in Fort Worth, Chicago, Denver, New York, Mexico, and Germany, all places that she used as settings for her short stories, which she referred to as outgrowths of her "constant exercise of memory." Her works, many of which are set in the rural South, are noted for their compression, intensity of emotion, and precise use of small details to reveal the complexities of the characters and their strained interrelationships. "Rope," which relates in part to the breakup of her second marriage, is set in an unspecified country location, whose isolation seems to intensify the animosity the husband and wife feel toward each other. Although little background information is given about the couple, the complex and shifting reactions of each to the length of rope bought by the husband reveal their characters and the nature of their mutual hostility.

# ROPE

On the third day after they moved to the country he came walking back from the village carrying a basket of groceries and a twenty-four-yard coil of rope. She came out to meet him, wiping her hands on her green smock. Her hair was tumbled, her nose was scarlet with sunburn; he told her that already she looked like a born country woman. His gray flannel shirt stuck to him, his heavy shoes were dusty. She assured him he looked like a rural character in a play.

Had he brought the coffee? She had been waiting all day long for coffee. They had forgot it when they ordered at the store the first day.

Gosh, no, he hadn't. Lord, now he'd have to go back. Yes, he would if it killed him. He thought, though, he had everything else. She reminded him it was only because he didn't drink coffee himself. If he did he would remember it quick enough. Suppose they ran out of cigarettes? Then she saw the rope. What was that for? Well, he thought it might do to hang clothes on, or something. Naturally she asked him if he thought they were going to run a laundry? They already had a fifty-foot line hanging right before his eyes? Why, hadn't he noticed it, really? It was a blot on the landscape to her.

He thought there were a lot of things a rope might come in handy for. She wanted to know what, for instance. He thought a few seconds, but nothing occurred. They could wait and see, couldn't they? You need all sorts of strange odds and ends around a place in the country. She said, yes, that was so; but she thought just at that time when every penny counted, it seemed funny to buy more rope. That was all. She hadn't meant anything else. She hadn't just seen, not at first, why he felt it was necessary.

Well, thunder, he had bought it because he wanted to, and that was all there was to it. She thought that was reason enough, and couldn't understand why he hadn't said so, at first. Undoubtedly it would be useful, twenty-four yards of rope, there were hundreds of things, she couldn't think of any at the moment, but it would come in. Of course. As he had said, things always did in the country.

But she was a little disappointed about the coffee, and oh, look, look, look at the eggs! Oh, my, they're all running! What had he put on top of them? Hadn't he known eggs mustn't be squeezed? Squeezed, who had squeezed them, he wanted to know. What a silly thing to say. He had simply brought them along in the basket with the other things. If they got broke it was the grocer's fault. He should know better than to put heavy things on top of eggs.

She believed it was the rope. That was the heaviest thing in the pack, she saw him plainly when he came in from the road, the rope was a big package on top of everything. He desired the whole wide world to witness that this was not a fact. He had carried the rope in one hand and the basket in the other, and what was the use of her having eyes if that was the best they could do for her?

Well, anyhow, she could see one thing plain: no eggs for breakfast. They'd have to scramble them now, for supper. It was too damned bad. She had planned to have steak for supper. No ice, meat wouldn't keep. He wanted to know why she couldn't finish breaking the eggs in a bowl and set them in a cool place.

Cool place! if he could find one for her, she'd be glad to set them there. Well, then, it seemed to him they might very well cook the meat at the same time they cooked the eggs and then warm up the meat for tomorrow. The idea simply choked her. Warmed-over meat, when they might as well have had it fresh. Second best and scraps and makeshifts, even to the meat! He rubbed her shoulder a little. It doesn't really matter so much, does it, darling? Sometimes when they were playful, he would rub her shoulder and she would arch and purr. This time she hissed and almost clawed. He was getting ready to say that they could surely manage somehow when she turned on him and said, if he told her they could manage somehow she would certainly slap his face.

10     He swallowed the words red hot, his face burned. He picked up the rope and started to put it on the top shelf. She would not have it on the top shelf, the jars and tins belonged there; positively she would not have the top shelf cluttered up with a lot of rope. She had borne all the clutter she meant to bear in the flat in town, there was space here at least and she meant to keep things in order.

Well, in that case, he wanted to know what the hammer and nails were doing up there? And why had she put them there when she knew very well he needed that hammer and those nails upstairs to fix the window sashes? She simply slowed down everything and made double work on the place with her insane habit of changing things around and hiding them.

She was sure she begged his pardon, and if she had had any reason to believe he was going to fix the sashes this summer she would have left the hammer and nails right where he put them; in the middle of the bedroom floor where they could step on them in the dark. And now if he didn't clear the whole mess out of there she would throw them down the well.

Oh, all right, all right — could he put them in the closet? Naturally not, there were brooms and mops and dustpans in the closet, and why couldn't he find a place for his rope outside her kitchen? Had he stopped to consider there were seven God-forsaken rooms in the house, and only one kitchen?

He wanted to know what of it? And did she realize she was making a complete fool of herself? And what did she take him for, a three-year-old idiot? The whole trouble with her was she needed something weaker than she was to heckle and tyrannize over. He wished to God now they had a couple of children she could take it out on. Maybe he'd get some rest.

15      Her face changed at this, she reminded him he had forgot the coffee and had bought a worthless piece of rope. And when she thought of all the things they actually needed to make the place even decently fit to live in, well, she could cry, that was all. She looked so forlorn, so lost and despairing he couldn't believe it was only a piece of rope that was causing all the racket. What *was* the matter, for God's sake?

Oh, would he please hush and go away, and *stay* away, if he could, for five minutes? By all means, yes, he would. He'd stay away indefinitely if she wished. Lord, yes, there was nothing he'd like better than to clear out and never come back. She couldn't for the life of her see what was holding him, then. It was a swell time. Here she was, stuck, miles from a railroad, with a half-empty house on her hands, and not a penny in her pocket, and everything on earth to do; it seemed the God-sent moment for him to get out from under. She was surprised he hadn't stayed in town as it was until she had come out and done the work and got things straightened out. It was his usual trick.

It appeared to him that this was going a little far. Just a touch out of bounds, if she didn't mind his saying so. Why the hell had he stayed in town the summer before? To do a half-dozen extra jobs to get the money he had sent her. That was it. She knew perfectly well they couldn't have done it otherwise. She had agreed with him at the time. And that was the only time so help him he had ever left her to do anything by herself.

Oh, he could tell that to his great-grandmother. She had her notion of what had kept him in town. Considerably more than a notion, if he wanted to know. So, she was going to bring all that up again, was she? Well, she could just think what she pleased. He was tired of explaining. It may have looked funny but he had simply got hooked in, and what could he do? It was impossible to believe that she was going to take it seriously. Yes, yes, she knew how it was with a man: if he was left by himself a minute, some woman was certain to kidnap him. And naturally he couldn't hurt her feelings by refusing!

Well, what was she raving about? Did she forget she had told him those two weeks alone in the country were the happiest she had known for four years? And how long had they been married when she said that? All right, shut up! If she thought that hadn't stuck in his craw.

20      She hadn't meant she was happy because she was away from him. She meant she was happy getting the devilish house nice and ready for him. That was what she had meant, and now look! Bringing up something she had said a year ago simply to justify himself for forgetting her coffee and breaking the eggs and buying a wretched piece of rope they couldn't afford. She really thought it was time to drop the subject, and now she wanted only two things in the world. She wanted him to get that rope from underfoot, and go back to the village and get her coffee, and if he could remember it, he might bring a metal mitt for the skillets, and two more curtain rods, and if there were any rubber gloves in the village, her hands were simply raw, and a bottle of milk of magnesia from the drugstore.

He looked out at the dark blue afternoon sweltering on the slopes, and mopped his forehead and sighed heavily and said, if only she could wait a minute for *anything*, he was going back. He had said so, hadn't he, the very instant they found he had overlooked it?

Oh, yes, well . . . run along. She was going to wash windows. The country was so beautiful. She doubted they'd have a moment to enjoy it. He meant to go, but he could not until he had said that if she wasn't such a hopeless melancholiac she might see that this was only for a few days. Couldn't she remember anything pleasant about the other summers? Hadn't they ever had any fun? She hadn't time to talk about it, and now would he please not leave that rope lying around for her to trip on? He picked it up, somehow it had toppled off the table, and walked out with it under his arm.

Was he going this minute? He certainly was. She thought so. Sometimes it seemed to her he had second sight about the precisely perfect moment to leave her ditched. She had meant to put the mattresses out to sun, if they put them out this minute they would get at least three hours, he must have heard her say that morning she meant to put them out. So of course he would walk off and leave her to it. She supposed he thought the exercise would do her good.

Well, he was merely going to get her coffee. A four-mile walk for two pounds of coffee was ridiculous, but he was perfectly willing to do it. The habit was making a wreck of her, but if she wanted to wreck herself there was nothing he could do about it. If he thought it was coffee that was making a wreck of her, she congratulated him: he must have a damned easy conscience.

25    Conscience or no conscience, he didn't see why the mattresses couldn't very well wait until tomorrow. And anyhow, for God's sake, were they living *in* the house, or were they going to let the house ride them to death? She paled at this, her face grew livid about the mouth, she looked quite dangerous, and reminded him that housekeeping was no more her work than it was his: she had other work to do as well, and when did he think she was going to find time to do it at this rate?

Was she going to start on that again? She knew as well as he did that his work brought in the regular money, hers was only occasional, if they depended on what *she* made — and she might as well get straight on this question once for all!

That was positively not the point. The question was, when both of them were working on their own time, was there going to be a division of the housework, or wasn't there? She merely wanted to know, she had to make her plans. Why, he thought that was all arranged. It was understood that he was to help. Hadn't he always, in summers?

Hadn't he, though? Oh, just hadn't he? And when, and where, and doing what? Lord, what an uproarious joke!

It was such a very uproarious joke that her face turned slightly purple, and she screamed with laughter. She laughed so hard she had to sit down, and finally a rush of tears spurted from her eyes and poured down into the lifted corners of her mouth. He dashed towards her and dragged her up to her feet and tried to pour water on her head. The dipper hung by a string on a nail and he broke it loose. Then he tried to pump water with one hand while she struggled in the other. So he gave it up and shook her instead.

30    She wrenched away, crying out for him to take his rope and go to hell, she had simply given him up: and ran. He heard her high-heeled bedroom slippers clattering and stumbling on the stairs.

He went out around the house and into the lane; he suddenly realized he had a blister on his heel and his shirt felt as if it were on fire. Things broke so suddenly you didn't know where you were. She could work herself into a fury about simply nothing. She was terrible, damn it: not an ounce of reason. You might as well talk to a sieve as that woman when she got going. Damned if he'd spend his life humoring her! Well, what to do now? He would take back the rope and exchange it for something else. Things accumulated, things were mountainous, you couldn't move them or sort them out or get rid of them. They just lay and rotted around. He'd take it back. Hell, why should he? He wanted it. What was it anyhow? A piece of rope. Imagine anybody caring more about a piece of rope than about a man's feelings. What earthly right had she to say a word about it? He remembered all the useless, meaningless things she bought for herself: Why? because I wanted it, that's why! He stopped and selected a large stone by the road. He would put the rope behind it. He would put it in the tool-box when he got back. He'd heard enough about it to last him a life-time.

When he came back she was leaning against the post box beside the road waiting. It was pretty late, the smell of broiled steak floated nose high in the cooling air. Her face was young and smooth and fresh-looking. Her unmanageable funny black hair was all on end. She waved to him from a distance, and he speeded up. She called out that supper was ready and waiting, was he starved?

You bet he was starved. Here was the coffee. He waved it at her. She looked at his other hand. What was that he had there?

Well, it was the rope again. He stopped short. He had meant to exchange it but forgot. She wanted to know why he should exchange it, if it was something he really wanted. Wasn't the air sweet now, and wasn't it fine to be here?

35    She walked beside him with one hand hooked into his leather belt. She pulled and jostled him a little as he walked, and leaned against him. He put his arm clear around her and patted her stomach. They exchanged wary smiles. Coffee, coffee for the Ootsum-Wootsums! He felt as if he were bringing her a beautiful present.

He was a love, she firmly believed, and if she had had her coffee in the morning, she wouldn't have behaved so funny... There was a whippoorwill still coming back, imagine, clear out of season, sitting in the crab-apple tree calling all by himself. Maybe his girl stood him up. Maybe she did. She hoped to hear him once more, she loved whippoorwills... He knew how she was, didn't he?

Sure, he knew how she was.

(1928)

# William Faulkner   (1897–1962)

In his 1950 acceptance speech for the Nobel Prize for literature, William Faulkner defined his subject matter as "the human heart in conflict with itself, which alone can make good writing because only that is worth writing about." Universal in their themes, most of his novels and short stories are set in Yoknapatawpha County, a fictionalized version of West Lafayette County, Mississippi, where he was born and lived most of his life. A major focus in many of his works is the central characters' awareness of the degeneration of their families from a once glorious past and their sense of imprisonment in memories of that past. In such novels as *Absalom, Absalom!* and *The Reivers*, Faulkner is as interested in attempts by the characters to understand the past as he is in that past itself. "A Rose for Emily," which begins after the death of the title character, presents an unnamed townsman's account and interpretation of details of Emily Grierson's life, many of which occurred before his birth, and the discovery he and the villagers make about her when they break into one of the rooms of her home after her funeral. With new knowledge, the narrator finally understands the recluse's character and her actions.

# A ROSE FOR EMILY

I

When Miss Emily Grierson died, our whole town went to her funeral: the men through a sort of respectful affection for a fallen monument, the women mostly out of curiosity to see the inside of her house, which no one save an old man-servant — a combined gardener and cook — had seen in at least ten years.

It was a big, squarish frame house that had once been white, decorated with cupolas and spires and scrolled balconies in the heavily lightsome style of the seventies, set on what had once been our most select street. But garages and cotton gins had encroached and obliterated even the august names of that neighborhood; only Miss Emily's house was left, lifting its stubborn and coquettish decay above the cotton wagons and the gasoline pumps — an eyesore among eyesores. And now Miss Emily had gone to join the representatives of those august names where they lay in the cedar-bemused cemetery among the ranked and anonymous graves of Union and Confederate soldiers[1] who fell at the battle of Jefferson.[2]

Alive, Miss Emily had been a tradition, a duty, and a care; a sort of hereditary obligation upon the town, dating from that day in 1894 when Colonel Sartoris, the mayor — he who fathered the edict that no Negro woman should appear on the streets without an apron — remitted her taxes, the dispensation dating from the death of her father on into perpetuity. Not that Miss Emily

---

1 soldiers who fought for the North and South, respectively, during the American Civil War.
2 Civil War battle fought in Mississippi; Jefferson is Faulkner's fictional name for Oxford, Mississippi.

would have accepted charity. Colonel Sartoris invented an involved tale to the effect that Miss Emily's father had loaned money to the town, which the town, as a matter of business, preferred this way of repaying. Only a man of Colonel Sartoris' generation and thought could have invented it, and only a woman could have believed it.

When the next generation, with its more modern ideas, became mayors and aldermen, this arrangement created some little dissatisfaction. On the first of the year they mailed her a tax notice. February came, and there was no reply. They wrote her a formal letter, asking her to call at the sheriff's office at her convenience. A week later the mayor wrote her himself, offering to call or to send his car for her, and received in reply a note on paper of an archaic shape, in a thin, flowing calligraphy in faded ink, to the effect that she no longer went out at all. The tax notice was also enclosed, without comment.

5  They called a special meeting of the Board of Aldermen. A deputation waited upon her, knocked at the door through which no visitor had passed since she ceased giving china-painting lessons eight or ten years earlier. They were admitted by the old Negro into a dim hall from which a stairway mounted into still more shadow. It smelled of dust and disuse — a close, dank smell. The Negro led them into the parlor. It was furnished in heavy, leather-covered furniture. When the Negro opened the blinds of one window, they could see that the leather was cracked; and when they sat down, a faint dust rose sluggishly about their thighs, spinning with slow motes in the single sun-ray. On a tarnished gilt easel before the fireplace stood a crayon portrait of Miss Emily's father.

They rose when she entered — a small, fat woman in black, with a thin gold chain descending to her waist and vanishing into her belt, leaning on an ebony cane with a tarnished gold head. Her skeleton was small and spare; perhaps that was why what would have been merely plumpness in another was obesity in her. She looked bloated, like a body long submerged in motionless water, and of that pallid hue. Her eyes, lost in the fatty ridges of her face, looked like two small pieces of coal pressed into a lump of dough as they moved from one face to another while the visitors stated their errand.

She did not ask them to sit. She just stood in the door and listened quietly until the spokesman came to a stumbling halt. Then they could hear the invisible watch ticking at the end of the gold chain.

Her voice was dry and cold. "I have no taxes in Jefferson. Colonel Sartoris explained it to me. Perhaps one of you can gain access to the city records and satisfy yourselves."

"But we have. We are the city authorities, Miss Emily. Didn't you get a notice from the sheriff, signed by him?"

10  "I received a paper, yes," Miss Emily said. "Perhaps he considers himself the sheriff... I have no taxes in Jefferson."

"But there is nothing on the books to show that, you see. We must go by the —"

"See Colonel Sartoris. I have no taxes in Jefferson."

"But, Miss Emily —"

"See Colonel Sartoris." (Colonel Sartoris had been dead almost ten years.) "I have no taxes in Jefferson. Tobe!" The Negro appeared. "Show these gentlemen out."

## II

So she vanquished them, horse and foot, just as she had vanquished their fathers thirty years before about the smell. That was two years after her father's death and a short time after her sweetheart — the one we believed would marry her — had deserted her. After her father's death she went out very little; after her sweetheart went away, people hardly saw her at all. A few of the ladies had the temerity to call, but were not received, and the only sign of life about the place was the Negro man — a young man then — going in and out with a market basket.

"Just as if a man — any man — could keep a kitchen properly," the ladies said; so they were not surprised when the smell developed. It was another link between the gross, teeming world and the high and mighty Griersons.

A neighbor, a woman, complained to the mayor, Judge Stevens, eighty years old.

"But what will you have me do about it, madam?" he said.

"Why, send her word to stop it," the woman said. "Isn't there a law?"

"I'm sure that won't be necessary," Judge Stevens said. "It's probably just a snake or a rat that nigger of hers killed in the yard. I'll speak to him about it."

The next day he received two more complaints, one from a man who came in diffident deprecation. "We really must do something about it, Judge. I'd be the last one in the world to bother Miss Emily, but we've got to do something." That night the Board of Aldermen met — three graybeards and one younger man, a member of the rising generation.

"It's simple enough," he said. "Send her word to have her place cleaned up. Give her a certain time to do it in, and if she don't . . ."

"Dammit, sir," Judge Stevens said, "will you accuse a lady to her face of smelling bad?"

So the next night, after midnight, four men crossed Miss Emily's lawn and slunk about the house like burglars, sniffing along the base of the brick-work and at the cellar openings while one of them performed a regular sowing motion with his hand out of a sack slung from his shoulder. They broke open the cellar door and sprinkled lime there, and in all the outbuildings. As they recrossed the lawn, a window that had been dark was lighted and Miss Emily sat in it, the light behind her, and her upright torso motionless as that of an idol. They crept quietly across the lawn and into the shadow of the locusts that lined the street. After a week or two the smell went away.

That was when people had begun to feel really sorry for her. People in our town, remembering how old lady Wyatt, her great-aunt, had gone completely crazy at last, believed that the Griersons held themselves a little too high for what they really were. None of the young men were quite good enough for Miss Emily and such. We had long thought of them as a tableau, Miss Emily a slender figure in white in the background, her father a spraddled silhouette in the foreground, his back to her and clutching a horsewhip, the two of them framed by the back-flung front door. So when she got to be thirty and was still single, we were not pleased exactly, but vindicated; even with insanity in the family she wouldn't have turned down all of her chances if they had really materialized.

When her father died, it got about that the house was all that was left to her; and in a way, people were glad. At last they could pity Miss Emily. Being left alone, and a pauper, she had become humanized. Now she too would know the old thrill and the old despair of a penny more or less.

The day after his death all the ladies prepared to call at the house and offer condolence and aid, as is our custom. Miss Emily met them at the door, dressed as usual and with no trace of grief on her face. She told them that her father was not dead. She did that for three days, with the ministers calling on her, and the doctors, trying to persuade her to let them dispose of the body. Just as they were about to resort to law and force, she broke down, and they buried her father quickly.

We did not say she was crazy then. We believed she had to do that. We remembered all the young men her father had driven away, and we knew that with nothing left, she would have to cling to that which had robbed her, as people will.

## III

She was sick for a long time. When we saw her again, her hair was cut short, making her look like a girl, with a vague resemblance to those angels in colored church windows — sort of tragic and serene.

30
    The town had just let the contracts for paving the sidewalks, and in the summer after her father's death they began the work. The construction company came with niggers and mules and machinery, and a foreman named Homer Barron, a Yankee — a big, dark, ready man, with a big voice and eyes lighter than his face. The little boys would follow in groups to hear him cuss the niggers, and the niggers singing in time to the rise and fall of picks. Pretty soon he knew everybody in town. Whenever you heard a lot of laughing anywhere about the square, Homer Barron would be in the center of the group. Presently we began to see him and Miss Emily on Sunday afternoons driving in the yellow-wheeled buggy and the matched team of bays from the livery stable.

At first we were glad that Miss Emily would have an interest, because the ladies all said, "Of course a Grierson would not think seriously of a Northerner, a day laborer." But there were still others, older people, who said that even grief could not cause a real lady to forget *noblesse oblige*[3] — without calling it *noblesse oblige*. They just said, "Poor Emily. Her kinsfolk should come to her." She had some kin in Alabama; but years ago her father had fallen out with them over the estate of old lady Wyatt, the crazy woman, and there was no communication between the two families. They had not even been represented at the funeral.

And as soon as the old people said, "Poor Emily," the whispering began. "Do you suppose it's really so?" they said to one another. "Of course it is. What else could..." This behind their hands; rustling of craned silk and satin behind jalousies closed upon the sun of Sunday afternoon as the thin, swift clop-clop-clop of the matched team passed: "Poor Emily."

3 the responsibility of privileged, high-born people to be honourable.

She carried her head high enough — even when we believed that she was fallen. It was as if she demanded more than ever the recognition of her dignity as the last Grierson; as if it had wanted that touch of earthiness to reaffirm her imperviousness. Like when she bought the rat poison, the arsenic. That was over a year after they had begun to say "Poor Emily," and while the two female cousins were visiting her.

"I want some poison," she said to the druggist. She was over thirty then, still a slight woman, though thinner than usual, with cold, haughty black eyes in a face the flesh of which was strained across the temples and about the eye-sockets as you imagine a lighthouse-keeper's face ought to look. "I want some poison," she said.

"Yes, Miss Emily. What kind? For rats and such? I'd recom —"

"I want the best you have. I don't care what kind."

The druggist named several. "They'll kill anything up to an elephant. But what you want is —"

"Arsenic," Miss Emily said. "Is that a good one?"

"Is ... arsenic? Yes, ma'am. But what you want —"

"I want arsenic."

The druggist looked down at her. She looked back at him, erect, her face like a strained flag. "Why, of course," the druggist said. "If that's what you want. But the law requires you to tell what you are going to use it for."

Miss Emily just stared at him, her head tilted back in order to look him eye for eye, until he looked away and went and got the arsenic and wrapped it up. The Negro delivery boy brought her the package; the druggist didn't come back. When she opened the package at home there was written on the box, under the skull and bones: "For rats."

## IV

So the next day we all said, "She will kill herself"; and we said it would be the best thing. When she had first begun to be seen with Homer Barron, we had said, "She will marry him." Then we said, "She will persuade him yet," because Homer himself had remarked — he liked men, and it was known that he drank with the younger men in the Elks' Club — that he was not a marrying man. Later we said, "Poor Emily" behind the jalousies as they passed on Sunday afternoon in the glittering buggy, Miss Emily with her head high and Homer Barron with his hat cocked and a cigar in his teeth, reins and whip in a yellow glove.

Then some of the ladies began to say that it was a disgrace to the town and a bad example to the young people. The men did not want to interfere, but at last the ladies forced the Baptist minister — Miss Emily's people were Episcopal[4] — to call upon her. He would never divulge what happened during that interview, but he refused to go back again. The next Sunday they again drove about the streets, and the following day the minister's wife wrote to Miss Emily's relations in Alabama.

So she had blood-kin under her roof again and we sat back to watch developments. At first nothing happened. Then we were sure that they were

4 the Anglican Church in the United States.

to be married. We learned that Miss Emily had been to the jeweler's and ordered a man's toilet set in silver, with the letters H.B. on each piece. Two days later we learned that she had bought a complete outfit of men's clothing, including a nightshirt, and we said, "They are married." We were really glad. We were glad because the two female cousins were even more Grierson than Miss Emily had ever been.

So we were not surprised when Homer Barron — the streets had been finished some time since — was gone. We were a little disappointed that there was not a public blowing-off, but we believed that he had gone on to prepare for Miss Emily's coming, or to give her a chance to get rid of the cousins. (By that time it was a cabal, and we were all Miss Emily's allies to help circumvent the cousins.) Sure enough, after another week they departed. And, as we had expected all along, within three days Homer Barron was back in town. A neighbor saw the Negro man admit him at the kitchen door at dusk one evening.

And that was the last we saw of Homer Barron. And of Miss Emily for some time. The Negro man went in and out with the market basket, but the front door remained closed. Now and then we would see her at a window for a moment, as the men did that night when they sprinkled the lime, but for almost six months she did not appear on the streets. Then we knew that this was to be expected too; as if that quality of her father which had thwarted her woman's life so many times had been too virulent and too furious to die.

When we next saw Miss Emily, she had grown fat and her hair was turning gray. During the next few years it grew grayer and grayer until it attained an even pepper-and-salt iron-gray, when it ceased turning. Up to the day of her death at seventy-four it was still that vigorous iron-gray, like the hair of an active man.

From that time on her front door remained closed, save for a period of six or seven years, when she was about forty, during which she gave lessons in china-painting. She fitted up a studio in one of the downstairs rooms, where the daughters and granddaughters of Colonel Sartoris' contemporaries were sent to her with the same regularity and in the same spirit that they were sent to church on Sundays with a twenty-five-cent piece for the collection plate. Meanwhile her taxes had been remitted.

50    Then the newer generation became the backbone and the spirit of the town, and the painting pupils grew up and fell away and did not send their children to her with boxes of color and tedious brushes and pictures cut from the ladies' magazines. The front door closed upon the last one and remained closed for good. When the town got free postal delivery, Miss Emily alone refused to let them fasten the metal numbers above her door and attach a mailbox to it. She would not listen to them.

Daily, monthly, yearly we watched the Negro grow grayer and more stooped, going in and out with the market basket. Each December we sent her a tax notice, which would be returned by the post office a week later, unclaimed. Now and then we would see her in one of the downstairs windows — she had evidently shut up the top floor of the house — like the carven torso of an idol in a niche, looking or not looking at us, we could never tell which. Thus she passed from generation to generation — dear, inescapable, impervious, tranquil, and perverse.

And so she died. Fell ill in the house filled with dust and shadows, with only a doddering Negro man to wait on her. We did not even know she was sick;

we had long since given up trying to get any information from the Negro. He talked to no one, probably not even to her, for his voice had grown harsh and rusty, as if from disuse.

She died in one of the downstairs rooms, in a heavy walnut bed with a curtain, her gray head propped on a pillow yellow and moldy with age and lack of sunlight.

## V

The Negro met the first of the ladies at the front door and let them in, with their hushed, sibilant voices and their quick, curious glances, and then he disappeared. He walked right through the house and out the back and was not seen again.

55     The two female cousins came at once. They held the funeral on the second day, with the town coming to look at Miss Emily beneath a mass of bought flowers, with the crayon face of her father musing profoundly above the bier and the ladies sibilant and macabre; and the very old men — some in their brushed Confederate uniforms — on the porch and the lawn, talking of Miss Emily as if she had been a contemporary of theirs, believing that they had danced with her and courted her perhaps, confusing time with its mathematical progression, as the old do, to whom all the past is not a diminishing road but, instead, a huge meadow which no winter ever quite touches, divided from them now by the narrow bottle-neck of the most recent decade of years.

Already we knew that there was one room in that region above stairs which no one had seen in forty years, and which would have to be forced. They waited until Miss Emily was decently in the ground before they opened it.

The violence of breaking down the door seemed to fill this room with pervading dust. A thin, acrid pall as of the tomb seemed to lie everywhere upon this room decked and furnished as for a bridal: upon the valance curtains of faded rose color, upon the rose-shaded lights, upon the dressing table, upon the delicate array of crystal and the man's toilet things backed with tarnished silver, silver so tarnished that the monogram was obscured. Among them lay a collar and tie, as if they had just been removed, which, lifted, left upon the surface a pale crescent in the dust. Upon a chair hung the suit, carefully folded; beneath it the two mute shoes and the discarded socks.

The man himself lay in the bed.

For a long while we just stood there, looking down at the profound and fleshless grin. The body had apparently once lain in the attitude of an embrace, but now the long sleep that outlasts love, that conquers even the grimace of love, had cuckolded him. What was left of him, rotted beneath what was left of the nightshirt, had become inextricable from the bed in which he lay; and upon him and upon the pillow beside him lay that even coating of the patient and biding dust.

60     Then we noticed that in the second pillow was the indentation of a head. One of us lifted something from it, and leaning forward, that faint and invisible dust dry and acrid in the nostrils, we saw a long strand of iron-gray hair.

(1930)

# Ernest Hemingway (1899–1961)

Like Stephen Crane, whose short stories he admired, Ernest Hemingway, a native of Oak Park, Illinois, began his writing career as a newspaper correspondent. The short sentences, crisp description of settings and actions, and relative lack of authorial comment that are distinguishing features of his mature style no doubt reflect his background in journalism. Hemingway's experiences in Italy during World War I, where he was injured while serving as an ambulance driver, and in Paris during the 1920s, where he was a member of the so-called Lost Generation (individuals who no longer believed in absolute moral or religious values), contributed to the development of his major theme: the need of the individual to live with control and dignity in a violent world devoid of spiritual meaning. Most fully developed in *The Sun Also Rises* (1926) and *A Farewell to Arms* (1929), two of his finest novels, these ideas are also expressed in "A Clean, Well-Lighted Place." The prose, which at first appears simply reportorial, implicitly develops the themes and symbols of the story.

# A CLEAN, WELL-LIGHTED PLACE

It was late and every one had left the café except an old man who sat in the shadow the leaves of the tree made against the electric light. In the day time the street was dusty, but at night the dew settled the dust and the old man liked to sit late because he was deaf and now at night it was quiet and he felt the difference. The two waiters inside the café knew that the old man was a little drunk, and while he was a good client they knew that if he became too drunk he would leave without paying, so they kept watch on him.

"Last week he tried to commit suicide," one waiter said.

"Why?"

"He was in despair."

5   "What about?"

"Nothing."

"How do you know it was nothing?"

"He has plenty of money."

They sat together at a table that was close against the wall near the door of the café and looked at the terrace where the tables were all empty except where the old man sat in the shadow of the leaves of the tree that moved slightly in the wind. A girl and a soldier went by in the street. The street light shone on the brass number on his collar. The girl wore no head covering and hurried beside him.

10   "The guard will pick him up," one waiter said.

"What does it matter if he gets what he's after?"

"He had better get off the street now. The guard will get him. They went by five minutes ago."

The old man sitting in the shadow rapped on his saucer with his glass. The younger waiter went over to him.

"What do you want?"

15    The old man looked at him. "Another brandy," he said.

"You'll be drunk," the waiter said. The old man looked at him. The waiter went away.

"He'll stay all night," he said to his colleague. "I'm sleepy now. I never get into bed before three o'clock. He should have killed himself last week."

The waiter took the brandy bottle and another saucer from the counter inside the café and marched out to the old man's table. He put down the saucer and poured the glass full of brandy.

"You should have killed yourself last week," he said to the deaf man. The old man motioned with his finger. "A little more," he said. The waiter poured on into the glass so that the brandy slopped over and ran down the stem into the top saucer of the pile. "Thank you," the old man said. The waiter took the bottle back inside the café. He sat down at the table with his colleague again.

20    "He's drunk now," he said.

"He's drunk every night."

"What did he want to kill himself for?"

"How should I know."

"How did he do it?"

25    "He hung himself with a rope."

"Who cut him down?"

"His niece."

"Why did she do it?"

"Fear for his soul."

30    "How much money has he got?"

"He's got plenty."

"He must be eighty years old."

"Anyway I should say he was eighty."

"I wish he would go home. I never get to bed before three o'clock. What kind of hour is that to go to bed?"

35    "He stays up because he likes it."

"He's lonely. I'm not lonely. I have a wife waiting in bed for me."

"He had a wife once too."

"A wife would be no good to him now."

"You can't tell. He might be better with a wife."

40    "His niece looks after him. You said she cut him down."

"I know."

"I wouldn't want to be that old. An old man is a nasty thing."

"Not always. This old man is clean. He drinks without spilling. Even now, drunk. Look at him."

"I don't want to look at him. I wish he would go home. He has no regard for those who must work."

45    The old man looked from his glass across the square, then over at the waiters.

"Another brandy," he said, pointing to his glass. The waiter who was in a hurry came over.

"Finished," he said, speaking with that omission of syntax stupid people employ when talking to drunken people or foreigners. "No more tonight. Close now."

"Another," said the old man.

"No. Finished." The waiter wiped the edge of the table with a towel and shook his head.

The old man stood up, slowly counted the saucers, took a leather coin purse from his pocket and paid for the drinks, leaving half a peseta tip.

The waiter watched him go down the street, a very old man walking unsteadily but with dignity.

"Why didn't you let him stay and drink?" the unhurried waiter asked. They were putting up the shutters. "It is not half-past two."

"I want to go home to bed."

"What is an hour?"

"More to me than to him."

"An hour is the same."

"You talk like an old man yourself. He can buy a bottle and drink at home."

"It's not the same."

"No, it is not," agreed the waiter with a wife. He did not wish to be unjust. He was only in a hurry.

"And you? You have no fear of going home before your usual hour?"

"Are you trying to insult me?"

"No, hombre, only to make a joke."

"No," the waiter who was in a hurry said, rising from pulling down the metal shutters. "I have confidence. I am all confidence."

"You have youth, confidence, and a job," the older waiter said. "You have everything."

"And what do you lack?"

"Everything but work."

"You have everything I have."

"No. I have never had confidence and I am not young."

"Come on. Stop talking nonsense and lock up."

"I am with those who like to stay late at the café," the older waiter said. "With all those who do not want to go to bed. With all those who need a light for the night."

"I want to go home and into bed."

"We are of two different kinds," the older waiter said. He was now dressed to go home. "It is not only a question of youth and confidence although those things are very beautiful. Each night I am reluctant to close up because there may be some one who needs the café."

"Hombre, there are bodegas open all night long."

"You do not understand. This is a clean and pleasant café. It is well lighted. The light is very good and also, now, there are shadows of the leaves."

"Good night," said the younger waiter.

"Good night," the other said. Turning off the electric light he continued the conversation with himself. It is the light of course but it is necessary that the place be clean and pleasant. You do not want music. Certainly you do not want music. Nor can you stand before a bar with dignity although that is all that is provided for these hours. What did he fear? It was not fear or dread. It was a nothing that he knew too well. It was all a nothing and a man was nothing too. It was only that and light was all it needed and a certain clean-ness and order. Some lived in it and never felt it but he knew it all was nada y pues nada y nada y pues nada.[1] Our nada who art in nada, nada be thy name thy kingdom nada thy will be nada in nada as it is in nada. Give us this nada our daily nada and nada us our nada as we nada our nadas and nada us not into nada but deliver us from nada; pues nada. Hail nothing full of nothing, nothing is with thee. He smiled and stood before a bar with a shining steam pressure coffee machine.

"What's yours?" asked the barman.

"Nada."

"Otro loco mas,"[2] said the barman and turned away.

80      "A little cup," said the waiter.

The barman poured it for him.

"The light is very bright and pleasant but the bar is unpolished," the waiter said.

The barman looked at him but did not answer. It was too late at night for conversation.

"You want another copita?"[3]

85      "No, thank you," said the waiter and went out. He disliked bars and bodegas. A clean, well-lighted café was a very different thing. Now, without thinking further, he would go home to his room. He would lie in the bed and finally, with daylight, he would go to sleep. After all, he said to himself, it is probably only insomnia. Many must have it.

(1933)

---

1 nothing, and therefore nothing.  2 another crazy one.  3 small cup.

# Sinclair Ross  (1908–1996)

Born on a farm near Prince Albert, Saskatchewan, Sinclair Ross, in his novel *As For Me and My House* (1941) and his first collection of short stories, *The Lamp at Noon* (1968), portrays life on the Canadian prairies during the "Dust Bowl" era of the 1930s. In addition to depicting the hardship and isolation, courage, and loneliness of his characters, Ross emphasizes the power of the land, which, as Margaret Laurence noted, appears "almost as a chief protagonist." In "The Lamp at Noon," the contrasting reactions of a husband and wife to a three-day dust storm that all but destroys their farm are presented in part by Ross's careful selection of physical symbols: the storm, the barren landscape, the barn to which the husband retreats, and the kitchen feebly illuminated by the lamp.

## THE LAMP AT NOON

A little before noon she lit the lamp. Demented wind fled keening past the house: a wail through the eaves that died every minute or two. Three days now without respite it had held. The dust was thickening to an impenetrable fog.

She lit the lamp, then for a long time stood at the window motionless. In dim, fitful outline the stable and oat granary still were visible; beyond, obscuring fields and landmarks, the lower of dust clouds made the farmyard seem an isolated acre, poised aloft above a sombre void. At each blast of wind it shook, as if to topple and spin hurtling with the dust-reel into space.

From the window she went to the door, opening it a little, and peering toward the stable again. He was not coming yet. As she watched there was a sudden rift overhead, and for a moment through the tattered clouds the sun raced like a wizened orange. It shed a soft, diffused light, dim and yellow as if it were the light from the lamp reaching out through the open door.

She closed the door, and going to the stove tried the potatoes with a fork. Her eyes all the while were fixed and wide with a curious immobility. It was the window. Standing at it, she had let her forehead press against the pane until the eyes were strained apart and rigid. Wide like that they had looked out to the depending ruin of the storm. Now she could not close them.

5　　The baby started to cry. He was lying in a homemade crib over which she had arranged a tent of muslin. Careful not to disturb the folds of it, she knelt and tried to still him, whispering huskily in a singsong voice that he must hush and go to sleep again. She would have liked to rock him, to feel the comfort of his little body in her arms, but a fear had obsessed her that in the dust-filled air he might contract pneumonia. There was dust sifting everywhere. Her own throat was parched with it. The table had been set less than ten minutes, and already a film was gathering on the dishes. The little cry continued, and with wincing, frightened lips she glanced around as if to find a corner where the air was less oppressive. But while the lips winced the eyes maintained their wide, immobile stare. "Sleep," she whispered again. "It's too soon for you to be hungry. Daddy's coming for his dinner."

He seemed a long time. Even the clock, still a few minutes off noon, could not dispel a foreboding sense that he was longer than he should be. She went to the door again — and then recoiled slowly to stand white and breathless in the middle of the room. She mustn't. He would only despise her if she ran to the stable looking for him. There was too much grim endurance in his nature ever to let him understand the fear and weakness of a woman. She must stay quiet and wait. Nothing was wrong. At noon he would come — and perhaps after dinner stay with her awhile.

Yesterday, and again at breakfast this morning, they had quarrelled bitterly. She wanted him now, the assurance of his strength and nearness, but he would stand aloof, wary, remembering the words she had flung at him in her anger, unable to understand it was only the dust and wind that had driven her.

Tense, she fixed her eyes upon the clock, listening. There were two winds: the wind in flight, and the wind that pursued. The one sought refuge in the eaves, whimpering, in fear; the other assailed it there, and shook the eaves apart to make it flee again. Once as she listened this first wind sprang inside the room, distraught like a bird that has felt the graze of talons on its wing; while furious the other wind shook the walls, and thudded tumbleweeds against the window till its quarry glanced away again in fright. But only to return — to return and quake among the feeble eaves, as if in all this dust-mad wilderness it knew no other sanctuary.

Then Paul came. At his step she hurried to the stove, intent upon the pots and frying pan. "The worst wind yet," he ventured, hanging up his cap and smock. "I had to light the lantern in the tool shed, too."

10   They looked at each other, then away. She wanted to go to him, to feel his arms supporting her, to cry a little just that he might soothe her, but because his presence made the menace of the wind seem less, she gripped herself and thought, "I'm in the right. I won't give in. For his sake, too, I won't."

He washed, hurriedly, so that a few dark welts of dust remained to indent upon his face a haggard strength. It was all she could see as she wiped the dishes and set the food before him: the strength, the grimness, the young Paul growing old and hard, buckled against a desert even grimmer than his will. "Hungry?" she asked, touched to a twinge of pity she had not intended. "There's dust in everything. It keeps coming faster than I can clean it up."

He nodded. "Tonight, though, you'll see it go down. This is the third day."

She looked at him in silence a moment, and then as if to herself muttered broodingly, "Until the next time. Until it starts again."

There was a dark resentment in her voice now that boded another quarrel. He waited, his eyes on her dubiously as she mashed a potato with her fork. The lamp between them threw strong lights and shadows on their faces. Dust and drought, earth that betrayed alike his labour and his faith, to him the struggle had given sternness, an impassive courage. Beneath the whip of sand his youth had been effaced. Youth, zest, exuberance — there remained only a harsh and clenched virility that yet became him, that seemed at the cost of more engaging qualities to be fulfilment of his inmost and essential nature. Whereas to her the same debts and poverty had brought a plaintive indignation, a nervous dread of what was still to come. The eyes were hollowed, the lips pinched dry and colourless. It was the face of a woman that had aged without maturing, that had loved the little vanities of life, and lost them wistfully.

15 "I'm afraid, Paul," she said suddenly. "I can't stand it any longer. He cries all the time. You will go, Paul — say you will. We aren't living here — not really living —"

The pleading in her voice now, after its shrill bitterness yesterday, made him think that this was only another way to persuade him. He answered evenly, "I told you this morning, Ellen; we keep on right where we are. At least I do. It's yourself you're thinking about, not the baby."

This morning such an accusation would have stung her to rage; now, her voice swift and panting, she pressed on, "Listen, Paul — I'm thinking of all of us — you, too. Look at the sky — what's happening. Are you blind? Thistles and tumbleweeds — it's a desert. You won't have a straw this fall. You won't be able to feed a cow or a chicken. Please, Paul, say we'll go away —"

"Go where?" His voice as he answered was still remote and even, inflexibly in unison with the narrowed eyes and the great hunch of muscle-knotted shoulder. "Even as a desert it's better than sweeping out your father's store and running his errands. That's all I've got ahead of me if I do what you want."

"And here —" she faltered. "What's ahead of you here? At least we'll get enough to eat and wear when you're sweeping out his store. Look at it — look at it, you fool. Desert — the lamp lit at noon —"

20 "You'll see it come back. There's good wheat in it yet."

"But in the meantime — year after year — can't you understand, Paul? We'll never get them back —"

He put down his knife and fork and leaned toward her across the table. "I can't go, Ellen. Living off your people — charity — stop and think of it. This is where I belong. I can't do anything else."

"Charity!" she repeated him, letting her voice rise in derision. "And this — you call this independence! Borrowed money you can't even pay the interest on, seed from the government — grocery bills — doctor bills —"

"We'll have crops again," he persisted. "Good crops — the land will come back. It's worth waiting for."

25 "And while we're waiting, Paul!" It was not anger now, but a kind of sob. "Think of me — and him. It's not fair. We have our lives, too, to live."

"And you think that going home to your family — taking your husband with you —"

"I don't care — anything would be better than this. Look at the air he's breathing. He cries all the time. For his sake, Paul. What's ahead of him here, even if you do get crops?"

He clenched his lips a minute, then, with his eyes hard and contemptuous, struck back, "As much as in town, growing up a pauper. You're the one who wants to go, it's not for his sake. You think that in town you'd have a better time — not so much work — more clothes —"

"Maybe —" She dropped her head defencelessly. "I'm young still. I like pretty things."

30 There was silence now — a deep fastness of it enclosed by rushing wind and creaking walls. It seemed the yellow lamplight cast a hush upon them. Through the haze of dusty air the walls receded, dimmed, and came again. At last she

raised her head and said listlessly, "Go on — your dinner's getting cold. Don't sit and stare at me. I've said it all."

The spent quietness in her voice was even harder to endure than her anger. It reproached him, against his will insisted that he see and understand her lot. To justify himself he tried, "I was a poor man when you married me. You said you didn't mind. Farming's never been easy, and never will be."

"I wouldn't mind the work or the skimping if there was something to look forward to. It's the hopelessness — going on — watching the land blow away."

"The land's all right," he repeated. "The dry years won't last forever."

"But it's not just dry years, Paul!" The little sob in her voice gave way suddenly to a ring of exasperation. "Will you never see? It's the land itself — the soil. You've plowed and harrowed it until there's not a root or fibre left to hold it down. That's why the soil drifts — that's why in a year or two there'll be nothing left but the bare clay. If in the first place you farmers had taken care of your land — if you hadn't been so greedy for wheat every year —"

35      She had taught school before she married him, and of late in her anger there had been a kind of disdain, an attitude almost of condescension, as if she no longer looked upon the farmers as her equals. He sat still, his eyes fixed on the yellow lamp flame, and seeming to know how her words had hurt him, she went on softly, "I want to help you, Paul. That's why I won't sit quiet while you go on wasting your life. You're only thirty — you owe it to yourself as well as me."

He sat staring at the lamp without answering, his mouth sullen. It seemed indifference now, as if he were ignoring her, and stung to anger again she cried, "Do you ever think what my life is? Two rooms to live in — once a month to town, and nothing to spend when I get there. I'm still young — I wasn't brought up this way."

"You're a farmer's wife now. It doesn't matter what you used to be, or how you were brought up. You get enough to eat and wear. Just now that's all I can do. I'm not to blame that we've been dried out five years."

"Enough to eat!" she laughed back shrilly. "Enough salt pork — enough potatoes and eggs. And look —" Springing to the middle of the room she thrust out a foot for him to see the scuffed old slipper. "When they're completely gone I suppose you'll tell me I can go barefoot — that I'm a farmer's wife — that it's not your fault we're dried out —"

"And what about these?" He pushed his chair away from the table now to let her see what he was wearing. "Cowhide — hard as boards — but my feet are so calloused I don't feel them any more."

40      Then he stood up, ashamed of having tried to match her hardships with his own. But frightened now as he reached for his smock she pressed close to him. "Don't go yet. I brood and worry when I'm left alone. Please, Paul — you can't work on the land anyway."

"And keep on like this? You start before I'm through the door. Week in and week out — I've troubles enough of my own."

"Paul — please stay —" The eyes were glazed now, distended a little as if with the intensity of her dread and pleading. "We won't quarrel any more. Hear it! I can't work — I just stand still and listen —"

The eyes frightened him, but responding to a kind of instinct that he must withstand her, that it was his self-respect and manhood against the

fretful weakness of a woman, he answered unfeelingly, "In here safe and quiet —
you don't know how well off you are. If you were out in it — fighting it —
swallowing it —"

"Sometimes, Paul, I wish I was. I'm so caged — if I could only break
away and run. See — I stand like this all day. I can't relax. My throat's so
tight it aches —"

45       With a jerk he freed his smock from her clutch. "If I stay we'll only keep
on all afternoon. Wait till tomorrow — we'll talk things over when the wind
goes down."

Then without meeting her eyes again he swung outside, and doubled low
against the buffets of the wind, fought his way slowly toward the stable. There
was a deep hollow calm within, a vast darkness engulfed beneath the tides of
moaning wind. He stood breathless a moment, hushed almost to a stupor by the
sudden extinction of the storm and the stillness that enfolded him. It was a long,
far-reaching stillness. The first dim stalls and rafters led the way into cavern-like
obscurity, into vaults and recesses that extended far beyond the stable walls. Nor
in these first quiet moments did he forbid the illusion, the sense of release
from a harsh, familiar world into one of peace and darkness. The contentious
mood that his stand against Ellen had roused him to, his tenacity and clenched
despair before the ravages of wind, it was ebbing now, losing itself in the cover
of darkness. Ellen and the wheat seemed remote, unimportant. At a whinny
from the bay mare, Bess, he went forward and into her stall. She seemed grateful for his presence, and thrust her nose deep between his arm and body. They
stood a long time motionless, comforting and assuring each other.

For soon again the first deep sense of quiet and peace was shrunken to the
battered shelter of the stable. Instead of release or escape from the assaulting
wind, the walls were but a feeble stand against it. They creaked and sawed as
if the fingers of a giant hand were tightening to collapse them; the empty loft
sustained a pipelike cry that rose and fell but never ended. He saw the
dust-black sky again, and his fields blown smooth with drifted soil.

But always, even while listening to the storm outside, he could feel the
tense and apprehensive stillness of the stable. There was not a hoof that
clumped or shifted, not a rub of halter against manger. And yet, though it
had been a strange stable, he would have known, despite the darkness, that
every stall was filled. They, too, were all listening.

From Bess he went to the big grey gelding, Prince. Prince was twenty
years old, with rib-grooved sides, and high, protruding hipbones. Paul ran his
hand over the ribs, and felt a sudden shame, a sting of fear that Ellen might be
right in what she said. For wasn't it true — nine years a farmer now on his
own land, and still he couldn't even feed his horses? What, then, could he
hope to do for his wife and son?

50       There was much he planned. And so vivid was the future of his planning, so real and constant, that often the actual present was but half felt, but
half endured. Its difficulties were lessened by a confidence in what lay beyond
them. A new house — land for the boy — land and still more land — or education, whatever he might want.

But all the time was he only a blind and stubborn fool? Was Ellen right?
Was he trampling on her life, and throwing away his own? The five years

since he married her, were they to go on repeating themselves, five, ten, twenty, until all the brave future he looked forward to was but a stark and futile past?

She looked forward to no future. She had no faith or dream with which to make the dust and poverty less real. He understood suddenly. He saw her face again as only a few minutes ago it had begged him not to leave her. The darkness round him now was as a slate on which her lonely terror limned itself. He went from Prince to the other horses, combing their manes and forelocks with his fingers, but always it was her face before him, its staring eyes and twisted suffering. "See Paul — I stand like this all day. I just stand still — My throat's so tight it aches —"

And always the wind, the creak of walls, the wild lipless wailing through the loft. Until at last as he stood there, staring into the livid face before him, it seemed that this scream of wind was a cry from her parched and frantic lips. He knew it couldn't be, he knew that she was safe within the house, but still the wind persisted as a woman's cry. The cry of a woman with eyes like those that watched him through the dark. Eyes that were mad now — lips that even as they cried still pleaded, "See, Paul — I stand like this all day. I just stand still — so caged! If I could only run!"

He saw her running, pulled and driven headlong by the wind, but when at last he returned to the house, compelled by his anxiety, she was walking quietly back and forth with the baby in her arms. Careful, despite his concern, not to reveal a fear or weakness that she might think capitulation to her wishes, he watched a moment through the window, and then went off to the tool shed to mend harness. All afternoon he stitched and riveted. It was easier with the lantern lit and his hands occupied. There was a wind whining high past the tool shed too, but it was only wind. He remembered the arguments with which Ellen had tried to persuade him away from the farm, and one by one he defeated them. There would be rain again — next year or the next. Maybe in his ignorance he had farmed his land the wrong way, seeding wheat every year, working the soil till it was lifeless dust — but he would do better now. He would plant clover and alfalfa, breed cattle, acre by acre and year by year restore to his land its fibre and fertility. That was something to work for, a way to prove himself. It was ruthless wind, blackening the sky with his earth, but it was not his master. Out of his land it had made a wilderness. He now, out of the wilderness, would make a farm and home again.

55   Tonight he must talk with Ellen. Patiently, when the wind was down, and they were both quiet again. It was she who had told him to grow fibrous crops, who had called him an ignorant fool because he kept on with summer fallow and wheat. Now she might be gratified to find him acknowledging her wisdom. Perhaps she would begin to feel the power and steadfastness of the land, to take a pride in it, to understand that he was not a fool, but working for her future and their son's.

And already the wind was slackening. At four o'clock he could sense a lull. At five, straining his eyes from the tool shed doorway, he could make out a neighbour's buildings half a mile away. It was over — three days of blight and havoc like a scourge — three days so bitter and so long that for a moment he stood still, unseeing, his senses idle with a numbness of relief.

But only for a moment. Suddenly he emerged from the numbness; suddenly the fields before him struck his eyes to comprehension. They lay black, naked. Beaten and mounded smooth with dust as if a sea in gentle swell had turned to stone. And though he had tried to prepare himself for such a scene, though he had known since yesterday that not a blade would last the storm, still now, before the utter waste confronting him, he sickened and stood cold. Suddenly like the fields he was naked. Everything that had sheathed him a little from the realities of existence: vision and purpose, faith in the land, in the future, in himself — it was all rent now, stripped away. "Desert," he heard her voice begin to sob. "Desert, you fool — the lamp lit at noon!"

In the stable again, measuring out their feed to the horses, he wondered what he would say to her tonight. For so deep were his instincts of loyalty to the land that still, even with the images of his betrayal stark upon his mind, his concern was how to withstand her, how to go on again and justify himself. It had not occurred to him yet that he might or should abandon the land. He had lived with it too long. Rather was his impulse still to defend it — as a man defends against the scorn of strangers even his most worthless kin.

He fed his horses, then waited. She too would be waiting, ready to cry at him, "Look now — that crop that was to feed and clothe us! And you'll still keep on! You'll still say 'Next year — there'll be rain next year'!"

But she was gone when he reached the house. The door was open, the lamp blown out, the crib empty. The dishes from their meal at noon were still on the table. She had perhaps begun to sweep, for the broom was lying in the middle of the floor. He tried to call, but a terror clamped upon his throat. In the wan, returning light it seemed that even the deserted kitchen was straining to whisper what it had seen. The tatters of the storm still whimpered through the eaves, and in their moaning told the desolation of the miles they had traversed. On tiptoe at last he crossed to the adjoining room; then at the threshold, without even a glance inside to satisfy himself that she was really gone, he wheeled again and plunged outside.

He ran a long time — distraught and headlong as a few hours ago he had seemed to watch her run — around the farmyard, a little distance into the pasture, back again blindly to the house to see whether she had returned — and then at a stumble down the road for help.

They joined him in the search, rode away for others, spread calling across the fields in the direction she might have been carried by the wind — but nearly two hours later it was himself who came upon her. Crouched down against a drift of sand as if for shelter, her hair in matted strands around her neck and face, the child clasped tightly in her arms.

The child was quite cold. It had been her arms, perhaps, too frantic to protect him, or the smother of dust upon his throat and lungs. "Hold him," she said as he knelt beside her. "So — with his face away from the wind. Hold him until I tidy my hair."

Her eyes were still wide in an immobile stare, but with her lips she smiled at him. For a long time he knelt transfixed, trying to speak to her, touching fearfully with his fingertips the dustgrimed cheeks and eyelids of the child. At last she said, "I'll take him again. Such clumsy hands — you don't know how to hold a baby yet. See how his head falls forward on your arm."

65    Yet it all seemed familiar — a confirmation of what he had known since noon. He gave her the child, then, gathering them up in his arms, struggled to his feet, and turned toward home.

It was evening now. Across the fields a few spent clouds of dust still shook and fled. Beyond, as if through smoke, the sunset smouldered like a distant fire.

He walked with a long dull stride, his eyes before him, heedless of her weight. Once he glanced down and with her eyes she still was smiling. "Such strong arms, Paul — and I was so tired just carrying him...."

He tried to answer, but it seemed that now the dusk was drawn apart in breathless waiting, a finger on its lips until they passed. "You were right, Paul...." Her voice came whispering, as if she too could feel the hush. "You said tonight we'd see the storm go down. So still now, and a red sky — it means tomorrow will be fine."

(1938)

# Eudora Welty (b. 1909)

Like fellow Mississippian William Faulkner, whose works she admires, Eudora Welty has set most of her short stories in and around the city where she was born and has lived most of her life: Jackson. Family and a sense of place are most important for her characters, for a place of one's own provides "a base of reference," and enables "individuals to put out roots." "Why I Live at the P.O.," which takes place on July 4, American Independence Day, traditionally a time of family reunions, focusses on the developing hostility the narrator feels toward her family and her own declaration of independence from them. Ironically, in its portrayal of the disintegrating interrelationships, the story provides a negative example of Welty's belief that "communication and hope of it are conditions of life itself."

# WHY I LIVE AT THE P.O.

I was getting along fine with Mama, Papa-Daddy and Uncle Rondo until my sister Stella-Rondo just separated from her husband and came back home again. Mr. Whitaker! Of course I went with Mr. Whitaker first, when he first appeared here in China Grove,[1] taking "Pose Yourself" photos, and Stella-Rondo broke us up. Told him I was one-sided. Bigger on one side than the other, which is a deliberate, calculated falsehood: I'm the same. Stella-Rondo is exactly twelve months to the day younger than I am and for that reason she's spoiled.

She's always had anything in the world she wanted and then she'd throw it away. Papa-Daddy gave her this gorgeous Add-a-Pearl necklace when she was eight years old and she threw it away playing baseball when she was nine, with only two pearls.

So as soon as she got married and moved away from home the first thing she did was separate! From Mr. Whitaker! This photographer with the popeyes she said she trusted. Came home from one of those towns up in Illinois and to our complete surprise brought this child of two.

Mama said she like to made her drop dead for a second. "Here you had this marvelous blonde child and never so much as wrote your mother a word about it," says Mama. "I'm thoroughly ashamed of you." But of course she wasn't.

5      Stella-Rondo just calmly takes off this *hat*, I wish you could see it. She says, "Why, Mama, Shirley-T.'s adopted, I can prove it."

"How?" says Mama, but all I says was, "H'm!" There I was over the hot stove, trying to stretch two chickens over five people and a completely unexpected child into the bargain, without one moment's notice.

"What do you mean —'H'm!'?" says Stella-Rondo, and Mama says, "I heard that, Sister."

I said that oh, I didn't mean a thing, only that whoever Shirley-T. was, she was the spit-image of Papa-Daddy if he'd cut off his beard, which of course he'd never do in the world. Papa-Daddy's Mama's papa and sulks.

---

1 town in central Mississippi.

Stella-Rondo got furious! She said, "Sister, I don't need to tell you you got a lot of nerve and always did have and I'll thank you to make no future reference to my adopted child whatsoever."

10 "Very well," I said. "Very well, very well. Of course I noticed at once she looks like Mr. Whitaker's side too. That frown. She looks like a cross between Mr. Whitaker and Papa-Daddy."

"Well, all I can say is she isn't."

"She looks exactly like Shirley Temple[2] to me," says Mama, but Shirley-T. just ran away from her.

So the first thing Stella-Rondo did at the table was turn Papa-Daddy against me.

"Papa-Daddy," she says. He was trying to cut up his meat. "Papa-Daddy!" I was taken completely by surprise. Papa-Daddy is about a million years old and's got this long-long beard. "Papa-Daddy, Sister says she fails to understand why you don't cut off your beard."

15 So Papa-Daddy l-a-y-s down his knife and fork! He's real rich. Mama says he is, he says he isn't. So he says, "Have I heard correctly? You don't understand why I don't cut off my beard?"

"Why," I says, "Papa-Daddy, of course I understand, I did not say any such of a thing, the idea!"

He says, "Hussy!"

I says, "Papa-Daddy, you know I wouldn't any more want you to cut off your beard than the man in the moon. It was the farthest thing from my mind! Stella-Rondo sat there and made that up while she was eating breast of chicken."

But he says, "So the postmistress fails to understand why I don't cut off my beard. Which job I got you through my influence with the government. 'Bird's nest'— is that what you call it?"

20 Not that it isn't the next to smallest P.O. in the entire state of Mississippi.

I says, "Oh, Papa-Daddy," I says, "I didn't say any such of a thing, I never dreamed it was a bird's nest, I have always been grateful though this is the next to smallest P.O. in the state of Mississippi, and I do not enjoy being referred to as a hussy by my own grandfather."

But Stella-Rondo says, "Yes, you did say it too. Anybody in the world could of heard you, that had ears."

"Stop right there," says Mama, looking at *me*.

So I pulled my napkin straight back through the napkin ring and left the table.

25 As soon as I was out of the room Mama says, "Call her back, or she'll starve to death," but Papa-Daddy says, "This is the beard I started growing on the Coast when I was fifteen years old." He would of gone on till nightfall if Shirley-T. hadn't lost the Milky Way she ate in Cairo.[3]

So Papa-Daddy says, "I am going out and lie in the hammock, and you can all sit here and remember my words: I'll never cut off my beard as long as I live, even one inch, and I don't appreciate it in you at all." Passed right by me in the hall and went straight out and got in the hammock.

2 American child movie star of the 1930s. 3 town in southern Illinois.

It would be a holiday. I wasn't five minutes before Uncle Rondo suddenly appeared in the hall in one of Stella-Rondo's flesh-colored kimonos, all cut on the bias, like something Mr. Whitaker probably thought was gorgeous.

"Uncle Rondo!" I says. "I didn't know who that was! Where are you going?"

"Sister," he says, "get out of my way, I'm poisoned."

30 "If you're poisoned stay away from Papa-Daddy," I says. "Keep out of the hammock. Papa-Daddy will certainly beat you on the head if you come within forty miles of him. He thinks I deliberately said he ought to cut off his beard after he got me the P.O., and I've told him and told him and told him, and he acts like he just don't hear me. Papa-Daddy must of gone stone deaf."

"He picked a fine day to do it then," says Uncle Rondo, and before you could say "Jack Robinson" flew out in the yard.

What he'd really done, he'd drunk another bottle of that prescription. He does it every single Fourth of July as sure as shooting, and it's horribly expensive. Then he falls over in the hammock and snores. So he insisted on zigzagging right on out to the hammock, looking like a half-wit.

Papa-Daddy woke up with this horrible yell and right there without moving an inch he tried to turn Uncle Rondo against me. I heard every word he said. Oh, he told Uncle Rondo I didn't learn to read till I was eight years old and he didn't see how in the world I ever got the mail put up at the P.O., much less read it all, and he said if Uncle Rondo could only fathom the lengths he had gone to to get me that job! And he said on the other hand he thought Stella-Rondo had a brilliant mind and deserved credit for getting out of town. All the time he was just lying there swinging as pretty as you please and looping out his beard, and poor Uncle Rondo was *pleading* with him to slow down the hammock, it was making him as dizzy as a witch to watch it. But that's what Papa-Daddy likes about a hammock. So Uncle Rondo was too dizzy to get turned against me for the time being. He's Mama's only brother and is a good case of a one-track mind. Ask anybody. A certified pharmacist.

Just then I heard Stella-Rondo raising the upstairs window. While she was married she got this peculiar idea that it's cooler with the windows shut and locked. So she has to raise the window before she can make a soul hear her outdoors.

35 So she raises the window and says, "*Oh!*" You would have thought she was mortally wounded.

Uncle Rondo and Papa-Daddy didn't even look up, but kept right on with what they were doing. I had to laugh.

I flew up the stairs and threw the door open! I says, "What in the wide world's the matter, Stella-Rondo? You mortally wounded?"

"No," she says, "I am not mortally wounded but I wish you would do me the favor of looking out that window there and telling me what you see."

So I shade my eyes and look out the window.

40 "I see the front yard," I says.

"Don't you see any human beings?" she says.

"I see Uncle Rondo trying to run Papa-Daddy out of the hammock," I says. "Nothing more. Naturally, it's so suffocating-hot in the house, with all the windows shut and locked, everybody who cares to stay in their right mind will have to go out and get in the hammock before the Fourth of July is over."

"Don't you notice anything different about Uncle Rondo?" asks Stella-Rondo.

"Why, no, except he's got on some terrible-looking flesh-colored contraption I wouldn't be found dead in, is all I can see," I says.

45 "Never mind, you won't be found dead in it, because it happens to be part of my trousseau, and Mr. Whitaker took several dozen photographs of me in it," says Stella-Rondo. "What on earth could Uncle Rondo *mean* by wearing part of my trousseau out in the broad open daylight without saying so much as 'Kiss my foot,' *knowing* I only got home this morning after my separation and hung my negligee up on the bathroom door, just as nervous as I could be?"

"I'm sure I don't know, and what do you expect me to do about it?" I says. "Jump out the window?"

"No, I expect nothing of the kind. I simply declare that Uncle Rondo looks like a fool in it, that's all," she says. "It makes me sick to my stomach."

"Well, he looks as good as he can," I says. "As good as anybody in reason could." I stood up for Uncle Rondo, please remember. And I said to Stella-Rondo, "I think I would do well not to criticize so freely if I were you and came home with a two-year-old child I had never said a word about, and no explanation whatever about my separation."

"I asked you the instant I entered this house not to refer one more time to my adopted child, and you gave me your word of honor you would not," was all Stella-Rondo would say, and started pulling out every one of her eyebrows with some cheap Kress tweezers.

50 So I merely slammed the door behind me and went down and made some green-tomato pickle. Somebody had to do it. Of course Mama had turned both the niggers loose; she always said no earthly power could hold one anyway on the Fourth of July, so she wouldn't even try. It turned out that Jaypan fell in the lake and came within a very narrow limit of drowning.

So Mama trots in. Lifts up the lid and says, "H'm! Not very good for your Uncle Rondo in his precarious condition, I must say. Or poor little adopted Shirley-T. Shame on you!"

That made me tired. I says, "Well, Stella-Rondo had better thank her lucky stars it was her instead of me came trotting in with that very peculiar-looking child. Now if it had been me that trotted in from Illinois and brought a peculiar-looking child of two, I shudder to think of the reception I'd of got, much less controlled the diet of an entire family."

"But you must remember, Sister, that you were never married to Mr. Whitaker in the first place and didn't go up to Illinois to live," says Mama, shaking a spoon in my face. "If you had I would of been just as overjoyed to see you and your little adopted girl as I was to see Stella-Rondo, when you wound up with your separation and came on back home."

"You would not," I says.

55 "Don't contradict me, I would," says Mama.

But I said she couldn't convince me though she talked till she was blue in the face. Then I said, "Besides, you know as well as I do that that child is not adopted."

"She most certainly is adopted," says Mama, stiff as a poker.

I says, "Why, Mama, Stella-Rondo had her just as sure as anything in this world, and just too stuck up to admit it."

"Why, Sister," said Mama. "Here I thought we were going to have a pleasant Fourth of July, and you start right out not believing a word your own baby sister tells you!"

60 "Just like Cousin Annie Flo. Went to her grave denying the facts of life," I remind Mama.

"I told you if you ever mentioned Annie Flo's name I'd slap your face," says Mama, and slaps my face.

"All right, you wait and see," I says.

"I," says Mama, "*I* prefer to take my children's word for anything when it's humanly possible." You ought to see Mama, she weighs two hundred pounds and has real tiny feet.

Just then something perfectly horrible occurred to me.

65 "Mama," I says, "can that child talk?" I simply had to whisper! "Mama, I wonder if that child can be — you know — in any way? Do you realize," I says, "that she hasn't spoken one single, solitary word to a human being up to this minute? This is the way she looks," I says, and I looked like this.

Well, Mama and I just stood there and stared at each other. It was horrible!

"I remember well that Joe Whitaker frequently drank like a fish," says Mama. "I believed to my soul he drank *chemicals*." And without another word she marches to the foot of the stairs and calls Stella-Rondo.

"Stella-Rondo? O-o-o-o-o! Stella-Rondo!"

"What?" says Stella-Rondo from upstairs. Not even the grace to get up off the bed.

70 "Can that child of yours talk?" asks Mama.

Stella-Rondo says, "Can she what?"

"Talk! Talk!" says Mama. "Burdyburdyburdyburdy!"

So Stella-Rondo yells back, "Who says she can't talk?"

"Sister says so," says Mama.

75 "You didn't have to tell me, I know whose word of honor don't mean a thing in this house," says Stella-Rondo.

And in a minute the loudest Yankee voice I ever heard in my life yells out, "OE'm Pop-OE the Sailor-r-r-r Ma-a-an!" and then somebody jumps up and down in the upstairs hall. In another second the house would of fallen down.

"Not only talks, she can tap-dance!" calls Stella-Rondo. "Which is more than some people I won't name can do."

"Why, the little precious darling thing!" Mama says, so surprised. "Just as smart as she can be!" Starts talking baby talk right there. Then she turns on me. "Sister, you ought to be thoroughly ashamed! Run upstairs this instant and apologize to Stella-Rondo and Shirley-T."

"Apologize for what?" I says. "I merely wondered if the child was normal, that's all. Now that she's proved she is, why, I have nothing further to say."

80 But Mama just turned on her heel and flew out, furious. She ran right upstairs and hugged the baby. She believed it was adopted. Stella-Rondo hadn't done a thing but turn her against me from upstairs while I stood there

helpless over the hot stove. So that made Mama, Papa-Daddy and the baby all on Stella-Rondo's side.

Next, Uncle Rondo.

I must say that Uncle Rondo has been marvelous to me at various times in the past and I was completely unprepared to be made to jump out of my skin, the way it turned out. Once Stella-Rondo did something perfectly horrible to him — broke a chain letter from Flanders Field[4] — and he took the radio back he had given her and gave it to me. Stella-Rondo was furious! For six months we all had to call her Stella instead of Stella-Rondo, or she wouldn't answer. I always thought Uncle Rondo had all the brains of the entire family. Another time he sent me to Mammoth Cave,[5] with all expenses paid.

But this would be the day he was drinking that prescription, the Fourth of July.

So at supper Stella-Rondo speaks up and says she thinks Uncle Rondo ought to try to eat a little something. So finally Uncle Rondo said he would try a little cold biscuits and ketchup, but that was all. So *she* brought it to him.

85     "Do you think it wise to disport with ketchup in Stella-Rondo's flesh-colored kimono?" I says. Trying to be considerate! If Stella-Rondo couldn't watch out for her trousseau, somebody had to.

"Any objections?" asks Uncle Rondo, just about to pour out all the ketchup.

"Don't mind what she says, Uncle Rondo," says Stella-Rondo. "Sister has been devoting this solid afternoon to sneering out my bedroom window at the way you look."

"What's that?" says Uncle Rondo. Uncle Rondo has got the most terrible temper in the world. Anything is liable to make him tear the house down if it comes at the wrong time.

So Stella-Rondo says, "Sister says, 'Uncle Rondo certainly does look like a fool in that pink kimono!'"

90     Do you remember who it was really said that?

Uncle Rondo spills out all the ketchup and jumps out of his chair and tears off the kimono and throws it down on the dirty floor and puts his foot on it. It had to be sent all the way to Jackson to the cleaners and re-pleated.

"So that's your opinion of your Uncle Rondo, is it?" he says. "I look like a fool, do I? Well, that's the last straw. A whole day in this house with nothing to do, and then to hear you come out with a remark like that behind my back!"

"I didn't say any such of a thing, Uncle Rondo," I says, "and I'm not saying who did, either. Why, I think you look all right. Just try to take care of yourself and not talk and eat at the same time," I says. "I think you better go lie down."

"Lie down my foot," says Uncle Rondo. I ought to of known by that he was fixing to do something perfectly horrible.

95     So he didn't do anything that night in the precarious state he was in — just played Casino with Mama and Stella-Rondo and Shirley-T. and gave Shirley-T. a nickel with a head on both sides. It tickled her nearly to death, and she

4 in Belgium, site of graves of World War I soldiers.  5 popular tourist attraction in Kentucky.

called him "Papa." But at 6:30 A.M. the next morning, he threw a whole five-cent package of some unsold one-inch firecrackers from the store as hard as he could into my bedroom and they every one went off. Not one bad one in the string. Anybody else, there'd be one that wouldn't go off.

Well, I'm just terribly susceptible to noise of any kind, the doctor has always told me I was the most sensitive person he had ever seen in his whole life, and I was simply prostrated. I couldn't eat! People tell me they heard it as far as the cemetery, and old Aunt Jep Patterson, that had been holding her own so good, thought it was Judgment Day and she was going to meet her whole family. It's usually so quiet here.

And I'll tell you it didn't take me any longer than a minute to make up my mind what to do. There I was with the whole entire house on Stella-Rondo's side and turned against me. If I have anything at all I have pride.

So I just decided I'd go straight down to the P.O. There's plenty of room there in the back, I says to myself.

Well! I made no bones about letting the family catch on to what I was up to. I didn't try to conceal it.

100     The first thing they knew, I marched in where they were all playing Old Maid and pulled the electric oscillating fan out by the plug, and everything got real hot. Next I snatched the pillow I'd done the needlepoint on right off the davenport from behind Papa-Daddy. He went "Ugh!" I beat Stella-Rondo up the stairs and finally found my charm bracelet in her bureau drawer under a picture of Nelson Eddy.[6]

"So that's the way the land lies," says Uncle Rondo. There he was, piecing on the ham. "Well, Sister, I'll be glad to donate my army cot if you got any place to set it up, providing you'll leave right this minute and let me get some peace." Uncle Rondo was in France.

"Thank you kindly for the cot and 'peace' is hardly the word I would select if I had to resort to firecrackers at 6:30 A.M. in a young girl's bedroom," I says back to him. "And as to where I intend to go, you seem to forget my position as postmistress of China Grove, Mississippi," I says. "I've always got the P.O."

Well, that made them all sit up and take notice.

I went out front and started digging up some four-o'clocks to plant around the P.O.

105     "Ah-ah-ah!" says Mama, raising the window. "Those happen to be my four-o'clocks. Everything planted in that star is mine. I've never known you to make anything grow in your life."

"Very well," I says. "But I take the fern. Even you, Mama, can't stand there and deny that I'm the one watered that fern. And I happen to know where I can send in a box top and get a packet of one thousand mixed seeds, no two the same kind, free."

"Oh, where?" Mama wants to know.

But I says, "Too late. You 'tend to your house, and I'll 'tend to mine. You hear things like that all the time if you know how to listen to the radio. Perfectly marvelous offers. Get anything you want free."

6 popular American singer on radio programs of the 1930s.

So I hope to tell you I marched in and got that radio, and they could of all bit a nail in two, especially Stella-Rondo, that it used to belong to, and she well knew she couldn't get it back, I'd sue for it like a shot. And I very politely took the sewing-machine motor I helped pay the most on to give Mama for Christmas back in 1929, and a good big calendar, with the first-aid remedies on it. The thermometer and the Hawaiian ukulele certainly were rightfully mine, and I stood on the step-ladder and got all my watermelon-rind preserves and every fruit and vegetable I'd put up, every jar. Then I began to pull the tacks out of the bluebird wall vases on the archway to the dining room.

110     "Who told you you could have those, Miss Priss?" says Mama, fanning as hard as she could.

"I bought 'em and I'll keep track of 'em," I says. "I'll tack 'em up one on each side the post-office window, and you can see 'em when you come to ask me for your mail, if you're so dead to see 'em."

"Not I! I'll never darken the door to that post office again if I live to be a hundred," Mama says. "Ungrateful child! After all the money we spent on you at the Normal."[7]

"Me either," says Stella-Rondo. "You can just let my mail lie there and *rot*, for all I care. I'll never come and relieve you of a single, solitary piece."

"I should worry," I says. "And who you think's going to sit down and write you all those big fat letters and postcards, by the way? Mr. Whitaker? Just because he was the only man ever dropped down in China Grove and you got him — unfairly — is he going to sit down and write you a lengthy correspondence after you come home giving no rhyme nor reason whatsoever for your separation and no explanation for the presence of that child? I may not have your brilliant mind, but I fail to see it."

115     So Mama says, "Sister, I've told you a thousand times that Stella-Rondo simply got homesick, and this child is far too big to be hers," and she says, "Now, why don't you all just sit down and play Casino?"

Then Shirley-T. sticks out her tongue at me in this perfectly horrible way. She has no more manners than the man in the moon. I told her she was going to cross her eyes like that some day and they'd stick.

"It's too late to stop me now," I says. "You should have tried that yesterday. I'm going to the P.O. and the only way you can possibly see me is to visit me there."

So Papa-Daddy says, "You'll never catch me setting foot in that post office, even if I should take a notion into my head to write a letter some place." He says, "I won't have you reachin' out of that little old window with a pair of shears and cuttin' off any beard of mine. I'm too smart for you!"

"We all are," says Stella-Rondo.

120     But I said, "If you're so smart, where's Mr. Whitaker?"

So then Uncle Rondo says, "I'll thank you from now on to stop reading all the orders I get on postcards and telling everybody in China Grove what you think is the matter with them," but I says, "I draw my own conclusions and will continue in the future to draw them." I says, "If people want to write their

7 teachers' college.

inmost secrets on penny postcards, there's nothing in the wide world you can do about it, Uncle Rondo."

"And if you think we'll ever *write* another postcard you're sadly mistaken," says Mama.

"Cutting off your nose to spite your face then," I says. "But if you're all determined to have no more to do with the U.S. mail, think of this: What will Stella-Rondo do now, if she wants to tell Mr. Whitaker to come after her?"

"Wah!" says Stella-Rondo. I knew she'd cry. She had a conniption fit right there in the kitchen.

125    "It will be interesting to see how long she holds out," I says. "And now — I am leaving."

"Good-bye," says Uncle Rondo.

"Oh, I declare," says Mama, "to think that a family of mine should quarrel on the Fourth of July, or the day after, over Stella-Rondo leaving old Mr. Whitaker and having the sweetest little adopted child! It looks like we'd all be glad!"

"Wah!" says Stella-Rondo, and has a fresh conniption fit.

*"He* left *her* — you mark my words," I says. "That's Mr. Whitaker. I know Mr. Whitaker. After all, I knew him first. I said from the beginning he'd up and leave her. I foretold every single thing that's happened."

130    "Where did he go?" asks Mama.

"Probably to the North Pole, if he knows what's good for him," I says.

But Stella-Rondo just bawled and wouldn't say another word. She flew to her room and slammed the door.

"Now look what you've gone and done, Sister," says Mama. "You go apologize."

"I haven't got time, I'm leaving," I says.

135    "Well, what are you waiting around for?" asks Uncle Rondo.

So I just picked up the kitchen clock and marched off, without saying "Kiss my foot" or anything, and never did tell Stella-Rondo goodbye.

There was a nigger girl going along on a little wagon right in front.

"Nigger girl," I says, "come help me haul these things down the hill, I'm going to live in the post office."

Took her nine trips in her express wagon. Uncle Rondo came out on the porch and threw her a nickel.

140    And that's the last I've laid eyes on any of my family or my family laid eyes on me for five solid days and nights. Stella-Rondo may be telling the most horrible tales in the world about Mr. Whitaker, but I haven't heard them. As I tell everybody, I draw my own conclusions.

But oh, I like it here. It's ideal, as I've been saying. You see, I've got everything cater-cornered, the way I like it. Hear the radio? All the war news. Radio, sewing machine, book ends, ironing board and that great big piano lamp — peace, that's what I like. Butter-bean vines planted all along the front where the strings are.

Of course, there's not much mail. My family are naturally the main people in China Grove, and if they prefer to vanish from the face of the earth, for all the mail they get or the mail they write, why, I'm not going to open my mouth.

Some of the folks here in town are taking up for me and some turned against me. I know which is which. There are always people who will quit buying stamps just to get on the right side of Papa-Daddy.

But here I am, and here I'll stay. I want the world to know I'm happy.

And if Stella-Rondo should come to me this minute, on bended knees, and *attempt* to explain the incidents of her life with Mr. Whitaker, I'd simply put my fingers in both my ears and refuse to listen.

(1941)

# Mavis Gallant (b. 1922)

Montreal-born novelist and short story writer Mavis Gallant has acknowledged the influence of James Joyce and Katherine Mansfield on both the style and themes of her short stories. Unlike most of her works, such as the stories in *The Other Paris*, which are set in Europe and often deal with rootless Canadian and American expatriates, "My Heart Is Broken" takes place in a remote construction camp in the Canadian bush. However, like her other stories, it deals with lonely individuals who feel alienated from the life around them. In the account of the short meeting between an older and a younger woman, Gallant's careful depiction of setting and presentation of the two people's emotionally intense dialogue reveals a great deal about their characters, their past lives, and their possible futures.

# MY HEART IS BROKEN

"When that Jean Harlow[1] died," Mrs. Thompson said to Jeannie, "I was on the 83 streetcar with a big, heavy paper parcel in my arms. I hadn't been married for very long, and when I used to visit my mother she'd give me a lot of canned stuff and preserves. I was standing up in the streetcar because nobody'd given me a seat. All the men were unemployed in those days, and they just sat down wherever they happened to be. You wouldn't remember what Montreal was like then. *You* weren't even on earth. To resume what I was saying to you, one of these men sitting down had an American paper — the *Daily News*, I guess it was — and I was sort of leaning over him, and I saw in big print 'JEAN HARLOW DEAD.' You can believe me or not, just as you want to, but that was the most terrible shock I ever had in my life. I never got over it."

Jeannie had nothing to say to that. She lay flat on her back across the bed, with her head toward Mrs. Thompson and her heels just touching the crate that did as a bedside table. Balanced on her flat stomach was an open bottle of coral-pink Cutex nail polish. She held her hands up over her head and with some difficulty applied the brush to the nails of her right hand. Her legs were brown and thin. She wore nothing but shorts and one of her husband's shirts. Her feet were bare.

Mrs. Thompson was the wife of the paymaster in a road-construction camp in northern Quebec. Jeannie's husband was an engineer working on the same project. The road was being pushed through country where nothing had existed until now except rocks and lakes and muskeg. The camp was established between a wild lake and the line of raw dirt that was the road. There were no towns between the camp and the railway spur, sixty miles distant.

Mrs. Thompson, a good deal older than Jeannie, had become her best friend. She was a nice, plain, fat, consoling sort of person, with varicosed legs,

1 American movie star and sex symbol of the 1930s.

shoes unlaced and slit for comfort, blue flannel dressing gown worn at all hours, pudding-bowl haircut, and coarse gray hair. She might have been Jeannie's own mother, or her Auntie Pearl. She rocked her fat self in the rocking chair and went on with what she had to say: "What I was starting off to tell you is you remind me of her, of Jean Harlow. You've got the same teeny mouth, Jeannie, and I think your hair was a whole lot prettier before you started fooling around with it. That peroxide's no good. It splits the ends. I know you're going to tell me it isn't peroxide but something more modern, but the result is the same."

5      Vern's shirt was spotted with coral-pink that had dropped off the brush. Vern wouldn't mind; at least, he wouldn't say that he minded. If he hadn't objected to anything Jeannie did until now, he wouldn't start off by complaining about a shirt. The campsite outside the uncurtained window was silent and dark. The waning moon would not appear until dawn. A passage of thought made Mrs. Thompson say, "Winter soon."

Jeannie moved sharply and caught the bottle of polish before it spilled. Mrs. Thompson was crazy; it wasn't even September.

"Pretty soon," Mrs. Thompson admitted. "Pretty soon. That's a long season up here, but I'm one person doesn't complain. I've been up here or around here every winter of my married life, except for that one winter Pops was occupying Germany."

"I've been up here seventy-two days," said Jeannie, in her soft voice. "Tomorrow makes seventy-three."

"Is that right?" said Mrs. Thompson, jerking the rocker forward, suddenly snappish. "Is that a fact? Well, who asked you to come up here? Who asked you to come and start counting days like you was in some kind of jail? When you got married to Vern, you must of known where he'd be taking you. He told you, didn't he, that he liked road jobs, construction jobs, and that? Did he tell you, or didn't he?"

10      "Oh, he told me," said Jeannie.

"You know what, Jeannie?" said Mrs. Thompson. "If you'd of just listened to me, none of this would have happened. I told you that first day, the day you arrived here in your high-heeled shoes, I said, 'I know this cabin doesn't look much, but all the married men have the same sort of place.' You remember I said that? I said, 'You just get some curtains up and some carpets down and it'll be home.' I took you over and showed you my place, and you said you'd never seen anything so lovely."

"I meant it," said Jeannie. "Your cabin is just lovely. I don't know why, but I never managed to make this place look like yours."

Mrs. Thompson said, "That's plain enough." She looked at the cold grease spattered behind the stove, and the rag of towel over by the sink. "It's partly the experience," she said kindly. She and her husband knew exactly what to take with them when they went on a job, they had been doing it for so many years. They brought boxes for artificial flowers, a brass door knocker, a portable bar decorated with sea shells, a cardboard fireplace that looked real, and an electric fire that sent waves of light rippling over the ceiling and walls. A concealed gramophone played the records they loved and cherished — the good old tunes. They had comic records that dated back to the year 1, and sad soprano records about shipwrecks and broken promises and babies' graves. The first time Jeannie heard one of the funny records, she was scared to death. She was paying a formal call, sitting straight in her chair, with her skirt pulled around her knees. Vern and Pops Thompson were talking about the Army.

"I wish to God I was back," said old Pops.

15 "Don't I?" said Vern. He was fifteen years older than Jeannie and had been through a lot.

At first there were only scratching and whispering noises, and then a mosquito orchestra started to play, and a dwarf's voice came into the room. "Little Johnnie Green, little Sallie Brown," squealed the dwarf, higher and faster than any human ever could. "Spooning in the park with the grass all around."

"Where is he?" Jeannie cried, while the Thompsons screamed with laughter and Vern smiled. The dwarf sang on: "And each little bird in the treetop high / Sang 'Oh you kid!' and winked his eye."

It was a record that had belonged to Pops Thompson's mother. He had been laughing at it all his life. The Thompsons loved living up north and didn't miss cities or company. Their cabin smelled of cocoa and toast. Over their beds were oval photographs of each other as children, and they had some Teddy bears and about a dozen dolls.

Jeannie capped the bottle of polish, taking care not to press it against her wet nails. She sat up with a single movement and set the bottle down on the bedside crate. Then she turned to face Mrs. Thompson. She sat cross-legged, with her hands outspread before her. Her face was serene.

20 "Not an ounce of fat on you," said Mrs. Thompson. "You know something? I'm sorry you're going. I really am. Tomorrow you'll be gone. You know that, don't you? You've been counting days, but you won't have to any more. I guess Vern'll take you back to Montreal. What do you think?"

Jeannie dropped her gaze, and began smoothing wrinkles on the bedspread. She muttered something Mrs. Thompson could not understand.

"Tomorrow you'll be gone," Mrs. Thompson continued. "I know it for a fact. Vern is at this moment getting his pay, and borrowing a jeep from Mr. Sherman, and a Polack driver to take you to the train. He sure is loyal to *you*. You know what I heard Mr. Sherman say? He said to Vern, 'If you want to send her off, Vern, you can always stay,' and Vern said, 'I can't very well do that, Mr. Sherman.' And Mr. Sherman said, 'This is the second time you've had to leave a job on account of her, isn't it?,' and then Mr. Sherman said, 'In my opinion, no man by his own self can rape a girl, so there were either two men or else she's invented the whole story.' Then he said, 'Vern, you're either a saint or a damn fool.' That was all I heard. I came straight over here, Jeannie, because I thought you might be needing me." Mrs. Thompson waited to hear she was needed. She stopped rocking and sat with her feet flat and wide apart. She struck her knees with her open palms and cried, "I *told* you to keep away from the men. I told you it would make trouble, all that being cute and dancing around. I said to you, I remember saying it, I said nothing makes trouble faster in a place like this than a grown woman behaving like a little girl. Don't you remember?"

"I only went out for a walk," said Jeannie. "Nobody'll believe me, but that's all. I went down the road for a walk."

"In high heels?" said Mrs. Thompson. "With a purse on your arm, and a hat on your head? You don't go taking a walk in the bush that way. There's no place to walk *to*. Where'd you think you were going? I could smell Evening in Paris a quarter mile away."

"There's no place to go," said Jeannie, "but what else is there to do? I just felt like dressing up and going out."

"You could have cleaned up your home a bit," said Mrs. Thompson. "There was always that to do. Just look at that sink. That basket of ironing's been under the bed since July. I know it gets boring around here, but you had the best of it. You had the summer. In winter it gets dark around three o'clock. Then the wives have a right to go crazy. I knew one used to sleep the clock around. When her Nembutal[2] ran out, she took about a hundred aspirin. I knew another learned to distill her own liquor, just to kill time. Sometimes the men get so's they don't like the life, and that's death for the wives. But here you had a nice summer, and Vern liked the life."

"He likes it better than anything," said Jeannie. "He liked the Army, but this was his favorite life after that."

"There," said Mrs. Thompson, "you had every reason to be happy. What'd you do if he sent you off alone, now, like Mr. Sherman advised? You'd be alone and you'd have to work. Women don't know when they're well off. Here you've got a good, sensible husband working for you and you don't appreciate it. You have to go and do a terrible thing."

"I only went for a walk," said Jeannie. "That's all I did."

"It's possible," said Mrs. Thompson, "but it's a terrible thing. It's about the worst thing that's ever happened around here. I don't know why you let it happen. A woman can always defend what's precious, even if she's attacked. I hope you remembered to think about bacteria."

"What d'you mean?"

"I mean Javel,[3] or something."

Jeannie looked uncomprehending and then shook her head.

"I wonder what it must be like," said Mrs. Thompson after a time, looking at the dark window. "I mean, think of Berlin and them Russians and all. Think of some disgusting fellow you don't know. Never said hello to, even. Some girls ask for it, though. You can't always blame the man. The man loses his job, his wife if he's got one, everything, all because of a silly girl."

Jeannie frowned, absently. She pressed her nails together, testing the polish. She licked her lips and said, "I was more beaten up, Mrs. Thompson. It wasn't exactly what you think. It was only afterwards I thought to myself, Why, I was raped and everything."

Mrs. Thompson gasped, hearing the word from Jeannie. She said, "Have you got any marks?"

"On my arms. That's why I'm wearing this shirt. The first thing I did was change my clothes."

2 brand of sleeping pill. 3 bleach solution.

Mrs. Thompson thought this over, and went on to another thing: "Do you ever think about your mother?"

"Sure."

40    "Do you pray? If this goes on at nineteen —"

"I'm twenty."

"— what'll you be by the time you're thirty? You've already got a terrible, terrible memory to haunt you all your life."

"I already can't remember it," said Jeannie. "Afterwards I started walking back to camp, but I was walking the wrong way. I met Mr. Sherman. The back of his car was full of coffee, flour, all that. I guess he'd been picking up supplies. He said, 'Well, get in.' He didn't ask any questions at first. I couldn't talk anyway."

"Shock," said Mrs. Thompson wisely.

45    "You know, I'd have to see it happening to know what happened. All I remember is that first we were only talking..."

"You and Mr. Sherman?"

"No, no, before. When I was taking my walk."

"Don't say who it was," said Mrs. Thompson. "We don't any of us need to know."

"We were just talking, and he got sore all of a sudden and grabbed my arm."

50    "Don't say the name!" Mrs. Thompson cried.

"Like when I was little, there was this Lana Turner movie. She had two twins. She was just there and then a nurse brought her in the two twins. I hadn't been married or anything, and I didn't know anything, and I used to think if I just kept on seeing the movie I'd know how she got the two twins, you know, and I went, oh, I must have seen it six times, the movie, but in the end I never knew any more. They just brought her the two twins."

Mrs. Thompson sat quite still, trying to make sense of this. "Taking advantage of a woman is a criminal offense," she observed. "I heard Mr. Sherman say another thing, Jeannie. He said, 'If your wife wants to press a charge and talk to some lawyer, let me tell you,' he said, 'you'll never work again anywhere,' he said. Vern said, 'I know that, Mr. Sherman.' And Mr. Sherman said, 'Let me tell you, if any reporters or any investigators start coming around here, they'll get their ... they'll never ...' Oh, he was mad. And Vern said, 'I came over to tell you I was quitting, Mr. Sherman.'" Mrs. Thompson had been acting this with spirit, using a quiet voice when she spoke for Vern and a blustering tone for Mr. Sherman. In her own voice, she said, "If you're wondering how I came to hear all this, I was strolling by Mr. Sherman's office window — his bungalow, that is. I had Maureen out in her pram." Maureen was the Thompsons' youngest doll.

Jeannie might not have been listening. She started to tell something else: "You know, where we were before, on Vern's last job, we weren't in a camp. He was away a lot, and he left me in Amos, in a hotel. I liked it. Amos isn't all that big, but it's better than here. There was this German in the hotel. He was selling cars. He'd drive me around if I wanted to go to a movie or anything. Vern didn't like him, so we left. It wasn't anybody's fault."

"So he's given up two jobs," said Mrs. Thompson. "One because he couldn't leave you alone, and now this one. Two jobs, and you haven't been married five months. Why should another man be thrown out of work? We don't need to know a thing. I'll be sorry if it was Jimmy Quinn," she went on slowly. "I like that boy. Don't say the name, dear. There's Evans. Susini. Palmer. But it might have been anybody, because you had them all on the boil. So it might have been Jimmy Quinn — let's say — and it could have been anyone else, too. Well, now let's hope they can get their minds back on the job."

55     "I thought they all liked me," said Jeannie sadly. "I get along with people. Vern never fights with me."

"Vern never fights with anyone. But he ought to have thrashed *you*."

"If he . . . you know. I won't say the name. If he'd liked me, I wouldn't have minded. If he'd been friendly. I really mean that. I wouldn't have gone wandering up the road, making all this fuss."

"Jeannie," said Mrs. Thompson, "you don't even know what you're saying."

"He could at least have liked me," said Jeannie. "He wasn't even friendly. It's the first time in my life somebody hasn't liked me. My heart is broken, Mrs. Thompson. My heart is just broken."

60     She has to cry, Mrs. Thompson thought. She has to have it out. She rocked slowly, tapping her foot, trying to remember how she'd felt about things when she was twenty, wondering if her heart had ever been broken, too.

(1961)

# Margaret Laurence (1926–1987)

Margaret Laurence's best-known novels and short stories are set in Manawaka, a fictionalized version of her home town of Neepawa, Manitoba. However, her first novel, *This Side Jordan* (1960), grew out of her experiences living in Africa during the 1950s and reflects her life-long concern with the repression of Native peoples. Later, in such novels as *The Stone Angel* (1964) and *A Jest of God* (1966), she depicted the social conflicts of the largely Scots-Presbyterian Manitoba community and the struggles of the women who grew up in it. "The Loons" is from *A Bird in the House* (1970), a collection of stories in which the portrayal of the maturation of Vanessa MacLeod is what Laurence called "fictionalized biography." In this story, the narrator examines the nature of her relationship to a Métis friend after the young woman's death.

## THE LOONS

Just below Manawaka, where the Wachakwa River ran brown and noisy over the pebbles, the scrub oak and grey-green willow and chokecherry bushes grew in a dense thicket. In a clearing at the centre of the thicket stood the Tonnerre family's shack. The basis of this dwelling was a small square cabin made of poplar poles and chinked with mud, which had been built by Jules Tonnerre some fifty years before, when he came back from Batoche[1] with a bullet in his thigh, the year that Riel was hung and the voices of the Metis entered their long silence.[2] Jules had only intended to stay the winter in the Wachakwa Valley, but the family was still there in the thirties, when I was a child. As the Tonnerres had increased, their settlement had been added to, until the clearing at the foot of the town hill was a chaos of lean-tos, wooden packing cases, warped lumber, discarded car tyres, ramshackle chicken coops, tangled strands of barbed wire and rusty tin cans.

The Tonnerres were French halfbreeds, and among themselves they spoke a *patois* that was neither Cree nor French. Their English was broken and full of obscenities. They did not belong among the Cree of the Galloping Mountain reservation, further north, and they did not belong among the Scots-Irish and Ukrainians of Manawaka, either. They were, as my Grandmother MacLeod would have put it, neither flesh, fowl, or good salt herring. When their men were not working at odd jobs or as section hands on the C.P.R., they lived on relief. In the summers, one of the Tonnerre youngsters, with a face that seemed totally unfamiliar with laughter, would knock at the doors of the town's brick houses and offer for sale a lard-pail full of bruised wild strawberries, and if he got as much as a quarter he would grab the coin and run before the customer had time to change her mind. Sometimes old Jules, or his son Lazarus, would get mixed up in a Saturday-night brawl, and would hit out at whoever was nearest, or howl drunkenly among the offended shoppers on

---

1 near Prince Albert, Saskatchewan; in 1855, the site of a major battle in the North-West Rebellion.
2 Louis Riel was the leader of the Métis people, who were of mixed white and Native blood.

Main Street, and then the Mountie would put them for the night in the barred cell underneath the Court House, and the next morning they would be quiet again.

Piquette Tonnerre, the daughter of Lazarus, was in my class at school. She was older than I, but she had failed several grades, perhaps because her attendance had always been sporadic and her interest in schoolwork negligible. Part of the reason she had missed a lot of school was that she had had tuberculosis of the bone, and had once spent many months in hospital. I knew this because my father was the doctor who had looked after her. Her sickness was almost the only thing I knew about her, however. Otherwise, she existed for me only as a vaguely embarrassing presence, with her hoarse voice and her clumsy limping walk and her grimy cotton dresses that were always miles too long. I was neither friendly nor unfriendly towards her. She dwelt and moved somewhere within my scope of vision, but I did not actually notice her very much until that peculiar summer when I was eleven.

"I don't know what to do about that kid," my father said at dinner one evening. "Piquette Tonnerre, I mean. The damn bone's flared up again. I've had her in hospital for quite a while now, and it's under control all right, but I hate like the dickens to send her home again."

5       "Couldn't you explain to her mother that she has to rest a lot?" my mother said.

"The mother's not there," my father replied. "She took off a few years back. Can't say I blame her. Piquette cooks for them, and she says Lazarus would never do anything for himself as long as she's there. Anyway, I don't think she'd take much care of herself, once she got back. She's only thirteen, after all. Beth, I was thinking — what about taking her up to Diamond Lake with us this summer? A couple of months rest would give that bone a much better chance."

My mother looked stunned.

"But Ewen — what about Roddie and Vanessa?"

"She's not contagious," my father said. "And it would be company for Vanessa."

10      "Oh dear," my mother said in distress, "I'll bet anything she has nits in her hair."

"For Pete's sake," my father said crossly, "do you think Matron would let her stay in the hospital for all this time like that? Don't be silly, Beth."

Grandmother MacLeod, her delicately featured face as rigid as a cameo, now brought her mauve-veined hands together as though she were about to begin a prayer.

"Ewen, if that half-breed youngster comes along to Diamond Lake, I'm not going," she announced. "I'll go to Morag's for the summer."

I had trouble in stifling my urge to laugh, for my mother brightened visibly and quickly tried to hide it. If it came to a choice between Grandmother MacLeod and Piquette, Piquette would win hands down, nits or not.

15      "It might be quite nice for you, at that," she mused. "You haven't seen Morag for over a year, and you might enjoy being in the city for a while. Well, Ewen dear, you do what you think best. If you think it would do Piquette some good, then we'll be glad to have her, as long as she behaves herself."

So it happened that several weeks later, when we all piled into my father's old Nash, surrounded by suitcases and boxes of provisions and toys for my ten-month-old brother, Piquette was with us and Grandmother MacLeod, miraculously, was not. My father would only be staying at the cottage for a couple of weeks, for he had to get back to his practice, but the rest of us would stay at Diamond Lake until the end of August.

Our cottage was not named, as many were, "Dew Drop Inn" or "Bide-a-Wee," or "Bonnie Doon." The sign on the roadway bore in austere letters only our name, MacLeod. It was not a large cottage, but it was on the lakefront. You could look out the windows and see, through the filigree of the spruce trees, the water glistening greenly as the sun caught it. All around the cottage were ferns, and sharp-branched raspberry bushes, and moss that had grown over fallen tree trunks. If you looked carefully among the weeds and grass, you could find wild strawberry plants which were in white flower now and in another month would bear fruit, the fragrant globes hanging like miniature scarlet lanterns on the thin hairy stems. The two grey squirrels were still there, gossiping at us from the tall spruce beside the cottage, and by the end of the summer they would again be tame enough to take pieces of crust from my hands. The broad moose antlers that hung above the back door were a little more bleached and fissured after the winter, but otherwise everything was the same. I raced joyfully around my kingdom, greeting all the places I had not seen for a year. My brother, Roderick, who had not been born when we were here last summer, sat on the car rug in the sunshine and examined a brown spruce cone, meticulously turning it round and round in his small and curious hands. My mother and father toted the luggage from car to cottage, exclaiming over how well the place had wintered, no broken windows, thank goodness, no apparent damage from storm-felled branches or snow.

Only after I had finished looking around did I notice Piquette. She was sitting on the swing, her lame leg held stiffly out, and her other foot scuffing the ground as she swung slowly back and forth. Her long hair hung black and straight around her shoulders, and her broad coarse-featured face bore no expression — it was blank, as though she no longer dwelt within her own skull, as though she had gone elsewhere. I approached her very hesitantly.

"Want to come and play?"

Piquette looked at me with a sudden flash of scorn.

"I ain't a kid," she said.

Wounded, I stamped angrily away, swearing I would not speak to her for the rest of the summer. In the days that followed, however, Piquette began to interest me, and I began to want to interest her. My reasons did not appear bizarre to me. Unlikely as it may seem, I had only just realised that the Tonnerre family, whom I had always heard called half-breeds, were actually Indians, or as near as made no difference. My acquaintance with Indians was not extensive. I did not remember ever having seen a real Indian, and my new awareness that Piquette sprang from the people of Big Bear and Poundmaker,[3] of Tecumseh,[4] of the Iroquois who had eaten Father Brebeuf's heart[5] — all this gave her an instant attraction in my eyes. I was a devoted reader of Pauline Johnson[6] at this age, and sometimes would orate aloud and in an exalted voice, *West Wind, blow from your prairie nest; Blow from the mountains, blow from the west—* and so on. It seemed to me that Piquette must be in some way a daughter of the forest, a kind of junior prophetess of the wilds, who might impart to me, if I took the right approach, some of the secrets which she undoubtedly knew — where the whippoorwill made her nest, how the coyote reared her young, or whatever it was that it said in Hiawatha.

I set about gaining Piquette's trust. She was not allowed to go swimming, with her bad leg, but I managed to lure her down to the beach — or rather, she came because there was nothing else to do. The water was always icy, for the lake was fed by springs, but I swam like a dog, thrashing my arms and legs around at such speed and with such an output of energy that I never grew cold. Finally, when I had had enough, I came out and sat beside Piquette on the sand. When she saw me approaching, her hand squashed flat the sand castle she had been building, and she looked at me sullenly, without speaking.

"Do you like this place?" I asked, after a while, intending to lead on from there into the question of forest lore.

25 Piquette shrugged. "It's okay. Good as anywhere."

"I love it," I said. "We come here every summer."

"So what?" Her voice was distant, and I glanced at her uncertainly, wondering what I could have said wrong.

"Do you want to come for a walk?" I asked her. "We wouldn't need to go far. If you walk just around the point there, you come to a bay where great big reeds grow in the water, and all kinds of fish hang around there. Want to? Come on."

She shook her head.

30 "Your dad said I ain't supposed to do no more walking than I got to."

I tried another line.

"I bet you know a lot about the woods and all that, eh?" I began respectfully.

Piquette looked at me from her large dark unsmiling eyes.

"I don't know what in hell you're talkin' about," she replied. "You nuts or somethin'? If you mean where my old man, and me, and all them live, you better shut up, by Jesus, you hear?"

35 I was startled and my feelings were hurt, but I had a kind of dogged perseverance. I ignored her rebuff.

"You know something, Piquette? There's loons here, on this lake. You can see their nests just up the shore there, behind those logs. At night, you can hear them even from the cottage, but it's better to listen from the beach. My dad says we should listen and try to remember how they sound, because in a few years when more cottages are built at Diamond Lake and more people come in, the loons will go away."

Piquette was picking up stones and snail shells and then dropping them again.

"Who gives a good goddamn?" she said.

6 early-twentieth-century Native writer.

It became increasingly obvious that, as an Indian, Piquette was a dead loss. That evening I went out by myself, scrambling through the bushes that overhung the steep path, my feet slipping on the fallen spruce needles that covered the ground. When I reached the shore, I walked along the firm damp sand to the small pier that my father had built, and sat down there. I heard someone else crashing through the undergrowth and the bracken, and for a moment I thought Piquette had changed her mind, but it turned out to be my father. He sat beside me on the pier and we waited, without speaking.

40      At night the lake was like black glass with a streak of amber which was the path of the moon. All around, the spruce trees grew tall and close-set, branches blackly sharp against the sky, which was lightened by a cold flickering of stars. Then the loons began their calling. They rose like phantom birds from the nests on the shore, and flew out onto the dark still surface of the water.

No one can ever describe that ululating sound, the crying of the loons, and no one who has heard it can ever forget it. Plaintive, and yet with a quality of chilling mockery, those voices belonged to a world separated by aeons from our neat world of summer cottages and the lighted lamps of home.

"They must have sounded just like that," my father remarked, "before any person ever set foot here."

Then he laughed. "You could say the same, of course, about sparrows, or chipmunks, but somehow it only strikes you that way with the loons."

"I know," I said.

45      Neither of us suspected that this would be the last time we would ever sit here together on the shore, listening. We stayed for perhaps half an hour, and then we went back to the cottage. My mother was reading beside the fireplace. Piquette was looking at the burning birch log, and not doing anything.

"You should have come along," I said, although in fact I was glad she had not.

"Not me," Piquette said. "You wouldn' catch me walkin' way down there jus' for a bunch of squawkin' birds."

Piquette and I remained ill at ease with one another. I felt I had somehow failed my father, but I did not know what was the matter, nor why she would not or could not respond when I suggested exploring the woods or playing house. I thought it was probably her slow and difficult walking that held her back. She stayed most of the time in the cottage with my mother, helping her with the dishes or with Roddie, but hardly ever talking. Then the Duncans arrived at their cottage, and I spent my days with Mavis, who was my best friend. I could not reach Piquette at all, and I soon lost interest in trying. But all that summer she remained as both a reproach and a mystery to me.

That winter my father died of pneumonia, after less than a week's illness. For some time I saw nothing around me, being completely immersed in my own pain and my mother's. When I looked outward once more, I scarcely noticed that Piquette Tonnerre was no longer at school. I do not remember seeing her at all until four years later, one Saturday night when Mavis and I were having Cokes in the Regal Café. The jukebox was booming like tuneful thunder, and beside it, leaning lightly on its chrome and its rainbow glass, was a girl.

50      Piquette must have been seventeen then, although she looked about twenty. I stared at her, astounded that anyone could have changed so much. Her

face, so stolid and expressionless before, was animated now with a gaiety that was almost violent. She laughed and talked very loudly with the boys around her. Her lipstick was bright carmine, and her hair was cut short and frizzily permed. She had not been pretty as a child, and she was not pretty now, for her features were still heavy and blunt. But her dark and slightly slanted eyes were beautiful, and her skin-tight skirt and orange sweater displayed to enviable advantage a soft and slender body.

She saw me, and walked over. She teetered a little, but it was not due to her once-tubercular leg, for her limp was almost gone.

"Hi, Vanessa." Her voice still had the same hoarseness. "Long time no see, eh?"

"Hi," I said. "Where've you been keeping yourself, Piquette?"

"Oh, I been around," she said. "I been away almost two years now. Been all over the place — Winnipeg, Regina, Saskatoon. Jesus, what I could tell you! I come back this summer, but I ain't stayin'. You kids goin' to the dance?"

55 "No," I said abruptly, for this was a sore point with me. I was fifteen, and thought I was old enough to go to the Saturday-night dances at the Flamingo. My mother, however, thought otherwise.

"Y'oughta come," Piquette said. "I never miss one. It's just about the on'y thing in this jerkwater town that's any fun. Boy, you couldn' catch me stayin' here. I don' give a shit about this place. It stinks."

She sat down beside me, and I caught the harsh over-sweetness of her perfume.

"Listen, you wanna know something, Vanessa?" she confided, her voice only slightly blurred. "Your dad was the only person in Manawaka that ever done anything good to me."

I nodded speechlessly. I was certain she was speaking the truth. I knew a little more than I had that summer at Diamond Lake, but I could not reach her now any more than I had then. I was ashamed, ashamed of my own timidity, the frightened tendency to look the other way. Yet I felt no real warmth towards her — I only felt that I ought to, because of that distant summer and because my father had hoped she would be company for me, or perhaps that I would be for her, but it had not happened that way. At this moment, meeting her again, I had to admit that she repelled and embarrassed me, and I could not help despising the self-pity in her voice. I wished she would go away. I did not want to see her. I did not know what to say to her. It seemed that we had nothing to say to one another.

60 "I'll tell you something else," Piquette went on. "All the old bitches an' biddies in this town will sure be surprised. I'm gettin' married this fall — my boyfriend, he's an English fella, works in the stockyards in the city there, a very tall guy, got blond wavy hair. Gee, is he ever handsome. Got this real classy name. Alvin Gerald Cummings — some handle, eh? They call him Al."

For the merest instant, then, I saw her. I really did see her, for the first and only time in all the years we had both lived in the same town. Her defiant face, momentarily, became unguarded and unmasked, and in her eyes there was a terrifying hope.

"Gee, Piquette —" I burst out awkwardly, "that's swell. That's really wonderful. Congratulations — good luck — I hope you'll be happy —"

As I mouthed the conventional phrases, I could only guess how great her need must have been, that she had been forced to seek the very things she so bitterly rejected.

When I was eighteen, I left Manawaka and went away to college. At the end of my first year, I came back home for the summer. I spent the first few days in talking non-stop with my mother, as we exchanged all the news that somehow had not found its way into letters — what had happened in my life and what had happened here in Manawaka while I was away. My mother searched her memory for events that concerned people I knew.

65    "Did I ever write you about Piquette Tonnerre, Vanessa?" she asked one morning.

"No, I don't think so," I replied. "Last I heard of her, she was going to marry some guy in the city. Is she still there?"

My mother looked perturbed, and it was a moment before she spoke, as though she did not know how to express what she had to tell and wished she did not need to try.

"She's dead," she said at last. Then, as I stared at her, "Oh, Vanessa, when it happened, I couldn't help thinking of her as she was that summer — so sullen and gauche and badly dressed. I couldn't help wondering if we could have done something more at that time — but what could we do? She used to be around in the cottage there with me all day, and honestly, it was all I could do to get a word out of her. She didn't even talk to your father very much, although I think she liked him, in her way."

"What happened?" I asked.

70    "Either her husband left her, or she left him," my mother said. "I don't know which. Anyway, she came back here with two youngsters, both only babies — they must have been born very close together. She kept house, I guess, for Lazarus and her brothers, down in the valley there, in the old Tonnerre place. I used to see her on the street sometimes, but she never spoke to me. She'd put on an awful lot of weight, and she looked a mess, to tell you the truth, a real slattern, dressed any old how. She was up in court a couple of times — drunk and disorderly, of course. One Saturday night last winter, during the coldest weather, Piquette was alone in the shack with the children. The Tonnerres made home brew all the time, so I've heard, and Lazarus said later she'd been drinking most of the day when he and the boys went out that evening. They had an old woodstove there — you know the kind, with exposed pipes. The shack caught fire. Piquette didn't get out, and neither did the children."

I did not say anything. As so often with Piquette, there did not seem to be anything to say. There was a kind of silence around the image in my mind of the fire and the snow, and I wished I could put from my memory the look that I had seen once in Piquette's eyes.

I went up to Diamond Lake for a few days that summer, with Mavis and her family. The MacLeod cottage had been sold after my father's death, and I did not even go to look at it, not wanting to witness my long-ago kingdom possessed now by strangers. But one evening I went down to the shore by myself.

The small pier which my father had built was gone, and in its place there was a large and solid pier built by the government, for Galloping Mountain was now a national park, and Diamond Lake had been re-named Lake Wapakata, for it was felt that an Indian name would have a greater appeal to tourists. The one store had become several dozen, and the settlement had all the attributes of a flourishing resort — hotels, a dance-hall, cafés with neon signs, the penetrating odours of potato chips and hot dogs.

I sat on the government pier and looked out across the water. At night the lake at least was the same as it had always been, darkly shining and bearing within its black glass the streak of amber that was the path of the moon. There was no wind that evening, and everything was quiet all around me. It seemed too quiet, and then I realized that the loons were no longer here. I listened for some time, to make sure, but never once did I hear that long-drawn call, half mocking and half plaintive, spearing through the stillness across the lake.

75    I did not know what had happened to the birds. Perhaps they had gone away to some far place of belonging. Perhaps they had been unable to find such a place, and had simply died out, having ceased to care any longer whether they lived or not.

I remembered how Piquette had scorned to come along, when my father and I sat there and listened to the lake birds. It seemed to me now that in some unconscious and totally unrecognised way, Piquette might have been the only one, after all, who had heard the crying of the loons.

(1966)

# Alice Munro (b. 1931)

Born in Wingham, Ontario, Alice Munro began writing short stories in high school but did not publish her first collection, *Dance of the Happy Shades*, winner of the Governor General's Award for fiction, until 1968. Like the American writer Eudora Welty, whose work she admires, Munro is essentially a regional writer, portraying girls and women from small-town western Ontario confronting the various stages of their lives and the nature of their relationships with other people. She has been praised for her precise depiction of the events and settings that are used to reveal aspects of the personalities of her characters. In "Dulse," a middle-aged, divorced woman vacationing in New Brunswick considers the failure of her most recent relationship in part by making hypotheses about the lives of the men staying at the same guest house.

# DULSE

At the end of the summer Lydia took a boat to an island off the southern coast of New Brunswick, where she was going to stay overnight. She had just a few days left until she had to be back in Ontario. She worked as an editor, for a publisher in Toronto. She was also a poet, but she did not refer to that unless it was something people knew already. For the past eighteen months she had been living with a man in Kingston. As far as she could see, that was over.

She had noticed something about herself, on this trip to the Maritimes. It was that people were no longer so interested in getting to know her. It wasn't that she had created such a stir, before, but something had been there that she could rely on. She was forty-five, and had been divorced for nine years. Her two children had started on their own lives, though there were still retreats and confusions. She hadn't got fatter or thinner, her looks had not deteriorated in any alarming way, but nevertheless she had stopped being one sort of woman and had become another, and she had noticed it on this trip. She was not surprised because she was in a new, strange condition at the time. She made efforts, one after the other. She set little blocks on top of one another and she had a day. Sometimes she almost could not do this. At other times the very deliberateness, the seeming arbitrariness, of what she was doing, the way she was living, exhilarated her.

She found a guest-house overlooking the docks, with their stacks of lobster traps, and the few scattered stores and houses that made up the village. A woman of about her own age was cooking dinner. This woman took her to a cheap, old-fashioned room upstairs. There were no other guests around, though the room next door was open and seemed to be occupied, perhaps by a child. Whoever it was had left several comic books on the floor beside the bed.

She went for a walk up the steep lane behind the guest-house. She occupied herself by naming shrubs and weeds. The goldenrod and wild aster were in bloom, and Japanese boxwood, a rarity in Ontario, seemed commonplace here. The grass was long and coarse and the trees were small. The Atlantic coast, which she had never seen before, was just as she had expected it to be. The bending grass; the bare houses; the sea light. She started wondering what it would be like to live there, whether the houses were still cheap or if people from the outside had started to buy them up. Often on this trip she had busied herself with calculations of this kind, and also with ideas of how she could make a living in some new way, cut off from everything she had done before. She did not think of making a living writing poetry, not only because the income would be so low but because she thought, as she had thought innumerable times in her life, that probably she would not write any more poems. She was thinking that she could not cook well enough to do it for pay but she could clean. There was at least one other guest-house besides the one where she was staying, and she had seen a sign advertising a motel. How many hours' cleaning could she get if she cleaned all three places, and how much an hour did cleaning pay?

5      There were four small tables in the dining room, but only one man was sitting there, drinking tomato juice. He did not look at her. A man who was probably the husband of the woman she had met earlier came in from the kitchen. He had a grayish-blond beard, and a downcast look. He asked Lydia's name and took her to the table where the man was sitting. The man stood up, stiffly, and Lydia was introduced. The man's name was Mr. Stanley and Lydia took him to be about sixty. Politely, he asked her to sit down.

Three men in work clothes came in and sat down at another table. They were not noisy in any self-important or offensive way, but just coming in and disposing themselves around the table, they created an enjoyable commotion. That is, they enjoyed it, and looked as if they expected others to. Mr. Stanley bowed in their direction. It really was a little bow, not just a nod of the head. He said good evening. They asked him what there was for supper, and he said he believed it was scallops, with pumpkin pie for dessert.

"These gentlemen work for the New Brunswick Telephone Company," he said to Lydia. "They are laying a cable to one of the smaller islands, and they stay here during the week."

He was older than she had thought at first. It did not show in his voice, which was precise and American, or in the movements of his hands, but in his small, separate, brownish teeth, and in his eyes, which had a delicate milky skin over the light-brown iris.

The husband brought their food, and spoke to the workmen. He was an efficient waiter, but rather stiff and remote, rather like a sleep-walker, in fact, as if he did not perform this job in his real life. The vegetables were served in large bowls, from which they helped themselves. Lydia was glad to see so much food: broccoli, mashed turnips, potatoes, corn. The American took small helpings of everything and began to eat in a very deliberate way, giving the impression that the order in which he lifted forkfuls of food to his mouth was not haphazard, that there was a reason for the turnip to follow the potatoes, and for the deep-fried scallops, which were not large, to be cut neatly in half. He looked up a couple of times as if he thought of saying something, but he did not do it. The workmen were quiet now, too, laying into the food.

10      Mr. Stanley spoke at last. He said, "Are you familiar with the writer Willa Cather?"[1]

1 early-twentieth-century American novelist noted for her portrayals of relationships between female characters.

"Yes." Lydia was startled, because she had not seen anybody reading a book for the past two weeks; she had not even noticed any paperback racks.

"Do you know, then, that she spent every summer here?"

"Here?"

"On this island. She had her summer home here. Not more than a mile away from where we are sitting now. She came here for eighteen years, and she wrote many of her books here. She wrote in a room that had a view of the sea, but now the trees have grown up and blocked it. She was with her great friend, Edith Lewis. Have you read *A Lost Lady*?"[2]

15          Lydia said that she had.

"It is my favorite of all her books. She wrote it here. At least, she wrote a great part of it here."

Lydia was aware of the workmen listening, although they did not glance up from their food. She felt that even without looking at Mr. Stanley or each other they might manage to communicate an indulgent contempt. She thought she did not care whether or not she was included in this contempt, but perhaps it was for that reason that she did not find anything much to say about Willa Cather, or tell Mr. Stanley that she worked for a publisher, let alone that she was any sort of writer herself. Or it could have been just that Mr. Stanley did not give her much of a chance.

"I have been her admirer for over sixty years," he said. He paused, holding his knife and fork over his plate. "I read and reread her, and my admiration grows. It simply grows. There are people here who remember her. Tonight, I am going to see a woman, a woman who knew Willa, and had conversations with her. She is eighty-eight years old but they say she has not forgotten. The people here are beginning to learn of my interest and they will remember someone like this and put me in touch.

"It is a great delight to me," he said solemnly.

20          All the time he was talking, Lydia was trying to think what his conversational style reminded her of. It didn't remind her of any special person, though she might have had one or two teachers at college who talked like that. What it made her think of was a time when a few people, just a few people, had never concerned themselves with being democratic, or ingratiating, in their speech; they spoke in formal, well-thought-out, slightly self-congratulating sentences, though they lived in a country where their formality, their pedantry, could bring them nothing but mockery. No, that was not the whole truth. It brought mockery, and an uncomfortable admiration. What he made Lydia think of, really, was the old-fashioned culture of provincial cities long ago (something she of course had never known, but sensed from books); the high-mindedness, the propriety; hard plush concert seats and hushed libraries. And his adoration of the chosen writer was of a piece with this; it was just as out-of-date as his speech. She thought that he could not be a teacher; such worship was not in style for teachers, even of his age.

"Do you teach literature?"

"No. Oh, no. I have not had that privilege. No. I have not even studied literature. I went to work when I was sixteen. In my day there was not so much choice. I have worked on newspapers."

2 1931 Willa Cather novel about life in seventeenth-century Quebec.

She thought of some absurdly discreet and conservative New England paper with a fusty prose style.

"Oh. Which paper?" she said, then realized her inquisitiveness must seem quite rude, to anyone so circumspect.

25 "Not a paper you would have heard of. Just the daily paper of an industrial town. Other papers in the earlier years. That was my life."

"And now, would you like to do a book on Willa Cather?" This question seemed not so out of place to her, because she was always talking to people who wanted to do books about something.

"No," he said austerely. "My eyes do not permit me to do any reading or writing beyond what is necessary."

That was why he was so deliberate about his eating.

"No," he went on, "I don't say that at one time I might not have thought of that, doing a book on Willa. I would have written something just about her life here on the island. Biographies have been done, but not so much on that phase of her life. Now I have given up the idea. I do my investigating just for my own pleasure. I take a camp chair up there, so I can sit underneath the window where she wrote and looked at the sea. There is never anybody there."

30 "It isn't being kept up? It isn't any sort of memorial?"

"Oh, no indeed. It isn't kept up at all. The people here, you know, while they were very impressed with Willa, and some of them recognized her genius — I mean the genius of her personality, for they would not be able to recognize the genius of her work — others of them thought her unfriendly and did not like her. They took offense because she was unsociable, as she had to be, to do her writing."

"It could be a project," Lydia said. "Perhaps they could get some money from the government. The Canadian government and the Americans too. They could preserve the house."

"Well, that isn't for me to say." He smiled; he shook his head. "I don't think so. No."

He did not want any other worshippers coming to disturb him in his camp chair. She should have known that. What would this private pilgrimage of his be worth if other people got into the act, and signs were put up, leaflets printed; if this guest-house, which was now called Sea View, had to be renamed Shadows on the Rock? He would let the house fall down and the grass grow over it, sooner than see that.

35 After Lydia's last attempt to call Duncan, the man she had been living with in Kingston, she had walked along the street in Toronto, knowing that she had to get to the bank, she had to buy some food, she had to get on the subway. She had to remember directions, and the order in which to do things: to open her checkbook, to move forward when it was her turn in line, to choose one kind of bread over another, to drop a token in the slot. These seemed to be the most difficult things she had ever done. She had immense difficulty reading the names of the subway stations, and getting off at the right one, so that she could go to the apartment where she was staying. She would have found it hard to describe this difficulty. She knew perfectly well which was the right stop,

she knew which stop it came after; she knew where she was. But she could not make the connection between herself and things outside herself, so that getting up and leaving the car, going up the steps, going along the street, all seemed to involve a bizarre effort. She thought afterwards that she had been seized up, as machines are said to be. Even at the time she had an image of herself. She saw herself as something like an egg carton, hollowed out in back.

When she reached the apartment she sat down on a chair in the hall. She sat for an hour or so, then she went to the bathroom, undressed, put on her nightgown, and got into bed. In bed she felt triumph and relief, that she had managed all the difficulties and got herself to where she was supposed to be and would not have to remember anything more.

She didn't feel at all like committing suicide. She couldn't have managed the implements, or aids, she couldn't even have thought which to use. It amazed her to think that she had chosen the loaf of bread and the cheese, which were now lying on the floor in the hall. How had she imagined she was going to chew and swallow them?

After dinner, Lydia sat out on the verandah with the woman who had cooked the meal. The woman's husband did the cleaning up.

"Well, of course we have a dishwasher," the woman said. "We have two freezers and an oversize refrigerator. You have to make an investment. You get the crews staying with you, you have to feed them. This place soaks up money like a sponge. We're going to put in a swimming pool next year. We need more attractions. You have to run to stay in the same place. People think what an easy nice life. Boy."

She had a strong, lined face, and long straight hair. She wore jeans and an embroidered smock and a man's sweater.

"Ten years ago I was living in a commune in the States. Now I'm here. I work sometimes eighteen hours a day. I have to pack the crew's lunch yet tonight. I cook and bake, cook and bake. John does the rest."

"Do you have someone to clean?"

"We can't afford to hire anybody. John does it. He does the laundry — everything. We had to buy a mangle for the sheets. We had to put in a new furnace. We got a bank loan. I thought that was funny, because I used to be married to a bank manager. I left him."

"I'm on my own now, too."

"Are you? You can't be on your own forever. I met John, and he was in the same boat."

"I was living with a man in Kingston, in Ontario."

"Were you? John and I are extremely happy. He used to be a minister. But when I met him he was doing carpentry. We both had sort of dropped out. Did you talk to Mr. Stanley?"

"Yes."

"Had you ever heard of Willa Cather?"

"Yes."

"That'd make him happy. I don't read hardly at all, it doesn't mean anything to me. I'm a visual person. But I think he's a wonderful character, old Mr. Stanley. He's a real old scholar."

"Has he been coming here for a long time?"

"No, he hasn't. This is just his third year. He says he's wanted to come here all his life. But he couldn't. He had to wait till some relative died, that he was looking after. Not a wife. A brother maybe. Anyway he had to wait. How old do you think he is?"

"Seventy? Seventy-five?"

"That man is eighty-one. Isn't that amazing? I really admire people like that. I really do. I admire people that keep going."

"The man I was living with — that is, the man I used to live with, in Kingston," said Lydia, "was putting some boxes of papers in the trunk of his car once, this was out in the country, at an old farmhouse, and he felt something nudge him and he glanced down. It was about dusk, on a pretty dark day. So he thought this was a big friendly dog, a big black dog giving him a nudge, and he didn't pay much attention. He just said go on, now, boy, go away now, good boy. Then when he got the boxes arranged he turned around. And he saw it was a bear. It was a black bear."

She was telling this later that same evening, in the kitchen.

"So what did he do then?" said Lawrence, who was the boss of the telephone work crew. Lawrence and Lydia and Eugene and Vincent were playing cards.

Lydia laughed. "He said, *excuse me*. That's what he claims he said."

"Papers all he had in the boxes? Nothing to eat?"

"He's a writer. He writes historical books. This was some material he needed for his work. Sometimes he has to go and scout out material from people who are very strange. That bear hadn't come out of the bush. It was a pet, actually, that had been let off its chain, for a joke. There were two old brothers there, that he got the papers from, and they just let it off its chain to give him a scare."

"That's what he does, collects old stuff and writes about it?" Lawrence said. "I guess that's interesting."

She immediately regretted having told this story. She had brought it up because the men were talking about bears. But there wasn't much point to it unless Duncan told it. He could show you himself, large and benign and civilized, with his courtly apologies to the bear. He could make you see the devilish old men behind their tattered curtains.

"You'd have to know Duncan," was what she almost said. And hadn't she told this simply to establish that she had known Duncan — that she had recently had a man, and an interesting man, an amusing and adventurous man? She wanted to assure them that she was not always alone, going on her aimless travels. She had to show herself attached. A mistake. They were not likely to think a man adventurous who collected old papers from misers and eccentrics, so that he could write books about things that had happened a hundred years ago. She shouldn't even have said that Duncan was a man she had lived with. All that could mean, to them, was that she was a woman who had slept with a man she was not married to.

Lawrence the boss was not yet forty, but he was successful. He was glad to tell about himself. He was a free-lance labor contractor and owned two houses in St. Stephen. He had two cars and a truck and a boat. His wife taught school. Lawrence was getting a thick waist, a trucker's belly, but he still looked alert and vigorous. You could see that he would be shrewd enough, in most situations, for his purposes; sure enough, ruthless enough. Dressed up, he might turn flashy. And certain places and people might be capable of making him gloomy, uncertain, contentious.

Lawrence said it wasn't all true — all the stuff they wrote about the Maritimes. He said there was plenty of work for people who weren't afraid to work. Men or women. He said he was not against women's lib, but the fact was, and always would be, that there was work men did better than women and work women did better than men, and if they would both settle down and realize that they'd be happier.

His kids were cheeky, he said. They had it too soft. They got everything — that was the way nowadays, what could you do? The other kids got everything too. Clothes, bikes, education, records. He hadn't had anything handed to him. He had got out and worked, driven trucks. He had got to Ontario, got as far as Saskatchewan. He had only got to grade ten in school but he hadn't let that hold him back. Sometimes, he wished, though, that he did have more of an education.

Eugene and Vincent, who worked for Lawrence, said they had never got past grade eight, when that was as far as you could go in the country schools. Eugene was twenty-five and Vincent was fifty-two. Eugene was French-Canadian from northern New Brunswick. He looked younger than his age. He had a rosy color, a downy, dreamy, look — a masculine beauty that was nevertheless soft-edged, sweet-tempered, bashful. Hardly any men or boys have that look nowadays. Sometimes you see it in an old photograph — of a bridegroom, a basketball player: the thick water-combed hair, the blooming boy's face on the new man's body. Eugene was not very bright, or perhaps not very competitive. He lost money at the game they were playing. It was a card game that the men called Skat. Lydia remembered playing it when she was a child, and calling it Thirty-one. They played for a quarter a game.

Eugene permitted Vincent and Lawrence to tease him about losing at cards, about getting lost in Saint John, about women he liked, and about being French-Canadian. Lawrence's teasing amounted to bullying. Lawrence wore a carefully good-natured expression, but he looked as if something hard and heavy had settled inside him — a load of self-esteem that weighed him down instead of buoying him up. Vincent had no such extra weight, and though he too was relentless in his teasing — he teased Lawrence as well as Eugene — there was no sense of cruelty or danger. You could see that his natural tone was one of rumbling, easy mockery. He was sharp and sly but not insistent; he would always be able to say the most pessimistic things and not sound unhappy.

70   Vincent had a farm — it was his family's farm, where he had grown up, near St. Stephen. He said you couldn't make enough to keep you nowadays, just from farming. Last year he put in a potato crop. There was frost in June, snow in September. Too short a season by a long shot. You never knew, he said, when you might get it like that. And the market is all controlled now, it is all run by the big fellows, the big interests. Everybody does what he can, rather than trust to farming. Vincent's wife works too. She took a course and learned to do

hair. His sons are not hardworking like their parents. All they want to do is roar around in cars. They get married and the first thing their wives want is a new stove. They want a stove that practically cooks the dinner by itself and puts it on the table.

It didn't used to be that way. The first time Vincent ever had boots of his own — new boots that hadn't been worn by anybody before him — was when he joined the army. He was so pleased he walked backwards in the dirt to see the prints they made, fresh and whole. Later on, after the war, he went to Saint John to look for work. He had been working at home on the farm for a while and he had worn out his army clothes — he had just one pair of decent pants left. In a beer parlor in Saint John a man said to him, "You want to pick up a good pair of pants cheap?" Vincent said yes, and the man said, "Follow me." So Vincent did. And where did they end up? At the undertaker's! For the fact was that the family of a dead man usually bring in a suit of clothes to dress him in, and he only needs to be dressed from the waist up, that's all that shows in the coffin. The undertaker sold the pants. That was true. The army gave Vince his first pair of new boots and a corpse donated the best pair of pants he ever wore, up to that time.

Vincent had no teeth. This was immediately apparent, but it did not make him look unattractive; it simply deepened his look of secrecy and humor. His face was long and his chin tucked in, his glance unchallenging but unfooled. He was a lean man, with useful muscles, and graying black hair. You could see all the years of hard work on him, and some years of it ahead, and the body just equal to it, until he turned into a ropy-armed old man, shrunken, uncomplaining, hanging on to a few jokes.

While they played Skat the talk was boisterous and interrupted all the time by exclamations, joking threats to do with the game, laughter. Afterwards it became more serious and personal. They had been drinking a local beer called Moose, but when the game was over Lawrence went out to the truck and brought in some Ontario beer, thought to be better. They called it "the imported stuff." The couple who owned the guest-house had long ago gone to bed, but the workmen and Lydia sat on in the kitchen, just as if it belonged to one of them, drinking beer and eating dulse, which Vincent had brought down from his room. Dulse was a kind of seaweed, greenish-brown, salty and fishy-tasting. Vincent said it was what he ate last thing at night and first thing in the morning — nothing could beat it. Now that they had found out it was so good for you, they sold it in the stores, done up in little wee packages at a criminal price.

The next day was Friday, and the men would be leaving the island for the mainland. They talked about trying to get the two-thirty boat instead of the one they usually caught, at five-thirty, because the forecast was for rough weather; the tail end of one of the tropical hurricanes was due to hit the Bay of Fundy before night.

"But the ferries won't run if it's too rough, will they?" said Lydia. "They won't run if it's dangerous?" She thought that she would not mind being cut off, she wouldn't mind not having to travel again in the morning.

"Well, there's a lot of fellows waiting to get off the island on a Friday night," Vincent said.

"Wanting to get home to their wives," said Lawrence sardonically. "There's always crews working over here, always men away from home." Then he began to talk in an unhurried but insistent way about sex. He talked about what he called the immorality on the island. He said that at one time the authorities had been going to put a quarantine around the whole island, on account of the V.D. Crews came over here to work and stayed at the motel, the Ocean Wave, and there'd be parties there all night every night, with drinking and young girls turning up offering themselves for sale. Girls fourteen and fifteen — oh, thirteen years of age. On the island, he said, it was getting so a woman of twenty-five could practically be a grandmother. The place was famous. Those girls would do anything for a price, sometimes for a beer.

"And sometimes for nothing," said Lawrence. He luxuriated in the telling.

They heard the front door open.

80 "Your old boyfriend," Lawrence said to Lydia.

She was bewildered for a moment, thinking of Duncan.

"The old fellow at the table," said Vincent.

Mr. Stanley did not come into the kitchen. He crossed the living room and climbed the stairs.

"Hey? Been down to the Ocean Wave?" said Lawrence softly, raising his head as if to call through the ceiling. "Old bugger wouldn't know what to do with it," he said. "Wouldn't've known fifty years ago any better than now. I don't let any of my crews go near that place. Do I, Eugene?"

85 Eugene blushed. He put on a solemn expression, as if he was being badgered by a teacher at school.

"Eugene, now, he don't have to," Vincent said.

"Isn't it true what I'm saying?" said Lawrence urgently, as if somebody had been disputing with him. "It's true, isn't it?"

He looked at Vincent, and Vincent said, "Yeah. Yeah." He did not seem to relish the subject as much as Lawrence did.

"You'd think it was all so innocent here," said Lawrence to Lydia. "Innocent! Oh, boy!"

90 Lydia went upstairs to get a quarter that she owed Lawrence from the last game. When she came out of her room into the dark hall, Eugene was standing there, looking out the window.

"I hope it don't storm too bad," he said.

Lydia stood beside him, looking out. The moon was visible, but misty.

"You didn't grow up near the water?" she said.

"No, I didn't."

95 "But if you get the two-thirty boat it'll be all right, won't it?"

"I sure hope so." He was quite childlike and unembarrassed about his fear. "One thing I don't like the idea of is getting drownded."

Lydia remembered that as a child she had said "drownded." Most of the adults and all the children she knew then said that.

"You won't," she said, in a firm, maternal way. She went downstairs and paid her quarter.

"Where's Eugene?" Lawrence said. "He upstairs?"

100 "He's looking out the window. He's worried about the storm."

Lawrence laughed. "You tell him to go to bed and forget about it. He's right in the room next to you. I just thought you ought to know in case he hollers in his sleep."

Lydia had first seen Duncan in a bookstore, where her friend Warren worked. She was waiting for Warren to go out to lunch with her. He had gone to get his coat. A man asked Shirley, the other clerk in the store, if she could find him a copy of *The Persian Letters*.[3] That was Duncan. Shirley walked ahead of him to where the book was kept, and in the quiet store Lydia heard him saying that it must be difficult to know where to shelve *The Persian Letters*. Should it be classed as fiction or as a political essay? Lydia felt that he revealed something, saying this. He revealed a need that she supposed was common to customers in the bookstore, a need to distinguish himself, appear knowledgeable. Later on she would look back on this moment and try to imagine him again so powerless, slightly ingratiating, showing a bit of neediness. Warren came back with his coat on, greeted Duncan, and as he and Lydia went outside Warren said under his breath, "The Tin Woodman."[4] Warren and Shirley livened up their days with nicknames for customers; Lydia had already heard of Marble-Mouth, and Chickpea and the Colonial Duchess. Duncan was the Tin Woodman. Lydia thought they must call him that because of the smooth gray overcoat he wore, and his hair, a bright gray which had obviously once been blond. He was not thin or angular and he did not look as if he would be creaky in the joints. He was supple and well-fleshed and dignified and pleasant; fair-skinned, freshly groomed, glistening.

She never told him about that name. She never told him that she had seen him in the bookstore. A week or so later she met him at a publisher's party. He did not remember ever seeing her before, and she supposed he had not seen her, being occupied with chatting to Shirley.

Lydia trusts what she can make of things, usually. She trusts what she thinks about her friend Warren, or his friend Shirley, and about chance acquaintances, like the couple who run the guest-house, and Mr. Stanley, and the men she has been playing cards with. She thinks she knows why people behave as they do, and she puts more stock than she will admit in her own unproved theories and unjustified suspicions. But she is stupid and helpless when contemplating the collision of herself and Duncan. She has plenty to say about it, given the chance, because explanation is her habit, but she doesn't trust what she says, even to herself; it doesn't help her. She might just as well cover her head and sit wailing on the ground.

105    She asks herself what gave him his power? She knows who did. But she asks what, and when — when did the transfer take place, when was the abdication of all pride and sense?

She read for half an hour after getting into bed. Then she went down the hall to the bathroom. It was after midnight. The rest of the house was in darkness.

---

3 taking the form of travel letters by two fictional characters from the Middle East, this work of eighteenth-century political philosopher Charles Montesquieu presents observations and satire of French society.
4 character without a heart in L. Frank Baum's 1900 children's fantasy *The Wonderful Wizard of Oz*.

She had left her door ajar, and coming back to her room, she did not turn on the hall light. The door of Eugene's room was also ajar, and as she was passing she heard a low, careful sound. It was like a moan, and also like a whisper. She remembered Lawrence saying Eugene hollered in his sleep, but this sound was not being made in sleep. She knew he was awake. He was watching from the bed in his dark room and he was inviting her. The invitation was amorous and direct and helpless-sounding as his confession of fear when he stood by the window. She went on into her own room and shut the door and hooked it. Even as she did this, she knew she didn't have to. He would never try to get in; there was no bullying spirit in him.

Then she lay awake. Things had changed for her; she refused adventures. She could have gone to Eugene, and earlier in the evening she could have given a sign to Lawrence. In the past she might have done it. She might, or she might not have done it, depending on how she felt. Now it seemed not possible. She felt as if she were muffled up, wrapped in layers and layers of dull knowledge, well protected. It wasn't altogether a bad thing — it left your mind unclouded. Speculation can be more gentle, can take its time, when it is not driven by desire.

She thought about what those men would have been like, as lovers. It was Lawrence who would have been her reasonable choice. He was nearest to her own age, and predictable, and probably well used to the discreet encounter. His approach was vulgar, but that would not necessarily have put her off. He would be cheerful, hearty, prudent, perhaps a bit self-congratulatory, attentive in a businesslike way, and he would manage in the middle of his attentions to slip in a warning: a joke, a friendly insult, a reminder of how things stood.

Eugene would never feel the need to do that, though he would have a shorter memory even than Lawrence (much shorter, for Lawrence, though not turning down opportunities, would carry afterward the thought of some bad consequence, for which he must keep ready a sharp line of defense). Eugene would be no less experienced than Lawrence; for years, girls and women must have been answering the kind of plea Lydia had heard, the artless confession. Eugene would be generous, she thought. He would be a grateful, self-forgetful lover, showing his women such kindness that when he left they would never make trouble. They would not try to trap him; they wouldn't whine after him. Women do that to the men who have held back, who have contradicted themselves, promised, lied, mocked. These are the men women get pregnant by, send desperate letters to, preach their own superior love to, take their revenge on. Eugene would go free, he would be an innocent, happy prodigy of love, until he decided it was time to get married. Then he would marry a rather plain, maternal sort of girl, perhaps a bit older than himself, a bit shrewder. He would be faithful, and good to her, and she would manage things; they would raise a large, Catholic family.

What about Vincent? Lydia could not imagine him as she easily imagined the others: their noises and movements and bare shoulders and pleasing warm skin; their power, their exertions, their moments of helplessness. She was shy of thinking any such things about him. Yet he was the only one whom she could think of now with real interest. She thought of his courtesy and reticence and humor, his inability to better his luck. She liked him for the very things that made him different from Lawrence and ensured that all his life he would be working for Lawrence — or for somebody like Lawrence — never the other way round. She liked him also for the things that made him different from Eugene: the irony, the patience, the self-containment. He was the sort of man she had known when she was a child living on a farm not so different from his, the sort of man who must have been in her family for hundreds of years. She knew his life. With him she could foresee doors opening, to what she knew and had forgotten; rooms and landscapes opening; *there*. The rainy evenings, a country with creeks and graveyards, and chokecherry and finches in the fence-corners. She had to wonder if this was what happened, after the years of appetite and greed — did you drift back into tender-hearted fantasies? Or was it just the truth about what she needed and wanted; should she have fallen in love with, and married, a man like Vincent, years ago; should she have concentrated on the part of her that would have been content with such an arrangement, and forgotten about the rest?

That is, should she have stayed in the place where love is managed for you, not gone where you have to invent it, and reinvent it, and never know if these efforts will be enough?

Duncan spoke about his former girlfriends. Efficient Ruth, pert Judy, vivacious Diane, elegant Dolores, wifely Maxine. Lorraine the golden-haired, full-breasted beauty; Marian the multilingual; Caroline the neurotic; Rosalie who was wild and gypsy-like; gifted, melancholy Louise; serene socialite Jane. What description would do now for Lydia? Lydia the poet. Morose, messy, unsatisfactory Lydia. The unsatisfactory poet.

One Sunday, when they were driving in the hills around Peterborough, he talked about the effects of Lorraine's beauty. Perhaps the voluptuous countryside reminded him. It was almost like a joke, he said. It was almost silly. He stopped for gas in a little town and Lydia went across the street to a discount store that was open Sundays. She bought makeup in tubes off a rack. In the cold and dirty toilet of the gas station she attempted a transformation, slapping buff-colored liquid over her face and rubbing green paste on her eyelids.

"What have you done to your face?" he said when she came back to the car.

"Makeup. I put some makeup on so I'd look more cheerful."

"You can see where the line stops, on your neck."

At such times she felt strangled. It was frustration, she said to the doctor later. The gap between what she wanted and what she could get. She believed that Duncan's love — love for her — was somewhere inside him, and that by gigantic efforts to please, or fits of distress which obliterated all those efforts, or tricks of indifference, she could claw or lure it out.

What gave her such an idea? He did. At least he indicated that he could love her, that they could be happy, if she could honor his privacy, make no demands upon him, and try to alter those things about her person and behavior which he did not like. He listed these things precisely. Some were very intimate in nature and she howled with shame and covered her ears and begged him to take them back or to say no more.

"There is no way to have a discussion with you," he said. He said he hated hysterics, emotional displays, beyond anything, yet she thought she saw a quiver of satisfaction, a deep thrill of relief, that ran through him when she finally broke under the weight of his calm and detailed objections.

120     "Could that be?" she said to the doctor. "Could it be that he wants a woman close but is so frightened of it he has to try to wreck her? Is that over-simplified?" she said anxiously.

"What about you?" said the doctor. "What do you want?"

"For him to love me?"

"Not for you to love him?"

She thought about Duncan's apartment. There were no curtains; he was higher than the surrounding buildings. No attempt had been made to arrange things to make a setting; nothing was in relation to anything else. Various special requirements had been attended to. A certain sculpture was in a corner behind some filing cabinets because he liked to lie on the floor and look at it in shadow. Books were in piles beside the bed, which was crossways in the room in order to catch the breeze from the window. All disorder was actually order, carefully thought out and not to be interfered with. There was a beau-tiful little rug at the end of the hall, where he sat and listened to music. There was one great, ugly armchair, a masterpiece of engineering, with all its attach-ments for the head and limbs. Lydia asked about his guests — how were they accommodated? He replied that he did not have any. The apartment was for himself. He was a popular guest, witty and personable, but not a host, and this seemed reasonable to him, since social life was other people's require-ment and invention.

125     Lydia brought flowers, and there was nowhere to put them except in a jar on the floor by the bed. She brought presents from her trips to Toronto: records, books, cheese. She learned pathways around the apartment and found places where she could sit. She discouraged old friends, or any friends, from phoning or coming to see her, because there was too much she couldn't explain. They saw Duncan's friends sometimes, and she was nervous with them, thinking they were adding her to a list, speculating. She didn't like to see how much he gave them of that store of presents — anecdotes, parodies, flattering wit — which were also used to delight her. He could not bear dullness. She felt that he despised people who were not witty. You needed to be quick to keep up with him, in con-versation, you needed energy. Lydia saw herself as a dancer on her toes, trem-bling delicately all over, afraid of letting him down on the next turn.

"Do you mean you think I don't love him?" she said to the doctor.

"How do you know you do?"

"Because I suffer so when he's fed up with me. I want to be wiped off the earth. It's true. I want to hide. I go out on the streets and every face I look at seems to despise me for my failure."

"Your failure to make him love you."

130     Now Lydia must accuse herself. Her self-absorption equals Duncan's, but is more artfully concealed. She is in competition with him, as to who can love best. She is in competition with all other women, even when it is ludi-crous for her to be so. She cannot stand to hear them praised or know they are well remembered. Like many women of her generation she has an idea of love which is ruinous but not serious in some way, not respectful. She is greedy. She talks intelligently and ironically and in this way covers up her

indefensible expectations. The sacrifices she made with Duncan — in living arrangements, in the matter of friends, as well as in the rhythm of sex and the tone of conversations — were violations, committed not seriously but flagrantly. That is what was not respectful, that was what was indecent. She made him a present of such power, then complained relentlessly to herself and finally to him, that he had got it. She was out to defeat him.

That is what she says to the doctor. But is it the truth?

"The worst thing is not knowing what is true about any of this. I spend all my waking hours trying to figure out about him and me and I get nowhere. I make wishes. I even pray. I throw money into those wishing wells. I think that there's something in him that's an absolute holdout. There's something in him that has to get rid of me, so he'll find reasons. But he says that's rubbish, he says if I could stop over-reacting we'd be happy. I have to think maybe he's right, maybe it is all me."

"When are you happy?"

"When he's pleased with me. When he's joking and enjoying himself. No. No. I'm never happy. What I am is relieved, it's as if I'd overcome a challenge, it's more triumphant than happy. But he can always pull the rug out."

135    "So, why are you with somebody who can always pull the rug out?"

"Isn't there always somebody? When I was married it was me. Do you think it helps to ask these questions? Suppose it's just pride? I don't want to be alone, I want everybody to think I've got such a desirable man? Suppose it's the humiliation, I want to be humiliated? What good will it do me to know that?"

"I don't know. What do you think?"

"I think these conversations are fine when you're mildly troubled and interested but not when you're desperate."

"You're desperate?"

140    She felt suddenly tired, almost too tired to speak. The room where she and the doctor were talking had a dark-blue carpet, blue-and-green-striped upholstery. There was a picture of boats and fishermen on the wall. Collusion somewhere, Lydia felt. Fake reassurance, provisional comfort, earnest deceptions.

"No."

It seemed to her that she and Duncan were monsters with a lot of heads, in those days. Out of the mouth of one head could come insult and accusation, hot and cold, out of another false apologies and slimy pleas, out of another just such mealy, reasonable, true-and-false chat as she had practised with the doctor. Not a mouth would open that had a useful thing to say, not a mouth would have the sense to shut up. At the same time she believed — though she didn't know she believed it — that these monster heads with their cruel and silly and wasteful talk could all be drawn in again, could curl up and go to sleep. Never mind what they'd said; never mind. Then she and Duncan with hope and trust and blank memories could reintroduce themselves, they could pick up the undamaged delight with which they'd started, before they began to put each other to other uses.

When she had been in Toronto a day she tried to retrieve Duncan, by phone, and found that he had acted quickly. He had changed to an unlisted number. He wrote to her in care of her employer, that he would pack and send her things.

Lydia had breakfast with Mr. Stanley. The telephone crew had eaten and gone off to work before daylight.

She asked Mr. Stanley about his visit with the woman who had known Willa Cather.

"Ah," said Mr. Stanley, and wiped a corner of his mouth after a bite of poached egg. "She was a woman who used to run a little restaurant down by the dock. She was a good cook, she said. She must have been, because Willa and Edith used to get their dinners from her. She would send it up with her brother, in his car. But sometimes Willa would not be pleased with the dinner — perhaps it would not be quite what she wanted, or she would think it was not cooked as well as it might be — and she would send it back. She would ask for another dinner to be sent." He smiled, and said in a confidential way, "Willa could be imperious. Oh, yes. She was not perfect. All people of great abilities are apt to be a bit impatient in daily matters."

Rubbish, Lydia wanted to say, she sounds a proper bitch.

Sometimes waking up was all right, and sometimes it was very bad. This morning she had wakened with the cold conviction of a mistake — something avoidable and irreparable.

"But sometimes she and Edith would come down to the café," Mr. Stanley continued. "If they felt they wanted some company, they would have dinner there. On one of these occasions Willa had a long talk with the woman I was visiting. They talked for over an hour. The woman was considering marriage. She had to consider whether to make a marriage that she gave me to understand was something of a business proposition. Companionship. There was no question of romance, she and the gentleman were not young and foolish. Willa talked to her for over an hour. Of course she did not advise her directly to do one thing or the other, she talked to her in general terms very sensibly and kindly and the woman still remembers it vividly. I was happy to hear that but I was not surprised."

"What would she know about it, anyway?" Lydia said.

Mr. Stanley lifted his eyes from his plate and looked at her in grieved amazement.

"Willa Cather lived with a woman," Lydia said.

When Mr. Stanley answered he sounded flustered, and mildly upbraiding.

"They were devoted," he said.

"She never lived with a man."

"She knew things as an artist knows them. Not necessarily by experience."

"But what if they don't know them?" Lydia persisted. "What if they don't?"

He went to eating his egg as if he had not heard that. Finally he said, "The woman considered Willa's conversation was very helpful to her."

Lydia made a sound of doubtful assent. She knew she had been rude, even cruel. She knew she would have to apologize. She went to the sideboard and poured herself another cup of coffee.

The woman of the house came in from the kitchen.

"Is it keeping hot? I think I'll have a cup, too. Are you really going today? Sometimes I think I'd like to get on a boat and go too. It's lovely here and I love it but you know how you get."

They drank their coffee standing by the sideboard. Lydia did not want to go back to the table, but knew that she would have to. Mr. Stanley looked frail and solitary, with his narrow shoulders, his neat bald head, his brown checked sports jacket which was slightly too large. He took the trouble to be clean and tidy, and it must have been a trouble, with his eyesight. Of all people he did not deserve rudeness.

"Oh, I forgot," the woman said.

She went into the kitchen and came back with a large brown-paper bag.

165   "Vincent left you this. He said you liked it. Do you?"

Lydia opened the bag and saw long, dark, ragged leaves of dulse, oily-looking even when dry.

"Well," she said.

The woman laughed. "I know. You have to be born here to have the taste."

"No, I do like it," said Lydia. "I was getting to like it."

170   "You must have made a hit."

Lydia took the bag back to the table and showed it to Mr. Stanley. She tried a conciliatory joke.

"I wonder if Willa Cather ever ate dulse?"

"Dulse," said Mr. Stanley thoughtfully. He reached into the bag and pulled out some leaves and looked at them. Lydia knew he was seeing what Willa Cather might have seen. "She would most certainly have known about it. She would have known."

But was she lucky or was she not, and was it all right with that woman? How did she live? That was what Lydia wanted to say. Would Mr. Stanley have known what she was talking about? If she had asked how did Willa Cather live, would he not have replied that she did not have to find a way to live, as other people did, that she was Willa Cather?

175   What a lovely, durable shelter he had made for himself. He could carry it everywhere and nobody could interfere with it. The day may come when Lydia will count herself lucky to do the same. In the meantime, she'll be up and down. "Up and down," they used to say in her childhood, talking of the health of people who weren't going to recover. "Ah. She's up and down."

Yet look how this present slyly warmed her, from a distance.

(1983)

# Jane Rule (b. 1931)

Born in Plainfield, New Jersey, Jane Rule taught creative writing for several years at the University of British Columbia, before moving to her present home on Galiano Island, British Columbia. Beginning with her first novel, *Desert of the Heart*, published in 1964, Rule has explored the complex nature of lesbian relationships. In novels, short stories, and critical essays, she examines not only the social pressures on such partnerships, but also the insecurities, vulnerabilities, and joys of the women involved. Her works have been praised for the sensitivity and compassion with which individuals are portrayed. Lesbianism is seen as a natural part of life, as are the relationships between other characters, often marginalized, that she creates. In "Inland Passage," a boat journey from Vancouver, through the narrow waterways between the British Columbia mainland and offshore islands, symbolizes the careful navigation two women who have recently lost loved ones must execute in the beginning stages of their new relationship. In the cramped quarters of their cabin, both Troy and Fido must "get [their] bearings" as individuals and potential partners.

# INLAND PASSAGE

"The other lady . . ." the ship's steward began.

"We're not together," a quiet but determined female voice explained from the corridor, one hand thrust through the doorway insisting that he take her independent tip for the bag he had just deposited on the lower bunk.

There was not room for Troy McFadden to step into the cabin until the steward had left.

"It's awfully small," Fidelity Munroe, the first occupant of the cabin, confirmed, shrinking down into her oversized duffle coat.

5    "It will do if we take turns," Troy McFadden decided. "I'll let you settle first, shall I?"

"I just need a place to put my bag."

The upper bunk was bolted against the cabin ceiling to leave headroom for anyone wanting to sit on the narrow upholstered bench below.

"Under my bunk," Troy McFadden suggested.

There was no other place. The single chair in the cabin was shoved in under the small, square table, and the floor of the minute closet was taken up with life jackets. The bathroom whose door Troy McFadden opened to inspect, had a coverless toilet, sink and triangle of a shower. The one hook on the back of the door might make dressing there possible. When she stepped back into the cabin, she bumped into Fidelity Munroe, crouching down to stow her bag.

10    "I'm sorry," Fidelity said, standing up, "But I can get out now."

"Let's both get out."

They sidled along the narrow corridor, giving room to other passengers in search of their staterooms.

Glancing into one open door, Troy McFadden said, "At least we have a window."

"Deck?" Fidelity suggested.

15    "Oh, yes."

Neither had taken off her coat. They had to shoulder the heavy door together before they could step out into the moist sea air. Their way was blocked to the raised prow of the ship where they might otherwise have watched the cars, campers, and trucks being loaded. They turned instead and walked to the stern of the ferry to find rows of wet, white empty benches facing blankly out to sea.

"You can't even see the Gulf Islands this morning," Troy McFadden observed.

"Are you from around here?"

"Yes, from North Vancouver. We should introduce ourselves, shouldn't we?"

20    "I'm Fidelity Munroe. Everyone calls me Fido."

"I'm Troy McFadden, and nearly everyone calls me Mrs. McFadden."

They looked at each other uncertainly, and then both women laughed.

"Are you going all the way to Prince Rupert?" Fidelity asked.

"And back, just for the ride."

25    "So am I. Are we going to see a thing?"

"It doesn't look like it," Troy McFadden admitted. "I'm told you rarely do on this trip. You sail into mist and maybe get an occasional glimpse of forest or the near shore or an island. Mostly you seem to be going nowhere."

"Then why...?"

"For that reason, I suppose," Troy McFadden answered, gathering her fur collar more closely around her ears.

"I was told it rarely gets rough," Fidelity Munroe offered.

30    "We're in open sea only two hours each way. All the rest is inland passage."

"You've been before then."

"No," Troy McFadden said. "I've heard about it for years."

"So have I, but I live in Toronto. There you hear it's beautiful."

"*Mrs.* Munroe?"

35    "Only technically," Fidelity answered.

"I don't think I can call you Fido."

"It's no more ridiculous than Fidelity once you get used to it."

"Does your mother call you Fido?"

"My mother hasn't spoken to me for years," Fidelity Munroe answered.

40    Two other passengers, a couple in their agile seventies, joined them on the deck.

"Well..." Troy McFadden said, in no one's direction, "I think I'll get my bearings."

She turned away, a woman who did not look as if she ever lost her bearings.

*You're not really old enough to be my mother*, Fidelity wanted to call after her, *Why take offense?* But it wasn't just that remark. Troy McFadden would be as daunted as Fidelity by such sudden intimacy, the risk of its smells as much as its other disclosures. She would be saying to herself, *I'm too old for this. Why on earth didn't I spend the extra thirty dollars?* Or she was on her way to the purser to see if she might be moved, if not into a single cabin then into one with someone less... more...

Fidelity looked down at Gail's much too large duffle coat, her own jeans and hiking boots. Well, there wasn't room for the boots in her suitcase, and, ridiculous as they might look for walking the few yards of deck, they might be very useful for exploring the places the ship docked.

45 *Up yours, Mrs. McFadden, with your fur collar and your expensive, sensible shoes and matching bag. Take up the whole damned cabin!*

All Fidelity needed for this mist-bound mistake of a cruise was a book out of her suitcase. She could sleep in the lounge along with the kids and the Indians, leave the staterooms (what a term!) to the geriatrics and Mrs. McFadden.

Fidelity wrenched the door open with her own strength, stomped back along the corridor like one of the invading troops, and unlocked and opened the cabin door in one gesture. There sat Troy McFadden, in surprised tears.

"I'm sorry..." Fidelity began, but she could not make her body retreat. Instead she wedged herself around the door and closed it behind her. Then she sat down beside Troy McFadden, took her hand, and stared quietly at their unlikely pairs of feet. A shadow passed across the window. Fidelity looked up to meet the eyes of another pasenger glancing in. She reached up with her free hand and pulled the small curtain across the window.

50 "I simply can't impose..." Troy finally brought herself to say.

"Look," Fidelity said, turning to her companion, "I may cry most of the way myself... it doesn't matter."

"I just can't make myself... walk into those public rooms... alone."

"How long have you been alone?" Fidelity asked.

"My husband died nearly two years ago... there's no excuse."

55 "Somebody said to me the other day, 'Shame's the last stage of grief.' 'What a rotten arrangement then,' I said. 'To be ashamed for the rest of my life.'"

"You've lost your husband?"

Fidelity shook her head, "Years ago. I divorced him."

"You hardly look old enough..."

"I know, but I am. I'm forty-one. I've got two grown daughters."

60 "I have two sons," Troy said. "One offered to pay for this trip just to get me out of town for a few days. The other thought I should lend him the money instead."

"And you'd rather have?"

"It's so humiliating," Troy said.

"To be alone?"

"To be afraid."

65 The ship's horn sounded.

"We're about to sail," Troy said. "I didn't even have the courage to get off the ship, and here I am, making you sit in the dark..."

"Shall we go out and get our bearings together?"

"Let me put my face back on," Troy said.

Only then did Fidelity let go of her hand so that she could take her matching handbag into the tiny bathroom and smoothe courage back into her quite handsome and appealing face.

70 Fidelity pulled her bag out from under the bunk, opened it and got out her own sensible shoes. If she was going to offer this woman any sort of reassurance, she must make what gestures she could to be a bird of her feather.

The prow of the ship had been lowered and secured, and the reverse engines had ceased their vibrating by the time the two women joined the bundled passengers on deck to see, to everyone's amazement, the sun breaking through, an ache to the eyes on the shining water.

Troy McFadden reached for her sunglasses. Fidelity Munroe had forgotten hers.

"This is your captain," said an intimate male voice from a not very loud speaker just above their heads. "We are sailing into a fair day."

The shoreline they had left remained hidden in clouds crowded up against the Vancouver mountains, but the long wooded line of Galiano Island and beyond it to the west the mountains of Vancouver Island lay in a clarity of light.

"I'm hungry," Fidelity announced. "I didn't get up in time to have breakfast."

"I couldn't eat," Troy confessed.

When she hesitated at the entrance to the cafeteria, Fidelity took her arm firmly and directed her into the short line that had formed.

"Look at that!" Fidelity said with pleasure. "Sausages, ham, bacon, pancakes. How much can we have?"

"As much as you want," answered the young woman behind the counter.

"Oh, am I ever going to pig out on this trip!"

Troy took a bran muffin, apple juice and a cup of tea.

"It isn't fair," she said as they unloaded their contrasting trays at a window table. "My husband could eat like that, too, and never gain a pound."

Fidelity, having taken off her coat, revealed just how light bodied she was.

"My kids call me bird bones. They have their father to thank for being human size. People think I'm their little brother."

"Once children tower over you, being their mother is an odd business," Troy mused.

"That beautiful white hair must help," Fidelity said.

"I've had it since I was twenty-five. When the boys were little, people thought I was their grandmother."

"I suppose only famous people are mistaken for themselves in public," Fidelity said, around a mouthful of sausage; so she checked herself and chewed instead of elaborating on that observation.

"Which is horrible in its way, too, I suppose," Troy said.

Fidelity swallowed. "I don't know. I've sometimes thought I'd like it: Mighty Mouse[1] fantasies."

She saw Troy try to smile and for a second lose the trembling control of her face. She hadn't touched her food.

"Drink your juice," Fidelity said, in the no-nonsense, cheerful voice of motherhood.

Troy's dutiful hand shook as she raised the glass to her lips, but she took a sip. She returned the glass to the table without accident and took up the much less dangerous bran muffin.

"I would like to be invisible," Troy said, a rueful apology in her voice.

"Well, we really are, aren't we?" Fidelity asked. "Except to a few people."

"Have you traveled alone a lot?"

---

1 cartoon character who uses super powers in his battles with cats.

"No," Fidelity said, "just about never. I had the girls, and they're still only semi-independent. And I had a friend, Gail. She and I took trips together. She died last year."

"I'm so sorry."

"Me, too. It's a bit like being a widow, I guess, except, nobody expects it to be. Maybe that helps."

100 "Did you live with Gail?"

"No, but we thought maybe we might...someday."

Troy sighed.

"So here we both are at someday," Fidelity said. "Day one of someday and not a bad day at that."

They both looked out at the coast, ridge after ridge of tall trees, behind which were sudden glimpses of high peaks of snow-capped mountains.

105 Back on the deck other people had also ventured, dressed and hatted against the wind, armed with binoculars for sighting of eagles and killer whales, for inspecting the crews of fishing boats, tugs, and pleasure craft.

"I never could use those things," Fidelity confessed. "It's not just my eyes. I feel like that woman in the Colville[2] painting."

"Do you like his work?" Troy asked.

"I admire it," Fidelity said. "There's something a bit sinister about it: all those figures seem prisoners of normality. That woman at the shore, about to get into the car..."

"With the children, yes," Troy said. "They seem so vulnerable."

110 "Here's Jonathan Seagull!" a woman called to her binocular-blinded husband, "Right here on the rail."

"I loathed that book," Troy murmured to Fidelity.

Fidelity chuckled. "In the first place, I'm no friend to seagulls."

Finally chilled, the two women went back inside. At the door to the largest lounge, again Troy hesitated.

"Take my arm," Fidelity said, wishing it and she were more substantial.

115 They walked the full length of that lounge and on into the smaller space of the gift shop where Troy was distracted from her nerves by postcards, travel books, toys and souvenirs.

Fidelity quickly picked up half a dozen postcards.

"I'd get home before they would," Troy said.

"I probably will, too, but everybody likes mail."

From the gift shop, they found their way to the forward lounge where tv sets would later offer a movie, on into the children's playroom, a glassed-in area heavily padded where several toddlers tumbled and stumbled about.

120 "It's like an aquarium," Fidelity said.

"There aren't many children aboard."

"One of the blessings of traveling in October," Fidelity said. "Oh, I don't feel about kids the way I do about seagulls, but they aren't a holiday."

"No," Troy agreed. "I suppose I really just think I miss mine."

Beyond the playroom they found the bar with only three tables of prelunch drinkers. Troy looked in, shook her head firmly and retreated.

2 twentieth-century Canadian artist whose paintings depict everyday events and scenes.

125    "Not a drinker?" Fidelity asked.

"I have a bottle of scotch in my case," Troy said. "I don't think I could ever...alone..."

"Mrs. McFadden," Fidelity said, taking her arm, "I'm going to make a hard point. You're not alone. You're with me, and we're both old enough to be grandmothers, and we're approaching the turn of the 21st not the 20th century, and I think we both could use a drink."

Troy McFadden allowed herself to be steered into the bar and settled at a table, but, when the waiter came, she only looked at her hands.

"Sherry," Fidelity decided. "Two sherries," and burst out laughing.

130    Troy looked over at her, puzzled.

"Sherry is my idea of what you would order. I've never tasted it in my life."

"You're quite right," Troy said. "Am I such a cliché?"

"Not a cliché, an ideal. I don't know, maybe they're the same thing when it comes down to it. You have style. I really admire that. If I ever got it together enough to have shoes and matching handbag, I'd lose one of the shoes."

"Is that really your coat?" Troy asked.

135    Fidelity looked down at herself. "No, it belonged to Gail. It's my Linus blanket."[3]

"I've been sleeping in my husband's old pajamas. I had to buy a night-gown to come on this trip," Troy confided. "I think it's marvelous the way you do what you want."

Fidelity bit her lip and screwed her face tight for a moment. Then she said, "But I don't want to cry any more than you do."

The waiter put their sherries before them, and Fidelity put a crumpled ten dollar bill on the table.

"Oh, you should let me," Troy said, reaching for her purse.

140    "Next round," Fidelity said.

Troy handled her glass more confidently than she had at breakfast, and, after her first sip, she said with relief, "Dry."

"This is your captain," the intimate male voice asserted again. "A pod of killer whales is approaching to starboard."

Fidelity and Troy looked out the window and waited. No more than a hundred yards away, a killer whale broke the water, then another, then another, their black backs arching, their bellies unbelievably white.

"They don't look real," Fidelity exclaimed.

145    Then one surfaced right alongside the ferry, and both women caught their breath.

"This trip is beginning to feel less like somebody else's day dream," Fidelity said. "Just look at that!"

For some moments after the whales had passed, the women continued to watch the water, newly interested in its possibilities for surprise. As if as a special reward for their attention, an enormous bird dropped out of the sky straight into the sea, then lifted off the water with a strain of great wings, a flash of fish in its talons.

---

3 security blanket clutched by a character in Charles Schultz's cartoon "Peanuts."

"What on earth was that?" Fidelity cried.

"A bald eagle catching a salmon," Troy replied.

150 The ship had slowed to navigate a quite narrow passage between the mainland and a small island, its northern crescent shore fingered with docks, reached by flights of steps going back up into the trees where the glint of windows and an occasional line of roof could be seen.

"Do people live there all year long?" Fidelity asked.

"Not many. They're summer places mostly."

"How do people get there?"

"Private boats or small planes."

155 "Ain't the rich wealthy?" Fidelity sighed.

Troy frowned.

"Did I make a personal remark by mistake?"

"Geoff and I had a place when the boys were growing up. We didn't *have* money, but he earned a good deal . . . law. He hadn't got around to thinking about . . . retiring. I'm just awfully grateful the boys had finished their education. It scares me to think what it might have been like if it had happened earlier. You just don't think . . . we didn't anyway. Oh, now that I've sold the house, I'm perfectly comfortable. When you're just one person . . ."

"Well, on this trip with the food all paid for, I'm going to eat like an army," Fidelity said. "Let's have lunch."

160 Though the ship wasn't crowded, there were more people in the cafeteria than there had been for breakfast.

"Let's not sit near the Jonathan Seagulls," Fidelity said, leading the way through the tables to a quiet corner where they could do more watching than being watched. Troy had chosen a seafood salad that Fidelity considered a first course to which she added a plate of lamb chops, rice and green beans.

"I really don't believe you could eat like that all the time," Troy said.

"Would if I could."

Fidelity tried not to let greed entirely overtake her, yet she needed to eat quickly not to leave Troy with nothing to do.

165 "See those two over there?" Fidelity said, nodding to a nondescript pair of middle-aged women. "One's a lady cop. The other's her prisoner."

"How did you figure that out?"

"Saw the handcuffs. That's why they're sitting side by side."

"They're both right handed," Troy observed critically.

"On their ankles."

170 "What's she done?"

"Blown up a mortgage company," Fidelity said.

"She ought to get a medal."

"A fellow anarchist, are you?"

"Only armchair," Troy admitted modestly.

175 "Mrs. McFadden, you're a fun lady. I'm glad we got assigned to the same shoe box."

"Do call me Troy."

"Only if you call me Fido."

"Will you promise not to bark?"

"No," Fidelity said and growled convincingly at a lamb chop but quietly enough not to attract attention.

"Fido, would it both antisocial and selfish of me to take a rest after lunch?"

"Of course not," Fidelity said. "I'll just come up and snag a book."

"Then later you could have a rest."

"I'm not good at them," Fidelity said. "I twitch and have horrible dreams if I sleep during the day. But, look, I do have to know a few intimate things about you, like do you play bridge or Scrabble or poker because I don't, but I could probably scout out some people who do..."

"I loathe games," Troy said. "In any case, please don't feel responsible for me. I do feel much better, thanks to you."

A tall, aging fat man nodded to Troy as they left the cafeteria and said, "Lovely day."

"Don't panic," Fidelity said out of the side of her mouth. "I bite too, that is, unless you're in the market for a shipboard romance."

"How about you?" Troy asked wryly.

"I'm not his type."

"Well, he certainly isn't mine!"

Fidelity went into the cabin first, struggled to get her case out from under the bunk and found her book, Alice Walker's[4] collection of essays.

"Is she good?" Troy asked, looking at the cover.

"I think she's terrific, but I have odd tastes."

"Odd?"

"I'm a closet feminist."

"But isn't that perfectly respectable by now?" Troy asked.

"Nothing about me is perfectly respectable."

"You're perfectly dear," Troy said and gave Fidelity a quick, hard hug before she went into the cabin.

Fidelity paused for a moment outside the closed door to enjoy that affectionate praise before she headed off to find a window seat in the lounge where she could alternately read and watch the passing scene. An occasional deserted Indian village was now the only sign of habitation on the shores of this northern wilderness.

The book lay instead neglected in her lap, and the scenery became a transparency through which Fidelity looked at her inner landscape, a place of ruins.

A man whose wife had died of the same cancer that had killed Gail said to Fidelity, "I don't even want to take someone out to dinner without requiring her to have a thorough physical examination first."

The brutality of that remark shocked Fidelity because it located in her her own denied bitterness, that someone as lovely and funny and strong as Gail could be not only physically altered out of recognition but so horribly transformed humanly until she seemed to have nothing left but anger, guilt, and fear, burdens she tried to shift, as she couldn't her pain, onto Fidelity's shoulders, until Fidelity found herself praying for Gail's death instead of her life. Surely she had

4 feminist African-American writer (see page 1172).

loved before she grew to dread the sight of Gail, the daily confrontations with her appalled and appalling fear. It was a face looking into hell Fidelity knew did not exist, and yet her love had failed before it. Even now it was her love she mourned rather than Gail, for without it she could not go back to the goodness between them, believe in it and go on.

She felt herself withdraw from her daughters as if her love for them might also corrupt and then fail them. In the way of adolescents they both noticed and didn't, excused her grief and then became impatient with it. They were anyway perched at the edge of their own lives, ready to be free of her.

"Go," she encouraged them, and they did.

"I guess I only think I miss them," Troy said. Otherwise this convention of parent abandonment would be intolerable, a cruel and unusual punishment for all those years of intimate attention and care.

205 And here she was, temporarily paired with another woman as fragile and shamed by self-pity as she was. At least they wouldn't be bleeding all over the other passengers. If they indulged in pitying each other, well, what was the harm in it?

Fidelity shifted uncomfortably. The possibility of harm was all around her.

"Why did you marry me then?" she had demanded of her hostile husband.

"I felt *sorry* for you," he said.

"That's a lie!"

210 "It's the honest truth."

So pity, even from someone else, is the seed of contempt.

Review resolutions for this trip: be cheerful, eat, indulge in Mighty Mouse fantasies, and enjoy the scenery.

An island came into focus, a large bird perched in a tree, another eagle no doubt, and she would not think of the fish except in its surprised moment of flight.

"This is your captain speaking..."

215 Fidelity plugged her ears and also shut her eyes, for even if she missed something more amazing than whales, she wanted to see or not see for herself.

"Here you are," Troy said. "What on earth are you doing?"

"Do you think he's going to do that all through the trip?" Fidelity demanded.

"Probably not after dark."

"Pray for an early sunset."

220 It came, as they stood watching it on deck, brilliantly red with promise, leaving the sky christened with stars.

"Tell me about these boys of yours," Fidelity said as they sat over a predinner drink in the crowded bar. "We've spent a whole day together without even taking out our pictures. That's almost unnatural."

"In this den of iniquity," Troy said, glancing around, "I'm afraid people will think we're exchanging dirty post-cards."

"Why oh why did I leave mine at home?"

Fidelity was surprised that Troy's sons were not better looking than they were, and she suspected Troy was surprised at how much better looking her daughters were than she had any right to expect. It's curious how really rare a handsome couple is. Beauty is either too vain for competition or indifferent to itself. Troy would have chosen a husband for his character. Fidelity had fallen for narcissistic good looks, for which her daughters were her only and lovely reward.

225    "Ralph's like his father," Troy said, taking back the picture of her older son, "conservative with some attractive independence of mind. So many of our friends had trouble with first children and blame it on their own inexperience. Geoff used to say, 'I guess the more we knew, the worse we did.'"

"What's the matter with Colin?" Fidelity asked.

"I've never thought there was anything the matter with him," Troy said, "except perhaps the world. Geoff didn't like his friends or his work (Colin's an actor). It was the only hard thing between Geoff and me, but it was very hard."

The face Fidelity studied was less substantial and livelier than Ralph's, though it was easy enough to tell that they were brothers.

"We ought to pair at least two of them off, don't you think?" Fidelity suggested flippantly. "Let's see. Is it better to put the conservative, responsible ones together, and let the scallywags go off and have fun, or should each kite have a tail?"

230    "Colin won't marry," Troy said. "He's homosexual."

Fidelity looked up from the pictures to read Troy's face. Her dark blue eyes held a question rather than a challenge.

"How lucky for him that you're his mother," Fidelity said. "Did you realize that I am, too?"

"I wondered when you spoke about your friend Gail," Troy said.

"Sometimes I envy people his age," Fidelity said. "There's so much less guilt, so much more acceptance."

235    "In some quarters," Troy said. "Geoff let it kill him."

"How awful!"

"That isn't true," Troy said. "It's the first time I've ever said it out loud, and it simply isn't true. But I've been so afraid Colin thought so, so angry, yes, *angry*. I always thought Geoff would finally come round. He was basically a fair-minded man. Then he had a heart attack and died. If he'd had any warning, if he'd had time . . ."

Fidelity shook her head. She did not want to say how easily that might have been worse. Why did people persist in the fantasy that facing death brought out the best in people when so often it did just the opposite?

"How does Colin feel about his father?"

240    "He always speaks of him very lovingly, remembering all the things he did with the boys when they were growing up. He never mentions those last, awful months when Geoff was remembering the same things but only so that he didn't have to blame himself."

"Maybe Colin's learning to let them go," Fidelity suggested.

"So why can't I?" Troy asked.

There was Fidelity's own question in Troy's mouth. *It's because they're dead*, she thought. *How do you go about forgiving the dead for dying?* Then, because she had no answer, she simply took Troy's hand.

"Is that why your mother doesn't speak to you?" Troy asked.

245    "That and a thousand other things," Fidelity said. "It used to get to me, but, as my girls have grown up, I think we're all better off for not trying to please

someone who won't be pleased. Probably it hasn't anything to do with me, just luck, that I like my kids, and they like me pretty well most of the time."

"Did they know about you and Gail?"

"Did and didn't. We've never actually talked about it. I would have, but Gail was dead set against it. I didn't realize just how much that had to do with her own hang-ups. Once she was gone, there didn't seem to be much point, for them."

"But for you?"

"Would you like another drink?" Fidelity asked as she signaled the waiter and, at Troy's nod, ordered two. "For myself, I'd like to tell the whole damned world, but I'm still enough of my mother's child to hear her say, 'Another one of your awful self-indulgences' and to think maybe she has a point."

250 "It doesn't seem to me self-indulgent to be yourself," Troy said.

Fidelity laughed suddenly. "Why that's exactly what it is! Why does everything to do with the *self* have such a bad press: self-pity, self-consciousness, self-indulgence, self-satisfaction, practices of selfish people, people being themselves?"

"The way we are," Troy said.

"Yes, and I haven't felt as good about myself in months."

"Nor I," Troy said, smiling.

255 "Are we going to watch the movie tonight, or are we going to go on telling each other the story of our lives?"

"We have only three days," Troy said. "And this one is nearly over."

"I suppose we'd better eat before the cafeteria closes."

They lingered long over coffee after dinner until they were alone in the room, and they were still there when the movie goers came back for a late night snack. Troy yawned and looked at her watch.

"Have we put off the evil hour as long as we can?" Fidelity asked.

260 "You're going to try to talk me out of the lower bunk."

"I may be little, but I'm very agile," Fidelity claimed.

The top bunk had been made up, leaving only a narrow corridor in which to stand or kneel, as they had to to get at their cases. Troy took her night-gown and robe and went into the bathroom. Fidelity changed into her flannel tent and climbed from the chair to the upper bunk, too close to the ceiling for sitting. She lay on her side, her head propped up on her elbow.

It occurred to her that this cabin was the perfect setting for the horrible first night of a honeymoon and she was about to tell Troy so as she came out of the bathroom but she looked both so modest and so lovely that an easy joke seemed instead tactless.

"I didn't have the courage for a shower," Troy confessed. "Really, you know, we're too old for this."

265 "I think that's beginning to be part of the fun."

When they had both settled and turned out their lights, Fidelity said, "Good night, Troy."

"Good night, dear Fido."

Fidelity did not expect to sleep at once, her head full of images and revelations, but the gentle motion of the ship lulled her, and she felt herself letting go and dropping away. When she woke, it was morning, and she could hear the shower running.

"You did it!" Fidelity shouted as Troy emerged fully dressed in a plum and navy pant suit, her night things over her arm.

270      "I don't wholeheartedly recommend it as an experience, but I do feel better for it."

Fidelity followed Troy's example. It seemed to her the moment she turned on the water, the ship's movement became more pronounced, and she had to hang onto a bar which might have been meant for a towel rack to keep her balance, leaving only one hand for the soaping. By the time she was through, the floor was awash, and she had to sit on the coverless toilet to pull on her grey and patchily soggy trousers and fresh wool shirt.

"We're into open water," Troy said, looking out their window.

"Two hours, you said?"

"Yes."

275      "I think I'm going to be better off on deck," Fidelity admitted, her normally pleasurable hunger pangs suddenly unresponsive to the suggestion of sausages and eggs. "Don't let me keep you from breakfast."

"What makes you think I'm such an old sea dog myself?"

Once they were out in the sun and air of a lovely morning, the motion of the open sea was exciting. They braced themselves against the railing and plunged with the ship, crossing from the northern tip of Vancouver Island to the mainland.

A crewman informed them that the ship would be putting in at Bella Bella to drop off supplies and pick up passengers.

"Will there be time to go ashore?" Fidelity asked.

280      "You can see everything there is to see from here," the crewman answered.

"No stores?"

"Just the Indian store ... for the Indians," he said, as he turned to climb to the upper deck.

"A real, lived-in Indian village!" Fidelity said. "Do you want to go ashore?"

"It doesn't sound to me as if we'd be very welcome," Troy said.

285      "Why not?"

"You're not aware that we're not very popular with the Indians?"

Fidelity sighed. She resented, as she always did, having to take on the sins and clichés of her race, nation, sex, and yet she was less willing to defy welcome at an Indian village than she was at the ship's bar.

They were able to see the whole of the place from the deck, irregular rows of raw wood houses climbing up a hill stripped of trees. There were more dogs than people on the dock. Several family groups, cheaply but more formally dressed than most of the other passengers, boarded.

"It's depressing," Fidelity said.

290      "I wish we knew how to expect something else and make it happen."

"I'm glad nobody else was living on the moon," Fidelity said, turning sadly away.

The Indian families were in the cafeteria where Troy and Fidelity went for their belated breakfast. The older members of the group were talking softly among themselves in their own language. The younger ones were chatting with the crew in a friendly enough fashion. They were all on their way to a great

wedding in Prince Rupert that night and would be back on board ship when
it sailed south again at midnight.

"Do you work?" Troy suddenly asked Fidelity as she put a large piece of ham
in her mouth.

Fidelity nodded as she chewed.

295    "What do you do?"

"I'm a film editor," Fidelity said.

"Something as amazing as that, and you haven't even bothered to tell
me?"

"It's nothing amazing," Fidelity said. "You sit in a dark room all by yourself, day after day, trying to make a creditable half hour or hour and a half out
of hundreds of hours of film."

"You don't like it at all?"

300    "Oh, well enough," Fidelity said. "Sometimes it's interesting. Once I did
a film on Haida carving that was shot up here in the Queen Charlottes, one
of the reasons I've wanted to see this part of the country."

"How did you decide to be a film editor?"

"I didn't really. I went to art school. I was going to be a great painter.
Mighty Mouse fantasy number ten. I got married instead. He didn't work; so
I had to. It was a job, and after a while I got pretty good at it."

"Did he take care of the children?"

"My mother did," Fidelity said, "until they were in school. They've had to
be pretty independent."

305    "Oh, Fido, you've done so much more with your life than I have."

"Got divorced and earned a living because I had to. Not exactly things to
brag about."

"But it's ongoing, something of your own to do."

"I suppose so," Fidelity admitted, "but you know, after Gail died, I looked
around me and realized that, aside from my kids, I didn't really have any
friends. I worked alone. I lived alone. I sometimes think now I should quit, do
something entirely different. I can't risk that until the girls are really independent, not just playing house with Mother's off-stage help. Who knows?
One of them might turn up on my doorstep as I did on my mother's."

"I'd love a job," Troy said, "but I'd never have the courage . . ."

310    "Of course you would," Fidelity said.

"Are you volunteering to take me by the hand as you did yesterday and say
to the interviewer, 'This is my friend, Mrs. McFadden. She can't go into strange
places by herself?'"

"Sure," Fidelity said. "I'll tell you what, let's go into business together."
"What kind of business?"

"Well, we could run a selling gallery and lose our shirts."

315    "Or a bookstore and lose our shirts . . . I don't really have a shirt to lose."

"Let's be more practical. How about a gay bar?"

"Oh, Fido," Troy said, laughing and shaking her head.

The ship now had entered a narrow inland passage, moving slowly and
carefully past small islands. The Captain, though he still occasionally pointed out
a deserted cannery, village or mine site, obviously had to pay more attention

to the task of bringing his ship out of this narrow reach in a nearly silent wilderness into the noise and clutter of the town of Prince Rupert.

A bus waited to take those passengers who had signed up for a tour of the place, and Troy and Fidelity were among them. Their driver and guide was a young man fresh from Liverpool, and he looked on his duty as bizarre, for what was there really to see in Prince Rupert but one ridge of rather expensive houses overlooking the harbor and a small neighborhood of variously tasteless houses sold to fishermen in seasons when they made too much money so that they could live behind pretentious front doors on unemployment all the grey winter long. The only real stop was a small museum of Indian artifacts and old tools. The present Indian population was large and poor and hostile.

320 "It's like being in Greece," Fidelity said, studying a small collection of beautifully patterned baskets. "Only here it's been over for less than a hundred years."

They ate delicious seafood at an otherwise unremarkable hotel and then skipped an opportunity to shop at a mall left open in the evening for the tour's benefit, business being what it was in winter. Instead they took a taxi back to the ship.

"I think it's time to open my bottle of scotch," Troy suggested.

They got ice from a vending machine and went back to their cabin, where Fidelity turned the chair so that she could put her feet up on the bunk and Troy could sit at the far end with her feet tucked under her.

"Cozy," Troy decided.

325 "I wish I liked scotch," Fidelity said, making a face.

By the time the steward came to make up the bunks, returning and new passengers were boarding the ship. Troy and Fidelity out on deck watched the Indians being seen off by a large group of friends and relatives who must also have been to the wedding. Fidelity imagined them in an earlier time getting into great canoes to paddle south instead of settling down to a few hours' sleep on the lounge floor. She might as well imagine herself and Troy on a sailing ship bringing drink and disease.

A noisy group of Australians came on deck.

"You call this a ship?" they said to each other. "You call those cabins?"

They had traveled across the States and had come back across Canada, and they were not happily prepared to spend two nights in cabins even less comfortable than Fidelity's and Troy's.

330 "Maybe the scenery will cheer them up," Fidelity suggested as they went back to their cabin.

"They sound to me as if they've already had more scenery than they can take."

True enough. The Australians paced the decks like prisoners looking at the shore only to evaluate their means of escape, no leaping whale or plummeting eagle compensation for this coastal ferry which had been described in their brochures as a "cruise ship." How different they were from the stoically settled Indians who had quietly left the ship at Bella Bella shortly after dawn.

Fidelity and Troy stayed on deck for the open water crossing to Port Hardy on Vancouver Island, went in only long enough to get warm, then back out into the brilliant sun and sea wind to take delight in every shape of island, contour of hill, the play of light on the water, the least event of sea life until even their cloud of complaining gulls seemed part of the festival of their last day.

"Imagine preferring something like The Love Boat,"[5] Troy said.

"Gail and I were always the ferry, barge, and freighter types," Fidelity said.

Film clips moved through her mind, Gail sipping ouso in a café in Athens, Gail hailing a cab in London, Gail . . . a face she had begun to believe stricken from her memory was there in its many moods at her bidding.

"What is it?" Troy asked.

"Some much better reruns in my head," Fidelity said, smiling. "I guess it takes having fun to remember how often I have."

"What time is your plane tomorrow?" Troy asked.

The question hit Fidelity like a blow.

"Noon," she managed to say before she excused herself and left Troy for the first time since she had pledged herself to Troy's need.

Back in their cabin, sitting on the bunk that was also Troy's bed, Fidelity was saying to herself, "You're such an idiot, such an idiot, such an idiot!"

Two and a half days playing Mighty Mouse better than she ever had in her life, and suddenly she was dissolving into a maudlin fool, into tears of a sort she hadn't shed since her delayed adolescence.

"I can't want her. I just can't," Fidelity chanted.

It was worse than coming down with a toothache, breaking out in boils, this stupid, sweet desire which she simply had to hide from a woman getting better and better at reading her face unless she wanted to wreck the last hours of this lovely trip.

Troy shoved open the cabin door.

"Did I say something . . .?"

Fidelity shook her head, "No, just my turn, I guess."

"You don't want to miss your last dinner, do you?"

"Of course not," Fidelity said, trying to summon up an appetite she could indulge in.

They were shy of each other over dinner, made conversation in a way they hadn't needed to from the first few minutes of their meeting. The strain of it made Fidelity both long for sleep and dread the intimacy of their cabin where their new polite reserve would be unbearable.

"Shall we have an early night?" Troy suggested. "We have to be up awfully early to disembark."

As they knelt together, getting out their night things, Troy said, mocking their awkward position, "I'd say a prayer of thanks if I thought there was anybody up there to pray to."

Fidelity *was* praying for whatever help there was against her every instinct.

"I'm going to find it awfully hard to say good-bye to you, Fido."

Fidelity had to turn then to Troy's lovely, vulnerable face.

"I just can't . . ." Fidelity began.

Then, unable to understand that it could happen, Fidelity was embracing Troy, and they moved into love-making as trustingly as they had talked.

5 television series in which passengers on a cruise ship often discover romance.

At six in the morning, when Troy's travel alarm went off, she said, "I don't think I can move."

Fidelity, unable to feel the arm that lay under Troy, whispered, "We're much too old for this."

"I was afraid you thought I was," Troy said as she slowly and painfully untangled herself, "and now I'm going to prove it."

"Do you know what I almost said to you the first night?" Fidelity asked, loving the sight of Troy's naked body in the light of the desk lamp she'd just turned on. "I almost said, 'what a great setting for the first horrible night of a honeymoon.'"

"Why didn't you?"

"You were so lovely, coming out of the bathroom," Fidelity explained, knowing it wasn't an explanation.

"You were wrong," Troy said, defying her painful stiffness to lean down to kiss Fidelity.

"Young lovers would skip breakfast," Fidelity said.

"But you're starved."

Fidelity nodded, having no easy time getting out of bed herself.

It occurred to her to disturb the virgin neatness of her own upper bunk only because it would have been the first thing to occur to Gail, a bed ravager of obsessive proportions. If it didn't trouble Troy, it would not trouble Fidelity.

As they sat eating, the sun rose over the Vancouver mountains, catching the windows of the apartment blocks on the north shore.

"I live over there," Troy said.

"Troy?"

"Will you invite me to visit you in Toronto?"

"Come with me."

"I have to see Colin . . . and Ralph. I could be there in a week."

"I was wrong about those two over there," Fidelity said. "They sit side by side because they're lovers."

"And you thought so in the first place," Troy said.

Fidelity nodded.

"This is your captain speaking . . ."

Because he was giving them instructions about how to disembark, Fidelity did listen but only with one ear, for she had to keep her own set of instructions clearly in her head. She, of course, had to see her children, too.

(1985)

# John Updike (b. 1932)

Born in Reading, Pennsylvania, and raised in Shillington, Pennsylvania, John Updike first attracted notice as a writer during the 1950s, when his stories and essays began appearing in *The New Yorker* magazine. In many of his short stories and in novels such as *Rabbit, Run* (1960) and *Couples* (1968), he portrays middle-class Americans confronting the moral complexities of their lives. "A & P" presents a brief yet significant episode in the life of the young hero. By carefully selecting the details reported by the narrator and faithfully depicting the narrator's reactions to the young women, the other customers, his co-worker, and the store manager, Updike transforms an incident of a few minutes into a story of the initiation of a young man into the complex and often unhappy realities of adulthood.

# A & P [1]

In walks these three girls in nothing but bathing suits. I'm in the third check-out slot, with my back to the door, so I don't see them until they're over by the bread. The one that caught my eye first was the one in the plaid green two-piece. She was a chunky kid, with a good tan and a sweet broad soft-looking can with those two crescents of white just under it, where the sun never seems to hit, at the top of the backs of her legs. I stood there with my hand on a box of HiHo crackers trying to remember if I rang it up or not. I ring it up again and the customer starts giving me hell. She's one of these cash-register-watchers, a witch about fifty with rouge on her cheekbones and no eyebrows, and I know it made her day to trip me up. She'd been watching cash registers for fifty years and probably never seen a mistake before.

By the time I got her feathers smoothed and her goodies into a bag — she gives me a little snort in passing, if she'd been born at the right time they would have burned her over in Salem [2] — by the time I get her on her way the girls had circled around the bread and were coming back, without a pushcart, back my way along the counters, in the aisle between the checkouts and the Special bins. They didn't even have shoes on. There was this chunky one, with the two-piece — it was bright green and the seams on the bra were still sharp and her belly was still pretty pale so I guessed she just got it (the suit) — there was this one, with one of those chubby berry-faces, the lips all bunched together under her nose, this one, and a tall one, with black hair that hadn't quite frizzed right, and one of these sunburns right across the eyes, and a chin that was too long — you know, the kind of girl other girls think is very "striking" and "attractive" but never quite makes it, as they very well know, which is why they like her so much — and then the third one, that wasn't quite so tall. She was the queen. She kind of led them, the other two peeking around and making their shoulders round. She didn't look around, not this

---

1 Great Atlantic and Pacific Tea Company, an eastern supermarket chain.  2 Massachusetts town, the site of the famous seventeenth-century witch trials.

queen, she just walked straight on slowly, on these long white prima-donna legs. She came down a little hard on her heels, as if she didn't walk in her bare feet that much, putting down her heels and then letting the weight move along to her toes as if she was testing the floor with every step, putting a little deliberate extra action into it. You never know for sure how girls' minds work (do you really think it's a mind in there or just a little buzz like a bee in a glass jar?) but you got the idea she had talked the other two into coming in here with her, and now she was showing them how to do it, walk slow and hold yourself straight.

She had on a kind of dirty-pink — beige maybe, I don't know — bathing suit with a little nubble all over it and, what got me, the straps were down. They were off her shoulders looped loose around the cool tops of her arms, and I guess as a result the suit had slipped a little on her, so all around the top of the cloth there was this shining rim. If it hadn't been there you wouldn't have known there could have been anything whiter than those shoulders. With the straps pushed off, there was nothing between the top of the suit and the top of her head except just *her*, this clean bare plane of the top of her chest down from the shoulder bones like a dented sheet of metal tilted in the light. I mean, it was more than pretty.

She had sort of oaky hair that the sun and salt had bleached, done up in a bun that was unravelling, and a kind of prim face. Walking into the A & P with your straps down, I suppose it's the only kind of face you *can* have. She held her head so high her neck, coming up out of those white shoulders, looked kind of stretched, but I didn't mind. The longer her neck was, the more of her there was.

5    She must have felt in the corner of her eye me and over my shoulder Stokesie in the second slot watching, but she didn't tip. Not this queen. She kept her eyes moving across the racks, and stopped, and turned so slow it made my stomach rub the inside of my apron, and buzzed to the other two, who kind of huddled against her for relief, and then they all three of them went up the cat-and-dog-food-breakfast-cereal-macaroni-rice-raisins-seasonings-spreads-spaghetti-soft-drinks-crackers-and-cookies aisle. From the third slot I look straight up this aisle to the meat counter, and I watched them all the way. The fat one with the tan sort of fumbled with the cookies, but on second thought she put the package back. The sheep pushing their carts down the aisle — the girls were walking against the usual traffic (not that we have one-way signs or anything) — were pretty hilarious. You could see them, when Queenie's white shoulders dawned on them, kind of jerk, or hop, or hiccup, but their eyes snapped back to their own baskets and on they pushed. I bet you could set off dynamite in an A & P and the people would by and large keep reaching and checking oatmeal off their lists and muttering "Let me see, there was a third thing, began with A, asparagus, no, ah, yes, applesauce!" or whatever it is they do mutter. But there was no doubt, this jiggled them. A few houseslaves in pin curlers even looked around after pushing their carts past to make sure what they had seen was correct.

You know, it's one thing to have a girl in a bathing suit down on the beach, where what with the glare nobody can look at each other much anyway, and another thing in the cool of the A & P, under the fluorescent lights, against all those stacked packages, with her feet paddling along naked over our checker-board green-and-cream rubber-tile floor.

"Oh Daddy," Stokesie said beside me. "I feel so faint."

"Darling," I said. "Hold me tight." Stokesie's married, with two babies chalked up on his fuselage already, but as far as I can tell that's the only difference. He's twenty-two, and I was nineteen this April.

"Is it done?" he asks, the responsible married man finding his voice. I forgot to say he thinks he's going to be manager some sunny day, maybe in 1990 when it's called the Great Alexandrov and Petrooshki Tea Company or something.

10      What he meant was, our town is five miles from a beach, with a big summer colony out on the Point, but we're right in the middle of town, and the women generally put on a shirt or shorts or something before they get out of the car into the street. And anyway these are usually women with six children and varicose veins mapping their legs and nobody, including them, could care less. As I say, we're right in the middle of town, and if you stand at our front doors you can see two banks and the Congregational church and the newspaper store and three real-estate offices and about twenty-seven old freeloaders tearing up Central Street because the sewer broke again. It's not as if we're on the Cape;[3] we're north of Boston and there's people in this town haven't seen the ocean for twenty years.

The girls had reached the meat counter and were asking McMahon something. He pointed, they pointed, and they shuffled out of sight behind a pyramid of Diet Delight peaches. All that was left for us to see was old McMahon patting his mouth and looking after them sizing up their joints. Poor kids, I began to feel sorry for them, they couldn't help it.

*****

Now here comes the sad part of the story, at least my family says it's sad, but I don't think it's so sad myself. The store's pretty empty, it being Thursday afternoon, so there was nothing much to do except lean on the register and wait for the girls to show up again. The whole store was like a pinball machine and I didn't know which tunnel they'd come out of. After a while they come around out of the far aisle, around the light bulbs, records at discount of the Caribbean Six or Tony Martin Sings or some such gunk you wonder they waste the wax on, sixpacks of candy bars, and plastic toys done up in cellophane that fall apart when a kid looks at them anyway. Around they come, Queenie still leading the way, and holding a little gray jar in her hand. Slots Three through Seven are unmanned and I could see her wondering between Stokes and me, but Stokesie with his usual luck draws an old party in baggy gray pants who stumbles up with four giant cans of pineapple juice (what do these bums *do* with all that pineapple juice? I've often asked myself) so the girls come to me. Queenie puts down the jar and I take it into my fingers icy cold. Kingfish Fancy Herring Snacks in Pure Sour Cream: 49¢. Now her hands are empty, not a ring or a bracelet, bare as God made them, and I wonder where the money's

3 Cape Cod, location of wealthy vacation homes and resorts.

coming from. Still with that prim look she lifts a folded dollar bill out of the hollow at the center of her nubbled pink top. The jar went heavy in my hand. Really, I thought that was so cute.

Then everybody's luck begins to run out. Lengel comes in from haggling with a truck full of cabbages on the lot and is about to scuttle into that door marked MANAGER behind which he hides all day when the girls touch his eye. Lengel's pretty dreary, teaches Sunday school and the rest, but he doesn't miss that much. He comes over and says, "Girls, this isn't the beach."

Queenie blushes, though maybe it's just a brush of sunburn I was noticing for the first time, now that she was so close. "My mother asked me to pick up a jar of herring snacks." Her voice kind of startled me, the way voices do when you see the people first, coming out so flat and dumb yet kind of tony, too, the way it ticked over "pick up" and "snacks." All of a sudden I slid right down her voice into her living room. Her father and the other men were standing around in ice-cream coats and bow ties and the women were in sandals picking up herring snacks on toothpicks off a big glass plate and they were all holding drinks the color of water with olives and sprigs of mint in them. When my parents have somebody over they get lemonade and if it's a real racy affair Schlitz in tall glasses with "They'll Do It Every Time" cartoons stencilled on.

15    "That's all right," Lengel said. "But this isn't the beach." His repeating this struck me as funny, as if it had just occurred to him, and he had been thinking all these years the A & P was a great big dune and he was the head lifeguard. He didn't like my smiling — as I say he doesn't miss much — but he concentrates on giving the girls that sad Sunday-school-superintendent stare.

Queenie's blush is no sunburn now, and the plump one in plaid, that I liked better from the back — a really sweet can — pipes up. "We weren't doing any shopping. We just came in for one thing."

"That makes no difference," Lengel tells her, and I could see from the way his eyes went that he hadn't noticed she was wearing a two-piece before. "We want you decently dressed when you come in here."

"We *are* decent," Queenie says suddenly, her lower lip pushing, getting sore now that she remembers her place, a place from which the crowd that runs the A & P must look pretty crummy. Fancy Herring Snacks flashed in her very blue eyes.

"Girls, I don't want to argue with you. After this come in here with your shoulders covered. It's our policy." He turns his back. That's policy for you. Policy is what the kingpins want. What the others want is juvenile delinquency.

20    All this while, the customers had been showing up with their carts but, you know, sheep, seeing a scene, they had all bunched up on Stokesie, who shook open a paper bag as gently as peeling a peach, not wanting to miss a word. I could feel in the silence everybody getting nervous, most of all Lengel, who asks me, "Sammy, have you rung up their purchase?"

I thought and said "No" but it wasn't about that I was thinking. I go through the punches, 4, 9, GROC, TOT—it's more complicated than you think, and after you do it often enough, it begins to make a little song, that you hear words to, in my case "Hello (*bing*) there, you (*gung*) hap-py *pee*-pul (*splat*)!" — the *splat* being the drawer flying out. I uncrease the bill, tenderly as you may imagine, it just having come from between the two smoothest scoops of vanilla

I had ever known were there, and pass a half and a penny into her narrow pink palm, and nestle the herrings in a bag and twist its neck and hand it over, all the time thinking.

The girls, and who'd blame them, are in a hurry to get out, so I say "I quit" to Lengel quick enough for them to hear, hoping they'll stop and watch me, their unsuspected hero. They keep right on going, into the electric eye; the door flies open and they flicker across the lot to their car, Queenie and Plaid and Big Tall Goony-Goony (not that as raw material she was so bad), leaving me with Lengel and a kink in his eyebrow.

"Did you say something, Sammy?"

"I said I quit."

"I thought you did."

"You didn't have to embarrass them."

"It was they who were embarrassing us."

I started to say something that came out "Fiddle-de-doo." It's a saying of my grandmother's, and I know she would have been pleased.

"I don't think you know what you're saying," Lengel said.

"I know you don't," I said. "But I do." I pull the bow at the back of my apron and start shrugging it off my shoulders. A couple customers that had been heading for my slot begin to knock against each other, like scared pigs in a chute.

Lengel sighs and begins to look very patient and old and gray. He's been a friend of my parents for years. "Sammy, you don't want to do this to your Mom and Dad," he tells me. It's true, I don't. But it seems to me that once you begin a gesture it's fatal not to go through with it. I fold the apron, "Sammy" stitched in red on the pocket, and put it on the counter, and drop the bow tie on top of it. The bow tie is theirs, if you've ever wondered. "You'll feel this for the rest of your life," Lengel says, and I know that's true, too, but remembering how he made that pretty girl blush makes me so scrunchy inside I punch the No Sale tab and the machine whirs "pee-pul" and the drawer splats out. One advantage to this scene taking place in summer, I can follow this up with a clean exit, there's no fumbling around getting your coat and galoshes, I just saunter into the electric eye in my white shirt that my mother ironed the night before, and the door heaves itself open, and outside the sunshine is skating around on the asphalt.

I look around for my girls, but they're gone, of course. There wasn't anybody but some young married screaming with her children about some candy they didn't get by the door of a powder-blue Falcon station wagon. Looking back in the big windows, over the bags of peat moss and aluminum lawn furniture stacked on the pavement, I could see Lengel in my place in the slot, checking the sheep through. His face was dark gray and his back stiff, as if he'd just had an injection of iron, and my stomach kind of fell as I felt how hard the world was going to be to me hereafter.

(1961)

# Elizabeth McGrath   (b. 1932)

A native of St. John's, Newfoundland, short story writer and English professor Elizabeth McGrath grew up in St. John's, St. Mary's, Harbour Grace, and Montreal. She studied and taught at several Canadian universities before returning to Newfoundland to teach at Memorial University. "Fogbound in Avalon," which first appeared in *The New Yorker* magazine, is based in part on her own experiences. In this short story, the narrator attempts, after the breakup of her marriage, to find focus in her life by returning to her home town and renewing old friendships. The fog that shrouds the airport and the rough landing it causes are physical foreshadowings of the psychological difficulties that the narrator will face.

# FOGBOUND IN AVALON [1]

Neither Laurel nor I will ever be certifiable, I imagine, though, having put in, between us, going on a hundred years in this world, we have inevitably had a brush or two with the darker side of things. So this will not be a story of alienation. And to put your mind at rest, right from the beginning, we have never been in love with each other, in spite of having been reared in the most repressive of girls' schools from the ages of five to eighteen.

Laurel and I, middle-aged, neurotic, still thin, still suffering, still fascinated by the world and ourselves in it, are friends. We were born on this rock, Newfoundland, and are fixed in the cracks of it, through and beyond the sparse topsoil, in a way that makes us neither want to nor be able to free ourselves, ever. Laurel, except for holidays in Europe and the Caribbean and occasional forays into New York, has been here all her life. I, Anne-Marie, onetime academic — Presentation Convent, Collège Sophie-Barat, Memorial, Oxford — am another kettle of fish.

For about twenty years we circled each other, meeting once a year when I came back from wherever I had been, tentative, polite, mildly admiring of each other, gradually spilling a bean here and a bean there until so many beans had been spilled that there was no going back from it. And we found ourselves, not unhappily, in that giggling communion characteristic of the passionate friendships of thirteen and a half. What we don't know about each other now you could put in your eye. What is more, what she and I don't know about the others on this rock isn't worth knowing. When we put our heads together, and we frequently do, we can pool enough of everyone's tatty little secrets to blackmail all the professions, including the oldest, the civil service, the clergy, and every House of Assembly back to 1855.

Just about everybody here is related by blood, marriage, or sheer tomfoolery to everybody else, and we all know our cousins to the third and fourth degree. At the rate we reproduce, emigrate, wander the world, and keep in

---

1 the most southeasterly peninsula of Newfoundland. In Celtic mythology, the blessed island of Avalon was believed to be the final resting place of King Arthur.

touch, there is no secret service that can approach us. What may be called ESP elsewhere can be nailed down here by genealogy, and we are all expert. Yesterday morning Laurel was telling me that when they were five she and her twin brother took the diapers off the minister's daughter to get a look at what was so carefully concealed. In the afternoon I called her and said, "Hey, remember Daphne Green?" "Remember her?" said Laurel. "She's the one Leonard and I took the diapers off. What in God's name made you ask about her?" "I've been hearing little baby voices all day," I said, "whispering to me 'Daphne Green, Daphne Green.'"

5     The truth is, I'd been warming a bench at Canada Manpower most of the afternoon with one of the other rock-born overeducated, bilingual unemployed and Daphne's name came up, the way names do, because I'd asked who his wife was. All you need in this town to get a reputation for extraordinary powers is a large acquaintance, a few elementary research skills, and coincidence. Laurel, of course, being a thoroughgoing romantic, wants to believe in the spookies and so she does. I don't, but I like to cater to her. My own reluctant rationalism is one of the things that keep me from going mad, but I do break out from time to time.

Fern, Laurel's husband — surgeon, reliable backbencher, utterly devoted to her (christened, unfortunately, Ferdinand, because his mother was a great reader of the lesser works of Lord Beaconsfield)[2] — is the only one of us who can pass muster as a healthy, well-integrated, well-adjusted dealer with life. If he weren't there to remind us unremittingly of health, sanity, hard work, and the old-fashioned values of the Church of England in Canada, I don't know where we'd be. He and Laurel have lived amid her storms and his calms for twenty years, and their daughters, both at college on the mainland, are beautiful and bright and loving and a credit to them. Actually, all our children are pretty good.

Though the men on this island are great talkers — never shutting up, as the rest of the country has cause to know — they don't talk much about themselves to women. If they do talk to each other of how they feel, they certainly don't let on about it. As a charter member of the Status of Women Council I should, I suppose, hack away at that, but I don't and won't. I am concerned with what people do. What they think in the inner recesses of their own beings is their own damned business. Unless they are moved to tell me, I will never know, and it is better not to ask. It wasn't very long ago that my children's father, Con O'Neill, told me what was in his head, at my request. It took him four and a half days, at the end of which I prevailed upon him to buy me four plane tickets from Vancouver to St. John's. I then resigned from the only really good job I have ever had and launched myself back to the rock, the Public Service Commission, Canada Manpower, the vagaries of Memorial University, and a dilapidated three-story frame dwelling fifty yards from where I had been born forty-two years before.

*****

2 Benjamin Disraeli, nineteenth-century British prime minister and novelist. Ferdinand is the hero of his novel *Henrietta Temple* (1837).

Not five hours out of Vancouver, coincidence and further disaster overtook me in the person of Hugh Forbes, run into at Halifax Airport as I shepherded three dazed and baffled kids off one flight and onto another. Hugh, asking loudly, "Jesus, Annie, what have you got there, a traveling circus?" Hugh, whom I hadn't seen since the winter I was twenty-one, changed almost beyond recall but merging into himself, Cape Shore[3] voice and all, as we talked on the two-seat side of the DC-9 and the kids slept, across the aisle, on the three-seat side.

I had braced myself for what had appeared to be only the first of many awkward but insignificant encounters with my past. After the usual stylized exchanges, I realized I had miscalculated.

10      "Going home on holiday, Annie?" asked Hugh.

"Not exactly," I said.

The feeling of being at a disadvantage with Hugh was familiar. Even the setting was eerily appropriate — Hugh and I, side by side in some vehicle, each wondering who would be the first to break the silence. I plunged in. "As a matter of fact, I am right this moment *leaving* home. I'm a bit punchy, so don't expect me to make too much sense."

"Annie, I don't remember your ever making too much sense. But I think I get the message. You blew it."

Lack of directness had never been one of Hugh's failings. I must have looked stricken, for he was immediately contrite and slightly embarrassed.

15      "Annie, I'm sorry. I didn't mean to be quite so blunt."

"It's all right," I said, making a face at him. "I find it reassuring that you haven't changed all that much."

He still looked embarrassed.

"Perhaps I'd better go sit somewhere else." He started to unbuckle his seat belt. "You'd probably rather not be bothered with me right now."

"Hugh, no," I said. "I'd like to talk. Please."

20      I looked at him. He seemed solid and friendly and, in spite of being annoyed with himself for his blunder, amused and curious. So I gave him fifteen minutes of the story of my life.

He listened without interrupting. As I talked, I watched his hands rebuckling the seat belt, unbuttoning his jacket, adjusting the tray, reaching for coffee from the stewardess, scratching his head, using a handkerchief, twisting his ring. Guilt and nostalgia flooded over me.

"Your hands," I said, "your arms, they're all right!"

He turned his palms upward, flexed his fingers, stretched his arms. "Yes," he said. "Good enough."

"How did you do it?"

25      "On hate, mostly."

There was a long silence. Nineteen fifty-nine had been the year of the last St. John's polio epidemic. Hugh, home from McGill, engineer's iron ring on his finger, job offer in his pocket, had found himself one August morning, after a weekend of pain and fever, flat on his back in the Fever Hospital with both arms immovable.

---

3 residents of the area between Placentia and Cape St. Mary's speak with a distinctive, almost Irish, accent.

"September," he said quietly, looking at me with a face devoid of expression. "All September I spent two hours a day watching my girl Annie making a public spectacle of herself on bloody television. I told myself that I was going to get my hands and arms back, if only to wring your neck. I hated and Ma prayed. It worked like a charm. By Christmas I was going to dances. My arms were in slings, but the fingers were good. By spring I had the slings off. After eighteen months I was able to work. After two years I was ready to pick a fight with Con O'Neill and break his jaw. After that I packed my bags and lit out for Ontario, all cured."

"None of it had anything to do with Con," I said.

"As I perceived it, it had a great deal to do with Con. And apart from everything else I was disgusted with your whole carry on."

30 "I was afraid of you," I said. "You scared me to death. All I could see was you beating around while I minded youngsters and forgot how to read and write."

"It wouldn't have been like that."

"Don't tell me," I said. "Anyway, what about my neck?"

"What?" He was momentarily puzzled.

"Do you want to wring it?"

35 "Hell, no, girl. I never wring ladies' necks when they're down and out. I kiss them instead. Better for everybody."

He leaned across and kissed me. The tears stung in my eyes.

"Oh my God, Annie, you're not still at that!"

"I always get tears in my eyes when in the grip of strong feeling," I said in my lecture-room voice.

He looked at me in amazed disbelief, then looked again and exploded into laughter. I could feel the hot blush climbing to my hairline.

40 "Dear Lord above! Every time I'd put my arm around you, you'd start to bawl. I thought you were afraid for your virtue. Well, I'm damned."

I blinked, sniffed, and smiled at him. "Well, now you know," I said. "Better late than never."

Hugh smiled back. "Thanks, Annie."

Sweetest Mother, I thought, I love him. "Hugh," I said quietly, "I think we scuttled the ship."

"Yes," he said. "We sure as hell did."

45 He turned to look out the window, then adjusted his seat to the horizontal and closed his eyes.

"My son Gerald," he said. "My wife Clare."

Again there was silence. He readjusted his seat to the vertical and turned back to face me. "Gerald died one night when he was six months old. Crib death, they called it; no explanation, no one's guilt, they said. Still, Clare took to the bottle and after three years of it I took to the girls. And there we are. But we're still married and we're going to stay married. Make no mistake."

I said nothing. Hugh's forthrightness had left me stunned.

"One thing more, Annie. If you and I are going to be friends, you will never refer to any of it again. But I want you to keep it in mind."

50 He pointed a thumb across the aisle at the sleeping children. "What about them? Were you good at it?"

"Yes," I said, clutching at a subject I could at least talk about. "Like falling off a log. It's in the blood."

He looked at me speculatively. "I should have stuffed you full of babies and stuck you down with Mom on Cape St. Mary's.[4] She'd have learned you the five sorrowful mysteries[5] all right."

"I learned," I said.

"I don't know. Seems to me you could still use some toughening up."

55    He took my hand, called the stewardess, ordered a bottle of champagne, and told her we had just got engaged.

"Forbes," she said, "if you get engaged on my flight one more time, I will personally drown you in champagne."

The landing was the worst I have ever had, even in Torbay fog.[6] Passengers I recognized as old hands showed in the rigid set of their shoulders what I myself felt — too much airspeed, the runway overshot, and a violent touchdown with too many rebounds off the tarmac. I was trying to remember if the runway ended at a cliff, a hill, or the woods, when we came to a shuddering stop. There was absolute quiet and then the captain's voice: "Ladies and gentlemen, as you may have noticed, we have just landed at St. John's."

A ripple of laughter ran through the aircraft and an audible communal sigh of relief. Hugh stood up, collected his briefcase and raincoat, and touched my shoulder with his free hand. "That time, Annie, it almost ended happily ever after." He smiled bleakly. "I'll call you."

I watched him as he headed up the aisle, and then I busied myself with the children. My sister Catherine met me in the crowded terminal. We went to Mother's, put the still groggy children to bed, took care of half a bottle of Captain Morgan,[7] and turned in ourselves. The next morning I was going to have to turf my tenants out of my house on St. Columb's Street and start job hunting.

*****

60    What happens when you bolt after sixteen years, four universities, three kids, the whole of Eng. Lit. read together, Paris, Florence, London, Oxford, Toronto, Lisbon, Washington, Vancouver, and hundreds of friends held in common? What I did was stash my books in Vancouver and go back home. I went because I wanted to do nothing else. I didn't want to face another city, another group of strangers. My ears hungered for the accents of the island. I wanted the smells and sights and sounds of St. John's Harbor, my father's grave, my mother's tenacious grip on life, old people I had known when they were young, middle-aged people I had known when they were children. I wanted my house on St. Columb's Street, groceries from Belbin's, gas from Fred and Eric Adams, vitamins from Stowe's Pharmacy, understanding from Laurel and Fern, and the children of my friends for my children. I wanted to terrify myself climbing up Barter's Hill in the sleet, to drive to Corner Brook and back in a night and a day, seeing if I could still evade the Mounties and not kill myself, to lie

4 the most southwesterly tip of the Avalon Peninsula. 5 grief of the Virgin Mary for the sufferings of Christ. 6 Torbay Airport, St. John's, is noted for its dense fogs. 7 brand of rum.

on the grass listening to the blessed silence in St. Mary's, and to breathe on the embers of old friendships and see if the flames would light my way out of the dark.

In spite of the encounter with Hugh, I was in good shape when I arrived. "Am I not the very picture of the wronged wife?" I said to Fern, and he laughed and hugged me and we all had a drink to celebrate. Five months later I had lost twenty-five pounds I could ill afford losing, my temper was unreliable, and I was still unemployed, but my children were happy and my house was looking less like a slum.

St. Columb's Street used to be solidly middle-class, occupied by people associated with the ships and stores of the port. My own house once belonged to a ship's chandler.[8] Some of the others were built by captains and shipowners who lived here because of the incomparable view of the town and the harbor — every ship that comes and goes can be seen from my kitchen window. Now many of the bigger houses have become "multiple-family dwellings," the pretty, decrepit terraces are occupied by the poor, and some foreign entrepreneur has put up a yellow brick apartment house directly opposite me. The roadway is potholed, the sidewalks crumbling and cracked. Rough-looking teen-agers skylark and catcall outside the corner stores, speaking a dialect that suggests a lengthy inheritance of infected adenoids and bad teeth.

But at the top of the street is the hospital where I was born: farther down is St. Columb's Church, which my grandmother's grandfather helped build; and beside it is St. Columb's Convent, which houses an elderly nun who taught me to read and write and made me, over six years, memorize the whole of Butler's *Catechism* and MacLaren and Campbell's *Grammar*.[9] These are the things I think about on the days when I struggle with the idea that I do not really belong here. And, try as I may, I cannot see myself old, with my grandchildren visiting, in this house on St. Columb's Street. It makes me unbearably, unutterably, sad. The Heritage Foundation is interested in us now and determined to improve us. I am afraid I may have to move, along with the other poor, since I cannot afford to be improved any further. Sooner or later someone with the money to repair the roof flashings and the rotting window frames and the exterior paint and the leaking laundry room will make me an offer and I will have to accept it.

The house — my house for the moment — is a narrow, plain three-story with bow windows and a peaked roof. It must have been intended for a large family with no servants, for the kitchen is the biggest room and there is only one bathroom and no back stairs. Built the year that I was born, it just misses being good, even of its kind. I suppose the ship's chandler ran out of money, too. The house has that look. The exterior walls and the floors are sound and strong and draftproof; the fireplaces are pleasant thirties neoclassical; the doors are paneled and the windows big and generously framed. But the walls are surfaced with painted or papered fiberboard instead of plaster, and the wainscoting and the additions made over the years are ill-conceived and cheap, running to plywood and wood-grained Arborite and acoustic tile.

8 merchant who sells supplies and equipment to ships. 9 standard religious and grammar texts in Newfoundland Catholic schools of the 1940s and 1950s.

65   How I acquired the house at all is an earnest of the emotional myopia with which I am afflicted. My marriage to Con had gone through one of its intermittent crises following a move from Toronto to Vancouver. Con suggested that since we hadn't much capital, certainly not enough to buy a house in expensive Vancouver, it would be sensible to invest in a house in an older part of St. John's, live in it for a summer, and then rent it. Our children would then have a base of operations, a home that would exist in their minds wherever they happened to be in actuality. To me the proposal made perfect sense. I had never seen myself as an emigrant, merely a traveler. The idea of a home on the island appealed to me and I liked the implicit promise that we would eventually all return. When the break came, the house was there, with boxes of old toys and baby clothes in the attic, discarded prams and pushchairs in the cellar, clothes hooks with the children's names on them in the bathroom, and odds and ends of furniture from my own childhood home in the bedrooms and living room.

By then responsibility for the house, for keeping it insured and tenanted, had gradually devolved on me. I was mildly mystified but not displeased. I saw the process as being one with the independence I was gaining as the children grew older and I settled, once again, into a fulltime job at the university. The years during which I had been, uncomfortably and resentfully, a financial dependent faded away and I assumed, along with the house on St. Columb's Street, responsibility for paying almost everything to do with myself and the children, except keeping the Vancouver roof over our heads. Food, clothing, dentistry, toys, Christmas, birthdays came out of my income from my job. We had been setting the stage for years. When the curtain went up, I said my lines and made my moves. We all did, even the children. "We knew it was a matter of time," my daughter said. "We just didn't know when. We thought it wouldn't be so soon." Nor did I.

\*\*\*\*\*

My first morning in St. John's, Laurel met me at Mother's and came with me to look at the house. All my tenants had been university students, so I assumed that not much housekeeping had been done. They had rented rooms to one another in a complex set of permutations that I had never tried to keep track of as long as they paid the rent punctually. Time and the salt air had worked their will on the exterior paint of the house, but it had been fairly shabby to begin with. When I opened the door, Laurel went rigid with shock. An effluvium of Victorian dimensions asssaulted us. The hall was crammed with old boots and dust-laden cartons of empty beer bottles. The windows were opaque with dirt, and where the panes had been broken, on either side of the door, pieces of plastic had been stretched over them and secured with bits of rough lath nailed into the moldings. The walls and floors had not been washed since I had left. The carpets were stained and felted with dog hair. Filthy and half furnished, without curtains or pictures, with its paint scabby, its wallpaper peeling, and its plastic tile discolored, the house was tawdry. "You cannot propose to live in this," Laurel said flatly. But I could and I did.

The children, when I moved them in, wept over their shattered fantasies. I attacked what I could with bucket and mop, Glass Wax and cloth, crowbar and paintbrush. The children, after their initial distress, channeled their energies and their disappointment into working with me. They took apart the broken fences and cut them into kindling. They lugged out sheets of wallboard and plywood and eight-foot two-by-fours as my crowbar did its work. They carried mattresses and bedsteads down from the attic and up from the cellar. I had not realized how strong ten- and twelve-year-olds can be when they have a job they want to do. When a semblance of normality had been achieved, they just quit and concentrated once again on their private concerns — school, games, hobbies, squabbling, television, and eating.

They were puzzled by my evident lack of pleasure in just being alive, in having a house to live in and enough to eat and wear and them to love me. I overheard one saying, "Why is she unhappy?" and another answering, "Life gave her a raw deal." I felt ashamed of not being happier and tried to smile more, but they asked me why I had that funny look on my face. I opted for the truth, which they found odd but uninteresting.

70     The process of recovering the house was alternately uplifting and depressing. "I refuse to lie here and watch you seesaw," said my mother, but did it nonetheless. When I had got one room fit for human habitation I persuaded her to stop for lunch on her way back from a visit to her doctor. "This is perfectly respectable," she said, on looking around my sitting room. "I fail to see what you are making such a fuss about." At that point, I found myself wanting not even to think about another tin of paint. I let the brushes dry and the children revert to their usual slovenly practices. I began, in spite of myself, to think of what it was going to mean to be on my own with no one to bitch at, no one to protect the kids from my habitual anxieties, no one to lean on, no one to sleep with, and, above all, no one to tell me, perhaps for the rest of my life, that I was essential to his breathing and being. Hugh? It was two months before Hugh turned up.

I was hammering palings into the front fence when a Land-Rover stopped at the curb and Hugh got out. I wanted to put my arms around him, but he had a very don't-touch-me look about him, so I just said it was good to see him and held on to my hammer for security. He said that he had just swung by to see how I was getting on and that I should write or call if there was anything he could do to help. I replied dryly that there were more accessible sources of help than his sweet self but that I would be glad to see him any time he got tired of doing whatever it was he did. He gave me his card, said he'd be back to share a dinner the following weekend, got into his Land-Rover, saluted, and drove off. I looked at the card and put it in my pocket. It had a Toronto address, and I thought how for seven years we had probably lived no more than fifteen blocks from each other in Don Mills.[10]

I threw down the hammer and went into the house to make tea. I drank it too fast, burned my tongue, and fired the mug viciously against the fireplace, smashing it and splattering tea over the newly scrubbed hearthrug. The mug had had a motto painted on the side. Later, I fitted the bits together, and read, "A house is made of bricks and stone but a home is made of love alone." I put the pieces on the hearth and bashed them to powder with the poker.

10 district in the City of North York, Ontario.

Hugh then appeared out of nowhere every two or three weeks, only to disappear into nowhere again. It seemed he did something with fish and oil and airplanes for the federal government. That made for a connection with Fern and Laurel. Sometimes he arrived on my doorstep monumentally plastered,[11] mirthful and bawdy, two quintals[12] and a fathom of black-hearted, cod-fed bayman.[13] Sometimes, rarely, he was sober and subtle, all civil servant and about as friendly as a cobra. I would hear his acquired Toronto accent overpowering the dental *t*'s and fog-soft vowels of the Cape Shore, and it served to remind me of what I would have preferred to forget.

I didn't ask questions of Hugh. He was there or he wasn't. He was sober or he wasn't. He loved me or he didn't. When he was drunk, I told him how beautiful he was and how I adored him. When he was sober, we talked politics and oil and mutual friends; I was careful not to show temper, and we tacitly avoided discussing how we felt. Either way, I was put into a state of elevation that sometimes lasted for days. The rest of my life the cats could have. But what was there to do? Making things happen was not my line. I watched, I listened, I cared. Nothing else was possible for me. I was through with moral imperatives: I care, therefore I am. I think, therefore I will make mistakes.

75        Though jobless, I was neither idle nor solitary. There was, if anything, too much to do, too many obligations, hordes of visiting children, and endless chores. I was ruthless about protecting my privacy, however, and my three hours of peace after the children were in bed and before midnight had overtaken me. I did not, except on very rare occasions, turn on television or stereo or take to drink. Except for smoking, I tried to do myself as little physical and spiritual harm as possible. Sometimes I even went to mass at St. Columb's, just in case. But I did, all the same, spend many days and nights in domestic squalor and intellectual tedium. I would go as much as six or eight weeks without balancing my checkbook, reading nothing but old copies of the *Atlantic* and the *Saturday Review*, washing the children's clothes in the bathwater and hanging them to dry on the bannister rails because I couldn't be bothered calling the repairman to fix the washer and dryer. I was sick to death of being bullied by ambition, concepts of efficiency, the demands of an academic conscience, fear at being out of work or even my own convenience.

Laurel held Hugh responsible for my otherwise unaccountable behaviour. I was a veteran of unrequited love, though, and surely familiar with its symptoms. I diagnosed, rather, some unease of the soul. Muddled and grubby, I read third-rate fiction and fourth-rate biography, thought fifth-rate thoughts, and felt sixth-rate emotions. And I was not at home on St. Columb's Street. I was instead, like a bird on a bush, waiting for whatever would happen next so that I would know what to do.

I talked a lot to Laurel. We were on the phone for at least thirty minutes a day. She visited me only rarely, for both the house and the neighborhood were in a world she did not care to inhabit and they made her uneasy. More frequently I visited her, early in the morning after I left the children off at school. I entered her world more easily than she did mine. We would sit in her ordered

11 drunk.  12 in Newfoundland, a measure of 112 pounds, or about 50.8 kilograms, usually of dried and salted cod fish.  13 usually a derogatory term for a rural or outport person.

living room (oh, the relief of it!), me in jeans and sweater, with untidy hair, she combed and brushed and tidily made up but in an ugly green fuzzy dressing gown, hands shaking from insomnia and cigarettes and not following the diet required by her mild diabetes. We would ask each other if we were, as people told us, eccentric or simply mad as hares. We considered our acquaintances and determined that by and large they were even more appalling than ourselves, apart from the few saints who were out of our league and therefore irrelevant to the discussion. We concluded that we did not want to be other than who we were. What we were was another question. We spent a scandalous amount of time talking it out. I talked about my past, my emotions, unemployment, the current state of my house, my mind, or my bank account. She talked about her depression, the causes of which had never emerged. I talked about my rages, the causes of which had been only too evident. We compared childhoods, holiday trips, attitudes, fantasies. I suggested that she got depressed because of hunger, perversity, boredom, and the indulgence of an excess of sensibility. She suggested that my malaise could be cured by Hugh. I told her that it was just as likely to be cured by the Atlantic Loto, the Riding of Placentia-St. Mary's, or the Henrietta Harvey Professorship.[14] Even as I said it, I thought it was probably not true. But if I had lived my life as Hugh said I should have done, I should now be like Laurel and be hankering after the kind of life I had had and botched.

Laurel knows that everyone assumes that she is lazy and self-indulgent and ought to have a job to do. But I am aware of how scared she is and how her mind and energy are drained by fear, so that she stays in bed for days and weeks at a time. Her concern for Fern makes her come awake long enough to straighten the house and get the meals, and she always seems to deal with any emergencies, including the most trivial social ones. Her usual waking time, though, is between three and eight in the morning, when she reads, makes notes, writes letters and poems in her head that never see the light of day, thinks of killing herself, and tries to stop the shakes by force of will. Her will power is irresistible, and sooner or later anyone who has much to do with her will be made to dance to her tune. Though she has had virtually every psychogenic symptom known to medicine, she succeeds always in looking as healthy as a chestnut in blossom.

Once Laurel actually did swallow sleeping pills and then, in her wayward fashion, followed them with a tin of anchovies and was sick all over the kitchen. She cleaned up while Fern continued to sleep the sleep of the just. As she tells it, he had one of his rare fits of furious exasperation when she refused to get up and prepare his breakfast. There is no questioning that in Laurel's life the farcical element continually intrudes.

80    All the same, her headlong emotionalism may be one of the things that make Laurel a superb political wife. She and Fern attract a variegated tribe of friends, because he is true blue and she is beautiful and amusing and enormously sympathetic. Some of her enthusiasms have led to dinner parties that could bring the government down, and Fern has learned to keep a covert eye on their guest list. Because Laurel takes everyone at face value, she is the repository of a multitude of confidences, which frequently inspire her to quixotic

14 distinguished professorship in the English Department of Memorial University of Newfoundland.

action. One Saturday, early on, she dropped in at my house without calling first and encountered Hugh. Hugh will inflict his adventures on anyone he can pin down, but even when well oiled[15] he tends to keep himself to himself. Laurel got more out of him in ten minutes than I had done in as many weeks.

After she had left, he turned to me indignantly and said, "Why do I tell Laurel all that stuff? I must be cracked."

"People do," I said, and shrugged. "They spend five minutes with her or get her when they've dialed a wrong number and she has their life stories, just like that."

"I suppose she knows enough of both of us now to write the book."

"No," I said. "But she has eyes in her head. And she loves me. She may try to help things along. I can't stop her, you know."

85   He made a particularly vulgar comment.

*****

When Laurel gets upset and concerned about someone, she has the gall of a robber's horse. Last February, I had an especially trying couple of weeks, with frozen water pipes, an ill-functioning furnace, kids home from school with the flu, and three job interviews at which I had been told I was overqualified. I was tense and miserable and jumpy. I had been expecting Hugh and looking forward to seeing him, but he hadn't turned up. Laurel called to say that she and Fern had met Hugh at a government function the previous night and that he had been in great form. One of the crosses I was having to bear was being unable to prevent Laurel from reporting on Hugh's whereabouts. I heard her out and then I ventilated for an hour and used some fairly extravagant language, including a reference to slitting my wrists Roman style[16] so that I wouldn't leave too much mess behind.

That evening Hugh was at my door. I had temporarily dismissed him from my mind and had been attempting to concentrate on sick, crotchety children and on the dirt and snow and oil handprints left by furnace men and plumbers. I needed a bath and was red-eyed and sleepless from nights of keeping coal fires going in the bedroom grates and was in no mood for dealing with Hugh's usual attitude of detached amusement at my ridiculous plight.

"Come in," I said. "If you can get in." A gust of icy wind accompanied him — and more snow. "Don't bother taking off your boots. The mess is past the point where I even care about it."

"You're all right, though?" he asked, looking at me warily.

90   "Sure," I said. "Dandy." I jammed my coal-blackened hands into the pockets of my jeans and leaned against the newel post.

"You look done in," he said.

"Beat to a rag. Want some coffee?"

"No thanks. I just took a notion to stop by. I've got a meeting to get back to. You're sure you're all right?"

15 drunk.  16 Roman suicides often slit their wrists while bathing.

"Perfectly fine." I tried what I hoped was a cheerful grin. "I'm cold, I'm tired, I'm unemployed, and the house is falling down. Don't expect Pollyanna[17] in this climate."

95 "Kids O.K.?"

"Sick as pigs," I said. "And crooked as sin."

"Anything I can do? You've only to ask."

"I know," I said, "I know. But there isn't anything, truly. I just need some sleep and a change in the weather."

"Don't overdo it, Annie." He put his hand under my chin and made me look at him. "Anything on your mind? You're sure you're all right?"

100 This sort of solicitude was unheard of from Hugh, who would normally only inquire about my state of being if he found me with my head under my arm like the ghost of Anne Boleyn.[18] I had a sudden shattering glimmer of understanding.

"Have you seen Fern lately?" I hazarded.

"Not this trip," he replied blandly. "Too busy." He looked at his watch. "I'd better get back. Take care, Annie."

"Sure," I said. "Pray for a thaw."

As soon as I'd closed the door on Hugh, I called Laurel.

105 "What did you tell him, Laurel?" I said. "That I was about to hang myself in my garters because he done me wrong?"

"An-nie, you puz-zle me," she said in her most nervous and distinct Bishop Spencer College[19] accents.

"And you are a damned liar," I said.

"You know I ne-ver tell an untruth, An-nie."

"Laurel," I said, "I can tell when you're lying within five syllables. I'll see you in the morning if I don't die of shame first." I hung up.

110 After another night of sleeplessness, half a bottle of Irish whiskey, and a packet of lethal American cigarettes from our all-night pizza parlor, I went to Laurel's to tell her to get off my case. It wasn't easy. In twenty years we had never had a serious difference. With the help of a couple of pints of Strongbow,[20] I managed to enlighten her on the enormity of what she had done. By lunchtime, when Fern got home, I was wandering the house barefoot, hugging the cider mug and humming a dirty song that I'd learned from Hugh when I was a freshman. Fern patted me on the head, said it must be great to have nothing to do, and went back to the hospital to see someone whose legs were in traction. Laurel took her telling-off better than I dealt it out, and promised never to interfere again.

Then she asked me how my life was going and how I thought it would all work out. I turned the question back to her, and she said she should never have thrown up the pills. I said that perhaps she and Hugh would be killed in a car crash when they wickedly, and in heedless contravention of all the ground rules of friendship, slipped off to Clarenville for a weekend, leaving me and Fern, given a decent interval of mourning, to console each other. Her eyes widened and she laughed with delight.

17 optimistic heroine in early-twentieth-century children's novels written by Eleanor Porter.  18 the second wife of Henry VIII of England, she was beheaded in 1536.  19 Protestant high school in St. John's, generally attended by students of wealthier families.  20 brand of alcoholic cider.

"An-nie, you are naugh-ty," she said. "How per-fect!" And I knew I had not been all that far from the truth.

"It won't work," I said. "It's a horrible cliché."

"No, no," she said, and laughed again. "I can't wait to tell Fern."

115    What actually did occur was one night in early spring, having read myself into a stupor, fully clothed in my bed, along with dirty ashtrays, my accounts and calculator, carbons of job applications, the phone, an alarm clock, unanswered letters, unsent Christmas cards, *The Oxford Book of Oxford*, unread, *The Pauper's Cook Book*, and an illustrated essay on the paintings of Edvard Munch,[21] I fell asleep smoking a cigarette and woke at dawn to find that I had burned a hole through two carbons, a book bill from Blackwell's, and my only pair of sheets.

For some minutes I stared at the burn without moving, then I headed for the bathroom. My hands were shaking and my eyes were large and dark and frightened. My impulse was to wrap myself in a blanket, crawl back into bed, and go to sleep — deeply, deeply to sleep — when one of the children knocked at the door and asked the time. I snapped to attention, cleaned out the sink, called the others, and went downstairs. I made an unusually big breakfast and insisted that it be eaten. After I had taken the children to school, I returned home, washed the dishes, then gathered up all the loose papers I could find — the year's small collection of books and the 1669 Donne[22] I had brought in my pocket from Vancouver. I put them in the ashcan, and carried it out to the sidewalk. I washed my hair, had a bath, and dressed in a silk shirt and a suit. I called my mother's cleaning woman and arranged for three days of her time. As I left the house again, the phone rang, and while I stood in the doorway, not answering it, I saw that the ashmen had been and gone. I got into the car and drove slowly down St. Columb's Street.

The fog was coming in through the Narrows, but the sun was still shining and the town and the harbor were brilliant with color and beautiful beyond the reaches of fantasy. My throat hurt and I could hardly see. I thought about my grandmother's grandfather leaning out over the unfinished walls of St. Columb's, watching the arrival of the White Fleet.[23] I thought about Sister Columba in her convent and about the day I was born in the hospital at the top of the street. I thought about Hugh and Laurel and Fern and the Heritage Foundation. My heart was breaking, for I knew inescapably that I had already, once again, set out on my travels.

(1980)

---

21 early-twentieth-century Norwegian expressionist artist whose paintings explored the depths of human feelings. 22 early and therefore valuable edition of the works of English poet John Donne.
23 the white-painted boats of the Portuguese fishing fleet would sail into St. John's harbour for supplies or to escape bad weather.

# Philip Roth (b. 1933)

Philip Roth, a native of Newark, New Jersey, achieved international attention in 1959 with the publication of his first book, *Goodbye, Columbus*, a collection of short stories. In many of these stories, as in such later novels as *Portnoy's Complaint* and *The Ghost Writer*, Roth explores the attempts by Jewish boys and men to reconcile individual desires with the conflicting forces of contemporary American society and their religious heritage. "The Conversion of the Jews," from his first book, focusses on the religious earnestness and inner rebelliousness of Ozzie Freedman. As he confronts his mother and the rabbi, Ozzie seeks answers to questions that deeply puzzle him; he also looks to achieve a kind of heroism in the eyes of his fellow students. The title may have been taken from a line in Andrew Marvell's seventeenth-century poem "To His Coy Mistress" (see page 68), referring to an event many people believed would not occur until the end of time.

## THE CONVERSION OF THE JEWS

"You're a real one for opening your mouth in the first place," Itzie said. "What do you open your mouth all the time for?"

"I didn't bring it up, Itz, I didn't," Ozzie said.

"What do you care about Jesus Christ for anyway?"

"I didn't bring up Jesus Christ. He did. I didn't even know what he was talking about. Jesus is historical, he kept saying. Jesus is historical." Ozzie mimicked the monumental voice of Rabbi Binder.

5     "Jesus was a person that lived like you and me," Ozzie continued. "That's what Binder said —"

"Yeah?... So what! What do I give two cents whether he lived or not. And what do you gotta open your mouth!" Itzie Lieberman favored closed-mouthedness, especially when it came to Ozzie Freedman's questions. Mrs. Freedman had to see Rabbi Binder twice before about Ozzie's questions and this Wednesday at four-thirty would be the third time. Itzie preferred to keep *his* mother in the kitchen; he settled for behind-the-back subtleties such as gestures, faces, snarls and other less delicate barnyard noises.

"He was a real person, Jesus, but he wasn't like God, and we don't believe he is God." Slowly, Ozzie was explaining Rabbi Binder's position to Itzie, who had been absent from Hebrew School the previous afternoon.

"The Catholics," Itzie said helpfully, "they believe in Jesus Christ, that he's God." Itzie Lieberman used "the Catholics" in its broadest sense — to include the Protestants.

Ozzie received Itzie's remark with a tiny head bob, as though it were a footnote, and went on. "His mother was Mary, and his father probably was Joseph," Ozzie said. "But the New Testament says his real father was God."

10     "His *real* father?"

"Yeah," Ozzie said, "that's the big thing, his father's supposed to be God."

"Bull."

"That's what Rabbi Binder says, that it's impossible —"

"Sure it's impossible. That stuff's all bull. To have a baby you gotta get laid," Itzie theologized. "Mary hadda get laid."

15     "That's what Binder says: 'The only way a woman can have a baby is to have intercourse with a man.'"

"He said *that*, Ozz?" For a moment it appeared that Itzie had put the theological question aside. "He said that, intercourse?" A little curled smile shaped itself in the lower half of Itzie's face like a pink mustache. "What you guys do, Ozz, you laugh or something?"

"I raised my hand."

"Yeah? Whatja say?"

"That's when I asked the question."

20     Itzie's face lit up. "Whatja ask about — intercourse?"

"No, I asked the question about God, how if He could create the heaven and earth in six days — the light especially, that's what always gets me, that He could make the light. Making fish and animals, that's pretty good —"

"That's damn good." Itzie's appreciation was honest but unimaginative: it was as though God had just pitched a one-hitter.[1]

"But making light . . . I mean when you think about it, it's really something," Ozzie said. "Anyway, I asked Binder if He could make all that in six days, and He could *pick* the six days He wanted right out of nowhere, why couldn't He let a woman have a baby without having intercourse."

"You said intercourse, Ozz, to Binder?"

25     "Yeah."

"Right in class?"

"Yeah."

Itzie smacked the side of his head.

"I mean, no kidding around," Ozzie said, "that'd really be nothing. After all that other stuff, that'd practically be nothing."

30     Itzie considered a moment. "What'd Binder say?"

"He started all over again explaining how Jesus was historical and how he lived like you and me but he wasn't God. So I said I under*stood* that. What I wanted to know was different."

What Ozzie wanted to know was always different. The first time he had wanted to know how Rabbi Binder could call the Jews "The Chosen People" if the Declaration of Independence claimed all men to be created equal. Rabbi Binder tried to distinguish for him between political equality and spiritual legitimacy, but what Ozzie wanted to know, he insisted vehemently, was different. That was the first time his mother had to come.

Then there was the plane crash. Fifty-eight people had been killed in a plane crash at La Guardia. In studying a casualty list in the newspaper his mother had discovered among the list of those dead eight Jewish names (his grandmother had nine but she counted Miller as a Jewish name); because of the eight she said the plane crash was "a tragedy." During free-discussion time on Wednesday Ozzie had brought to Rabbi Binder's attention this matter of "some of his relations" always picking out the Jewish names. Rabbi Binder had begun to explain cultural unity and some other things when Ozzie stood up at his seat

---

1 baseball game in which the pitcher yields only one base hit.

and said that what he wanted to know was different. Rabbi Binder insisted that he sit down and it was then that Ozzie shouted that he wished all fifty-eight were Jews. That was the second time his mother came.

"And he kept explaining about Jesus being historical, and so I kept asking him. No kidding, Itz, he was trying to make me look stupid."

35 "So what he finally do?"

"Finally he starts screaming that I was deliberately simple-minded and a wise guy, and that my mother had to come, and this was the last time. And that I'd never get bar-mitzvahed if he could help it. Then, Itz, then he starts talking in that voice like a statue, real slow and deep, and he says that I better think over what I said about the Lord. He told me to go to his office and think it over." Ozzie leaned his body towards Itzie. "Itz, I thought it over for a solid hour, and now I'm convinced God could do it."

*****

Ozzie had planned to confess his latest transgression to his mother as soon as she came home from work. But it was a Friday night in November and already dark, and when Mrs. Freedman came through the door she tossed off her coat, kissed Ozzie quickly on the face, and went to the kitchen table to light the three yellow candles, two for the Sabbath[2] and one for Ozzie's father.

When his mother lit the candles she would move her two arms slowly towards her, dragging them through the air, as though persuading people whose minds were half made up. And her eyes would get glassy with tears. Even when his father was alive Ozzie remembered that her eyes had gotten glassy, so it didn't have anything to do with his dying. It had something to do with lighting the candles.

As she touched the flaming match to the unlit wick of a Sabbath candle, the phone rang, and Ozzie, standing only a foot from it, plucked it off the receiver and held it muffled to his chest. When his mother lit candles Ozzie felt there should be no noise; even breathing, if you could manage it, should be softened. Ozzie pressed the phone to his breast and watched his mother dragging whatever she was dragging, and he felt his own eyes get glassy. His mother was a round, tired, gray-haired penguin of a woman whose gray skin had begun to feel the tug of gravity and the weight of her own history. Even when she was dressed up she didn't look like a chosen person. But when she lit candles she looked like something better; like a woman who knew momentarily that God could do anything.

40 After a few mysterious minutes she was finished. Ozzie hung up the phone and walked to the kitchen table where she was beginning to lay the two places for the four-course Sabbath meal. He told her that she would have to see Rabbi Binder next Wednesday at four-thirty, and then he told her why. For the first time in their life together she hit Ozzie across the face with her hand.

All through the chopped liver and chicken soup part of the dinner Ozzie cried; he didn't have any appetite for the rest.

*****

2 celebration of the Jewish Sabbath begins at sundown Friday.

On Wednesday, in the largest of the three basement classrooms of the synagogue, Rabbi Marvin Binder, a tall, handsome, broad-shouldered man of thirty
with thick strong-fibered black hair, removed his watch from his pocket and
saw that it was four o'clock. At the rear of the room Yakov Blotnik, the
seventy-one-year-old custodian, slowly polished the large window, mumbling
to himself, unaware that it was four o'clock or six o'clock, Monday or Wednesday. To most of the students Yakov Blotnik's mumbling, along with his
brown curly beard, scythe nose, and two heel-trailing black cats, made him an
object of wonder, a foreigner, a relic, towards whom they were alternately
fearful and disrespectful. To Ozzie the mumbling had always seemed a monotonous, curious prayer; what made it curious was that old Blotnik had been
mumbling so steadily for so many years, Ozzie suspected he had memorized
the prayers and forgotten all about God.

"It is now free-discussion time," Rabbi Binder said. "Feel free to talk about
any Jewish matter at all — religion, family, politics, sports —"

There was silence. It was a gusty, clouded November afternoon and it did
not seem as though there ever was or could be a thing called baseball. So
nobody this week said a word about that hero from the past, Hank Greenberg[3] —
which limited free discussion considerably.

45    And the soul-battering Ozzie Freedman had just received from Rabbi
Binder had imposed its limitation. When it was Ozzie's turn to read aloud
from the Hebrew book the rabbi had asked him petulantly why he didn't read
more rapidly. He was showing no progress. Ozzie said he could read faster but
that if he did he was sure not to understand what he was reading. Nevertheless,
at the rabbi's repeated suggestion Ozzie tried, and showed a great talent, but in
the midst of a long passage he stopped short and said he didn't understand a
word he was reading, and started in again at a drag-footed pace. Then came the
soul-battering.

Consequently when free-discussion time rolled around none of the students
felt too free. The rabbi's invitation was answered only by the mumbling of
feeble old Blotnik.

"Isn't there anything at all you would like to discuss?" Rabbi Binder asked
again, looking at his watch. "No questions or comments?"

There was a small grumble from the third row. The rabbi requested that
Ozzie rise and give the rest of the class the advantage of his thought.

Ozzie rose. "I forget it now," he said, and sat down in his place.

50    Rabbi Binder advanced a seat towards Ozzie and poised himself on the edge
of the desk. It was Itzie's desk and the rabbi's frame only a dagger's-length
away from his face snapped him to sitting attention.

"Stand up again, Oscar," Rabbi Binder said calmly, "and try to assemble
your thoughts."

Ozzie stood up. All his classmates turned in their seats and watched as he
gave an unconvincing scratch to his forehead.

"I can't assemble any," he announced, and plunked himself down.

"Stand up!" Rabbi Binder advanced from Itzie's desk to the one directly
in front of Ozzie; when the rabbinical back was turned Itzie gave it five-fingers

3 all-star player for the Detroit Tigers baseball team in the 1930s and 1940s.

off the tip of his nose, causing a small titter in the room. Rabbi Binder was too absorbed in squelching Ozzie's nonsense once and for all to bother with titters. "Stand up, Oscar. What's your question about?"

55     Ozzie pulled a word out of the air. It was the handiest word. "Religion."

"Oh, now you remember?"

"Yes."

"What is it?"

Trapped, Ozzie blurted the first thing that came to him. "Why can't He make anything he wants to make!"

60     As Rabbi Binder prepared an answer, a final answer, Itzie, ten feet behind him, raised one finger on his left hand, gestured it meaningfully towards the rabbi's back, and brought the house down.

Binder twisted quickly to see what had happened and in the midst of the commotion Ozzie shouted into the rabbi's back what he couldn't have shouted to his face. It was a loud, toneless sound that had the timbre of something stored inside for about six days.

"You don't know! You don't know anything about God!"

The rabbi spun back towards Ozzie. "What?"

"You don't know — you don't —"

65     "Apologize, Oscar, apologize!" It was a threat.

"You don't —"

Rabbi Binder's hand flicked out at Ozzie's cheek. Perhaps it had only meant to clamp the boy's mouth shut, but Ozzie ducked and the palm caught him squarely on the nose.

The blood came in a short, red spurt on to Ozzie's shirt front.

The next moment was all confusion. Ozzie screamed, "You bastard, you bastard!" and broke for the classroom door. Rabbi Binder lurched a step backwards, as though his own blood had started flowing violently in the opposite direction, then gave a clumsy lurch forward and bolted out the door after Ozzie. The class followed after the rabbi's huge blue-suited back, and before old Blotnik could turn from his window, the room was empty and everyone was headed full speed up the three flights leading to the roof.

*****

70     If one should compare the light of day to the life of man: sunrise to birth; sunset — the dropping down over the edge — to death; then as Ozzie Freedman wiggled through the trapdoor of the synagogue roof, his feet kicking backwards bronco-style at Rabbi Binder's outstretched arms — at that moment the day was fifty years old. As a rule, fifty or fifty-five reflects accurately the age of late afternoons in November, for it is in that month, during those hours, that one's awareness of light seems no longer a matter of seeing, but of hearing: light begins clicking away. In fact, as Ozzie locked shut the trapdoor in the rabbi's face, the sharp click of the bolt into the lock might momentarily have been mistaken for the sound of the heavier gray that had just throbbed through the sky.

With all his weight Ozzie kneeled on the locked door; any instant he was certain that Rabbi Binder's shoulder would fling it open, splintering the wood into shrapnel and catapulting his body into the sky. But the door did not move and below him he heard only the rumble of feet, first loud then dim, like thunder rolling away.

A question shot through his brain. "Can this be *me?*" For a thirteen-year-old who had just labeled his religious leader a bastard, twice, it was not an improper question. Louder and louder the question came to him — "Is it me?" "Is it me?" — until he discovered himself no longer kneeling, but racing crazily towards the edge of the roof, his eyes crying, his throat screaming, and his arms flying everywhichway as though not his own!

"Is it me? Is it me ME ME ME! It has to be me — but is it!"

It is the question a thief must ask himself the night he jimmies open his first window, and it is said to be the question with which bridegrooms quiz themselves before the altar.

75    In the few wild seconds it took Ozzie's body to propel him to the edge of the roof, his self-examination began to grow fuzzy. Gazing down at the street, he became confused as to the problem beneath the question: was it, is-it-me-who-called-Binder-a-bastard? or, is-it-me-prancing-around-on-the-roof? However, the scene below settled all, for there is an instant in any action when whether it is you or somebody else is academic. The thief crams the money in his pockets and scoots out the window. The bridegroom signs the hotel register for two. And the boy on the roof finds a streetful of people gaping at him, necks stretched backwards, faces up, as though he were the ceiling of the Hayden Planetarium. Suddenly you know it's you.

"Oscar! Oscar Freedman!" A voice rose from the center of the crowd, a voice that, could it have been seen, would have looked like the writing on scroll. "Oscar Freedman, get down from there. Immediately!" Rabbi Binder was pointing one arm stiffly up at him; and at the end of that arm, one finger aimed menacingly. It was the attitude of a dictator, but one — the eyes confessed all — whose personal valet had spit neatly in his face.

Ozzie didn't answer. Only for a blink's length did he look towards Rabbi Binder. Instead his eyes began to fit together the world beneath him, to sort out people from places, friends from enemies, participants from spectators. In little jagged starlike clusters his friends stood around Rabbi Binder, who was still pointing. The topmost point on a star compounded not of angels but of five adolescent boys was Itzie. What a world it was, with those stars below, Rabbi Binder below... Ozzie, who a moment earlier hadn't been able to control his own body, started to feel the meaning of the word control: he felt Peace and he felt Power.

"Oscar Freedman, I'll give you three to come down."

Few dictators give their subjects three to do anything; but, as always, Rabbi Binder only looked dictatorial.

80    "Are you ready, Oscar?"

Ozzie nodded his head yes, although he had no intention in the world — the lower one or the celestial one he'd just entered — of coming down even if Rabbi Binder should give him a million.

"All right then," said Rabbi Binder. He ran a hand through his black Samson hair as though it were the gesture prescribed for uttering the first digit. Then, with his other hand cutting a circle out of the small piece of sky around him, he spoke. "One!"

There was no thunder. On the contrary, at that moment, as though "one" was the cue for which he had been waiting, the world's least thunderous person appeared on the synagogue steps. He did not so much come out of the synagogue door as lean out, onto the darkening air. He clutched at the doorknob with one hand and looked up at the roof.

"Oy!"

85     Yakov Blotnik's old mind hobbled slowly, as if on crutches, and though he couldn't decide precisely what the boy was doing on the roof, he knew it wasn't good — that is, it wasn't-good-for-the-Jews. For Yakov Blotnik life had fractioned itself simply: things were either good-for-the-Jews or no-good-for-the-Jews.

He smacked his free hand to his in-sucked cheek, gently. "Oy, Gut!"[4] And then quickly as he was able, he jacked down his head and surveyed the street. There was Rabbi Binder (like a man at an auction with only three dollars in his pocket, he had just delivered a shaky "Two!"); there were the students, and that was all. So far it-wasn't-so-bad-for-the-Jews. But the boy had to come down immediately, before anybody saw. The problem: how to get the boy off the roof?

Anybody who has ever had a cat on the roof knows how to get him down. You call the fire department. Or first you call the operator and you ask her for the fire department. And the next thing there is great jamming of brakes and clanging of bells and shouting of instructions. And then the cat is off the roof. You do the same thing to get a boy off the roof.

That is, you do the same thing if you are Yakov Blotnik and you once had a cat on the roof.

*****

When the engines, all four of them, arrived, Rabbi Binder had four times given Ozzie the count of three. The big hook-and-ladder swung around the corner and one of the firemen leaped from it, plunging headlong towards the yellow fire hydrant in front of the synagogue. With a huge wrench he began to unscrew the top nozzle. Rabbi Binder raced over to him and pulled at his shoulder.

90     "There's no fire..."

The fireman mumbled back over his shoulder and, heatedly, continued working at the nozzle.

"But there's no fire, there's no fire..." Binder shouted. When the fireman mumbled again, the rabbi grasped his face with both his hands and pointed it up at the roof.

To Ozzie it looked as though Rabbi Binder was trying to tug the fireman's head out of his body, like a cork from a bottle. He had to giggle at the picture they made: it was a family portrait — rabbi in black skullcap, fireman in red fire hat, and the little yellow hydrant squatting beside like a kid brother, bareheaded. From the edge of the roof Ozzie waved at the portrait, a one-handed, flapping, mocking wave; in doing it his right foot slipped from under him. Rabbi Binder covered his eyes with his hands.

---

4 Yiddish expression signifying dismay.

Firemen work fast. Before Ozzie had even regained his balance, a big, round, yellowed net was being held on the synagogue lawn. The firemen who held it looked up at Ozzie with stern, feelingless faces.

95     One of the firemen turned his head towards Rabbi Binder. "What, is the kid nuts or something?"

Rabbi Binder unpeeled his hands from his eyes, slowly, painfully, as if they were tape. Then he checked: nothing on the sidewalk, no dents in the net.

"Is he gonna jump, or what?" the fireman shouted.

In a voice not at all like a statue, Rabbi Binder finally answered, "Yes, yes, I think so . . . He's been threatening to . . ."

Threatening to? Why, the reason he was on the roof, Ozzie remembered, was to get away: he hadn't even thought about jumping. He had just run to get away, and the truth was that he hadn't really headed for the roof as much as he'd been chased there.

100     "What's his name, the kid?"

"Freedman," Rabbi Binder answered. "Oscar Freedman."

The fireman looked up at Ozzie. "What is it with you, Oscar? You gonna jump, or what?"

Ozzie did not answer. Frankly, the question had just arisen.

"Look, Oscar, if you're gonna jump, jump — and if you're not gonna jump, don't jump. But don't waste our time, willya?"

105     Ozzie looked at the fireman and then at Rabbi Binder. He wanted to see Rabbi Binder cover his eyes one more time.

"I'm going to jump."

And then he scampered around the edge of the roof to the corner, where there was no net below, and he flapped his arms at his sides, swishing the air and smacking his palms to his trousers on the downbeat. He began screaming like some kind of engine, "Wheeeee . . . wheeeeee," and leaning way out over the edge with the upper half of his body. The firemen whipped around to cover the ground with the net. Rabbi Binder mumbled a few words to Somebody and covered his eyes. Everything happened quickly, jerkily, as in a silent movie. The crowd, which had arrived with the fire engines, gave out a long, Fourth-of-July fireworks oooh-aahhh. In the excitement no one had paid the crowd much heed, except, of course, Yakov Blotnik, who swung from the door now counting heads. "Fier und tsvansik . . . finf und tsvansik.[5] Oy, Gut!" It wasn't like this with the cat.

Rabbi Binder peeked through his fingers, checked the sidewalk and net. Empty. But there was Ozzie racing to the other corner. The firemen raced with him but were unable to keep up. Whenever Ozzie wanted to he might jump and splatter himself upon the sidewalk, and by the time the firemen scooted to the spot all they could do with their net would be to cover the mess.

"Wheeeee . . . wheeeeee . . ."

110     "Hey, Oscar," the winded fireman yelled, "What the hell is this, a game or something?"

"Wheeeee . . . wheeeee . . ."

"Hey, Oscar —"

5 Twenty-four . . . twenty-five.

But he was off now to the other corner, flapping his wings fiercely. Rabbi Binder couldn't take it any longer — the fire engines from nowhere, the screaming suicidal boy, the net. He fell to his knees, exhausted, and with his hands curled together in front of his chest like a little dome, he pleaded, "Oscar, stop it, Oscar. Don't jump, Oscar. Please come down... Please don't jump."

And further back in the crowd a single voice, a single young voice, shouted a lone word to the boy on the roof.

115    "Jump!"

It was Itzie. Ozzie momentarily stopped flapping.

"Go ahead, Ozz — jump!" Itzie broke off his point of the star and courageously, with the inspiration not of a wise-guy but of a disciple, stood alone. "Jump, Ozz, jump!"

Still on his knees, his hands still curled, Rabbi Binder twisted his body back. He looked at Itzie, then, agonizingly, back to Ozzie.

"OSCAR, DON'T JUMP! PLEASE, DON'T JUMP... PLEASE, PLEASE..."

120    "Jump! This time it wasn't Itzie but another point of the star. By the time Mrs. Freedman arrived to keep her four-thirty appointment with Rabbi Binder, the whole little upside down heaven was shouting and pleading for Ozzie to jump, and Rabbi Binder no longer was pleading with him not to jump, but was crying into the dome of his hands.

*****

Understandably Mrs. Freedman couldn't figure out what her son was doing on the roof. So she asked.

"Ozzie, my Ozzie, what are you doing? My Ozzie, what is it?"

Ozzie stopped wheeeeeing and slowed his arms down to a cruising flap, the kind birds use in soft winds, but he did not answer. He stood against the low, clouded, darkening sky — light clicked down swiftly now, as on a small gear — flapping softly and gazing down at the small bundle of a woman who was his mother.

"What are you doing, Ozzie?" She turned towards the kneeling Rabbi Binder and rushed so close that only a paper-thickness of dust lay between her stomach and his shoulders.

125    "What is my baby doing?"

Rabbi Binder gaped up at her but he too was mute. All that moved was the dome of his hands; it shook back and forth like a weak pulse.

"Rabbi, get him down! He'll kill himself. Get him down, my only baby..."

"I can't," Rabbi Binder said, "I can't..." and he turned his handsome head towards the crowd of boys behind him. "It's them. Listen to them."

And for the first time Mrs. Freedman saw the crowd of boys, and she heard what they were yelling.

130    "He's doing it for them. He won't listen to me. It's them." Rabbi Binder spoke like one in a trance.

"For them?"

"Yes."

"Why for them?"

"They want him to..."

135    Mrs. Freedman raised her two arms upward as though she were conducting the sky. "For them he's doing it!" And then in a gesture older than pyramids, older than prophets and floods, her arms came slapping down to her
sides. "A martyr I have. Look!" She tilted her head to the roof. Ozzie was still
flapping softly. "My martyr."

       "Oscar, come down, *please*," Rabbi Binder groaned.

       In a startling even voice Mrs. Freedman called to the boy on the roof.
"Ozzie, come down, Ozzie. Don't be a martyr, my baby."

       As though it were a litany, Rabbi Binder repeated her words. "Don't be a
martyr, my baby. Don't be a martyr."

       "Gawhead, Ozz — be a Martin!" It was Itzie. "Be a Martin, be a Martin,"
and all the voices joined in singing for Martindom, whatever *it* was. "Be a
Martin, be a Martin..."

                          *****

140    Somehow when you're on a roof the darker it gets the less you can hear. All
Ozzie knew was that two groups wanted two new things: his friends were spir-
ited and musical about what they wanted; his mother and the rabbi were
eventoned, chanting, about what they didn't want. The rabbi's voice was
without tears now and so was his mother's.

       The big net stared up at Ozzie like a sightless eye. The big, clouded sky
pushed down. From beneath it looked like a gray corrugated board. Suddenly,
looking up into that unsympathetic sky, Ozzie realized all the strangeness of what
these people, his friends, were asking: they wanted him to jump, to kill himself;
they were singing about it now — it made them happy. And there was an even
greater strangeness: Rabbi Binder was on his knees, trembling. If there was a question to be asked now it was not "Is it me?" but rather "Is it us?... Is it us?"

       Being on the roof, it turned out, was a serious thing. If he jumped would
the singing become dancing? Would it? What would jumping stop? Yearningly,
Ozzie wished he could rip open the sky, plunge his hands through, and pull out
the sun; and on the sun, like a coin, would be stamped JUMP or DON'T JUMP.

       Ozzie's knees rocked and sagged a little under him as though they were
setting him for a dive. His arms tightened, stiffened, froze, from shoulders to fin-
gernails. He felt as if each part of his body were going to vote as to whether he
should kill himself or not — and each part as though it were independent of *him*.

       The light took an unexpected click down and the new darkness, like a gag,
hushed the friends singing for this and the mother and rabbi chanting for that.

145    Ozzie stopped counting votes, and in a curiously high voice, like one who
wasn't prepared for speech, he spoke.

       "Mamma?"

       "Yes, Oscar."

       "Mamma, get down on your knees, like Rabbi Binder."

       "Oscar —"

150    "Get down on your knees," he said, "or I'll jump."

       Ozzie heard a whimper, then a quick rustling, and when he looked down
where his mother had stood he saw the top of a head and beneath that a circle
of dress. She was kneeling beside Rabbi Binder.

He spoke again. "Everybody kneel." There was the sound of everybody kneeling.

Ozzie looked around. With one hand he pointed towards the synagogue entrance. "Make *him* kneel."

There was a noise, not of kneeling, but of body-and-cloth stretching. Ozzie could hear Rabbi Binder saying in a gruff whisper, " . . . or he'll *kill* himself," and when next he looked there was Yakov Blotnik off the doorknob and for the first time in his life upon his knees in the Gentile[6] posture of prayer.

155 As for the firemen — it is not as difficult as one might imagine to hold a net taut while you are kneeling.

Ozzie looked around again; and then he called to Rabbi Binder.

"Rabbi?"

"Yes, Oscar."

"Rabbi Binder, do you believe in God?"

160 "Yes."

"Do you believe God can do Anything?" Ozzie leaned his head out into the darkness. "Anything?"

"Oscar, I think —"

"Tell me you believe God can do Anything."

There was a second's hesitation. Then: "God can do Anything."

165 "Tell me you believe God can make a child without intercourse."

"He can."

"Tell me!"

"God," Rabbi Binder admitted, "can make a child without intercourse."

"Mamma, you tell me."

170 "God can make a child without intercourse," his mother said.

"Make *him* tell me." There was no doubt who *him* was.

In a few moments Ozzie heard an old comical voice say something to the increasing darkness about God.

Next, Ozzie made everybody say it. And then he made them all say they believed in Jesus Christ — first one at a time, then all together.

When the catechizing was through it was the beginning of evening. From the street it sounded as if the boy on the roof might have sighed.

175 "Ozzie?" A woman's voice dared to speak. "You'll come down now?"

There was no answer, but the woman waited, and when a voice finally did speak it was thin and crying, and exhausted as that of an old man who has just finished pulling the bells.

"Mamma, don't you see — you shouldn't hit me. He shouldn't hit me. You shouldn't hit me about God, Mamma. You should never hit anybody about God —"

"Ozzie, please come down now."

"Promise me, promise me you'll never hit anybody about God."

180 He had asked only his mother, but for some reason everyone kneeling in the street promised he would never hit anybody about God.

---

6 non-Jewish people; generally refers to Christians.

Once again there was silence.

"I can come down now, Mamma," the boy on the roof finally said. He turned his head both ways as though checking the traffic lights. "Now I can come down..."

And he did, right into the center of the yellow net that glowed in the evening's edge like an overgrown halo.

(1959)

# Austin C. Clarke (b. 1934)

Barbadian-born novelist and short story writer Austin Clarke, who moved to Toronto in 1955, has chronicled the lives of his compatriots both in the Caribbean and in Canada, the latter often referred to as "that cold, ungodly place" by his characters. His acclaimed Toronto trilogy, *The Meeting Point, Storm of Fortune,* and *The Bigger Light,* portrays the tensions that exist among poor men and women who have travelled to Toronto in search of better lives and found low-paying jobs and racial prejudice. "The Motor Car" uses the familiar initiation journey structure, tracing the move of a young man from a small town to a big city. The result of Calvin's search for happiness, which involves an attempt to deny his past and to find materialistic well-being through ownership of an automobile, symbolizes the lot of the immigrant in modern Canadian society. The story exemplifies the author's sensitive understanding of his characters, the gentle humour with which he depicts their situations, and his accurate reproduction of the dialect and rhythms of Barbadian speech.

# THE MOTOR CAR

That Canadian thing you see lying down there in that bed is Calvin woman, I mean *was* Calvin woman. Calvin wash motor cars back in Barbados till his back hurt and his belly burn, and when the pain stop in the body it start up fresh in his mind. Good thing Calvin was a God-faring man, cause if not he would have let go some real bad curse words that would have blow way the garage itself. But instead o' talking to the customers bout the hard work, instead o' talking to the boss bout the slave work he was making Calvin do in 1968 in these modern days, Calvin talk to God. Calvin didn' know if God did really hear him, cause the more he talk to God every morning before he went to work on his old Raleigh green three-speed bicycle, and after work when his head hit that pillow, the more the work did get harder. One day Calvin take in with a bout o' bad-feels, and the moment he come outta the fit or the trance, or the *hellucinations* as his boss call it, right that very second Calvin swear blind to God that he leffing Barbados. One time. For good. First chance. Is only the governorship or the governor-generalship that could get Calvin to stay in Barbados. That is the kind o' swearing he put pon God. And it ain't really clear, even at this time, if God really understand the kind o' message that Calvin put to him. But Calvin didn't care. Calvin decide already. Calvin start to work hard, more harder than he ever work in his life, from the very day after he decide that he pulling outta Barbados. And is to Canada he coming. Now the problems start falling pon top o' Calvin head like rainwater. First problem: he can't get a Canadian visa. He seeing Canadian tourisses morning noon and night all bout his island, walking bout like if they own the blasted place, and if you don't look out they getting on as if they want to own Calvin too. Calvin hit a low point o' studyation. The work done now and he pack already, two big big imitation leather valises; and he manage to buy the ticket too, although there is a regulation down there in the island that say a black man can't buy a ticket pon *Air Canada* saving he have a job and a roof to come to in Canada, or he have family here, or some kind o' support, cause Trudeau[1] get vex vex as hell bout supporting the boys when they come up here and can't find proper ployment. Calvin walking bout Bridgetown the capital all day telling people he pulling out next week for Canada. Next week come and he still walking bout Bridgetown. He ain't pull out in trute, yuh: he ain't like he pulling out at all, man; that is what the boys was beginning to think. They start laughing at Calvin behind his back, and Calvin grinning and telling them, "Gorblummuh, you laugh! *laugh!* he who laugh last, laugh..." And for purpose, he won't finish the saying at all, he only ordering a next round o' steam for his friends, and his mind focus-on pon a new shining motto-car that he going buy up in Canada before he even living there a year. He done make up his mind that he going work at two car-wash places, and if the Lord hear his prayers, and treat he nice, he going hustle a next job on top o' them two, too. Well, the more the boys laugh, the more Calvin decide with a piece o' real bad-mind that he going buy a brand-new Chevvy, perhaps even a custom-build *Galaxie*. And then, all of a sudden, one night when the fellas drink three free-round o' rum offa Calvin, Calvin really start to laugh. He push he hand inside his pocket, and he pull out a thing that look real important and official, and all he say is, "I taking off at nine in the morning." Calvin then throw a new-brand twenty dollar bill pon Marcus rum shop counter, and the fellas gone wild, be-Christ, cause is now real drinking going begin. Calvin stand up like a man. Every one that his best friend Willy fire, Calvin fire one, too. Willy, who didn' lick he mouth too much gainst Calvin going way, when he reach the fifth straight *Mount Gay*, Calvin was right there with him. Is rum for rum. Drink for drink. They start eating raw salt fish, and Calvin iamming the cod fish as if he catch it himself off the banks o' Newfoundland in the same Canada that he heading out to. The fellas eat off all o' Marcus bad half-rotten salt fish, and then start-on pon a tin o' corn beef and raw onions and you would have think that Calvin was pon a real religious fast during the time he was worrying bout the Canadian visa. "I going tell you fellas something," Willy say, for no conceivable reason at all, cause they just then telling Calvin that he ain' going see no good cricket when he get up in that cold ungodly place call Canada. "I going tell you fellas something now," Willy say, after he clear his throat for effect, and to make the fellas stop drinking and eating and listen to him. "Godblummuh! Calvin is the most luckiest one o' we, yuh! Calvin lucky-lucky-lucky as shite!" He say the last two "lucky" like if they was one word. Anyhow, he went on, "Calvin is a king to we!" Now, nobody ain' know what the arse Willy trying to say, cause Willy is a man who does try to talk big and talk a lot o' shite in the bargain. But this time, solemn occasion as it be, the fellas decide to give Willy a listen. "We lis'ning, man, so talk yuh talk. We lis'ning." Willy take a long pull pon the rum bottle, and he stuff bout a half-pound o' corn beef inside his mouth, with the biscuits flying bout the place like big drops o' spit. "You see that salt fish that we just put way? Well, it make up in Canada. Tha's where Calvin here going. Now understand this when I say it. I only say that to say this. Comprehend? The salt fish that we does

<hr>

1 Pierre Elliott Trudeau, prime minister of Canada from 1968 to 1979 and 1980 to 1984.

get down here, send-down by Canada, is the same quality o' salt fish that they uses to send down here to feed we when we was slaves. It smell stink. You could tell when a woman cooking salt fish. We even invent a term to go long with this kind o' salt fish and this kind o' stinkingness. We does say to a person who uses *profine* words, 'Yuh mouth smell like a fucking salt-fish barrel,' Unnerstand? I going to lay a bet pon any one o' you bitches in here now, drinking this rum. I going wager five dollars gainst a quarter that the brand o' salt fish Calvin going get to buy and eat up in that place call Canada is a better quality o' salt fish. It rass-hole bound to be, cause that is where it produce. And if you ever study Marx, you would understand the kind o' social-ism I talking bout." Nobody ain' answer Willy for a time, all they do is laugh. "Laugh! laugh!" Willy say with scorn, "cause godblindme!..." And then Calvin say, like if he didn' really want to say the words at-all, "Be-Jesus Christ, when you see me leff this blasted backwards place, call Barbados, that is the last time I eating salt fish. I eating steaks!"

Well, they poured Calvin on pon the *Air Canada*, next morning, nine sharp, drunk as a flying-fish. Good thing Calvin mother did pack the fry dolphin steak, a bottle o' Cod Liver Oil, in case the bowels do a thing and give trouble in that cold ungodly climate, as she call Canada; and she pack some Phensic for headache, just in case; she pack some miraculous bush, for medi-cine, "cause they ain' have doctor no place under the sun who know the good-ness in this mirac'lous bush-tea as we does, so you tek it along with you, son; you going up in that strange savage place, and you far from me, and I ain' near enough no more to run to you and rub your face with a lime and some Limacol, and tie it up with oil-leaves and candle-grease..."; and she put in half dozen limes and two bottle o' Limacol; man, is a good-good thing that Calvin mother had the presence o' mind to pack these things for Calvin whilst Calvin was walking bout Broadstreet in Bridgetown like if he was one o' them Canadian tourisses. Calvin mother do a real good job, and when she done pack the things, and she inspect the clothes that Calvin carrying way, she tie-up the two valises with a strong piece o' string, although they had brand-new locks pon them. "Good!" is the last thing she say to Calvin, as she was holding over the kitchen door, whilst Willy was revving up the hired car and blowing the horn — which, of course, Calvin pay for, the hired car I mean — plus dropping a ten dollar bill inside Willy hand for old times sake. "Go long in the name o' the Lord, and make yuh fortune, son." A tear or two drop outta she eye, too; but she was glad-glad in she heart that she boy-child was leffing Barbados. "Too much foreigners and tourisses and crooks living here with we, now, son. Canada more brighter than here." Calvin get vex-vex when he see the water in his mother eye, and he was embarrass as hell, cause he always use to brag how nothing he do, or don't do, could make his mother belly burn she. Good thing Willy had the car motor revving, cause Calvin get in such a state over the tears and heart-break on the part of his mother that he almost forget that deep-down he is a christian-minded man and say a bad word, whiching as he did know full-well, God would be vex as hell with him for. The motto-car was making good time moving like hell going up the airport road, and every-body Calvin know, and everybody that he barely know in the twenty-nine years he born and living in Barbados, he hold half of his body out through the car window, and yell out, "Boy, I going this morning! Canada, in your arse!" All the people who see and hear, wave back and grin their teet', if they could hear from the distance and through the speed; and some o' them say, "Bless." If everybody in Barbados, down Broadstreet, at the airport didn' know that Calvin pulling out for Canada at quarter-to-nine that morning, by nine o'clock the whole world did know. Friend or no friend, every time he see a face, or a hand, he saying, "Well, I won't be see you for a while, man, I going up." And they did all know what he meant, cause it was a time when all the young boys and young girls was pulling outta the island and going to Amer'ca, Britain, although Britain begin to tighten up things for the fellas because o' Powell; and some o' them start running up in Canada. And they was more *Air Canada* planes all bout Seawell Airport in Barbados in them days that you would have think that Barbados did own *Air Canada*. But is the other way round. Anyhow, drunk as Calvin was when he step pon that plane, and the white lady smile at him and say, "Good morning, sir" — first time in Calvin life white woman ever call him that, that way — well, Calvin know long time that he make the right move. Canada nice, he say in his heart; and he end it up with "Praise God." Canada now gone straight to Calvin head, long time and with a kind o' power, that when the airplane start up Calvin imagine that he own the whole blasted plane along with the white ladies who tell him, "Good morning, sir"; he feel that the plane is the big motto-car he intend to own one year after he land pon Canadian soil. The plane making time fast fast, and Calvin drink rum after rum till he went fast asleep and didn' even know he was in Toronto. The white lady come close to him, and tap him soft soft pon his new tropical suit and say, "Sir?", like if she asking some important question, when all she want is to wake up Calvin outta the white man plane. Well, Calvin wake up. He stretch like how he uses to stretch when he wake up in his mother bed. He yawn so hard that the white lady move back a step or two, after she see the pink inside his mouth and the black and blue gums running round them white pearly teets. Calvin eyes red red as a cheery from lack o' sleep and too much rum drinking, and the body tired like how it uses to get tired and wrap-up like a old motto-car fender. But is Canada, old man, and in a jiffy, before the white lady get to the front o' the plane to put down the last glass, Calvin looking out through the window. "Toronto in your arse!" he went to say to himself, but it come out too loud, as if he was saying it to Willy and the boys who didn' think he was really going to come through. "Toronto in your arse, man!" The plane touch down, and the first man outta the plane is, well, no need to tell you who it was. Calfuckingvin! And he pass through the customs like if he was born in Toronto. The white man didn' even ask him a question. Something like it was wrong, cause Calvin did know as far away as in Barbados that the Immigration and Customs men in Toronto is the roughest in the world, when they see a black face in front o' them. But this white gentleman must have been down in the islands recently, cause all he tell Calvin was, "Don't tell me! Don't tell me! You're a Bajun!" For years after, Calvin wondering how the hell this white man know so much bout black people. Before the first week come and gone, Calvin take up pen and paper and send off a little thing to Willy and the boys: . . . *and I am going to tell you something, this place is the greatest place for a working man to live. I hear some things about this place, but*

*I isn't a man to complain, because while I know I am a man, and I won't take no shit from no Canadian, white, black or red, I still have another piece of knowledge which says that I didn't born here. So I controls myself to suit, and make the white man money. The car only a couple of months off. I see one already that I got my eyes on. And if God willing, by the next two months, DV, I sitting down in the drivers seat. The car I got my eyes on is a red one, with white tires. The steering wheel as you know is on the left hand side, and we drives on the right hand side of the road up here, not like back in Barbados where you drive on the left hand. Next week, I taking out my licents. I not found a church I like yet, mainly because I see some strange things happening up here in churches. You don't know, man, Willy, but black people can't or don't go in the same church as white people. God must be have two colours then. One for black people and one for white people. And a next thing. There is some fellas up here from the islands who talking a lot of shite about Black Power, and I hear that one of them is a Barbadian. But I am one man who don't want to hear no shit about Black Power. I am here working for a living and a motor car and if my mother herself come in my way and be an obstacle against me getting them two things, a living and a motor car, I would kill her by Christ...* Calvin was going to write more: about the room he was renting for twenty dollars a week, which a white fellow tell him was pure robbery, because he was paying ten dollars for a more larger room on the ground floor in the same house; and he didn' write Willy bout the car-wash job he got the next day down Spadina Avenue, working for a dollar a hour, and when the first three hours pass he felt he been working for three days, the work was so hard; he didn' tell Willy that a certain kind of white people in Canada didn' sit too close to him on the street car, that they didn' speak to him on the street... lots o' things he didn' worry to tell Willy, cause he did want Willy to think that he was really a king to the boys back home, a champion for emigrading to Canada. Willy send back a post card with a mauby[2] woman on the colour side selling mauby, and on the writing side, in his scribbly handwriting, "*As man!*" But be-Christ, Calvin didn' care what they do, he was here for two purpose; one, living, and number two, motto-car. If they touch my motto-car, now, well, that would be something else... and Calvin work hard, man, Calvin work more harder than when he was washing-off cars back in Barbados. The money was good too. Sal'ry and tips. From the two car-wash jobs he uses to clear a hundred dollars a week, and that is two hundred back home, and not even Dipper does make that kind o' money, and he is the fucking prime minister! The third job, Calvin land like a dream; nightwatchman with a big big important company which put him in big big important uniform and thing, big leather belt like what he uses to envy the officers in the Volunteer Force back home wearing pon a Queen Birthday parade on the Garrison Savannah, shoes the company people even provide, and the only thing that was missing, according to what Calvin figure out some months afterwards, was that the holster at his side, join-on to the leather belt, didn' have in no blasted gun. He tell it to a next Barbadian he make friends with, and the Bajan just laugh and say, "They think you going rass-hole shoot yourself, boy!" But Calvin did already become Canadified enough to know that the only people he see in them uniforms with guns in the leather

---

2 West Indian herbal beverage.

holster was certain white people, and he know he wasn' Canadified so much that he did turn white overnight. "Once it don't stop me from getting that *Galaxie!*" Work work work, a occasional postcard to Willy, cause envelopes was costing too much all of a sudden, and postage stamps was going up too, no pleasure for Calvin: he went down by the *Tropics Club* where they play calypsoes and dance, one time, and he never went back cause the ugly Grenadian fellow at the door ask him for "Three dollars to come in!", and he curse the fellow and leff. But the bank account was mounting and climbing like a woman belly when she in the family-way. Quick-quick so, Calvin have a thousand dollars pon the bank. Fellas who get to know Calvin and who Calvin won't sociate with because "sociating does cost money, boy!", them fellas so who here donkey years, still borrowing money to help pay their rent, fellas gambling like hell, throwing dice every Fridee night right into Mondee morning early, missing work and getting fired from work, fellas playing poker and betting, "Forty dollars more for these two fours, in your rass, sah! I *raise!*", them brand o' Trinidadian, Bajan, Jamaician, Grenadian and thing, them so can't understand at-all how Calvin just land and he get rich so fast. "I bet all-yuh Calvin selling pussy!" one fella say. A next bad-minded fella say, "He peddling his arse to white boys down Yonge Street," and a third fella who did just bet fifty dollars 'pon a pair o' deuces, and get broke at the poker game, say quick-quick before the words fall-out o' the other fella mouth, "I going peddle mine too, then! Bread is bread." Calvin start slacking up on the first car wash work, and he humming as he shine the white people car, he skinning his teet in the shine and he smiling, and the white people thinking he smiling because he like the work and them, cause his hands never tarried whilst he was car-dreaming, they drop a little dollar bill pon Calvin as a tip, and a regular twenty-five cent piece, and Calvin pinching pon the groceries, eating a lotta pigs feet and chicken necks and salt fish… "I gotta write Willy and tell him bout the brand o' salt fish in this place. Willy was right!"… Calvin won't spend thirty cents pon a beer with a sinner, only time he even reading is when he clean out a car in the car wash and it happen to have a used paper inside it, or a throw-away paperback book. But Calvin decide long time that he didn' come here for eddication. He come for a living and a motto-car. A new one, too! And he intend to get both. And by the look o' things, be-Christ, both almost in his hand. Only now waiting to see the right model o' motor car, with the right colour inside it, and the right mileage and thing. The motto-car must have the right colour o' tires, right colour o' gear shift and in the handle too. And it have to have-in radio; and he see a fella in the car wash with a thing inside his Cadillac, and Calvin gone crazy over Cadillacs until he walk down by Bay Street and price the price of a old one. He bawl for murder. "Better stick to the *Galaxie*, boy!" he tell himself; and he do that. But he really like the thing inside the white man Cadillac and he ask the man one morning what it was, and the man tell Calvin. Now Calvin *must* have red *Galaxie*, with not more than 20,000 miles on the register, black upholstery, red gear shift, radio, AM *and FM and a tellyfone*… Them last three things is what the man had inside his Cadillac. Calvin working even on a Sundee, bank holidays ain' touching Calvin, and the Old Queen back home who send a occasional letter asking Calvin to remember the house rent and the Poor Box in the Nazarene Church where he was a testifying brother, preaching and thing, and also to remember "who birthed him", well, Calvin tell the Old Queen, his own-own mother; *Things hard up here, mother. Don't let nobody fool you that because a man emigrade it mean that he elevate. That isn't true. But I am sending this Canadian money order for five dollars, which is ten dollars back home, and I hope that next week I would find myself a nice job, and then I am going to send you a little something more. Your loving son, Calvin. P.S. Pray for me.* Calvin start thinking that maybe the Old Queen had a bad mind for him; he start one long stewpsing, and the fellas at work even had to ask him if he sick or something, he even stop laughing and chumming around with the Canadians at work; he refuse to play Frisbee and throw the ball in the other fellas mittens, he even stop begging the German fella for a lift home after work. Calvin start getting ingrown like a toenail: pressure in Calvin arse. The studyation take a hold o' him and one weekend it capsize him in bed, Fridee night, Sardah morning and Sardah night, Sundee and right into Mondee morning half hour before he is to leff for work. Landlady couldn' even come in and change the filthy linens and bed sheets. But Calvin make sure he went to work that Mondee. "Can't lose that money now, boy!" Willy was the next joker at this time o' hardship and studyation. Willy send a letter registered and thing, in a real pretty envelope with the colours o' the Union Jack, to Calvin: *. . . and if it isn't asking too much, Calvin, I wonder if you can see your way in sending me down a piece of change. I am thinking about emigrading too, because Barbados is at a standstill for people like me, people who don't have no high school education, no big kind of skills and no kiss-me-arse godfather in big jobs in the civil service. My kind of man in Barbados is loss. I hope I am not imposing when I ask you if you could see your way in lending me the passage money, one way, and I am going to open a new bank account with it and take a picture of it and show it to the Canadian immigration people down here, because another fellow promise to do the same thing for me with the return part of the passage money. The Canadian high commission place in Trinidad giving the fellows a hard time. But we smarter than any number of Canadian immigration people they send down here. So I asking this favour for old times sake, because not that I hard on you, but I don't want to remind you of the time when you had the accident with the motor car that didn't belongst to you, and you was in hospital, and you know who help you out, so . . .* Calvin get in a bad bad mood straightaway, thinking that everybody back home think he is a millionaire, everybody back there getting on like crabs, willing to pull him down the moment he come up for breath. "Be-Christ, not me!" and in that frame o' mind Calvin take up a piece o' stationery he borrow from a Jamaican fellow who had a job in the General Hospital, and a envelope to match, with the hospital name on both, and he ask a next fellow who had a typewriter to write this letter back to Willy: *Dear Willy, I have been laid up in this hospital for two months now. I am getting a friend who is in the hospital too, but who is not confine to bed and who can barely walk around, to post this letter to you for me. Things really bad, man . . .* because all my friends back home think I is a arse or something, they see me emigrade to this place and they think that I get rich overnight, or that I don't work hard as hell for my money, but that ain't true. Willy didn' answer back immediately, but a month and a half later, two days before Calvin decide he see the right automobile, a card drop through the door where Calvin living, address to Calvin: *What are you doing up there, then?*

*Canadians buying out all the island. You standing for that? Send down a couple of dollars and let me invest it in a piece of beach land for you, Brother. Power to the people! Salaam and love. Willy X.* Calvin get so blasted vex, so damn vex, cause he sure now that Willy gone mad too, like everybody else he been reading bout in the States and in England; black people gone mad, Calvin say; and he get more vex when he think that it was the landlady, Mistress Silvermann who take up the post card from the linoleum and hand it to him, and he swear blind that she hand it to him after she done read the thing: and now she must be frighten like hell for Calvin, cause Calvin getting letters from these political extremists, and birds of a feather does flock together, she thinking now that Calvin perhaps is some kind o' political maniac, crying Black Power! all this damn foolishness bout Power to the People, and signing his name Willy X, when everybody in Barbados know that that damn fool's name is really William Fortesque: Calvin get shame-shame-shame that the landlady thinking different bout him, because sometimes she does be in the house alone all night with Calvin, and she must be even thinking bout giving him notice, which would be a damn bad thing to happen right now, cause the motto-car just two days off, the room he renting now is a nice one, the rent come down like the temperature in May when he talk plain to Mistress Silvermann bout how he paying twice as much as other tenants, but what really get Calvin really vex-vex-vex as hell is that a little Canadian thing in the room over his head come downstairs one night in a mini-dress and thing, bubbies jumping bout inside her bosom, free and thing and looking juicy, and giggling all the time and calling sheself a women liberation, all her skin at the door, and the legs nice and fat just as Calvin like his meats, and Calvin already gone thinking that this thing is the right woman to drive-bout in his new automobile with, this Canadian thing coming downstairs every night for the past month, and out of the blue asking him, "You'll like a coffee?" When she say so the first time, coffee was as far from Calvin mind as lending Willy twenty-five cents for the downpayment for the house spot pon the beach back home. Now, be-Christ, Willy X, or whatever the hell that bastard calling himself nowadays, is going to stay right there down in Barbados and mash up Calvin life so! Just so? Simple so? Oh God, no, man! But the landlady couldn' read English, she did only uses to pretend she is a genius; the Canadian girl is who tell Calvin not to worry; one night when they was drinking the regular coffee in the communal kitchen, the Canadian girl say, "Missis Silvermann is only a D.P.[3] She can't read English." Calvin take courage. The bank book walking bout with him, inside his trousers all the time, he counting the digits going to work, coming from work, in the back seat alone, pon the street car, while waiting for the subway early on a morning at the Ossington Station, and then he make a plan. He plan it down to a T. Every penny organize for the proper thing, every nickel with its own work to do: the bottle of wine that the Canadian girl gave him the name to; the new suit from Eaton's that he see in the display window one night when he get hold of the girl and he get bold bold as hell and decide to take she for a lover's walk down Yonge Street; the new shoes, brown-brown till they look red to match the car; and the shirt and tie — every-blasted-thing matching-up like if he is a new bride

3 Displaced Person; derogatory term for a post–World War II European refugee or immigrant.

stepping down the aisle to the wedding march. And he even have a surprise up his sleeve for the thing, too. He isn' no longer a stingy man, cause he see his goal; and his goal is like gold. The car delivery arrange for three o'clock, Sardah; no work; the ice box in his room have in a beer or two, plus the wine; and he have a extra piece o' change in his pocket... "I going have to remember to change the money from this pocket," he tell himself, as if he was talking to somebody else in the room with him, "to the next pocket in the new suit" ...and he have Chinese food now on his mind because the Canadian thing mention a nice Chinese restaurant down in Chinatown near Elizabeth Street. Calvin nervous as arse all Fridee night; all Fridee night the thing in Calvin room (here of late she behaving as if she live in Calvin room!), and Calvin is a man with ambitions: one night she tantalize Calvin head so much that he start talking bout high-rise apartment; perhaps, if she behave sheself he might even put a little gold thing pon her pretty little pink finger... the girl start asking Calvin if he want *some*; not in them exact words, but that is what she did mean; and Calvin turn shame-shame and nearly blush, only thing, as you know black people can't show really if they blushing or if they mad as shite with a white person, and Calvin turn like a virgin on the night before she getting hang in church and in marriage, and he saying all the time because his mind pon the mileage in the motto-car, "Want some o' what?" And the girl laugh, and she throw back she head and show she gold fillings and she pink tongue and the little speck o' dirt under she neck; and she laugh and say to sheself, "This one is a real gentleman, not like what my girlfriend say to expect from West Indian men, at all...". And you know something? She start one big confessing: "...and do you know what, Calvin? Would you like to hear something that I been thinking..." Calvin thinking bout motto-car and this blasted white woman humbugging him bout sex! Calvin get vex, he play he get vex bout something different from the woman and she sex, and he send she flying back upstairs to she own room. He get in bed too, but he ain' sleeping, he wide awake in the dark like a thief, and he eyes open wide-wide-wide like a owl eyes, and in that darkness in that little little room that only have one small window way up by the ceiling and facing the clothes-lines and the dingy sheets that the landlady does spend all week washing, Calvin see the whole o' Toronto standing up and watching him drive by in his new motto-car — with the Canadian thing beside o' him in the front seat! — dream turn into different dream that Fridee night, because he was free to dream as much as he like since Sardah wasn' no work. Sardah is car day. He have everything plan. Go for the motto-car, pick it up, drive it home, pick up the Canadian thing, go for a spin down Bloor as far as Yonge, swing back up by Harbord, turn left at Spadina, take in College Street, and every West Indian in Toronto bound to see him in new car, before he get back home. Park she in front o' the house, *let everybody see me getting outta she, come in, have a little bite, change, change into the new suit, give the Canadian thing the surprise, and whilst she dressing, I sit down in the car*... "And I hope she take a long time dressing so I would have to press the car-horn, press the horn just a little, a soft little thing, and call she outside, to see me in the..." Morning break nice. It was a nice morning round the middle o' September, fall time in the air, everybody stretching and holding up their head cause the weather nice.

Even the cops have a smile on their fissiogomy.[4] Calvin get up at five, take a quick look at the alarm clock, curse the clock for being so damn slow, went back to sleep, had a dream in which he see Willy as the garage mechanic at the car-place taking too long over the *Galaxie*; he curse Willy in the dream and nearly didn' get up in time, then turn round and curse Willy for coming into his dream; he left without tea, travelling with the Canadian thing half-sleep beside him, and gone fast pon the subway at Ossington down Danforth for the machine. The salesman-man smile and shake Calvin hand strong, and give Calvin the history of the bird although Calvin did already hear the bird history before. The salesman-man come outta the office still smiling, holding the motto-car keys between the index finger and the big thumb, and he drop them in Calvin hand. Calvin make a shiver. A shiver o' pride and ownership. "*Galaxie in your arse!*" He say that in his mind, and he thinking o' Willy and the boys back in Marcus rum shop. He get in the car. He shuffle bout a bit in the leather seat. He straighten he trouser seams. He touch the leather. He start up the motor. Listen to the motor. It ticking over like a fucking charm. He put the thing in gear. And he make a little thing through the car park, and he would have gone straight back up Danforth if the Canadian thing didn' wave she handbag to remind Calvin that she come with he, cause Calvin did forget she standing up there looking at a white convertible Cadillac, which she say is the car for Calvin, that there is lots o' "Negro-men driving cars, even in Nova Scotia where I come from," that Calvin should have buy one o' them. "You start spending my blasted money already, woman! This is *mine*!" He didn' tell she out loud in words what he was really thinking bout she, but he was thinking so, though. The Canadian gash get in the motto-car, cause driving in a *Galaxie* more better than walking behind a Cadillac, and she sit down so comfortable that it look like if she own the car and she was giving Calvin a chance to try she out, and that it wasn' Calvin own-own money that pay-down pon the car. Calvin didn't like that at all: he want she to sit down in the front seat like if *he* own the motto-car. But Calvin gone up Danforth with new motto-car and white woman beside o' him, like if he going to a funeral: "got to break she in gently, man"; and the Canadian thing not too please that Calvin didn' listen to her advice as a woman should advise a man, and buy the Cadillac, but she still please and proud that Calvin get the *Galaxie*. She sitting in it like if she belong there by birth. And Calvin don't really mind, cause he have the car, and it driving like oil pon a tar road back home. He make a thing along Danforth as far as Bloor, turn pon Yonge and gone as far as Harbord . . . the itinerary ain' exactly as he first think it out, but it would do . . . make a thing along Harbord and meet up with Spadina, and continue according to plan. And in all this time so, not one blasted West Indian or black person in sight to look at Calvin new car and make a thing with his head, or laugh, or wave. When he make a right pon College at the corner o' Spadina, a woman with a bag mark HONEST ED'S start walking through the green light, drop a tomato, and she bend down to pick it up, and Calvin now, whether he looking for the woman tomato or he looking the wrong way, nearly run-over she. Blam! Brakes on, and the Canadian thing nearly break she

---

4 physiognomy, or face.

blasted neck 'gainst the windshield. Calvin rattle bad like a snake. Police come. Police look inside the car, see Calvin, turn he eyes pon the Canadian thing who get frighten as hell, and he say, "Okay, move along now, buster!" Calvin shaking till he get the *Galaxie* in front o' the landlady rooming house, and he ain' remember nothing bout what he plan to do when he bring home the prize of a motto-car; the police upset him and he trembling bad. "Give me a drink o' water," he say to the Canadian thing. She rubbing she neck all the time like if it really break in truth, and she get out, and she didn' even look back at the new car, whiching as you would understand is what Calvin expect any man who just have a new motto-car, to do: yuh have to walk out of the door, close the door soft-soft because it ain' the same thing as getting out of a taxi, make sure the door close, and when you know it close, open it again to show yuhself that it close proper, and then really close it a next time; then walk off, look at the car, turn yuh head right and left like if you escaping from a light jab to the head, rub yuh hand over the chrome, walk round to the door where the passenger does sit down, open that door too, close it, and open it, and then, lock it. Then yuh does have to forget something inside the car, so yuh could have a chance to open the doors a next time and play with the car, hoping in the meantime that somebody who never see you before with a car, see you now with this new one and would say something like, "My! How much horsepower?", because according to Calvin, a "Car in some ways is like a woman, yuh does have to care she!" Calvin do all these things, and he didn't forget to walk to the back o' the *Galaxie*, stoop down and play he looking at the tires, give them a little kick with his shoes to see if they got in enough air, look under the car to see what the muffler look like, and things like that, although he know full-well that he don't know one blasted thing bout motto-cars except to wash them off, or that yuh does drive them. He do the same thing when he walk round to the front o' the car. The Canadian thing gone inside the house long time; and Calvin remember the glass o' water and he walking up the front steps. Not one blasted person on the whole street look out at Calvin new motto-car. Then the landlady, Mistress Silvermann walk out, "Don't forget Mr. Kingston, today your rent is due." Calvin tell her in his mind something bad, and she look at the car as she reach the sidewalk, without looking back, she say, "Do you know the owner of this car, Mr. Kingston? Tell him to move it please...I don't want cars blocking my driveway..." Well, Calvin gone mad now. He walk in the house, and he catch the Canadian thing sitting down in his room, with the glass o' water in she hand, as if she dreaming, just sitting and looking at the air. He drink the water, but it was like drinking miraculous bush-tea the Old Queen uses to make when the bowels was giving trouble back in Barbados. Calvin think bout the Old Queen, put the Old Queen outta his head, and start dressing. He noticed that something was wrong with his dresser: perhaps the landlady was looking for she rent; perhaps the Canadian thing was..."That's why she didn' come back outside with the water! Anyhow..." He put on his clothes, the new suit, shoes and tie and shirt new and matching the *Galaxie* outside shining in the sun, and meantime the Canadian thing gone upstairs. Calvin finish dress, take up a old kerchief..."Gotta have a shammy-cloth, gotta buy one Mondee!"...and he gone outside polishing the motto-car. Back inside, he gone up to the Canadian thing room, knock soft, the door open, and out from behind his back he take a thing, and say in a sweet loving voice, "I buy this for you." Ohhhhhhh! Myyyyyyyyyyyyyyyy! "You shouldn't reallllllllyyyyyyy!" But all the time she did know it was dress Calvin buy for she for the occasion, cause when she went inside for the water, she start searching all the man things, and she had a nice peep at the dress. She even know it cost twenty-nine dollars without tax: and she wonder if Calvin really love she so much. Well, they dress-off and they coming out like husband and wife going to church. The *Galaxie* smiling so, like if the *Galaxie* itself in love with the two o' them, too. The dress nearly red like the car, everybody in red, and looking nice. Calvin steal a peep at the Canadian thing and she look good-good-good, like something to eat! He inspect the tires a next time, though he just done looking at them, but what the hell it is his motto-car; and then he check the gas tank and the tank say, "Let's go for a long one, man!", and Calvin get in, fix the seams in the new trousers, adjust the tie, look at the knot in the mirror, fix the mirror two times, and then ask the Canadian thing if she comfortable. "I'm fine, thank you!" Calvin rev-up the thing, she turn over nice, and he ready to go. "You not nervous?" She smile. A dimple and a gold filling show when she smile. Nice. She ain' nervous. "Don't mind what happen just now by Spadina, eh?" She smile nice again. She ain' mind what happen by Spadina. Darling come to she lips with the smile. Calvin happy as hell now. He think he might treat this Canadian thing nice, and do the right thing with a gold ring even. "I take those things in my stride usually, but now it seems like an omen," she say, just as they turn into Bloor. Calvin ain' thinking bout omen, cause the only omen he know bout is that he pray for a *Galaxie* and he get a *Galaxie*! And the horses under the bonnet roaring like hell. Well, they drive and drive like if they was two explorers exploring Toronto: through Rosedale where the Canadian thing say she would *just love* to own a house; and in his mind, Calvin promise she she going get one in Rosedale; through the Bridle Path where she say the cheapest house cost a million dollars; through Don Mills where they see the big tall Foresters' Building, all up there by IBM; "You should get a job at IBM, dear" ("Doing wha'? Cleaning out the closets?" . . . this Canadian thing like she is the wrong kind o' woman for me, Calvin thinking: I hads better get a black woman!); all this she talk as they driving back on the Don Valley Parkway. The highway nice. The motto-car open a new whole life to Calvin, and he love Canada even better. Damn good thing he left Barbados! The *Galaxie* like a horse, prancing pon the white man road. Night fall long time as they travel-ling, and Calvin experimenting with the dip-lights and the high beam. It nice to play with. The FM radio thing ain' working good, cause Calvin never play one o' them radios before, and he forget to practise pon it when he was vis-iting the car in the lot after he pay-down something pon it, so that the sales-man would keep it for him. So he working the AM thing overtime. A nice tune come on. Before the tune come on, he thinking again that the Canadian thing maybe the right woman for him: she nice, she tidy and she quiet. And he raise-up liking quiet women; his mother tell him never married a woman who ain' quiet, and like church. The tune is a calypso, man. "It's a nice calypso," Calvin say. "Sparrow, in you arse!" he shout, and he beg the Canadian pardon, he excited because it is the first time he hear a calypso on the radio. He start liking Canada bad bad again. "Look at me, though! New car! A *Galaxie*, and you beside me..." The Canadian thing start working up she behind beside o' Calvin; she start saying she been going down in the islands for years now, that she have more calypso records than any white woman in Toronto, and she wish she had the money to take them outta storage and play one or two for Calvin. She start singing the tune, and Calvin vex as hell, cause he don't like no woman who does sing calypso, his Old Queen didn' even let him sing calypso when he was a boy in Barbados. And he was a *man*! Besides, the calypso that the Canadian thing singing now is a thing bout "...*three white women travelling through Africa!*", and something bout "*Uh never had a white meat, yet!*", and this nice woman, the simple-looking Canadian girl know all the words, and she enjoying sheself too, and Calvin thinking that Sparrow watching him from through the AM radio thing, and laughing at him, and he vex as shite, cause the calypso mean that certain white women like black men to lash them, and..."Don't sing that!" he order the thing, as if he talking to his wife; and the Canadian thing tell him, in a sharp voice, that she isn' his damn wife, so "Don't you be uppity with me, buster!" Well, who tell she she could talk-back to a Bajan man like Calvin? Calvin slam on the brakes. The motto-car cry out, *screeennnnchhhhh!* The Canadian thing head hit the windshield, bram! and she neck like it break this time, in truth. The motto-car half-way in the middle o' the highway. Traffics whizzing by, and the wind from them like it want to smash-up Calvin new *Galaxie*. Calvin vex as shite but he can't do nothing cause he trembling like hell: the woman in the front seat turning white-white-white like a piece o' paper, and the blood gone outta she face; Calvin ain' see no dimples in she face; and she ain' moving, she ain' talking, not a muscle ain' shiver. Traffics whizzing by and one come so damn close that Calvin close he eyes, and pray. "Look my blasted crosses! And my *Galaxie* ain' a fucking day old yet!" He try to start-up the motor and the motor only coughing like it have consumption. The woman like she sleeping or dead or something. The calypso still blaring over the AM radio, and Calvin so jittery he can't find the right button to turn the blasted thing off. And sudden so, one of the traffics flying by is a police. Calvin hear, *weeeeeeeeeeeeeeeeeeennnnnnnnnnnnnnnnnnnnnnnn!* Sirens! A police car in the rear-view mirror. Calvin stop shaking sudden-sudden. He start thinking. White woman deading in his new motto-car, the car new, and he is a stranger in Canada. He jump out, and lift-up the hood, and he back his new jacket, and he touching this and touching that, playing he is a mechanic. The police stop. He face red as a beet. "What's holding you up, boy!" Calvin hear the "boy", and he get vex, but he can't say nothing, cause they is two against his one, and he remember that he black. But he ain' no damn fool. He talk fast and sweet, and soft, and he impress the police: "...and officer I *just-now-now-now* give this lady a lift as I pass she on the highway, she say she feeling bad, and I was taking she to the hospital, cause as a West Indian I learn how to be a good samaritan, and..." The police ask for the licents, and when he see that the ownership papers say that Calvin only had the car this morning, he smile, and say, "Help me with her in the cruiser. You *are* a good samaritan, fellow. Wish our coloured people were more like you West Indians..." They lift the Canadian thing with she neck half-popped outta the *Galaxie*, and into the cruiser, and

Calvin even had a tear in his eye too. But the police take she way, and the sireen start-up again, weeeeeeennnnnnn . . . Calvin manage to get the *Galaxie* outta the middle o' the road, the traffics still flying by, but now the new motto-car safe at the side o' the road. He put back on his jacket, and he shrug the jacket in shape and in fit pon his shoulders, he turn off the AM radio thing with the calypso, another calypso it was playing now, and fix the seams in his trousers, look back on the highway in the rear view mirror, start-up the *Galaxie*. He driving slow slow on the highway and the traffics blowing their horn to tell him get the fuck outta the road, nigger, but all the time he smiling and holding his hand outta the window and waving them on. He hold over outta habit to say something to the Canadian thing beside him, forgetting that she ain' there no more, and he still say, "This *Galaxie* is car for so! And godblummuh, look what a close shave I had!" He see the Canadian thing handbag open on the seat beside o' him, and he run his hand through it, searching. It had in five single dollar bills. He snap the handbag shut, leaving the money, touch the automatic window-winder, and throw the blasted handbag out on the Don Valley Parkway road.

(1971)

# Jack Hodgins   (b. 1939)

Born in a logging community on Vancouver Island, Jack Hodgins has set the stories in his collections *Spit Delaney's Island* (1976) and *The Barclay Family Theatre* (1981), from which this story is taken, in the rural area in which he grew up. Like William Faulkner and Margaret Laurence, whose writings have influenced him, Hodgins has not only used a specific region as setting, but has also dealt with the interrelationships among family members, in this case both within the large extended Barclay family and between the family and the rest of the community. In "The Concert Stages of Europe," Hodgins sensitively portrays the young hero's problems growing up in a small town. The narrator displays the dislike most boys have of piano lessons, and he also experiences the difficulties finding his own identity when confronted with the pressures of his parents' expectations.

# THE CONCERT STAGES OF EUROPE

Now I know Cornelia Horncastle would say I'm blaming the wrong person. I know that. I know too that she would say thirty years is a long time to hold a grudge, and that if I needed someone to blame for the fact that I made a fool of myself in front of the whole district and ruined my life in the process, then I ought to look around for the person who gave me my high-flown ideas in the first place. But she would be wrong; because there is no doubt I'd have led a different sort of life if it weren't for her, if it weren't for that piano keyboard her parents presented her with on her eleventh birthday. And everything — everything would have been different if that piano keyboard hadn't been the kind made out of stiff paper that you unfolded and laid out across the kitchen table in order to do your practising.

I don't suppose there would have been all that much harm in her having the silly thing, if only my mother hadn't got wind of it. What a fantastic idea, she said. You could learn to play without even making a sound! You could practise your scales without having to hear that awful racket when you hit a wrong note! A genius must have thought of it, she said. Certainly someone who'd read his Keats: *Heard melodies are sweet, but those unheard are sweeter.*[1] "And don't laugh," she said, "because Cornelia Horncastle is learning to play the piano and her mother doesn't even have to miss an episode of *Ma Perkins*[2] while she does it."

That girl, people had told her, would be giving concerts in Europe some day, command performances before royalty, and her parents hadn't even had to fork out the price of a piano. It was obvious proof, if you needed it, that a person didn't have to be rich to get somewhere in this world.

In fact, Cornelia's parents hadn't needed to put out even the small amount that paper keyboard would have cost. A piano teacher named Mrs. Humphries

1 lines from "Ode on a Grecian Urn" by nineteenth-century English poet John Keats (see page 171).
2 popular radio soap opera of the 1940s.

had moved onto the old Dendoff place and, discovering that almost no one in the district owned a piano, gave the keyboard to the Horncastles along with a year's free lessons. It was her idea, apparently, that when everyone heard how quickly Cornelia was learning they'd be lining up to send her their children for lessons. She wanted to make the point that having no piano needn't stop anyone from becoming a pianist. No doubt she had a vision of paper keyboards in every house in Waterville, of children everywhere thumping their scales out on the kitchen table without offending anyone's ears, of a whole generation turning silently into Paderewskis[3] without ever having played a note.

5      They would, I suppose, have to play a real piano when they went to her house for lessons once a week, but I was never able to find out for myself, because all that talk of Cornelia's marvellous career on the concert stages of Europe did not prompt my parents to buy one of those fake keyboards or sign me up for lessons with Mrs. Humphries. My mother was born a Barclay, which meant she had a few ideas of her own, and Cornelia's glorious future prompted her to go one better. We would buy a *real* piano, she announced. And I would be sent to a teacher we could trust, not to that newcomer. If those concert stages of Europe were ever going to hear the talent of someone from the stump ranches of Waterville, it wouldn't be Cornelia Horncastle, it would be Barclay Desmond. Me.

My father nearly choked on his coffee. "But Clay's a boy!"

"So what?" my mother said. *All* those famous players used to be boys. What did he think Chopin was? Or Tchaikovsky?

My father was so embarrassed that his throat began to turn a dark pink. Some things were too unnatural even to think about.

But eventually she won him over. "Think how terrible you'd feel," she said, "if he ended up in the bush, like you. If Mozart's father had worked for the Comox Logging Company and thought piano-playing was for sissies, where would the world be today?"

10     My father had no answer to that. He'd known since before his marriage that though my mother would put up with being married to a logger, expecting every day to be made a widow, she wouldn't tolerate for one minute the notion that a child of hers would follow him up into those hills. The children of Lenora Barclay would enter the professions.

She was right, he had to agree; working in the woods was the last thing in the world he wanted for his sons. He'd rather they take up ditch-digging or begging than have to work for that miserable logging company, or take their orders from a son-of-a-bitch like Tiny Beechman, or get their skulls cracked open like Stanley Kirck. It was a rotten way to make a living, and if he'd only had a decent education he could have made something of himself.

Of course, I knew he was saying all this just for my mother's benefit. He didn't really believe it for a minute. My father loved his work. I could tell by the way he was always talking about Ab Jennings and Shorty Cresswell, the men he worked with. I could tell by the excitement that mounted in him every year as the time grew near for the annual festival of loggers' sports where he usually won the bucking contest. It was obvious, I thought, that the man

3 early-twentieth-century Polish classical pianist.

really wanted nothing more in this world than that one of his sons should follow in his footsteps. And much as I disliked the idea, I was sure that I was the one he'd set his hopes on. Kenny was good in school. Laurel was a girl. I was the obvious choice. I even decided that what he'd pegged me for was high-rigger.[4] I was going to be one of those men who risked their necks climbing hundreds of feet up the bare lonely spar tree to hang the rigging from the top. Of course I would fall and kill myself the first time I tried it, I knew that, but there was no way I could convey my hesitation to my father since he would never openly admit that this was really his goal for me.

And playing the piano on the concert stages of Europe was every bit as unattractive. "Why not Kenny?" I said, when the piano had arrived, by barge, from Vancouver.

"He's too busy already with his school work," my mother said. Kenny was hoping for a scholarship, which meant he got out of just about everything unpleasant.

15    "What about Laurel?"

"With her short fat fingers?"

In the meantime, she said, though she was no piano-player herself (a great sigh here for what might have been), she had no trouble at all identifying which of those ivory keys was the all-important Middle C and would show it to me, to memorize, so that I wouldn't look like a total know-nothing when I showed up tomorrow for my first lesson. She'd had one piano lesson herself as a girl, she told me, and had learned all about Mister Middle C, but she'd never had a second lesson because her time was needed by her father, outside, helping with the chores. Seven daughters altogether, no sons, and she was the one who was the most often expected to fill the role of a boy. The rest of them had found the time to learn chords and chromatic scales and all those magic things she'd heard them practising while she was scrubbing out the dairy and cutting the runners off strawberry plants. They'd all become regular show-offs in one way or another, learning other instruments as well, putting on their own concerts and playing in dance bands and earning a reputation all over the district as entertaining livewires — The Barclay Sisters. And no one ever guessed that all the while she was dreaming about herself at that keyboard, tinkling away, playing beautiful music before huge audiences in elegant theatres.

"Then it isn't me that should be taking lessons," I said. "It's you."

"Don't be silly." But she walked to the new piano and pressed down one key, a black one, and looked as if I'd tempted her there for a minute. "It's too late now," she said. And then she sealed my fate: "But I just know that you're going to be a great pianist."

20    When my mother "just knew" something, that was as good as guaranteeing it already completed. It was her way of controlling the future and, incidentally, the rest of us. By "just knowing" things, she went through life commanding the future to fit into certain patterns she desired while we scurried around making sure that it worked out that way so she'd never have to be disappointed. She'd had one great disappointment as a girl — we were never

4 logger who climbs to the top of trees to cut off their tips.

quite sure what it was, since it was only alluded to in whispers with far-off looks — and it was important that it never happen again. I was trapped.

People were always asking what you were going to be when you grew up. As if your wishes counted. In the first six years of my life the country had convinced me it wanted me to grow up and get killed fighting Germans and Japanese. I'd seen the coils of barbed wire along the beach and knew they were there just to slow down the enemy while I went looking for my gun. The teachers at school obviously wanted me to grow up and become a teacher just like them, because as far as I could see nothing they ever taught me could be of any use or interest to a single adult in the world except someone getting paid to teach it to someone else. My mother was counting on my becoming a pianist with a swallow-tail coat and standing ovations. And my father, despite all his noises to the contrary, badly wanted me to climb into the crummy every morning with him and ride out those gravelly roads into mountains and risk my life destroying forests.

I did not want to be a logger. I did not want to be a teacher. I did not want to be a soldier. And I certainly did not want to be a pianist. If anyone had ever asked me what I did want to be when I grew up, in a way that meant they expected the truth, I'd have said quite simply that what I wanted was to be a Finn.

Our new neighbours, the Korhonens, were Finns. And being a Finn, I'd been told, meant something very specific. A Finn would give you the shirt off his back, a Finn was as honest as the day is long, a Finn could drink anybody under the table and beat up half a dozen Germans and Irishmen without trying, a Finn was not afraid of work, a Finn kept a house so clean you could eat off the floors. I knew all these things before ever meeting our neighbours, but as soon as I had met them I was able to add a couple more generalizations of my own to the catalogue: Finnish girls were blonde and beautiful and flirtatious, and Finnish boys were strong, brave, and incredibly intelligent. These conclusions were reached immediately after meeting Lilja Korhonen, whose turned-up nose and blue eyes fascinated me from the beginning, and Larry Korhonen, who was already a teenager and told me for starters that he was actually Superman, having learned to fly after long hours of practice off their barn roof. Mr. and Mrs. Korhonen, of course, fitted exactly all the things my parents had told me about Finns in general. And so I decided my ambition in life was to be just like them.

I walked over to their house every Saturday afternoon and pretended to read their coloured funnies. I got in on the weekly steam-bath with Larry and his father in the sauna down by the barn. Mr. Korhonen, a patient man whose eyes sparkled at my eager attempts, taught me to count to ten — *yksi, kaksi, kolme, nelja, viisi, kuusi, seitseman, kahdeksan, yhdeksan, kymmenen.* I helped Mrs. Korhonen scrub her linoleum floors and put down newspapers so no one could walk on them, then I gorged myself on cinnamon cookies and *kala loota* and coffee sucked through a sugar cube. If there was something to be caught from just being around them, I wanted to catch it. And since being a Finn seemed to be a full-time occupation, I didn't have much patience with my parents, who behaved as if there were other things you had to prepare yourself for.

25      The first piano teacher they sent me to was Aunt Jessie, who lived in a narrow, cramped house up a gravel road that led to the mountains. She'd

learned to play as a girl in Toronto, but she had no pretensions about being a real teacher, she was only doing this as a favour to my parents so they would-n't have to send me to that Mrs. Humphries, an outsider. But one of the prob-lems was that Aunt Jessie — who was no aunt of mine at all, simply one of those family friends who somehow get saddled with an honorary family title — was exceptionally beautiful. She was so attractive, in fact, that even at the age of ten I had difficulty keeping my eyes or my mind on the lessons. She exuded a dreamy sort of delicate femininity; her soft, intimate voice made the hair on the back of my neck stand on end. Besides that, her own playing was so much more pleasant to listen to than my own stumbling clangs and clunks that she would often begin to show me how to do something and become so carried away with the sound of her own music that she just kept right on playing through the rest of my half-hour. It was a simple matter to per-suade her to dismiss me early every week so that I'd have a little time to play in the creek that ran past the back of her house, poling a homemade raft up and down the length of her property while her daughters paid me nickels and candies for a ride. At the end of a year my parents suspected I wasn't pro-gressing as fast as I should. They found out why on the day I fell in the creek and nearly drowned, had to be revived by a distraught Aunt Jessie, and was driven home soaked and shivering in the back seat of her old Hudson.

Mr. Korhonen and my father were huddled over the taken-apart cream sep-arator on the verandah when Aunt Jessie brought me up to the door. My father, when he saw me, had that peculiar look on his face that was halfway between amusement and concern, but Mr. Korhonen laughed openly. "That boy lookit like a drowny rat."

I felt like a drowned rat too, but I joined his laughter. I was sure this would be the end of my piano career, and could hardly wait to see my mother roll her eyes to the ceiling, throw out her arms, and say, "I give up."

She did nothing of the sort. She tightened her lips and told Aunt Jessie how disappointed she was. "No wonder the boy still stumbles around on that key-board like a blind-folded rabbit; he's not going to learn the piano while he's out risking his life on the *river!*"

When I came downstairs in dry clothes Aunt Jessie had gone, no doubt wishing she'd left me to drown in the creek, and my parents and the Korhonens were all in the kitchen drinking coffee. The Korhonens sat at either side of the table, smoking hand-rolled cigarettes and squinting at me through the smoke. Mrs. Korhonen could blow beautiful white streams down her nostrils. They'd left their gumboots on the piece of newspaper just inside the door, of course, and wore the same kind of grey work-socks on their feet that my father always wore on his. My father was leaning against the wall with both arms folded across his chest inside his wide elastic braces, as he sometimes did, swishing his mug gently as if he were trying to bring something up from the bottom. My mother, however, was unable to alight anywhere. She slammed wood down into the firebox of the stove, she rattled dishes in the sink water, she slammed cupboard doors, she went around the room with the coffee pot, refilling mugs, and all the while she sang the song of her betrayal, cursing her own stupidity for sending me to a friend instead of to a professional teacher, and suddenly in a flash of inspiration dumping all the blame on my father: "If you hadn't made me feel it was somehow pointless I wouldn't have felt guilty about spending more money!"

From behind the drifting shreds of smoke Mr. Korhonen grinned at me. Sucked laughter between his teeth. "Yust *teenk*, boy, looks like-it you're saved!"

Mrs. Korhonen stabbed out her cigarette in an ashtray, picked a piece of tobacco off her tongue, and composed her face into the most serious and lady-like expression she could muster. "Yeh! Better he learn to drive the tractor." And swung me a conspirator's grin.

"Not on your life," my mother said. Driving a machine may have been a good enough ambition for some people, she believed, but the Barclays had been in this country for four generations and she knew there were a few things higher. "What we'll do is send him to a real teacher. Mrs. Greensborough."

Mrs. Greensborough was well known for putting on a public recital in town once a year, climaxing the program with her own rendition of Grieg's Piano Concerto — so beautiful that all went home, it was said, with tears in their eyes. The problem with Mrs. Greensborough had nothing to do with her teaching. She was, as far as I could see, an excellent piano teacher. And besides, there was something rather exciting about playing on her piano, which was surrounded and nearly buried by a thousand tropical plants and dozens of cages full of squawking birds. Every week's lesson was rather like putting on a concert in the midst of the Amazon jungle. There was even a monkey that swung through the branches and sat on the top of the piano with the metronome between its paws. And Mrs. Greensborough was at the same time warm and demanding, complimentary and hard to please — though given a little, like Aunt Jessie, to taking off on long passages of her own playing, as if she'd forgotten I was there.

It took a good hour's hard bicycling on uphill gravel roads before I could present myself for the lesson — past a dairy farm, a pig farm, a turkey farm, a dump, and a good long stretch of bush — then more washboard road through heavy timber where driveways disappeared into the trees and one dog after another lay in wait for its weekly battle with my right foot. Two spaniels, one Irish setter, and a bulldog. But it wasn't a spaniel or a setter or even a bulldog that met me on the driveway of the Greensboroughs' chicken farm, it was a huge German shepherd that came barking down the slope the second I had got the gate shut, and stuck its nose into my crotch. And kept it there, growling menacingly, the whole time it took me to back him up to the door of the house. There was no doubt in my mind that I would come home from piano lesson one Saturday minus a few parts. Once I had got to the house, I tried to get inside quickly and shut the door in his face, leaving him out there in the din of cackling hens; but he always got his nose between the door and the jamb, growled horribly and pushed himself inside so that he could lie on the floor at my feet and watch me hungrily the whole time I sat at the kitchen table waiting for Ginny Stamp to finish off her lesson and get out of there. By the time my turn came around my nerves were too frayed for me to get much benefit out of the lesson.

Still, somehow I learned. That Mrs. Greensborough was a marvellous teacher, my mother said. The woman really knew her stuff. And I was such a fast-learning student that it took less than two years for my mother to begin thinking it was time the world heard from me.

"Richy Ryder," she said, "is coming to town."

"What?"

"Richy Ryder, CJMT. *The Talent Show.*"

I'd heard the program. Every Saturday night Richy Ryder was in a different town somewhere in the province, hosting his one-hour talent contest from the stage of a local theatre and giving away free trips to Hawaii.

40 Something rolled over in my stomach.

"And here's the application form right here," she said, whipping two sheets of paper out of her purse to slap down on the table.

"No thank you," I said. If she thought I was going in it, she was crazy.

"Don't be silly. What harm is there in trying?" My mother always answered objections with great cheerfulness, as if they were hardly worth considering.

"I'll make a fool of myself."

45 "You play beautifully," she said. "It's amazing how far you've come in only two years. And besides, even if you don't win, the experience would be good for you."

"You have to go door-to-door ahead of time, begging for pledges, for money."

"Not begging," she said. She plunged her hands into the sink, peeling carrots so fast I couldn't see the blade of the vegetable peeler. "Just giving people a chance to vote for you. A dollar a vote." The carrot dropped, skinned naked, another one was picked up. She looked out the window now toward the barn and, still smiling, delivered the argument that never failed. "I just know you'd win it if you went in, I can feel it in my bones."

"Not this time!" I shouted, nearly turning myself inside out with the terror. "Not this time. I just can't do it."

Yet somehow I found myself riding my bicycle up and down all the roads around Waterville, knocking at people's doors, explaining the contest, and asking for their money and their votes. I don't know why I did it. Perhaps I was doing it for the same reason I was tripping over everything, knocking things off tables, slamming my shoulder into doorjambs; I just couldn't help it, everything had gone out of control. I'd wakened one morning that year and found myself six feet two inches tall and as narrow as a fence stake. My feet were so far away they seemed to have nothing to do with me. My hands flopped around on the ends of those lanky arms like fish, something alive. My legs had grown so fast the bones in my knees parted and I had to wear elastic bandages to keep from falling apart. When I turned a corner on my bicycle, one knee would bump the handlebar, throwing me into the ditch. I was the same person as before, apparently, saddled with this new body I didn't know what to do with. Everything had gone out of control. I seemed to have nothing to do with the direction of my own life. It was perfectly logical that I should end up playing the piano on the radio, selling myself to the countryside for a chance to fly off to Hawaii and lie on the sand under the whispering palms.

50 There were actually two prizes offered. The all-expense, ten-day trip to Hawaii would go to the person who brought in the most votes for himself, a dollar a vote. But lest someone accuse the radio station of getting its values confused, there was also a prize for the person judged by a panel of experts to have the most talent. This prize, which was donated by Nelson's Hardware, was a leatherette footstool.

"It's not the prize that's important," people told me. "It's the chance to be heard by all those people."

I preferred not to think of all those people. It seemed to me that if I were cut out to be a concert pianist it would be my teacher and not my parents encouraging me in this thing. Mrs. Greensborough, once she'd forked over her two dollars for two votes, said nothing at all. No doubt she was hoping I'd keep her name out of it.

But it had taken no imagination on my part to figure out that if I were to win the only prize worth trying for, the important thing was not to spend long hours at the keyboard, practising, but to get out on the road hammering at doors, on the telephone calling relatives, down at the General Store approaching strangers who stopped for gas. Daily piano practice shrank to one or two quick run-throughs of "The Robin's Return", school homework shrank to nothing at all, and home chores just got ignored. My brother and sister filled in for me, once in a while, so the chickens wouldn't starve to death and the woodbox would never be entirely empty, but they did it grace-lessly. It was amazing, they said, how much time a great pianist had to spend out on the road, meeting his public. Becoming famous, they said, was more work than it was worth.

And becoming famous, I discovered, was what people assumed I was after. "You'll go places," they told me. "You'll put this place on the old map." I was a perfect combination of my father's down-to-earth get-up-and-go and my mother's finer sensitivity, they said. How wonderful to see a young person with such high ambition!

"I always knew this old place wouldn't be good enough to hold you," my grandmother said as she fished out a five-dollar bill from her purse. But my mother's sisters, who appeared from all parts of the old farmhouse in order to contribute a single collective vote, had some reservations to express. Eleanor, the youngest, said she doubted I'd be able to carry it off, I'd probably freeze when I was faced with a microphone, I'd forget what a piano was for. Christina announced she was betting I'd faint, or have to run out to the bathroom right in the middle of my piece. And Mabel, red-headed Mabel who'd played accor-dion once in an amateur show, said she remembered a boy who made such a fool of himself in one of these things that he went home and blew off his head. "Don't be so morbid," my grandmother said. "The boy probably had no talent. Clay here is destined for higher things."

From behind her my grandfather winked. He seldom had a chance to contribute more than that to a conversation. He waited until we were alone to stuff a five-dollar bill in my pocket and squeeze my arm.

I preferred my grandmother's opinion of me to the aunts'. I began to feed people lies so they'd think that about me — that I was destined for dizzying heights. I wanted to be a great pianist, I said, and if I won that trip to Hawaii I'd trade it in for the money so that I could go off and study at the Toronto Conservatory. I'd heard of the Toronto Conservatory only because it was printed in big black letters on the front cover of all those yellow books of finger exercises I was expected to practise.

I don't know why people gave me their money. Pity, perhaps. Maybe it was impossible to say no to a six-foot-two-inch thirteen-year-old who trips over his own bike in front of your house, falls up your bottom step, blushes red with embarrassment when you open the door, and tells you he wants your money for a talent contest so he can become a Great Artist. At any rate, by the day of the contest I'd collected enough money to put me in the third spot. I would have to rely on pledges from the studio audience and phone-in pledges from the radio audience to rocket me up to first place. The person in second place when I walked into that theatre to take my seat down front with the rest of the contestants was Cornelia Horncastle.

I don't know how she managed it so secretly. I don't know where she found the people to give her money, living in the same community as I did, unless all those people who gave me their dollar bills when I knocked on their doors had just given her two the day before. Maybe she'd gone into town, canvassing street after street, something my parents wouldn't let me do on the grounds that town people already had enough strangers banging on their doors every day. Once I'd got outside the vague boundaries of Waterville I was to approach only friends or relatives or people who worked in the woods with my dad, or stores that had — as my mother put it — done a good business out of us over the years. Cornelia Horncastle, in order to get herself secretly into that second place, must have gone wild in town. Either that or discovered a rich relative.

60    She sat at the other end of the front row of contestants, frowning over the sheets of music in her hands. A short nod and a quick smile were all she gave me. Like the other contestants, I was kept busy licking my dry lips, rubbing my sweaty palms together, wondering if I should whip out to the bathroom one last time, and rubbernecking to get a look at people as they filled up the theatre behind us. Mrs. Greensborough, wearing dark glasses and a big floppy hat, was jammed into the far corner at the rear, studying her program. Mr. and Mrs. Korhonen and Lilja came partway down the aisle and found seats near the middle. Mr. Korhonen winked at me. Larry, who was not quite the hero he had once been, despite the fact that he'd recently beat up one of the teachers and set fire to the bus shelter, came in with my brother Kenny — both of them looking uncomfortable — and slid into a back seat. My parents came all the way down front, so they could look back up the slope and pick out the seats they wanted. My mother smiled as she always did in public, as if she expected the most delightful surprise at any moment. They took seats near the front. Laurel was with them, reading a book.

My mother's sisters — with husbands, boyfriends, a few of my cousins — filled up the entire middle section of the back row. Eleanor, who was just a few years older than myself, crossed her eyes and stuck out her tongue when she saw that I'd turned to look. Mabel pulled in her chin and held up her hands, which she caused to tremble and shake. Time to be nervous, she was suggesting, in case I forgot. Bella, Christina, Gladdy, Frieda — all sat puffed up like members of a royal family, or the owners of this theatre, looking down over the crowd as if they believed every one of these people had come here expressly to watch their nephew and for no other reason. "Look, it's the Barclay girls," I heard someone behind me say. And someone else: "Oh, *them*." The owner of the first voice giggled. "It's a wonder they aren't all entered in this thing, you know how they like to perform." A snort. "They *are* performing, just watch them." I could tell by the muffled "Shhh" and the rustling of clothing that one of them was nudging the other and pointing at me, at the back of my neck. "One of them's son." When I turned again, Eleanor stood up in the aisle by her seat, did a few steps of a tap dance, and quickly sat down. In case I was tempted to take myself seriously.

When my mother caught my eye, she mouthed a silent message: stop gawking at the audience, I was letting people see how unusual all this was to me, instead of taking it in my stride like a born performer. She indicated with her head that I should notice the stage.

As if I hadn't already absorbed every detail. It was exactly as she must have hoped. A great black concert grand with the lid lifted sat out near the front of the stage, against a painted backdrop of palm trees along a sandy beach, and — in great scrawled letters — the words "Richy Ryder's CJMT Talent Festival". A long blackboard leaned against one end of the proscenium arch, with all the contestants' names on it and the rank order of each. Someone named Brenda Roper was in first place. On the opposite side of the stage, a microphone seemed to have grown up out of a heap of pineapples. I felt sick.

Eventually Richy Ryder came out of whatever backstage room he'd been hiding in and passed down the row of contestants, identifying us and telling us to get up onto the stage when our turns came without breaking our necks on those steps. "You won't be nervous, when you get up there," he said. "I'll make you feel at ease." He was looking off somewhere else as he said it, and I could see his jaw muscles straining to hold back a yawn. And he wasn't fooling me with his "you won't be nervous" either, because I knew without a doubt that the minute I got up on that stage I would throw up all over the piano.

65   Under the spotlight, Richy Ryder acted like a different person. He did not look the least bit like yawning while he told the audience the best way of holding their hands to get the most out of applause, cautioned them against whistling or yelling obscenities, painted a glorious picture of the life ahead for the talented winner of this contest, complimented the audience on the number of happy, shiny faces he could see out there in the seats, and told them how lucky they were to have this opportunity of showing off the fine young talent of the valley to all the rest of the province. I slid down in my seat, sure that I would rather die than go through with this thing.

The first contestant was a fourteen-year-old girl dressed up like a gypsy, singing something in a foreign language. According to the blackboard she was way down in ninth place, so I didn't pay much attention until her voice cracked open in the middle of a high note and she clutched at her throat with both hands, a look of incredulous surprise on her face. She stopped right there, face a brilliant red, and after giving the audience a quick curtsey hurried off the stage. A great beginning, I thought. If people were going to fall to pieces like that through the whole show no one would even notice my upchucking on the Heintzman. I had a vision of myself dry-heaving the whole way through "The Robin's Return".

Number two stepped up to the microphone and answered all of Richy Ryder's questions as if they were some kind of test he had to pass in order to be allowed to perform. Yes sir, his name was Roger Casey, he said with a face drawn long and narrow with seriousness, and in case that wasn't enough he added that his father was born in Digby, Nova Scotia, and his mother was born Esther Romaine in a little house just a couple blocks up the street from the theatre, close to the Native Sons' Hall, and had gone to school with the mayor though she'd dropped out of Grade Eight to get a job at the Safeway cutting meat. And yes sir, he was going to play the saxophone because he'd taken lessons for four years from Mr. D. P. Rowbottom on Seventh Street though he'd actually started out on the trumpet until he decided he didn't like it all that much. He came right out to the edge of the stage, toes sticking over, leaned back like a rooster about to crow, and blasted out "Softly As in a Morning Sunrise" so loud and hard that I thought his bulging eyes would pop right out of his head and his straining lungs would blast holes through that red-and-white shirt. Everyone moved forward, tense and straining, waiting for something terrible to happen — for him to fall off the stage or explode or go sailing off into the air from the force of his own fantastic intensity — but he stopped suddenly and everyone fell back exhausted and sweaty to clap for him.

The third contestant was less reassuring. A kid with talent. A smart-aleck ten-year-old with red hair, who told the audience he was going into show business when he grew up, started out playing "Swanee River" on his banjo, switched in the middle of a bar to a mouth organ, tap-danced across the stage to play a few bars on the piano, and finished off on a trombone he'd had stashed away behind the palm tree. He bowed, grinned, flung himself around the stage as if he'd spent his whole life on it, and looked as if he'd do his whole act again quite happily if the audience wanted him to. By the time the tremendous applause had died down my jaw was aching from the way I'd been grinding my teeth the whole time he was up there. The audience would not have gone quite so wild over him, I thought, if he hadn't been wearing a hearing aid and a leg brace.

Then it was my turn. A strange calm fell over me when my name was called, the kind of calm that I imagine comes over a person about to be executed when his mind finally buckles under the horror it has been faced with, something too terrible to believe in. I wondered for a moment if I had died. But no, my body at least hadn't died, for it transported me unbidden across the front of the audience, up the staircase (with only a slight stumble on the second step, hardly noticeable), and across the great wide stage of the theatre to stand facing Richy Ryder's enormous expanse of white smiling teeth, beside the microphone.

70 "And you are Barclay Philip Desmond," he said.

"Yes," I said.

And again "yes", because I realized that not only had my voice come out as thin and high as the squeal of a dry buzz-saw, but the microphone was at least a foot too low. I had to bend my knees to speak into it.

"You don't live in town, do you?" he said. He had no intention of adjusting that microphone. "You come from a place called . . . Waterville. A logging and farming settlement?"

"Yes," I said.

75 And again "yes" because while he was speaking my legs had straightened up, I'd returned to my full height and had to duck again for the microphone.

He was speaking to me but his eyes, I could see, were busy keeping all that audience gathered together, while his voice and his mind were obviously concentrated on the thousands of invisible people who were crouched inside that microphone, listening, the thousands of people who — I imagined now — were pulled up close to their sets all over the province, wondering if I was actually a pair of twins or if my high voice had some peculiar way of echoing itself, a few tones lower.

"Does living in the country like that mean you have to milk the cows every morning before you go to school?"

"Yes."

And again "yes".

I could see Mrs. Greensborough cowering in the back corner. I promise not to mention you, I thought. And the Korhonens, grinning. I had clearly passed over into another world they couldn't believe in.

"If you've got a lot of farm chores to do, when do you find the time to practise the piano?"

He had me this time. A "yes" wouldn't be good enough. "Right after school," I said, and ducked to repeat. "Right after school. As soon as I get home. For an hour."

"And I just bet," he said, throwing the audience an enormous wink, "that like every other red-blooded country kid you hate every minute of it. You'd rather be outside playing baseball."

The audience laughed. I could see my mother straining forward; she still had the all-purpose waiting-for-the-surprise smile on her lips but her eyes were frowning at the master of ceremonies. She did not approve of the comment. And behind that face she was no doubt thinking to herself "I just know he's going to win" over and over so hard that she was getting pains in the back of her neck. Beside her, my father had a tight grin on his face. He was chuckling to himself, and sliding a look around the room to see how the others were taking this.

Up at the back, most of my aunts — and their husbands, their boyfriends — had tilted their chins down to their chests, offering me only the tops of their heads. Eleanor, however, had both hands behind her neck. She was laughing harder than anyone else.

Apparently I was not expected to respond to the last comment, for he had another question as soon as the laughter had died, "How old are you, son?"

"Thirteen."

For once I remembered to duck the first time.

"Thirteen. Does your wife like the idea of your going on the radio like this?"

Again the audience laughed. My face burned. I felt tears in my eyes. I had no control over my face. I tried to laugh like everyone else but realized I probably looked like an idiot. Instead, I frowned and looked embarrassed and kicked at one shoe with the toe of the other.

"Just a joke," he said, "just a joke." The jerk knew he'd gone too far. "And now seriously, one last question before I turn you loose on those ivories over there."

My heart had started to thump so noisily I could hardly hear him. My hands, I realized, had gone numb. There was no feeling at all in my fingers. How was I ever going to play the piano?

"What are you going to be when you grow up?"

The thumping stopped. My heart stopped. A strange, cold silence settled over the world. I was going to die right in front of all those people. What I was going to be was a corpse, dead of humiliation, killed in a trap I hadn't seen being set. What must have been only a few seconds crawled by while something crashed around in my head, trying to get out. I sensed the audience, hoping for some help from them. My mother had settled back in her seat and for the first time that surprise-me smile had gone. Rather, she looked confident, sure of what I was about to say.

And suddenly, I was aware of familiar faces all over that theatre. Neighbours. Friends of the family. My aunts. People who had heard me answer that question at their doors, people who thought they knew what I wanted.

There was nothing left of Mrs. Greensborough but the top of her big hat. My father, too, was looking down at the floor between his feet. I saw myself falling from that spar tree, high in the mountains.

"Going to be?" I said, turning so fast that I bumped the microphone with my hand, which turned out after all not to be numb.

I ducked.

"Nothing," I said. "I don't know. Maybe . . . maybe nothing at all."

I don't know who it was that snorted when I screwed up the stool, sat down, and stood up to screw it down again. I don't know how well I played, I wasn't listening. I don't know how loud the audience clapped, I was in a hurry to get back to my seat. I don't know what the other contestants did, I wasn't paying any attention, except when Cornelia Horncastle got up on the stage, told the whole world she was going to be a professional pianist, and sat down to rattle off Rachmaninoff's Rhapsody on a Theme of Paganini as if she'd been playing for fifty years. As far as I know it may have been the first time she'd ever heard herself play it. She had a faint look of surprise on her face the whole time, as if she couldn't quite get over the way the keys went down when you touched them.

As soon as Cornelia came down off the stage, smiling modestly, and got back into her seat, Richy Ryder announced a fifteen-minute intermission while the talent judges made their decision and the studio audience went out into the lobby to pledge their money and their votes. Now that the talent had been displayed, people could spend their money according to what they'd heard rather than according to who happened to come knocking on their door. Most of the contestants got up to stretch their legs but I figured I'd stood up once too often that night and stayed in my seat. The lower exit was not far away; I contemplated using it; I could hitch-hike home and be in bed before any of the others got out of there.

I was stopped, though, by my father, who sat down in the seat next to mine and put a greasy carton of popcorn in my lap.

"Well," he said, "that's that."

His neck was flushed. This must have been a terrible evening for him. He had a carton of popcorn himself and tipped it up to gather a huge mouthful.

I had never before in my life, I realized, seen my father eat popcorn. It must have been worse for him than I thought.

105     Not one of the aunts was anywhere in sight. I could see my mother standing in the far aisle, talking to Mrs. Korhonen. Still smiling. She would never let herself fall apart in public, no matter what happened. My insides ached with the knowledge of what it must have been like right then to be her. I felt as if I had just betrayed her in front of the whole world. Betrayed everyone.

"Let's go home," I said.

"Not yet. Wait a while. Might as well see this thing to the end."

True, I thought. Wring every last drop of torture out of it.

He looked hard at me a moment, as if he were trying to guess what was going on in my head. And he did, he did, he always knew. "My old man wanted me to be a doctor," he said. "My mother wanted me to be a florist. She liked flowers. She thought if I was a florist I'd be able to send her a bouquet every week. But what does any of that matter now?"

110     Being part of a family was too complicated. And right then I decided I'd be a loner. No family for me. Nobody whose hearts could be broken every time I opened my mouth. Nobody *expecting* anything of me. Nobody to get me all tangled up in knots trying to guess who means what and what is it that's really going on inside anyone else. No temptations to presume I knew what someone else was thinking or feeling or hoping for.

When the lights had flickered and dimmed, and people had gone back to their seats, a young man with a beard came out onto the stage and changed the numbers behind the contestants' names. I'd dropped to fifth place, and Cornelia Horncastle had moved up to first. She had also, Richy Ryder announced, been awarded the judges' footstool for talent. The winner of the holiday in sunny Hawaii would not be announced until the next week, he said, when the radio audience had enough time to mail in their votes.

"And that," my mother said when she came down the aisle with her coat on, "is the end of a long and tiring day." I could find no disappointment showing in her eyes, or in the set of her mouth. Just relief. The same kind of relief that I felt myself. "You did a good job," she said, "and thank goodness it's over."

As soon as we got in the house I shut myself in the bedroom and announced I was never coming out. Lying on my bed, I tried to read my comic books but my mind passed from face to face all through the community, imagining everyone having a good laugh at the way my puffed-up ambition had got its reward. My face burned. Relatives, the aunts, would be ashamed of me. Eleanor would never let me forget. Mabel would remind me of the boy who'd done the only honourable thing, blown off his head. Why wasn't I doing the same? I lay awake the whole night, torturing myself with these thoughts. But when morning came and the hunger pains tempted me out of the bedroom as far as the breakfast table, I decided the whole wretched experience had brought one benefit with it: freedom from ambition. I wouldn't worry any more about becoming a pianist for my mother. Nor would I worry any more about becoming a high-rigger for my father. I was free at last to concentrate on pursuing the only goal that ever really mattered to me: becoming a Finn.

Of course I failed at that too. But then neither did Cornelia Horncastle become a great pianist on the concert stages of Europe. In fact, I understand that once she got back from her holiday on the beaches of Hawaii she announced to her parents that she was never going to touch a piano again as long as she lived, ivory, or cardboard, or any other kind. She had already, she said, accomplished all she'd ever wanted from it. And as far as I know, she's kept her word to this day.

(1978)

# Margaret Atwood   (b. 1939)

Ottawa-born poet, novelist, short story writer, and critic Margaret Atwood is one of Canada's best-known authors, both at home and abroad. Such novels as *Surfacing* (1972) and *Cat's Eye* (1988) have been praised for their portrayal of introspective, contemporary women examining their pasts and their relationships as they search for new directions in their lives. In "The Resplendent Quetzal," the growing alienation between a childless husband and wife is revealed during a vacation tour of Mexico. Their separate reactions to a visit to ancient ruins emphasize the lovelessness of their relationship, which began to disintegrate when their baby died at birth. (See also the introduction to Margaret Atwood's poetry, page 414.)

# THE RESPLENDENT QUETZAL

Sarah was sitting near the edge of the sacrificial well. She had imagined something smaller, more like a wishing well, but this was huge, and the water at the bottom wasn't clear at all. It was mud-brown; a few clumps of reeds were growing over to one side, and the trees at the top dangled their roots, or were they vines, down the limestone walls into the water. Sarah thought there might be some point to being a sacrificial victim if the well were nicer, but you would never get her to jump into a muddy hole like that. They were probably pushed, or knocked on the head and thrown in. According to the guidebook the water was deep but it looked more like a swamp to her.

Beside her a group of tourists were being rounded up by the guide, who obviously wanted to get the whole thing over with so he could cram them back onto their pink-and-purple-striped *turismo* bus and relax. These were Mexican tourists, and Sarah found it reassuring that other people besides Canadians and Americans wore big hats and sunglasses and took pictures of everything. She wished she and Edward could make these excursions at a less crowded time of year, if they had to make them at all, but because of Edward's teaching job they were limited to school holidays. Christmas was the worst. It would be the same even if he had a different job and they had children, though; but they didn't have any.

The guide shooed his charges back along the gravel path as if they were chickens, which was what they sounded like. He himself lingered beside Sarah, finishing his cigarette, one foot on a stone block, like a conquistador.[1] He was a small dark man with several gold teeth, which glinted when he smiled. He was smiling at Sarah now, sideways, and she smiled back serenely. She liked it when these men smiled at her or even when they made those juicy sucking noises with their mouths as they walked behind her on the street; so long as they didn't touch. Edward pretended not to hear them. Perhaps they did it so much because she was blonde: blondes were rare here. She didn't think of herself as beautiful, exactly; the word she had chosen for herself some time ago was "comely." Comely to look upon. You would never use that word for a thin woman.

---

1 Spanish invader of Mexico and Peru.

The guide tossed his cigarette butt into the sacrificial well and turned to follow his flock. Sarah forgot about him immediately. She'd felt something crawling up her leg, but when she looked nothing was there. She tucked the full skirt of her cotton dress in under her thighs and clamped it between her knees. This was the kind of place you could get flea bites, places with dirt on the ground, where people sat. Parks and bus terminals. But she didn't care, her feet were tired and the sun was hot. She would rather sit in the shade and get bitten than rush around trying to see everything, which was what Edward wanted to do. Luckily the bites didn't swell up on her the way they did on Edward.

5    Edward was back along the path, out of sight among the bushes, peering around with his new Leitz binoculars. He didn't like sitting down, it made him restless. On these trips it was difficult for Sarah to sit by herself and just think. Her own binoculars, which were Edward's old ones, dangled around her neck; they weighed a ton. She took them off and put them into her purse.

His passion for birds had been one of the first things Edward had confided to her. Shyly, as if it had been some precious gift, he'd shown her the lined notebook he'd started keeping when he was nine, with its awkward, boyish printing — ROBIN, BLUE JAY, KINGFISHER — and the day and the year recorded beside each name. She'd pretended to be touched and interested, and in fact she had been. She herself didn't have compulsions of this kind; whereas Edward plunged totally into things, as if they were oceans. For a while it was stamps; then he took up playing the flute and nearly drove her crazy with the practising. Now it was pre-Columbian[2] ruins, and he was determined to climb up every heap of old stones he could get his hands on. A capacity for dedication, she guessed you would call it. At first Edward's obsessions had fascinated her, since she didn't understand them, but now they merely made her tired. Sooner or later he'd dropped them all anyway, just as he began to get really good or really knowledgeable; all but the birds. That had remained constant. She herself, she thought, had once been one of his obsessions.

It wouldn't be so bad if he didn't insist on dragging her into everything. Or rather, he had once insisted; he no longer did. And she had encouraged him, she'd let him think she shared or at least indulged his interests. She was becoming less indulgent as she grew older. The waste of energy bothered her, because it was a waste, he never stuck with anything, and what use was his encyclopaedic knowledge of birds? It would be different if they had enough money, but they were always running short. If only he would take all that energy and do something productive with it, in his job, for instance. He could be a principal if he wanted to, she kept telling him that. But he wasn't interested, he was content to poke along doing the same thing year after year. His Grade Six children adored him, the boys especially. Perhaps it was because they sensed he was a lot like them.

He'd started asking her to go birding, as he called it, shortly after they'd met, and of course she had gone. It would have been an error to refuse. She hadn't complained, then, about her sore feet or standing in the rain under the dripping bushes trying to keep track of some nondescript sparrow, while Edward thumbed through his Peterson's Field Guide as if it were the Bible or

2 before Columbus arrived in the New World in 1492.

the bird were the Holy Grail.[3] She'd even become quite good at it. Edward was nearsighted, and she was quicker at spotting movement than he was. With his usual generosity he acknowledged this, and she'd fallen into the habit of using it when she wanted to get rid of him for a while. Just now, for instance.

"There's something over there." She'd pointed across the well to the tangle of greenery on the other side.

"Where?" Edward had squinted eagerly and raised his binoculars. He looked a little like a bird himself, she thought, with his long nose and stilt legs.

"That thing there, sitting in that thing, the one with the tufts. The sort of bean tree. It's got orange on it."

Edward focused. "An oriole?"

"I can't tell from here. Oh, it just flew." She pointed over their heads while Edward swept the sky in vain.

"I think it lit back there, behind us."

That was enough to send him off. She had to do this with enough real birds to keep him believing, however.

Edward sat down on the root of a tree and lit a cigarette. He had gone down the first side-path he'd come to; it smelled of piss, and he could see by the decomposing Kleenexes further along that this was one of the places people went when they couldn't make it back to the washroom behind the ticket counter.

He took off his glasses, then his hat, and wiped the sweat off his forehead. His face was red, he could feel it. Blushing, Sarah called it. She persisted in attributing it to shyness and boyish embarrassment; she hadn't yet deduced that it was simple rage. For someone so devious she was often incredibly stupid.

She didn't know, for instance, that he'd found out about her little trick with the birds at least three years ago. She'd pointed to a dead tree and said she saw a bird in it, but he himself had inspected that same tree only seconds earlier and there was nothing in it at all. And she was very careless: she described oriole-coloured birds behaving like kingbirds, woodpeckers where there would never be any woodpeckers, mute jays, neckless herons. She must have decided he was a total idiot and any slipshod invention would do.

But why not, since he appeared to fall for it every time? And why did he do it, why did he chase off after her imaginary birds, pretending he believed her? It was partly that although he knew what she was doing to him, he had no idea why. It couldn't be simple malice, she had enough outlets for that. He didn't want to know the real reason, which loomed in his mind as something form-less, threatening and final. Her lie about the birds was one of the many lies that propped things up. He was afraid to confront her, that would be the end, all the pretences would come crashing down and they would be left standing in the rubble, staring at each other. There would be nothing left to say and Edward wasn't ready for that.

She would deny everything anyway. "What do you mean? Of course I saw it. It flew right over there. Why would I make up such a thing?" With her level gaze, blonde and stolid and immoveable as a rock.

3 sacred cup used by Christ at the Last Supper.

Edward had a sudden image of himself, crashing out of the undergrowth like King Kong, picking Sarah up and hurling her over the edge, down into the sacrificial well. Anything to shatter that imperturbable expression, bland and pale and plump and smug, like a Flemish Madonna's.[4] Self-righteous, that's what it was. Nothing was ever her fault. She hadn't been like that when he'd met her. But it wouldn't work: as she fell she would glance at him, not with fear but with maternal irritation, as if he'd spilled chocolate milk on a white tablecloth. And she'd pull her skirt down. She was concerned for appearances, always.

Though there would be something inappropriate about throwing Sarah into the sacrificial well, just as she was, with all her clothes on. He remembered snatches from the several books he'd read before they came down. (And that was another thing: Sarah didn't believe in reading up on places beforehand. "Don't you want to understand what you're looking at?" he'd asked her. "I'll see the same thing in any case, won't I?" she said. "I mean, knowing all those facts doesn't change the actual statue or whatever." Edward found this attitude infuriating; and now that they were here, she resisted his attempts to explain things to her by her usual passive method of pretending not to hear.

("That's a Chac-Mool,[5] see that? That round thing on the stomach held the bowl where they put the hearts, and the butterfly on the head means the soul flying up to the sun."

("Could you get out the suntan lotion, Edward? I think it's in the tote bag, in the left-hand pocket."

25    And he would hand her the suntan lotion, defeated once again.)

No, she wouldn't be a fit sacrifice, with or without lotion. They only threw people in — or perhaps they jumped in, of their own free will — for the water god, to make it rain and ensure fertility. The drowned were messengers, sent to carry requests to the god. Sarah would have to be purified first, in the stone sweat-house beside the well. Then, naked, she would kneel before him, one arm across her breast in the attitude of submission. He added some ornaments: a gold necklace with a jade medallion, a gold circlet adorned with feathers. Her hair, which she usually wore in a braid coiled at the back of her head, would be hanging down. He thought of her body, which he made slimmer and more taut, with an abstract desire which was as unrelated as he could make it to Sarah herself. This was the only kind of desire he could feel for her any more: he had to dress her up before he could make love to her at all. He thought about their earlier days, before they'd married. It was almost as if he'd had an affair with another woman, she had been so different. He'd treated her body then as something holy, a white-and-gold chalice, to be touched with care and tenderness. And she had liked this; even though she was two years older than he was and much more experienced she hadn't minded his awkwardness and reverence, she hadn't laughed at him. Why had she changed?

Sometimes he thought it was the baby, which had died at birth. At the time he'd urged her to have another right away, and she'd said yes, but nothing had happened. It wasn't something they talked about. "Well, that's that," she

4 painting of the Virgin Mary in the style of sixteenth-century artists from Flanders, in Belgium.
5 Mayan and Toltec statues of the rain god.

said in the hospital afterwards. A perfect child, the doctor said; a freak accident, one of those things that happen. She'd never gone back to university
either and she wouldn't get a job. She sat at home, tidying the apartment,
looking over his shoulder, towards the door, out the window, as if she was
waiting for something.

Sarah bowed her head before him. He, in the feathered costume and
long-nosed, toothed mask of the high priest, sprinkled her with blood drawn
with thorns from his own tongue and penis. Now he was supposed to give her
the message to take to the god. But he couldn't think of anything he wanted
to ask for.

And at the same time he thought: what a terrific idea for a Grade Six
special project! He'd have them build scale models of the temples, he'd show
the slides he'd taken, he'd bring in canned tortillas and tamales for a Mexican
lunch, he'd have them make little Chac-Mools out of papier-mâché . . . and the
ball game where the captain of the losing team had his head cut off, that
would appeal to them, they were bloodthirsty at that age. He could see himself
up there in front of them, pouring out his own enthusiasm, gesturing, postur-
ing, acting it out for them, and their response. Yet afterwards he knew he
would be depressed. What were his special projects anyway but a substitute for
television, something to keep them entertained? They liked him because he
danced for them, a funny puppet, inexhaustible and a little absurd. No wonder
Sarah despised him.

30 Edward stepped on the remains of his cigarette. He put his hat back on,
a wide-brimmed white hat Sarah had bought for him at the market. He had
wanted one with a narrower brim, so he could look up through his binoculars
without the hat getting in his way; but she'd told him he would look like an
American golfer. It was always there, that gentle, patronizing mockery.

He would wait long enough to be plausible; then he would go back.

*****

Sarah was speculating about how she would be doing this whole trip if Edward
had conveniently died. It wasn't that she wished him dead, but she couldn't
imagine any other way for him to disappear. He was omnipresent, he pervaded
her life like a kind of smell; it was hard for her to think or act except in reference to him. So she found it harmless and pleasant to walk herself through the
same itinerary they were following now, but with Edward removed, cut neatly
out of the picture. Not that she would be here at all if it wasn't for him. She
would prefer to lie in a deck chair in, say, Acapulco, and drink cooling drinks.
She threw in a few dark young men in bathing suits, but took them out: that
would be too complicated and not relaxing. She had often thought about
cheating on Edward — somehow it would serve him right, though she wasn't
sure what for — but she had never actually done it. She didn't know anyone
suitable, any more.

Suppose she was here, then, with no Edward. She would stay at a better
hotel, for one thing. One that had a plug in the sink; they had not yet stayed
in a hotel with a plug. Of course that would cost more money, but she thought
of herself as having more money if Edward were dead: she would have all of his

salary instead of just part of it. She knew there wouldn't be any salary if he really were dead, but it spoiled the fantasy to remember this. And she would travel on planes, if possible, or first-class buses, instead of the noisy, crowded second-class ones he insisted on taking. He said you saw more of the local colour that way and there was no point going to another country if you spent all your time with other tourists. In theory she agreed with this, but the buses gave her headaches and she could do without the closeup tour of squalor, the miserable thatched or tin-roofed huts, the turkeys and tethered pigs.

He applied the same logic to restaurants. There was a perfectly nice one in the village where they were staying, she'd seen it from the bus and it didn't look that expensive; but no, they had to eat in a seedy linoleum-tiled hutch, with plastic-covered tablecloths. They were the only customers in the place. Behind them four adolescent boys were playing dominoes and drinking beer, with a lot of annoying laughter, and some smaller children watched television, a program that Sarah realized was a re-run of *The Cisco Kid*, with dubbed voices.

35     On the bar beside the television set there was a crèche, with three painted plaster Wise Men, one on an elephant, the others on camels. The first Wise Man was missing his head. Inside the stable a stunted Joseph and Mary adored an enormous Christ Child which was more than half as big as the elephant. Sarah wondered how the Mary could possibly have squeezed out this colossus; it made her uncomfortable to think about it. Beside the crèche was a Santa Claus haloed with flashing lights, and beside that a radio in the shape of Fred Flintstone, which was playing American popular songs, all of them ancient.

"*Oh someone help me, help me, plee-ee-ee-eeze...*"

"Isn't that Paul Anka?"[6] Sarah asked.

But this wasn't the sort of thing Edward could be expected to know. He launched into a defence of the food, the best he'd had in Mexico, he said. Sarah refused to give him the consolation of her agreement. She found the restaurant even more depressing than it should have been, especially the crèche. It was painful, like a cripple trying to walk, one of the last spastic gestures of a religion no one, surely, could believe in much longer.

Another group of tourists was coming up the path behind her, Americans by the sound of them. The guide was Mexican, though. He scrambled up onto the altar, preparing to give his spiel.

40     "Don't go too near the edge, now."

"Who me, I'm afraid of heights. What d'you see down there?"

"Water, what am I supposed to see?"

The guide clapped his hands for attention. Sarah only half-listened: she didn't really want to know anything more about it.

"Before, people said they threw nothing but virgins in here," the guide began. "How they could tell that, I do not know. It is always hard to tell." He waited for the expected laughter, which came. "But this is not true. Soon, I will tell you how we have found this out. Here we have the altar to the rain god Tlaloc..."

45     Two women sat down near Sarah. They were both wearing cotton slacks, high-heeled sandals and wide-brimmed straw hats.

6 popular Ottawa-born singer of the 1950s.

"You go up the big one?"

"Not on your life. I made Alf go up, I took a picture of him at the top."

"What beats me is why they built all those things in the first place."

"It was their religion, that's what he said."

50 "Well, at least it would keep people busy."

"Solve the unemployment problem." They both laughed.

"How many more of these ruins is he gonna make us walk around?"

"Beats me. I'm about ruined out. I'd rather go back and sit on the bus."

"I'd rather go shopping. Not that there's much to buy."

55 Sarah, listening, suddenly felt indignant. Did they have no respect? The sentiments weren't that far from her own of a moment ago, but to hear them from these women, one of whom had a handbag decorated with tasteless straw flowers, made her want to defend the well.

"Nature is very definitely calling," said the woman with the handbag. "I couldn't get in before, there was such a lineup."

"Take a Kleenex," the other woman said. "There's no paper. Not only that, you just about have to wade in. There's water all over the floor."

"Maybe I'll just duck into the bushes," the first woman said.

Edward stood up and massaged his left leg, which had gone to sleep. It was time to go back. If he stayed away too long, Sarah would be querulous, despite the fact that it was she herself who had sent him off on this fool's expedition.

60 He started to walk back along the path. But then there was a flash of orange, at the corner of his eye. Edward swivelled and raised his binoculars. They were there when you least expected it. It was an oriole, partly hidden behind the leaves; he could see the breast, bright orange, and the dark barred wing. He wanted it to be a hooded oriole, he had not yet seen one. He talked to it silently, begging it to come out into the open. It was strange the way birds were completely magic for him the first time only, when he had never seen them before. But there were hundreds of kinds he would never see; no matter how many he saw there would always be one more. Perhaps this was why he kept looking. The bird was hopping further away from him, into the foliage. *Come back*, he called to it wordlessly, but it was gone.

Edward was suddenly happy. Maybe Sarah hadn't been lying to him after all, maybe she had really seen this bird. Even if she hadn't, it had come anyway, in answer to his need for it. Edward felt he was allowed to see birds only when they wanted him to, as if they had something to tell him, a secret, a message. The Aztecs thought hummingbirds were the souls of dead warriors, but why not all birds, why just warriors? Or perhaps they were the souls of the unborn, as some believed. "A jewel, a precious feather," they called an unborn baby, according to *The Daily Life of the Aztecs*. *Quetzal*, that was *feather*.

"This is the bird I want to see," Sarah said when they were looking through *The Birds of Mexico* before coming down.

"The Resplendent Quetzal," Edward said. It was a green-and-red bird with spectacular iridescent-blue tail plumes. He explained to her that Quetzal Bird meant Feather Bird. "I don't think we're likely to see it," he said. He looked up the habitat. "*Cloud forests*. I don't think we'll be in any cloud forests."

"Well, that's the one I want," Sarah said. "That's the only one I want."

Sarah was always very determined about what she wanted and what she didn't want. If there wasn't anything on a restaurant menu that appealed to her, she would refuse to order anything; or she would permit him to order for her and then pick around the edges, as she had last night. It was no use telling her that this was the best meal they'd had since coming. She never lost her temper or her self-possession, but she was stubborn. Who but Sarah, for instance, would have insisted on bringing a collapsible umbrella to Mexico in the dry season? He'd argued and argued, pointing out its uselessness and the extra weight, but she'd brought it anyway. And then yesterday afternoon it had rained, a real cloudburst. Everyone else had run for shelter, huddling against walls and inside the temple doorways, but Sarah had put up her umbrella and stood under it, smugly. This had infuriated him. Even when she was wrong, she always managed, somehow, to be right. If only just once she would admit... what? That she could make mistakes. This was what really disturbed him: her assumption of infallibility.

And he knew that when the baby had died she had blamed it on him. He still didn't know why. Perhaps it was because he'd gone out for cigarettes, not expecting it to be born so soon. He wasn't there when she was told; she'd had to take the news alone.

"It was nobody's fault," he told her repeatedly. "Not the doctor's, not yours. The cord was twisted."

"I know," she said, and she had never accused him; nevertheless he could feel the reproach, hanging around her like a fog. As if there was anything he could have done.

"I wanted it as much as you did," he told her. And this was true. He hadn't thought of marrying Sarah at all, he'd never mentioned it because it had never occurred to him she would agree, until she told him she was pregnant. Up until that time, she had been the one in control; he was sure he was just an amusement for her. But the marriage hadn't been her suggestion, it had been his. He'd dropped out of Theology, he'd taken his public-school teaching certificate that summer in order to support them. Every evening he had massaged her belly, feeling the child move, touching it through her skin. To him it was a sacred thing, and he included her in his worship. In the sixth month, when she had taken to lying on her back, she had begun to snore, and he would lie awake at night listening to these gentle snores, white and silver they seemed to him, almost songs, mysterious talismans. Unfortunately Sarah had retained this habit, but he no longer felt the same way about it.

When the child had died, he was the one who had cried, not Sarah. She had never cried. She got up and walked around almost immediately, she wanted to get out of the hospital as quickly as possible. The baby clothes she'd been buying disappeared from the apartment; he never found out what she'd done with them, he'd been afraid to ask.

Since that time he'd come to wonder why they were still married. It was illogical. If they'd married because of the child and there was no child, and there continued to be no child, why didn't they separate? But he wasn't sure he wanted this. Maybe he was still hoping something would happen, there would be another child. But there was no use demanding it. They came when they wanted to, not when you wanted them to. They came when you least expected it. A jewel, a precious feather.

"Now I will tell you," said the guide. "The archaeologists have dived down into the well. They have dredged up more than fifty skeletons, and they have found that some of them were not virgins at all but men. Also, most of them were children. So as you can see, that is the end of the popular legend." He made an odd little movement from the top of the altar, almost like a bow, but there was no applause. "They do not do these things to be cruel," he continued. "They believe these people will take a message to the rain god, and live forever in his paradise at the bottom of the well."

The woman with the handbag got up. "Some paradise," she said to her friend. "I'm starting back. You coming?"

In fact the whole group was moving off now, in the scattered way they had. Sarah waited until they had gone. Then she opened her purse and took out the plaster Christ Child she had stolen from the crèche the night before. It was inconceivable to her that she had done such a thing, but there it was, she really had.

75     She hadn't planned it beforehand. She'd been standing beside the crèche while Edward was paying the bill, he'd had to go into the kitchen to do it as they were very slow about bringing it to the table. No one was watching her: the domino-playing boys were absorbed in their game and the children were riveted to the television. She'd just suddenly reached out her hand, past the Wise Men and through the door of the stable, picked the child up and put it into her purse.

She turned it over in her hands. Separated from the dwarfish Virgin and Joseph, it didn't look quite so absurd. Its diaper was cast as part of it, more like a tunic, it had glass eyes and a sort of pageboy haircut, quite long for a newborn. A perfect child, except for the chip out of the back, luckily where it would not be noticed. Someone must have dropped it on the floor.

You could never be too careful. All the time she was pregnant, she'd taken meticulous care of herself, counting out the vitamin pills prescribed by the doctor and eating only what the books recommended. She had drunk four glasses of milk a day, even though she hated milk. She had done the exercises and gone to the classes. No one would be able to say she had not done the right things. Yet she had been disturbed by the thought that the child would be born with something wrong, it would be a mongoloid or a cripple, or a hydrocephalic with a huge liquid head like the ones she'd seen taking the sun in their wheelchairs on the lawn of the hospital one day. But the child had been perfect.

She would never take that risk, go through all that work again. Let Edward strain his pelvis till he was blue in the face; "trying again," he called it. She took the pill every day, without telling him. She wasn't going to try again. It was too much for anyone to expect of her.

What had she done wrong? She hadn't done anything wrong, that was the trouble. There was nothing and no one to blame, except, obscurely, Edward; and he couldn't be blamed for the child's death, just for not being there. Increasingly since that time he had simply absented himself. When she no longer had the child inside her he had lost interest, he had deserted her. This, she realized, was what she resented most about him. He had left her alone with the corpse, a corpse for which there was no explanation.

80 "*Lost*," people called it. They spoke of her as having lost the child, as though it was wandering around looking for her, crying plaintively, as though she had neglected it or misplaced it somewhere. But where? What limbo had it gone to, what watery paradise? Sometimes she felt as if there had been some mistake, the child had not been born yet. She could still feel it moving, ever so slightly, holding on to her from the inside.

Sarah placed the baby on the rock beside her. She stood up, smoothing out the wrinkles in her skirt. She was sure there would be more flea bites when she got back to the hotel. She picked up the child and walked slowly towards the well, until she was standing at the very brink.

Edward, coming back up the path, saw Sarah at the well's edge, her arms raised above her head. My God, he thought, she's going to jump. He wanted to shout to her, tell her to stop, but he was afraid to startle her. He could run up behind her, grab her ... but she would hear him. So he waited, paralyzed, while Sarah stood immobile. He expected her to hurtle downwards, and then what would he do? But she merely drew back her right arm and threw something into the well. Then she turned, half stumbling, towards the rock where he had left her and crouched down.

"Sarah," he said. She had her hands over her face; she didn't lift them. He kneeled so he was level with her. "What is it? Are you sick?"

She shook her head. She seemed to be crying, behind her hands, soundlessly and without moving. Edward was dismayed. The ordinary Sarah, with all her perversity, was something he could cope with, he'd invented ways of coping. But he was unprepared for this. She had always been the one in control.

85 "Come on," he said, trying to disguise his desperation, "you need some lunch, you'll feel better." He realized as he said this how fatuous it must sound, but for once there was no patronizing smile, no indulgent answer.

"This isn't like you," Edward said, pleading, as if that was a final argument which would snap her out of it, bring back the old calm Sarah.

Sarah took her hands away from her face, and as she did so Edward felt cold fear. Surely what he would see would be the face of someone else, someone entirely different, a woman he had never seen before in his life. Or there would be no face at all. But (and this was almost worse) it was only Sarah, looking much as she always did.

She took a Kleenex out of her purse and wiped her nose. It is like me, she thought. She stood up and smoothed her skirt once more, then collected her purse and her collapsible umbrella.

"I'd like an orange," she said. "They have them, across from the ticket office. I saw them when we came in. Did you find your bird?"

(1977)

# Bharati Mukherjee  (b. 1940)

Born in Calcutta, India, Bharati Mukherjee lived in Canada from 1966 to 1980. She then moved to the United States because, as she stated in her introduction to her short story collection *Darkness* (1985), she found most Canadians extremely prejudiced against East Asian women. In her short stories and such novels as *Wife*, she examines the constraints placed on Indian women, both in their homeland and abroad. Maya Sanyal, the central character of "The Tenant," is, as the title implies, without roots. Her race, her social position as a divorced woman, and her professional lack of status as an untenured professor all contribute to the deep inner loneliness and restlessness that she has experienced since leaving her family and heritage in India.

# THE TENANT

Maya Sanyal has been in Cedar Falls, Iowa, less than two weeks. She's come, books and clothes and one armchair rattling in the smallest truck that U-Haul would rent her, from New Jersey. Before that she was in North Carolina. Before that, Calcutta, India. Every place has something to give. She is sitting at the kitchen table with Fran drinking bourbon for the first time in her life. Fran Johnson found her the furnished apartment and helped her settle in. Now she's brought a bottle of bourbon which gives her the right to stay and talk for a bit. She's breaking up with someone named Vern, a pharmacist. Vern's father is also a pharmacist and owns a drugstore. Maya has seen Vern's father on TV twice already. The first time was on the local news when he spoke out against the selling of painkillers like Advil and Nuprin in supermarkets and gas stations. In the matter of painkillers, Maya is a universalist. The other time he was in a barbershop quartet. Vern gets along all right with his father. He likes the pharmacy business, as business goes, but he wants to go back to graduate school and learn to make films. Maya is drinking her first bourbon tonight because Vern left today for San Francisco State.

"I understand totally," Fran says. She teaches Utopian Fiction and a course in Women's Studies and worked hard to get Maya hired. Maya has a Ph.D. in Comparative Literature and will introduce writers like R. K. Narayan and Chinua Achebe[1] to three sections of sophomores at the University of Northern Iowa. "A person has to leave home. Try out his wings."

Fran has to use the bathroom. "I don't feel abandoned." She pushes her chair away from the table. "Anyway, it was a sex thing totally. We were good together. It'd be different if I'd loved him."

Maya tries to remember what's in the refrigerator. They need food. She hasn't been to the supermarket in over a week. She doesn't have a car yet and so she relies on a corner store — a longish walk — for milk, cereal, and frozen dinners. Someday these exigencies will show up as bad skin and collapsed muscle tone. No folly is ever lost. Maya pictures history as a net, the kind of

---

1 Indian and Nigerian writers, respectively.

safety net travelling trapeze artists of her childhood fell into when they were inattentive, or clumsy. Going to circuses in Calcutta with her father is what she remembers vividly. It is a banal memory, for her father, the owner of a steel company, is a complicated man.

5     Fran is out in the kitchen long enough for Maya to worry. They need food. Her mother believed in food. What is love, anger, inner peace, etc., her mother used to say, but the brain's biochemistry. Maya doesn't want to get into that, but she is glad she has enough stuff in the refrigerator to make an omelette. She realizes Indian women are supposed to be inventive with food, whip up exotic delights to tickle an American's palate, and she knows she should be meeting Fran's generosity and candor with some sort of bizarre and effortless countermove. If there's an exotic spice store in Cedar Falls or in neighboring Waterloo, she hasn't found it. She's looked in the phone book for common Indian names, especially Bengali, but hasn't yet struck up culinary intimacies. That will come — it always does. There's a six-pack in the fridge that her landlord, Ted Suminski, had put in because she'd be thirsty after unpacking. She was thirsty, but she doesn't drink beer. She probably should have asked him to come up and drink the beer. Except for Fran she hasn't had anyone over. Fran is more friendly and helpful than anyone Maya has known in the States since she came to North Carolina ten years ago, at nineteen. Fran is a Swede, and she is tall, with blue eyes. Her hair, however, is a dull, darkish brown.

"I don't think I can handle anything that heavy-duty," Fran says when she comes back to the room. She means the omelette. "I have to go home in any case." She lives with her mother and her aunt, two women in their mid-seventies, in a drafty farmhouse. The farmhouse now has a computer store catty-corner from it. Maya's been to the farm. She's been shown photographs of the way the corner used to be. If land values ever rebound, Fran will be worth millions.

Before Fran leaves she says, "Has Rab Chatterji called you yet?"

"No." She remembers the name, a good, reliable Bengali name, from the first night's study of the phone book. Dr. Rabindra Chatterji teaches Physics.

"He called the English office just before I left." She takes car keys out of her pocketbook. She reknots her scarf. "I bet Indian men are more sensitive than Americans. Rab's a Brahmin,[2] that's what people say."

10     A Chatterji has to be a Bengali Brahmin — last names give ancestral secrets away — but Brahminness seems to mean more to Fran than it does to Maya. She was born in 1954, six full years after India became independent. Her India was Nehru's India: a charged, progressive place.

"All Indian men are wife beaters," Maya says. She means it and doesn't mean it. "That's why I married an American." Fran knows about the divorce, but nothing else. Fran is on the Hiring, Tenure, and Reappointment Committee.

Maya sees Fran down the stairs and to the car which is parked in the back in the spot reserved for Maya's car, if she had owned one. It will take her several months to save enough to buy one. She always pays cash, never borrows. She tells herself she's still recovering from the U-Haul drive halfway

---

2 member of the politically powerful priestly and intellectual Hindu caste.

across the country. Ted Suminski is in his kitchen watching the women. Maya waves to him because waving to him, acknowledging him in that way, makes him seem less creepy. He seems to live alone though a sign, THE SUMINSKIS, hangs from a metal horse's head in the front yard. Maya hasn't seen Mrs. Suminski. She hasn't seen any children either. Ted always looks lonely. When she comes back from campus, he's nearly always in the back, throwing darts or shooting baskets.

"What's he like?" Fran gestures with her head as she starts up her car. "You hear these stories."

Maya doesn't want to know the stories. She has signed a year's lease. She doesn't want complications. "He's all right. I keep out of his way."

15    "You know what I'm thinking? Of all the people in Cedar Falls, you're the one who could understand Vern best. His wanting to try out his wings, run away, stuff like that."

"Not really." Maya is not being modest. Fran is being impulsively democratic, lumping her wayward lover and Indian friend together as headstrong adventurers. For Fran, a utopian and feminist, borders don't count. Maya's taken some big risks, made a break with her parents' ways. She's done things a woman from Ballygunge Park Road doesn't do, even in fantasies. She's not yet shared stories with Fran, apart from the divorce. She's told her nothing of men she picks up, the reputation she'd gained, before Cedar Falls, for "indiscretions." She has a job, equity, three friends she can count on for emergencies. She is an American citizen. But.

Fran's Brahmin calls her two nights later. On the phone he presents himself as Dr. Chatterji, not Rabindra or Rab. An old-fashioned Indian, she assumes. Her father still calls his closest friend, "Colonel." Dr. Chatterji asks her to tea on Sunday. She means to say no but hears herself saying, "Sunday? Fiveish? I'm not doing anything special this Sunday."

Outside, Ted Suminski is throwing darts into his garage door. The door has painted-on rings: orange, purple, pink. The bull's-eye is gray. He has to be fifty at least. He is a big, thick, lonely man about whom people tell stories. Maya pulls the phone cord as far as it'll go so she can look down more directly on her landlord's large, bald head. He has his back to her as he lines up a dart. He's in black running shoes, red shorts, he's naked to the waist. He hunches his right shoulder, he pulls the arm back; a big, lonely man shouldn't have so much grace. The dart is ready to cut through the September evening. But Ted Suminski doesn't let go. He swings on worn rubber soles, catches her eye in the window (she has to have imagined this), takes aim at her shadow. Could she have imagined the noise of the dart's metal tip on her windowpane?

Dr. Chatterji is still on the phone. "You are not having any mode of transportation, is that right?"

20    Ted Suminski has lost interest in her. Perhaps it isn't interest, at all; perhaps it's aggression. "I don't drive," she lies, knowing it sounds less shameful than not owning a car. She has said this so often she can get in the right degree of apology and Asian upper-class helplessness. "It's an awful nuisance."

"Not to worry, please." Then, "It is a great honor to be meeting Dr. Sanyal's daughter. In Calcutta business circles he is a legend."

On Sunday she is ready by four-thirty. She doesn't know what the afternoon holds; there are surely no places for "high tea" — a colonial tradition — in Cedar Falls, Iowa. If he takes her back to his place, it will mean he has invited other guests. From his voice she can tell Dr. Chatterji likes to do things correctly. She has dressed herself in a peach-colored nylon georgette sari, jade drop-earrings and a necklace. The color is good on dark skin. She is not pretty, but she does her best. Working at it is a part of self-respect. In the mid-seventies, when American women felt rather strongly about such things, Maya had been in trouble with her women's group at Duke.[3] She was too feminine. She had tried to explain the world she came out of. Her grandmother had been married off at the age of five in a village now in Bangladesh. Her great-aunt had been burned to death over a dowry problem. She herself had been trained to speak softly, arrange flowers, sing, be pliant. If she were to seduce Ted Suminski, she thinks as she waits in the front yard for Dr. Chatterji, it would be minor heroism. She has broken with the past. But.

Dr. Chatterji drives up for her at about five ten. He is a hesitant driver. The car stalls, jumps ahead, finally slams to a stop. Maya has to tell him to back off a foot or so; it's hard to leap over two sacks of pruned branches in a sari. Ted Suminski is an obsessive pruner and gardener.

"My sincerest apologies, Mrs. Sanyal," Dr. Chatterji says. He leans across the wide front seat of his noisy, very old, very used car and unlocks the door for her. "I am late. But then, I am sure you're remembering that Indian Standard Time is not at all the same as time in the States." He laughs. He could be nervous — she often had that effect on Indian men. Or he could just be chatty. "These Americans are all the time rushing and rushing but where it gets them?" He moves his head laterally once, twice. It's the gesture made famous by Peter Sellers. When Peter Sellers did it, it had seemed hilarious. Now it suggests that Maya and Dr. Chatterji have three thousand years plus civilization, sophistication, moral virtue, over people born on this continent. Like her, Dr. Chatterji is a naturalized American.

"Call me Maya," she says. She fusses with the seat belt. She does it because she needs time to look him over. He seems quite harmless. She takes in the prominent teeth, the eyebrows that run together. He's in a blue shirt and a beige cardigan with the K-Mart logo that buttons tightly over the waist. It's hard to guess his age because he has dyed his hair and his moustache. Late thirties, early forties. Older than she had expected. "Not Mrs. Sanyal."

This isn't the time to tell about ex-husbands. She doesn't know where John is these days. He should have kept up at least. John had come into her life as a graduate student at Duke, and she, mistaking the brief breathlessness of sex for love, had married him. They had stayed together two years, maybe a little less. The pain that John had inflicted all those years ago by leaving her had subsided into a cozy feeling of loss. This isn't the time, but then she doesn't want to be a legend's daughter all evening. She's not necessarily on Dr. Chatterji's

25

3 university located in Chapel Hill, North Carolina.

side is what she wants to get across early; she's not against America and Americans. She makes the story — of marriage outside the Brahminic pale, the divorce — quick, dull. Her unsentimentality seems to shock him. His stomach sags inside the cardigan.

"We've each had our several griefs," the physicist says. "We're each required to pay our karmic debts."

"Where are we headed?"

"Mrs. Chatterji has made some Indian snacks. She is waiting to meet you because she is knowing your cousin-sister who studied in Scottish Church College. My home is okay, no?"

30    Fran would get a kick out of this. Maya has slept with married men, with nameless men, with men little more than boys, but never with an Indian man. Never.

The Chatterjis live in a small blue house on a gravelly street. There are at least five or six other houses on the street; the same size but in different colors and with different front yard treatments. More houses are going up. This is the cutting edge of suburbia.

Mrs. Chatterji stands in the driveway. She is throwing a large plastic ball to a child. The child looks about four, and is Korean or Cambodian. The child is not hers because she tells it, "Chung-Hee, ta-ta, bye-bye. Now I play with guest," as Maya gets out of the car.

Maya hasn't seen this part of town. The early September light softens the construction pits. In that light the houses too close together, the stout woman in a striped cotton sari, the child hugging a pink ball, the two plastic lawn chairs by a tender young tree, the sheets and saris on the clothesline in the back, all seem miraculously incandescent.

"Go home now, Chung-Hee. I am busy." Mrs. Chatterji points the child homeward, then turns to Maya, who has folded her hands in traditional Bengali greeting. "It is an honor. We feel very privileged." She leads Maya indoors to a front room that smells of moisture and paint.

35    In her new, deliquescent mood, Maya allows herself to be backed into the best armchair — a low-backed, boxy Goodwill item draped over with a Rajasthani bedspread — and asks after the cousin Mrs. Chatterji knows. She doesn't want to let go of Mrs. Chatterji. She doesn't want husband and wife to get into whispered conferences about their guest's misadventures in America, as they make tea in the kitchen.

The coffee table is already laid with platters of mutton croquettes, fish chops, onion pakoras, ghugni with puris, samosas, chutneys. Mrs. Chatterji has gone to too much trouble. Maya counts four kinds of sweetmeats in Corning casseroles on an end table. She looks into a see-through lid; spongy, white dumplings float in rosewater syrup. Planets contained, mysteries made visible.

"What are you waiting for, Santana?" Dr. Chatterji becomes imperious, though not unaffectionate. He pulls a dining chair up close to the coffee table. "Make some tea." He speaks in Bengali to his wife, in English to Maya. To Maya he says, grandly, "We are having real Indian Green Label Lipton. A nephew is bringing it just one month back."

His wife ignores him. "The kettle's already on," she says. She wants to know about the Sanyal family. Is it true her great-grandfather was a member of the Star Chamber[4] in England?

Nothing in Calcutta is ever lost. Just as her story is known to Bengalis all over America, so are the scandals of her family, the grandfather hauled up for tax evasion, the aunt who left her husband to act in films. This woman brings up the Star Chamber, the glories of the Sanyal family, her father's philanthropies, but it's a way of saying, *I know the dirt.*

40    The bedrooms are upstairs. In one of those bedrooms an unseen, tormented presence — Maya pictures it as a clumsy ghost that strains to shake off the body's shell — drops things on the floor. The things are heavy and they make the front room's chandelier shake. Light bulbs, shaped like tiny candle flames, flicker. The Chatterjis have said nothing about children. There are no tricycles in the hallway, no small sandals behind the doors. Maya is too polite to ask about the noise, and the Chatterjis don't explain. They talk just a little louder. They flip the embroidered cover off the stereo. What would Maya like to hear? Hemanta Kumar? Manna Dey? Oh, that young chap, Manna Dey! What sincerity, what tenderness he can convey!

Upstairs the ghost doesn't hear the music of nostalgia. The ghost throws and thumps. The ghost makes its own vehement music. Maya hears in its voice madness, self-hate.

Finally the water in the kettle comes to a boil. The whistle cuts through all fantasy and pretense. Dr. Chatterji says, "I'll see to it," and rushes out of the room. But he doesn't go to the kitchen. He shouts up the stairwell. "Poltoo, kindly stop this nonsense straightaway! We're having a brilliant and cultured lady-guest and you're creating earthquakes?" The kettle is hysterical.

Mrs. Chatterji wipes her face. The face that had seemed plump and cheery at the start of the evening now is flabby. "My sister's boy," the woman says.

So this is the nephew who has brought with him the cartons of Green Label tea, one of which will be given to Maya.

45    Mrs. Chatterji speaks to Maya in English as though only the alien language can keep emotions in check. "Such an intelligent boy! His father is government servant. Very highly placed."

Maya is meant to visualize a smart, clean-cut young man from south Calcutta, but all she can see is a crazy, thwarted, lost graduate student. Intelligence, proper family guarantee nothing. Even Brahmins can do self-destructive things, feel unsavory urges. Maya herself had been an excellent student.

"He was First Class First in B.Sc. from Presidency College," the woman says. "Now he's getting Master's in Ag. Science at Iowa State."

The kitchen is silent. Dr. Chatterji comes back into the room with a tray. The teapot is under a tea cozy, a Kashmiri one embroidered with the usual chinar leaves, loops, and chains. "*Her* nephew," he says. The dyed hair and dyed moustache are no longer signs of a man wishing to fight the odds. He is a vain man, anxious to cut losses. "Very unfortunate business."

---

4 powerful English judicial court, believed to favour the authorities in the cases it tried, which was abolished in 1641. The term is used for trials that favour the authorities.

The nephew's story comes out slowly, over fish chops and mutton croquettes. He is in love with a student from Ghana.

50    "Everything was A-Okay until the Christmas break. Grades, assistant-
ship for next semester, everything."

"I blame the college. The office for foreign students arranged a Christmas
party. And now, *baapre baap!* Our poor Poltoo wants to marry a Negro Muslim."

Maya is known for her nasty, ironic one-liners. It has taken her friends
weeks to overlook her malicious, un-American pleasure in others' misfor-
tunes. Maya would like to finish Dr. Chatterji off quickly. He is pompous;
he is reactionary; he wants to live and work in America but give back nothing
except taxes. The confused world of the immigrant — the lostness that Maya
and Poltoo feel — that's what Dr. Chatterji wants to avoid. She hates him. But.

Dr. Chatterji's horror is real. A good Brahmin boy in Iowa is in love with an
African Muslim. It shouldn't be a big deal. But the more she watches the physicist, the more she realizes that "Brahmin" isn't a caste; it's a metaphor. You
break one small rule, and the constellation collapses. She thinks suddenly that
John Cheever[5]— she is teaching him as a "world writer" in her classes,
cheek-by-jowl with Africans and West Indians — would have understood Dr.
Chatterji's dread. Cheever had been on her mind, ever since the late afternoon
light slanted over Mrs. Chatterji's drying saris. She remembers now how full of
a soft, Cheeverian light Durham had been the summer she had slept with John
Hadwen; and how after that, her tidy graduate-student world became monstrous, lawless. All men became John Hadwen; John became all men. Outwardly,
she retained her poise, her Brahminical breeding. She treated her crisis as a literary event; she lost her moral sense, her judgment, her power to distinguish. Her
parents had behaved magnanimously. They had cabled from Calcutta: WHAT'S
DONE IS DONE. WE ARE CONFIDENT YOU WILL HANDLE NEW SITUATION WELL.
ALL LOVE. But she knows more than do her parents. Love is anarchy.

Poltoo is Mrs. Chatterji's favorite nephew. She looks as though it is her fault
that the Sunday has turned unpleasant. She stacks the empty platters methodically. To Maya she says, "It is the goddess who pulls the strings. We are puppets.
I know the goddess will fix it. Poltoo will not marry that African woman."
Then she goes to the coat closet in the hall and staggers back with a harmonium, the kind sold in music stores in Calcutta, and sets it down on the car-
peted floor. "We're nothing but puppets," she says again. She sits at Maya's feet,
her pudgy hands on the harmonium's shiny, black bellows. She sings, beautifully, in a virgin's high voice, "Come, goddess, come, muse, come to us hapless
peoples' rescue."

55    Maya is astonished. She has taken singing lessons at Dakshini Academy
in Calcutta. She plays the sitar and the tanpur, well enough to please Bengalis,
to astonish Americans. But stout Mrs. Chatterji is a devotee, talking to God.

A little after eight, Dr. Chatterji drops her off. It's been an odd evening and they
are both subdued.

"I want to say one thing," he says. He stops her from undoing her seat
belt. The plastic sacks of pruned branches are still at the corner.

---

5 American author John Cheever (1912–82) was noted for his depiction of modern suburban life.

"You don't have to get out," she says.

"Please. Give me one more minute of your time."

60 "Sure."

"Maya is my favorite name."

She says nothing. She turns away from him without making her embarrassment obvious.

"Truly speaking, it is my favorite. You are sometimes lonely, no? But you are lucky. Divorced women can date, they can go to bars and discos. They can see mens, many mens. But inside marriage there is so much loneliness." A groan, low, horrible, comes out of him.

She turns back toward him, to unlatch the seat belt and run out of the car. She sees that Dr. Chatterji's pants are unzipped. One hand works hard under his Jockey shorts; the other rests, limp, penitential, on the steering wheel.

65 "Dr. Chatterji — *really!*" she cries.

The next day, Monday, instead of getting a ride home with Fran — Fran says she *likes* to give rides, she needs the chance to talk, and she won't share gas expenses, absolutely not — Maya goes to the periodicals room of the library. There are newspapers from everywhere, even from Madagascar and New Caledonia. She thinks of the periodicals room as an asylum for homesick aliens. There are two aliens already in the room, both Orientals, both absorbed in the politics and gossip of their far-off homes.

She goes straight to the newspapers from India. She bunches her raincoat like a bolster to make herself more comfortable. There's so much to catch up on. A village headman, a known Congress-Indira party worker, has been shot at by scooter-riding snipers. An Indian pugilist has won an international medal — in Nepal. A child drawing well water — the reporter calls the child "a neo-Buddhist, a convert from the now-outlawed untouchable caste" — has been stoned. An editorial explains that the story about stoning is not a story about caste but about failed idealism; a story about promises of green fields and clean, potable water broken, a story about bribes paid and wells not dug. But no, thinks Maya, it's about caste.

Out here, in the heartland of the new world, the India of serious newspapers unsettles. Maya longs again to feel what she had felt in the Chatterjis' living room: virtues made physical. It is a familiar feeling, a longing. Had a suitable man presented himself in the reading room at that instant, she would have seduced him. She goes on to the stack of *India Abroads*, reads through matrimonial columns, and steals an issue to take home.

Indian men want Indian brides. Married Indian men want Indian mistresses. All over America, "handsome, tall, fair" engineers, doctors, data processors — the new pioneers — cry their eerie love calls.

70 Maya runs a finger down the first column; her fingertip, dark with newsprint, stops at random.

> Hello! Hi! Yes, you *are* the one I'm looking for. You are the new emancipated Indo-American woman. You have a zest for life. You are at ease in USA and yet your ethics are rooted in Indian tradition. The man of your

dreams has come. Yours truly is handsome, ear-nose-throat specialist, well-settled in Connecticut. Age is 41 but never married, physically fit, sportsmanly, and strong. I adore idealism, poetry, beauty. I abhor smugness, passivity, caste system. Write with recent photo. Better still, call!!!

Maya calls. Hullo, hullo, hullo! She hears immigrant lovers cry in crowded shopping malls. Yes, you who are at ease in both worlds, you are the one. She feels she has a fair chance.

A man answers. "Ashoke Mehta speaking."

She speaks quickly into the bright-red mouthpiece of her telephone. He will be in Chicago, in transit, passing through O'Hare. United counter, Saturday, two p.m. As easy as that.

75   "Good," Ashoke Mehta says. "For these encounters I, too, prefer a neutral zone."

On Saturday at exactly two o'clock the man of Maya's dreams floats toward her as lovers used to in shampoo commercials. The United counter is a loud, harassed place but passengers and piled-up luggage fall away from him. Full-cheeked and fleshy-lipped, he is handsome. He hasn't lied. He is serene, assured, a Hindu god touching down in Illinois.

She can't move. She feels ugly and unworthy. Her adult life no longer seems miraculously rebellious; it is grim, it is perverse. She has accomplished nothing. She has changed her citizenship but she hasn't broken through into the light, the vigor, the *hustle* of the New World. She is stuck in dead space.

"Hullo, Hullo!" Their fingers touch.

Oh, the excitement! Ashoke Mehta's palm feels so right in the small of her back. Hullo, hullo, hullo. He pushes her out of the reach of anti-Khomeini Iranians, Hare Krishnas, American Fascists, men with fierce wants, and guides her to an empty gate. They have less than an hour.

80   "What would you like, Maya?"

She knows he can read her mind, she knows her thoughts are open to him. *You*, she's almost giddy with the thought, with simple desire. "From the snack bar," he says, as though to clarify. "I'm afraid I'm starved."

Below them, where the light is strong and hurtful, a Boeing is being serviced. "Nothing," she says.

He leans forward. She can feel the nap of his scarf — she recognizes the Cambridge colors — she can smell the wool of his Icelandic sweater. She runs her hand along the scarf, then against the flesh of his neck. "Only the impulsive ones call," he says.

The immigrant courtship proceeds. It's easy, he's good with facts. He knows how to come across to a stranger who may end up a lover, a spouse. He makes over a hundred thousand. He owns a house in Hartford, and two income properties in Newark. He plays the market but he's cautious. He's good at badminton but plays handball to keep in shape. He watches all the sports on television. Last August he visited Copenhagen, Helsinki and Leningrad. Once upon a time he collected stamps but now he doesn't have hobbies, except for reading. He counts himself an intellectual, he spends too much on books.

Ludlum, Forsyth, MacInnes;[6] other names she doesn't catch. She suppresses a smile, she's told him only she's a graduate student. He's not without his vices. He's a spender, not a saver. He's a sensualist: good food — all foods, but easy on the Indian — good wine. Some temptations he doesn't try to resist.

85     And I, she wants to ask, do I tempt?

"Now tell me about yourself, Maya." He makes it easy for her. "Have you ever been in love?"

"No."

"But many have loved you, I can see that." He says it not unkindly. It is the fate of women like her, and men like him. Their karmic duty, to be loved. It is expected, not judged. She feels he can see them all, the sad parade of need and demand. This isn't the time to reveal all.

And so the courtship enters a second phase.

90     When she gets back to Cedar Falls, Ted Suminski is standing on the front porch. It's late at night, chilly. He is wearing a down vest. She's never seen him on the porch. In fact there's no chair to sit on. He looks chilled through. He's waited around a while.

"Hi." She has her keys ready. This isn't the night to offer the six-pack in the fridge. He looks expectant, ready to pounce.

"Hi." He looks like a man who might have aimed the dart at her. What has he done to his wife, his kids? Why isn't there at least a dog? "Say, I left a note upstairs."

The note is written in Magic Marker and thumb-tacked to her apartment door. DUE TO PERSONAL REASONS, NAMELY REMARRIAGE, I REQUEST THAT YOU VACATE MY PLACE AT THE END OF THE SEMESTER.

Maya takes the note down and retacks it to the kitchen wall. The whole wall is like a bulletin board, made of some new, crumbly building-material. Her kitchen, Ted Suminski had told her, was once a child's bedroom. Suminski in love: the idea stuns her. She has misread her landlord. The dart at her window speaks of no twisted fantasy. The landlord wants the tenant out.

95     She gets a glass out of the kitchen cabinet, gets out a tray of ice, pours herself a shot of Fran's bourbon. She is happy for Ted Suminski. She is. She wants to tell someone how moved she'd been by Mrs. Chatterji's singing. How she'd felt in O'Hare, even about Dr. Rab Chatterji in the car. But Fran is not the person. No one she's ever met is the person. She can't talk about the dead space she lives in. She wishes Ashoke Mehta would call. Right now.

Weeks pass. Then two months. She finds a new room, signs another lease. Her new landlord calls himself Fred. He has no arms, but he helps her move her things. He drives between Ted Suminski's place and his twice in his station wagon. He uses his toes the way Maya uses her fingers. He likes to do things. He pushes garbage sacks full of Maya's clothes up the stairs.

"It's all right to stare," Fred says. "Hell, I would."

That first afternoon in Fred's rooming house, they share a Chianti. Fred wants to cook her pork chops but he's a little shy about Indians and meat. Is it

6 authors of popular modern spy novels.

beef, or pork? Or any meat? She says it's okay, any meat, but not tonight. He has an ex-wife in Des Moines, two kids in Portland, Oregon. The kids are both normal; he's the only freak in the family. But he's self-reliant. He shops in the supermarket like anyone else, he carries out the garbage, shovels the snow off the sidewalk. He needs Maya's help with one thing. Just one thing. The box of Tide is a bit too heavy to manage. Could she get him the giant size every so often and leave it in the basement?

The dead space need not suffocate. Over the months, Fred and she will settle into companionship. She has never slept with a man without arms. Two wounded people, he will joke during their nightly contortions. It will shock her, this assumed equivalence with a man so strikingly deficient. She knows she is strange, and lonely, but being Indian is not the same, she would have thought, as being a freak.

100   One night in spring, Fred's phone rings. "Ashoke Mehta speaking." None of this "do you remember me?" nonsense. The god has tracked her down. He hasn't forgotten. "Hullo," he says, in their special way. And because she doesn't answer back, "Hullo, hullo, hullo." She is aware of Fred in the back of the room. He is lighting a cigarette with his toes.

"Yes," she says, "I remember."

"I had to take care of a problem," Ashoke Mehta says. "You know that I have my vices. That time at O'Hare I was honest with you."

She is breathless.

"Who is it, May?" asks Fred.

105   "You also have a problem," says the voice. His laugh echoes. "You will come to Hartford, I know."

When she moves out, she tells herself, it will not be the end of Fred's world.

(1986)

# Thomas King   (b. 1943)

Thomas King, who is of Greek, German, and Cherokee ancestry, has taught at the University of Lethbridge and the University of Minnesota, where he is director of the Native Studies program. His fiction, in which, he says, comedy is used to present often tragic themes, is set in southern Alberta. "I am," he comments, "this Native writer who's out there in the middle, not of nowhere." This quality is found in many of his characters. *Medicine River*, a novel created out of the related stories of several people, focusses on a half-Blackfoot photographer who returns to his home town for his mother's funeral and discovers his own identity. In *Green Grass, Running Water*, five Native people engage in a similar quest. "Borders," from King's collection *One Good Story, That One*, presents the theme of Native people's situation in the modern world in the comic encounter between the narrator's proud mother and Canadian and American immigration officials. The invisible border dividing the two countries symbolizes the many divisions in the story among individuals and between cultures.

# BORDERS

When I was twelve, maybe thirteen, my mother announced that we were going to go to Salt Lake City to visit my sister who had left the reserve, moved across the line, and found a job. Laetitia had not left home with my mother's blessing, but over time my mother had come to be proud of the fact that Laetitia had done all of this on her own.

"She did real good," my mother would say.

Then there were the fine points to Laetitia's going. She had not, as my mother liked to tell Mrs. Manyfingers, gone floating after some man like a balloon on a string. She hadn't snuck out of the house, either, and gone to Vancouver or Edmonton or Toronto to chase rainbows down alleys. And she hadn't been pregnant.

"She did real good."

5    I was seven or eight when Laetitia left home. She was seventeen. Our father was from Rocky Boy on the American side.

"Dad's American," Laetitia told my mother, "so I can go and come as I please."

"Send us a postcard."

Laetitia packed her things, and we headed for the border. Just outside of Milk River,[1] Laetitia told us to watch for the water tower.

"Over the next rise. It's the first thing you see."

10    "We got a water tower on the reserve," my mother said. "There's a big one in Lethbridge, too."

"You'll be able to see the tops of the flagpoles, too. That's where the border is."

---

1 river originating in northern Montana that flows north into Alberta before flowing south to the Missouri River.

When we got to Coutts, my mother stopped at the convenience store and bought her and Laetitia a cup of coffee. I got an Orange Crush.

"This is real lousy coffee."

"You're just angry because I want to see the world."

"It's the water. From here on down, they got lousy water."

"I can catch the bus from Sweetgrass. You don't have to lift a finger."

"You're going to have to buy your water in bottles if you want good coffee."

There was an old wooden building about a block away, with a tall sign in the yard that said "Museum." Most of the roof had been blown away. Mom told me to go and see when the place was open. There were boards over the windows and doors. You could tell that the place was closed, and I told Mom so, but she said to go and check anyway. Mom and Laetitia stayed by the car. Neither one of them moved. I sat down on the steps of the museum and watched them, and I don't know that they ever said anything to each other. Finally, Laetitia got her bag out of the trunk and gave Mom a hug.

I wandered back to the car. The wind had come up, and it blew Laetitia's hair across her face. Mom reached out and pulled the strands out of Laetitia's eyes, and Laetitia let her.

"You can still see the mountain from here," my mother told Laetitia in Blackfoot.

"Lots of mountains in Salt Lake," Laetitia told her in English.

"The place is closed," I said. "Just like I told you."

Laetitia tucked her hair into her jacket and dragged her bag down the road to the brick building with the American flag flapping on a pole. When she got to where the guards were waiting, she turned, put the bag down, and waved to us. We waved back. Then my mother turned the car around, and we came home.

We got postcards from Laetitia regular, and, if she wasn't spreading jelly on the truth, she was happy. She found a good job and rented an apartment with a pool.

"And she can't even swim," my mother told Mrs. Manyfingers.

Most of the postcards said we should come down and see the city, but whenever I mentioned this, my mother would stiffen up.

So I was surprised when she bought two new tires for the car and put on her blue dress with the green and yellow flowers. I had to dress up, too, for my mother did not want us crossing the border looking like Americans. We made sandwiches and put them in a big box with pop and potato chips and some apples and bananas and a big jar of water.

"But we can stop at one of those restaurants, too, right?"

"We maybe should take some blankets in case you get sleepy."

"But we can stop at one of those restaurants, too, right?"

The border was actually two towns, though neither one was big enough to amount to anything. Coutts was on the Canadian side and consisted of the convenience store and gas station, the museum that was closed and boarded up, and a motel. Sweetgrass was on the American side, but all you could see was an overpass that arched across the highway and disappeared into the prairies. Just hearing the names of these towns, you would expect that Sweetgrass, which is a nice name and sounds like it is related to other places such as

Medicine Hat and Moose Jaw and Kicking Horse Pass, would be on the Canadian side, and that Coutts, which sounds abrupt and rude, would be on the American side. But this was not the case.

Between the two borders was a duty-free shop where you could buy cigarettes and liquor and flags. Stuff like that.

We left the reserve in the morning and drove until we got to Coutts.

"Last time we stopped here," my mother said, "you had an Orange Crush. You remember that?"

"Sure," I said. "That was when Laetitia took off."

"You want another Orange Crush?"

"That means we're not going to stop at a restaurant, right?"

My mother got a coffee at the convenience store, and we stood around and watched the prairies move in the sunlight. Then we climbed back in the car. My mother straightened the dress across her thighs, leaned against the wheel, and drove all the way to the border in first gear, slowly, as if she were trying to see through a bad storm or riding high on black ice.

The border guard was an old guy. As he walked to the car, he swayed from side to side, his feet set wide apart, the holster on his hip pitching up and down. He leaned into the window, looked into the back seat, and looked at my mother and me.

"Morning, ma'am."

"Good morning."

"Where you heading?"

"Salt Lake City."

"Purpose of your visit?"

"Visit my daughter."

"Citizenship?"

"Blackfoot,"[2] my mother told him.

"Ma'am?"

"Blackfoot," my mother repeated.

"Canadian?"

"Blackfoot."

It would have been easier if my mother had just said "Canadian" and had been done with it, but I could see she wasn't going to do that. The guard wasn't angry or anything. He smiled and looked towards the building. Then he turned back and nodded.

"Morning, ma'am."

"Good morning."

"Any firearms or tobacco?"

"No."

"Citizenship?"

"Blackfoot."

He told us to sit in the car and wait, and we did. In about five minutes, another guard came out with the first man. They were talking as they came, both men swaying back and forth like two cowboys headed for a bar or a gunfight.

2 the Blackfoot Nation has reserves in both Alberta and Montana.

60 "Morning, ma'am."

"Good morning."

"Cecil tells me you and the boy are Blackfoot."

"That's right."

"Now, I know that we got Blackfeet on the American side and the Canadians got Blackfeet on their side. Just so we can keep our records straight, what side do you come from?"

65 I knew exactly what my mother was going to say, and I could have told them if they had asked me.

"Canadian side or American side?" asked the guard.

"Blackfoot side," she said.

It didn't take them long to lose their sense of humor, I can tell you that. The one guard stopped smiling altogether and told us to park our car at the side of the building and come in.

We sat on a wood bench for about an hour before anyone came over to talk to us. This time it was a woman. She had a gun, too.

70 "Hi," she said. "I'm Inspector Pratt. I understand there is a little misunderstanding."

"I'm going to visit my daughter in Salt Lake City," my mother told her. "We don't have any guns or beer."

"It's a legal technicality, that's all."

"My daughter's Blackfoot, too."

The woman opened a briefcase and took out a couple of forms and began to write on one of them. "Everyone who crosses our border has to declare their citizenship. Even Americans. It helps us keep track of the visitors we get from the various countries."

75 She went on like that for maybe fifteen minutes, and a lot of the stuff she told us was interesting.

"I can understand how you feel about having to tell us your citizenship, and here's what I'll do. You tell me, and I won't put it down on the form. No-one will know but you and me."

Her gun was silver. There were several chips in the wood handle and the name "Stella" was scratched into the metal butt.

We were in the border office for about four hours, and we talked to almost everyone there. One of the men bought me a Coke. My mother brought a couple of sandwiches in from the car. I offered part of mine to Stella, but she said she wasn't hungry.

I told Stella that we were Blackfoot and Canadian, but she said that that didn't count because I was a minor. In the end, she told us that if my mother didn't declare her citizenship, we would have to go back to where we came from. Then we got back in the car and drove to the Canadian border, which was only about a hundred yards away.

80 I was disappointed. I hadn't seen Laetitia for a long time, and I had never been to Salt Lake City. When she was still at home, Laetitia would go on and on about Salt Lake City. She had never been there, but her boyfriend Lester Tallbull had spent a year in Salt Lake at a technical school.

"It's a great place," Lester would say. "Nothing but blondes in the whole state."

Whenever he said that, Laetitia would slug him on his shoulder hard enough to make him flinch. He had some brochures on Salt Lake and some maps, and every so often the two of them would spread them out on the table.

"That's the temple. It's right downtown. You got to have a pass to get in."

"Charlotte says anyone can go in and look around."

85 "When was Charlotte in Salt Lake? Just when the hell was Charlotte in Salt Lake?"

"Last year."

"This is Liberty Park. It's got a zoo. There's good skiing in the mountains."

"Got all the skiing we can use," my mother would say. "People come from all over the world to ski at Banff. Cardston's got a temple, if you like those kinds of things."

"Oh, this one is real big," Lester would say. "They got armed guards and everything."

90 "Not what Charlotte says."

"What does she know?"

Lester and Laetitia broke up, but I guess the idea of Salt Lake stuck in her mind.

The Canadian border guard was a young woman, and she seemed happy to see us. "Hi," she said. "You folks sure have a great day for a trip. Where are you coming from?"

"Standoff."

95 "Is that in Montana?"

"No."

"Where are you going?"

"Standoff."

The woman's name was Carol and I don't guess she was any older than Laetitia. "Wow, you both Canadians?"

100 "Blackfoot."

"Really? I have a friend I went to school with who is Blackfoot. Do you know Mike Harley?"

"No."

"He went to school in Lethbridge, but he's really from Browning."[3]

It was a nice conversation and there were no cars behind us, so there was no rush.

105 "You're not bringing any liquor back, are you?"

"No."

"Any cigarettes or plants or stuff like that?"

"No."

"Citizenship?"

110 "Blackfoot."

"I know," said the woman, "and I'd be proud of being Blackfoot if I were Blackfoot. But you have to be American or Canadian."

---

3 town in northern Montana that is the American headquarters of the Blackfoot Nation.

When Laetitia and Lester broke up, Lester took his brochures and maps with him, so Laetitia wrote to someone in Salt Lake City, and, about a month later, she got a big envelope of stuff. We sat at the table and opened up all the brochures, and Laetitia read each one out loud.

"Salt Lake City is the gateway to some of the world's most magnificent skiing.

"Salt Lake City is the home of one of the newest professional basketball franchises, the Utah Jazz.

115    "The Great Salt Lake is one of the natural wonders of the world."

It was kind of exciting seeing all those color brochures on the table and listening to Laetitia read all about how Salt Lake City was one of the best places in the entire world.

"That Salt Lake City place sounds too good to be true," my mother told her.

"It has everything."

"We got everything right here."

120    "It's boring here."

"People in Salt Lake City are probably sending away for brochures of Calgary and Lethbridge and Pincher Creek right now."

In the end, my mother would say that maybe Laetitia should go to Salt Lake City, and Laetitia would say that maybe she would.

We parked the car to the side of the building and Carol led us into a small room on the second floor. I found a confortable spot on the couch and flipped through some back issues of *Saturday Night* and *Alberta Report*.

When I woke up, my mother was just coming out of another office. She didn't say a word to me. I followed her down the stairs and out to the car. I thought we were going home, but she turned the car around and drove back towards the American border, which made me think we were going to visit Laetitia in Salt Lake City after all. Instead she pulled into the parking lot of the duty-free store and stopped.

125    "We going to see Laetitia?"

"No."

"We going home?"

Pride is a good thing to have, you know. Laetitia had a lot of pride, and so did my mother. I figured that someday, I'd have it, too.

"So where are we going?"

130    Most of that day, we wandered around the duty-free store, which wasn't very large. The manager had a name tag with a tiny American flag on one side and a tiny Canadian flag on the other. His name was Mel. Towards evening, he began suggesting that we should be on our way. I told him we had nowhere to go, that neither the Americans nor the Canadians would let us in. He laughed at that and told us that we should buy something or leave.

The car was not very comfortable, but we did have all that food and it was April, so even if it did snow as it sometimes does on the prairies, we wouldn't freeze. The next morning my mother drove to the American border.

It was a different guard this time, but the questions were the same. We didn't spend as much time in the office as we had the day before. By noon, we were back at the Canadian border. By two we were back in the duty-free shop parking lot.

The second night in the car was not as much fun as the first, but my mother seemed in good spirits, and, all in all, it was as much an adventure as an inconvenience. There wasn't much food left and that was a problem, but we had lots of water as there was a faucet at the side of the duty-free shop.

One Sunday, Laetitia and I were watching television. Mom was over at Mrs. Manyfingers's. Right in the middle of the program, Laetitia turned off the set and said she was going to Salt Lake City, that life around here was too boring. I had wanted to see the rest of the program and really didn't care if Laetitia went to Salt Lake City or not. When Mom got home, I told her what Laetitia had said.

135   What surprised me was how angry Laetitia got when she found out that I had told Mom.

"You got a big mouth."

"That's what you said."

"What I said is none of your business."

"I didn't say anything."

140   "Well, I'm going for sure, now."

That weekend, Laetitia packed her bags, and we drove her to the border.

Mel turned out to be friendly. When he closed up for the night and found us still parked in the lot, he came over and asked us if our car was broken down or something. My mother thanked him for his concern and told him that we were fine, that things would get straightened out in the morning.

"You're kidding," said Mel. "You'd think they could handle the simple things."

"We got some apples and a banana," I said, "but we're all out of ham sandwiches."

145   "You know, you read about these things, but you just don't believe it. You just don't believe it."

"Hamburgers would be even better because they got more stuff for energy."

My mother slept in the back seat. I slept in the front because I was smaller and could lie under the steering wheel. Late that night, I heard my mother open the car door. I found her sitting on her blanket leaning against the bumper of the car.

"You see all those stars," she said. "When I was a little girl, my grand-mother used to take me and my sisters out on the prairies and tell us stories about all the stars."

"Do you think Mel is going to bring us any hamburgers?"

150   "Every one of those stars has a story. You see that bunch of stars over there that look like a fish?"

"He didn't say no."

"Coyote[4] went fishing, one day. That's how it all started." We sat out under the stars that night, and my mother told me all sorts of stories. She was

---

4 trickster figure in the mythology of several Native peoples of the northern plains.

serious about it, too. She'd tell them slow, repeating parts as she went, as if she expected me to remember each one.

Early the next morning, the television vans began to arrive, and guys in suits and women in dresses came trotting over to us, dragging microphones and cameras and lights behind them. One of the vans had a table set up with orange juice and sandwiches and fruit. It was for the crew, but when I told them we hadn't eaten for a while, a really skinny blonde woman told us we could eat as much as we wanted.

They mostly talked to my mother. Every so often one of the reporters would come over and ask me questions about how it felt to be an Indian without a country. I told them we had a nice house on the reserve and that my cousins had a couple of horses we rode when we went fishing. Some of the television people went over to the American border, and then they went to the Canadian border.

155     Around noon, a good-looking guy in a dark blue suit and an orange tie with little ducks on it drove up in a fancy car. He talked to my mother for a while, and, after they were done talking, my mother called me over, and we got into our car. Just as my mother started the engine, Mel came over and gave us a bag of peanut brittle and told us that justice was a damn hard thing to get, but that we shouldn't give up.

I would have preferred lemon drops, but it was nice of Mel anyway.

"Where are we going now?"

"Going to visit Laetitia."

The guard who came out to our car was all smiles. The television lights were so bright they hurt my eyes, and, if you tried to look through the windshield in certain directions, you couldn't see a thing.

160     "Morning, ma'am."

"Good morning."

"Where you heading?"

"Salt Lake City."

"Purpose of your visit?"

165     "Visit my daughter."

"Any tobacco, liquor, or firearms?"

"Don't smoke."

"Any plants or fruit?"

"Not any more."

170     "Citizenship?"

"Blackfoot."

The guard rocked back on his heels and jammed his thumbs into his gun belt. "Thank you," he said, his fingers patting the butt of the revolver. "Have a pleasant trip."

My mother rolled the car forward, and the television people had to scramble out of the way. They ran alongside the car as we pulled away from the border, and, when they couldn't run any farther, they stood in the middle of the highway and waved and waved and waved.

We got to Salt Lake City the next day. Laetitia was happy to see us, and, that first night, she took us out to a restaurant that made really good soups. The list of pies took up a whole page. I had cherry. Mom had chocolate. Laetitia said that she saw us on television the night before and, during the meal, she had us tell her the story over and over again.

175     Laetitia took us everywhere. We went to a fancy ski resort. We went to the temple. We got to go shopping in a couple of large malls, but they weren't as large as the one in Edmonton, and Mom said so.

After a week or so, I got bored and wasn't at all sad when my mother said we should be heading back home. Laetitia wanted us to stay longer, but Mom said no, that she had things to do back home and that, next time, Laetitia should come up and visit. Laetitia said she was thinking about moving back, and Mom told her to do as she pleased, and Laetitia said that she would.

On the way home, we stopped at the duty-free shop, and my mother gave Mel a green hat that said "Salt Lake" across the front. Mel was a funny guy. He took the hat and blew his nose and told my mother that she was an inspiration to us all. He gave us some more peanut brittle and came out into the parking lot and waved at us all the way to the Canadian border.

It was almost evening when we left Coutts. I watched the border through the rear window until all you could see were the tops of the flagpoles and the blue water tower, and then they rolled over a hill and disappeared.

(1993)

# Alice Walker   (b. 1944)

Born in Eatonton in rural Georgia, where her parents were poor sharecrop-
pers, Alice Walker published her first book—a collection of poems entitled
*Once*—in 1968, shortly after graduating from Sarah Lawrence College in New
York. Active in Mississippi during the civil rights movement of the 1960s, she has
published several books: poetry, short stories, essays, and four novels, of which
the best known, *The Color Purple* (1982), was made into a motion picture. In all
her writing, Walker celebrates the lives of African-American women and their heritage. "Everyday Use" contrasts characters' attitudes toward an old quilt to
reveal the differences between, on the one hand, the narrator and her daughter Maggie, both of whom live simple lives close to the land, and, on the other,
Dee, who has developed a superficial sophistication. In her essay "In Search
of Our Mothers' Gardens," Walker writes of quilts, now often preserved in
museums, as creations of people who possessed "powerful imagination and
deep spiritual feeling."

# EVERYDAY USE

## FOR YOUR GRANDMAMA

I will wait for her in the yard that Maggie and I made so clean and wavy yesterday afternoon. A yard like this is more comfortable than most people know.
It is not just a yard. It is like an extended living room. When the hard clay is
swept clean as a floor and the fine sand around the edges lined with tiny,
irregular grooves, anyone can come and sit and look up into the elm tree and
wait for the breezes that never come inside the house.

Maggie will be nervous until her sister goes: she will stand hopelessly in
corners, homely and ashamed of the burn scars down her arms and legs, eying
her sister with a mixture of envy and awe. She thinks her sister has held life
always in the palm of one hand, that "no" is a word the world never learned to
say to her.

You've no doubt seen those TV shows where the child who has "made it" is confronted, as a surprise, by her own mother and father, tottering in weakly from
backstage. (A pleasant surprise, of course: What would they do if parent
and child came on the show only to curse out and insult each other?) On TV
mother and child embrace and smile into each other's faces. Sometimes the
mother and father weep, the child wraps them in her arms and leans across the
table to tell how she would not have made it without their help. I have seen
these programs.

Sometimes I dream a dream in which Dee and I are suddenly brought
together on a TV program of this sort. Out of a dark and soft-seated limousine
I am ushered into a bright room filled with many people. There I meet a
smiling, gray, sporty man like Johnny Carson who shakes my hand and tells me
what a fine girl I have. Then we are on the stage and Dee is embracing me with

tears in her eyes. She pins on my dress a large orchid, even though she has told me once that she thinks orchids are tacky flowers.

5     In real life I am a large, big-boned woman with rough, man-working hands. In the winter I wear flannel nightgowns to bed and overalls during the day. I can kill and clean a hog as mercilessly as a man. My fat keeps me hot in zero weather. I can work outside all day, breaking ice to get water for washing; I can eat pork liver cooked over the open fire minutes after it comes steaming from the hog. One winter I knocked a bull calf straight in the brain between the eyes with a sledge hammer and had the meat hung up to chill before nightfall. But of course all this does not show on television. I am the way my daughter would want me to be: a hundred pounds lighter, my skin like an uncooked barley pancake. My hair glistens in the hot bright lights. Johnny Carson has much to do to keep up with my quick and witty tongue.

But that is a mistake. I know even before I wake up. Who ever knew a Johnson with a quick tongue? Who can even imagine me looking a strange white man in the eye? It seems to me I have talked to them always with one foot raised in flight, with my head turned in whichever way is farthest from them. Dee, though. She would always look anyone in the eye. Hesitation was no part of her nature.

"How do I look, Mama?" Maggie says, showing just enough of her thin body enveloped in pink skirt and red blouse for me to know she's there, almost hidden by the door.

"Come out into the yard," I say.

Have you ever seen a lame animal, perhaps a dog run over by some care-less person rich enough to own a car, sidle up to someone who is ignorant enough to be kind to him? That is the way my Maggie walks. She has been like this, chin on chest, eyes on ground, feet in shuffle, ever since the fire that burned the other house to the ground.

10     Dee is lighter than Maggie, with nicer hair and a fuller figure. She's a woman now, though sometimes I forget. How long ago was it that the other house burned? Ten, twelve years? Sometimes I can still hear the flames and feel Maggie's arms sticking to me, her hair smoking and her dress falling off her in little black papery flakes. Her eyes seemed stretched open, blazed open by the flames reflected in them. And Dee. I see her standing off under the sweet gum tree she used to dig gum out of; a look of concentration on her face as she watched the last dingy gray board of the house fall in toward the red-hot brick chimney. Why don't you do a dance around the ashes? I'd wanted to ask her. She had hated the house that much.

I used to think she hated Maggie, too. But that was before we raised the money, the church and me, to send her to Augusta[1] to school. She used to read to us without pity; forcing words, lies, other folks' habits, whole lives upon us two, sitting trapped and ignorant underneath her voice. She washed us in a river of make-believe, burned us with a lot of knowledge we didn't necessarily need to know. Pressed us to her with the serious way she read, to shove us away at just the moment, like dimwits, we seemed about to understand.

---

1 city in Georgia southeast of Atlanta.

Dee wanted nice things. A yellow organdy dress to wear to her graduation from high school; black pumps to match a green suit she'd made from an old suit somebody gave me. She was determined to stare down any disaster in her efforts. Her eyelids would not flicker for minutes at a time. Often I fought off the temptation to shake her. At sixteen she had a style of her own: and knew what style was.

I never had an education myself. After second grade the school was closed down. Don't ask me why: in 1927 colored asked fewer questions than they do now. Sometimes Maggie reads to me. She stumbles along good-naturedly but can't see well. She knows she is not bright. Like good looks and money, quickness passed her by. She will marry John Thomas (who has mossy teeth in an earnest face) and then I'll be free to sit here and I guess just sing church songs to myself. Although I never was a good singer. Never could carry a tune. I was always better at a man's job. I used to love to milk till I was hooked in the side in '49. Cows are soothing and slow and don't bother you, unless you try to milk them the wrong way.

I have deliberately turned my back on the house. It is three rooms, just like the one that burned, except the roof is tin; they don't make shingle roofs any more. There are no real windows, just some holes cut in the sides, like portholes in a ship, but not round and not square, with rawhide holding the shutters up on the outside. This house is in a pasture, too, like the other one. No doubt when Dee sees it she will want to tear it down. She wrote me once that no matter where we "choose" to live, she will manage to come see us. But she will never bring her friends. Maggie and I thought about this and Maggie asked me, "Mama, when did Dee ever *have* any friends?"

15      She had a few. Furtive boys in pink shirts hanging about on washday after school. Nervous girls who never laughed. Impressed with her they worshiped the well-turned phrase, the cute shape, the scalding humor that erupted like bubbles in lye. She read to them.

When she was courting Jimmy T she didn't have much time to pay to us, but turned all her faultfinding power on him. He *flew* to marry a cheap city girl from a family of ignorant flashy people. She hardly had time to recompose herself.

When she comes I will meet — but there they are!

Maggie attempts to make a dash for the house, in her shuffling way, but I stay her with my hand. "Come back here," I say. And she stops and tries to dig a well in the sand with her toe.

It is hard to see them clearly through the strong sun. But even the first glimpse of leg out of the car tells me it is Dee. Her feet were always neat-looking, as if God himself had shaped them with a certain style. From the other side of the car comes a short, stocky man. Hair is all over his head a foot long and hanging from his chin like a kinky mule tail. I hear Maggie suck in her breath. "Uhnnnh," is what it sounds like. Like when you see the wriggling end of a snake just in front of your foot on the road. "Uhnnnh."

20      Dee next. A dress down to the ground, in this hot weather. A dress so loud it hurts my eyes. There are yellows and oranges enough to throw back the

light of the sun. I feel my whole face warming from the heat waves it throws out. Earrings gold, too, and hanging down to her shoulders. Bracelets dangling and making noises when she moves her arm up to shake the folds of the dress out of her armpits. The dress is loose and flows, and as she walks closer, I like it. I hear Maggie go "Uhnnnh" again. It is her sister's hair. It stands straight up like the wool on a sheep. It is black as night and around the edges are two long pigtails that rope about like small lizards disappearing behind her ears.

"Wa-su-zo-Tean-o!"[2] she says, coming on in that gliding way the dress makes her move. The short stocky fellow with the hair to his navel is all grinning and he follows up with "Asalamalakim,[3] my mother and sister!" He moves to hug Maggie but she falls back, right up against the back of my chair. I feel her trembling there and when I look up I see the perspiration falling off her chin.

"Don't get up," says Dee. Since I am stout it takes something of a push. You can see me trying to move a second or two before I make it. She turns, showing white heels through her sandals, and goes back to the car. Out she peeks next with a Polaroid. She stoops down quickly and lines up picture after picture of me sitting there in front of the house with Maggie cowering behind me. She never takes a shot without making sure the house is included. When a cow comes nibbling around the edge of the yard she snaps it and me and Maggie *and* the house. Then she puts the Polaroid in the back seat of the car, and comes up and kisses me on the forehead.

Meanwhile Asalamalakim is going through motions with Maggie's hand. Maggie's hand is as limp as a fish, and probably as cold, despite the sweat, and she keeps trying to pull it back. It looks like Asalamalakim wants to shake hands but wants to do it fancy. Or maybe he don't know how people shake hands. Anyhow, he soon gives up on Maggie.

"Well," I say. "Dee."

25 "No, Mama," she says. "Not 'Dee,' Wangero Leewanika Kemanjo!"

"What happened to 'Dee'?" I wanted to know.

"She's dead," Wangero said. "I couldn't bear it any longer, being named after the people who oppress me."

"You know as well as me you was named after your aunt Dicie," I said. Dicie is my sister. She named Dee. We called her "Big Dee" after Dee was born.

"But who was *she* named after?" asked Wangero.

30 "I guess after Grandma Dee," I said.

"And who was she named after?" asked Wangero.

"Her mother," I said, and saw Wangero was getting tired. "That's about as far back as I can trace it," I said. Though, in fact, I probably could have carried it back beyond the Civil War through the branches.

"Well," said Asalamalakim, "There you are."

"Uhnnnh," I heard Maggie say.

35 "There I was not," I said, "before 'Dicie' cropped up in our family, so why should I try to trace it that far back?"

2 Islamic greeting popular among some African Americans in the 1960s.  3 Islamic greeting also popular during the 1960s.

He just stood there grinning, looking down on me like somebody inspecting a Model A car. Every once in a while he and Wangero sent eye signals over my head.

"How do you pronounce this name?" I asked.

"You don't have to call me by it if you don't want to," said Wangero.

"Why shouldn't I?" I asked. "If that's what you want us to call you, we'll call you."

40     "I know it might sound awkward at first," said Wangero.

"I'll get used to it," I said. "Ream it out again."

Well, soon we got the name out of the way. Asalamalakim had a name twice as long and three times as hard. After I tripped over it two or three times he told me to just call him Hakim-a-barber. I wanted to ask him was he a barber, but I didn't really think he was, so I didn't ask.

"You must belong to those beef-cattle peoples down the road," I said. They said "Asalamalakim" when they met you, too, but they didn't shake hands. Always too busy: feeding the cattle, fixing the fences, putting up salk-lick shelters, throwing down hay. When the white folks poisoned some of the herd the men stayed up all night with rifles in their hands. I walked a mile and a half just to see the sight.

Hakim-a-barber said, "I accept some of their doctrines, but farming and raising cattle is not my style." (They didn't tell me, and I didn't ask, whether Wangero (Dee) had really gone and married him.)

45     We sat down to eat and right away he said he didn't eat collards and pork was unclean. Wangero, though, went on through the chitlins and corn bread, the greens and everything else. She talked a blue streak over the sweet potatoes. Everything delighted her. Even the fact that we still used the benches her daddy made for the table when we couldn't afford to buy chairs.

"Oh, Mama!" she cried. Then turned to Hakim-a-barber. "I never knew how lovely these benches are. You can feel the rump prints," she said, running her hands underneath her and along the bench. Then she gave a sigh and her hand closed over Grandma Dee's butter dish. "That's it!" she said. "I knew there was something I wanted to ask you if I could have." She jumped up from the table and went over in the corner where the churn stood, the milk in it clabber by now. She looked at the churn and looked at it.

"This churn top is what I need," she said. "Didn't Uncle Buddy whittle it out of a tree you all used to have?"

"Yes," I said.

"Uh huh," she said happily. "And I want the dasher, too."

50     "Uncle Buddy whittle that, too?" asked the barber.

Dee (Wangero) looked up at me.

"Aunt Dee's first husband whittled the dash," said Maggie so low you almost couldn't hear her. "His name was Henry, but they called him Stash."

"Maggie's brain is like an elephant's," Wangero said, laughing. "I can use the churn top as a centrepiece for the alcove table," she said, sliding a plate over the churn, "and I'll think of something artistic to do with the dasher."

When she finished wrapping the dasher the handle stuck out. I took it for a moment in my hands. You didn't even have to look to see where hands pushing the dasher up and down to make butter had left a kind of sink in the wood. In fact, there were a lot of small sinks; you could see where thumbs and fingers had sunk into the wood. It was beautiful light yellow wood, from a tree that grew in the yard where Big Dee and Stash had lived.

After dinner Dee (Wangero) went to the trunk at the foot of my bed and started rifling through it. Maggie hung back in the kitchen over the dishpan. Out came Wangero with two quilts. They had been pieced by Grandma Dee and then Big Dee and me had hung them on the quilt frames on the front porch and quilted them. One was in the Lone Star pattern. The other was Walk Around the Mountain. In both of them were scraps of dresses Grandma Dee had worn fifty and more years ago. Bits and pieces of Grandpa Jarrell's Paisley shirts. And one teeny faded blue piece, about the size of a penny matchbox, that was from Great Grandpa Ezra's uniform that he wore in the Civil War.

"Mama," Wangero said sweet as a bird. "Can I have these old quilts?"

I heard something fall in the kitchen, and a minute later the kitchen door slammed.

"Why don't you take one or two of the others?" I asked. "These old things was just done by me and Big Dee from some tops your grandma pieced before she died."

"No," said Wangero. "I don't want those. They are stitched around the borders by machine."

"That'll make them last better," I said.

"That's not the point," said Wangero. "These are all pieces of dresses Grandma used to wear. She did all this stitching by hand. Imagine!" She held the quilts securely in her arms, stroking them.

"Some of the pieces, like those lavender ones, come from old clothes her mother handed down to her," I said, moving up to touch the quilts. Dee (Wangero) moved back just enough so that I couldn't reach the quilts. They already belonged to her.

"Imagine!" she breathed again, clutching them closely to her bosom.

"The truth is," I said, "I promised to give them quilts to Maggie, for when she marries John Thomas."

She gasped like a bee had stung her.

"Maggie can't appreciate these quilts!" she said. "She'd probably be backward enough to put them to everyday use."

"I reckon she would," I said. "God knows I been saving 'em for long enough with nobody using 'em. I hope she will!" I didn't want to bring up how I had offered Dee (Wangero) a quilt when she went away to college. Then she had told me they were old-fashioned, out of style.

"But they're *priceless*!" she was saying now, furiously; for she has a temper. "Maggie would put them on the bed and in five years they'd be in rags. Less than that!"

"She can always make some more," I said. "Maggie knows how to quilt."

Dee (Wangero) looked at me with hatred. "You just will not understand. The point is these quilts, *these* quilts!"

"Well," I said, stumped. "What would *you* do with them?"

"Hang them," she said. As if that was the only thing you *could* do with quilts.

Maggie by now was standing in the door. I could almost hear the sound her feet made as they scraped over each other.

"She can have them, Mama," she said, like somebody used to never winning anything, or having anything reserved for her. "I can 'member Grandma Dee without the quilts."

75    I looked at her hard. She had filled her bottom lip with checkerberry snuff and it gave her face a kind of dopey, hangdog look. It was Grandma Dee and Big Dee who taught her how to quilt herself. She stood there with her scarred hands hidden in the folds of her skirt. She looked at her sister with something like fear but she wasn't mad at her. This was Maggie's portion. This was the way she knew God to work.

When I looked at her like that something hit me in the top of my head and ran down to the soles of my feet. Just like when I'm in church and the spirit of God touches me and I get happy and shout. I did something I never had done before: hugged Maggie to me, then dragged her on into the room, snatched the quilts out of Miss Wangero's hands and dumped them into Maggie's lap. Maggie just sat there on my bed with her mouth open.

"Take one or two of the others," I said to Dee.

But she turned without a word and went out to Hakim-a-barber.

"You just don't understand," she said, as Maggie and I came out to the car.

80    "What don't I understand," I wanted to know.

"Your heritage," she said. And then she turned to Maggie, kissed her, and said, "You ought to try to make something of yourself, too, Maggie. It's really a new day for us. But from the way you and Mama still live you'd never know it."

She put on some sunglasses that hid everything above the tip of her nose and her chin.

Maggie smiled; maybe at the sunglasses. But a real smile, not scared. After we watched the car dust settle I asked Maggie to bring me a dip of snuff. And then the two of us sat there just enjoying, until it was time to go in the house and go to bed.

(1973)

# Greg Hollingshead (b. 1947)

A professor of eighteenth-century literature and creative writing at the University of Alberta, Greg Hollingshead was born in Toronto and studied at the Universities of Toronto and London. In three collections of short stories and a novel, *Spin Dry*, Hollingshead examines the mystery and absurdity that lurk beneath the surface of apparently "ordinary" modern life. A student of the eighteenth-century philosopher George Berkeley, he considers writing "an ongoing perception of process and discovery. For me, narrative is philosophy as we actually live it, day by day, all our lives. Each event in a story conveys an understanding of those that precede it. Each raises and addresses the question 'Why?'" "The Naked Man" is from Hollingshead's most recent collection, *The Roaring Girl* (1995), winner of the Governor General's Award for fiction. Like "Rappaccini's Daughter" and "The Motor Car," its central character is a young man who has left his family home. Unlike Giovanni and Calvin, however, Dennis returns. The ambiguous feelings both he and his family experience are, in part, reflected in their attitudes toward his Studebaker, an ornate, chromium-decorated car popular in the 1950s.

# THE NAKED MAN

By the time I was eighteen it was getting hard to live at home. Instead of moving out I bought a Studebaker. I loved the Studebaker, but it made no difference, so I left it with my parents and went to Australia. My parents had a double garage with so much junk in it there was hardly room for the family Chev. By stacking the junk higher up the walls I made room for a Studebaker too. This was fine with my parents, but I was uneasy for my car.

When I called home there was always some problem about it. Even just sitting in the garage. Of course, it made parking the Chev tighter, and I heard about that. A few times I hung up with the impression there had been some scraping. My father had talked me into leaving the keys for safety reasons. The first definite thing that happened was they lost the keys.

"Tell me again why you need them," I said to my father.

"Safety reasons," he replied.

5      Reluctantly I explained about the spare key under the front fender. He listened dubiously.

Another time I called he told me the Studebaker was leaking oil.

"It always did," I said. "It's not a leak. It's just a little drip."

"That car of yours is making a terrible mess out there," my mother said when she came on.

"So put a piece of carpeting under it," I said.

10      "A *what?*"

The next time I called they had got in a mechanic to see about the leak.

"He says you need a new clutch," my father told me. "He says you should have arranged to have it started at least every two weeks."

"What'd he say about the leak?"

"There's nothing he can do about the leak. The leak is the least of your worries. Do you realize what this car of yours is costing me?"

15     I told them to just leave the car alone.

After a while it stopped coming up. Sometimes this was how things would happen. Their lives had moved on. As a kind of joke I would say, "So how's my car?" and in a resigned voice my father would say, "Well, it's still there," or, "You realize your mother won't park in the garage any more, don't you."

When I got back from Australia it was six in the morning about a year later, and I had no money at all. But my parents lived twenty minutes from the airport, so I waited until seven and called home.

"Hello —" My father's voice was damaged and incredulous with sleep.

"Hi, Dad, it's Dennis."

20     There was a pause. "Dennis — ?"

"Your son, Dennis,"

"It's Dennis!" my mother cried in the background. She grabbed the phone. "Dennis, you sound so close! Where are you?"

An hour later the Chev pulled up at the Arrivals door with my father clinging to the wheel like a shipwreck victim. His hair fanned straight out at the side, and he was still breathing hard from sleep. I threw my bags in the back seat and got in beside him.

"So how was Australia?" he said. "Are they ahead of us or behind? It was dawn there too?"

25     "Australia was great. It's hard to know where to start —"

"Feed it out slowly, over time." And he told me how with the way interest rates were going it looked like we'd lose the house.

As we turned into the driveway I asked, "So how's the car?"

"It runs, doesn't it? It's not as if I could afford a new one."

My mother was at the foot of the driveway with her coat on, waiting impatiently for the Chev. She had an eight-thirty hair appointment and made us get out immediately.

30     We walked to the house. As soon as we were inside, my father called a cab. "Think I'll slide over to the track," he said, standing in the middle of the kitchen eating a bowl of cornflakes. "Now that I'm up."

As soon as he left I flopped down on the living-room chesterfield and passed out.

I woke up badly disoriented. I was on a different chesterfield, and for a long time I thought I was still in Australia, but I couldn't figure out which city. The only thing worse than waking up from sleeping too long at the wrong time is waking up in a different place from where you fell asleep.

It was my parents' main-floor guest room. When I tried to get up my body was completely without tonus. I fell back on the bed. "Hey Denny." It was my younger sister Sophie, passing the door. She shot me the six-gun salute.

"Sophie!" my mother called from the kitchen. "Why don't you give Dennis a tour of the house?"

35     "No time!" Sophie shouted from the bathroom. "Nothing ever changes!" She was washing her face.

I stepped out the French doors to the garage to take a look at my car. It was not there.

I checked the driveway and the other side of the house. From the darkness of the garage I watched Sophie's ride for work stop out front and pick her up. I waved, but she didn't see me. When I turned on the garage light I saw that I had tracked oil from the puddle where the Studebaker had been.

My mother was in the living room with her hair done, sitting next to a beautiful young woman I had never seen before. I said my name and we shook hands.

"You know Lori," my mother said.

40 "I never saw Lori before in my life."

"Get off it," my mother said.

Lori worked nearby with disturbed children.

"Lori's staying in the spare room downstairs," my mother explained.

"I didn't know there was a spare room downstairs," I said. There was only my room.

45 "Well, there isn't now," my mother said.

At that moment a naked man walked past the doorway down the hall between the main-floor bedrooms. A door closed.

"Excuse me," I said quietly, my heart going. "I think there's someone else in the house."

My mother was listing the people she had invited to a party we were having that night. She paused, looking at me. "I know," she said. "It can be kind of a Welcome Home Dennis party."

"What was it before?" I asked with a smile at Lori, who smiled back.

50 "A naked man just walked past the door," I said more loudly, pointing.

My mother was continuing with her list. "Susan and Ed, and Effie, and the Rauches (the Cy and Doris Rauches, that is), and Aunt B.J., and Wade of course, and the Chatterjees —"

"Who's Wade?" I asked.

"Lori's friend. And Dave Arkett, and Tony and his wife, and —"

I asked if there was a bed I could use.

55 "Of course there's a bed you can use," my mother said irritably. "Why do you have to put an edge on everything?" There was Dave's old room upstairs, she said. And could I please clear my bags out of the front hall. She didn't want our guests tripping over them.

Dave's bed was a double. I turned back the covers and checked around until I came up with two shades of pubic hair. I dropped these down behind the headboard and brushed away absently at the sheet. I sat on the edge of the mattress and rubbed my shanks. After a while I went to take a shower, but there was somebody in there.

I returned to the living room in Dave's dressing gown. Lori and my mother looked at me expectantly.

"I was going to take a shower, but there's somebody in there," I said.

"I thought you told us you were going to bed," my mother said.

60 "Can't I shower first?"

"Not if somebody's in there."

"It's not Sophie," I said. "Sophie went to work."

"Nonsense."

"I think she did, Mrs. Weatherall," Lori put in softly. "I heard the door."

"Well, I'm sure I don't know who it could be in that case," my mother said with impatience, refusing to be held accountable for strangers in the house.

"By the way," I said. "I've been meaning to ask. Where's my car?"

"What car?"

"The one I left in the garage."

"There's no car in the garage."

"That's what I'm saying. What did you do with it?"

"Why are you asking me? I haven't been able to park in my own garage for a year. You'll have to talk to your father."

"Well, I guess the bathroom's free now," I said, but it wasn't.

Instead of returning to the living room, I went on to the kitchen where I made myself a toasted bacon and tomato sandwich. I ate this standing in the middle of the kitchen like my father, I noticed, and then I went to bed.


When I came downstairs again it was dark. Lori was sitting in the same place in the living room, only now she was alone, smoking a cigarette and wearing a sequined gown with a generous neckline.

"Hi," I said.

"Hi."

"I guess I should change."

"You don't have to."

"I look like a bum."

"You look very nice."

My father entered from the kitchen with a couple of bowls of chips and dip. To Lori he said, "If that dress had slits you could call it a strange sequins of vents."

To me he said, "Help out a little."

In the kitchen my mother was mixing nuts in a bowl. She gave my father and me a look that said, *They'll be here any minute.*

"Right," my father said and rubbed his hands together while glancing around in vague anticipation.

She shot us another look that said, *You don't think you're greeting our guests dressed like that, do you?*

My father looked down at himself with his hands at his sides, spread and turned outward in a gesture that said, *What's wrong with the way I'm dressed?*

My mother made no reply.

My father grew silent as if musing. Finally he rubbed his jaw and murmured, "Maybe I'll shave."

An hour later my father had a bar set up on a card table in a corner of the dining room, telling women who ordered their drinks on the rocks, "I only have ice for you," and describing their Bristol Creams as rhapsodies in goo.

When he noticed me watching him, my father told me to take over. "Wade's shirking his responsibilities on all fronts," he said from the corner of his mouth.

"Which one's Wade?"

"The shifty one."

As soon as I was behind the bar, people started talking to me. Most of them when they heard I was a Weatherall thought I was my younger brother Dave, at that time in Hawaii. A few thought I was my dead brother Joe.

From behind the bar I could see Lori sitting completely alone in her place on the chesterfield, drinking soda water. As I poured my mother her usual — Silent Sam, a cloud of Pepsi, no ice — I asked what was wrong with Lori.

95      "It's Wade," my mother said, scarcely moving her lips. "He's ignored the poor kid all night. She's completely heartbroken."

"Which one is he?"

"Downstairs. Playing table tennis with Gwen Dermott."

"Who's Gwen Dermott?"

"You tell me. She tagged along with the Freibergs."

100      When the men had been drinking long enough to approach Lori and engage her in conversation, she talked and smiled but always sooner or later looked sadly into the distance as she took a long drag on her cigarette, and the men moved soberly away. A few minutes later, during a crush at the bar, as Lou Destaffo stepped in beside me to pour his own drink, I caught a glimpse of sequins in the hall.

"Thanks for taking over, Lou."

I was knocking on the main-floor guest-room door.

"Come in?"

Lori's voice was high and soft with expectation. When she saw who it was, her head pitched back onto the coats. She must have been lying on fifty coats, her body slightly arched. When I approached, she moved over a little to make room. I imagined her rolling down between the bed and wall and becoming lodged there. I took off my shoes and sat alongside her with my heels dug into the edge of the bed.

105      "Look," I said. "I'm really sorry about Wade."

"No, I'm the one who should be sorry."

"You don't have to be sorry."

There was a muffled crash at the door, and my mother rushed in with a cup and saucer. I could see it dripping across the floor. "Coffee!" she cried. "It's all right!" The cup and saucer clattered down on the bedside table and my mother dashed from the room.

"You must like him a lot," I said.

110      The front door slammed, hard. The blow of it shook the house.

"He's all right."

Suddenly there came a violent hammering on the window behind us. I twisted around to see. Nothing. More hammering. A fist! A flash of wild face at the window, mad-eyed and snarling. It fell away. Reappeared. Fell away. Reappeared. Heathcliff on a trampoline. More hammering. For a better look, I turned off the bedside lamp. Immediately the frequency and violence of the hammering increased. At any moment a fist would smash through.

"You'd better turn the light back on," Lori said. "I think he's jealous."

As I switched on the lamp there was a knock at the door. It opened, and my father beckoned. When I went to the door he put an arm around my shoulder and walked me forcibly into the TV room and closed the door behind us.

115 "Where's my car?" I said.

"Listen, Dennis. We've got a kid out here who's pretty much in love." My father looked away. The cartilage in his jaw danced. "Don't spoil it."

I shrugged out of his arm and went back to Lori. I asked her why she put up with it.

"Up with what?"

My mother rushed in holding an ashtray way out in front of her. "Ow by iddoo ums?" she cried breathlessly to no one. Keeping her face averted as if Lori and I were physically making love, she snatched up the unused ashtray from the bedside table and banged the other down in its place. She rushed away. Like a spun plate the ashtray took a long time to settle. *Wrowr wrowr wrowr wrowr* — I was stopping it with my hand when the window hammering resumed. And then my mother was back for the cup and saucer. "All right?" she cried on her way out, spilling coffee again. Immediately then, both my parents were at the door.

120 "Dennis!"

"No! Go away!"

But already they were inside the room, with people from the party peering over their shoulders like idle villagers. I sprang forward and tried to push everybody out, but once I got them into the hall my mother slipped past me into the guest room and locked the door.

"You're on the bar," my father said. His lips were thin and he was holding my arm in a vice grip.

My mother of course would not let me back into the guest room.

125 "My shoes are in there," I said.

"Socks are fine," my father said.

I returned to the bar, where people were helping themselves.

I was carrying more mix up from the basement when my father drew me aside, "Better come with me. We've got a major crisis on our hands out here."

Wade had disappeared.

130 "You check the driveway," my father said.

The driveway was all cars. It was a cold night, and I was wearing my father's galoshes without shoes. I didn't know what I was looking for.

When I got back to the house my father came around the corner. "Is it there?" he asked.

"Is what there?"

"His car."

135 "How would I know his car?"

"He's using the Studebaker."

"Who said you could lend out my car?" I cried.

"Relax," my father said. "We couldn't all use the Chev." He was looking over his shoulder into the darkness. "The river!" he cried suddenly and headed off at a jog across the lawn.

"Dad! The river's frozen!"

140 He stopped and walked back with his hands in his blazer pockets. "Let's go inside," he said. "It's cold out here."

In the kitchen my mother was waiting by the oven for a tray of hors d'oeuvres.

"Where's Lori?" I asked her.

"Where's that big platter? I want you to help me serve."

"Did you leave Lori alone?"

"Here it is. Never you mind about Lori. Lori's just fine." She handed me the platter. "Here. Arrange them nicely."

I passed around the platter, and then I started to drink. Eventually I went to bed. Some time in the night I staggered naked to the bathroom to throw up. The party was over. I slumped on the edge of the bed with my head in my hands, wondering if I was going to throw up again. But I must have thought I was sleeping in my old room and taken a wrong turn from the bathroom. I heard a stir behind me. I was practically sitting on my mother.

"Wade —" my father said.

"George, it's not Wade," my mother whispered. "I think it's Dave, I mean —"

"Dave, go back to your room."

"Dennis?" my mother said.

When I came downstairs the next day Lori was at her usual place. She was wearing jeans and a pale blue cashmere sweater. A cigarette was going in the ashtray alongside her hand.

"Is Wade still asleep?" I asked.

Lori shook her head. "Thanks for being so nice last night. Wade can be such a pain."

"Is he around? I never got a chance to meet him."

"I know. I think you'd really like each other, too. He was hoping he'd see you this morning, but he got a call first thing about his car."

"The Studebaker?"

"That's right. He lent it to somebody he didn't know all that well."

"Somebody who drove it drunk and stoned with a suspended licence and no insurance and the car's a write-off?"

"I think he might have still had his licence," Lori said.

(1995)

# INTERVIEW
## *with Greg Hollingshead*

Q. *How did your childhood influence your writing? Have elements of your early life played a role?*

A. I grew up in a rough neighbourhood, and I didn't have a particularly happy home life. I spent a lot of time alone, I had time to fantasize. I developed an elaborate interior world, filled with secrets and stories. Then the problem arose how to connect this inner world with the one outside. From the age of about eleven to nineteen I wrote poetry; I didn't write stories as such. When I was in Grade 12, I first read the modern short story writers — Joyce, Conrad, Woolf, Chekhov. I had never experienced writing at that level of intensity before then.

Q. *What about your reading as a college student? I know that you studied the philosophers of the eighteenth century, which was a time of balance and control. Did these writers influence you?*

A. I studied the eighteenth century so that I'd have an academic field of expertise far away from the last half of the twentieth century. I studied literary history, not theory. I loved Swift, Sterne, Pope, Fielding. Later I focussed on Berkeley, who was interested in how to talk about the connection between in here and out there — a concern close to my heart. Berkeley said that the essence of reality lies in the experience of it. He was speaking directly to me.

Q. *Like some of the authors of the later eighteenth century, you have stories of manners, also of the grotesque, the absurd, like Swift, and you have a sense of exuberance like Sterne and Fielding. Do you think that these qualities of eighteenth-century fiction find their way into your stories?*

A. I hope they do. One eighteenth-century value I am conscious of is the way I try to make things clear. Clarity is very important to me, especially if I'm dealing with off-kilter people or complex situations. I want the language crisp and precise so that we have a sense of respect for the significance of the situation and the world of the consciousness of the characters.

Q. *You once said that writing is salvage. What is that? How are your stories a salvage operation?*

A. In my short story collection *White Buick* a lot of the stories are based on documentation, so there was a way in which I was rewriting texts. I was taking historical documents and making them into stories. That was a kind of salvage. In a larger sense, my writing is salvage in that it is increasingly concerned with real experience, real bits of stories that have happened to people I know or actual people I have read about. So I think of myself as a collector of fragments and pieces, always looking for ways to put them together to make a compelling narrative. I'm a retriever. In a still larger sense — coming back now to my anxieties as a child — writing has always been for me a way of salvaging experience. Early on, my anxiety about being out of touch with the outside world turned into an anxiety about experience as fleeting, as disappearing very fast down the sink of time. I try to get some things in focus as a way of holding on to them, before they disappear completely.

Q. *That's somewhat like some of the characters in your stories — they wake up and things are gone. They're not successful salvagers.*

A. No, they're not. The author is doing the work they should be doing.

Q. *How did the story "The Naked Man" develop into the finished product?*

A. That's simple to answer. It's an early story, based on personal experience. I came home from England one time to find a young woman living in my room. Her boyfriend also seemed to be an item of the household. This story as it first appeared in the late 1970s had a different ending. There was no car, and when I came to rewrite it for *The Roaring Girl* I didn't like the way I had done it. In the original version, the boyfriend in his jealousy hits her, and the story ends with the girl still in love, saying, "Yes [he hit me], but did you see his eyes?" It was all wrong, the wrong note. It turned the attention on her instead of the narrator. The car became a way of saying somthing more to the point.

Q. *The Studebaker in "The Naked Man" and the white Buick are similar: ornate, glitzy, big, attention-drawing cars; they both get damaged, those two big American 1950s cars.*

A. I see them as images of the male ego, a recreation of internal needs. They are showy, vulnerable — highly vulnerable — they promise mobility; they relate to males as sexual predators. In "White Buick" the car also signifies the immigrant's attempt to fit into this new society. In both stories there are elements of glory and absurdity to the car. In "The Naked Man" it's at the same time in the way and not there — just like the narrator.

Q. *There is a basic situation in many of your works: a social gathering that is almost like the mad tea party in Alice's Adventures in Wonderland. These gatherings aren't social minuets; everyone is going at cross purposes.*

**A.** You get the crispness, the sense of hearing people talk. But the people aren't connecting. Those gatherings, party situations, are about lack of connection. Mavis Gallant calls it "the dialogue of the deaf."

**Q.** *There seems to be a young person at a gathering, and he's lost. It's as if he never got to the party. It almost seems like a reflection of his existential situation.*

**A.** Yes. There are two things I wanted to put together in "The Naked Man." One was the old story of the child who comes to understand that his family can carry on without him, that in some sense he's expendable, that they'll close ranks when he leaves. The family does not revolve around him. He no longer has a place. But also, these particular parents have no sense of boundaries. This is where the comedy comes in. They simultaneously encroach on him (or his car) and are always letting inappropriate people into their own space. I thought those two dynamics would make an interesting combination.

**Q.** *When I read your stories I don't end up feeling despairing, the way I would if I read Camus. The characters are still struggling, still working at keeping their noses above water. I get the idea that there's hope in these stories.*

**A.** I certainly want there to be. I wanted *The Roaring Girl* to have enough comedy, enough buoyancy, in the treatment of the situations — however dark or pessimistic they may be — so that they would not seem hopeless.

**Q.** *There seems to be a lot of felt life — as novelist Henry James called it — it's as if the more you're involved with the characters, the more felt life emerges.*

**A.** There are writers who don't seem to like their characters, they seem to be a long way above them. As a reader I find that can wear me down. One thing I am increasingly aware of is the compassion I feel for my characters. I care about them; I'm not going to do anything rash with them. There was sometimes a kind of heartlessness, a youthful anger, in my earlier work. Balance is what I'm after now. It seemed to work for Shakespeare.

**Q.** *Is it sort of like being a parent, in the sense that when the kid reaches a certain age, you still care, but you have to let him go, all you can give is your love?*

**A.** Yes, that's a good analogy. In the writing process, there is a point you reach where you're sitting around waiting for the characters to make up their minds about what they're going to do next. Your heart's with them, you're hoping they do something worthwhile, something good for themselves. But you never know — you can't force them. Most of James Joyce's characters are far beneath him socially and intellectually, but he cared for them, and he did it without sentimentality, and that is a very difficult balance to achieve.

Q.  *You don't stand god-like above your characters in a judgemental way; you see both sides of their stories.*

A.  I try to do that, for the poise. I try to write about characters who are my equals. As divided as I am.

# Guy Vanderhaeghe (b. 1951)

Born in Esterhazy, Saskatchewan, Guy Vanderhaeghe has twice won the Governor General's Award for fiction, for *Man Descending* (1982), a collection of short stories, and for *The Englishman's Boy* (1996), a novel. Influenced by the works of Margaret Laurence and Sinclair Ross, most of the short stories in *Man Descending* are about men and boys working on the Prairies. In one of them, "Cages," the young narrator expresses his anger and love for his brother and father, and reveals their feelings for him. The central symbol, introduced in the title, develops many meanings as the story progresses.

# CAGES

Here it is, 1967, the Big Birthday. Centennial Year[1] they call it. The whole country is giving itself a pat on the back. Holy shit, boys, we made it.

I made it too for seventeen years, a spotless life, as they say, and for presents I get, in my senior year of high school, my graduating year for chrissakes, a six-month suspended sentence for obstructing a police officer, and my very own personal social worker.

The thing is I don't *need* this social worker woman. She can't tell me anything I haven't already figured out for myself. Take last Wednesday, Miss Krawchuk, who looks like the old widow chicken on the Bugs Bunny Show, the one who's hot to trot for Foghorn Leghorn, says to me: "You know, Billy, your father loves you just as much as he does Gene. He doesn't have a favourite."

Now I can get bullshit at the poolroom any time I want it — and without having to keep an appointment. Maybe Pop *loves* me as much as he does Gene, but Gene is still his favourite kid. Everybody has a favourite kid. I knew that much already when I was only eight and Gene was nine. I figured it out right after Gene almost blinded me.

Picture this. There the two of us were in the basement. It was Christmas holidays and the old man had kicked us downstairs to huck darts at this board he'd give us for a present. Somehow I must've had horseshoes up my ass, I'd beat Gene six games straight. And was he pissed off! He never loses to me at nothing ever. And me being in such a real unique situation, I was giving him the needle-rooney.

"What's that now?" I said. "Is that six or seven that I won?"

"Luck," Gene said, and he sounded like somebody was slowly strangling him. "Luck. Luck. Luck." He could hardly get it out.

And that's when I put the capper on it. I tossed a bull's-eye. "Read 'er and weep," I told him. That's what the old man says whenever he goes out at rummy. It's his needle-rooney. "Read 'er and weep."

That did it. The straw what broke the frigging camel's back. All I saw was his arm blur when he let fly at me. I didn't even have time to *think* about ducking. Bingo. Dead centre in the forehead, right in the middle of the old noggin he drills me with a dart. And there it stuck. Until it loosened a bit. Then it sagged down real slow between my eyes, hung for a second, slid off my nose, and dropped at my feet. I hollered bloody blue murder, you better believe it.

10      For once, Pop didn't show that little bastard any mercy. He took after him from room to room whaling him with this extension cord across the ass, the back of the legs, the shoulders. Really hard. Gene, naturally, was screaming and blubbering and carrying on like it was a goddamn axe murder or something. He'd try to get under a bed, or behind a dresser or something, and get stuck halfway. Then old Gene would really catch it. He didn't know whether to plough forward, back up, shit, or go blind. And all the time the old man was lacing him left and right and saying in this sad, tired voice: "You're the oldest. Don't you know no better? You could of took his eye out, you crazy little bugger."

But that was only justice. He wasn't all that mad at Gene. Me he was mad at. If that makes any sense. Although I have to admit he didn't lay a hand on me. But yell? Christ, can that man yell. Especially at me. Somehow I'm the one that drives him squirrelly.

"Don't you *never, never* tease him again!" he bellowed and his neck started to swell. When the old man gets mad you can see it swell, honest. "You know he can't keep a hold of himself. One day you'll drive him so goddamn goofy with that yap of yours he'll do something terrible! Something he'll regret for the rest of his life. And it'll all be your fault!" The old man had to stop there and slow down or a vein would've exploded in his brain, or his arsehole popped inside out, or something. "So smarten up," he said, a little quieter, finally, "or you'll be the death of me and all my loved ones."

So there you are. I never pretended the world was fair, and I never bitched because it wasn't. But I do resent the hell out of being forced to listen to some dried-up old broad who gets paid by the government to tell me it is. Fuck her. She never lived in the Simpson household with my old man waiting around for Gene to do that *terrible thing*. It spoils the atmosphere. Makes a person edgy, you know?

Of course, Gene has done a fair number of *bad things* while everybody was waiting around for him to do the one great big *terrible thing*; and he's done them in a fair number of places. That's because the old man is a miner, and for a while there he was always telling some foreman to go piss up a rope. So we moved around a lot. That's why the Simpson household has a real history. But Gene's is the best of all. In Elliot Lake he failed grade three; in Bombertown[2] he got picked up for shoplifting; in Flin Flon[3] he broke some snotty kid's nose and got sent home from school. And every grade he goes higher, it gets a little worse. Last year, when we were both in grade eleven, I'm sure the old man was positive Gene was finally going to pull off the *terrible thing* he's been worrying about as long as I can remember.

15      It's crazy. Lots of times when I think about it, I figure I don't get on with the old man because I treat him nice. That I try too hard to make him like me. I'm not the way Gene is, I respect Pop. He slogs it out, shift after shift, on a shitty job he hates. Really hates. In fact, he told me once he would have liked

---

2 mining towns in northern Ontario. 3 mining town in Manitoba.

to been a farmer. Which only goes to show you how crazy going down that hole day after day makes you. Since we moved to Saskatchewan I've seen lots of farmers, and if you ask me, being one doesn't have much to recommend it.

But getting back to that business of being nice to Dad. Last year I started waiting up for him to come home from the afternoon shift. The one that runs from four p.m. in the afternoon until midnight. It wasn't half bad. Most nights I'd fall asleep on the chesterfield with the TV playing after Mom went to bed. Though lots of times I'd do my best to make it past the national news to wait for Earl Cameron[4] and his collection of screwballs. Those guys kill me. They're always yapping off because somebody or something rattled their chain. Most of those characters with all the answers couldn't pour piss out of a rubber boot if they read the instructions printed on the sole. They remind me of Gene; he's got all the answers too. But still, quite a few of them are what you'd call witty. Which Gene is in his own way too.

But most times, as I say, I'd doze off. Let me give you a sample evening. About twelve-thirty the lights of his half-ton would come shooting into the living-room, bouncing off the walls, scooting along the ceiling when he wheeled into the driveway like a madman. It was the lights flashing in my eyes that woke me up most nights, and if that didn't do it there was always his grand entrance. When the old man comes into the house, from the sound of it you'd think he never heard of door knobs. I swear sometimes I'm sure he's taking a battering-ram to the back door. Then he thunks his lunch bucket on the kitchen counter and bowls his hard hat into the landing. This is because he always comes home from work mad. Never once in his life has a shift ever gone right for that man. Never. They could pack his pockets with diamonds and send him home two hours early and he'd still bitch. So every night was pretty much the same. He had a mad on. Like in my sample night.

He flicked on the living-room light and tramped over to his orange recliner with the bottle of Boh. "If you want to ruin your eyes, do it on school-books, not on watching TV in the goddamn dark. It's up to somebody in this outfit to make something of themselves."

"I was sleeping."

20    "You ought to sleep in bed." *Keerash!* He weighs two hundred and forty-four pounds and he never sits down in a chair. He falls into it. "Who's that? Gary Cooper?" he asked. He figures any movie star on the late show taller than Mickey Rooney is Cooper. He doesn't half believe you when you tell him they aren't.

"Cary Grant."

"What?"

"Cary Grant. Not Gary Cooper. Cary Grant."

"Oh." There he sat in his recliner, big meaty shoulders sagging, belly propped up on his belt buckle like a pregnant pup's. Eyes red and sore, hair all mussed up, the top of his beer bottle peeking out of his fist like a little brown nipple. He has cuts all over those hands of his, barked knuckles and raspberries that never heal because the salt in the potash ore keeps them open, eats right down to the bone sometimes.

25    "How'd it go tonight?"

4 host of the Canadian Broadcasting Corporation's National News during the 1960s.

"Usual shit. We had a breakdown." He paused. "Where's your brother? In bed?"

"Out."

"Out? Out? *Out?* What kind of a goddamn answer is that? Out where?"

I shrugged.

30 "Has he got his homework done?" That's the kind of question I get asked. *Has your brother got his homework done?*

"How the hell would I know?"

"I don't know why you don't help him with his schoolwork," the old man said, peeved as usual.

"You mean do it for him."

"Did I say that? Huh? I said help him. Didn't I say that?" he griped, getting his shirt in a knot.

35 He thinks it's that easy. Just screw the top off old Gene and pour it in. No problem. Like an oil change.

"He's got to be around to help," I said.

That reminded him. He jumped out of the chair and gawked up and down the deserted street. "It's almost one o'clock. On a school night. I'll kick his ass." He sat down and watched the screen for a while and sucked on his barley sandwich.

Finally, he made a stab at acting civilized. "So how's baseball going?"

"What?"

40 "Baseball. For chrissakes clean out your ears. How's it going?"

"I quit last year. Remember?"

"Oh yeah." He didn't say nothing at first. Then he said: "You shouldn't have. You wasn't a bad catcher."

"The worst. No bat and no arm — just a flipper. They stole me blind."

"But you had the head," said the old man. And the way he said it made him sound like he was pissed at me for mean-mouthing myself. That surprised me. I felt kind of good about that. "You had the head," he repeated, shaking his own. "I never told you but Al came up to me at work and said you were smart back there behind the plate. He said he wished Gene had your head."

45 I can't say that surprised me. Gene is one of those cases of a million-dollar body carrying around a ten-cent head. He's a natural. Flop out his glove and, smack, the ball sticks. He's like Mickey Mantle. You know those stop-action photos where they caught Mickey with his eyes glommed onto the bat, watching the ball jump off the lumber? That's Gene. And he runs like a Negro, steals bases like Maury Wills for chrissake.

But stupid and conceited? You wouldn't believe the half of it. Give him the sign to bunt to move a runner and he acts as if you're asking him to bare his ass in public. Not him. He's a big shot. He swings for the fence. Nothing less. And old Gene is always in the game, if you know what I mean? I don't know what happens when he gets on base, maybe he starts thinking of the hair pie in the stands admiring him or something, but he always dozes off at the wheel. Once he even started to comb his hair at first base. Here it is, a 3 and 2 count with two men out, and my brother forgets to run on the pitch because he's combing his hair. I could have died. Really I could have. The guy is such an embarrassment sometimes.

"He can have my head," I said to Pop. "If I get his girls."

That made the old man wince. He's sure that Gene is going to knock up one of those seat-covers he takes out and make him a premature grandpa.

"You pay attention to school. There's plenty of time later for girls." And up he jumped again and stuck his nose against the window looking for Gene again. Mom has to wash the picture window once a week; he spots it all up with nose grease looking for Gene.

50   "I don't know why your mother lets him out of the house," he said. "Doesn't she have any control over that boy?"

That's what he does, blames everybody but himself. Oh hell, maybe nobody's to blame. Maybe Gene is just Gene, and there's nothing to be done about it.

"I don't know what she's supposed to do. You couldn't keep him in if you parked a tank in the driveway and strung barbed wire around the lot."

Of course that was the wrong thing to say. I usually say it.

"Go to bed!" he yelled at me. "You're no better than your brother. I don't see you in bed neither. What'd I do, raise alley cats or kids? Why can't you two keep hours like human beings!"

55   And then the door banged and we knew the happy wanderer was home. Gene makes almost as much noise as the old man does when he comes in. It's beneath his dignity to sneak in like me.

Dad hoisted himself out of the chair and steamed off for the kitchen. He can move pretty quick for a big guy when he wants to. Me, I was in hot pursuit. I don't like to miss much.

Old Gene was hammered, and grinning from ass-hole to ear-lobes. The boy's got a great smile. Even when he grins at old ladies my mother's age you can tell they like it.

"Come here and blow in my face," said my father.

"Go on with you," said Gene. All of a sudden the smile was gone and he was irritated. He pushed past Pop, took the milk out of the fridge and started to drink out of the container.

60   "Use a glass."

Gene burped. He's a slob.

"You stink of beer," said the old man. "Who buys beer for a kid your age?"

"I ain't drunk," said Gene.

"Not much. Your eyes look like two piss-holes in the snow."

65   "Sure, sure," said Gene. He lounged, he swivelled over to me and lifted my Players out of my shirt pocket. "I'll pay you back tomorrow," he said, taking out a smoke. I heard that one before.

"I don't want to lose my temper," said Dad, being patient with him as usual, "so don't push your luck, sunshine." The two of them eyeballed it, hard. Finally Gene backed down, looked away and fiddled with his matches. "I don't ride that son of a bitch of a cage up and down for my health. I do it for you two," Dad said. "But I swear to God, Gene, if you blow this year of school there'll be a pair of new work boots for you on the back step, come July 1. Both of you know my rules. Go to school, work, or pack up. I'm not having bums put their feet under my table."

"I ain't scared of work," said Gene. "Anyways, school's a pain in the ass."

"Well, you climb in the cage at midnight with three hours of sleep and see if *that* ain't a pain in the ass. Out there nobody says, please do this, please do that. It ain't school out there, it's life."

"Ah, I wouldn't go to the mine. The mine sucks."

"Just what the hell do you think you'd do?"

"He'd open up shop as a brain surgeon," I said. Of course, Gene took a slap at me and grabbed at my shirt. He's a tough guy. He wasn't really mad, but he likes to prevent uppityness.

"You go to bed!" the old man hollered. "You ain't helping matters!"

So off I went. I could hear them wrangling away even after I closed my door. You'd wonder how my mother does it, but she sleeps through it all. I think she's just so goddamn tired of the three of us she's gone permanently deaf to the sound of our voices. She just don't hear us any more.

The last thing I heard before I dropped off was Pop saying: "I've rode that cage all my life, and take it from me, there wasn't a day I didn't wish I'd gone to school and could sit in an office in a clean white shirt." Sometimes he can't remember what he wants to be, a farmer or a pencil-pusher.

The cage. He's always going on about the cage. It's what the men at the mine call the elevator car they ride down the shaft. They call it that because it's all heavy reinforced-steel mesh. The old man has this cage on the brain. Ever since we were little kids he's been threatening us with it. *Make something of yourself*, he'd warn us, *or you'll end up like your old man, a monkey in a cage! Or: What's this, Gene? Failed arithmetic? Just remember, dunces don't end up in the corner. Hell no, they end up in the cage! Look at me!* My old man really hates that cage and the mine. He figures it's the worst thing you can threaten anybody with.

I was in the cage, once. A few years ago, when I was fourteen, the company decided they'd open the mine up for tours. It was likely the brainstorm of some public relations tit sitting in head office in Chicago. In my book it was kind of like taking people into the slaughterhouse to prove you're kind to the cows. Anyway, Pop offered to take us on one of his days off. As usual, he was about four years behind schedule. When we were maybe eleven we might have been nuts about the idea, but just then it didn't thrill us too badly. Gene, who is about as subtle as a bag of hammers, said flat out he wasn't interested. I could see right away the old man was hurt by that. It isn't often he plays the buddy to his boys, and he probably had the idea he could whiz us about the machines and stuff. Impress the hell out of us. So it was up to me to slobber and grin like some kind of half-wit over the idea, to perk him up, see? Everybody suffers when the old man gets into one of his moods.

Of course, like always when I get sucked into this good-turn business, I shaft myself. I'd sort of forgotten how much I don't like tight places and being closed in. When we were younger, Gene used to make me go berserk by holding me under the covers, or stuffing a pillow in my face, or locking me in the garage whenever he got the chance. The jerk.

To start with, they packed us in the cage with twelve other people, which didn't help matters any. Right away my chest got tight and I felt like I couldn't breathe. Then the old cables started groaning and grinding and this fine red dust like chili powder sprinkled down through the mesh and dusted our hard hats with the word GUEST stencilled on them. It was rust. Kind of makes you think.

"Here we go," said Pop.

80     We went. It was like all of a sudden the floor fell away from under my boots. That cage just dropped in the shaft like a stone down a well. It rattled and creaked and banged. The bare light bulb in the roof started to flicker, and all the faces around me started to dance and shake up and down in the dark. A wind twisted up my pant-legs and I could hear the cables squeak and squeal. It made me think of big fat fucking rats.

"She needs new brake shoes," said this guy beside me and he laughed. He couldn't fool me. He was scared shitless too, in his own way.

"It's not the fall that kills you," his neighbour replied. "It's the sudden stop." There's a couple of horses' patoots in every crowd.

We seemed to drop forever. Everybody got quieter and quieter. They even stopped shuffling and coughing. Down. Down. Down. Then the cage started to slow, I felt a pressure build in my knees and my crotch and my ears. The wire box started to shiver and clatter and shake. *Bang!* We stopped. The cage bobbed a little up and down like a yo-yo on the end of a string. Not much though, just enough to make you queasy.

"Last stop, Hooterville!" said the guide, who thought he was funny, and threw back the door. Straight ahead I could see a low-roofed big open space with tunnels running from it into the ore. Every once in a while I could see the light from a miner's helmet jump around in the blackness of one of those tunnels like a firefly flitting in the night.

85     First thing I thought was: *What if I get lost? What if I lose the group? There's miles and miles and miles of tunnel under here.* I caught a whiff of the air. It didn't smell like air up top. It smelled used. You could taste the salt. *I'm suffocating,* I thought. *I can't breathe this shit.*

I hadn't much liked the cage but this was worse. When I was in the shaft I knew there was a patch of sky over my head with a few stars in it and clouds and stuff. But all of a sudden I realized how deep we were. How we were sort of like worms crawling in the guts of some dead animal. Over us were billions, no trillions, of tons of rock and dirt and mud pressing down. I could imagine it caving in and falling on me, crushing my chest, squeezing the air out slowly, dust fine as flour trickling into my eyes and nostrils, or mud plugging my mouth so I couldn't even scream. And then just lying there in the dark, my legs and arms pinned so I couldn't even twitch them. For a long time maybe. Crazy, lunatic stuff was what I started to think right on the spot.

My old man gave me a nudge to get out. We were the last.

"No," I said quickly and hooked my fingers in the mesh.

"We get out here," said the old man. He hadn't caught on yet.

90     "No, I can't," I whispered. He must have read the look on my face then. I think he knew he couldn't have pried me off that mesh with a gooseneck and winch.

Fred, the cage operator, lifted his eyebrows at Pop. "What's up, Jack?"

"The kid's sick," said Pop. "We'll take her up. He don't feel right." My old man was awful embarrassed.

Fred said, "I wondered when it'd happen. Taking kids and women down the hole."

"Shut your own goddamn hole," said the old man. "He's got the flu. He was up all last night."

95 Fred looked what you'd call sceptical.

"Last time I take you any place nice," the old man said under his breath.

\*\*\*\*\*

The last day of school has always got to be some big deal. By nine o'clock all the dipsticks are roaring their cars up and down main street with their goofy broads hanging out their windows yelling, and trying to impress on one another how drunk they are.

Dad sent me to look for Gene because he didn't come home for supper at six. I found him in the poolroom playing dollar-a-hand poker pool.

"Hey, little brother," he waved to me from across the smoky poolroom, "come on here and I'll let you hold my cards!" I went over. He grinned to the goofs he was playing with. "You watch out now, boys," he said, "my little brother always brings me luck. Not that I need it," he explained to me, winking.

100 Yeah, I always brought him luck. *I* kept track of the game. *I* figured out what order to take the balls down. *I* reminded him not to put somebody else out and to play the next guy safe instead of slamming off some cornball shot. When *I* did all that Gene won — because I brought him luck. Yeah.

Gene handed me his cards. "You wouldn't believe these two," he said to me out of the corner of his mouth, "genuine plough jockeys. These boys couldn't find their ass in the dark with both hands. I'm fifteen dollars to the good."

I admit they didn't look too swift. The biggest one, who was *big*, was wearing an out-of-town team jacket, a Massey-Ferguson cap, and shit-kicker wellingtons. He was maybe twenty-one, but his skin hadn't cleared up yet by no means. His pan looked like all-dressed pizza, heavy on the cheese. His friend was a dinky little guy with his hair designed into a duck's ass. The kind of guy who hates the Beatles. About two feet of a dirty comb was sticking out of his ass pocket.

Gene broke the rack and the nine went down. His shot.

"Dad's looking for you. He wants to know if you passed," I said.

105 "You could've told him."

"Well, I didn't."

"Lemme see the cards." I showed him. He had a pair of treys, a six, a seven, and a lady. Right away he stopped to pocket the three. I got a teacher who always talks about thought processes. Gene doesn't have them.

"Look at the table," I said. "Six first and you can come around up here." I pointed.

"No coaching," said Pizza Face. I could see this one was a poor loser.

110 Gene shifted his stance and potted the six.

"What now?" he asked.

"The queen, and don't forget to put pants on her." I paused. "Pop figured you were going to make it. He really did, Gene."

"So tough titty. I didn't. Who the hell cares? He had your suck card to slobber over, didn't he?" He drilled the lady in the side pocket. No backspin. He'd hooked himself on the three. "Fuck."

"The old man is on graveyard shift. You better go home and face the music before he goes to work. It'll be worse in the morning when he needs sleep," I warned him.

115    "Screw him."

I could see Gene eyeballing the four. He didn't have any four in his hand, so I called him over and showed him his cards. "You can't shoot the four. It's not in your hand."

"Just watch me." He winked. "I've been doing it all night. It's all pitch and no catch with these prizes." Gene strolled back to the table and coolly stroked down the four. He had shape for the three which slid in the top pocket like shit through a goose. He cashed in on the seven. "That's it, boys," he said. "That's all she wrote."

I was real nervous. I tried to bury the hand in the deck but the guy with the runny face stopped me. He was getting tired of losing, I guess. Gene doesn't even cheat smart. You got to let them win once in a while.

"Gimme them cards," he said. He started counting the cards off against the balls, flipping down the boards on the felt. "Three." He nodded. "Six, seven, queen. I guess you got them all," he said slowly, with a look on his face like he was pissing ground glass.

120    That's when Duck Ass chirped up. "Hey, Marvin," he said, "that guy shot the four. He shot the four."

"Nah," said Gene.

Marvin studied on this for a second, walked over to the table and pulled the four ball out of the pocket. Just like little Jack Horner lifting the plum out of the pie. "Yeah," he said. "You shot the four."

"Jeez," said Gene, "I guess I did. Honest mistake. Look, here's a dollar for each of you." He took two bills out of his shirt pocket. "You got to pay for your mistakes is what I was always taught."

"I bet you he's been cheating all along," said Duck Ass.

125    "My brother don't cheat," I said.

"I want all my money back," said Marvin. Quite loud. Loud enough that some heads turned and a couple of tables stopped playing. There was what you would call a big peanut gallery, it being the beginning of vacation and the place full of junior high kids and stags.

"You can kiss my ass, bozo," said Gene. "Like my brother here said, I never cheated nobody in my life."

"You give us our money back," threatened Marvin, "or I'll pull your head off, you skinny little prick."

Guys were starting to drift towards us, curious. The manager, Fat Bert, was easing his guts out from behind the cash register.

130    "Give them their money, Gene," I said, "and let's get out of here."

"No."

Well, that was that. You can't change his mind. I took a look at old Marvin. As I said before, Marvin was *big*. But what was worse than that was that he had this real determined look people who aren't too bright get when they finally dib on to the fact they've been hosed and somebody has been laughing up his sleeve at them. They don't like it too hot, believe me.

"Step outside, shit-head," said Marvin.

"Fight," somebody said encouragingly. A real clump of ringsiders was starting to gather. "Fight." Bert came hustling up, bumping his way through the kids with his bay window. "Outside, you guys. I don't want nothing broke in here. Get out or I'll call the cops."

135　　Believe me, was I tense. Real tense. I know Gene pretty well and I was sure that he had looked at old Marvin's muscles trying to bust out everywhere. Any second I figured he was going to even the odds by pasting old Marv in the puss with his pool cue, or at least sucker-punching him.

But Gene is full of surprises. All of a sudden he turned peacemaker. He laid down his pool cue (which I didn't figure was too wise) and said: "You want to fight over this?" He held up the four ball. "Over this? An honest mistake?"

"Sure I do," said Marvin. "You're fucking right I do, cheater."

"Cheater, cheater," said Duck Ass. I was looking him over real good because I figured if something started in there I'd get him to tangle with.

Gene shrugged and even kind of sighed, like the hero does in the movies when he has been forced into a corner and has to do something that is against his better nature. He tossed up the four ball once, looked at it, and then reached behind him and shoved it back into the pocket. "All right," he said, slouching a little and jamming his hands into his jacket pockets. "Let's go, sport."

140　　That started the stampede. "Fight! Fight!" The younger kids, the ones thirteen and fourteen, were really excited; the mob kind of swept Marvin and Gene out the door, across the street and into the OK Economy parking lot where most beefs get settled. There's lots of dancing-room there. A nice big ring.

Marvin settled in real quick. He tugged the brim of his Massey-Ferguson special a couple of times, got his dukes up and started to hop around like he'd stepped right out of the pages of *Ring* magazine. He looked pretty stupid, especially when Gene just looked at him, and kept his hands rammed in his jacket pockets. Marvin kind of clomped from foot to foot for a bit and then he said, "Get 'em up."

"You get first punch," said Gene.

"What?" said Marv. He was so surprised his yap fell open.

"If I hit you first," said Gene, "you'll charge me with assault. I know your kind."

145　　Marvin stopped clomping. I suspect it took too much coordination for him to clomp and think at the same time. "Oh no," he said, "I ain't falling for that. If I hit *you* first, you'll charge *me* with assault." No flies on Marvin. "*You* get the first punch."

"Fight. Come on, fight," said some ass-hole, real disgusted with all the talk and no action.

"Oh no," said Gene. "I ain't hitting *you* first."

Marvin brought his hands down. "Come on, come on, let fly."

"You're sure?" asked Gene.

150　　"Give her your best shot," said Marvin. "You couldn't hurt a fly, you scrawny shit. Quit stalling. Get this show on the road."

Gene uncorked on him. It looked like a real pansy punch. His right arm whipped out of his jacket pocket, stiff at the elbow like a girl's when she slaps.

It didn't look like it had nothing behind it, sort of like Gene had smacked him kind of contemptuous in the mouth with the flat of his hand. That's how it looked. It *sounded* like he'd hit him in the mouth with a ball-peen hammer. Honest to God, you could hear the teeth crunch when they broke.

Big Marvin dropped on his knees like he'd been shot in the back of the neck. His hands flew up to his face and the blood just ran through his fingers and into his cuffs. It looked blue under the parking-lot lights. There was an awful lot of it.

"Get up, you dick licker," said Gene.

Marvin pushed off his knees with a crazy kind of grunt that might have been a sob. I couldn't tell. He came up under Gene's arms, swept him off his feet and dangled him in the air, crushing his ribs in a bear hug.

"*Waauugh!*" said Gene. I started looking around right smartly for something to hit the galoot with before he popped my brother like a pimple.

But then Gene lifted his fist high above Marvin's head and brought it down on his skull, hard as he could. It made a sound like he was banging coconuts together. Marvin sagged a little at the knees and staggered. *Chunk! Chunk!* Gene hit him two more times and Marvin toppled over backwards. My brother landed on top of him and right away started pasting him left and right. Everybody was screaming encouragement. There was no invitation to the dick licker to get up this time. Gene was still clobbering him when I saw the cherry popping on the cop car two blocks away. I dragged him off Marvin.

"Cops," I said, yanking at his sleeve. Gene was trying to get one last kick at Marvin. "Come on, fucker," he was yelling. "Fight now!"

"Jesus," I said, looking at Gene's jacket and shirt, "you stupid bugger, you're all over blood." It was smeared all over him. Marvin tried to get up. He only made it to his hands and knees. There he stayed, drooling blood and saliva on the asphalt. The crowd started to edge away as the cop car bounced up over the curb and gave a long, low whine out of its siren.

I took off my windbreaker and gave it to Gene. He pulled off his jacket and threw it down. "Get the fuck out of here," I said. "Beat it."

"I took the wheels off his little red wagon," said Gene. "It don't pull so good now." His hands were shaking and so was his voice. He hadn't had half enough yet. "I remember that other guy," he said. "Where's his friend?"

I gave him a shove. "Get going." Gene slid into the crowd that was slipping quickly away. Then I remembered his hockey jacket. It was wet with blood. It also had flashes with his name and number on it. It wouldn't take no Sherlock Holmes cop to figure out who'd beat on Marvin. I picked it up and hugged it to my belly. Right away I felt something hard in the pocket. Hard and round. I started to walk away. I heard a car door slam. I knew what was in that pocket. The controversial four ball old Gene had palmed when he pretended to put it back. He likes to win.

I must have been walking too fast or with a guilty hunch to my shoulders, because I heard the cop call, "Hey you, the kid with the hair." Me, I'm kind of a hippy for this place, I guess. Lots of people mention my hair.

I ran. I scooted round the corner of the supermarket and let that pool ball fly as hard as I could, way down the alley. I never rifled a shot like that in my life. If coach Al had seen me trigger that baby he'd have strapped me into a belly pad himself. Of course, a jacket don't fly for shit. The bull came storming around the corner just as I give it the heave-ho. I was kind of caught with shit on my face, if you know what I mean?

*****

Now a guy with half a brain could have talked his way out of that without too much trouble. Even a cop understands how somebody would try to help his brother. They don't hold it too much against you. And I couldn't really protect Gene. That geek Marvin would have flapped his trap if I hadn't. And it wasn't as if I hadn't done old Gene *some* good. After all, they never found out about that pool ball. The judge would have pinned Gene's ears back for him if he'd known he was going around thwacking people with a hunk of shatter-proof plastic. So Gene came out smelling like a rose, same suspended sentence as me, and a reputation for having hands of stone.

165 But at a time like that you get the nuttiest ideas ever. I watched them load Marvin in a squad car to drive him to the hospital while I sat in the back seat of another. And I thought to myself: *I'll play along with this. Let the old man come down to the cop shop over me for once. Me he takes for granted. Let him worry about Billy for a change. It wouldn't hurt him.*

So I never said one word about not being the guy who bopped Marvin. It was kind of fun in a crazy way, making like a hard case. At the station I was real rude and lippy. Particularly to a sergeant who was a grade A dink if I ever saw one. It was only when they took my shoe-laces and belt that I started to get nervous.

"Ain't you going to call my old man?" I asked.

The ass-hole sergeant gave me a real smile. "In the morning," he said. "All in good time."

"In the morning?" And then I said like a dope: "Where am I going to sleep?"

170 "Show young Mr. Simpson where he's going to sleep," said the sergeant. He smiled again. It looked like a ripple on a slop pail. The constable who he was ordering around like he was his own personal slave took me down into the basement of the station. Down there it smelled of stale piss and old puke. I kind of gagged. I got a weak stomach.

Boy, was I nervous. I saw where he was taking me. There were four cells. They weren't even made out of bars, just metal strips riveted into a cross hatch you couldn't stick your hand through. They were all empty.

"Your choice," said the corporal. He was real humorous too, like his boss.

"You don't have to put me in one of them, sir," I said. "I won't run away."

"That's what all the criminals say." He opened the door. "Entrez-vous."

175 I was getting my old crazy feeling really bad. Really bad. I felt kind of dizzy. "I got this thing," I said, "about being locked up. It's torture."

"Get in."

"No — please," I said. "I'll sit upstairs. I won't bother anybody."

"You think you got a choice? You don't have a choice. Move your ass."

I was getting ready to cry. I could feel it. I was going to bawl in front of a cop. "I didn't do it," I said. "I never beat him up. Swear to Jesus I didn't."

180 "I'm counting three," he said, "and then I'm applying the boots to your backside."

It all came out. Just like that. *"It was my fucking ass-hole brother, Gene!"* I screamed. The only thing I could think of was, if they put me in there I'll be off my head by morning. I really will. *"I didn't do nothing! I never do nothing! You can't put me in there for him!"*

\*\*\*\*\*

They called my old man. I guess I gave a real convincing performance. Not that I'm proud of it. I actually got sick on the spot from nerves. I just couldn't hold it down.

Pop had to sign for me and promise to bring Gene down in the morning. It was about twelve-thirty when everything got cleared up. He'd missed his shift and his ride in the cage.

When we got in the car he didn't start it. We just sat there with the windows rolled down. It was a beautiful night and there were lots of stars swimming in the sky. This town is small enough that street-lights and neon don't interfere with the stars. It's the only thing I like about this place. There's plenty of sky and lots of air to breathe.

185 "Your brother wasn't enough," he said. "You I trusted."

"I only tried to help him."

"You goddamn snitch." He needed somebody to take it out on, so he belted me. Right on the snout with the back of his hand. It started to bleed. I didn't try to stop it. I just let it drop on those goddamn furry seat-covers that he thinks are the cat's ass. "They were going to put me in this place, this cage, for him, for that useless shit!" I yelled. I'd started to cry. "No more, Pop. He failed! He failed on top of it all! So is he going to work? You got the boots ready on the back step? Huh? Is he going down in the fucking cage?"

"Neither one of you is going down in the cage. Not him, not you," he said.

"Nah, I didn't think so," I said, finally wiping at my face with the back of my hand. "I didn't think so."

190 "I don't have to answer to you," he said. "You just can't get inside his head. You were always the smart one. I didn't have to worry about you. You always knew what to do. But Gene…" He pressed his forehead against the steering-wheel, hard. "Billy, I see him doing all sorts of stuff. Stuff you can't imagine. I see it until it makes me sick." He looked at me. His face was yellow under the street-light, yellow like a lemon. "I try so hard with him. But he's got no sense. He just does things. He could have killed that other boy. He wouldn't even think of that, you know." All of a sudden the old man's face got all crumpled and creased like paper when you ball it up. "What's going to happen to him?" he said, louder than he had to. "What's going to happen to Eugene?" It was sad. It really was.

I can never stay mad at my old man. Maybe because we're so much alike, even though he can't see it for looking the other way. Our minds work alike. I'm a chip off the old block. Don't ever doubt it.

"Nothing."

"Billy," he said, "you mean it?"

I knew what he was thinking. "Yes," I said. "I'll do my best."

(1982)

# Amy Tan (b. 1952)

Born in Oakland, California, Amy Tan visited her ancestral homeland of China when she was 35. This visit, during which she met her sisters from her mother's first marriage, inspired the writing of her first book, *The Joy Luck Club*, a series of interrelated stories about Chinese mothers and their American-born daughters. "Two Kinds" depicts the conflicts, based on cultural differences and expectations, between one of these pairs. Like the narrator of Jack Hodgins's "The Concert Stages of Europe" (see page 1127), the young girl resists her mother's hopes of her achieving musical celebrity. The title, which refers explicitly to the piece the girl plays at the recital, implicitly refers to the many tensions the narrator feels within herself and between herself and her mother.

# TWO KINDS

My mother believed you could be anything you wanted to be in America. You could open a restaurant. You could work for the government and get good retirement. You could buy a house with almost no money down. You could become rich. You could become instantly famous.

"Of course you can be prodigy, too," my mother told me when I was nine. "You can be best anything. What does Auntie Lindo know? Her daughter, she is only best tricky."

America was where all my mother's hopes lay. She had come here in 1949 after losing everything in China: her mother and father, her family home, her first husband, and two daughters, twin baby girls. But she never looked back with regret. There were so many ways for things to get better.

*****

We didn't immediately pick the right kind of prodigy. At first my mother thought I could be a Chinese Shirley Temple.[1] We'd watch Shirley's old movies on TV as though they were training films. My mother would poke my arm and say, "*Ni kan*" — You watch. And I would see Shirley tapping her feet, or singing a sailor song, or pursing her lips into a very round O while saying, "Oh my goodness."

5     "*Ni Kan*," said my mother as Shirley's eyes flooded with tears. "You already know how. Don't need talent for crying!"

Soon after my mother got this idea about Shirley Temple, she took me to a beauty training school in the Mission district[2] and put me in the hands of a student who could barely hold the scissors without shaking. Instead of getting big fat curls, I emerged with an uneven mass of crinkly black fuzz. My mother dragged me off to the bathroom and tried to wet down my hair.

"You look like Negro Chinese," she lamented, as if I had done this on purpose.

---

1 popular child actor in motion pictures of the 1930s. 2 fashionable residential district of San Francisco.

The instructor of the beauty training school had to lop off these soggy clumps to make my hair even again. "Peter Pan is very popular these days," the instructor assured my mother. I now had hair the length of a boy's, with straight-across bangs that hung at a slant two inches above my eyebrows. I liked the haircut and it made me actually look forward to my future fame.

In fact, in the beginning, I was just as excited as my mother, maybe even more so. I pictured this prodigy part of me as many different images, trying each one on for size. I was a dainty ballerina girl standing by the curtains, waiting to hear the right music that would send me floating on my tiptoes. I was like the Christ child lifted out of the straw manger, crying with holy indignity. I was Cinderella stepping from her pumpkin carriage with sparkly cartoon music filling the air.

10    In all of my imaginings, I was filled with a sense that I would soon become perfect. My mother and father would adore me. I would be beyond reproach. I would never feel the need to sulk for anything.

But sometimes the prodigy in me became impatient. "If you don't hurry up and get me out of here, I'm disappearing for good," it warned. "And then you'll always be nothing."

Every night after dinner, my mother and I would sit at the Formica kitchen table. She would present new tests, taking her examples from stories of amazing children she had read in *Ripley's Believe It or Not*, or *Good Housekeeping*, *Reader's Digest*, and a dozen other magazines she kept in a pile in our bathroom. My mother got these magazines from people whose houses she cleaned. And since she cleaned many houses each week, we had a great assortment. She would look through them all, searching for stories about remarkable children.

The first night she brought out a story about a three-year-old boy who knew the capitals of all the states and even most of the European countries. A teacher was quoted as saying the little boy could also pronounce the names of the foreign cities correctly.

"What's the capital of Finland?" my mother asked me, looking at the magazine story.

15    All I knew was the capital of California, because Sacramento was the name of the street we lived on in Chinatown. "Nairobi!" I guessed, saying the most foreign word I could think of. She checked to see if that was possibly one way to pronounce "Helsinki"[3] before showing me the answer.

The tests got harder — multiplying numbers in my head, finding the queen of hearts in a deck of cards, trying to stand on my head without using my hands, predicting the daily temperatures in Los Angeles, New York, and London.

One night I had to look at a page from the Bible for three minutes and then report everything I could remember. "Now Jehoshaphat[4] had riches and honor in abundance and . . . that's all I remember, Ma," I said.

And after seeing my mother's disappointed face once again, something inside of me began to die. I hated the tests, the raised hopes and failed expectations. Before going to bed that night, I looked in the mirror above the bathroom sink

---

3 Nairobi is the capital city of Kenya; Helsinki, the capital of Finland.    4 king of Judah in the ninth century B.C.

and when I saw only my face staring back — and that it would always be this ordinary face — I began to cry. Such a sad, ugly girl! I made high-pitched noises like a crazed animal, trying to scratch out the face in the mirror.

And then I saw what seemed to be the prodigy side of me — because I had never seen that face before. I looked at my reflection, blinking so I could see more clearly. The girl staring back at me was angry, powerful. This girl and I were the same. I had new thoughts, willful thoughts, or rather thoughts filled with lots of won'ts. I won't let her change me, I promised myself. I won't be what I'm not.

20    So now on nights when my mother presented her tests, I performed listlessly, my head propped on one arm. I pretended to be bored. And I was. I got so bored I started counting the bellows of the foghorns out on the bay while my mother drilled me in other areas. The sound was comforting and reminded me of the cow jumping over the moon. And the next day, I played a game with myself, seeing if my mother would give up on me before eight bellows. After a while I usually counted only one, maybe two bellows at most. At last she was beginning to give up hope.

Two or three months had gone by without any mention of my being a prodigy again. And then one day my mother was watching *The Ed Sullivan Show*[5] on TV. The TV was old and the sound kept shorting out. Every time my mother got halfway up from the sofa to adjust the set, the sound would go back on and Ed would be talking. As soon as she sat down, Ed would go silent again. She got up, the TV broke into loud piano music. She sat down. Silence. Up and down, back and forth, quiet and loud. It was like a stiff embraceless dance between her and the TV set. Finally she stood by the set with her hand on the sound dial.

She seemed entranced by the music, a little frenzied piano piece with this mesmerizing quality, sort of quick passages and then teasing lilting ones before it returned to the quick playful parts.

"*Ni kan*," my mother said, calling me over with hurried hand gestures, "Look here."

I could see why my mother was fascinated by the music. It was being pounded out by a little Chinese girl, about nine years old, with a Peter Pan haircut. The girl had the sauciness of a Shirley Temple. She was proudly modest like a proper Chinese child. And she also did this fancy sweep of a curtsy, so that the fluffy skirt of her white dress cascaded slowly to the floor like the petals of a large carnation.

25    In spite of these warning signs, I wasn't worried. Our family had no piano and we couldn't afford to buy one, let alone reams of sheet music and piano lessons. So I could be generous in my comments when my mother bad-mouthed the little girl on TV.

"Play note right, but doesn't sound good! No singing sound," complained my mother.

"What are you picking on her for?" I said carelessly. "She's pretty good. Maybe she's not the best, but she's trying hard." I knew almost immediately I would be sorry I said that.

5 popular television variety show of the 1950s and 1960s.

"Just like you," she said. "Not the best. Because you not trying." She gave a little huff as she let go of the sound dial and sat down on the sofa.

The little Chinese girl sat down also to play an encore of "Anitra's Dance" by Grieg.[6] I remember the song, because later on I had to learn how to play it.

30     Three days after watching *The Ed Sullivan Show*, my mother told me what my schedule would be for piano lessons and piano practice. She had talked to Mr. Chong, who lived on the first floor of our apartment building. Mr. Chong was a retired piano teacher and my mother had traded housecleaning services for weekly lessons and a piano for me to practice on every day, two hours a day, from four until six.

When my mother told me this, I felt as though I had been sent to hell. I whined and then kicked my foot a little when I couldn't stand it anymore.

"Why don't you like me the way I am? I'm *not* a genius! I can't play the piano. And even if I could, I wouldn't go on TV if you paid me a million dollars!" I cried.

My mother slapped me. "Who ask you be genius?" she shouted. "Only ask you be your best. For you sake. You think I want you be genius? Hnnh! What for! Who ask you!"

"So ungrateful," I heard her mutter in Chinese. "If she had as much talent as she has temper, she would be famous now."

35     Mr. Chong, whom I secretly nicknamed Old Chong, was very strange, always tapping his fingers to the silent music of an invisible orchestra. He looked ancient in my eyes. He had lost most of the hair on top of his head and he wore thick glasses and had eyes that always looked tired and sleepy. But he must have been younger than I thought, since he lived with his mother and was not yet married.

I met Old Lady Chong once and that was enough. She had this peculiar smell like a baby that had done something in its pants. And her fingers felt like a dead person's, like an old peach I once found in the back of the refrigerator; the skin just slid off the meat when I picked it up.

I soon found out why Old Chong had retired from teaching piano. He was deaf. "Like Beethoven!" he shouted to me. "We're both listening only in our head!" And he would start to conduct his frantic silent sonatas.

Our lessons went like this. He would open the book and point to different things, explaining their purpose. "Key! Treble! Bass! No sharps or flats! So this is C major! Listen now and play after me!"

And then he would play the C scale a few times, a simple chord, and then, as if inspired by an old, unreachable itch, he gradually added more notes and running trills and a pounding bass until the music was really something quite grand.

40     I would play after him, the simple scale, the simple chord, and then I just played some nonsense that sounded like a cat running up and down on top of garbage cans. Old Chong smiled and applauded and then said, "Very good! But now you must learn to keep time!"

So that's how I discovered that Old Chong's eyes were too slow to keep up with the wrong notes I was playing. He went through the motions in half-time.

6 nineteenth-century Norwegian composer noted for his nationalistic music.

To help me keep rhythm, he stood behind me, pushing down on my right shoulder for every beat. He balanced pennies on top of my wrists so I would keep them still as I slowly played scales and arpeggios.[7] He had me curve my hand around an apple and keep that shape when playing chords. He marched stiffly to show me how to make each finger dance up and down, staccato like an obedient little soldier.

He taught me all these things, and that was how I also learned I could be lazy and get away with mistakes, lots of mistakes. If I hit the wrong notes because I hadn't practiced enough, I never corrected myself. I just kept playing in rhythm. And Old Chong kept conducting his own private reverie.

So maybe I never really gave myself a fair chance. I did pick up the basics pretty quickly, and I might have become a good pianist at that young age. But I was so determined not to try, not to be anybody different that I learned to play only the most ear-splitting preludes, the most discordant hymns.

Over the next year, I practiced like this, dutifully in my own way. And then one day I heard my mother and her friend Lindo Jong both talking in a loud bragging tone of voice so others could hear. It was after church, and I was leaning against the brick wall wearing a dress with stiff white petticoats. Auntie Lindo's daughter, Waverly, who was about my age, was standing farther down the wall about five feet away. We had grown up together and shared all the closeness of two sisters squabbling over crayons and dolls. In other words, for the most part, we hated each other. I thought she was snotty. Waverly Jong had gained a certain amount of fame as "Chinatown's Littlest Chinese Chess Champion."

45   "She bring home too many trophy," lamented Auntie Lindo that Sunday. "All day she play chess. All day I have no time do nothing but dust off her winnings." She threw a scolding look at Waverly, who pretended not to see her.

"You lucky you don't have this problem," said Auntie Lindo with a sigh to my mother.

And my mother squared her shoulders and bragged: "Our problem worser than yours. If we ask Jing-mei wash dish, she hear nothing but music. It's like you can't stop this natural talent."

And right then, I was determined to put a stop to her foolish pride.

A few weeks later, Old Chong and my mother conspired to have me play in a talent show which would be held in the church hall. By then, my parents had saved up enough to buy me a secondhand piano, a black Wurlitzer spinet with a scarred bench. It was the showpiece of our living room.

50   For the talent show, I was to play a piece called "Pleading Child" from Schumann's *Scenes from Childhood*.[8] It was a simple, moody piece that sounded more difficult than it was. I was supposed to memorize the whole thing, playing the repeat parts twice to make the piece sound longer. But I dawdled over it, playing a few bars and then cheating, looking up to see what notes followed. I never really listened to what I was playing. I daydreamed about being somewhere else, about being someone else.

---

7 playing the notes of a musical chord in succession instead of simultaneously; a standard exercise for piano students.  8 series of short, simple piano pieces by the nineteenth-century German composer Robert Schumann.

The part I liked to practice best was the fancy curtsy: right foot out, touch the rose on the carpet with a pointed foot, sweep to the side, left leg bends, look up and smile.

My parents invited all the couples from the Joy Luck Club to witness my debut. Auntie Lindo and Uncle Tin were there. Waverly and her two older brothers had also come. The first two rows were filled with children both younger and older than I was. The littlest ones got to go first. They recited simple nursery rhymes, squawked out tunes on miniature violins, twirled Hula Hoops, pranced in pink ballet tutus, and when they bowed or curtsied, the audience would sigh in unison, "Awww," and then clap enthusiastically.

When my turn came, I was very confident. I remember my childish excitement. It was as if I knew, without a doubt, that the prodigy side of me really did exist. I had no fear whatsoever, no nervousness. I remember thinking to myself, This is it! This is it! I looked out over the audience, at my mother's blank face, my father's yawn, Auntie Lindo's stiff-lipped smile, Waverly's sulky expression. I had on a white dress layered with sheets of lace, and a pink bow in my Peter Pan haircut. As I sat down I envisioned people jumping to their feet and Ed Sullivan rushing up to introduce me to everyone on TV.

And I started to play. It was so beautiful. I was so caught up in how lovely I looked that at first I didn't worry how I would sound. So it was a surprise to me when I hit the first wrong note and I realized something didn't sound quite right. And then I hit another and another followed that. A chill started at the top of my head and began to trickle down. Yet I couldn't stop playing, as though my hands were bewitched. I kept thinking my fingers would adjust themselves back, like a train switching to the right track. I played this strange jumble through two repeats, the sour notes staying with me all the way to the end.

55   When I stood up, I discovered my legs were shaking. Maybe I had just been nervous and the audience, like Old Chong, had seen me go through the right motions and had not heard anything wrong at all. I swept my right foot out, went down on my knee, looked up and smiled. The room was quiet, except for Old Chong, who was beaming and shouting, "Bravo! Bravo! Well done!" But then I saw my mother's face, her stricken face. The audience clapped weakly, and as I walked back to my chair, with my whole face quivering as I tried not to cry, I heard a little boy whisper loudly to his mother, "That was awful," and the mother whispered back, "Well, she certainly tried."

And now I realized how many people were in the audience, the whole world it seemed. I was aware of eyes burning into my back. I felt the shame of my mother and father as they sat stiffly throughout the rest of the show.

We could have escaped during intermission. Pride and some strange sense of honor must have anchored my parents to their chairs. And so we watched it all: the eighteen-year-old boy with a fake mustache who did a magic show and juggled flaming hoops while riding a unicycle. The breasted girl with white makeup who sang from *Madama Butterfly*[9] and got honorable mention.

---

9 early twentieth-century opera by Giacomo Puccini about a Japanese woman abandoned by her American husband.

And the eleven-year-old boy who won first prize playing a tricky violin song that sounded like a busy bee.

After the show, the Hsus, the Jongs, and the St. Clairs from the Joy Luck Club came up to my mother and father.

"Lots of talented kids," Auntie Lindo said vaguely, smiling broadly.

"That was somethin' else," said my father, and I wondered if he was referring to me in a humorous way, or whether he even remembered what I had done.

Waverly looked at me and shrugged her shoulders. "You aren't a genius like me," she said matter-of-factly. And if I hadn't felt so bad, I would have pulled her braids and punched her stomach.

But my mother's expression was what devastated me: a quiet, blank look that said she had lost everything. I felt the same way, and it seemed as if everybody were now coming up, like gawkers at the scene of an accident, to see what parts were actually missing. When we got on the bus to go home, my father was humming the busy-bee tune and my mother was silent. I kept thinking she wanted to wait until we got home before shouting at me. But when my father unlocked the door to our apartment, my mother walked in and then went to the back, into the bedroom. No accusations. No blame. And in a way, I felt disappointed. I had been waiting for her to start shouting, so I could shout back and cry and blame her for all my misery.

I assumed my talent-show fiasco meant I never had to play the piano again. But two days later, after school, my mother came out of the kitchen and saw me watching TV.

"Four clock," she reminded me as if it were any other day. I was stunned, as though she were asking me to go through the talent-show torture again. I wedged myself more tightly in front of the TV.

"Turn off TV," she called from the kitchen five minutes later.

I didn't budge. And then I decided. I didn't have to do what my mother said anymore. I wasn't her slave. This wasn't China. I had listened to her before and look what happened. She was the stupid one.

She came out from the kitchen and stood in the arched entryway of the living room. "Four clock," she said once again, louder.

"I'm not going to play anymore," I said nonchalantly. "Why should I? I'm not a genius."

She walked over and stood in front of the TV. I saw her chest was heaving up and down in an angry way.

"No!" I said, and I now felt stronger, as if my true self had finally emerged. So this was what had been inside me all along.

"No! I won't!" I screamed.

She yanked me by the arm, pulled me off the floor, snapped off the TV. She was frighteningly strong, half pulling, half carrying me toward the piano as I kicked the throw rugs under my feet. She lifted me up and onto the hard bench. I was sobbing by now, looking at her bitterly. Her chest was heaving even more and her mouth was open, smiling crazily as if she was pleased I was crying.

"You want me to be someone that I'm not!" I sobbed. "I'll never be the kind of daughter you want me to be!"

"Only two kinds of daughters," she shouted in Chinese. "Those who are obedient and those who follow their own mind! Only one kind of daughter can live in this house. Obedient daughter!"

75 "Then I wish I wasn't your daughter. I wish you weren't my mother," I shouted. As I said these things I got scared. It felt like worms and toads and slimy things crawling out of my chest, but it also felt good, as if this awful side of me had surfaced, at last.

"Too late change this," said my mother shrilly.

And I could sense her anger rising to its breaking point. I wanted to see it spill over. And that's when I remembered the babies she had lost in China, the ones we never talked about. "Then I wish I'd never been born!" I shouted. "I wish I were dead! Like them."

It was as if I had said the magic words. Alakazam!—and her face went blank, her mouth closed, her arms went slack, and she backed out of the room, stunned, as if she were blowing away like a small brown leaf, thin, brittle, lifeless.

*****

It was not the only disappointment my mother felt in me. In the years that followed, I failed her so many times, each time asserting my own will, my right to fall short of expectations. I didn't get straight As. I didn't become class president. I didn't get into Stanford. I dropped out of college.

80 For unlike my mother, I did not believe I could be anything I wanted to be. I could only be me.

And for all those years, we never talked about the disaster at the recital or my terrible accusations afterward at the piano bench. All that remained unchecked, like a betrayal that was now unspeakable. So I never found a way to ask her why she had hoped for something so large that failure was inevitable.

And even worse, I never asked her what frightened me the most: Why had she given up hope?

For after our struggle at the piano, she never mentioned my playing again. The lessons stopped. The lid to the piano was closed, shutting out the dust, my misery, and her dreams.

So she surprised me. A few years ago, she offered to give me the piano, for my thirtieth birthday. I had not played in all those years. I saw the offer as a sign of forgiveness, a tremendous burden removed.

85 "Are you sure?" I asked shyly. "I mean, won't you and Dad miss it?"

"No, this your piano," she said firmly. "Always your piano. You only one can play."

"Well, I probably can't play anymore," I said. "It's been years."

"You pick up fast," said my mother, as if she knew this was certain. "You have natural talent. You could been genius if you want to."

"No I couldn't."

90 "You just not trying," said my mother. And she was neither angry nor sad. She said it as if to announce a fact that could never be disproved. "Take it," she said.

But I didn't at first. It was enough that she had offered it to me. And after that, every time I saw it in my parents' living room, standing in front of the bay windows, it made me feel proud, as if it were a shiny trophy I had won back.

Last week I sent a tuner over to my parents' apartment and had the piano reconditioned, for purely sentimental reasons. My mother had died a few months before and I had been getting things in order for my father, a little bit at a time. I put the jewelry in special silk pouches. The sweaters she had knitted in yellow, pink, bright orange — all the colors I hated — I put those in moth-proof boxes. I found some old Chinese silk dresses, the kind with the little slits up the sides. I rubbed the old silk against my skin, then wrapped them in tissue and decided to take them home with me.

After I had the piano tuned, I opened the lid and touched the keys. It sounded even richer than I remembered. Really, it was a very good piano. Inside the bench were the same exercise notes with handwritten scales, the same secondhand music books with their covers held together with yellow tape.

I opened up the Schumann book to the dark little piece I had played at the recital. It was on the left-hand side of the page, "Pleading Child." It looked more difficult than I remembered. I played a few bars, surprised at how easily the notes came back to me.

95     And for the first time, or so it seemed, I noticed the piece on the right-hand side. It was called "Perfectly Contented." I tried to play this one as well. It had a lighter melody but the same flowing rhythm and turned out to be quite easy. "Pleading Child" was shorter but slower; "Perfectly Contented" was longer, but faster. And after I played them both a few times, I realized they were two halves of the same song.

(1989)

# WRITING ESSAYS ABOUT LITERATURE

## PUTTING THE JOB IN PERSPECTIVE

Writing well on any academic subject is demanding work, and writing about literature is among the most demanding kinds of academic writing. It helps to remember, however, that confronting the task seriously will improve not only the way you express what you think but your ability to think, as well. Mastering the critical and interpretive essays required in English courses will prepare you to handle other writing jobs with comparative ease. Whether you are committed to specializing in English or interested mainly in doing as well as you can in a required English course before going on to other areas of study, the advice that follows will help you make your choices sensibly and get the most from the work you do.

Writing about literature often starts with a feeling — you either like something or not — or an intuition about how a piece of writing works. In expressing these inklings in writing, you clarify them for yourself, identify the assumptions behind them, and learn how well they are grounded in the work you are considering. In the process, you not only come to understand better how literature works, but you also discover a good deal about how you think. Writing about literature is challenging for the same reasons it is rewarding — because it requires you to confront yourself as well as what you read.

When you explore literature in essays, you will rarely be looking for answers that are absolutely right or wrong. Depending on the approach taken and the questions asked, a wide variety of conclusions can be drawn about an individual work of literature, and because of the personal element in responses, even writers approaching questions in similar ways will often come up with quite different answers. Think of your essays about literature as part of an ongoing search for understanding, a process that begins when an author, poet, or playwright confronts his or her perceptions about the world in writing and that continues as long as somebody is reading and writing about the original creation. Remembering that you are taking part in a continuing dialogue rather than solving a problem with a single, predetermined answer will help you resist obvious conclusions and make your confrontation with a demanding subject less intimidating.

But again, "less intimidating" does not mean easy. The lack of pat answers, though reassuring in some ways, is no excuse for either slack thinking or sloppy writing. On the contrary, because your essays will be judged more by the quality of thought and expression they demonstrate than by how close they come to some established position, care is especially important. Originality is a start, but your original perceptions have to be supported scrupulously with evidence from the work in question; you must impress your audience by convincing it.

## PREPARING TO WRITE

An essay about a literary work should say something illuminating about it, and an illumination depends on focus as well as initial brilliance. Thoughtful insights take time to develop, and an essential step in writing about literature involves clarifying for yourself what it is you want to say. Only when you are sure of your message can you decide how best to present it clearly and convincingly to your readers. The work cannot be rushed at this stage, so it is essential to leave yourself adequate time, not only to draft and revise, but to think, to plan, and to criticize your own ideas, as well.

---

### PROCESS IN SUMMARY

### Preparing to Write

Step 1:   Prepare for writing assignments in advance by reading all assigned texts in a course as early as possible and by including speculation about potential lines of argument in your notes.

Step 2:   Once you receive a writing assignment, evaluate it carefully to determine special requirements and anticipate problems.

Step 3:   Choose a subject that interests you.

Step 4:   Choose a topic you can handle well in the time available.

Step 5:   If you are confused about any aspect of an assignment or if you anticipate deviating in any way from the directions, check with your instructor.

Step 6:   Review the primary works you are writing about carefully, taking notes and identifying key passages as you read.

Step 7:   Read whatever background material you consider necessary.

### Drafting

Step 1:   Begin generating ideas in writing while you still have more time than you need to complete your essay.

Step 2:   Focus your ideas into a manageable thesis and state this thesis clearly in a single sentence.

Step 3:   Prepare a simple, tentative outline. Do not spend a lot of time on this outline because it will probably have to be modified later. Repeat Step 2 if necessary.

Step 4:   Working from your outline and keeping your thesis statement clearly in mind, complete a rough draft of the entire essay without stopping to revise.

*(continued)*

### Revising and Editing

Step 1:   Review your essay to identify any parts that do not relate clearly to your thesis; cut or adapt these as necessary.

Step 2:   Add support at any point where your conclusions seem to need it.

Step 3:   Revise your opening to ensure that the main points of your essay are clear and supply any additional information your reader may need to follow your approach.

Step 4:   When you are satisfied with the content of your essay, continue revising it for clarity and style until you are satisfied that it is the best you can make it or until the deadline requires you to commit yourself to a final version.

Step 5:   When you are rested and free from distractions, proofread your essay carefully, making neat changes on the manuscript where necessary.

## Reading with Awareness

The most fundamental preparation for writing about literature is reading. Read the piece you intend to write about, and then reread it. Read not just superficially to get a basic idea of what the piece says, but carefully, with an awareness of implications beneath the surface and of how the way it is written determines the way it affects you. Taking English courses and studying what others write about literature will teach you the kinds of things to look for, but you will need more. Serious reading, like serious writing, takes practice and cannot be rushed: putting off thinking about literature in general until you are required to write about a particular piece is like putting off training for a race until just before you have to run it. Developing the habit of reading seriously will put you far ahead of students who read only when forced to by an assignment, and it will also yield a great deal of satisfaction in itself.

## Taking Notes

While reading thoughtfully is essential, it is not enough. You will find that your reading translates more readily into essays if you record your responses. Take notes as you read, perhaps on the text itself if it is your own copy and an inexpensive one. Marking particularly interesting passages will be a great help when you come back later to sort out evidence for an idea you are developing in an essay. When taking notes in class, record not only what your instructor says but the ideas that occur to you as well. If what is said about one work suggests comparison with another, take note of the possibility. Remark contradictions and unanswered questions. Your dissenting opinions, which you might well forget if you neglected to write them down at the time, will often provide the foundation for your most original essays and may in the long run prove to be the most valuable material you record in class.

An excellent practice for bridging the gap between the sketchy notes you write in class and fully developed essays is to extend your notes in a journal. Rather than reviewing class notes only when you are preparing for an exam, take time between classes to review and expand on the ideas your notes record. Consider which of your ideas may yield topics for essays, and test the manageability of these topics by sketching outlines. Elaborate in a paragraph or two on ideas you have had time to record in only a sentence. If you have recorded questions in your notes, attempt to answer them yourself in writing. The best time to develop your notes into something more useful occurs when the ideas they record are still fresh in your mind. While keeping a literary journal is not so different from taking notes, it allows you time to develop your ideas more thoughtfully and provides practice that will help you become more comfortable with critical writing.

## Evaluating Assignments

Before attempting a writing assignment, you must first determine exactly what it requires and whether you can carry out any approach you are considering in the time available. The time you invest in evaluating assignments is rarely wasted. However eager you may be to get started, be cautious; enthusiasm is great, but you will win few races by sprinting off in the wrong direction.

Be especially careful when choosing topics from a list, a point at which the work of a few minutes can make the difference between success and failure. While you can assume that your instructor considers all suggested topics suitable for some students in your class, you cannot assume that all the topics will be suitable for all the students. Resist the temptation to commit yourself to the first topic that catches your interest. Evaluate all your options, eliminating the obvious impossibilities first. It will usually be clear that some works and some approaches are too difficult for you to manage. Personal taste is also an important consideration: until you gain more experience as a critic, you will rarely write successful essays about literary works you dislike. Once you have narrowed the choice to a few possibilities, sketch brief outlines to give yourself a better idea of where you might go with each topic. Determine whether you can meet all the requirements in each case. For example, even though you admire a certain poem, you may not be capable of handling a topic that requires you to produce a successful essay about how that poem's metrical patterns reinforce its meaning. While there can be long-term benefits in taking the extra time required to prepare for specialized topics, be sure you can manage the workload. Be wary of ambitious failures.

Once you find an assignment you think you can handle well, consider its wording carefully. Are you sure what all the terms mean? If not, ask your instructor to explain. Is there anything about the approach you are considering that seems at odds with the assignment as stated? Perhaps, for example, an assignment asks you to compare characterization in two stories, only one of which particularly impresses you. It may be permissible to concentrate on the one you like while using the other to illuminate by contrast what you admire in your favourite, but, then again, your instructor may want a more balanced comparison. Find out before you devote a lot of time to a questionable approach. Similarly, even though you plan no deviations from the stated requirements, you may find an assignment ambiguous in some respect. If you are told to compare two poems, for example, does this mean you are obligated to consider all aspects of the two poems? Or will you be permitted to devote most of your comparison to some aspect that seems especially revealing? While the more focussed approach may seem more interesting to you, your instructor may have left the comparison general to test your understanding of a variety of elements in the poems. Any number of misunderstandings can occur, and you will be wise to anticipate them while you still have plenty of time to adapt.

Think early. Check early. Doing so can save you time, effort, and disappointment.

## Research

In a very limited sense, any essay you write on a literary subject will involve research: you will have to read the works you intend to write about very carefully, probably a number of times, and even with an assignment that does not formally require research, you will often read other works by the same writer and explore his or her personal and historical background.

In a formal research paper, however, you will also be expected to find and evaluate what others have written about your subject. In this case, finding and properly acknowledging your debt to secondary material — writings about literature rather than the literature itself — will be a major part of your job. A detailed explanation of research methods and the format for acknowledging sources is beyond the scope of this chapter, but most college-level writing textbooks cover such material thoroughly. If you plan to take more than a few English courses, *The MLA Handbook for Writers of Research Papers*, which provides an exhaustive guide to the standard format used in English essays, is a good investment. Here it will suffice to provide a few general hints that can save you a lot of time and trouble.

Many students get into difficulty by confusing random sampling with research. They find the call number of a book on their topic, go to the specified shelf in the library, pull out several books on the same general subject, and consider their search complete. The one advantage of this approach — speed — cannot compensate for the problems it will almost certainly create. Books chosen at random rarely provide more than brief, general comment on an essay topic; what relevant comment they do include is often slanted according to their focal concerns. In addition, books stay on library shelves long after what they say has been qualified by later observations, and the material you find in a random selection will certainly not be the most recent available. This is not to say that books are of no value; the point is that books must be chosen carefully and supplemented by reference to up-to-date articles from scholarly journals.

The annotated bibliographies and the periodical indexes available in reference libraries will allow you to find material relevant to your topic quickly, and they will also give you an overview of the kinds of approaches to the work in question that others have found useful. But, as valuable as they are in saving you the trouble of reviewing irrelevant or barely relevant material, these resources will not solve all your problems. Often, they will list far more apparently relevant resources than you have time to consult. How are you to choose? In some cases your instructor will make suggestions, but such advice may still leave you guessing about which comments are most important and influential. One of the easiest ways into ongoing critical debates is to look first at the most recent writings you can find on your topic, taking careful note of the earlier works these cite. When two or three recent sources refer to an older one, it will usually be worth your while to check what it says directly. No method of sampling is a substitute for an exhaustive review of criticism, but methods that allow you to make an informed selection should be sufficient for most of your essays. They will certainly serve you better than random choice.

Seeking out the most pertinent material is not the only challenge in research, however. When you set out to research critical comment, remember that you are in at least as much danger from what you find as from what you miss. Discovering a source that carries on your line of argument so well that it leaves you little to add will take the satisfaction out of your work as well as the challenge, and you will learn little from basing your essay on such a source. Moreover, depending heavily on a source increases the chances of unintentional plagiarism — not making it entirely clear which ideas are really yours and which are borrowed. Thus, finding a published essay that covers much of what you intend to say about a topic is a good reason to consider changing topics or at least modifying your approach.

Much more serious than occasional reliance on secondary sources for ideas is developing a habit of dependency. It is all too easy to drift into a pattern of reviewing criticism before you begin to form your own ideas, thereby allowing others to shape your views. Always keep in mind when dealing with critical opinions that they are just that — opinions. Be impressed if you like, but never be intimidated. Even the best critics are human and therefore fallible. They are influenced by the prevailing critical assumptions of their times and often by specific theoretical affiliations. You have every right to disagree with published critics or, for that matter, with your instructors, provided you state your case clearly and support it conscientiously with references to the text in question. Consider other views carefully and with the respect any honest effort to advance understanding deserves, but then, when writing your essays, think for yourself.

## STARTING TO WRITE

In contrast with the many difficulties involved in completing a good critical essay on time, putting off getting started is one of the easiest things you will ever do — easy and risky. It is human nature to put off the more difficult of competing tasks until the straightforward ones are out of the way, but with writing, the difficult jobs are precisely the ones to start first. Start early. Leave yourself time to explore blind alleys and, when you feel you are getting nowhere, to allow your subconscious mind to work on the problem while you are consciously engaged with other concerns. You will almost always find that ten hours invested in a writing project over a week will yield better results than a single ten-hour stretch of writing immediately before the deadline for submission.

## Writer's Block

Unfortunately, even when you are well aware of the advantages of an early start, you may be held up by a psychological quirk commonly referred to as "writer's block."

Writer's block usually sets in at the earliest stages of a project, making it impossible to begin writing at all or, at best, to carry on past the first page or two. Because fear of failure is part of the cause, writer's block often strikes when you can least afford it — when you are involved in an especially important project or working under pressure. If you have never experienced writer's block, you may find the idea amusing, but sooner or later it affects most writers, and when it does, it can be both unpleasant and costly. Moreover, the anxiety created by one experience can lead to others, creating a steadily worsening problem. It makes sense, therefore, to prepare for writer's block before it strikes by experimenting with methods of resistance in order to determine which work best for you.

The methods described below are primarily intended to help you generate and shape ideas, but because they also encourage you to start writing early, not just when you have time to complete a project but when you have time to waste, they help eliminate writer's block as well. So, even if you find it fairly easy to think of things to say without writing, writing will usually help, and it will certainly make your work no harder.

## Questions

Perhaps the most straightforward way to clarify what you think about a subject is to ask yourself questions about it. In order to avoid writer's block, not to mention loss and confusion, keep a record of your questions and answers in writing.

Beginning with very general questions, such as why you like or dislike something, progress gradually to questions that are more specific, quickly abandoning lines of inquiry that lead away from manageable topics. If you need help devising questions, you will find the lists included in writing textbooks many and varied, and most of them will work adequately up to a point. Watch for that point. At first, any question that forces you to examine your ideas will be better than none, but the further you carry on with a ready-made list, the more likely the questions are to limit your answers. As soon as a suggested line of inquiry begins to get in the way of your developing ideas, abandon it and strike off on your own. Such lists are generally more useful for getting started than for leading you to conclusions.

Be wary also of lists of questions not designed for students of literature. For example, lists are often based on the journalistic standard: Who? What? Where? When? Why? How? While such lists encourage thoroughness in getting at the facts of a situation, an essay about literature is, of course, far more subtle than a news story. Normally, your readers will be familiar with the facts of the works you are discussing and will not require a review. Thus you will be wise to pass quickly over the Who? What? Where? and When? and concentrate on questions concerned with Why? and How? More often than not, you will begin forming a useful argument only when you begin addressing these last two.

## Interaction

If asking and answering questions by yourself seems lonely work, you may prefer to involve others. Approaches vary according to circumstances and temperament.

One common method of generating ideas, sometimes called brainstorming, involves gathering a group together, with tape recorder running or one member taking notes, and throwing out ideas. The exchange is kept as informal as possible to avoid inhibiting creativity. This sort of exercise works better in developing advertising slogans than critical essays, and a lot of what results will be useless, but finding and rejecting inappropriate approaches to a subject will often help you progress toward forming better ones. At least such an exchange of ideas will get you started.

If you lack the informed group required for brainstorming, you can sometimes develop ideas and free yourself from writer's block by talking to a single listener. Even if this person knows little about your subject, his or her responses can help you decide where your views lack clarity or need support. Remember, however, that in the end it should be you who judges and refines the ideas: using another person as a sounding board for your own ideas is not the same thing as allowing another person to tell you what to think. For the sake of honesty and your development as a critical thinker, avoid working with someone whose superior knowledge of your subject may make it hard to rely on your own judgement.

## Free Writing

One of the most reliable ways of breaking writer's block is called "free writing." Free writing is a way of freeing yourself from worry about imperfections in expression that can inhibit the flow of ideas early in a project. It involves committing yourself to writing for a predetermined period of time. You simply sit down in a place where you will not be interrupted and, keeping your subject in mind, write until the time is up. Resist pausing for reflection or stopping to revise. At best, you will be well into a rough draft by the time you finish. At worst, what you produce will be only vaguely relevant to your subject, but, even if the written result is of little value, you will still have broken your writer's block and moved closer to understanding what you want to say. You can always begin a second session of free writing by reacting to the shortcomings of your first.

## FOCUSSING

Once you put your early inhibitions behind you and begin accumulating ideas, you will soon find yourself with more than you can hope to bring together in a paper. This is the time to turn your attention from generating ideas to pruning and focussing. Handling the focussing stage of a writing project well can save you a great deal of time later on, but it takes discipline. Piling up ideas becomes so easy once you get started that it is tempting to carry on too long, deluding yourself that you are accomplishing something when in fact you are rambling out of control. While writing anything is better than writing nothing at the start of the writing process, this does not remain true throughout. Avoid the common mistake of trying to substitute quantity for quality.

You can approach the job of focussing from two general directions — working from a thesis or toward one. If you are lucky, you will discover one particularly interesting line of argument early along. Stating your main ideas as a proposition to be proved — a proposition often referred to as a "thesis" and commonly announced near the beginning of an essay in a sentence termed a "thesis statement" — will provide you with a guide as you write, a premise to refer to as you choose which of your secondary ideas to expand, which to subordinate, and which to cut. If no clear thesis has emerged by the time you are ready to start focussing, you can develop one by grouping the most promising ideas and then pruning obvious loose ends. The more loose ends you cut, the more clearly you will see the best potential lines of argument. By the time you have narrowed the possibilities to two or three, you will not only be in a good position to choose the best, but you will also have developed a general idea of how best to support the one you choose.

Be certain, however, that you do not stop before the job is done. Just as it is important to begin focussing before you are overwhelmed with an unmanageable accumulation of ideas, it is also vital to carry on to the desired end — a single, supportable thesis:

> **Not** "Although Andrew Marvell's 'To His Coy Mistress' is manipulative to some extent in taking advantage of flattery, sophistry, and shocking images of mutability, it sometimes reveals a genuine regard for the object of passion and leaves the reader wondering how fully the object of Marvell's affection — or lust — would be capable of appreciating what is going on in the poem."

> **But** "In 'To His Coy Mistress,' Andrew Marvell is addressing a well-educated woman whose intelligence he respects."

> **Or** "Andrew Marvell's most compelling means of seduction in 'To His Coy Mistress' is neither flattery nor shock, but logic."

The first statement above has more than its share of interesting ideas, but it would likely yield either two or three papers tacked loosely together or, worse still, a muddled blend. Parting with ideas can be hard, but attempting to fit more notions into an essay than you can explain and support adequately will be much harder. Saving a few minutes by rushing the focussing stage can cost you many hours later on.

## Outlines

Quite a few writing textbooks advise preparing a detailed outline before attempting the first draft, a practice that is usually less effective for critical arguments than expository essays. In essays devoted mainly to reviewing large amounts of factual information, information that is readily gathered and organized in advance of writing, a detailed outline will prove an invaluable tool, one that can greatly speed the process of writing and revision. In more speculative essays, however, the kind of essays commonly written about literature, the difficulty of deciding what you are going to say, and in what order, without a certain amount of groping on paper will often make a detailed outline harder to produce than a draft.

Therefore, using outlines for essays on literature requires flexibility. If planning is one of your strengths, beginning your writing with an outline will definitely speed the work that follows. But if you find preparing outlines more difficult than diving in and writing a draft without one, you will be wise not to spend too much time struggling to follow advice that is more appropriate for some types of writers and for some types of writing than others. Do what works for you.

## Tree-Diagramming

If you like working from an outline yet find outlines difficult to organize while you are still generating ideas, try "tree-diagramming," a method that can help you form an outline in something the same way free writing helps you progress toward a first draft. Place a word or phrase representing your central idea in the middle of a large sheet of paper and work outward, connecting related ideas through a series of branches. Though the result of this exercise will rarely resemble a tree, it will provide you with an overview of relationships, revealing both dead ends and useful lines of inquiry quickly. (See Figures 1 and 2.)

## WRITING AND REVISING

If you start early and use your time efficiently, you should have developed and focussed your ideas several days before your essay is due. At this point, you will have at least a general idea of how your essay will be organized to support your thesis, and will probably have done some drafting. The next step, completing your first draft, should be fairly straightforward if you resist the temptation to stop and polish style.

Once you have a completed draft that makes sense and includes all your main points, distance yourself from what you have written by leaving it alone

**Figure 1**  Writer's Block: First Tree Diagram

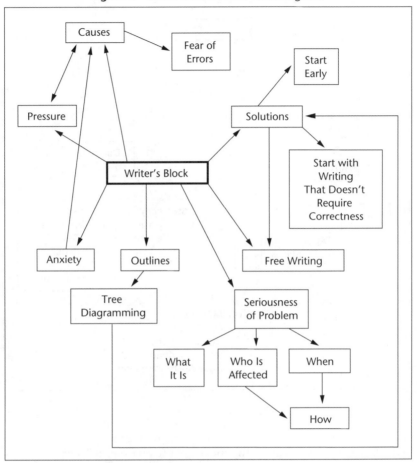

for a day or two. Then, coming back to the project relatively fresh, you will be able to decide more quickly and reliably whether what you have written needs cutting, expansion, or restructuring. After you are satisfied with the form and the essential content, it will be time for polishing style and fine-tuning your argument.

Remember: an essay you write over a week or ten days will almost always be better than one you produce in a single marathon effort, even though you invest the same number of hours in total.

## Audience

As you revise your essay, you will have two main concerns — making your argument clear and forceful, and maintaining one consistent appropriate

**Figure 2**   Writer's Block: Second Tree Diagram

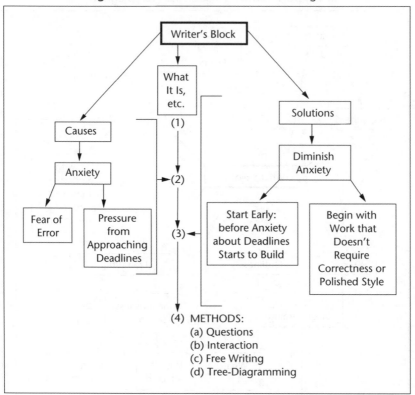

style throughout. Style can be the trickier of the two, especially when you try to affect it. Do not assume an overly sophisticated, erudite style which may not be appropriate even for literary critics. You will find that an unnatural style will be very difficult to maintain for an entire essay. A much easier and more reliable approach is to let your audience and your relationship with it control your style automatically, as they would your voice if you were speaking.

What audience do you write for? The answer is less obvious than you might think. While you probably want most to impress the instructor who will eventually give your work a grade, you may well find that writing with another audience in mind makes this easier. Consider the unnaturalness of explicating literature for someone who knows a great deal more about it than you and who has probably encountered views similar to yours many times before. Will this situation inspire you with confidence? Or is it more likely to make you adopt an apologetic tone and be slightly dismissive about your ideas? How do you feel about writing for someone who can be expected to note technical errors and lower your grade in consequence? Will this audience encourage a confident, forceful style? Hardly.

It makes more sense to write for an audience you can persuade and enlighten, one at about your own level of ability. An audience made up of the better students in your class is a sensible choice. You know this audience well, you can assume it will be familiar with the works you are considering, and you can be confident that it will find your insights fresh and interesting. Writing for an audience of equals will also make it easier for you to adopt a natural, unpretentious style — your own.

In addition to helping you find an appropriate style, writing for an audience of equals will also help you decide what needs to be explained and what does not. For example, since your audience has read and understood the surface meaning of the works you are writing about, you will not need to summarize plot or review other obvious facts. When you need to make specific references to plot or character in support of your developing argument, you will keep these references brief — reminders, rather than revelations. On the other hand, you cannot assume that your audience has seen reasoning similar to yours before, and you should therefore make your line of thinking and the connections between evidence and the conclusions you draw from it more explicit than you might if you were writing exclusively for your instructor.

## Openings

Inexperienced writers often get into trouble by working on the assumption that the parts of an essay should be finished one at a time from first to last. This assumption is wrong on two counts. First, if you have the time, it is almost always easier to improve all the parts of an essay at about the same rate as you work through a series of drafts. Second, when lack of time makes a series of drafts impossible and you have to finish sections in sequence, it is usually easier to write the rest of the essay before you put the finishing touches on the opening.

If you are like most student writers, you have more difficulty with openings than with any other part of your essays. Your opening paragraphs may be wordy, vague, and repetitive, even though they receive more attention line for line than other sections. The problem is poor timing. While good essays generally require several drafts, inexperienced writers working under pressure hope to arrive at a final version in as few drafts as possible. In this hope, they attempt to produce a final, polished version when they have only an incomplete or very rough draft to revise, and they naturally start with the opening, struggling to introduce what they will say before they are sure of precisely what this will be. The time-consuming tinkering with wording and groping for ideas that ensue can take more time than revising the whole essay less meticulously. Even worse, having put so much effort into the opening, they are reluctant to make necessary changes once they finish the rest of the essay. The result: a vague, inflated introduction followed by a hastily composed argument that had to be dashed off because of all the time wasted in introducing it. There is nothing wrong with including an opening paragraph containing a clear thesis statement in your first draft; in fact it helps to keep your argument on topic. But, having done that, you will usually find it easiest to leave the opening rough until the rest of your essay is polished to its conclusion.

At this point, you will have a much more certain idea of what you want to introduce in the opening, and you will find writing it much easier in consequence.

Keep in mind as you complete your opening that it should actually accomplish something — excite your reader's interest, persuade your reader of the value of your approach, prepare your reader to grasp what follows. You can achieve these aims only when you yourself fully understand where your essay is going.

## Revising for Correctness

While your first concerns throughout most of the writing process should be to make sense and express yourself in an appropriate, consistent style, you cannot afford to ignore correctness — following the accepted conventions of grammar, punctuation, and spelling. While correctness cannot in itself guarantee success, carelessness or incompetence in handling basic writing will certainly ensure failure.

Fortunately, whether they believe it or not, most students who are penalized for errors know enough about grammar and punctuation to write correctly. Attitude more than ignorance is the cause. If you tend to make a lot of mistakes, do not let discouragement or frustration exaggerate your weakness. Convincing yourself that you lack the ability to write correctly is simply an excuse for not investing the time and the work required to master correctness. Seriously confronted, the job of revising for correctness will become easier and less time-consuming with practice.

---

### TEN COMMON MISTAKES TO AVOID IN WRITING ABOUT LITERATURE

Occasionally, even when you start early and work conscientiously, you will still get into difficulty in writing an essay about literature. More often than not this stems from one of the common errors below. While being on guard against these mistakes cannot guarantee success, it will greatly increase your chances.

#### 1. Taking On Unrealistically Ambitious Projects
Be realistic in choosing topics. Avoid topics that will take more space, time, specialized knowledge, or research than you can put into them. If you are not sure whether your plans are manageable, check with your instructor.

#### 2. Plagiarizing by Mistake
Be careful not to drift into plagiarism by keeping sloppy records of your research. Record complete information for references immediately upon

*(continued)*

---

encountering a source you may want to refer to later. When taking notes, make a clear distinction between recorded information, paraphrases, and quotations.

## 3. Retaining Irrelevant Material from Early Drafts

If sections of an essay seem loosely connected with each other or with the controlling thesis, try to put the essay in order by supplying clear transitions showing the reader how each part relates to the whole. If you find it difficult to justify a section, cut or shorten it. The ideas that could produce two or three good essays will usually make one bad one.

## 4. Attempting to Polish Style Too Early

Do not attempt to perfect style while you are still unsure of what you want to say. Be especially wary of polishing openings before you have a clear idea of what will follow.

## 5. Writing about Yourself Rather than Your Topic

Concentrate on your topic rather than your feelings, doubts, or difficulties as you write. Avoid such redundant insertions as "it seems to me that" and "I think that"; your reader will know you are doing the thinking that goes into your essay without constantly being reminded.

## 6. Summarizing Plot and Explaining the Obvious

Avoid boring your reader by summarizing what happens in literary works and reviewing obvious facts at length. Assume an audience of intelligent readers familiar with the works you are analyzing and supply only the information this audience will need to evaluate your argument.

Do not be influenced by the summaries provided in various publications termed "notes." These summaries do not constitute serious criticism and should not be imitated.

## 7. Confusing Verb Tenses

Keep the sequences of verb tenses within long sentences as simple as possible, and avoid shifting tenses unnecessarily. Using the conventional present tense to describe characters, circumstances, and events in literary works will help greatly.

## 8. Inflating Style

Inflated style is no substitute for good ideas. Impress your readers with the clarity and sense of your thinking rather than the sophistication of your presentation. Strive to write in your own voice; keep your sentence structure as straightforward as you can without being choppy and repetitive;

*(continued)*

use only those literary terms that you understand. If you work with a thesaurus, use it to find the most accurate and readily understood terms available rather than as a shortcut to pretentiousness and obscurity.

## 9. Failing to Follow Conventions of Manuscript Form

Follow the accepted conventions for presenting your work on the page and acknowledging sources. It helps to remember that these conventions are not merely decorative; rather, they are an essential code for communicating information efficiently and accurately.

## 10. Proofreading Inattentively

Proofread when you are rested, preferably after a good night's sleep, rather than immediately after you finish an essay. Proofread in a place free from distractions, and give the job the full attention it requires. The half hour or so you take to proofread an essay properly will often have more effect on the grade than any other half hour of work you invest in the project.

Time is the key factor. To write correctly you must know your limitations and allow yourself time to compensate for them. If you find yourself penalized for errors regularly, understand why. Is it carelessness in the final stages of writing? Or do you lack the background in the basics of writing? If you know what you are doing but make careless mistakes, you need merely improve your proofreading skills and find an appropriate proofreading time, which is to say a time when you will not be too tired to concentrate or likely to be distracted. If your problem is more serious and you are uncertain of what is correct in some cases, budget the extra time you will need to check. Checking your own work is a good way to learn, and you will probably find once you confront the problem of errors that you know more than you think you do. Like most students who are penalized for errors, you probably make the same types of errors again and again, although you handle most elements correctly. Take note of the types of things that go wrong and concentrate on these. Make a checklist of things to watch for. Review the relevant rules as you approach the final stages of writing. Ignorance, in this case, is no excuse: all the information you need about grammar and punctuation can be found easily in writing handbooks, and spelling can, of course, be checked in a dictionary — provided you allow yourself time to do the work.

Once you are satisfied that your own writing is correct, turn your attention to another aspect of your essay that requires care. Most instructors consider the format and accuracy of quotations and references to be just as important as the correctness of your own writing, so check these carefully before submitting your essay. Have you provided all the requirements, such as a title and title page, that are mentioned in the assignment? Are all your quotations recorded exactly? Have you consistently followed the correct format in supplying notes and bibliographical references? Taking care with such details shows that you are serious about your work; allowing even a few mistakes can call the accuracy of all your work into question.

One further word of warning, however: remember that timing is just as important as taking time in correcting your essays. It is as serious a mistake to let your concern with correctness preoccupy you during the earlier stages of writing as it is to neglect correctness later on. Worrying about errors early along will distract you from the important work of forming ideas, and it may also encourage you to adopt an overly cautious style aimed more at avoiding errors than communicating. So leave the job of checking for correctness till the end of your project, and then take it seriously.

*****

While you cannot avoid the basic fact that writing well about literature involves hard work, you can, by following the advice supplied here, avoid wasting the work you do and ensure that your hard work yields the good results it deserves. But be sceptical: this advice is a basis, not a formula, for success. Keep in mind that writing is a personal endeavour and that no one method will work best for every person and every occasion. Treat this and all advice on writing critically, measuring its usefulness against your experience of what works best for you as you continue to grow as a writer.

# GLOSSARY OF LITERARY TERMS

**accent**  The stress that makes a syllable more emphatic or prominent in pronunciation than neighbouring syllables.

**act**  A main division of a drama.

**action**  What happens in a drama; the physical activity represented on the stage, but also the mental activity stimulated in a reader or audience.

**alliteration**  The repetition of consonant sounds, particularly at the beginning of words close to one another.

**allusion**  A reference to characters, places, events, or objects from history, religion, mythology, or literature, which the reader is supposed to recognize and connect to the subject of the work in which the allusion appears.

**ambiguity**  The presence of multiple meanings in a word or phrase, whether intentional or accidental.

**amphibrach (amphibrachic)**  A poetic foot of three syllables, only the middle one being accented. See FOOT and Table 1, "The Metrical Feet," in the Introduction to Poetry.

**amphimacer (amphimacric)**  A poetic foot of three syllables, the first and last being accented; also called a cretic. See FOOT and Table 1, "The Metrical Feet," in the Introduction to Poetry.

**anapest (anapestic)**  A poetic foot of three syllables, only the last being accented. See FOOT and Table 1, "The Metrical Feet," in the Introduction to Poetry.

**antagonist**  Any character who opposes another; most often applied to one opposing the main character (the protagonist).

**apostrophe**  An address to an absent or dead person, to an object, or to an abstraction.

**archetype**  A character type, symbol, plot, or theme that appears frequently in works of literature and therefore seems to have universal meaning.

**aside**  Words delivered by one character to another or to the audience, and understood not to be heard by other characters on the stage.

**assonance**  Repetition of similar vowel sounds.

**ballad**  A form of narrative poetry used continuously since medieval times, consisting of four-line stanzas usually alternating iambic tetrameter and iambic trimeter and rhyming *abcb*, often characterized by repetition and repeated refrains. Ballads are usually classed as either popular or literary ballads. Popular ballads were transmitted orally and were frequently intended to be sung; they originated with anonymous authors among the folk, or common people of rural society. Literary ballads are conscious imitations of these popular ballads and are intended to be read or recited, not sung. Because they are often composed by individuals familiar with literary traditions, however, they may employ complex symbolism lacking in the popular ballads.

**blank verse** Lines of unrhymed iambic pentameter.

**blocking** The planning of movement on the stage for a production of a drama.

**caesura** A pause within a poetic line, created by punctuation, by the phrasing of ideas, or by the manipulation of metre.

**carpe diem** A Latin phrase, meaning "seize the day," often used to describe poems that urge the enjoyment of the moment because time is fleeting.

**character** A person in a work of literature or one of the *dramatis personae* of a play; also the moral, psychological, and intellectual traits of such a person. A *round* character possesses the complexities, contradictions, and subtle depths of personality associated with actual human beings. A *flat* character, in contrast, seems relatively two dimensional: the character is presented briefly and has little depth of personality. Both kinds may be *dynamic*— a character who changes, for better or worse, during the course of a literary work — or *static*, a character who undergoes no development.

**characterization** The techniques used to depict the traits of a character in a literary work. See CHARACTER.

**chorus** In ancient Greek drama, a group of characters who comment in unison upon and sometimes take part in the action of a drama.

**classic** A work considered to be the best of its class.

**classical literature** The literature of ancient Greece and Rome.

**classicism** The application of artistic principles supposedly derived from the classical literatures of Greece and Rome, including formal control, proportion, simplicity, unity, and rationality. Classicism emerged in the Continent and England among the humanists of the fifteenth and sixteenth centuries. See NEOCLASSICISM.

**climax** The crucial or high point of tension, understanding, or recognition in a plot and the turning point of the action.

**closed couplet** See COUPLET.

**comedy** A literary mode, especially in drama, that ends happily, with the resolution of difficulties, the restoration of fortunes, and the unity of the community, often symbolized by one or more marriages. Comedy can celebrate or satirize the values of a society or individual, but it affirms life through its presentation of good fortune, positive pleasures, meaningful societal values, and individuals as significant parts of society.

**complication** The problem near the beginning of a story or drama that causes the conflict.

**conceit**  An elaborate or extended comparison, whether simile or metaphor; known as Petrarchan conceits (after Petrarch, the poet who popularized them in his sonnets) when they are conventional, as with the comparison of a lover to a ship, and as metaphysical conceits (after the metaphysical poets of the seventeenth century) when they are elaborate or ingenious comparisons of things not traditionally linked, as with the comparison of separated lovers to a compass.

**conflict**  The opposition of forces within a character, or the struggles either between characters (protagonists) and other characters (antagonists) or between characters and natural or supernatural forces.

**connotation**  The implications of a word; that is, the feelings, ideas, or associations suggested by a word in addition to its denotation, or dictionary meaning.

**consonance**  Repetition of consonants within or at the end of words.

**contextual symbol**  See SYMBOL.

**convention**  A technique or feature included frequently in specific types of literature or in literature from a particular historical period. The Petrarchan conceit is a conventional feature in some Renaissance poetry; the use of heroic couplets is a conventional technique in eighteenth-century poetry.

**conventional symbol**  See SYMBOL.

**couplet**  Two adjacent lines of poetry that rhyme; called a closed couplet when the pair is end-stopped by significant punctuation and contains a complete thought; called a heroic couplet when the rhymed lines are in iambic pentameter.

**cretic**  See AMPHIMACER.

**dactyl (dactylic)**  A poetic foot of three syllables, only the first being accented. See FOOT and Table 1, "The Metrical Feet," in the Introduction to Poetry.

**dactylic rhyme**  See RHYME.

**denotation**  The dictionary meaning of a word, which depends significantly on context, without reference to its implications and associations.

**dénouement**  See RESOLUTION.

**deus ex machina**  Literally, "the god out of the machine"; the descent of a god, represented by an actor lowered to the main level of the stage in a mechanical device, to intercede and conclude an ancient Greek drama; by extension, any contrived and improbable ending.

**dialogue**  The direct presentation of the spoken words of characters in a story or play.

**diction**  The choice of types of words, specific words, and levels of language. Levels may be formal (lofty language such as that used in epics and in the speeches of nobles in Shakespearean drama), informal (the speech and idiom of daily life), or colloquial (the speech and idioms of particular social classes or groups, such as the Cockneys in England).

**dimeter** A term of poetic measurement indicating a line containing two feet. See FOOT, METRE, and Table 2, "Line Lengths," in the Introduction to Poetry.

**double rhyme** See RHYME.

**dramatic monologue** A form of poetry in which a character speaks to a definite but silent listener and thereby reveals his or her own character.

**dramatis personae** Literally, "the characters of the drama"; a descriptive list of characters prefixed to a drama; see CHARACTER.

**dynamic character** See CHARACTER.

**elegy** In classical Greece, a poem on any serious theme that was written in a couplet form known as elegiac metre; since the Renaissance, used to refer to a lyric that laments a death.

**end rhyme** See RHYME.

**end-stopped line** A line terminated with a relatively strong pause, usually indicated by the presence of a comma, semicolon, dash, or period; the opposite of enjambment.

**enjambment** The running over of meaning from one line to another unhindered by punctuation or syntactical pauses; the opposite of an end-stopped line.

**epic** A long narrative poem recounting in elevated language the deeds of heroes; settings are vast, sometimes extending beyond earth, and episodes may involve the gods or other supernatural beings.

**epilogue** The concluding, summarizing section of a drama in which all the strands of the plot are drawn together; sometimes the epilogue is an actual addition.

**epiphany** A religious term meaning a "manifestation" or "showing forth"; western Christianity celebrates the Feast of the Epiphany on January 6 to mark Christ's manifestation of divinity to the Magi; James Joyce applied the term to short fiction to describe the moment when events show forth their meaning, bringing illumination or revelation to a character.

**exeunt** The plural form of the Latin "*exit*"; literally, "they go out"; a stage direction signalling the exit of all characters in a scene; sometimes expressed as "*exeunt omnes*" ("all go out"); when names or categories follow the term, as in "*exeunt* Lords," only the named group leaves the stage.

**exposition** The presentation, usually at or near the beginning of a narrative or drama, of necessary background information about characters and situations.

**expressionism** An early-twentieth-century artistic movement that emphasized the inner world of emotions and thought and projected this inner world through distortions of real-world objects; unlike impressionism, expressionist literature and drama distorts and abstracts the external world, creating works that are symbolic, anti-realistic, and often nightmarish in vision; in prose, stream of consciousness narration is one of its major techniques.

**eye rhyme**   See RHYME.

**feminine rhyme**   See RHYME.

**figurative language**   Language that uses figures of speech (such as metaphors or similes) so that it means more than the simple denotation of the words and, therefore, must be understood in more than a literal way.

**flashback**   An interruption of the chronological sequence of events to present an event that occurred at an earlier time.

**flat character**   See CHARACTER.

**foot**   The basic metrical unit in poetry, consisting of one or more syllables, usually with one stressed or accented; a basic pattern of stressed and unstressed syllables commonly identified by names derived from Greek poetics, the most common being the iamb, the trochee, the dactyl, the anapest, and the spondee. See METRE and Glossary entries for each kind, or see Table 1, "The Metrical Feet," in the Introduction to Poetry for a list.

**foreshadowing**   The presentation of incidents, characters, or objects that hint at important events that will occur later.

**free verse**   Poetry that is free of regular rhythm, rhyme pattern, and verse form; often called *vers libre*.

**Freytag's Pyramid**   A structural diagram, resembling a pyramid in shape, devised by the nineteenth-century German playwright and critic Gustav Freytag to illustrate the rising and falling action of a five-act drama:

3. Climax

2. Rising Action      4. Falling Action

1. Exposition            5. Resolution

**genre**   A classification of literature into separate kinds, such as drama, poetry, and prose fiction; a major literary form that sometimes contains other related forms, which are known as subgenres.

**heptameter**   A term of poetic measurement indicating a line containing seven feet. See FOOT, METRE, and Table 2, "Line Lengths," in the Introduction to Poetry.

**heroic couplet**   See COUPLET.

**heroic quatrain**   See QUATRAIN.

**hexameter**   A term of poetic measurement indicating a line containing six feet. See FOOT, METRE, and Table 2, "Line Lengths," in the Introduction to Poetry.

**hyperbole**   A figure of speech depending on exaggeration, the overstatement of the literal situation, to achieve dramatic or comic effects.

**iamb (iambic)** A poetic foot of two syllables, the second being accented. See FOOT and Table 1, "The Metrical Feet," in the Introduction to Poetry.

**image** See IMAGERY.

**imagery** At its most basic, the verbal creation of images, or pictures, in the imagination; also applied to verbal appeals to any of the senses.

**imperfect rhyme** See RHYME.

**internal rhyme** See RHYME.

**irony** A figure of speech that creates a discrepancy between appearance and reality, expectation and result, or surface meaning and implied meaning; traditionally categorized as verbal irony (a reversal of denotative meaning in which the thing stated is not the thing meant), dramatic irony (in which the discrepancy is between what a character believes or says and the truth possessed by the reader or audience), and situational irony (in which the result of a situation is the reverse of what a character expects).

**Italian sonnet** See SONNET AND SONNET, PETRARCHAN.

**leitmotif** A recurring word, phrase, situation, or theme running through a literary work. Also see MOTIF.

**line length** See Table 2, "Line Lengths," in the Introduction to Poetry for a list; consult this Glossary for descriptions of individual kinds.

**lyric** A form of poetry that is relatively short and that emphasizes emotions, moods, and thoughts, rather than story.

**masculine rhyme** See RHYME.

**metaphor** A figure of speech that makes a comparison by equating things, as in "His heart is a stone."

**metaphysical conceit** See CONCEIT.

**metaphysical poets** Seventeenth-century poets who linked physical with metaphysical or spiritual elements in their poetry.

**metonymy** A figure of speech that substitutes one idea or object for a related one, such as saying "the Crown" when referring to the monarchy or the government.

**metre** A measure of the feet in a line of poetry, and thus a term expressing the number of feet in a line and the pattern of the predominant feet in that line; the rhythmic pattern of a line. See Table 1, "The Metrical Feet," in the Introduction to Poetry.

**Miltonic sonnet** See SONNET, MILTONIC.

**modernism** An artistic movement of the early twentieth century that deliberately broke from the reliance on established forms and insisted that individual consciousness, not something objective or external, was the source of truth; modernist literature may be structurally fragmented; its themes tend to emphasize the philosophy of existentialism, the alienation of the individual, and the despair inherent in modern life.

**monometer** A term of poetic measurement indicating a line containing one foot. See FOOT, METRE, and Table 2, "Line Lengths," in the Introduction to Poetry.

**mood** A general emotional atmosphere created by the characters and setting and by the language chosen to present these.

**motif** An image, character, object, setting, situation, or theme recurring in many works. Also see LEITMOTIF.

**motivation** The psychological reason behind a character's words or actions.

**myth** A traditional story embodying ideas or beliefs of a people; also a story setting forth the ideas or beliefs of an individual writer.

**narration** The recounting, in summarized form, of events and conversations.

**narrative poem** A poem that tells a story.

**narrator** The person telling a story, either a fictional character or the implied author of the work; see POINT OF VIEW.

**naturalism** A literary movement based on philosophical determinism, the belief that the lives of ordinary people are determined by biological, economic, and social factors; naturalists tend to use the techniques of realism in order to present a tragic vision of the fate of individuals crushed by forces they cannot control.

**near rhyme** See RHYME.

**neoclassicism** The principles of those writers who emerged with the restoration of Charles II to the throne of England in 1660 and who sought to restore classical restraint in all areas of life. The literature of the Neoclassical Period, which extends until about the 1798 publication of Wordsworth and Coleridge's *Lyrical Ballads*, was highly formal (frequently being based on the heroic couplet), praised reason over emotion, and often used satire and irony to criticize deviations from decorum and propriety. See CLASSICISM.

**oblique rhyme** See RHYME.

**octameter** A term of poetic measurement indicating a line containing eight feet. See FOOT, METRE, and Table 2, "Line Lengths," in the Introduction to Poetry.

**octave** An eight-line stanza in any metre or any rhyme scheme; any eight-line unit of poetry, rhymed or unrhymed; the initial eight lines of a sonnet united by the rhyme scheme.

**ode** A long, often elaborate, lyric poem that uses a dignified tone and style in treating a lofty or serious theme; regular forms not frequently used in English include the Greek Pindaric ode, which was divided into three repeated types of stanzas (strophe, antistrophe, and epode), each with its own metrical pattern, and the Horatian ode, which retained a single pattern throughout every stanza.

**off rhyme**  See RHYME.

**onomatopoeia**  Words that imitate the sounds that they describe.

**oxymoron**  An ironic figure of speech containing an overt contradiction, as in the word *oxymoron* itself, which means "sharp stupidity" in Greek, or in such phrases as "fearful joy" or "paper coin"; see IRONY and PARADOX.

**paradox**  An apparent contradiction that, upon deeper analysis, contains a degree of truth.

**parody**  A humorous imitation that mocks a given literary work by exaggerating or distorting some of its salient features.

**pentameter**  A term of poetic measurement indicating a line containing five feet. See FOOT, METRE, and Table 2, "Line Lengths," in the Introduction to Poetry.

**persona**  Literally, the mask; the speaking personality through which the author delivers the words in a poem or other literary work; the fictional "I" who acts as the actual author's mouthpiece in a literary work.

**personification**  The attribution of human traits to inanimate objects or abstract concepts.

**Petrarchan conceit**  See CONCEIT.

**Petrarchan sonnet**  See SONNET and SONNET, PETRARCHAN.

**plot**  The arrangement of actions in a drama or story, often in a sequence according to cause and effect.

**point of view**  The angle of vision or perspective from which a story is told. The point of view may be first person (in which the narrator is a character within the story), third person (a character or an implied author outside the story), or, very rarely, second person (in which the narrator, as in "choose-your-adventure" books, addresses the reader as "you"). Narrative point of view also involves questions of knowledge and reliability. Narrators may be omniscient, knowing both external events and internal thoughts and motivations, or they may be limited to some degree, knowing only some external details. Reliable narrators (a category that includes omniscient narrators) tell the truth completely. Unreliable narrators have personal limitations, such as youth or lack of education, that make them misunderstand what they narrate.

**prologue**  The preface or introduction to a play, often containing a plot summary.

**protagonist**  The main character of a drama or story.

**pyrrhic**  A poetic foot of two syllables, neither of which is accented. See FOOT and Table 1, "The Metrical Feet," in the Introduction to Poetry.

**quatrain**  A four-line stanza in any metre or any rhyme scheme, except the heroic quatrain, which is in iambic pentameter and rhymes *abab*; any four-line unit of poetry, rhymed or unrhymed; four lines of a sonnet united by the rhyme scheme.

**quintet**  A five-line stanza in any metre or any rhyme scheme; any five-line unit of poetry, rhymed or unrhymed.

**realism**  The attempt to represent accurately the actual world; a literary movement that developed in reaction to the artificialities of romantic literature and melodramatic drama and that tended to focus on the lives of ordinary people, to use the language of daily speech, and to develop themes that offered social criticism and explored the problems of mundane life.

**resolution**  A portion of a story or drama occurring after the climax that reveals the consequences of the plot and resolves conflicts.

**rhyme (rime)**  The repetition of identical or similar final sounds in words, particularly at the end of lines of poetry. Single, or masculine, rhymes repeat only the last syllable of the words; double, or feminine, rhymes (also sometimes called trochaic rhymes) repeat identical sounds in both an accented syllable and the following unaccented syllable; triple, or dactylic, rhymes repeat identical sounds in an accented syllable and the two following unaccented syllables. End rhyme occurs when the rhyming words are at the end of their respective lines; internal rhyme occurs when one or both of the rhyming words are within a line. Most rhyme involves the exact repetition of sounds; near rhyme (also known as slant, off, imperfect, or oblique rhyme) depends upon the approximation, rather than duplication, of sounds: it repeats either the final consonant (but not the preceding vowels) or the vowels (but not the following consonants) of the words. Eye, or sight, rhyme depends on the similar spelling of words, not their pronunciation, as in *gone* and *lone*.

**rhythm**  The flow of stressed and unstressed syllables; the patterned repetition of beats.

**rising action**  The progression of events and development of the conflict of a story or play up to the point of the climax.

**romanticism**  A literary movement that began in England sometime around the 1798 publication of Wordsworth and Coleridge's *Lyrical Ballads* and was a reaction to the restraint and order of neoclassicism. The Romantics praised emotion over reason and celebrated the imagination; their literature used a diction that was less formal and elevated than that of the classicists (see CLASSICISM), employed themes based on the supernatural, nature and nature's influence on human beings, and the power of the liberated imagination. "Romantic" and "romanticism" are applied to works that exhibit emotional and imaginative exuberance or that use such themes, whether or not written during the Romantic period.

**round character**  See CHARACTER.

**satire**  A literary form that uses wit and humour to ridicule persons, things, and ideas, frequently with the declared purpose of effecting a reformation of vices or follies.

**scansion**  The analysis and marking of the metres and feet in a poem; see METRE and FOOT; see also Table 1, "The Metrical Feet," and Table 2, "Line Lengths," in the Introduction to Poetry.

**septet** A seven-line stanza in any metre or any rhyme scheme; any seven-line unit of poetry, rhymed or unrhymed.

**sestet** A six-line stanza in any metre or any rhyme scheme; any six-line unit of poetry, rhymed or unrhymed; the final six lines of a Petrarchan sonnet, which are united by the rhyme scheme.

**setting** Emotional, physical, temporal, and cultural context in which the action of the story or play takes place.

**Shakespearean sonnet** See SONNET and SONNET, ENGLISH.

**sight rhyme** See RHYME.

**simile** A figure of speech making a direct comparison between things by using *like* or *as* or similar words, as in "His heart is like a stone."

**single rhyme** See RHYME.

**slant rhyme** See RHYME.

**soliloquy** The thoughts and impulses of a character, voiced aloud on stage and shared with the audience.

**sonnet** A lyric form of fourteen lines, traditionally of iambic pentameter and following one of several established rhyme schemes; see SONNET, ENGLISH; SONNET, MILTONIC; SONNET, PETRARCHAN.

**sonnet, English** Also called the Shakespearean sonnet; a sonnet consisting of three quatrains and a couplet, rhyming *abab cdcd efef gg*; when the quatrains employ linked rhyme (*abab bcbc cdcd ee*), known as the Spenserian sonnet.

**sonnet, Miltonic** A variation of the Petrarchan sonnet that eliminates the pause at the end of the octave; thus, the *volta*, when it occurs, usually appears in the middle of the ninth line.

**sonnet, Petrarchan** Also called the Italian sonnet: the first eight lines (the octave) state a problem, and the final six lines (the sestet) frequently begin with a *volta*, or turn, such as *but*, *yet*, or *however*, and resolve or comment on the problem; originally limited to five rhymes, with the rhyme scheme of the octave usually being *abba abba* (thus dividing into two quatrains), and the rhyme scheme of the sestet varying, but generally being either *cde cde* (thus dividing into two tercets, or three-line units) or *cdcdcd*.

**Spenserian sonnet** See SONNET, ENGLISH.

**spondee (spondaic)** A poetic foot of two syllables, both of which are accented. See FOOT and Table 1, "The Metrical Feet," in the Introduction to Poetry.

**stanza** A division of a poem into a group of lines; traditionally, a grouping of lines according to rhyme scheme, number of lines, or metrical pattern that frequently is repeated in each stanza; a unit of two or more lines that are grouped together visually in any poem by being separated from preceding and following lines. See Table 3, "Names of Stanzas and Line Groupings," and Table 4, "Notable Fixed and Complex Forms," in the Introduction to Poetry.

**static character** See CHARACTER.

**stream of consciousness** A narrative presenting the flow of thoughts and emotions of a character.

**structure** The arrangement of elements within a work; the organization of and relationship between parts of a work; the plan, design, or form of a work.

**style** A writer's selection and arrangement of words.

**suspense** The anxiety created by a situation in which the outcome is uncertain.

**symbol** A figure of speech that links a person, place, object, or action to a meaning that is not necessarily inherent in it; a word so charged with implication that it means itself and also suggests additional meanings, which are the product of convention (the culture traditionally associates a particular image with a particular meaning) or of context (the placement of the image in a work and the details and emphases within that work add suggestiveness to the image, making it symbolic).

**synecdoche** A figure of speech in which a part stands for the whole or the whole stands for the part, as when the term "hands" signifies "sailors."

**tercet** A three-line stanza in any metre or any rhyme scheme, but usually called a triplet when all three lines rhyme; any three-line unit of poetry, rhymed or unrhymed; three lines united by the rhyme scheme in the sestet of a Petrarchan sonnet.

**tetrameter** A term of poetic measurement indicating a line containing four feet. See FOOT, METRE, and Table 2, "Line Lengths," in the Introduction to Poetry.

**theme** The central idea or meaning of a work; a generalization, or statement of underlying ideas, suggested by the concrete details of language, character, setting, and action in a work.

**tone** The speaker's attitude toward the subject matter or audience, as revealed by the choice of language and the rhythms of speech.

**tragedy** A literary work, especially a drama, presenting the failure and downfall of a character. Tragedy is a serious form demonstrating moral choice, error of judgement, and, in many cases, heroic death, as well as the enlightened understanding resulting from such considerations. Tragedy tends to deal with right and wrong, life and death, and the remorselessness of the universe in relationship to the puniness of human beings.

**trimeter** A term of poetic measurement indicating a line containing three feet. See FOOT, METRE, and Table 2, "Line Lengths," in the Introduction to Poetry.

**triple rhyme** See RHYME.

**triplet** A tercet; usually applied to one in which all three lines rhyme.

**trochaic rhyme** See RHYME.

**trochee (trochaic)** A poetic foot of two syllables, the first being accented. See FOOT and Table 1, "The Metrical Feet," in the Introduction to Poetry.

**understatement** A figure of speech, the opposite of exaggeration, that intensifies meaning ironically by deliberately minimizing, or underemphasizing, the importance of ideas, emotions, and situations.

**unity** The cohesiveness of a literary work in which all the parts and elements harmonize.

**vers libre** See FREE VERSE.

**volta** The turn of thought in a poem, especially after the octave of a Petrarchan sonnet.

# CREDITS

**Anonymous Medieval Lyrics** "Western Wind" from *Early English Lyrics*, 1967, published by October House. "The Cuckoo Song" and "Alison" from *One Hundred Middle English Lyrics*, edited by R.D. Stevick (Indianapolis: The Bobbs-Merrill Company/Macmillan Publishing Company, 1964).

**Anonymous Medieval Popular Ballads** "Sir Patrick Spens," "Lord Randal," and "The Twa Corbies" from *The Oxford Book of Ballads*, edited by Arthur Quiller-Couch (London Oxford University Press, 1910).

**Arnold, Matthew** "Dover Beach" from *Arnold: Poetical Works*, edited by C.B. Tinker and H.F. Lowry (Oxford: Oxford University Press, 1950).

**Atwood, Margaret** "Progressive Insanities of a Pioneer," "The Animals in That Country," "Further Arrivals," "Variations on the Word *Love*," "A Women's Issue," and "Interlunar" from *Selected Poems 1966–1984*. Copyright © 1990. Reprinted with the permission of Oxford University Press Canada. "you fit into me" from *Power Politics* (Toronto: House of Anansi Press, 1971). Reprinted by permission of Stoddart Publishing Co: Limited, Don Mills, Ontario. "Helen of Troy Does Counter Dancing" from *Morning in the Burned House*. "The Resplendent Quetzal" from *Dancing Girls and Other Stories*. Used by permission of the Canadian Publishers, McClelland & Stewart, Toronto.

**Auden, W.H.** "The Unknown Citizen," "In Memory of W.B. Yeats," "Musée des Beaux Arts," and "After Reading a Child's Guide to Modern Physics" from *Collected Poems of W.H. Auden*, edited by Edward Mendelson (London: Faber and Faber, 1976). Reprinted by permission of Faber and Faber Limited.

**Behn, Aphra** *The Rover*, reprinted from *The Works of Aphra Behn* (6 vols.), edited by Montague Summers (London: Heinemann, 1915).

**Birney, Earle** "Vancouver Lights," "Anglosaxon Street," "Bushed," and "The Bear on the Delhi Road" from *Collected Poems of Earle Birney*. Used by permission of the Canadian Publishers, McClelland & Stewart, Toronto.

**Blake, William** Songs of Innocence: "The Lamb," "The Little Black Boy," "The Chimney Sweeper (1789)," "Holy Thursday (1789)," and "Nurse's Song (1789)," and Songs of Experience: "The Tyger," "The Chimney Sweeper (1794)," "Holy Thursday (1794)," "Nurse's Song (1794)," "The Sick Rose," "London," and "Auguries of Innocence" from *The Complete Poetry and Prose of William Blake*, revised edition, edited by David V. Erdman (New York: Doubleday, 1962).

**Bradstreet, Anne** "The Author to her Book," "To my Dear and loving Husband," and "Upon the burning of our house, July 10, 1666" from *Poems of Anne Bradstreet*, edited by Robert Hutchinson (New York: Dover Publications, 1969).

**Brand, Dionne** "Blues Spiritual for Mammy Prater" copyright © 1990 by Dionne Brand from *No Language Is Neutral*. Reprinted by permission of Coach House Press.

**Browning, Elizabeth Barrett** From Sonnets from the Portuguese: "XLIII (How do I love thee?)," "Hiram Powers's Greek Slave," and "A Musical Instrument" from *The Complete Works of Elizabeth Barrett Browning* (New York: T.Y. Crowell, 1900).

**Browning, Robert** "My Last Duchess," "The Bishop Orders His Tomb at Saint Praxed's Church," and "'Childe Roland to the Dark Tower Came'" from *Robert Browning: The Poems*, vol. 1, edited by J. Pettigrew (New Haven: Yale University Press, 1981).

**Byron, George Gordon, Lord** "She Walks in Beauty" and "On This Day I Complete My Thirty-Sixth Year" from *The Poetical Works of Byron*, edited by Robert F. Gleckner (Boston: Houghton Mifflin, 1975).

**Chopin, Kate** "The Story of an Hour" from *The Complete Works of Kate Chopin*, vol. 1 (Baton Rouge: Louisiana State University Press, 1969).

**Clarke, Austin C.** "The Motor Car" from *When He Was Free and Young and He Used to Wear Silks*, 1971: House of Anansi (Canada); 1973: Little, Brown (U.S.). Reprinted by permission of the author via The Bukowski Agency.

**Cohen, Leonard** "I Have Not Lingered in European Monasteries," "For E.J.P.," and "Suzanne Takes You Down" from *Selected Poems 1950–1975.* "Closing Time" from *Stranger Music: Selected Poems and Songs.* Used by permission of the Canadian Publishers, McClelland & Stewart, Toronto.

**Coleridge, Samuel Taylor** "Kubla Khan," "The Rime of the Ancient Mariner," and "Dejection: An Ode" from *Coleridge: The Complete Poetical Works*, Volume 1, edited by Ernest Hartley Coleridge (Oxford: Oxford University Press, 1912).

**Conrad, Joseph** "An Outpost of Progress" from *The Medallion Edition of the Works of Joseph Conrad*, vol. 1 (London: Gresham Publishing, 1925).

**Crane, Stephen** "The Open Boat" from *The Open Boat and Other Stories* (London: Heinemann, 1898).

**Cummings, E.E.** "it may not always be so;and i say" and "in Just- spring" copyright 1923, 1951, © 1991 by the Trustees for the E.E. Cummings Trust. Copyright © 1976 by George James Firmage. "next to of course god america i" copyright 1926, 1954, © 1991 by the Trustees for the E.E. Cummings Trust. Copyright © 1985 by George James Firmage from *Complete Poems: 1904–1962*, edited by George J. Firmage. Reprinted by permission of Liveright Publishing Corporation.

**Dawe, Tom** "The Bear" from *Hemlock Cove and After* (Portugal Cove, Nfld.: Breakwater Books, 1975). Reprinted with the permission of Breakwater Books. "The Naked Man" from *Island Spell* (St. John's, Nfld.: Harry Cuff Publications, 1981). Reprinted by permission of Harry Cuff Publications.

**Dickinson, Emily** "There's a certain Slant of light," "I'm Nobody! Who are you?," "The Soul selects her own Society —," "A Bird came down the Walk —," "I heard a Fly buzz — when I died —," "I started Early — Took my Dog —," and "As imperceptibly as Grief" from *The Poems of Emily Dickinson*, edited by Thomas H. Johnson. Cambridge, Mass: The Belknap Press of Harvard University Press, Copyright © 1951, 1955, 1979, 1983 by the President and Fellows of Harvard College. Reprinted by permission of the publishers and the Trustees of Amherst College.

**Donne, John** "Song (Go, and catch a falling star)," "The Bait," "A Valediction: Forbidding Mourning," "The Canonization," "The Flea," "Holy Sonnet X (Death be not proud)," "Holy Sonnet XIV (Batter my heart)," and "Elegy XIX: To His Mistress Going to

Bed" from *John Donne: The Complete English Poems*, edited by A.J. Smith (Harmonds-worth: Penguin, 1971).

**Eliot, T.S.** "The Love Song of J. Alfred Prufrock," "The Hollow Men," and "Journey of the Magi" from *Collected Poems 1909–1962* (London: Faber and Faber, 1964). Reprinted by permission of Faber and Faber Limited.

**Faulkner, William** "A Rose for Emily" from *Collected Stories of William Faulkner*. Copyright © 1930 and renewed 1958 by William Faulkner. Reprinted by permission of Random House, Inc.

**French, David** *Leaving Home* (Toronto: New Press, 1972). Copyright © 1972 by David French. Reprinted by permission of Stoddart Publishing Co. Limited, Don Mills, Ontario.

**Frost, Robert** "After Apple-Picking," "An Old Man's Winter Night," "Stopping by Woods on a Snowy Evening," "Acquainted with the Night," and "Design" from *The Poetry of Robert Frost*, edited by Edward Connery Lathem. Copyright 1936, © 1951, 1956 by Robert Frost. Copyright © 1964 by Lesley Frost Ballantine. Copyright 1923, 1928, © 1969 by Henry Holt and Company, Inc. Reprinted by permission of Henry Holt and Company, Inc.

**Fugard, Athol** *"MASTER HAROLD" . . . and the boys*. Copyright © 1982 by Athol Fugard. Reprinted by permission of Alfred A. Knopf, Inc.

**Gallant, Mavis** "My Heart Is Broken." Copyright © 1957 by Mavis Gallant. Reprinted by permission of Georges Borchardt, Inc. for the author.

**Gilman, Charlotte Perkins** "The Yellow Wallpaper" from *The Charlotte Perkins Gilman Reader*, Volume 1 (New York: Pantheon, 1980). Reprinted by permission of Pantheon, a division of Random House, Inc.

**Gray, Thomas** "Elegy Written in a Country Church-Yard" from *The Complete Poems of Thomas Gray*, edited by H.W. Starr and J.R. Hendrickson (Oxford: Clarendon Press, 1966).

**Hardy, Thomas** "The Ruined Maid," "The Darkling Thrush," and "The Convergence of the Twain" from *The Complete Poems of Thomas Hardy*, edited by James Gibson, 1976. Reprinted by permission of Macmillan, London.

**Heaney, Seamus** "Death of a Naturalist" from *Death of a Naturalist* (London: Faber and Faber, 1969). "The Otter," "The Singer's House," "The Harvest Bow," and "Casualty" from *Field Work* (London: Faber and Faber, 1980). Reprinted by permission of Faber and Faber Limited.

**Hecht, Anthony** "The Dover Bitch: A *Criticism of Life*" from *Collected Earlier Poems*. Copyright © 1990 by Anthony E. Hecht. Reprinted by permission of Alfred A. Knopf, Inc.

**Hemingway, Ernest** "A Clean, Well-Lighted Place" from *The Complete Short Stories of Ernest Hemingway*. Copyright 1933 by Charles Scribner's Sons. Copyright renewed © 1961 by Mary Hemingway. Reprinted by permission of Scribner, a division of Simon & Schuster.

**Herbert, George** "The Altar," "Easter Wings," and "The Collar" from *The Poetical Works of George Herbert* (Oxford: Oxford University Press, 1941).

**Herrick, Robert** "To the Virgins, To Make Much of Time," and "Upon Julia's Clothes" from *Herrick's Poetical Works*, Volume 1 (Boston: Houghton Mifflin, 1854).

**Hodgins, Jack** "The Concert Stages of Europe" from *The Barclay Family Theatre*. Copyright © 1981. Reprinted by permission of Macmillan Canada.

**Hollingshead, Greg** "The Naked Man" from *The Roaring Girl* (Toronto: Somerville House Books, 1995). Reprinted by permission of Somerville House Books.

**Hopkins, Gerard Manley** "Pied Beauty," "God's Grandeur," and "The Windhover: To Christ our Lord" reprinted from *The Poems of Gerard Manley Hopkins*, edited by W.H. Gardiner and N.H. Mackenzie (Oxford: Oxford University Press, 1967).

**Howard, Henry, Earl Of Surrey** "Love that doth reign" from *The Poems of Henry Howard, Earl of Surrey*, edited by F.M. Padelford (Seattle: University of Washington Press, 1928).

**Housman, A.E.** "Loveliest of trees, the cherry now," "When I was one-and-twenty," and "To an Athlete Dying Young" from *Collected Poems*. Reprinted by permission of The Society of Authors as the literary representative of the Estate of A.E. Housman.

**Hughes, Ted** "Pike" and "Hawk Roosting" from *Selected Poems 1957–1967*. Copyright © 1972 by Ted Hughes. Reprinted by permission of Faber and Faber Limited.

**Jonson, Ben** "Song: To Celia" and "On My First Son" from *Ben Jonson: Selected Works*, edited by Harry Levin (New York: Random House, 1938).

**Joyce, James** "Araby" from *Dubliners*. Copyright 1916 by B.W. Huebsch. Definitive text copyright © 1967 by the Estate of James Joyce. Reprinted by permission of Viking Penguin, a division of Penguin Books USA Inc.

**Keats, John** "On First Looking into Chapman's Homer," "When I have fears," "Ode to a Nightingale," "Ode on a Grecian Urn," "To Autumn," and "La Belle Dame sans Merci: A Ballad" from *The Poetical Works of John Keats*, edited by H.W. Garrod (Oxford: Clarendon Press, 1958).

**King, Thomas** "Borders" from *One Good Story, That One*, copyright © 1993 by Thomas King. Published in Canada by HarperCollins Publishers Ltd. Reprinted with permission.

**Klein, A.M.** "Heirloom" and "Portrait of the Poet as Landscape" from *Complete Poems*, edited by Zailig Pollock. Copyright © 1990 by University of Toronto Press. Reprinted by permission of University of Toronto Press Incorporated.

**Lampman, Archibald** "Heat," "In November" (1888), "In November" (1895), "Winter Evening," and "The City of the End of Things" from *The Poems of Archibald Lampman*, 2nd edition (Toronto: G.N. Morang, 1900).

**Larkin, Philip** "Lines on a Young Lady's Photograph Album," "Next, Please," "Church Going," and "Toads" from *The Less Deceived*. Reprinted by permission of The Marvell Press, England and Australia.

**Lau, Evelyn** "What We Do in the Name of Money" from *You Are Not Who You Claim* (Vancouver: Beach Holme Publishing, 1990). Reprinted with permission of Beach Holme Publishing. "Nineteen" © by Evelyn Lau, from *Oedipal Dreams* (Toronto: Coach House Press, 1992). "My Tragic Opera" from *In the House of Slaves* (Toronto: Coach House Press, 1994). Reprinted by permission of the author.

**Laurence, Margaret** "The Loons" from *A Bird in the House*. Used by permission of the Canadian Publishers, McClelland & Stewart, Toronto.

**Lawrence, D.H.** "Snake" from *The Complete Poems of D.H. Lawrence* (London: Heinemann, 1964, 1972). "The Horse Dealer's Daughter" from *The Collected Short Stories of D.H. Lawrence* (London: Heinemann, 1955). Reprinted by permission of Laurence Pollinger Limited, Authors' Agents, and the Estate of Frieda Lawrence Ravagli.

**Page, P.K.** "The Stenographers" and "Stories of Snow" from *The Glass Air: Selected Poems* (Toronto: Oxford University Press, 1985). "The Landlady" from *Poems Selected and New* (Toronto: House of Anansi, 1974). Copyright © P.K. Page. Reprinted by permission of the author.

**Plath, Sylvia** "Spider," "Daddy," and "Lady Lazarus" from *Ariel* (London: Faber and Faber, 1966). Reprinted by permission of Faber and Faber Limited.

**Pollock, Sharon** *Blood Relations* from *Blood Relations and Other Plays*. Reprinted by permission of NeWest Publishers Limited, Edmonton.

**Pope, Alexander** "The Rape of the Lock; An Heroi-Comical Poem" from *The Rape of the Lock and Other Poems*, edited by Geoffrey Tillotson (London: Methuen, 1962).

**Porter, Katherine Anne** "Rope" from *Flowering Judas and Other Stories*, copyright 1930 and renewed 1958 by Katherine A. Porter. Reprinted by permission of Harcourt Brace & Company.

**Pound, Ezra** "The River-Merchant's Wife: A Letter," "In a Station of the Metro," and "Ancient Music" from *Personae*. Copyright © 1926 by Ezra Pound. Reprinted by permission of New Directions Publishing Corporation.

**Pratt, E.J.** "The Shark," "From Stone to Steel," and "The Truant" from *E.J. Pratt: Complete Poems*, edited by Sandra Djwa and R.G. Moyles. Copyright © 1989 by University of Toronto Press. Reprinted by permission of University of Toronto Press Incorporated.

**Purdy, Al** "The Country North of Belleville," "Lament for the Dorsets," and "Wilderness Gothic" from *Being Alive: Poems 1958–1978*, McClelland & Stewart, Toronto. Reprinted by permission of the author.

**Rich, Adrienne** "Aunt Jennifer's Tigers," "Living in Sin," and "Diving into the Wreck" from *The Fact of a Doorframe: Poems Selected and New, 1950–1984*. Copyright © 1984. Copyright © 1975, 1978 by W.W. Norton & Company, Inc. Copyright © 1981 by Adrienne Rich. "What Kind of Times Are These" and "In Those Years" from *Dark Fields of the Republic: Poems 1991–1995*. Copyright © 1995 by Adrienne Rich. Reprinted by permission of W.W. Norton & Company, Inc.

**Roberts, Sir Charles G.D.** "Tantramar Revisited," "The Potato Harvest," "The Winter Fields," and "The Herring Weir" from *The Collected Poems of Sir Charles G.D. Roberts* (Wolfville, N.S.: The Wombat Press, 1985). Copyright © by Mary Pacey and Lady Joan Roberts. Reprinted by permission of The Wombat Press.

**Roethke, Theodore** "Root Cellar," copyright 1943 by Modern Poetry Association, Inc. "My Papa's Waltz" from *The Collected Poems of Theodore Roethke*, copyright 1942 by Hearst Magazines, Inc. "The Waking" from *The Waking Poems: 1933–53*, (New York: Doubleday, 1954). Used by permission of Doubleday, a division of Bantam Doubleday Dell Publishing Group, Inc.

**Rosenberg, Isaac** "Break of Day in the Trenches" from *The Collected Poems of Isaac Rosenberg*, edited by Gordon Bottomley and Denys Harding (London: Chatto and Windus, 1949). Reprinted by permission of the Estate of Isaac Rosenberg and Chatto and Windus Publishers.

**Ross, Sinclair** "The Lamp at Noon" from *The Lamp at Noon and Other Stories*. Used by permission of the Canadian Publishers, McClelland & Stewart, Toronto.

# INDEX OF AUTHORS

# INDEX OF TITLES
# AND FIRST LINES*

* includes first lines of poetry selections only; first lines of drama and short fiction selections are
not included.

## READER REPLY CARD

We are interested in your reaction to *The Harbrace Anthology of Literature*, Second Edition, edited by Jon C. Stott, Raymond E. Jones, and Rick Bowers. With your comments, we can improve this book in future editions. Please help us by completing this questionnaire.

1. Please indicate which version of this anthology you used:

   ❑ literature          ❑ poetry          ❑ short fiction

2. What was your reason for using this book?

   ❑ university course          ❑ college course
   ❑ continuing education course          ❑ personal interest
   ❑ professional development          ❑ other _____

3. If you are a student, please identify your school and the course in which you used this book.


4. What did you like best about this book?


5. What did you like least about this book?


6. Did you use the section "Writing Essays about Literature"? If yes, did you find it helpful? Why or why not?


7. Did you find the interviews with Evelyn Lau, Ken Mitchell, and Greg Hollingshead useful? Why or why not?


8. Please add any comments or suggestions.


9. May we contact you for further information?

   Name: _____

   Address: _____

   _____

   Phone: _____

(fold here and tape shut)

------------------------------------------------------------------------

Larry Gillevet
Director of Product Development
HARCOURT BRACE & COMPANY, CANADA
55 HORNER AVENUE
TORONTO, ONTARIO
M8Z 9Z9